RISK   ENQUIRY   THE DANGER

Dick Francis, former National Hunt jockey, is the king of
thriller writers, with thirty-two brilliant bestselling novels
acclaimed across the world. In 1989 he received the Crime
Writers' Association's prestigious award, the Cartier
Diamond Dagger, in recognition of his outstanding
contribution to the crime genre, and in May 1991 Tufts
University of Boston awarded him an honorary Doctorate of
Humane Letters.

Dick Francis

RISK
ENQUIRY
THE DANGER

PAN BOOKS
LONDON, SYDNEY AND AUCKLAND

Risk first published 1977 by Michael Joseph Ltd
and first published by Pan Books Ltd 1979
Enquiry first published 1969 by Michael Joseph Ltd
and first published by Pan Books Ltd 1971
The Danger first published 1983 by Michael Joseph Ltd
and first published by Pan Books Ltd 1983

This combined edition published 1994 by Pan Books
an imprint of Macmillan General Books
Cavaye Place London SW10 9PG
and Basingstoke

Associated companies throughout the world

ISBN 0 330 34148 0

9 8 7 6 5 4 3 2 1

A CIP catalogue record for this book is available from
the British Library

Printed and bound in Great Britain by
Cox & Wyman Ltd, Reading, Berkshire

RISK

To the memory of
Lionel Vick
first a professional steeplechase jockey,
then a certified accountant;
always a brave man.
And my thanks to his associate,
Michael Foote

1

Thursday, March 17th, I spent the morning in anxiety, the afternoon in ecstasy, and the evening unconscious.

Thursday night, somewhere between dark and dawn, I slowly surfaced into a nightmare which would have been all right if I'd been asleep.

It took me a good long time to realize I was actually awake. Half awake, anyway.

There was no light. I thought my eyes were open, but the blackness was absolute.

There was a lot of noise. Different noises, loud and confusing. A heavy engine. Rattling noises. Creaks. Rushing noises. I lay in a muzzy state and felt battered by too much sound.

Lay . . . I was lying on some sort of mattress. On my back. Cold, sick and stiff. Aching. Shivering. Physically wretched and mentally bewildered.

I tried to move. Couldn't for some reason lift either hand to my face. They seemed to be stuck to my legs. Very odd.

An interminable time passed. I grew colder, sicker, stiffer, and wide awake.

Tried to sit up. Banged my head on something close above. Lay down again, fought a sudden spurt of panic, and made myself take it step by step.

Hands. Why couldn't I move my hands? Because my wrists seemed to be fastened to my trousers. It didn't make sense, but that was what it felt like.

Space. What of space? I stiffly moved my freezing feet, exploring. Found I had no shoes on. Only socks. On the immediate left, a wall. Close above, a ceiling. On the immediate right, a softer barrier. Possibly cloth.

I shifted my whole body a fraction to the right, and felt with my fingers. Not cloth, but netting. Like a tennis net. Pulled tight. Keeping me in. I pushed my fingers through the mesh, but could feel nothing at all on the far side.

Eyes. If I hadn't gone suddenly blind (and it didn't feel like it), I was lying somewhere where no light penetrated. Brilliant deduction. Most constructive. Ha bloody ha.

Ears. Almost the worst problem. Constant din assaulted them, shutting me close in the narrow black box, preventing me hearing any further than the powerful, nearby, racketing engine. I had a frightening feeling that even if I screamed no one would hear me. I had a sudden even more frightening feeling of *wanting* to scream. To make someone come. To make someone tell me where I was, and why I was there, and what on earth was happening.

I opened my mouth and yelled.

I yelled 'Hey' and 'Come here' and 'Bloody bastard, come and let me out', and thrashed about in useless rage, and all that happened was that my voice and fear bounded back in the confined space and made things worse. Chain reaction. One-way trip to exhaustion.

In the end I stopped shouting and lay still. Swallowed. Ground my teeth. Tried to force my mind into holding on to sense. Disorientation was the road to gibbering.

Concentrate, I told myself. *Think*.

That engine . . .

A big one. Doing a job of work. Situated somewhere close, but not where I was. The other side of a wall. Perhaps behind my head.

If it would only stop, I thought numbly, I would feel less sick, less pulverized, less panicky, less threatened.

The engine went right on hammering, its vibration reaching me through the walls. Not a turbine engine: not smooth enough, and no whine. A piston engine. Heavy duty, like a tractor . . . or a lorry. But I wasn't in a lorry. There was no feeling of movement; and the engine never altered its rate. No slowing or accelerating. No changes of gear. Not a lorry..

A generator. It's a generator, I thought. Making electricity.

I was lying tied up in the dark and on a sort of shelf near an electric generator. Cold, sick and frightened. And where?

As to how I'd got there . . . well, I knew that, up to a point. I remembered the beginning, well enough. I would never forget Thursday, March 17th.

The most shattering questions were those to which I could think of no answer at all.

Why? What for? And *what next*?

2

That Thursday morning a client with his life in ruins kept me in the office in Newbury long after I should have left for Cheltenham races, and it seemed churlish to say, 'Yes, Mr Wells, terribly sorry about your agony, but I can't stop to help you now because I want to nip off and enjoy myself.' Mr Wells, staring-eyed and suicidal, simply had to be hauled in from his quicksand.

It took three and a half hours of analysis, sympathy, brandy, discussion of ways and means, and general pep-talk, to restore the slightest hope to his horizon, and I wasn't his doctor, priest, solicitor or other assorted hand-holder, but only the accountant he'd engaged in a frenzy the night before.

Mr Wells had bitten the dust in the hands of a crooked financial adviser. Mr Wells, frantic, desperate, had heard that Roland Britten, although young, had done other salvage jobs. Mr Wells on the telephone had offered double fees, tears, and lifelong gratitude as inducements: and Mr Wells was a confounded nuisance.

For the first and probably the only time in my life I was that day going to ride in the Cheltenham Gold Cup, the race which ranked next to the Grand National in the lives of British steeplechase riders. No matter that the tipsters gave my mount little chance or the bookies were offering ante-post odds of forty-to-one, the fact remained that for a part-time amateur like myself the offer of a ride in the Gold Cup was as high as one could go.

Thanks to Mr Wells I did not leave the office calmly and early after a quick shuffle through the day's mail. Not until a quarter to one did I begin to unstick his leech-like dependence and get him moving, and only then by promising another long session on the following Monday. Half-way through the door, he froze yet again. Was I sure we had covered every angle. Couldn't I give him the afternoon? Monday, I said firmly. Wasn't there anyone else he could see, then?

'Sorry,' I said. 'My senior partner is away on holiday.'

'Mr King?' he asked, pointing to the neat notice 'King and Britten' painted on the open door.

I nodded, reflecting gloomily that my senior partner, if he hadn't been touring somewhere in Spain, would have been most insistent that I got off to Cheltenham in good time. Trevor King, big, silver-haired, authoritative and worldly, had my priorities right.

We had worked together for six years, ever since he'd enticed me, from the city office where I'd been trained, with the one inducement I couldn't refuse: flexible working hours which allowed time to go racing. He already had five or six clients from the racing world, Newbury being central for many of the racing stables strung out along the Berkshire Downs, and, needing a replacement for a departing assistant, he'd reckoned that if he engaged me he might acquire a good deal more business in that direction. Not that he'd ever actually said so, because he was not a man to use two words where one would do; but his open satisfaction as his plan had gradually worked made it obvious.

All he had apparently done towards checking my ability as an accountant, as opposed to amateur jockey, was to ask my former employers if they would offer me a substantial raise in salary in order to keep me. They said yes, and did so. Trevor, it seemed, had smiled like a gentle shark, and gone away. His subsequent offer to me had been for a full partnership and lots of racing time; the partnership would cost me ten thousand pounds and I could pay it to him over several years out of my earnings. What did I think?

I'd thought it might turn out just fine; and it had.

In some ways I knew Trevor no better than on that first day. Our real relationship began and ended at the office door, social contact outside being confined to one formal dinner party each year, to which I was invited by letter by his wife. His house was opulent: building and contents circa nineteen twenties, with heavy plate glass cut to fit the top surfaces of polished furniture, and an elaborate bar built into the room he called his 'snug'. Friends tended to be top management types or county councillors, worthy substantial citizens like Trevor himself.

On the professional level, I knew him well. Orthodox establishment outlook, sober and traditional. Patriarchal, but not pompous. Giving the sort of gilt-edged advice that still appeared sound even if in hindsight it turned out not to be.

Something punitive about him, perhaps. He seemed to me sometimes to get a positive pleasure from detailing the extent of a client's tax liabilities, and watching the client droop.

Precise in mind and method, discreetly ambitious, pleased to be a noted local personage, and at his charming best with rich old ladies. His favourite clients were prosperous companies; his least favourite, incompetent individuals with their affairs in a mess.

I finally got rid of the incompetent Mr Wells and took my tensions down to the office car park. It was sixty miles from Newbury to Cheltenham and on the way I chewed my finger-nails through two lots of roadworks and an army convoy, knowing also that near the course the crawling racegoing jams would mean half an hour for the last mile. There had been enough said already about the risks of putting up an amateur ('however good' some kind columnist had written) against the top brass of the professionals on the country's best horses in the most important race of the season's most prestigious meeting. 'The best thing Roland Britten can do is to keep Tapestry out of everyone else's way' was the offering of a less kind writer, and although I more or less agreed with him I hadn't meant to do it by not arriving in time. Of all possible unprofessional behaviour, that would be the worst.

Lateness was the last and currently the most acute of a whole list of pressures. I had been riding as an amateur in jump races since my sixteenth birthday, but was now, with thirty-two in sight, finding it increasingly difficult to keep fit. Age and desk work were nibbling away at a stamina I'd always taken for granted: it now needed a lot of effort to do what I'd once done without thought. The hour and a half I spent early every morning riding exercise for a local trainer were no longer enough. Recently, in a couple of tight finishes, I'd felt the strength draining like bathwater from my creaking muscles, and had lost at least one race because of it. I couldn't swear to myself that I was tuned up tight for the Gold Cup.

Work in the office had multiplied to the point where doing it properly was a problem in itself. Half-days off for racing had begun to feel like treachery. Saturdays were fine, but impatient clients viewed Wednesdays at Ascot or Thursday at Stratford-upon-Avon with irritation. That I worked at home in the evenings to make up for it satisfied Trevor, but no one else. And my case load, as jargon would put it, was swamping me.

Apart from Mr Wells, there had been other jobs I should have done that morning. I should have sent an appeal against a top jockey's tax assessment; I should have signed a certificate for a solicitor; and there had been two summonses for clients to appear before the Tax Commissioners, which needed instant action, even if only evasive.

'I'll apply for postponements,' I told Peter, one of our two assistants. 'Ring both of those clients, and tell them not to worry, I'll start on their cases at once. And check that we've all the papers we need. Ask them to send any that are missing.'

Peter nodded sullenly, unwillingly, implying that I was always giving him too much work. And maybe I was.

Trevor's plans to take on another assistant had been so far halted by an offer which was currently giving both of us headaches. A big London firm wanted to move in on us, merge, amalgamate, and establish a large branch of itself on our patch, with us inside. Materially, we would benefit, as at present the steeply rising cost of overheads like office rent, electricity and secretarial wages was coming straight out of our pockets. We would also be under less stress, as at present when one of us was ill or on holiday, the burden on the other was heavy. But Trevor agonized over the prospect of demotion from absolute boss, and I over the threat of loss of liberty. We had postponed a decision until Trevor's return from Spain in two weeks' time, but at that point bleak realities would have to be faced.

I drummed my fingers on the steering wheel of my Dolomite and waited impatiently for the roadworks' traffic lights to turn green. Looked at my watch for the hundredth time. 'Come on,' I said aloud. 'Come *on*.' Binny Tomkins would be absolutely furious.

Binny, Tapestry's trainer, didn't want me on the horse. 'Not in the Gold Cup,' he'd said positively, when the owner had proposed it. They'd faced each other belligerently outside the weighing room of Newbury racecourse, where Tapestry had just obliged in the three mile 'chase: Mrs Moira Longerman, small, blonde and bird-like, versus sixteen stone of frustrated male.

'. . . just because he's your *accountant*,' Binny was saying in exasperation when I rejoined them after weighing-in. 'It's bloody ridiculous.'

'Well, he won today, didn't he?' she said.

Binny threw his arms wide, breathing heavily. Mrs Longerman had offered me the Newbury ride on the spur of the moment when the stable jockey had broken his ankle in a fall in the previous race. Binny had accepted me as a temporary arrangement with fair grace, but Tapestry was the best horse in his yard, and for a middle-ranker like him a runner in the Gold Cup was an event. He wanted the best professional jockey he could get. He did not want Mrs Longerman's accountant who rode in thirty races in a year, if he was lucky. Mrs Longerman, however, had murmured something about removing Tapestry to a more accommodating trainer, and I had not been unselfish enough to decline the offer, and Binny had fumed in vain.

Mrs Longerman's previous accountant had for years let her pay to the Inland Revenue a lot more tax than she'd needed, and I'd got her a refund of thousands. It wasn't the best grounds for choosing a jockey to ride for you in the Gold Cup, but I understood she was thanking me by giving me something beyond price. I quite passionately did not want to let her down; and that, too, was a pressure.

I was worried about making a reasonable show, but not about falling. When one worried about falling, it was time to stop racing: it would happen to me one day, I supposed, but it hadn't yet. I worried about being unfit, unwanted, and late. Enough to be going on with.

Binny was spluttering like a lit fuse when I finally arrived, panting, in the weighing room.

'Where the hell have you been?' he demanded. 'Do you realize the first race is over already and in another five minutes you'd be fined for not turning up?'

'Sorry.'

I carried my saddle, helmet, and bag of gear through into the changing room, sat down thankfully on the bench, and tried to stop sweating. The usual bustle went on around me; jockeys dressing, undressing, swearing, laughing, accepting me from long acquaintance as a part of the scenery. I did the accounts for thirty-two jockeys and had unofficially filled in tax assessment forms for a dozen more. I was also to date employed as accountant by thirty-one trainers, fifteen stud farms, two Stewards of the Jockey Club, one racecourse, thirteen bookmakers, two horse-transport firms, one blacksmith, five forage merchants, and upwards of forty people who owned racehorses. I probably knew more about the private financial affairs of the racing world than any other single person on the racecourse.

In the parade ring Moira Longerman twittered with happy nerves, her button nose showing kittenishly just above a fluffy upstanding sable collar. Below the collar she snuggled into a coat to match, and on the blonde curls floated a fluffy sable hat. Her middle-aged blue eyes brimmed with excitement, and in the straightforward gaiety of her manner one could see why it was that so many thousands of people spent their hobby money on owning racehorses. Not just for the gambling, nor the display: more likely for the kick from extra adrenalin, and the feeling of being involved. She knew well enough that the fun could turn to disappointment, to tears. The lurking valleys made the mountaintops more precious.

'Doesn't Tapestry look *marvellous*?' she said, her small gloved hands fluttering in the horse's direction as he plodded round the ring under the gaze of the ten-deep banks of intent spectators.

'Great,' I said truthfully.

Binny scowled at the cold sunny sky. He had produced the horse with a gloss seldom achieved by his other runners: impeccably plaited mane and tail, oiled hooves, a new rug, gleamingly polished leather tack, and an intricate geometric pattern brushed into the well-groomed hairs of the hindquarters. Binny was busy telling the world that if his horse failed it would not be from lack of preparation. Binny was going to use me for evermore as his reason for not having won the Gold Cup.

12

I can't say that it disturbed me very much. Like Moira Longerman, I was feeling the throat-catching once-in-a-lifetime thrill of a profound experience waiting just ahead. Disaster might follow, but whatever happened I would have had my ride in the Gold Cup.

There were eight runners, including Tapestry. We mounted, walked out on to the course, paraded in front of the packed and noisy stands, cantered down to the start. I could feel myself trembling, and knew it was stupid. Only a cool head could produce a worthy result. Tell that to the adrenal glands.

I could pretend, anyway. Stifle the butterfly nerves and act as if races of this calibre came my way six times a season. None of the other seven riders looked anxious or strung up, yet I guessed that some of them must be. Even for the top pros, this was an occasion. I reckoned that their placid expressions were nearly as phoney as mine, and felt better.

We advanced to the tapes in a bouncing line, restraining the eager heads on short reins, and keeping the weight still back in the saddle. Then the starter pressed his lever and let the tapes fly up, and Tapestry took a great bite of air and practically yanked my arms out of their sockets.

Most three and a quarter mile 'chases started moderately, speeded up a mile from home, and maybe finished in a decelerating procession. The Gold Cup field that day set off as if to cover the whole distance in record Derby time, and Moira Longerman told me later that Binny used words she'd never heard before when I failed to keep Tapestry close in touch.

By the time we'd swept over the first two fences, by the stands, I was last by a good six lengths, a gap not much in itself but still an I-told-you-so sort of distance so early in the proceedings. I couldn't in fact make up my mind. Should I go faster? Stick closer to the tails in front? Tapestry had set off at a greater speed already than when he'd won with me at Newbury. If I let him zip along with the others he could be exhausted and tailed off at half-way. If I held him up, we might at least finish the race.

Over the third fence and over the water I saw the gap lengthening and still dithered about tactics. I hadn't expected the others to go off so fast. I didn't know if they hoped to maintain that speed throughout, or whether they would slow and come back to me later. I couldn't decide which was more likely.

But what would Binny say if I guessed wrong and was last the whole way? What wouldn't he say?

What was I doing in this race, out of my class?

Making an utter fool of myself.

Oh God, I thought, why did I try it?

Accountants are held to be cautious by nature but at that point I threw caution to the winds. Almost anything would be better than starting last and staying last. Prudence would get me nowhere. I gave Tapestry a kick which he didn't expect and he shot forward like an arrow.

'Steady,' I gasped. 'Steady, dammit.'

Shorten the gap, I thought, but not too fast. Spurt too fast and I'd use the reserves we'd need for the last stretch uphill. If we ever got there. If I didn't fall off. If I didn't let Tapestry meet a fence wrong, or run out, or refuse to jump at all.

Only a mile done, and I'd lived a couple of lifetimes.

I was still last by the end of the first circuit, but no longer a disgrace. Once more round . . . and maybe we'd pass one or two before we'd done. I began at that point to enjoy myself, a background feeling mostly smothered by anxious concentration, but there all the same, and I knew from other days that it would be the enjoyment I remembered most afterwards, not the doubts.

Over the water-jump, still last, the others all in a group just ahead. Open ditch next; Tapestry met it just right and we pegged it back a length in mid-air. Landed nose to tail with the horse in front. Stayed there to the next fence, and again won ground in flight, setting off that time beside the next horse, not behind.

Great. I was no longer last. Just joint last. Whatever I might fear about Tapestry staying to the end, he was surging over the jumps meanwhile with zest and courage.

It was at the next fence, on the far side of the course, that the race came apart. The favourite fell, and the second favourite tripped over him. Tapestry swerved violently as he landed among the rolling bodies and crashed into the horse alongside. The rider of that horse fell off.

It happened so fast. One second, an orderly Gold Cup. Next second, a shambles. Three down, the high hopes of owners,

14

trainers, lads and punters blown to the wind. Tapestry forged his way out like a bull, but when we tackled the hill ahead, we again lay last.

Never try to accelerate uphill, they say, because the horses you pass will pass you again on the way down. Save your strength, don't waste it. I saved Tapestry's strength in last place up the hill and it seemed to me that at the crest the others suddenly swooped away from me, piling on every ounce of everything they had, shooting off while I was still freewheeling.

Come on, I thought urgently, come on, it's now or never. Now, or absolutely never. Get on, Tapestry. Get going. I went down the hill faster than I'd ever ridden in my life.

A fence half-way down. A fractional change of stride. A leap to shame the chamoix.

Another jockey lay on the ground there, curled in a ball to avoid being kicked. Hard luck . . . Too bad . . .

Three horses in front. Two fences to go. I realized abruptly that the three horses in front were all there were. Not far in front, either. My God, I thought, almost laughing, just supposing I can pass one, I'll finish third. Third in the Gold Cup. A dream to last till death.

I urged Tapestry ever faster, and amazingly, he responded. This was the horse whose finishing speed was doubtful, who had to be nursed. This horse, thundering along like a sprinter.

Round the bend . . . only one fence to go . . . I was approaching it faster than the others . . . took off alongside the third horse, landed in front . . . with only the last taxing uphill stretch to the post. I'm third, I thought exultantly. I'm *bloody* third.

Some horses find the Cheltenham finish a painful struggle. Some wander sideways from tiredness, swish their tails and falter when in front, slow to a leaden all-spent pace that barely takes them to the post.

Nothing like that happened to Tapestry, but it did to both of the horses in front. One of them wavered up the straight at a widening angle. The other seemed to be stopping second by second. To my own and everyone else's disbelief, Tapestry scorched past both of them at a flat gallop and won the Gold Cup.

I didn't give a damn that everyone would say (and did say)

that if the favourite and second favourite hadn't fallen, I wouldn't have had a chance. I didn't care a fig that it would go down in history as a 'bad' Gold Cup. I lived through such a peak of ecstasy on the lengthy walk round from the winning post to the unsaddling enclosure that nothing after, I thought, could ever match it.

It was impossible . . . and it had happened. Mrs Longerman's accountant had brought her a tax-free capital gain.

A misty hour later, changed into street clothes, with champagne flowing in the weighing room and all the hands I'd ever want slapping me on the shoulder, I was still so wildly happy that I wanted to run up the walls and laugh aloud and turn handsprings. Speeches, presentations, Moira Longerman's excited tears, Binny's incredulous embarrassment, all had passed in a jumble which I would sort out later. I was high on the sort of glory wave which would put poppies out of business.

Into this ball of a day came a man in a St John's Ambulance uniform, asking for me.

'You Roland Britten?' he said.

I nodded over a glass of bubbles.

'There's a jockey wanting you. In the ambulance. Says he won't go off to hospital before he's talked to you. Proper fussed, he is. So would you come?'

'Who is it?' I asked, putting my drink down.

'Budley. Fell in the last race.'

'Is he badly hurt?'

We walked out of the weighing room and across the crowded stretch of tarmac towards the ambulance which stood waiting just outside the gates. It was five minutes before the time for the last race of the day, and thousands were scurrying about, making for the stands, hurrying to put on the last bet of the meeting. The ambulance man and I walked in the counter-current of those making for the car park before the greater rush began.

'Broken leg,' said the ambulance man.

'What rotten luck.'

I couldn't imagine what Bobby Budley wanted me for. There had been nothing wrong with his last annual accounts and we'd had them agreed by the Inspector of Taxes. He shouldn't have had any urgent problems.

We reached the back doors of the white ambulance, and the St John's man opened them.

'He's inside,' he said.

Not one of the big ambulances, I thought, stepping up. More like a white van, with not quite enough headroom to stand upright. They were short of regular ambulances, I supposed, on race days.

Inside there was a stretcher, with a figure on it under a blanket. I went a step towards it, head bent under the low roof.

'Bobby?' I said.

It wasn't Bobby. It was someone I'd never seen before. Young, agile, and in no way hurt. He sprang upwards off the stretcher shedding dark grey blanket like a cloud.

I turned to retreat. Found the ambulance man up beside me, inside the van. Behind him the doors were already shut. His expression was far from gentle and when I tried to push him out of the way he kicked my shin.

I turned again. The stretcher case was ripping open a plastic bag which seemed to contain a hand-sized wad of damp cotton wool. The ambulance man caught hold of one of my arms and the stretcher case the other, and despite fairly desperate heavings and struggles on my part they managed between them to hold the damp cotton wool over my nose and mouth.

It's difficult to fight effectively when you can't stand up straight and every breath you draw is pure ether. The last thing I saw in a greying world was the ambulance man's peaked cap falling off. His light brown hair tumbled out loose into a shaggy mop and turned him from an angel of mercy into a straightforward villain.

I had left racecourses once or twice before on a stretcher, but never fast asleep.

Awake in the noisy dark I could make no sense of it.

Why should they take me? Did it have anything to do with winning the Gold Cup? And if so, what?

It seemed to me that I had grown colder, and still sicker, and

17

that the peripheral noises of creaks and rushing sounds had grown louder. There was also now an uncoordinated feeling of movement: yet I was not in a lorry.

Where, then? In an aeroplane?

The sickness suddenly identified itself into being not the aftermath of ether, as I'd vaguely thought, but a familiar malaise I'd suffered on and off from childhood.

I was seasick.

On a boat.

3

I was lying, I realized, on a bunk. The tight net across the open side on my right was to prevent me from falling off. The rushing noises were from the waves washing against the hull. The creaks and rattles were the result of a solid body being pushed by an engine through the resistance of water.

To have made at least some sense of my surroundings was an enormous relief. I could relate myself to space again, and visualize my condition. On the other hand, sorting out the most disorientating part of the mystery left me feeling more acutely the physical discomforts. Cold. Hands tied to legs. Muscles stiff from immobility: and knowing I was on a boat, and knowing boats always made me sick, was definitely making me feel a lot sicker.

Ignorance was a great tranquillizer, I thought. The intensity of a pain depended on the amount of attention one gave it, and one never felt half as bad talking to people in daylight as alone in the dark. If someone would come and talk to me I might feel less cold and less miserable and less quite horribly sick.

No one came for a century or so.

The motion of the boat increased, and my queasiness with it. I could feel my weight rolling slightly from side to side, and had an all too distinct impression that I was also pitching lengthwise, first toe down, then head down, as the bows lifted and fell with the waves.

18

Out at sea, I thought helplessly. It wouldn't be so rough on a river.

I tried for a while with witticisms like 'Press-ganged, by God', and 'Shanghaied!' and 'Jim lad, Long John Silver's got you', to put a twist of lightness into the situation. Not a deafening success.

In time also I gave up trying to work out why I was there. I gave up feeling apprehensive. I gave up feeling cold and uncomfortable. Finally I was concentrating only on not actually vomiting, and the fact that I'd eaten nothing since breakfast was all that helped.

Breakfast . . . ? I had lost all idea of time. I didn't know how long I'd been unconscious, or even how long I'd lain awake in the dark. Unconscious long enough to be shipped from Cheltenham to the coast, and to be carried on board. Awake long enough to long for sleep.

The engine stopped.

The sudden quiet was so marvellous that I only fully realized then how exhausting had been the assault of noise. I actively feared that it would start again. And was this, I wondered, the basis of brainwashing?

There was a new noise, suddenly, from overhead. Dragging sounds, and then metallic sounds, and then, devastatingly, a shaft of daylight.

I shut my dark-adjusted eyes, wincing, and opened them again slowly. Above my head, the shaft had grown to a square. Someone had opened a hatch.

Fresh air blew in like a shower, cold and damp. Without much enthusiasm I glanced around, seeing a small world through a wide-meshed white net.

I was in what one might call the sharp end. In the bows. The bunk where I lay grew narrower at my feet, the side walls of the cabin angling to meet in the centre, like an arrowhead.

The bunk was about two feet wide, and had another bunk above it. I was lying on a cloth-covered mattress; navy blue.

Most of the rest of the cabin was taken up by two large, open-topped, built-in, varnished wooden bins. For stowing sails, I thought. I was in the sail locker of a sailing boat.

Behind my right shoulder a door, now firmly shut, presumably led back to warmth, life, the galley and the saloon.

The matter of my wrists, too, became clear. They were indeed tied to my trousers, one on each side. From what I could see, someone had punched a couple of holes through the material in the region of each side pocket, threaded something which looked like bandage through the holes, and effectively tied each of my wrists to a bunch of cloth.

A good pair of trousers ruined: but then all disasters were relative.

A head appeared above me, framed by the hatch. Indistinctly, seeing him through the net and silhouetted against the grey sky, I got the impression he was fairly young and uncompromisingly tough.

'Are you awake?' he said, peering down.

'Yes,' I said.

'Right.'

He went away, but presently returned, leaning head and shoulders into the hatch.

'If you act sensible, I'll untie you,' he said.

His voice had the bossy strength of one accustomed to dictate, not cajole. A voice which had come up the hard way, gathering aggression on the journey.

'Have you got any dramamine?' I asked.

'No,' he said. 'There's a toilet in the cabin. You can throw up into that. You're going to have to agree you'll act quiet if I come down and untie you. Otherwise I won't. Right?'

'I agree,' I said.

'Right.'

Without more ado he lowered himself easily through the hatch and stood six feet three in his canvas shoes, practically filling all available space. His body moved in effortless balance in the boat's tossing.

'Here,' he said, lifting the lid of what had looked like a built-in varnished box. 'Here's the head. You open the stop-cock and pump sea water through with that lever. Turn the water off when you've done, or you'll have a flood.' He shut the lid and opened a locker door on the wall above. 'In here there's a bottle of drinking water and some paper cups. You'll get your meals when we get ours.' He fished deep into one of the sail bins, which otherwise seemed empty. 'Here's a blanket. And a pillow.' He lifted them out, showed them to me, both dark blue, dropped them back.

He looked upwards to the generous square of open sky above him.

'I'll fix you the hatch so you'll have air and light. You won't be able to get out. And there's nothing to get out for. We're out of sight of land.'

He stood for a moment, considering, then began to unfasten the net, which was held simply by chrome hooks slotted into eyelets on the bunk above.

'You can hook the net up if it gets rough,' he said.

Seen without intervening white meshes, he was not reassuring. A strong face with vigorous bones. Smallish eyes, narrow-lipped mouth, open air skin and straight brown floppy hair. My own sort of age: no natural kinship, though. He looked down at me without any hint of sadistic enjoyment, for which I was grateful, but also without apology or compassion.

'Where am I?' I said. 'Why am I here? Where are we going? And who are you?'

He said, 'If I untie your hands and you try anything, I'll bash you.'

You must be joking, I thought. Six foot three of healthy muscle against a cold, stiff, seasick five foot ten. No thank you very much.

'What *is* this all about?' I said. Even to my ears, it sounded pretty weak. But then, pretty weak was exactly how I felt.

He didn't answer. He merely bent down, leaned in and over me, and unknotted the bandage from my left wrist. Extracting himself from the small space between the bunks, he repeated the process on the right.

'Stay lying down until I'm out of here,' he said.

'Tell me what's going on.'

He put a foot on the edge of the sail bins, and his hands on the sides of the hatch, and pulled himself halfway up into the outside world.

'I'll tell you,' he said unemotionally, looking down, 'that you're a bloody nuisance to me. I'm having to stow all the sails on deck.'

21

He gave a heave, a wriggle, and a kick, and hauled himself out.

'Tell me,' I shouted urgently. 'Why am I here?'

He didn't answer. He was fiddling with the hatch. I swung my feet over the side of the bunk and rolled in an exceedingly wobbly fashion to my feet. The pitching of the boat promptly threw me off balance and I ended in a heap on the floor.

'Tell me,' I shouted, pulling myself up again and holding onto things. 'Tell me, God dammit.'

The hatch cover slid over and shut out most of the sky. This time, though, it was not clamped down tight, but rested on metal stays, which left a three-inch gap all round: like a lid held three inches above a box.

I put a hand up through the gap and yelled again 'Tell me.'

The only reply I got was the sound of the hatch being made secure against any attempt of mine to dislodge it. Then even those sounds ceased, and I knew he'd gone away; and a minute or two later the engine started again.

The boat rolled and tossed wildly, and the sickness won with a rush. I knelt on the floor with my head over the lavatory bowl and heaved and retched as if trying to rid myself of my stomach itself. I hadn't eaten for so long that all that actually came up was bright yellow bile, but that made nothing any better. The misery of seasickness was that one's body never seemed to realize that there was nothing left to vomit.

I dragged myself onto the bunk and lay there both sweating and shivering, wanting to die.

Blanket and pillow, I thought. In the sail bin.

A terrible effort to get up and get them. I leaned down to pick them up, and my head whirled alarmingly.

Another frightful session over the bowl. Curse the blanket and pillow. But I was so cold.

I got them at the second attempt. Wrapped myself closely in the thick navy wool and put my head thankfully on the navy pillow. There was mercy somewhere, it seemed. I had a bed and a blanket and light and air and a water closet, and a lot of shipboard prisoners before me would have given their souls for all that. It seemed unreasonable to want an explanation as well.

The day passed with increasing awfulness. Anyone who has

been comprehensively seasick won't need telling. Head ached and swam, skin sweated, stomach heaved, entire system felt unbelievably ill. If I opened my eyes it was worse.

How long, I thought, will this be going on? Were we crossing the Channel? Surely this relentless churning would soon end. Wherever we were going, it couldn't be far.

At some point he came back and undid the hatch.

'Food,' he said, shouting to be heard against the engine's din.

I didn't answer; couldn't be bothered.

'Food,' he shouted again.

I flapped a weak hand in the air, making go away signals.

I could swear he laughed. Extraordinary how funny seasickness is to those who don't have it. He pushed the hatch into place again and left me to it.

The light faded to dark. I slid in and out of dreams which were a good deal more comforting than reality; and during one of those brief sleeps someone came and fastened the hatch. I didn't care very much. If the boat had sunk, I would have looked upon drowning as a blessed release.

The next time the engine stopped it was only a minor relief compared with the general level of misery. I had supposed it was only in my imagination that the boat was tossing in a storm, but when the engine stopped I rolled clean off the bunk.

Climbing clumsily to my feet, holding on with one hand to the upper bunk, I felt for the door and the light switch beside it. Found the switch, and pressed it. No light. No damned light. Bloody stinking sods, giving me no light.

I fumbled my way back to the lower bunk in the blackness. Tripped over the blanket. Rolled it around me and lay down, feeling most insecure. Felt around for the net: fastened a couple of the hooks, groaning and grunting; not tidily, but enough to do the job.

From the next lot of noises from the outside world, I gathered that someone was putting up sails. On a sailing boat that merely made sense. There were rattlings and flappings and indistinct shouts, about none of which I cared a drip. It seemed vaguely strange someone should be sluicing the decks with buckets of water at such a time, until it dawned on me that the heavy intermittent splashes were made by waves breaking over the bows. The tight-closed hatch made sense. I had never wished for anything more passionately than to get my feet on warm, steady, dry land.

I entirely lost touch of time. Life became merely a matter of total wretchedness, seemingly without end. I would quite have liked a drink of water, but partly couldn't raise the energy to search for it, and partly feared to spill it in the dark, but mostly I didn't bother because every time I lifted my head the whirling bouts of sickness sent me retching to my knees. Water would be no sooner down than up.

He came and undid the hatch: not wide, but enough to let in some grey daylight and a flood of fresh air. He did not, it seemed, intend me to die of suffocation.

It was raining hard outside: or maybe it was spray. I saw the bright shine of his yellow oilskins as a shower of heavy drops spattered in through the narrow gap.

His voice came to me, shouting. 'Do you want food?'

I lay apathetically, not answering.

He shouted again. 'Wave your hand if you are all right.'

I reckoned all right was a relative term, but raised a faint flap.

He said something which sounded like 'Gale', and shut the hatch again.

Bloody hell, I thought bitterly. Where were we going that we should run into gales? Out into the Atlantic? And *what for*?

The old jingle about seasickness ran through my head: 'one minute you're afraid you're dying, next minute you're afraid you're not'. For hours through the storm I groaned miserably into the pillow, incredibly ill from nothing but motion.

I woke from a sunny dream, the umpteenth awakening into total darkness.

Something different, I thought hazily. Same wild weather outside, the bows crashing against the seas and shipping heavy waves over the deck. Same creaking and slapping of wind-strained rigging. But inside, in me, something quite different.

I breathed deeply from relief. The sickness was going, subsiding slowly like an ebb tide, leaving me acclimatized to an alien environment. I lay for a while in simple contentment, while normality crept back like a forgotten luxury: but then,

24

insistently, other troubles began to surface instead. Thirst, hunger, exhaustion, and an oppressive headache which I eventually put down to dehydration and a dearth of fresh air. A sour taste. An itching stubble of beard. A sweaty feeling of having worn the same clothes for a month. But worse than physical pinpricks, the mental rocks.

Confusion had had its points. Clarity brought no comfort at all. The more I was able to think straight, the less I liked the prospects.

There had to be a reason for any abduction, but the most usual reason made least sense. Ransom . . . it couldn't be. There was no one to pay a million for my release: no parents, rich or poor. Hostage . . . but hostages were mostly taken at random, not elaborately, from a public place. I had no political significance and no special knowledge: I couldn't be bartered, didn't know any secrets, had no access to Government papers or defence plans or scientific discoveries. No one would care more than a passing pang whether I lived or died, except perhaps Trevor, who would count it a nuisance to have to find a replacement.

I considered as dispassionately as possible the thought of death, but eventually discarded it. If I was there to be murdered, it would already have been done. The cabin had been made ready for a living prisoner, not a prospective corpse. Once out at sea, a weighted heave-ho would have done the trick. So, with luck, I was going to live.

However unrealistic it seemed to me, the only reason I could raise which made any sense at all was that I was there for revenge.

Although the majority of mankind think of auditing accountants as dry-as-dust creatures burrowing dimly into columns of boring figures, the dishonest regard them as deadly enemies.

I had had my share of uncovering frauds. I'd lost a dozen people their jobs and set the Revenue onto others, and seen five embezzlers go to prison, and the spite in some of those eyes had been like acid.

If Connaught Powys, for instance, had arranged this trip, my troubles had hardly started. Four years ago, when I'd last seen him, in court and newly convicted, he'd sworn to get even. He would be out of Leyhill about now. If by getting even he meant the full four years in a sail locker . . . well, it couldn't be that. It couldn't. I swallowed, convincing myself that from the solely practical viewpoint, it was impossible.

My throat was dry. From thirst, I told myself firmly: not from fear. Fear would get me nowhere.

I eased myself out of the bunk and onto the small patch of floor, holding on tight to the upper bunk. The black world went on corkscrewing around, but the vertigo had really gone. The fluid in my ears' semi-circular canals had finally got used to sloshing about chaotically: a pity it hadn't done it with less fuss.

I found the catch of the wall locker, opened it, and felt around inside. Paper cups, as promised. Bottle of water, ditto. Big plastic bottle with a screw cap. It was hopeless in the dark to use one of the cups: I wedged myself on the only available seat, which was the lowered lid of the loo, and drank straight from the bottle. Even then, with the violent rolling and pitching, a good deal of it ran down my neck.

I screwed the cap on again carefully and groped my way back to the bunk, taking the bottle with me. Hooked up the net again. Lay on my back with my head propped up on the pillow, holding the water on my chest and whistling 'Oh Susanna' to prove I was alive.

A long time passed during which I drank a good deal and whistled every tune I could think of.

After that I stood up and banged on the cabin door with my fists and the bottle, and shouted at the top of my voice that I was awake and hungry and furious at the whole bloody charade. I used a good deal of energy and the results were an absolute zero.

Back in the bunk I took to swearing instead of whistling. It made a change.

The elements went on giving the boat a bad time. I speculated fruitlessly about where we were, and how big the boat was, and how many people were sailing it, and whether they were any good. I thought about hot sausages and crusty bread and red wine, and for a fairly cheerful hour I thought about winning the Gold Cup.

At about the time that I began to wonder seriously if everyone except me had been washed overboard, the hatch-opening noises returned. He was there, still in his oilskins. I gulped in the refreshing blast of cold air and wondered just how much of a stinking fug was rushing out to meet him.

I unhooked the net and stood up, holding on and swaying. The wind outside shrieked like starlings.

He shouted, 'Do you want food?'

'Yes,' I yelled. 'And more water.' I held the nearly empty bottle up to him, and he reached down for it.

'Right.'

He shut the hatch and went away, but not before I had a terrifying glimpse of the outside world. The boat rolled heavily as usual to one side, to the left, and before it rolled back to the right I saw the sea. A huge uneven wave, towering to obliterate the sky, charcoal grey, shining, swept with gusts of spray. The next heavy crash of water over the hatch made me think happier thoughts of my dry cabin.

He came back, opened the hatch a few inches, and lowered in a plastic carrier bag on a loop of rope. He shouted down at me.

'Next time I bring you food, you give me back this carrier. Understand?'

'Yes,' I shouted back, untying the rope. 'What time is it?'

'Five o'clock. Afternoon.'

'What day?'

'Sunday.' He pulled the rope up and began to shut the hatch.

'Give me some light,' I yelled.

He shouted something which sounded like 'Batteries' and put me back among the blind. Yes, well . . . one could live perfectly well without sight. I slid back onto the bunk, fastened the net, and investigated the carrier bag.

The water bottle, full; an apple; and a packet of two thick sandwiches, faintly warm. They turned out to be hamburgers in bread, not buns; and very good too. I ate the lot.

Five o'clock on Sunday. Three whole damned days since I'd stepped into the white van.

I wondered if anyone had missed me seriously enough to go to the police. I had disappeared abruptly from the weighing room, but no one would think it sinister. The changing room valet might be surprised that I hadn't collected from him my wallet and keys and watch, which he'd been holding as usual in safe keeping while I raced, and that I hadn't in fact paid him, either: but he would have put my absentmindedness down to excitement. My car would still, I supposed, be standing in the jockeys' car park, but no one yet would have begun to worry about it.

I lived alone in a cottage three miles outside Newbury: my next-door neighbour would merely think I was away celebrating for the weekend. Our two office assistants, one boy, one girl, would have made indulgent allowances, or caustic allowances perhaps, when I hadn't turned up for work on Friday. The clients I had been supposed to see would have been irritated, but no more.

Trevor was away on his holidays. So no one, I concluded, would be looking for me.

On Monday morning, the bankrupt Mr Wells might make a fuss. But even if people began to realize I had vanished, how would they ever find me? The fact had to be faced that they wouldn't. Rescue was unlikely. Unless I escaped, I would be staying in the sail locker until someone chose to let me out.

Sunday to Monday was a long cold, wild, depressing night.

4

On Monday, March 21st the hatch opened twice to let in air, food, sprays of water, and brief views of constantly grey skies. On each occasion I demanded information, and got none. The oilskins gave merely an impression that the crew had more than enough to do with sailing the boat in those conditions, and had no time to answer damn fool questions.

I was used to being alone. I lived alone and to a great extent worked alone; solitary by nature, and seldom lonely. An only child, long accustomed to my own company, I tended often to feel oppressed by the constant companionship of a large number of people, and to seek escape as soon as possible. All the same, as the hours dragged on, I found life alone in the sail locker increasingly wearing.

Limbo existence, I thought. Lying in a black capsule, endlessly tossing. How long did it take for the human mind to disintegrate, left alone in uncertainty in the rattling, corkscrewing dark.

A bloody long time, I answered myself rebelliously. If the purpose of all this incarceration was to reduce me to a crying wreck, then it wasn't going to succeed. Tough thoughts, tough words . . . I reckoned more realistically that it depended on the true facts. I could survive another week of it passably, and two weeks with difficulty. After that . . . unknown territory.

Where could we be going? Across the Atlantic? Or, if the idea really was to break me up, maybe just up and down the Irish Sea? They might reckon that any suitable stretch of rough water would do the trick.

And who were 'they'?

Not him in the oilskins. He looked upon me as a nuisance, not a target for malice. He probably had instructions regarding me, and was carrying them out. How unfunny if his instructions were to take me home once I'd gone mad.

Dammit, I thought. Dammit to bloody hell. He'd have a bloody long job. Bugger him. Bugger and sod him.

There was a great sane comfort to be found in swearing.

At some long time after my second Monday glimpse of the outside, it seemed that the demented motion of the boat was slowly steadying. Standing up out of the bunk was no longer quite such a throw-around affair. Holding on was still necessary, but not holding on for dear life. The bows crashed more gently against the waves. The thuds of water over the hatch diminished in number and weight. There were shouts on deck and a good deal of pulley noise, and I guessed they were resetting the sails.

I found also that for the first time since my first awakening, I was no longer cold.

I was still wearing the clothes I had put on in the far off world of sanity: charcoal business suit, sleeveless waistcoat-shaped pullover underneath, pale blue shirt, underpants, and socks. Somewhere on the floor in the dark was my favourite Italian silk tie, worn to celebrate the Gold Cup. Shoes had vanished altogether. From being inadequate even when reinforced by a blanket, the long-suffering ensemble was suddenly too much.

I took off my jacket and rolled it into a tidy ball. As gent's natty suiting it was already a past number: as an extra pillow it added considerably to life's luxuries. Amazing how deprivation made the smallest extras marvellous.

Time had become a lost faculty. Drifting in and out of sleep with no external references was a queer business. I mostly couldn't tell whether I'd been asleep for minutes or hours. Dreams occurred in a semi-waking state, sometimes in such short snatches that I could have counted them in seconds. Other dreams were deeper and longer, and I knew that they were the product of sounder sleep. None of them seemed to have anything to do with my present predicament, and not one came up with any useful subconscious information as to why I should be there. In my innermost soul, it seemed, I didn't know.

Tuesday morning – it must have been Tuesday morning – he came without the oilskins. The air which flowed in through the open hatch was as always fresh and clean, but now dry and faintly warm. The sky was pale blue. I could see a patch of white sail and hear the hissing of the hull as it cut through the water.

'Food,' he said, lowering one of the by now familiar plastic carriers.

'Tell me why I'm here,' I said, untying the knot.

He didn't answer. I took the carrier off, and tied on the empty one, and held onto the rope.

'Who are you? What is this boat? Why am I here?' I said.

His face showed no response except faint irritation.

'I'm not here to answer your questions.'

'Then what *are* you here for?' I said.

'None of your business. Let go of the rope.'

I held on to it. 'Please tell me why I'm here,' I said.

He stared down, unmoved. 'If you ask any more questions, and you don't leave go of the rope, you'll get no supper.'

The simplicity of the threat, and the simplicity of the mind that made it, was a bit of a stunner. I let go of the rope, but I made one more try.

'Then please just tell me how long you're going to keep me here.'

He gave me a stubborn scowl as he pulled up the carrier.

'You'll get no supper,' he said, withdrawing his head out of sight, and beginning to shut the hatch.

'Leave the hatch open,' I shouted.

I got no joy from that either. He firmly fastened me back in the dark. I stood swaying with the boat, holding onto the upper bunk, and trying to fight down a sudden overwhelming tide of furious anger. How *dared* they abduct me and imprison me in this tiny place and treat me like a naughty child. How dared they give me no reasons and no horizons. How dared they thrust me into the squalor of my own unwashed, unbrushed, unshaven state. There was a great deal of insulted pride and soaring temper in the fiery outrage with which I literally shook.

I could go berserk and smash up the place, I thought, or calm down again and eat whatever he'd brought in the carrier: and the fact that I'd recognized the choice made it certain I'd choose the latter. The bitter, frustrated fury didn't exactly go away, but at least with a sigh I had it back under control.

The intensity of what I'd felt, and its violent, unexpected onset, both alarmed me. I would have to be careful, I thought. There were so many roads to destruction, and rage, it seemed, was one of them.

If a psychiatrist had been shut up like this, I wondered, would he have had any safety nets that I hadn't? Would his knowledge of what might happen to the mind of someone in this position help him to withstand the symptoms when they occurred? Probably I should have studied psychology, not accountancy. More useful if one were kidnapped. Stood to reason.

The carrier contained two de-shelled hard boiled eggs, an apple, and three small foil-wrapped triangles of processed cheese. I saved one of the eggs and two pieces of cheese for later, in case he meant it about no supper.

He did mean it. Uncountable hours passed. I ate the second egg and the rest of the cheese. Drank some water. As the day's total entertainment, hardly a riot.

When the hatch was next opened, it was dark outside, though dark with a luminous greyness quite unlike the black inside the cabin. No carrier of food materialized, and I gathered that the respite was only so that I shouldn't asphyxiate. He had opened the hatch and gone before I got round to risking any more questions.

Gone.

The hatch was wide open. Out on the deck there were voices and a good deal of activity with ropes and sails.

'Let go.'

'You're letting the effing thing fall into the sea . . .'

'Catch that effing sheet . . . Move, can't you . . .'

'You'll have to stow the gennie along the rail . . .'

Mostly his voice, from close by, directing things.

I put one foot on the thigh-high rim of the sail bin, as he had done, and hooked my hands over the side of the hatch, and heaved. My head popped out into the free world and it was about two whole seconds before he noticed.

'Get back,' he said brusquely, punctuating his remark by stamping on my fingers. 'Get down and stay down.' He kicked at my other hand. 'Do you want a bash on the head?' He was holding a heavy chromium winch handle, and he swung it in an unmistakable gesture.

'There's no land in sight,' he said, kicking again. 'So get down.'

I dropped back to the floor, and he shut the hatch. I hugged my stinging fingers and counted it fortunate that no one went sailing in hob-nailed boots.

Two seconds uninterrupted view of the boat had been worth it, though. I sat on the lid of the loo with my feet on the side of the lower bunk opposite, and thought about the pictures still alive on my retinas. Even in night light, with eyes adjusted to a deeper darkness, I'd been able to see a good deal.

For a start, I'd seen three men.

The one I knew, who seemed to be not only in charge of me but of the whole boat. Two others, both young, hauling in a voluminous sail which hung half over the side, pulling it in with outstretched arms and trying to stop it billowing again once they'd got it on deck.

There might be a fourth one steering: I hadn't been able to see. About ten feet directly aft of the hatch the single mast rose majestically skywards, and with all the cleats and pulleys and ropes clustered around its base it had formed a block to any straight view towards the stern. There might have been a helmsman and three or four crewmen resting below. Or there might have been automatic steering and all hands visible on deck. It seemed a huge boat, though, to be managed by three.

From the roughest of guesses and distant gleams from chromium winches I would have put it at about a cricket pitch long. Say sixty-five feet. Or say, if you preferred it, nineteen point eight one metres. Give or take an octave.

Not exactly a nippy little dinghy for Sunday afternoons on the Thames. An ocean racer, more like.

I had had a client once who had bought himself a second-hand ocean racer. He'd paid twenty-five thousand for thirty feet of adventure, and beamed every time he thought of it. His voice came back over the years: 'The people who race seriously have to buy new boats every year. There's always something new. If they don't get a better boat they can't possibly win, and the possibility of winning is what it's all about. Now me, all I want is to be able to sail round Britain comfortably at weekends in the summer. So I buy one of the big boys' cast-offs, because they're well built boats, and just the job.' He had once invited me to Sunday lunch on board. I had enjoyed looking over his pride and joy, but privately had been most relieved when a sudden gale had prevented us leaving the moorings at his yacht club for the promised afternoon's sail.

Highly probable, I thought, that I was now being entertained on some other big boy's cast-off. The great question was, at whose expense?

The improvement in the weather was a mixed blessing, because the engine started again. The din seemed an even worse assault on my nerves than it had at the beginning. I lay on the bunk and tried to shut my ears with the pillow and my fingers, but the roaring vibration easily by-passed such frivolous barriers. I'd either got to get used to it and ignore it, I thought, or go raving, screaming bonkers.

I got used to it.

*

Wednesday. Was it Wednesday? I got food and air twice. I said nothing to him, and he said nothing to me. The constant noise of the engine made talking difficult. Wednesday was a black desert.

Thursday. I'd been there a week.

When he opened the hatch, I shouted 'Is it Thursday?'

He looked surprised. Hesitated, then shouted back, 'Yes.' He looked at his watch. 'Quarter to eleven.'

He was wearing a blue cotton tee shirt, and the day outside seemed fine. The light tended to hurt my eyes.

I untied the carrier and fastened on the previous one, which as usual contained an empty water bottle. I looked up at him as he pulled it out, and he stared down at my face. He looked his normal unsmiling self: a hard young man, unfeeling rather than positively brutal.

I didn't consciously ask him, but after a pause, during which he seemed to be inspecting the horizon, he began to fix the hatch as he had done on the first day, so that it was a uniform three inches above the deck, letting in continuous air and light.

The relief at not being locked back in the dark was absolutely shattering. I found I was trembling from head to foot. I swallowed, trying to guard against the possibility that he would change his mind. Trying to tell myself that even if it proved to be only for five minutes, I should be grateful for that.

He finished securing the hatch and went away. I took some shaky deep breaths and gave myself an ineffective lecture about stoical responses, come dark, come shine.

After a while I sat on the lid of the loo and ate the first shipboard meal that I could actually see. Two hard boiled eggs, some crispbread, three triangles of cheese and an apple. Never much variety in the diet, but at least no one intended me to starve.

He came back about half an hour after he'd gone away.

Hell, I thought. Half an hour. Be grateful for that. I had at least talked myself into facing another dose of darkness without collapsing into rubble.

He didn't, however, shut the hatch. Without altering the way it was fixed, he slid another plastic carrier through the gap. It was not this time tied to a rope, because when he let go of it, it fell to the floor; and before I could raise any remark, he had gone again.

I picked up the carrier, which seemed light and almost empty, and looked inside.

For God's sake, I thought. Laugh. Laugh, but don't bloody snivel. An ounce of kindness was more devastating than a week of misery.

He'd given me a pair of clean socks and a paperback novel.

I spent a good deal of the day trying to look out of the gap. With one foot on the rim of the sail bins, and my hands grasping the hatch opening, I could get my head up to the top well enough, but the view would have been more comprehensive if either the gap had been a couple of inches deeper or my eyes had been located half way up my forehead. What I did see, mostly by tilting my head and applying one eye at a time, was a lot of ropes, pulleys, and rolled up sails, a lot of green sea, and a dark line of land on the horizon ahead.

None of these things changed all day except that the smudge of land grew slowly thicker, but I never tired of looking.

At closer quarters I also looked at the fittings of the hatch itself, which, I realized after a time, had been modified slightly for my visit. The metal props which held it open were hinged, and folded down inside the cabin when the hatch was closed. Out on deck the hatch cover was mounted on two heavier extending hinges, which allowed it to open outwards completely and lie flat on its back.

Inside the cabin there were two sturdy clips for securing the hatch shut from below, and outside there were two others, for securing the hatch from above.

So far, all as planned by the ship builders. What had been added, though, was extra provision to prevent someone inside the cabin from pushing the hatch wide open after releasing it from the hinged props. Normally, one could have done this. Sail locker hatches were supposed to open easily and wide, so that the sails could be pulled in and out. There was no point in ordinary circumstances in making things difficult. But now, outside, crossing from fore to aft and from port to starboard over the top of the hatch cover, were two lengths of chain, each secured at both ends to cleats which to my eyes looked newly screwed to the deck. The chains held the hatch cover down on the props like guy ropes, taut and forceful. If I could dislodge those chains, I thought, I could get out. If I had anything to dislodge them with. A couple of Everest-sized ifs. I could get my hands out through the three inch gap, but not much arm. Not enough to reach the cleats, let alone undo the chains. As for levers, screwdrivers, hammers and files, all I had were paper cups, a flimsy carrier and a plastic water bottle. Tantalizing, all those hours looking out at unreachable freedom.

In between the long bouts of balancing up by the ceiling I sat on the loo lid and read the book, which was an American private-eye thriller with a karate-trained hero who would have chopped his way out of a sail locker in five minutes.

Inspired by him, I had another go at the cabin door. It withstood my efforts like a stolid wall. Obviously I should have studied karate as well as psychiatry. Better luck next time.

The day whizzed past. The light began to fade. Outside the smudge of land had grown into an approaching certainty, and I had no idea what land it was.

He came back, lowered the carrier, and waited while I tied on the empty ones.

'Thank you,' I shouted, as he pulled them up, 'for the books and socks.'

He nodded, and began to close the hatch.

'Please don't,' I shouted.

He paused and looked down. It seemed to be still be-kind-to-prisoners day, because he provided his first explanation.

'We are going into port. Don't waste your breath making a noise when we stop. We'll be anchored. No one will hear you.'

He shut the hatch. I ate sliced tinned ham and a hot baked potato in the noisy stupefying dark, and to cheer myself up thought that now that the journey was ending they surely wouldn't keep me there much longer. Tomorrow, perhaps, I would be out. And after that I might get some answers.

I stifled the gloomy doubts.

*

The engine slowed, the first time it had changed its note. There were footsteps on deck, and shouts, and the anchor went over with a splash. The anchor chain rattled out, sounding as if it were passing practically through the sail locker; behind the panelling, no doubt.

The engine was switched off. There was no sound from anywhere. The creakings and rushing noises had stopped. No perceptible motion any more. I had expected the peace to be a relief, but as time passed it was the opposite. Even aggravating stimuli, it seemed, were better than none at all. I slept in disjointed snatches and lay emptily awake for hours and hours wondering if one really could go mad from too much nothing.

When he next opened the hatch it was full daylight outside. Friday; mid-morning. He lowered the carrier, waited for the exchange, raised the rope, and began to close the hatch.

I made involuntarily a vague imploring gesture with my hands. He paused, looking down.

'I can't let you see where we are,' he said.

It was the nearest he had come to an apology, the nearest to admitting that he might have treated me better, if he didn't have his orders.

'Wait,' I yelled, as he pulled the hatch over.

He paused again: prepared at least to listen.

'Can't you put screens round if you don't want me to see the land?' I said. 'Leave the hatch open . . .'

He considered it. 'I'll see,' he said, 'later.'

It seemed an awfully long time later, but he did come back, and he did open the hatch. While he was fastening it, I said 'When are you going to let me out?'

'Don't ask questions.'

'I *must*,' I said explosively. 'I have to know.'

'Do you want me to shut the hatch?'

'No.'

'Then don't ask questions.'

It may have been spineless of me, but I didn't ask any more. He hadn't given me one useful answer in eight days, and if I persevered, all I would get would be no light and no supper and an end to the new era of partial humanity.

When he'd gone I climbed up for a look, and found he had

surrounded the hatch area with bulging bolsters of rolled sails. My field of vision had come down to about eighteen inches.

I lay on the top bunk for a change, and tried to imagine what it was about the port, so hopelessly near, that I might recognize. The sky was pale blue, with sun shining through high, hazy cloud. It was warm, like a fine spring day. There were even sea-gulls.

It evoked in me such a strong picture that I became convinced that if I could only see over the sail bolsters, I would be looking at the harbour and beaches where I'd played as a child. Maybe all that frantic sailing had been nowhere but up and down the English Channel, and we were now safe back home in Ryde, Isle of Wight.

I shook the comforting dream away. All one could actually tell for sure was that it was not in the Arctic Circle.

There were occasional sounds from outside, but all distant, and nothing of any use. I read the American thriller again, and thought a good deal about escape.

When the day was fading he came back with supper, but this time, after I'd swopped the carriers, he didn't shut the hatch. That evening I watched the light die to dusk and night, and breathed sweet air. Small mercies could be huge mercies, I thought.

Saturday, March 26th. The morning carrier contained fresh bread, fresh cheese, fresh tomatoes: someone had been shopping ashore. It also contained an extra bottle of water and a well-worn piece of soap. I looked at the soap and wondered if it was there from kindness or because I stank; and then with wildly leaping hope wondered if it was there so that I should at least be clean when they turned me loose.

I took off all my clothes and washed from head to foot, using a sock as a sponge. After the week's desultory efforts with salt water from the loo, the lather was a fantastic physical delight. I washed my face and ears and neck and wondered what I looked like with a beard.

After that, dressed in shirt and underpants which were both long overdue for the same treatment, I ate the morning meal.

38

After that, I tidied the cabin, folding the blanket and my extra clothes and stacking everything neatly.

After that, I still couldn't face for a long time that my soaring hope was unfounded. No one came to let me out.

It was odd how soon the most longed-for luxury became commonplace and not enough. In the dark, I had ached for light. Now that I had light, I took it for granted and ached for room to move.

The cabin was triangular, its three sides each about six feet long. The bunks on the port side, and the loo and sail bins on the starboard side, took up most of the space. The floor area in the centre was roughly two feet wide by the cabin door, but narrowed to a point about four feet in, where the bunks and the forward sail bin met. There was room to take two small paces, or one large. Any attempt at knees-bend-arms-stretch involved unplanned contact with the surrounding woodwork. There was more or less enough space to stand on one's head by the cabin door. I did that a couple of times. It just shows how potty one can get. The second time I bashed my ankle on the edge of the sail bin coming down, and decided to give Yoga a miss. If I'd tried the Lotus position, I'd have been wedged for life.

I felt a continuous urge to scream and shout. I knew that no one would hear me, but the impulse had nothing to do with reason. It stemmed from frustration, fury and induced claustrophobia. I knew that if I gave way to it, and yelled and yelled, I would probably end up sobbing. The thought that maybe that was precisely what someone wanted to happen to me was an enormous support. I couldn't stop the screaming and shouting from going on inside my head, but at least it didn't get out.

After I'd finally come to terms with the thought that it wasn't Exodus day, I spent a good deal of time contemplating the loo. Not metaphysically: mechanically.

Everything in the cabin was either built-in, or soft. From the beginning I'd been given no possible weapons, no possible implements. All the food had been for eating with my fingers, and came wrapped only in paper or plastic, if at all. No plates. Nothing made of metal, china or glass. The light bulb had not only been unscrewed from its socket, but the glass cover for it, which I guessed should be there, was not.

39

The pockets of my suit had been emptied. The nail file I usually carried in my breast pocket was no longer there: nor were my pens clipped inside: and my penknife had gone from my trousers.

I sat on the floor, lifted the lid, and at close quarters glared at the loo's mechanics.

Bowl, flushing lever, pump. A good deal of tubing. The stopcock for turning the sea water on and off. Everything made with the strength and durability demanded by the wild motions of the sea, which shook flimsy contraptions to pieces.

The lever was fastened at the back, hinged to the built-in casing of the fitment. At the front, it ended in a wooden handle. Attached at about a third of the way back was the rod which led directly down into the pump, to pull the piston there up and down. The whole lever, from handle to hinge, measured about eighteen inches.

I lusted for that lever like a rapist, but I could see no way, without tools, of getting it off. The hinge and the piston linkage were each fastened with a nut and bolt, and appeared to have been tightened by Atlas. Nut versus thumb and finger was no contest. I had tried on and off for two days.

A spanner. My kingdom for a spanner, I thought.

Failing a spanner, what else?

I tried with my shirt. The cloth saved the pressure on skin and bones, but gave no extra purchase. The nuts sat there like rocks. It was like trying to change a wheel with only fingers and a handkerchief.

Trousers? The cloth itself tended to slip more easily than my shirt. I tried the waistband, and found it a great deal better. Around the inside of the waist was a strip with two narrow rows of rough-surfaced rubber let into it. The real purpose of the strip was to help belt-less trousers stay up by providing a friction grip against a tucked-in shirt. Applying trouser-band to nut gave a good grip and slightly more hope, but despite a lot of heavy effort, no results.

The day ground on. I went on sitting on the floor futilely trying to unscrew nuts which wouldn't unscrew, simply because there was nothing else to do.

*

Tinned ham again for supper. I carefully peeled off all the fat, and ate the lean.

The hatch stayed open.

I said thanks for the soap, and asked no questions.

Sunday. Another Sunday. How *could* anyone keep me locked up so long without explanation? The whole modern world was churning along outside, and there I was cooped up like the man in the iron mask, or as near as dammit.

I applied the strips of ham fat to the nuts, to see if grease would have any effect. I spent most of the day warming the piston-rod nut in my fingers, rubbing fat round its edges, and hauling at it with my trousers.

Nothing happened.

Now and again I stood up and stretched, and climbed up to see if the sail bolsters were still obstructing the view, which they always were. I read bits of the thriller again. I closed the loo lid and sat on it, and looked at the walls. I listened to the seagulls.

My ordinary life seemed far removed. Reality was inside the sail locker. Reality was a mystery. Reality was mind-cracking acres of empty time.

Sunday night drifted in and darkened and slowly became Monday. He came much earlier than usual with my breakfast, and when he had lifted out the exchange carrier, he began to close the hatch.

'Don't,' I yelled.

He paused only briefly, staring down unmoved.

'Necessary,' he said.

I went on yelling for him to open it for a long time after he'd gone away and left me in the dark. Once I'd started making a noise, I found it difficult to stop: all the stifled screams and shouts were trying to burst out through the hole in the dam. If the dam broke up, so would I. I stuffed the pillow into my mouth to make myself shut up, and resisted a desire to bang my head against the door instead.

The engine started. Din and vibration and darkness, all as before. It's too much, I thought. Too much. But there were only two basic alternatives. Stay sane or go crazy. Sanity was definitely getting harder.

Think rational thoughts, I told myself. Repeat verses, do mental arithmetic, remember all the tricks that other solitary prisoners have used to see them through weeks and months and years.

I tore my mind away from such impossible periods and directed it to the present.

The engine ran on fuel. It had used a good deal of fuel on the journey. Therefore if the boat was going far, it would need more.

Engines were always switched off during refuelling. If I made the most colossal racket when we refuelled, just possibly someone might hear. I didn't honestly see how any noise I could make would attract enough attention, but I could try.

The chain rattled back through its hidden chute as the anchor came up, and I presumed the boat was moving, although there was no feeling of motion.

Then someone came and put a radio on top of the hatch, and turned the volume up loud. The music fought a losing battle against the engine for a while, but shortly I felt the boat bump, and almost at once the engine switched off.

I knew we were refuelling. I could hear only loud pop music. And no one on the quayside, whatever I did, could possibly have heard *me*.

After a fairly short while the engine started again. There were a few small thuds outside, felt through the hull, and then nothing. Someone came and collected the radio: I yelled for the hatch to be opened, but might as well not have bothered.

Motion slowly returned to the boat, bringing hopeless recognition with it.

Going out to sea again.

Out to sea, in the noise and the dark. Still not knowing why I was there, or for how long. Growing less fit from lack of exercise and less able to deal with mental pressure. Starting last week's torments all over again.

I sat on the floor with my back against the cabin door, and folded my arms over my knees, and put my head on my arms, and wondered how I could possibly endure it.

Monday I spent in full-blown despair.

On Tuesday, I got out.

5

Monday night the boat was anchored somewhere, but it stopped after I got my supper and started again before Tuesday mid-morning. It rained most of the time, drumming on the hatch. I was glad of the respite from the engine but in general the misery level was a pain.

When he brought the morning food he fixed the hatch open. The extent of my relief was pathetic.

Shortly after, they stopped the engine and put up the sails, and the grey sky outside slowly cleared to blue.

I ate the hard boiled eggs and the apple and thought about the thick slice of bread, upon which, for the first time, he had given me butter. Then I pulled a button off my shirt to use as a scraper, and transferred as much of the butter as I could to the stubborn nuts and bolts on the flushing lever. Then I ate the bread. Then I sat on the floor and one after the other warmed the nuts with my hand in the hope that the butter and ham fat would melt into the screw threads.

After that I ripped a length of the rubberized waistband from my trousers, and fished out of the bottom of one of the sail bins the white net which I had stored there after the storms.

It was activity for activity's sake, more than any real hope. I wound the waistband twice round the piston-rod nut, because it was the nearest, and fitted over that the chromium hook which had attached the net to the upper berth. Then I tugged the net.

After a second of gripping, the hook slid round on the cloth and fell off. I tried again, folding the waistband so that it had an elasticated side against the hook as well as against the nut. That time the hook stayed in place; but so did the nut.

I tugged several times. If I tugged very hard, hook, waistband

and all came off. Nothing else happened. I slung the net back into the sail bin in depression.

After that I sat for ages with my hand on the piston-rod nut, until it was as warm as a handful of pennies clutched by a child. Then I wound the strip of waistband round quickly three times, to make the nut larger to grip, and then I tried it with all my remaining muscle power.

The waistband turned in my hand.

Damn it to hell, I thought hopelessly. I pulled it off and wound it on again, trying to grip it more tightly.

It turned again.

It may seem ridiculous, but it was not until it turned more easily the third time that I realized I was turning the nut on the bolt, not the waistband on the nut.

Unbelievable. I sat there looking idiotic, with my mouth open. Excitement fluttered in my throat like a stifled laugh. If I could get one off, what about the other?

Time hadn't mattered for the first one. I'd had nothing else to do. For the second one, the hinge, I was feverishly impatient.

I warmed the nut, and wound on the waistband, and heaved; and nothing happened.

Heaved again.

A blob.

It had to move, I thought furiously. It simply had to. After several more useless attempts, I went back to basics.

Perhaps after all the tugging session with the hook had had some effect. I scooped out the net and applied it to the hinge nut, and tugged away with enthusiasm, replacing the hook every time it fell off. Then I made myself warm the nut as thoroughly as I had the other one, so that the heat from my hand was conducted right to the inside, where the melted grease and the minute heat-expansion of the metal could do their work. Then I wound on the waistband again and practically tore all the ligaments in my arm and back with a long and mighty heave.

And that time, the waistband turned. That time again I couldn't be sure until the third turn, when the nut started moving more freely, that I'd really done it.

I climbed up on the sail bin and squinted out at the free world.

44

To the left all I could see was sky and a sparkle of sun on the water. I turned my head to the right and nearly fell off my perch. To the right there was a sail, and shining below it, green and rocky and moderately close, there was land.

I thought that if he came along at that moment to shut the hatch I would perversely be grateful.

Only desperation made me do what I did next, because I was sure that if he caught me in mid-escape he'd tie my hands and leave me in the dark on starvation rations.

The risk that I wouldn't get out unseen was appalling. My present conditions were just about bearable; my future afterwards wouldn't be.

Yet if I hadn't meant to risk it, why had I laboured so long on the nuts?

I went back to the loo and unscrewed the nuts completely. I knocked the bolts out, and pulled the whole lever free.

Without it, no one could flush the loo. I thought grimly that it would be an added complication if I found myself back in the cabin with it gone.

There was no sign of anyone on deck, and as usual I couldn't see if the boat was on automatic steering or whether there was anyone at the helm.

Hesitation was only in my mind. Looking back, it seemed as if I did everything very fast.

I pulled the hinged props of the hatch down inside the cabin, which one would do in the normal way if one wanted to shut the hatch oneself from the inside. This had the effect of slackening the guy-rope action of the chains crossed over the top.

Through the much reduced gap, little more than a slit, I poked the lever, aiming at where a link of chain was hooked over the top.

Long hours of inspection had given me the impression that those chains had no other fastening. Putting a link over the hook of the cleat must have seemed safe enough, because they were certain I had no means of dislodging them. I stuck the lever into the chain on the right, wedged it securely, and pushed. With almost miraculous elegance the whole chain slid loosely outwards, and the link fell off the cleat.

Without pausing for anything but mental hip-hoorays I

applied the lever again, this time to where the fore and aft chain was fastened on the bow side. Again, with no more fuss, the link slid off.

I was committed. I couldn't get the chains back on again. I had to open the hatch now, and climb out. There was no retreat.

I took the lever with me as a last resort against recapture, putting it out first onto the deck. Then with both hands I released the hatch from the hinged props and pushed it wide. Eased it down gently until it lay flat, fearing to let it crash open and bring them running.

I snaked out onto the deck on my stomach. Rolled to the right, under the jib sail. Reached the railing, grabbed it with both hands, and bunny-hopped fast over the side, going down into the sea straight and feet first, like a pillar.

It wasn't the safest way of disembarking, but I survived it, staying down under the surface until my lungs protested. Surfacing was one of the most anxious moments of my life, but when I cautiously lifted mouth, nose and eyes above the water, there was the boat a hundred yards away, steadily sailing on.

With a great intake of air I sank down again and began to swim underwater towards the shore; gently, so as to make no notice-attracting splash.

The water was chilly, but not as cold as I'd expected. The shore, when I came up again, looked about a mile away, though distances at sea were deceptive.

The boat sailed on peacefully. It must have had a name on it, I supposed, though in the flurry I hadn't seen one. I wondered how long it would be before they found I had gone. Supper time, with luck.

The land ahead looked a most promising haven. To the left it was rocky, with grassy cliffs, but straight ahead lay a much greener part, with houses and hotels, and a strip of sand. Civilization, hot baths, freedom and a razor. I swam towards them steadily, taking rests. A mile was a long way for a moderate swimmer, and I was nothing like as strong as I had been twelve days earlier.

I looked back at the boat. It had gone a good way along the coast: growing smaller.

The big mainsail was sagging down the mast.

46

God, I thought, my heart lurching, if they're taking down the sails they'll see the open hatch.

Time had run out. They knew I had gone.

I ploughed for the shore until I felt dizzy with the effort. Swam until I had grey dots before the eyes and even greyer dots in the mind.

I wasn't going back into that dark hole. I absolutely couldn't.

When I next looked back all the sails were down and the boat was turning.

The hotels ahead were in a sandy bay. Two big hotels, white, with rows of balconies, and a lot of smaller buildings all around. There were some people on the beach, and four or five standing in the water.

Five hundred yards, perhaps.

It would take me years to swim five hundred yards.

I pushed my absolutely useless muscles into frantic efforts. If I could only reach the other bathers, I would be just one more head.

The boat had not been travelling very fast under sail. They would motor back faster. I feared to look around; to see them close. My imagination heard him shouting and pointing, and steering the boat to intercept me, felt them grabbing me with boathooks and pulling me in. When in the end I did nerve myself for a look, it was bad enough, but still too far to distinguish anyone clearly.

Next time I looked, it was alarming. They were catching up like hares. The nearest point of land was still about three hundred yards away, and it was uneven rock, not easy shelving beach. The sand lay in the centre of the bay: the curving arms were shallow cliffs. I would never reach the sand, I thought.

And yet . . . sailing boats had deep keels. They wouldn't be able to motor right up to the beach. Perhaps, after all, I could get there.

I had never felt so tired, so leaden. The hardest steeplechase had never demolished me so completely, even those I'd lost from being unfit. My progress through the water grew slower and slower, when speed was all that mattered. In the end it took me all my time to stay afloat.

There was a current, which I hadn't noticed at first, carrying me to the left, drifting me off my line to the beach. Nothing fierce; but simply sapping. I hadn't enough kick left to overcome it.

Another look back.

Literally terrifying. I could see him on deck, standing in the bows, shading his eyes with his hand. He had come back on a course closer to the shore than when I'd jumped, and it was the shoreline he seemed to be scouring most closely.

I swam on with feeble, futile strokes. I could see that I was not going to reach the sand. The current was taking me inexorably towards the higher, left hand side of the bay, where there were trees to within ten feet of the waterline, and rocks below the trees.

When I'd got to the numb stage of thinking drowning would be preferable to recapture, and doubting if one *could* drown oneself in cold blood, I found suddenly that I could no longer see for miles along the coast. I had at last got within the embracing arms of the bay. When I looked back, I couldn't see the boat.

It didn't stay out of sight long. It crept along in a straight line until it reached the centre of the bay, and there dropped anchor. I watched it in sick glimpses over my shoulder. Saw them unbuckle a black rubber dinghy and lower it over the side. Caught an impression of them lowering an outboard engine, and oars, and of two of them climbing down into the boat.

I heard the outboard splutter into life. Only about thirty feet to go to touch the land. It seemed like thirty miles.

There was a man-made strip of concrete set into the rocks ahead of me at the water's edge. I glanced along the shore towards the beach, and saw that there were others. Aids to bathers. The most heartening aid in the world to the bather approaching at snail's pace with the hounds of hell at his back.

The dinghy pulled away from the anchored boat and pointed its bulky black shape towards the shore.

I reached the strip of concrete. It was a flat step, set only inches above the water.

No grips for hauling oneself out. Just a step. I put one hand flat on it and raised a foot to it, and used jelly muscles to flounder up onto my stomach.

Not enough. Not enough. The dinghy would come while I was lying there.

My heart was pounding. Effort and fear in equal measures. Utter desperation took me to hands and knees and set me crawling up the rocks to find shelter.

Ordinarily it would have been easy. It was a gentle shore, undemanding. A child could have jumped where I laboured. I climbed up about six feet of tumbled rocks and found a shallow gully, half full of water. I rolled into the hollow and lay there panting, hopelessly exhausted, listening to the outboard engine grow steadily louder.

They must have seen me, I thought despairingly. Seen me climbing up out of the sea. Yet if I'd stayed at the water's edge they would have found me just as surely. I lay in defeated misery and wondered how on earth I could live through whatever was coming.

The dinghy approached. I kept my head down. They were going to have to come and find me and carry me, and if I could raise enough breath I'd yell until some of the people on the beach took notice, except that they were far enough away to think it was all a game.

The engine died and I heard his voice, raised but not exactly shouting.

He said, 'Excuse me, but have you seen a friend of ours swim in from the sea? We think he fell overboard.'

A woman's voice answered him, from so close to me that I almost fainted.

'No, I haven't seen anybody.'

He said, 'He takes drugs. He might have been acting funny.'

'Serves him right, then,' she said, sanctimoniously. 'I've been reading. I haven't seen him. Have you come from that boat?'

'That's right. We think he fell overboard about here. We heard a splash, but we thought it was just a fish. Till after.'

'Sorry,' she said. 'Why don't you ask along the beach.'

'Just starting this side,' he said. 'We'll work round.'

There was a noise of oars being fitted into rowlocks, and the splash and squeak as they pulled away. I stayed where I was without moving, hoping she wouldn't have hysterics when she saw me, dreading that she would call them back.

I could hear him, away along the shore, loudly asking the same question of someone else.

Her voice said, 'Don't be frightened. I know you're there.'

I didn't answer her. She'd taken away what was left of my breath.

After a pause she said, 'Do you take drugs?'

'No,' I said. It was little more than a whisper.

'What did you say?'

'No.'

'Hm. Well, you'd better not move. They're methodical. I think I'll go on reading.'

Incredulously, I took her advice, lying half in and half out of the water, feeling heart and lungs subside slowly to a more manageable rhythm.

'They've landed on the beach,' she said.

My heart stirred up again. 'Are they searching?' I said anxiously.

'No. Asking questions, I should think.' She paused. 'Are they criminals?'

'I don't know.'

'But . . . would they take you from here by force? With people watching?'

'Yes. You heard them. If I shouted for help, they'd say I was crazy with drugs. No one would stop them.'

'They're walking round the far side of the bay,' she said. 'Asking people.'

'My name is Roland Britten,' I said. 'I live in Newbury, and I'm an accountant. I was kidnapped twelve days ago, and they've kept me on that boat ever since, and I don't know why. So please, whoever you are, if they do manage to get me back there, will you tell the police? I really do most desperately need help.'

There was a short silence. I thought that I must have over-done it; that she didn't believe me. Yet I'd had to tell her, as a precaution.

She apparently made up her mind. 'Well then,' she said briskly, 'time for you to vanish '

'Where to?'

'My bedroom,' she said.

She was a great one for punches in the mental solar plexus. In spite of the grimness of things in general, I almost laughed.

'Can you see me?' I said.

'I can see your feet. I saw all of you when you climbed out of the sea and scrambled up here.'

'And how do I get to your bedroom dressed in a wet shirt and underpants and nothing else?'

'Do you want to avoid those men, or don't you?'

There was no answer to that.

'Stay still,' she said sharply, though I had not in fact moved. 'They're looking this way. Someone over there seems to be pointing in this direction.'

'Oh God.'

'Stay still.' There was a longish pause, then she said, 'They are walking back along the beach, towards their boat. If they don't stop there, but come on this way, we will go.'

I waited dumbly, and more or less prayed.

'There's a path above us,' she said. 'I will hand you a towel. Wrap it round you, and climb up to the path.'

'Are they coming?'

'Yes.'

A triangle of brightly striped bathing towel appeared over the rock by my head. There was little I'd ever wanted to do less than stand up out of my secure hiding place. My nerves were all against it.

'Hurry up,' she said. 'Don't look back.'

I stood up, dripping, with my back to the sea. Pulled the towel towards me, wrapped it round like a sarong, and tackled the rocky upgrade to the path. The respite in the gully had given me back a surprising amount of energy: or perhaps it was plain fear. In any case I climbed the second stage a great deal more nimbly than the first.

'I'm behind you,' her voice said. 'Don't look back. Turn right when you reach the path. And don't run.'

'Yes ma'am,' I said under my breath. Never argue with a guardian angel.

The path was fringed on both sides with trees, with a mixture of sand and bare rock underfoot. The sunshine dappled through the branches and at any other time would have looked pretty.

When the path widened she fell into step beside me, between me and the sea.

'Take the branch path to the left,' she said, drawing level. 'And don't walk too fast.'

I glanced at her, curious to see what she looked like. She matched her voice: a no-nonsense middle-aged lady with spectacles and a practical air. Self-confident. Tall: almost six feet. Thin, and far from a beauty.

She was wearing a pale-pink blouse, fawn cotton trousers, and sandshoes, and she carried a capacious canvas beach bag.

Beach. Swimming. In March.

'Where is this place?' I said.

'Cala St Galdana.'

'Where's that?'

'Minorca, of course.'

'Where?'

'Don't stop walking. Minorca.'

'Island next to Majorca?'

'Of course.' She paused. 'Didn't you know?'

I shook my head. The branch path reached the top of a shallow gradient and began to descend through more trees on the far side.

She peered to the right as we went over the brow.

'Those men are just coming along the lower path, heading towards where I was sitting. I think it would be a good idea to hurry a little now, don't you?'

'Understatement,' I said.

Hurrying meant stubbing my bare toes on various half-buried stones and feeling the dismal weakness again make rubber of my legs.

'While they are looking for you on the rocks, we will reach my hotel,' she said.

I shuffled along and saved my breath. Glanced over my shoulder. Only empty path. No pursuing furies. So why did I feel that they could see through earth and trees and know exactly where to find me?

'Over that little bridge, and across the road. Over there.' She pointed. 'That's the hotel.'

It was one of the two big white ones. We reached the wide

glass doors and went inside. Made it unchallenged across the hall and into the lift. Rose to the fifth floor. She scooped some keys out of her beach bag, and let us into 507.

We had seen almost nobody on the way. Still enough warm sun for holidaymakers to be out on the beach and for the staff to be sleeping.

507 had a sea-view balcony, twin beds, two armchairs, a yellow carpet, and orange and brown curtains. Regulation hotel room, with almost none of my saviour's belongings in sight.

She walked over to the glass door, which was wide open, and half stepped onto the balcony.

'Do you want to watch?' she said.

I looked cautiously over her shoulder. From that height one could see the whole panorama of the bay. There was the boat, anchored in the centre. There was the dinghy on the sand. The headland where I'd crawled out of the sea was to the right, the path leading to it from the beach showing clearly through the trees like a dappled yellow snake.

Along the path came the two men, my familiar warder in front, making for the sand. They trudged slowly across to the dinghy, still looking continually around, and pushed it into the sea.

They both climbed in. They started the outboard. They steered away from the beach.

I felt utterly drained.

'Do you mind if I sit down?' I said.

6

Thanks to telephones, consul, bank, and friends, I flew back to England the following evening, but not before I had collected further unforgettable memories of Miss Hilary Margaret Pinlock.

She asked me my measurements, descended to the local boutiques, and returned with new clothes.

She lent me her bathroom, inspected me cleaned and dressed,

and decided to go shopping for a razor. I protested. She went. It was as easy to stop Miss Pinlock as an avalanche.

With some relief I scratched the twelve days' scruffy dark stubble off my face, one glance in the looking glass having persuaded me that I was not going to look better in a beard. The twelve days of indoor life had left me thin and pale, with grey hollows in cheeks and eye sockets which I didn't remember having before. Nothing that a little freedom wouldn't fix.

On her second expedition she had also bought bread, cheese and fruit, explaining that she was there on a package holiday, and that the hotel didn't cater for random visitors.

'I'll go down to dinner at seven as usual,' she said. 'You can eat here.'

Throughout all her remarks and actions ran the positive decision-making of one accustomed to command.

'Are you a children's nurse?' I asked curiously.

'No,' she said, unsmiling. 'A headmistress.'

'Oh.'

The smile came, briefly. 'Of a girls-only comprehensive, in Surrey.'

With a touch of sardonic humour she watched me reassess her in the light of that revelation. Not a do-gooding bossy spinster, but a fulfilled career woman of undoubted power.

'Yes. Well . . .' she shrugged. 'If you give me the numbers, I'll ask the switchboard for your calls.'

'And I need a bedroom,' I said.

'Your friends might return and ask about strangers needing bedrooms,' she said.

It had occurred to me too. 'Yes, but . . .' I said.

She pointed to one of the twin beds. 'You can sleep there. I am here alone. The friend who was coming with me had to cry off at the last minute.'

'But . . .' I stopped.

She waited calmly.

'All right,' I said. 'Thank you.'

When she returned from dinner she brought with her a piece of news and a bottle of wine.

'Your friend from the boat was downstairs in the lobby, asking everyone who speaks English if they saw a crazy young man

54

come ashore today. Everyone said no. He looks extremely worried.'

'Probably thinks I drowned.'

The boat had gone from the bay. He must have reached another mooring and returned to Cala St Galdana by road. I wondered how long and how thoroughly he would persevere in his search: the more he feared whoever he was working for, the less he would give up.

The evening air was chilly. Miss Pinlock shut the glass door against the night sky and expertly opened her bottle of Marqués de Riscal.

'Tell me about your journey,' she said, handing me a glass.

I told her the beginning and the end, and not much of the middle.

'Extraordinary,' she said.

'When I get home I'll have a go at finding out what it was all about . . .'

She looked at me gravely. 'It may not be over.'

She had an uncomfortable habit of putting my worst fears into speech.

We drank the excellent wine and she told me a little of her busy life.

'I enjoy it,' she said positively.

'Yes, I see that.'

There was a pause. She looked carefully at the wine in her glass.

She said, 'Will you go to bed with me?'

I suppose I sat in an ungentlemanly heap with my mouth open. I closed it, conscious of the insult it conveyed.

When I'd got over the first shock, she looked up. Her face was calm and businesslike as before, but also suddenly there was vulnerability and self-consciousness. A blush started on her neck, and spread painfully upwards.

She was between forty-two and forty-six, I guessed. She had dark brown wavy hair, going grey, cut with shape but not much style. A broad, lined forehead, large nose, mouth turning down naturally at the corners, and small chin. Behind her glasses her eyes were brown and looked small, probably the effect of the lenses. Wrinkles grew where wrinkles grow; and there was no glow to her skin. A face of character, but not sexually attractive, at least not to me.

'Why?' I said, which was a pretty stupid question.

She blushed a little deeper and shook her head.

'Look,' I said, 'it isn't as simple as that. I can't . . . I mean, one can't just sort of switch that sort of thing on and off, like a tap.'

We sat in awkward silence. She put down her glass, and said, 'I'm sorry. It was a ridiculous thing to say. Please try and forget it.'

'You said it because it was in your mind. So . . . well . . . you must have meant it.'

She half smiled, ruefully. 'It's been in my mind, now and again, for a long time. You will find it extraordinary, but I have never . . . so to speak, slept with a man.'

'In this permissive age?' I said.

'There you are, you see. You find it hard to believe. But I've never been pretty, even as a child. And also I've always been, well . . . able to do things. Learn. Teach. Organize. Administrate. All the unfeminine things. All my life people have relied on me, because I was capable. I've always had health and energy, and I've enjoyed getting on, being given senior posts, and five years ago, being offered a headship. In most ways my life has been absorbing and gratifyingly successful.'

'But?' I suggested.

She nodded. 'But. I was never interested in boys when I was in my teens, and then I thought them callow, and at university I worked all hours to get a First, and after that I've always taught in girls' schools because frankly it is usually a man who's given the headship in a mixed school, and I've never fancied the role of male-ego-massager in second place. Nothing I've ever been or done has been geared to romance.'

'So why *now*?'

'I hope you won't be angry, but it is mostly curiosity, and the pursuit of knowledge.'

I wasn't angry. Just astounded.

Her blush had subsided as fast as it had risen. She was back on surer ground.

'For some time I've thought I ought to have had the experience. Of sexual intercourse, that is. It didn't come my way when I was young, but I didn't expect it, you see. I think now that I should have tried to find a man, but then, when I was at college, I was half scared of it, and I didn't have any great urge, and I was engrossed in my work. Afterwards for years it didn't bother me, until I was thirty or so, and of course by that time all the men one meets are married, and in any case, teaching among women, one rarely meets any men, except officials, and so on. I go to many official functions, of course, but people tend not to ask unmarried women to private social occasions.'

'What changed your mind?' I asked, fascinated.

'Oh, having to cope with highly-sexed young girls. The modern lot are so clued up. So brash and outspoken. I like them. But I have to arrange their sex-education lessons, and in my time I've even taught them, from text books. I feel it would be a great deal better if I knew . . . what the sex act felt like. I feel at a disadvantage with many of the older girls, particularly as this last term I had to advise a pregnant fourteen-year-old. Fourteen! She knows more than I do. How can I advise her?'

'Catholic priests don't have this problem,' I commented.

'Catholic priests may be respected for virginity, but schoolmistresses are not.' She paused, hesitating, and went on. 'To be honest, I also find myself at a disadvantage with the married members of my staff. Some of them have a tendency to patronize me, even unconsciously. I don't like it. I would be able to cope with it perfectly, though, if I actually knew what they know.'

'Am I,' I said slowly, 'the first man you have asked?'

'Oh yes.' She smiled slightly and drank some wine. 'There are practically no men one *can* ask. Especially if one is a headmistress, and widely known. I certainly wouldn't jeopardize my job.'

'I can see that it would be difficult,' I said, thinking about it.

'So of course holidays are the only possibility,' she said. 'I've been on archaeological cruises to Greece, and all that sort of thing, and I've seen other couples join up, but it never happened to me. And then I've heard that some lonely women throw themselves at ski-instructors and waiters and men who perform for money, but somehow that isn't what I want. I mean, I don't want to despise myself. I want knowledge without guilt or shame.'

57

'The dream of Eden,' I said.

'What? Oh, yes.'

'What about your friend?' I said, pointing to the second bed. She smiled twistedly. 'No friend, just an excuse for having come alone.'

'Friends being death to the pursuit of knowledge?'

'Exactly.'

We drank some more wine.

'I've been here since last Saturday,' she said. 'I always take a complete break straight after the end of term, and then go back refreshed for the new work.'

'A perfect system,' I said absently. 'Why didn't you ... er ... throw me back, when the men in the dinghy came after me?'

'If you mean, did I immediately see you as a ... *possible* ... then no, of course not. I was fascinated, in a way. I'd never seen anyone in such terror before. I watched you from quite a long way out. Swimming, and looking back. It wasn't until you reached the concrete step, though, and I saw your face clearly, that I realized that you were being *hunted*. It would take a certain mentality to point the hounds at an exhausted quarry gone to ground, and I don't have it.'

'And thank God for that,' I said.

I stood up, and opened the glass door, and went out onto the balcony. The cool night was clear, with bright stars over the ageless Mediterranean. Waves rippled softly round the edges of the bay, and the gentle moonlight shone on the wide, empty expanse where the boat had been anchored.

It was the weirdest of debts. She had saved me from recapture. I certainly owed her my wholeness of mind, if not life itself. If the only payment she wanted was something I didn't much want to give, then that was simply too bad. One extreme favour, I thought sardonically, deserved another.

I went in, and sat down. Drank some wine with a dry mouth.

'We'll try, if you like,' I said.

She sat very still. I had a swift impression that now I'd agreed she was hastily retreating: that the half-fear of her student days was definitely still there.

'You don't have to,' she said.

'No. I want to.' Heaven forgive all liars.

58

She said, as if speaking to herself, and not to me: 'I'll never have another chance.'

The voice of longing teetering on the brink of the leap in the dark. Her strength of mind, I saw, would carry her through. I admired her. I determined to make Hilary Pinlock's leap something that at least she wouldn't regret: if I could.

'First of all,' I said, 'we'll switch off the lights and sit by the window for a while, and talk about it.'

We sat facing each other in dim reflected moonlight, and I asked her some fairly medical questions, to which she gave straightforward replies.

'What if you get pregnant?' I said.

'I'd solve that later.'

'You want to go ahead?'

She took a deep breath. 'If you do.'

If I *can*, I thought.

'Then I think the best thing to do first would be to get undressed,' I said. 'Do you have a nightdress? And could you lend me a dressing gown?'

I reflected, as I put on her blue candlewick in the privacy of the bathroom, that deep physical tiredness was a rotten basis for the matter in hand. I yawned. I wanted above all to go to sleep.

When I went out she was sitting by the window in a long cotton nightgown which had a frill round the neckline, but was not, of course, transparent.

'Come on,' I said. 'We'll sit on the bed.'

She stood up. The nightgown accentuated her height and thinness, and revealed long narrow feet. I pulled back the bedclothes, sat on the white sheet, and held my hand out towards her. She came, gripped my hand, and sat beside me.

'Right,' I said. 'Now, if at any point you want to stop, you've only got to say so.'

She nodded.

'Lie down, then,' I said, 'and imagine you are twenty.'

'Why?'

'Because this is not a brain matter. It's about the stimulation of nerve endings. About feeling, not thinking. If you think all the time of who you are, you may find it inhibiting. Age doesn't exist in the dark. If you imagine you are twenty, you will *be* twenty, and you'll find it liberating.'

'You're a most unusual man.'

'Oh sure,' I said. 'And you're a most unusual woman. So lie down.'

She gave a small unexpected chuckle, and did as I said.

'Take off your glasses,' I said, and she put them without comment on the bedside table. In the dim light her eyes looked larger, as I'd guessed, and her big nose smaller, and her determined mouth softer. I leaned over and kissed her lips, and if it was basically a nephew-to-aunt gesture it brought a smile to her face and a grin to my own.

It was the strangest love-making, but it did work. I looked back afterwards to the moment when she first took pleasure in the sensation of my stroking her skin; the ripple of surprise when she felt with her hands the size of an erect man; the passion with which she finally responded; and the stunning release into gasping incredulity.

'Is that,' she said, out of breath, 'is that what every woman feels?'

I knew she had reached a most satisfactory climax. 'I guess so,' I said. 'On good days.'

'Oh my goodness,' she said in a sort of exultation. 'So now I *know*.'

7

Thursday morning I went back to the office and tried to take up my life where it had left off.

The same smell of typewriters, filing cabinets, reams of paper. Same bustle, adding machines, telephones. Same heaps of too much work. All familiar, all unreal.

Our two assistants, Debbie and Peter, had had a rough time, they said aggrievedly, trying to account to everyone for my unaccountable absence. They had reported my disappearance to the police, who had said I was over twenty-one and had the right to duck out if I wanted to, and that they would look for me only if I'd committed a crime, or was clearly a missing victim. They had thought I had merely gone off on a celebratory binge after winning the Gold Cup.

'We told them you wouldn't have gone away for so long,' Peter said. 'But they didn't show much interest.'

'We wanted them to get in touch with Mr King, through Interpol,' Debbie complained. 'And they laughed at the idea.'

'I expect they would,' I said. 'So Trevor is still on his holiday?'

'He's not due back until Monday,' Peter said, surprised that I should have forgotten something I knew so well.

'Oh yes . . .'

I spent the morning re-organizing the time-table and getting Peter to make new appointments to replace those I'd missed, and the afternoon discovering that as far as the police were concerned, my troubles were still of little interest. I was back home, wasn't I? Unharmed. Without having to pay a ransom? Was there any form of extortion? No. Was I starved? No. Beaten? No. Tied with ropes, straps, shackles? No. Was I sure it wasn't a practical joke? They would look into it, they said: but one of them remarked that *he* wouldn't mind a free fortnight's trip to the Mediterranean, and his colleague laughed. I gathered that if I seriously wanted to get to know, I would have to do the investigating myself.

I did want to know. Not knowing felt dangerously unsafe, like standing behind a bad-tempered horse. If I didn't know why I'd been taken the first time, how was I to stop it happening again?

Thursday evening I collected my Dolomite, which had been moved to the Cheltenham racecourse manager's front drive. ('Where on earth have you been? We traced that it was your car through the police.') Next I drove to the house of the racecourse valet to pick up my wallet and keys and racing saddle. ('Where on earth have you been? I gave the racecourse manager your car keys, I hope that's all right.') Then I drove back to my cottage (having spent the previous night in an airport hotel), and with faint-hearted caution let myself in.

No one was waiting there in the dark, with coshes or ether or one-way tickets to sail lockers. I switched on all the lights and poured myself a stiff Scotch and told myself to calm down and take a better grip.

I telephoned to the trainer I regularly rode early morning exercise for ('Where on earth have you been?') and arranged to start again on Monday: and I rang a man who had asked me to ride in a hunter 'chase, to apologize for not turning up. I saw no reason not to answer the questions about where I'd been, so I told them all: abducted and taken on a boat to Minorca, and I didn't know why. I thought at least that someone might come up with a possible explanation, but everyone I told sounded as flummoxed as I felt.

There wasn't much food in the cottage, and the steak in the fridge had grown whiskers. I decided on spaghetti, with chopped up cheese melting on it, but before starting to cook I went upstairs to change new jacket for old sweater, and to make a detour to the bathroom.

I glanced casually out of the bathroom window and spent a frozen instant in pure panic.

There was a man in the garden, looking towards the downstairs rooms of the cottage. The light from the sitting-room window fell brightly on his face.

I hadn't consciously remembered him, but I knew him at once, in one heart-stopping flash of the inner eye. He was the fake St John's Ambulance man from Cheltenham races.

Behind him, in the road, stood a car, with gleams of light edging its roof and windows. A second man was levering himself out of the passenger's seat, carrying what looked like a plastic bag containing cotton wool. A third figure, dimly seen, was heading through the garden to the back of the house.

They couldn't, I thought: surely they couldn't think they would trick me again. But with three of them, they hardly needed tricks.

The St John's man waved his arm to the man by the car, and pointed, and the two of them took up positions, one on each side of my front door, out of sight of anyone opening it from the inside. The St John's man stretched out an arm and rang my bell.

I unfroze.

Wonderful how terror sharpened the wits. There was only

one place I could hide, and that was in my bedroom. The speed with which I'd gone over the side of the boat was nothing compared with my disappearance inside the cottage.

Downstairs in the sitting-room the huge old fireplace had at one side incorporated a bread-oven, which the people living there before me had removed, constructing instead a head-high alcove with display shelves. Wanting a safe place in which to keep valuables, they had opened the upper part of the bread-oven space into the bedroom above, where it formed a sort of box below the floor of the built-in wardrobe. Not having much in the way of valuables, I stored my two suitcases in there instead.

I opened the wardrobe door, and pulled up the hinged flap of flooring, and hauled out the cases.

The door bell rang again, insistently.

Lowering myself into the space took seconds, and I had the wardrobe door shut and the flap of floor almost in place when they burst in through the front door.

They rampaged through the place, opening and slamming doors, and shouting, and finally gathering all together downstairs.

'He must be bloody here.'

'Britten! Britten, come out, we know you're here.'

'The effing bastard's scarpered.'

I could hear every loud word through the chipboard partition between my hiding place and the sitting-room. It felt horribly vulnerable sitting there, level with the picture over the mantelshelf, practically in the room with them, hidden only by a thin piece of wall.

'He couldn't have seen us coming.'

'He never got out of the back, I'll tell you that for sure.'

'Then where the bleeding hell is he?'

'How about those suitcases of his upstairs?'

'No. He ain't in them. They're too small. And I looked.'

'He must be meaning to bleeding scarper.'

'Yeah.'

'Take another butcher's upstairs. He must be here somewhere.'

They searched the whole house again, crashing about with heavy boots.

One of them opened the wardrobe above me for the second time, and saw nothing but clothes, as before. I sat under their feet and sweated, and felt my pulse shoot up to the hundreds.

'Look under the bed,' he said.

'Can't. The bed's right on the floor.

'How about the other bedroom, then?'

'I looked. He ain't there.'

'Well, bleeding well look again.'

The wardrobe door closed above me. I wiped the sweat out of my eyes and tried to ease my legs without scraping my shoes on the wall and making a noise. I was half sitting, half lying, in a recess about three feet long by two feet deep, and just wide enough for my shoulders. My knees were bent acutely, with my heels against the backs of my thighs. It was a bad position for every muscle I could think of.

Two of them came into the sitting-room, one after the other.

'What you got there? Here, let me see.'

'None of your bleeding business.'

'It's his wallet. You've got his wallet.'

'Yeah. Well, it was in his bedroom.'

'Well, bleeding well put it back.'

'Not likely, he's got thirty quid in it.'

'You'll effing well do as I say. You know the orders, same as I do. Don't steal nothink, don't break nothink. I told you.'

'You can have half, then.'

'Give it to me. I'll put it back. I don't trust you.' It was the St John's man talking, I thought.

'It's bloody stupid, not nicking what we can get.'

'You want the fuzz on our necks? They didn't bloody look for him last time, and they won't bloody look for him this time, either, but they will if they find his place has been turned over. Use your bloody loaf.'

'We ain't got him yet.'

'Matter of time. He's round here some place. Bound to be.'

'He won't come back if he sees us in here.'

'No, you got a point there. Tell you what, we'll turn the lights off and wait for him, and jump him, like.'

'He left all the lights on, himself. He won't come in if they're— off.'

'Best if one of us waits in the kitchen, like, and the other two in the garden. Then when he gets here we can jump him from both sides, right, just as he's coming back through the door.'

'Yeah.'

Into these plans there suddenly came a fresh voice, female and enquiring.

'Mr Britten? Mr Britten, are you there?'

I heard her push the front door open and take the step into the sitting-room.

The voice of my next-door neighbour.

Yes, Mrs Morris, I'm here, I thought. And it would take more than me and a small plump senior citizen to fight off my unwanted guests.

'Who are you?' she said.

'Friends of his. Calling on him, like.'

'He's away,' she said sharply.

'No he's not. He's back. His car's round the side. And he's having a drink, see? Whisky.'

'Then where is he? Mr Britten?' she called.

'Ain't no use, lady. He's out. We're waiting for him, like.'

'I don't think you should be in here.' A brave lady, old Mrs Morris.

'We're friends of his, see.'

'You don't look like his friends,' she said.

'Know his friends, then, do yer?'

A certain nervousness crept into her voice, but the resolution was still there.

'I think you'd better wait ouside.'

There was a pause, then the St John's man said, 'Where do you think he could be? We've searched all over for him.'

Let her not know about this hiding place, I prayed. Let her not think of it.

'He might've gone to the pub,' she said. 'Why don't you go down there? To the Fox.'

'Yeah, maybe.'

'Anyway, I think I'll just see you out.'

Intrepid little Mrs Morris. I heard them all go out, and shut the front door behind them. The lock clicked decisively. The cottage was suddenly still.

I lay quiet, listening for their car to start.

Nothing happened.

They were still there, I thought. Outside. Round my house. Waiting.

On the mantelshelf, the clock ticked.

I cautiously pushed up the flap over my head, and sat up, straightening knees, back and neck, with relief.

The light in my bedroom was still on, shining in a crack under the wardrobe door. I left the door shut. If they saw so much as a shadow move they would know for sure I was inside the house.

I reflected that I had had a good deal too much practice at passing uncertain hours in small dark places.

The lock clicked on my front door.

One gets to know the noises of one's own house so well that sight is unnecessary for interpretation. I heard the unmistakeable sound of the hinges, and the gritty sound of a shoe on the bare flagstones of the entrance hall. Then there were quiet noises in the sitting-room itself, and low voices, and the squeak of the door to the kitchen. They had come back in a way that would not bring Mrs Morris.

I sat rigidly, wondering whether to slide down into the smaller space and risk them hearing my movements, or stay with head and shoulders above floor level and risk them searching my clothes cupboard yet again. If I coughed or sneezed, or as much as knocked the chipboard with my elbow as I slid down into the safer hiding place, they would hear me. I sat immobile, stretching my own ears and wondering despairingly how long they would stay.

Breathing evenly was difficult, controlling my heartbeat was impossible. Acute anxiety over a period of hours was highly shattering to the nerves.

From time to time I could hear them moving and murmuring, but could no longer distinctly hear their words. I supposed that they too were hiding, waiting out of sight for me to come home. It was almost funny when one thought of it: them hiding behind the furniture and me within the walls.

Unfunny if they found me. More like unfaceable.

I took a deep, shaky breath, one of many.

Someone began to come quietly upstairs. The familiar creaks of the old treads fizzed through my body like electric shocks. The risk of moving had to be taken. I tucked my elbows in and bent my knees, and eased myself back under the floor. The flap came down hard on my hair and I thought wildly that they must have heard it: but no one arrived with triumphant shouts, and the awful suspense just went on and on.

I got pains from being bent up, and I got cramps, but there was nothing I could do about that except surrender.

One of them spent a good time in my bedroom. I could hear his footfall through the floorboards, and the small thuds of drawers shutting. Guessed he was no longer looking for me, but at what I owned. It didn't make his nearness to me any safer.

The fear seemed endless; but everything ends. I heard them murmuring again in the sitting-room, and shutting the kitchen door. The man upstairs went down again. More murmurings: a chorus. Then silence for a while. Then a step or two in the hall, and the click of the front door closing.

I waited, thinking that only one of them had gone out.

Their car started. Shifted quietly into gear. Drove off.

I still lay without moving, not trusting that it was over, that it wasn't a trick: but the absolute quietness persisted, and in the end I pushed up the flap of the floor and levered myself with much wincing and pins-and-needles onto my bedroom carpet.

The lights were still on, but the black square of window was grey. The whole night had passed. It was dawn.

I threw a few things into one of the suitcases and left the cottage ten minutes later.

The Yale lock on the front door showed no signs of forcing, and I guessed they must have opened it with a credit card, as I myself had done once when I'd locked myself out. My car stood untouched where I'd left it, and even my half-drunk glass of Scotch was still on the sitting-room table.

Feeling distinctly unsettled I had a wash, shave and breakfast at the Chequers Hotel, and then went to the police.

'Back again?' they said.

They listened, made notes, asked questions.

'Do you know who they were?'

'No.'

'Any evidence of a forced entry?'

'No.'

'Anything stolen?'

'No.'

'Nothing we can do, sir.'

'Look,' I said, 'these people are trying to abduct me. They've succeeded once, and they're trying again. Can't you do a damn thing to help?'

They seemed fairly sympathetic, but the answer was no. They hadn't enough men or money to mount a round-the-clock guard on anyone for an indefinite period without a very good reason.

'Isn't the threat of abduction a very good reason?'

'No. If you believe the threat, you could hire yourself a private bodyguard.'

'Thanks very much,' I said. 'But if anyone reports me missing again, I won't have gone by choice, and you might do me a favour and start looking.'

'If they do, sir, we will.'

I went to the office and sat at my desk and watched my hands shake. Whatever I normally had in the way of mental and physical stamina was at a very low ebb.

Peter came in with a cable and his usual expression of not quite grasping the point, and handed me the bad news. CAR BROKEN DOWN RETURNING WEDNESDAY APOLOGIES TREVOR.

'You read this?' I asked Peter.

'Yes.'

'Well, you'd better fetch Mr King's list, for next week, and his appointment book.'

He went on the errand and I sat and looked blankly at the cable. Trevor had sent it from some town I'd never heard of in France, and had given no return address. He wouldn't be worried, wherever he was. He would be sure I could take his extra few days in my stride.

Peter came back with the list and I laced my fingers together to keep them still. What did people take for tranquillizers?

'Get me some coffee,' I said to Peter. His eyebrows rose. 'I know it's only a quarter past nine,' I said, 'but get me some coffee . . . please.'

When he brought the coffee I sent him to fetch Debbie, so that I could share between them the most urgent jobs. Neither of them had a good brain, but they were both persistent, meticulous plodders, invaluable qualities in accountants' assistants. In many offices the assistants were bright and actively studying to become accountants themselves, but Trevor for some reason seemed always to prefer working with the unambitious sort. Peter was twenty-two, Debbie twenty-four. Peter, I thought, was a latent homosexual who hadn't quite realized it. Debbie, mousy-haired, big-busted, and pious, had a boyfriend working in a hardware shop. Peter occasionally made jokes about screws, which shocked her.

They sat opposite my desk with notebooks poised, both of them looking at me with misgiving.

'You really look awfully ill,' Debbie said. 'Worse even than yesterday. Grey, sort of.' There seemed to be more ghoulish relish in her voice than concern.

'Yes, well, never mind that,' I said. 'I've looked at Mr King's list, and there are a few accounts that won't wait until he gets back.' There were two he should have seen to before he went, but no one was perfect. 'Certificate for the solicitors, Mr Crest, and Mr Grant. I'm afraid they are already overdue. Could you bring all the papers for those two in here, Debbie? Later, I mean. Not this instant. Then there are the two summonses to appear before the Commissioners next Thursday. I'll apply for postponements for those, but you'd better bring all the books in here, Debbie, anyway, and I'll try and make a start on them.'

'That's the Axwood stables, is it? And Millrace Stud?'

'Not the stud; that's the week after. Mr King can deal with that. The Axwood stables, yes, and those corn merchants, Coley Young.'

'The Coley Young books aren't here yet,' Peter said.

'Well, for crying out loud, didn't you do what I said two weeks ago, and tell them to send them?' I could hear the scratch in my voice and did my best to stop it. 'OK,' I said slowly. 'Did you ask them to send them?'

'Yes, I did.' Peter tended to look sulky. 'But they haven't come.'

'Ring them again, would you? And what about the Axwood stables?'

'You checked those yourself, if you remember.'

'Did I?' I looked back as if to a previous existence. The two summonses to appear before the Commissioners were not particularly serious. We seldom actually went. The summonses were issued when the Inland Revenue thought a particular set of accounts were long overdue: a sort of goad to action. It meant that Trevor or I asked for a postponement, did the accounts, and sent them in before the revised date. End of drama. The two summonses in question had arrived after Trevor had left for his holidays, which was why he hadn't dealt with them himself.

'You said the petty cash book hadn't arrived,' Peter said.

'Did I? Did you ask them to send it?'

'Yes, I did, but it hasn't come.'

I sighed. 'Ring them again.'

A great many clients saw no urgency at all in getting their accounts done, and requests from us for further information or relevant papers were apt to be ignored for weeks.

'Tell them both they really will have to go before the Commissioners if they don't send those books.'

'But they won't really, will they?' Peter said. Not the brightest of boys, I thought.

'I'll get adjournments anyway,' I said patiently, 'but Trevor will need those books to hand the second he gets back.'

Debbie said, 'Mr Wells rang three times yesterday afternoon.'

'Who is Mr Wells? Oh yes. Mr Wells.'

'He says one of his creditors is applying to have him made bankrupt and he wants to know what you're going to do about it.'

I'd forgotten all the details of Mr Wells' troubles. 'Where are his books?' I asked.

'In one of those boxes,' Debbie said, pointing. A three-high row of large cardboard boxes ran along the wall under the window. Each box had the name of the client on it, in large black letters, and each contained the cash books, invoices, receipts, ledgers, paying-in books, bank statements, petty cash records, stocktakings and general paraphernalia needed for the assessment of taxes. Each of the boxes represented a task I had yet to do.

It took me an average of two working days to draw up the annual accounts for each client. Some audits took longer. I had roughly two hundred clients. The thing was impossible.

Trevor had collared the bigger firms and liked to spend nearly a week on each. He dealt with seven clients. No wonder Commissioners' summonses fell on us like snow.

Peter and Debbie did most of the routine work, checking bank statements against cheque numbers, and against invoices paid. Someone extra to share that work would only help Trevor and me to a certain extent. Taking a third, fully equal partner would certainly reduce the pressure, but it would also entail dividing the firm's profits into three instead of two, which would mean a noticeable drop in income. Trevor was totally opposed. Amalgamation with the London firm meant Trevor not being boss and me not going racing . . . a fair sized impasse, all in all.

'Debbie and I didn't get our pay cheques last week,' Peter said. 'Nor did Bess.' Bess was the typist.

'And the water-heater in the washroom is running cold,' Debbie added. 'And you did say I could go to the dentist this afternoon at three-thirty.'

'Sorry about all the extra work,' Peter said, not sounding it, 'but I'm afraid it's my Friday for the Institute of Accounting Staff class.'

'Mm,' I said. 'Peter, telephone to Leyhill Prison and ask if Connaught Powys is still there.'

'What?'

'Leyhill Prison. Somewhere in Gloucestershire. Get the number from directory enquiries.'

'But . . . '

'Just go and do it,' I said. 'Connaught Powys. Is he still there.'

He went out looking mystified, but then he, like Debbie, dated from after the searchingly difficult court case. Debbie went to fetch the first batch of the papers I needed, and I began on the solicitors' certificates.

Since embezzlement of clients' trust monies had become a flourishing industry, laws had been passed to ensure that auditors checked every six months to see that the cash and securities which were supposed to be in a solicitor's care, actually were there. If they weren't, Nemesis swiftly struck the solicitor off the Roll. If they were, the auditor signed the certificate and pocketed his fee.

Peter returned as if he'd come from a dangerous mission, looking noble.

'The prison said he was released six weeks ago, on February 16th.'

'Thanks.'

'I had a good deal of trouble in getting through.'

'Er . . . well done,' I said. He still looked as if he thought more praise was due, but he didn't get it.

If Connaught Powys had been out for six weeks, he would have had a whole month to fix me up with a voyage. I tried hard to concentrate on the checking for the certificates but the sail locker kept getting in the way.

Solicitor Grant's affair tallied at about the third shot, but I kept making errors with Denby Crest's. I realized I'd always taken clarity of mind for granted, like walking: one of those things you don't consciously value until you've lost it. Numbers, from my infancy, had been like a second language, understood without effort. I checked Denby Crest's figures five times and kept getting a fifty thousand pounds' discrepancy, and knowing him, as he occasionally did work for us, it was ridiculous. Denby Crest was no crook, I thought in exasperation. It's my useless muddle-headed thought processes. Somewhere I was transposing a decimal point, making a mountain out of a molehill discrepancy of probably five pounds or fifty pence.

In the end I telephoned his office and asked to speak to him.

'Look, Denby,' I said, 'I'm most awfully sorry, but are you sure we've got all the relevant papers?'

'I expect so,' he said, sounding impatient. 'Why don't you leave it for Trevor? He gets back to England tomorrow, doesn't he?'

I explained about the broken-down car. 'He won't be back in the office until Wednesday or Thursday.'

'Oh.' He sounded disconcerted and there was a perceptible pause. 'All the same,' he said, 'Trevor is used to our ways. Please leave our certificate until he gets back.'

'But it's overdue,' I said.

'Tell Trevor to call me,' he said. 'And now, I'm sorry, but I have a client with me. So if you'll excuse me . . .'

He disconnected. I shuffled his papers together thankfully and thought that if he wanted to risk waiting for Trevor it was certainly all right by me.

At twelve-thirty Peter and Debbie went out to lunch, but I didn't feel hungry. I sat in shirtsleeves before the newly tackled sea of Mr Wells' depressing papers: put my elbows on the desk, and propped my forehead on the knuckles of my right hand, and shut my eyes. Thought a lot of rotten thoughts and wondered about buying myself a one-way ticket to Antarctica.

A voice said, 'Are you ill, asleep or posing for Rodin?'

I looked up, startled.

She was standing in the doorway. Young, fair, slender pretty.

'I'm looking for Trevor,' she said.

One couldn't have everything, I supposed.

8

'Don't I know you?' I said, puzzled, standing up.

'Sure.' She looked resigned, as if this sort of thing happened often. 'Cast your mind back to long hair, no lipstick, dirty jeans and ponies.'

I looked at the short bouncy bob, the fashionable make-up, the swirling brown skirt topped by a neat waist-length fur-fabric jacket. Someone's daughter, I thought; recently and satisfactorily grown up.

'Whose daughter?' I said.

'My own woman.'

'Reasonable.'

She was enjoying herself, pleased with her impact on men.

'Jossie Finch, actually.'

'Wow,' I said.

'Every grub spreads its wings.'

'To where will you fly?'

'Yes,' she said, 'I've heard you were smooth.'

'Trevor isn't here, I'm afraid.'

'Mm. Still on his hols?'

I nodded.

'Then I was to deliver the same message to you, if you were here instead.'

'Sit down?' I suggested, gesturing to a chair.

'Can't stop. Sorry. Message from Dad. What are you doing about the Commissioners? He said he was absolutely not going before any so-and-so Commissioners next Thursday, or lurid words to that effect.'

'No, he won't have to.'

'He also says he would have sent the Petty Cash book, or whatever, in with me this morning, but his secretary is sick, and if you ask me she's the sickest thing that ever broke fingernails on a typewriter, and she has not done something or other with petty cash receipts or vouchers, or whatever it is you need. However . . .' she paused, drawing an exaggerated breath. 'Dad says, if you would like to drop in this evening you could go round the yard with him at evening stables, and have a noggin afterwards, and he will personally press into your hot little palms the book your assistant has been driving him mad about.'

'I'd like that,' I said.

'Good. I'll tell him.'

'And will you be there?'

'Ah,' she said, her eyes laughing, 'a little uncertainty is the HP sauce on the chips.'

'And the spice of life to you, too.'

She gave me an excellent smile, spun on her heel so that the skirt swirled and the hair bounced, and walked out of the office.

Jossie Finch, daughter of William Finch, master of Axwood Stables. I knew her father in the way all long-time amateur riders knew all top trainers; enough to greet and chat to at the races. Since his was one of the racing accounts which pre-dated my arrival in the firm, and which Trevor liked to do himself, I had never before actually visited his yard.

I was interested enough to want to go, in spite of all my troubles. He had approximately ninety horses in his care, both

74

jumpers and flat racers, and winners were taken for granted. Apart from Tapestry, most of the horses I usually rode were of moderate class, owned with more hope than expectation. To see a big stableful of top performers was always a feast. I would be safe from abduction there. And Jossie looked a cherry on the top.

When Peter and Debbie came back I laid into them for going out and leaving the outer door unlocked, and they adopted put-upon expressions and said they thought it was all right, as I was there, which would stop people sneaking in to steal things.

My fault, I thought more reasonably. I should have locked it after them myself. I would have to reshape a lot of habits. It could easily have been the enemy who walked in, not Jossie Finch.

I spent part of the afternoon on Mr Wells, but more of it trying to trace Connaught Powys.

We had his original address on file, left over from the days when he had rigged the computer and milked his firm of a quarter of a million pounds in five years. The firm's audit was normally Trevor's affair, but one year, when Trevor was away a great deal with an ulcer, I had done it instead, and by some fluke had discovered the fraud. It had been one of those things you don't believe even when it is in front of your eyes. Connaught Powys had been an active director, and had paid his taxes on a comfortable income. The solid, untaxed lolly had disappeared without trace, but Connaught himself hadn't been quick enough.

I tried his old address. A sharp voice on the telephone told me the new occupants knew nothing of the Powys' whereabouts, and wished people would stop bothering them, and regretted the day they'd ever moved into a crook's house.

I tried his solicitors, who froze when they heard who was trying to find him. They could not, they said, divulge his present address without his express permission: which, their tone added, he was as likely to give as Shylock to a church bazaar.

I tried Leyhill Prison. No good.

I tried finally a racing acquaintance called Vivian Iverson who ran a gambling club in London and always seemed to know of corruption scandals before the stories publicly broke.

'My dear Ro,' he said, 'you're fairly non gratis in that quarter, don't you know.'

'I could guess.'

'You put the shivers up embezzlers, my friend. They're leaving the Newbury area in droves.'

'Oh sure. And I pick the Derby winner every year.'

'You may well jest, my dear chap, but the whisper has gone round.' He hesitated. 'Those two little dazzlers, Glitberg and Ownslow, have been seen talking to Powys, who has got rid of his indoor pallor under a sun lamp. The gist, so I'm fairly reliably told, was a hate-Britten chorus.'

'With vengeance intended?'

'No information, my dear chap.'

'Could you find out?'

'I only *listen*, my dear Ro,' he said. 'If I hear the knives are out, I'll tell you.'

'You're a pet,' I said dryly.

He laughed. 'Connaught Powys comes here to play, most Fridays.'

'What time?'

'You do ask a lot, my dear chap. After dinner to dawn.'

'How about making me an instant member?'

He sighed heavily. 'If you are bent on suicide, I'll tell the desk to let you in.'

'See you,' I said. 'And thanks.'

I put down the receiver and stared gloomily into space. Glitberg and Ownslow. Six years apiece, reduced for good behaviour . . . They could have met Connaught Powys in Leyhill, and it would have been no joy to any of them that I had put them all there.

Glitberg and Ownslow had served on a local council and robbed the ratepayers blind, and I'd turned them up through some dealings they'd done with one of my clients. My client had escaped with a fine, and had removed his custom from me with violent curses.

I wondered how much time all the embezzlers and bent solicitors and corrupted politicians in Leyhill Prison spent in think-

76

ing up new schemes for when they got out. Glitberg and Ownslow must already have been out for about six months.

Debbie had gone to the dentist and Peter to his Institute of Accounting Staff class, and this time I did lock the door behind them.

I felt too wretchedly tired to bother any further with Mr Wells. The shakes of the morning had gone, but even the swift tonic of Jossie Finch couldn't lift the persistent feeling of threat. I spent an hour dozing in the armchair we kept for favoured clients and when it was time, locked the filing cabinets and my desk and every door in the office, and went down to my car.

There was no one hiding behind the front seats. No one lurking round the edges of the car park. Nothing in the boot except the suitcase I'd stowed there that morning. I started up and drove out into the road, assaulted by nothing but my own nerves.

William Finch's yard lay south-west of Newbury: a huge spread of buildings sheltering in a hollow, with a creeper-covered Victorian mansion rising on the hillside above. I arrived at the house just as Finch was coming out of it, and we walked down together to the first cluster of boxes.

'Glad you could come,' he said.

'It's a treat.'

He smiled with easy charm. A tall man, going grey at about fifty, very much in command of himself and everything else. He had a broad face, fine well-shaped mouth, and the eyes of experience. Horses and owners thrived in his care, and years of success had given him a stature he plainly enjoyed.

We went from box to box, spending a couple of minutes in each. Finch told me which horse we were looking at, with some of its breeding and form. He held brief reassurance conversations in each case with the lad holding the horse's head, and with his head lad, who walked round with us. If all was well, he patted the horse's neck and fed him a carrot from a bag which his head lad carried. A practised important routine evening inspection, as carried out by every trainer in the country.

We came to an empty box in a full row. Finch gestured to it with a smile.

'Ivansky. My National runner. He's gone up to Liverpool.'

I almost gaped like an idiot. I'd been out of touch with the normal world so much that I had completely forgotten that the Grand National was due that Saturday.

I cleared my throat. 'He should . . . er . . . have a fair chance at the weights.' It seemed a fairly safe comment, but he disagreed.

'Ten twelve is far too much on his Haydock form. He's badly in with Wasserman, don't you think?'

I raked back for all the opinions I'd held in the safe and distant life of three weeks ago. Nothing much surfaced.

'I'm sure he'll do well,' I said.

He nodded as if he hadn't noticed the feebleness of the remark, and we went on. The horses were truly an impressive bunch, glowing with good feeding, thorough grooming and well-judged exercise. I ran out of compliments long before he ran out of horses.

'Drink?' he said, as the head lad shut the last door.

'Great.'

We walked up to the house, and he led the way into a sitting-room-cum-office. Chintz-covered sofa and chairs, big desk, table with drinks and glasses, walls covered with framed racing photographs. Normal affluent trainer ambience.

'Gin?' he said.

'Scotch, if you have it.'

He gave me a stiff one and poured gin like water for himself.

'Your health,' he said.

'And yours.'

We drank the ritual first sip, and he gestured to me to sit down.

'I've found that damned cash book for you,' he said, opening a drawer in the desk. 'There you are. Book, and file of petty cash receipts.'

'That's fine.'

'And what about these Commissioners?'

'Don't worry, I've applied for a postponement.'

'But will they grant it?'

'Never refused us yet,' I said. 'They'll set a new date about a month ahead, and we'll do your accounts and audit before then.'

He relaxed contentedly over his draught of gin. 'We can expect Trevor here next week, then? Counting hay bales and saddles?' There was humour in his voice at the thoroughness ahead.

'Well,' I said, 'maybe at the end of the week, or the one after. He won't be back until Wednesday or Thursday.' Did 'Returning Wednesday', I wondered, mean *travelling* Wednesday, or turning up for work. 'I'll do a lot of the preliminary paperwork for him, to save time.'

Finch turned to the drinks table and unscrewed the gin. 'I thought he was due back on Monday.'

'His car's broken down somewhere in France.'

'That'll please him.' He drank deeply. 'Still, if you make a start on things, the audit should get done in time.'

'Don't worry about the Commissioners,' I said; but everyone did worry when the peremptory summons dropped through their door. If one neither asked for a postponement nor attended at the due hour, the Commissioners would fix one's year's tax at whatever figure they cared to, and to that assessment there was no appeal. As such assessments were customarily far higher than the amount of tax actually due, one avoided them like black ice.

To my pleasure, the swirly brown skirt and bouncy fair hair made a swooping entrance. She was holding a marmalade cat which was trying to jump out of her arms.

'Damn thing,' she said, 'why won't he be *stroked*.'

'It's a mouser,' said her father, unemotionally.

'You'd think it would be glad of a cuddle.'

The cat freed itself and bolted. Jossie shrugged. 'Hello,' she said to me. 'So you got here.'

'Mm.'

'Well,' she said to her father, 'what did he say?'

'Eh? Oh . . . I haven't asked him yet.'

She gave him a fond exasperated smile and said to me, 'He wants to ask you to ride a horse for him.'

Finch shook his head at her, and I said, 'When?'

'Tomorrow,' Jossie said. 'At Towcester.'

'Er,' I said, 'I'm not really ultra fit.'

'Nonsense. You won the Gold Cup a fortnight ago. You must be.'

'Josephine,' her father said. 'Clam up.' He turned to me. 'I'm flying up to Liverpool in the morning, but I have this horse in at Towcester, and to be blunt he's still entered there only because someone forgot to scratch him by the eleven o'clock deadline this morning . . .'

'The chronically sick secretary,' muttered Jossie.

'So we've either got to run him after all or pay a fine, and I was toying with the idea of sending him up there, if I could get a suitable jockey.'

'Most of them having gone to the National,' Jossie added.

'Which horse?' I said.

'Notebook. Novice hurdler. Four-year-old chestnut gelding, in the top yard.'

'The one with the flaxen mane and tail?'

'That's right. He's run a couple of times so far. Shows promise, but still green.'

'Last of twenty-six at Newbury,' Jossie said cheerfully. 'It won't matter a curse if you're not fit.' She paused. 'I've been delegated to saddle it up, so you might do us a favour and come and ride it.'

'Up to you,' Finch said.

The delegated saddler was a powerful attraction, even if Notebook himself was nothing much.

'Yes,' I said weakly. 'OK.'

'Good.' Jossie gave me a flashing smile. 'I'll drive you up there, if you like.'

'I would like,' I said regretfully, 'but I'll be in London tonight. I'll go straight to Towcester from there.'

'I'll meet you outside the weighing room, then. He's in the last race, by the way. He would be.'

Novice hurdles were customarily first or last (or both), on a day's programme: the races a lot of racegoers chose to miss through lunch or leaving early to avoid the crush. The poor-relation races for the mediocre majority, where every so often a new blazing star scorched out of the ruck on its way to fame.

Running horses in novice hurdles meant starting from home early or getting back late; but there were far more runners in novice hurdles than in any other type of race.

When I left it was Jossie who came back with me through the

entrance hall to see me off. As we crossed a vast decrepit Persian rug I glanced at the large dark portraits occupying acres of wall-space.

'Those are Nantuckets, of course,' she said, following my gaze. 'They came with the house.'

'Po-faced lot,' I said.

'You did know that Dad doesn't actually own all this?'

'Yes, I actually did know.' I smiled to myself, but she saw it.

She said defensively, 'All right, but you'd be surprised how many people make up to me, thinking that they'll marry the trainer's daughter and step into all this when he retires.'

'So you like to establish the ground rules first?'

'OK, greyhound-brain, I'd forgotten you'd know from Trevor.'

I knew in general that Axwood Stables Ltd belonged to an American family, the Nantuckets, who rarely took much personal interest in the place except as a business asset. It had been bought and brought to greatness in the fifties by a rumbustious tycoon thrown up atypically from prudent banking stock. Old Naylor Nantucket had brought his energies and enterprise to England, had fallen in love with English racing, had built a splendid modern stable yard and filled it with splendid horses. He had engaged the young William Finch to train them for him, and the middle-aged William Finch was still doing it for his heirs, except that nowadays nine tenths of the horses belonged to other owners, and the young Nantuckets, faintly ashamed of Uncle Naylor, never crossed the Atlantic to see their own horses perform.

'Doesn't your father ever get tired of training for absent owners?' I said.

'No. They don't argue. They don't ring him up in the middle of the night. And when they lose, they don't complain. He says training would be a lot easier if *all* owners lived in New York.'

She stood on the doorstep to wave me goodbye, assured and half-mocking, a girl with bright brown eyes, graceful neck, and neat nose and mouth in between.

I booked into the Gloucester Hotel, where I'd never stayed before, and ate a leisurely and much needed dinner in a nearby restaurant. I shouldn't have accepted the ride on Notebook, I thought ruefully; I'd hardly enough strength to cut up a steak.

A strong feeling of walking blindfold towards a precipice dragged at my feet all the way to Vivian Iverson's gambling club. I didn't know which way the precipice lay: ahead, behind, or all round. I only suspected that it was still there, and if I did nothing about finding it, I could walk straight over.

The Vivat Club proved as suave and well-manicured as its owner, and was a matter of interconnecting small rooms, not open expanses like casinos. There were no croupiers in eye-shades with bright dramatic spotlights over the tables, and no ladies tinkling with diamonds in half shadow. There were how-ever two or three discreet chandeliers, a good deal of cigar smoke, and a sort of reverent hush.

Vivian, good as his word, had left a note for me to be let in, and as an extra, treated as a guest. I walked slowly from room to room, balloon glass of brandy in hand, looking for his ele-gant shape, and not finding it.

There were a good many businessmen in lounge suits earnestly playing chemin-de-fer, and women among them with eyes that flicked concentratedly from side to side with every delivered card. I'd never had an urge towards betting for hours on the turn of a card, but everyone to his own poison.

'Ro, my dear fellow,' Vivian said behind me. 'Come to play?'

'On an accountant's earnings?' I said, turning to him and smiling. 'What are the stakes?'

'Whatever you can afford to lose, my dear fellow.'

'Life, liberty, and a ticket to the Cup Final.'

His eyes didn't smile as thoroughly as his mouth. 'Some people lose honour, fortunes, reputation, and their heads.'

'Does it disturb you?' I asked.

He made a small waving gesture towards the chemin-de-fer. 'I provide a pastime to cater for an impulse. Like bingo.'

He put his hand on my shoulder as if we were long-lost friends and steered me towards a further room. There were heavy gold links in his cuffs, and a silk cord edging to his blue velvet jacket. Dark glossy hair on a well-shaped head, flat stomach, faint smell of fresh talc. About thirty-five, and shrewdly succeeding where others had fallen to bailiffs.

There was a green baize raised-edge gaming table in the further room, but no one was playing cards.

Behind the table, in the club's ubiquitous wooden-armed, studded-leather armchairs, sat three men.

They were all large, smoothly dressed, and unfriendly. I knew them, from way back.

Connaught Powys. Glitberg. Ownslow.

'We hear you're looking for us,' Connaught Powys said.

9

I stood still. Vivian closed the door behind me and sat in another armchair on the edge of my left-hand vision. He crossed one leg elegantly over the other and eased the cloth over the knee with a languid hand.

Ownslow watched with disfavour.

'Piss off,' he said.

Vivian's answer was an extra-sophisticated drawl. 'My dear fellow, I may have set him up, but you've no licence to knock him down.'

There were several other empty chairs, pulled back haphazardly from the centre table. I sat unhurriedly in one of them and did my best with Vivian's leg-crossing ritual, hoping that casualness would reduce the atmosphere from bash-up to boardroom. Ownslow's malevolent stare hardly persuaded me that I'd succeeded.

Ownslow and Glitberg had run a flourishing construction racket for years, robbing the ratepayers of literally millions. Like all huge frauds, theirs had been done on paper, with Glitberg in the council's Planning Office, and Ownslow in the Works and Maintenance. They had simply invented a large number of buildings: offices, flats and housing estates. The whole council having approved the buildings in principle, Glitberg, in his official capacity, advertised for tenders from developers. The lowest good-looking tender often came from a firm called National Construction (Wessex) Ltd and the council confidently entrusted the building to them.

National Construction (Wessex) Ltd did not exist except as expensively produced lettterheads. The sanctioned buildings were never built. Huge sums of money were authorized and paid to National Construction (Wessex) Ltd, and regular reports of the buildings' progress came back as Glitberg, from Planning, made regular inspections. After the point when the buildings were passed as ready for occupation the Maintenance department took over. Ownslow's men maintained bona-fide buildings, and Ownslow also requistioned huge sums for the maintenance of the well-documented imaginary lot.

All the paperwork had been punctiliously, even brilliantly, completed. There were full records of rents received from the imaginary buildings, and rates paid by the imaginary tenants; but as all councils took it for granted that council buildings had to be heavily subsidised, the permament gap between revenue and expenditure was accepted as normal.

Like many big frauds it had been uncovered by accident, and the accident had been my digging a little too deeply into the affairs of one of the smaller operators sharing in the crumbs of the greater rip-off.

The council, when I'd informed them, had refused to believe me. Not, that was, until they toured their area in detail, and found weedy grass where they had paid for, among other things, six storeys of flats for low-income families, a cul-de-sac of maisonettes for single pensioners, and two roadfuls of semi-detached bungalows for the retired and handicapped.

Blind-eye money had obviously been passed to various council members, but bribery in cash was hard to prove. The council had been publicly embarrassed and had not forgiven me. Glitberg and Ownslow, who had seen that the caper could not continue for ever, had been already preparing a quiet departure when the police descended on them in force on a Sunday afternoon. They had not exactly forgiven me either.

In line with all their other attention to detail, neither of them had made the mistake of living above his legal income. The huge sums they had creamed off had been withdrawn from the National Construction (Wessex) Ltd bank account over the years as a stream of cheques and cash which had aroused no suspicion at the bank, and had then apparently vanished into thin air. Of the million-plus which they had each stolen, not a pound had been recovered.

'Whatever you want from us,' Glitberg said, 'you're not going to get.'

'You're a danger to us,' Connaught Powys said.

'And like a wasp, you'll get swatted,' said Ownslow.

I looked at their faces. All three showed the pudgy roundness of self-indulgence, and all three had the sharp, wary eyes of guilt. Separately, Connaught Powys, with his sun-lamp tan and smoothly brushed hair, looked a high-up City gent. Heavy of body, in navy blue pin-stripes. Pale grey silk tie. Overall air of power and opulence, and not a whisper of cell-fug and slopping-out in the mornings.

Ownslow in jail was an easier picture. Fairish hair straggled to his collar from a fringe round a bald dome. Thick neck, bull shoulders, hands like baseball gloves. A hard, tough man whose accent came from worlds away from Connaught Powys.

Glitberg, in glasses, had short bushy grey hair and a fanned-out spread of white side-whiskers, which made him look like a species of ape. If Connaught Powys was power, and Ownslow was muscle, Glitberg was venom.

'Have you already tried?' I said.

'Tried what?' Ownslow said.

'Swatting.'

They stared, all three of them, without expression, at some point in the air between myself and Vivian.

'Someone has,' I said.

Connaught Powys smiled very slightly. 'Whatever we have done, or intend to do, about you,' he said, 'we are not going to be so insane as to admit it in front of a witness.'

'You'll be looking over your shoulder for the rest of your life,' Glitberg said, with satisfaction.

'Don't go near building sites on a dark night,' Ownslow said. 'There's a bit of advice, free, gratis and for nothing.'

'How about a sailing boat on a dark night?' I said. 'An ocean-going sailing boat.'

I wished at once that I hadn't said it. The unfriendliness on all three faces hardened to menace, and the whole room became very still.

Into the silence came Vivian's voice, relaxed and drawling. 'Ro . . . time you and I had a drink together, don't you think?'

He unfolded himself from his chair, and I, feeling fairly weak at the knees, stood up from mine.

Connaught Powys, Glitberg, and Ownslow delivered a collective look of such hatred that even Vivian began to look nervous. His hand fumbled with the door knob, and as he left the room, behind me, he almost tripped over his own feet.

'Whew,' he said in my ear. 'You do play with big rough boys, my dear fellow.' He steered me this time into a luxurious little office; three armchairs, all safely unoccupied. He waved me to one of them and poured brandy into two balloons.

'It's not what they say,' he said, 'as how they say it.'

'And what they don't say.'

He looked at me speculatively over his glass.

'Did you get what you wanted? I mean, was it worth your while, running under their guns?'

I smiled twistedly. 'I think I got an answer.'

'Well then.'

'Yes. But it was to a question I didn't ask.'

'I don't follow you.'

'I'm afraid,' I said slowly, 'that I've made everything a great deal worse.'

I slept soundly at the Gloucester, but more from exhaustion than an easy mind.

From the racing page of the newspaper delivered under my door in the morning I saw that my name was down in the list of runners as the rider of Notebook in the last race at Towcester. I sucked my teeth. I hadn't thought of asking William Finch not to include me in his list for the press, and now the whole world would learn where I would be that afternoon at four-thirty. If, that was, they bothered to turn to an insignificant race at a minor meeting on Grand National day.

'You'll be looking over your shoulder for the rest of your life,' Glitberg had said.

I didn't intend to. Life would be impossible if I feared for demons in every shadow. I wouldn't climb trustingly into any ambulances at Towcester, but I would go and ride there. There was an awfully thin line, it seemed to me, between cowardice and caution.

Jossie, waiting outside the weighing room, sent the heeby-jeebies flying.

'Hello,' she said. 'Notebook is here, looking his usual noble self and about to turn in his standard useless performance.'

'Charming.'

'The trainer's orders to the jockey,' she said, 'are succinct. Stay on, and stay out of trouble. He doesn't want you getting hurt.'

'Nor do I,' I said with feeling.

'He doesn't want anything to spoil the day if Ivansky wins the National.'

'Ah,' I said. 'Does he think he will?'

'He flew off in the air-taxi this morning in the usual agonized euphoria,' she said, with affection. 'Hope zigzagging from conviction to doubt.'

Finch had sent two horses to Towcester, the second of them, Stoolery, being the real reason for Jossie's journey. I helped her saddle it for the two mile handicap 'chase, and cheered with her on the stands when it won. The Grand National itself was transmitted on television all over the racecourse straight afterwards, so that Jossie was already consoled when Ivansky finished fifth.

'Oh well.' She shrugged. 'That's that. Dad will feel flat, the owners will feel flat, the lads will get gloomily drunk, and then they'll all start talking about next year.'

We strolled along without much purpose and arrived at the door to the bar.

'Like a drink?' I asked.

'Might pass the time.'

The bar was crowded with people dissecting the National result, and the elbowing customers jockeying for service were four deep.

'Don't let's bother,' Jossie said.

I agreed. We turned to leave, and a thin hand stretched out

from the tight pressed ranks and gripped my wrist hard.

'What do you want?' a voice shouted over the din. 'I've just got served. What do you want? Quick!'

The hand, I saw, belonged to Moira Longerman, and beyond her, scowling as usual, stood Binny Tomkins.

'Jossie?' I said.

'Fruit juice. Grapefruit if poss.'

'Two grapefruit juice,' I said.

The hand let go and disappeared, shortly to reappear with a glass in it. I took it, and also the next issue, and finally Moira Longerman herself, followed by Binny, fought her way out of the throng, holding two glasses high to avoid having the expensive thimblefuls knocked flying.

'How super! ' she said. 'I saw you in the distance just now. I've been trying to telephone you for weeks and now I hear some extraordinary story about you being kidnapped.'

I introduced Jossie who was looking disbelievingly at what Moira had said.

'Kidnapped?' Her eyebrows rose comically. 'You?'

'You may well laugh,' I said ruefully.

Moira handed a glass to Binny, who nodded a scant thanks. Graceless man, I thought. Extraordinary to leave any woman to fight her way to get him a drink, let alone the owner of the most important horse in his yard. She was paying, of course.

'My *dear*,' Moira Longerman said to Jossie. 'Right after Ro won the Gold Cup on my darling Tapestry, someone kidnapped him from the racecourse. Isn't that right?' She beamed quizzically up at my face, her blue eyes alight with friendly interest.

'Sure is,' I agreed.

Binny scowled some more.

'How's the horse?' I said.

Binny gave me a hard stare and didn't answer, but Moira Longerman was overflowing with news and enthusiasm.

'I do so want you to ride Tapestry in all his races from now on, Ro, so I hope you will. He's ready for Ascot next Wednesday, Binny says, and I've been trying and trying to get hold of you to see if you'll ride him.'

Binny said sourly, 'I've already engaged another jockey.'

'Then disengage him, Binny dear.' Underneath the friendly birdlike brightness there was the same touch of steel which had got me the Gold Cup ride in the first place. Moira might be half Binny's physical weight but she had twice the mental muscle.

'It might be better to let this other chap ride . . .' I began.

'No, no,' she interrupted. 'It's you I want, Ro. I won't have anyone else. I told Binny that, quite definitely, the very moment after you'd won the Cup. Now you're back and safe again it will either be you on my horse or I won't run him.' She glanced defiantly at Binny, impishly at Jossie, and with a determined nod of her blonde curly head, expectantly turned to me. 'Well? What do you say?'

'Er,' I said, which was hardly helpful.

'Oh go on,' Jossie said. 'You'll have to.'

Binny's scowl switched targets. Jossie caught the full blast and showed no discomfiture at all.

'He did win the Gold Cup,' she said. 'You can't say he isn't capable.'

'He does say that, my dear,' beamed Moira Longerman happily. 'Isn't it odd?'

Binny muttered something blackly of which the only audible word was 'amateurs'.

'I think that what Binny really means,' said Moira sweetly and distinctly, 'is that Ro, like most amateurs, always tries very hard to win, and won't listen to propositions to the contrary.'

Binny's face turned a dark red. Jossie practically giggled. Moira looked at me with limpid blue eyes as if not quite aware of what she'd said, and I chewed around helplessly for a sensible answer.

'Like most *jockeys*,' I said finally.

'You're so nice, Ro,' she said. 'You think everyone's honest.'

I tended, like most accountants, to think exactly the opposite, but as it happened I had never much wondered about Binny. To train a horse like Tapestry should have been enough, without trying to rig his results.

Binny himself had decided to misunderstand what Moira had said, and was pretending that he hadn't seen the chasm that was opening at his feet. Moira gave him a mischievous glance and allowed him no illusions about her power to push him in.

'Binny dear,' she said, 'I'll never desert the man who trained a Gold Cup winner for me. Not as long as he keeps turning out my horses beautifully fit, and I choose who rides them.'

Jossie cleared her throat in the following silence and said encouragingly to Binny, 'I expect you had a good bet in the Gold Cup? My father always puts a bit on in the Cup and the National. Too awful if you win, and you haven't. Makes you look such an ass, he says.'

If she had tried to rub salt into his raw wounds, it appeared she couldn't have done a better job. Moira Longerman gave a delighted laugh.

'You naughty girl,' she said, patting Jossie's arm. 'Poor Binny had so little faith, you see, that not only did he not back Tapestry to win, but I've heard he unfortunately laid it to lose. Such a pity. Poor Binny, winning the Gold Cup and ending up out of pocket.'

Binny looked so appalled that I gathered the extent of her information was a nasty shock to him.

'Never mind,' Moira said kindly. 'What's past is past. And if Ro rides Tapestry next Wednesday, all will be well.'

Binny looked as if everything would be very far from well. I wondered idly if he could possibly have already arranged that Tapestry should lose on Wednesday. On his first outing after a Gold Cup win, any horse would start at short odds. Many a bookmaker would be grateful to know for certain that he wouldn't have to pay out. Binny could already have sold that welcome information, thinking that I wasn't around to upset things. Binny was having a thoroughly bad time.

I reflected that I simply couldn't afford to take Wednesday off. The mountains of undone work made me feel faintly sick.

'Ro?' Moira said persuasively.

'Yes,' I said. 'Nothing I'd like better in the world.'

'Oh goody!' Her eyes sparkled with pleasure. 'I'll see you at Ascot, then. Binny will ring you, of course, if there's a change of plan.'

Binny scowled.

*

'Tell me all,' Jossie demanded as we walked across to the trainers' stand to watch the next race. 'All this drama about you being kidnapped.'

I told her briefly, without much detail.

'Do you mean they just popped you on a boat and sailed off with you to the Med?'

'That's right.'

'What a lark.'

'It was inconvenient,' I said mildly.

'I'll bet.' She paused. 'You said you escaped. How did you do that?'

'Jumped overboard.'

Her mouth twisted with sympathy. I reflected that it was only four days since that frantic swim. It seemed another world.

Jossie was of the real, sensible world, where things were understandable, if not always pleasant. Being with her made me feel a great deal more settled, more normal, and safer.

'How about dinner,' I said, 'on the way home?'

'We've got two cars,' she said.

'Nothing to prevent them both stopping at the same place.'

'How true.'

She was again wearing swirly clothes: a soft rusty red, this time. There was nothing tailored about her, and nothing untidy. An organized girl, amusing and amused.

'There's a fair pub near Oxford,' I said.

'I'll follow you, then.'

I changed in due course for Notebook's race, and weighed out, and gave my lightest saddle to the Axwood travelling head lad, who was waiting for it by the door.

'Carrying overweight, are you?' he said sardonically.

'Four pounds.'

He made an eyes-to-heaven gesture, saying louder than words that trainers should put up professionals in novice hurdle races, not amateurs who couldn't do ten stone six. I didn't mention that on Gold Cup day I'd weighed eight pounds more.

When I went out to the parade ring, he and Jossie were waiting, while a lad led the noble Notebook round and round, now wearing my saddle over a number cloth. Number thirteen. So who was superstitious?

'He bucks a bit,' said the travelling head lad, with satisfaction.

'When you get home,' Jossie said to him, 'please tell my father I'm stopping on the way back for dinner with Roland. So that he doesn't worry about car crashes.'

'Right.'

'Dad fusses,' Jossie said.

The travelling head lad gave me another look which needed no words, and which speculated on whether I would get her into bed. I wasn't so sure that I cared all that much for the travelling head lad.

A good many people had already gone home, and from the parade ring one could see a steady drift to the gate. There were few things as disheartening, I thought, as playing to a vanishing audience. On the other hand, if one made a frightful mess, the fewer who saw it, the better.

'They said "jockeys get mounted" half an hour ago,' Jossie said.

'Two seconds,' I said. 'I was listening.'

The travelling head lad gave me a leg up. Notebook gave a trial buck.

'Stay out of trouble,' Jossie said.

'It's underneath me,' I said, feeling the noble animal again try to shoot me off.

She grinned unfeelingly. Notebook bounced away, hiccupped sideways down to the start, and then kept everyone waiting while he did a circus act on his hind legs. 'Bucks a bit', I thought bitterly. I'd fall off before the tapes went up, if I wasn't careful.

The race started, and Notebook magnanimously decided to take part, setting off at an uncoordinated gallop which involved a good deal of head-shaking and yawing from side to side. His approach to the first hurdle induced severe loss of confidence in his rider, as he seemed to be trying to jump it sideways, like a crab.

As I hadn't taken the precaution of dropping him out firmly at the back, always supposing I could actually have managed it, as he was as strong as he was wilful, his diagonal crossing of the flight of hurdles harvested a barrage of curses from the other jockeys. 'Sorry' was a useless word in a hurdle race, particularly from an unfit amateur who should have known better than to be led astray by a pretty girl. I yanked Notebook's head straight at the next hurdle with a force which would have had the Cruelty to Animals people swooning. He retaliated by screwing his hindquarters sideways in mid-air and landing on all four feet at once, pointing east-north-east to the rails.

This manoeuvre at least dropped him out into last place, which he tried to put right by running away with me up the stretch in front of the stands. As we fought each other on the way outwards round the mile-and-half circuit I understood the full meaning of the trainer's orders to his jockey. 'Stay on, and stay out of trouble.' My God.

I was not in the least surprised that Notebook had finished last of twenty-six at Newbury. He would have been last of a hundred and twenty-six, if his jockey had had any sense. Last place on Notebook was not exactly safe, but if one had to be anywhere on him, last place was wisest. No one, however, had got the message through to the horse.

The circuit at Towcester went out downhill from the stands, flattened into a straight stretch on the far side, and ended with a stamina-sapping uphill pull to the finishing straight and the winning post. Some of the world's slowest finishes had been slogged out there on muddy days at the end of three-mile 'chases. Notebook however set off downhill on firm going at a graceless rush, roller-coastered over the most distant hurdles, and only began to lose interest when he hit the sharply rising ground on the way back.

By that time the nineteen other runners were ahead as of right, as Notebook's stop-go and sideways type of jumping lost at every flight the lengths he made up on the flat.

I suppose I relaxed a little. He met the next hurdle all wrong, ignored my bid to help him, screwed wildly in mid-air, and landed with his nose on the turf and all four feet close together behind it. Not radically different from six other landings, just more extreme.

Being catapulted off at approximately thirty miles an hour is a kaleidoscopic business. Sky, trees, rails and grass somersaulted around my vision in a disjointed jumble, and if I tucked my head in it was from instinct, not thought. The turf smacked me sharply in several places, and Notebook delivered a parting kick on the thigh. The world stopped rolling, and half a ton of horse had not come crashing down on top of me. Life would go on.

I sat up slowly, all breath knocked out, and watched the noble hindquarters charge heedlessly away.

An ambulance man ran towards me, in the familiar black St John's uniform. I felt a flood of panic. A conditioned reflex. He had a kind face: a total stranger.

'All right, mate?' he said.

I nodded weakly.

'You came a proper purler.'

'Mm.' I unclipped my helmet, and pulled it off. Speech was impossible. My chest heaved from lack of air. He put a hand under one of my armpits and helped me as far as my knees, and from there, once I could breathe properly, to my feet.

'Bones OK?'

I nodded.

'Just winded,' he said cheerfully.

'Mm.'

A Land Rover arrived beside us with a jerk, and the vet inside it said that as there were no injured horses needing his attention, he could offer me a lift back to the stands.

'You fell off,' Jossie observed, as I emerged with normal breath and clean bill of health from the doctor in the First Aid room.

I smiled, 'Granted.'

She gave me a sideways glance from the huge eyes.

'I thought all jockeys were frightfully touchy about being told they fell off,' she said. 'All that guff about it's the horse that falls, and the jockey just goes down with the ship.'

'Quite right,' I said.

'But Notebook didn't actually fall, so you fell off.' Her voice was lofty, teasing.

'I don't dispute it.'

'No, aren't you boring.' She smiled. 'They caught Notebook in the next parish, so while you change I'll go along to the stables and see he's OK, and I'll meet you in the car park.'

'Fine.'

I changed into street clothes, fixed with the valet to take my

94

saddles, helmet, and other gear to Ascot for the following Wednesday, and walked the short distance to the car park.

The crowds had gone, and only the stragglers like me were leaving now in twos and threes. The cars still remaining stood singly, haphazardly scattered instead of in orderly rows.

I looked into the back of mine, behind the front seats.

No one there.

I wondered with a shiver what I would have done if there had been. Run a mile, no doubt. I stood leaning on my car waiting for Jossie, and no one looked in the least like trying to carry me off. A quiet spring-like Saturday evening in the Northamptonshire countryside, as friendly as beer.

10

She followed me in her pale blue Midget to the pub on the south side of Oxford, and chose a long cold drink with fruit on the top and a kick in the tail.

'Dad has schooled Notebook until he's blue in the face,' she said, pursing her lips to the straw which stuck up like a mast from the log-jam of fruit.

'Some of them never learn,' I said.

She nodded. Polite transaction achieved, I thought: she had obliquely apologized for the horse's frightful behaviour, and I had accepted that her father had done his best to teach him to jump. Some trainers, but not those of William Finch's standing, seemed to think that the best place for a green novice to learn to jump was actually in a race: rather like urging a child up the Eiger without showing him how to climb.

'What made you become an accountant?' she said. 'It's such a dull sort of job.'

'Do you think so?'

She gave me the full benefit of the big eyes. 'You obviously don't,' she said. She tilted her head a little, considering. 'You don't *look* boring and stuffy, and you don't *act* boring and stuffy, so give.'

'Judges are sober, nurses are dedicated, miners are heroes, writers drink.'

'Or in other words, don't expect people to fit the image?'

'As you say,' I said.

She smiled. 'I've known Trevor since I was six.'

A nasty one. Trevor, without any stretch of imagination, could fairly be classed as stuffy and boring.

'Carry on,' she said. 'Why?'

'Security. Steady employment. Good pay. The usual inducements.'

She looked at me levelly. 'You're lying.

'What makes you think so?'

'People who risk their necks for nothing in jump races are not hell-bent on security, steady employment, and money.'

'Because of me Mum, then,' I said flippantly.

'She bossed you into it?'

'No.' I hesitated, because in fact I never had told anyone why I'd grown up with a fiery zeal as powerful as a vocation. Jossie waited with quizzical expectation.

'She had a rotten accountant,' I said. 'I promised her that when I grew up I would take over. As corny as that.'

'And did you?'

'No. She died.'

'Sob story.'

'Yes, I told you. Pure corn.'

She stirred the fruit with her straw, looking less mocking. 'You're afraid I'll laugh at you.'

'Sure of it,' I said.

'Try me, then.'

'Well . . . she was a rotten businesswoman, my Mum. My father got killed in a pointless sort of accident, and she was left having to bring me up alone. She was about thirty. I was nine.' I paused. Jossie was not actually laughing, so I struggled on. 'She rented a house just off the sea-front at Ryde and ran it as a holiday hotel, half a step up from a boarding house. Comfortable, but no drinks licence; that sort of thing. So she could be there when I got home from school, and in the holidays.'

'Brave of her,' Jossie said. 'Go on.'

'You can guess.'

She sucked down to the dregs of her glass and made a bubbling noise through the straw. 'Sure,' she said. 'She was good at cooking and welcoming people and lousy at working out how much to charge.'

'She was also paying tax on money she should have claimed as expenses.'

'And that's bad?'

'Crazy.'

'Well, go on,' she said encouragingly. 'Digging a story out of you is worse than looking for mushrooms.'

'I found her crying sometimes, mostly in the winter when there weren't any guests. It's pretty upsetting for a kid of ten or so to find his mother crying, so you can say I was upset. Protective also, probably. Anyway, at first I thought it was still because of losing Dad. Then I realized she always cried when she'd been seeing Mr Jones, who was her accountant. I tried to get her to open up on her troubles, but she said I was too young.'

I stopped again. Jossie sighed with exasperation and said, 'Do get *on* with it.'

'I told her to ditch Mr Jones and get someone else. She said I didn't understand, I was too young. I promised her that when I got older I would be an accountant, and I'd put her affairs to rights.' I smiled lopsidedly. 'When I was thirteen she went down to Boots one morning and bought two hundred aspirins. She stirred them into a glass of water, and drank them. I found her lying on her bed when I came home from school. She left me a note.'

'What did it say?'

'It said "Dear Ro, Sorry, Love, Mum." '

'Poor girl.' Jossie blinked. Not laughing.

'She'd made a will,' I said. 'One of those simple things on a form from the stationers. She left me everything, which was actually nothing much except her own personal things. I kept all the account books and bank statements. I got shuttled around uncles and aunts for a few years, but I kept those account books safe, and then I got another accountant to look at them. He told me Mr Jones seemed to have thought he was working for the Inland Revenue, not his client. I told him I wanted to be an accountant, and I got him to show me exactly what Mr Jones had done wrong. So there you are. That's all.'

'Are you still killing Mr Jones to dry your mother's tears?' The teasing note was back, but gentler.

I smiled, 'I enjoy accountancy. I might never have thought of it if it hadn't been for Mr Jones.'

'So God bless villains.'

'He was ultra-righteous. A smug pompous ass. There are still a lot of Mr Joneses around, not pointing out to their clients all the legitimate ways of avoiding tax.'

'Huh?'

'It's silly to pay tax when you don't have to.'

'That's obvious.'

'A lot of people do, though, from ignorance or bad advice.'

I ordered refill drinks and told Jossie it was her turn to unbutton with the family skeletons.

'My Ma?' she said in surprise. 'I thought the whole world knew about my Ma. She canoes up and down the Amazon like a yo-yo, digging up ancient tribes. Sends back dispatches in the shape of earnest papers to obscure magazines. Dad and I haven't seen her for years. We get telegrams in January saying Happy Christmas.'

Revelation dawned. 'Christabel Saffray Finch! Intrepid female explorer, storming about in rain forests?'

'Ma,' Jossie nodded.

'Good heavens.'

'Good grief, more like.'

'Trevor never told me,' I said. 'But then he wouldn't, I suppose.'

Jossie grinned. 'Trevor disapproves. Trevor also always disapproves of Dad's little consolations. Aunts, I used to call them. Now I call them Lida and Sandy.'

'He's very discreet.' Even on the racecourse, where gossip was a second occupation, I hadn't heard of Lida and Sandy. Or that Christabel Saffray Finch, darling of anthropological documentaries, was William's wife.

'Sandy is his ever-sick secretary,' Jossie said, 'perpetually shuttling between bronchitis, backache and abortion.'

I laughed. 'And Lida?'

Jossie made a face, suddenly vulnerable under all the bright froth.

'Lida's got her hooks into him like a tapeworm. I can't stand her. Let's talk about food; I'm starving.'

We read the menu and ordered, and finished our drinks, and went in to dinner in the centuries-old dining-room: stone walls, uncovered oak beams, red velvet and soft lights.

Jossie ate as if waistlines never expanded, which was refreshing after the finicky picker I'd taken out last.

'Luck of the draw,' she said complacently, smothering a baked-in-the-skin potato with a butter mountain. I reflected that she'd drawn lucky in more ways than metabolism. A quick mind, fascinating face, tall, slender body: there was nothing egalitarian about nature.

Most of the tables around us were filled with softly chattering groups of twos and fours, but over by a far wall a larger party were making the lion's share of the noise.

'They keep looking over here,' Jossie said. 'Do you know them?'

'It looks like Sticks Elroy with his back to us.'

'Is it? Celebrating his winner?'

Sticks Elroy, named for the extreme thinness of his legs, had studiously avoided me in the Towcester changing room, and must have been thoroughly disconcerted to find me having dinner in his local pub. He was one of my jockey clients, but for how much longer was problematical. I was not currently his favourite person.

The noise, however, was coming not from him but from the host of the party, a stubborn-looking man with a naturally loud voice.

'Avert your gaze,' I said to Jossie.

The large eyes regarded me over salad and steak.

'An ostrich act?' she said.

I nodded. 'If we bury our heads, maybe the storm won't notice us.'

The storm, however, seemed to be gathering force. Words like 'bastard' rose easily above the prevailing clatter and the uninvolved majority began to look interested.

'Trouble,' Jossie said without visible regret, 'is on its feet and heading this way.'

'Damn.'

She grinned. 'Faint heart.'

Trouble arrived with the deliberate movements of the slightly drunk. Late forties, I judged. About five feet eight, short dark hair, flushed cheeks and aggressive eyes. He stood four-square and ignored Jossie altogether.

'My son tells me you're that bastard Roland Britten.' His voice, apart from fortissimo, was faintly slurred.

To ignore him was to invite a punch-up. I laid down my knife and fork. Leaned back in my chair. Behaved as if the enquiry was polite.

'Is Sticks Elroy your son?'

'Too right, he bloody is,' he said.

'He had a nice winner today,' I said. 'Well done.'

It stopped him for barely two seconds.

'He doesn't need your bloody "well done".'

I waited mildly, without answering. Elroy senior bent down, breathed alcohol heavily, and pointed an accusing finger under my nose.

'You leave my son alone, see? He isn't doing anyone any harm. He doesn't want any bastard like you snitching on him to the bloody tax man. Judas, that's what you are. Going behind his back. Bloody informer, that's what you are.'

'I haven't informed on him.'

'What's that?' He wagged the finger to and fro, belligerently. 'Costing him hundreds, aren't you, with the bloody tax man. Bastard like you ought to be locked up. Serve you bloody well right.'

The head waiter arrived smoothly at Elroy's shoulder.

'Excuse me, sir,' he began.

Elroy turned on him like a bull. 'You trot off. You major-domo, or whatever you are. You trot off. I'll have my say, and when I've had my say I'll sit down, see? Not before.'

The head waiter cravenly retired, and Elroy returned to his prime target. Jossie's eyes stared at him with disfavour, which deflected him not at all.

'I hear someone locked you up for ten days or so just now,

and you got out. Bloody shame. You deserve to be locked up, you do. Bastard like you. Whoever it was locked you up had the right idea.'

I said nothing. Elroy half turned away, but he had by no means finished. Merely addressing a wider audience.

'You know what this bastard did to my son?' The audience removed its eyes in thoroughly British embarrassment, but they got told the answer whether they liked it or not.

'This boot-licking, creeping bastard went crawling to the tax man and told him my son had some cash he hadn't paid taxes on.'

'I didn't,' I said to Jossie.

He swung round to me again and poked the finger rigidly under my nose. 'Bloody liar. Locking up's too bloody good for bastards like you.'

The manager arrived, with the head waiter hovering behind.

'Mr Elroy,' the manager said courteously. 'A bottle of wine for your party, compliments of the management.' He beckoned a finger to the head waiter, who deftly proffered a bottle of claret.

The manager was young and well-dressed, and reminded me of Vivian Iverson. His unexpected oil worked marvels on the storm, which abated amid a few extra 'bastards' and went back to its table muttering under its breath.

The people at the other tables watched from the cover of animated conversation, while the head waiter drew the cork for Elroy and poured the free wine. The manager drifted casually back to Jossie and me.

'There will be no charge for your dinner, sir.' He paused delicately. 'Mr Elroy is a valued customer.' He bowed very slightly and drifted on without waiting for an answer.

'How cool of him,' Josie said, near explosion.

'How professional.'

She stared at me. 'Do you often sit still and let people call you a bastard?'

'Once a week and twice on Sundays.'

'Spineless.'

'If I'd stood up and slogged him, our steaks would have gone cold.'

'Mine has, anyway.'

'Have another,' I said. I started to eat again where I had left off, and so, after a moment or two, did Jossie.

'Go on,' she said. 'I'm all agog. Just what was that all about?' She looked round the restaurant. 'You are now the target of whispers, and the consensus looks unfavourable.'

'In general,' I said, spearing lettuce, 'people shouldn't expect their accountants to help them break the law.'

'Sticks?'

'And accountants unfortunately cannot discuss their clients.'

'Are you being serious?'

I sighed. 'A client who wants his accountant to connive at a massive piece of tax-dodging is not going to be madly pleased when the accountant refuses to do it.'

'Mm.' She chewed cheerfully. 'I do see that.'

'And,' I went on, 'an accountant who advises such a client to declare the loot and pay the tax, because otherwise the nasty Revenue men will undoubtedly find out, and the client will have to pay fines on top of tax and will end up very poorly all round, because not only will he get it in the neck for that one offence, but every tax return he makes in the future will be inspected with magnifying glasses and he'll be hounded for evermore over every penny and have inspectors ransacking every cranny of his house at two in the morning . . .' I took a breath. '. . . such an accountant may be unpopular.'

'Unreasonable.'

'And an accountant who refuses to break the law, and says that if his client insists on doing so he will have to take his custom somewhere else, such an accountant may possibly be called a bastard.'

She finished her steak and laid down her knife and fork. 'Does this hypothetical accountant snitch to the tax man?'

I smiled. 'If the client is no longer his client, he doesn't know whether his ex-client is tax-dodging or not. So no, he doesn't snitch.'

'Elroy had it all wrong, then.'

'Er,' I said, 'it was he who set up the scheme from which Sticks drew the cash. That's why he is so furious. And I shouldn't be telling you that.'

'You'll be struck off, or strung up, or whatever.'

'Sky high.' I drank some wine. 'It's quite extraordinary how many people try to get their accountants to help them with tax fiddles. I reckon if someone wants to fiddle, the last person he should tell should be his accountant.'

'Just get on with it, and keep quiet?'

'If they want to take the risk.'

She half laughed. 'What risk? Tax-dodging is a national sport.'

People never understood about taxation, I thought. The ruthlessness with which tax could be collected put Victorian landlords in the shade, and the Revenue people now had frightening extra powers of entry and search.

'It's much safer to steal from your employer than the tax man,' I said.

'You must be joking.'

'Have some profiteroles,' I said.

Jossie eyed the approaching trolley of super-puds and agreed on four small cream-filled buns smothered in chocolate sauce.

'Aren't you having any?' she demanded.

'Think of Tapestry on Wednesday.'

'No wonder jockeys get fat when they finally let themselves eat.' She spooned up the dark brown goo with satisfaction. 'Why is it safer to steal from your employer?'

'He can't sell your belongings to get his money back.'

The big eyes widened.

'Golly!' she said.

'If you run up debts, the courts can send bailiffs to take your furniture. If you steal instead, they can't.'

She paused blankly in mid-mouthful, then went on chewing, and swallowed. 'Carry right on,' she said. 'I'm riveted.'

'Well . . . it's theft which is the national sport, not tax-dodging. Petty theft. Knocking off. Nicking. Most shop-lifting is done by the staff, not the customers. No one really blames a girl who sells tights all day if she tucks a pair into her handbag when she goes home. Pinching from employers is almost regarded as a rightful perk, and if ever a manufacturing firm puts an efficient checker on the staff exits there's practically a riot until he's removed.'

'Because he stops the outward march of spanners and fork-lift trucks?'

I grinned. 'You could feed an army on what disappears from the fridges of hotels.'

'Accountants,' she said, 'shouldn't find it amusing.'

'Especially as they spend their lives looking for fraud.'

'Do you?' she said, surprised. 'Do you really? I thought accountants just did sums.'

'The main purpose of an audit is to turn up fiddles.'

'I thought it was . . . well . . . to add up the profit or loss.'

'Not really.'

She thought. 'But when Trevor comes to count the hay and saddles and stuff, that's stocktaking.'

I shook my head. 'More like checking on behalf of your father that he hasn't got a stable lad selling the odd bale or bridle on the quiet.'

'Good heavens.' She was truly astounded. 'I'll have to stop thinking of auditors as fuddy-duddies. Change their image to fraud squad policemen.'

'Not that, either.'

'Why not?'

'If an auditor finds that a firm is being swindled by its cashier, for instance, he simply tells the firm. He doesn't arrest the cashier. He leaves it to the firm to decide whether to call in the handcuffs.'

'But surely they always do.'

'Absolutely not. Firms get red faces and tend to lose business if everyone knows their cashier took them for a ride. They sack the cashier and keep quiet, mostly.'

'Are you bored with telling me all this?'

'No,' I said truthfully.

'Then tell me a good fraud.'

I laughed. 'Heard any good frauds lately?'

'Get on with it.'

'Um . . .' I thought. 'A lot of the best frauds are complicated juggling with figures. It's the paperwork which deceives the eye, like a three card trick. I paused, then smiled. 'I know a good one, though they weren't my clients, thank God. There was a manager of a broiler-chicken factory farm which sold thousands of chickens every week to a freezing firm. The manager was also quietly selling a hundred a week to a butcher who didn't know the chickens had fallen off the back of a lorry, so to speak. No one could ever tell how many chickens there actually were on the farm, because the turnover was so huge and fast, and baby chicks tend to die. The manager pocketed a neat little untaxed regular income, and like most good frauds it was discovered by accident.'

'What accident?'

'The butcher used to pay the manager by cheque, made out in the manager's name. One day he happened to meet one of the directors of the firm which owned the chicken farm, and to save postage he got out his chequebook, wrote a cheque in the manager's name, and asked the director to give it to him, to pay for that month's delivery of chickens.'

'And the lid blew off.'

'With a bang. They sacked the manager.'

'No prosecution?'

'No. The last I heard, he was selling rose bushes by mail order.'

'And you wondered for whose nursery he was working?'

I grinned and nodded. She was quick and funny, and it seemed incredible that I'd met her only the day before.

We drank coffee and talked about horses. She said she had been trying her hand at three-day-eventing, but would be giving it up soon.

'Why?' I asked.

'Lack of talent.'

'What will you do instead?'

'Marry.'

'Oh.' I felt obscurely disappointed. 'Who?'

'I've no idea. Someone will turn up.'

'Just like that?'

'Of course just like that. One finds husbands in the oddest places.'

'What are you doing tomorrow?' I said.

Her eyes gleamed with light and life. 'Visiting a girl friend. What will you do instead?'

'Sums, I expect.'

'But tomorrow's Sunday.'

'And I can have the office to myself all day, without any interruption. I often work on Sundays. Nearly always.'

'Good grief.'

We went out to where the Midget and the Dolomite stood side by side in the car park.

'Thanks for the grub,' Jossie said.

'And for your company.'

'Do you feel all right?'

'Yes,' I said, surprised. 'Why?'

'Just checking,' she said. 'Dad'll ask. It looked such a crunching fall.'

I shook my head. 'A bruise or two.'

'Good. Well, goodnight.'

'Goodnight.' I kissed her cheek.

Her eyes glinted in the dim light from the pub's windows. I kissed her mouth, rather briefly, with closed lips. She gave me the same sort of kiss in return.

'Hm,' she said, standing back. 'That wasn't bad. I do hate wet slobbers.'

She slid expertly into the Midget and started the engine.

'See you in the hay,' she said. 'Counting it.'

She was smiling as she drove away, probably with a mirror expression of my own. I unlocked my car door, and, feeling slightly silly, I looked into the dark area behind the front seats.

No one there.

I sat in the car and started it, debating whether or not to risk going home to the cottage. Friday and Saturday had passed safely enough; but maybe the cats were still watching the mousehole. I decided that another night away would be prudent, and from the pub drove northwards around Oxford again, to the anonymity of the large motel and service station built beside a busy route-connecting roundabout.

The place as usual was bright with lights and bustle: flags flying on tall poles and petrol pumps rattling. I booked in at the reception office, took the key, and drove round to the slightly quieter wing of bedrooms at the rear.

Sleep would be no problem, I thought. The constant rumble of traffic would be soporific. A lullaby.

I yawned, took out my suitcase, locked the car, and fitted the key into the bedroom door.

Something hit me very hard between the shoulders. I fell against the still closed door, and something immediately hit me very hard on the head.

This time, it was brutal. This time, no ether.

I slid in a daze down the door and saw only dark unrecognizable figures bending over to punch and kick. The thuds shuddered through my bones, and another bang on the head slid me deep into peaceful release.

11

I awoke in the dark. Black, total darkness.

I couldn't make out why I should be lying on a hard surface in total darkness, aching all over.

A fall, I thought. I had a fall at Towcester. Why couldn't I remember?

I felt cold. Chilled through and through. When I moved, the aches were worse.

I suddenly remembered having dinner with Jossie. Remembered it all clearly, down to kissing her goodnight in the car park.

So then what?

I tried to sit up, but raising my head was as far as I got. The result was whirling nausea and a pile-driving headache. I inched my fingers tentatively through my hair and found a wince-making area of swelling. I let my head down again, gingerly.

There was no sound except the rustle of my clothes. No engine. No creakings or rushings or water noises. I was not lying on a bunk, but on a larger surface, hard and flat.

I might not be in a sail locker, but I was certainly still in the dark. In the dark in every sense. Weak frustrated anger mocked me that in four days of freedom I hadn't found out enough to save me from the gloomy present.

Every movement told me what I still couldn't remember. I

knew only that the fall off Notebook could not be the source of the soreness all over my body. There would have been a few bruises which would have stiffened up overnight, but nothing like the overall feeling of having been kneaded like dough. I rolled with a grunt on to my stomach and put my head on my folded arms. The only good thing that I could think of was that they hadn't tied my hands.

They. Who were *they?*

When my head stopped hammering, I thought, I would have enough energy to find out where I was and try to get out. Meanwhile it was enough just to lie still and wait for things to get better.

Another thing to be grateful for, I thought. The hard flat surface I was lying on was not swaying about. With luck, I was not on a boat. I wasn't going to be sick. A bruised body was absolutely nothing compared with the agonies of seasickness.

I had no shoes on, just socks. When I squinted at my wrist there was no luminous dial there: no watch. I couldn't be bothered to check all my pockets. I was certain they'd be empty.

After a while I remembered deciding to go to the motel, and after that, bit by bit, I remembered booking in, and the affray on the doorstep.

They must have followed me all the way from Towcester, I thought. Waited through dinner with Jossie. Followed me to the motel. I hadn't spotted them once. I hadn't even heard their footsteps behind me, against the constant noise of traffic.

My instinctive feeling of being safe with Jossie had been dead right.

Ages passed.

The racket inside my skull gradually subsided. Nothing else happened.

I had a feeling that it was nearly dawn, and time to wake up. It had been ten-thirty when I'd been knocked out. There was no telling how long I'd been unconscious, or lain feebly in my present state, but the body had its own clock, and mine was saying six in the morning.

The dawn feeling stirred me to some sort of action, though if there was dawn outside it was not making its way through to me. Perhaps, I thought uneasily, I was wrong about the time. It was still night outside. I prayed for it to be still night outside.

I had another go at sitting up. One couldn't say that I felt superbly healthy. Concussion took a while to go away, and cold was notoriously bad for bruised muscles. The combination made every movement a nuisance. A familiar sort of pain, because of racing falls in the past. Just worse.

The surface beneath me was dirty: I could feel the gritty dust. It smelled faintly of oil. It was flat and smooth and not wood.

I felt around me in all directions, and on my left connected with a wall. Slithering on one hip, I inched that way and cautiously explored with my fingers.

Another smooth flat surface, at right angles to the floor. I banged it gently with my fist, and got back the noise and vibration of metal.

I thought that if I sat for a while with my back against the wall it would soon get light, and it would be easy then to see where I was. It had to get light, I thought forlornly. It simply had to.

It didn't, of course.

When they'd given me light on the boat, I'd escaped. A mistake to be avoided.

It had to be faced. The darkness was deliberate, and would go on. It was no good, I told myself severely, sitting in a miserable huddle feeling sorry for myself.

I made a further exploration into unmapped territory, and found that my world was a good deal smaller than Columbus's. It seemed prudent to move while still sitting down, on the flat-earth theory that one might fall over the edge; but two feet of shuffling to the right brought me to a corner.

The adjacent wall was also flat, smooth, and metal. I shifted my spine round on to it, and set off again to the right.

The traverse was short. I came almost at once to another corner. I found that if I sat in the centre of the wall I could reach both side walls at once quite easily with my finger-tips. Five feet, approximately, from side to side.

I shuffled round the second corner and pressed on. Three feet down that side, I knew where I was. The flatness of the metal wall was broken there by a big rounded bulge, whose meaning was as clear to my touch as if I'd been seeing it.

It was the semi-circular casing over a wheel; and I was inside a van.

I had a powerful, immediate picture of the fake ambulance I'd climbed into at Cheltenham. A white van, of a standard pattern, with the doors opening outwards at the rear. If I continued past the wheel, I would come to the rear doors.

And I would feel a proper fool, I thought, if all I had to do was open the doors and step out.

I wouldn't have minded feeling a proper fool. The doors were firmly shut, and likely to remain so. There was no handle on the inside.

In the fourth corner I came across what I'had this time been given in the way of life support systems, and if my spirits had already been at zero, at that point they went way below.

There was a five-gallon plastic jerry-can full of liquid, and a large carrier bag.

I unscrewed the cap of the jerry-can and sniffed at the contents. No smell. Sloshed some of the liquid out on to my hand, and tasted it.

Water.

I screwed the cap on again, fumbling in the dark.

Five gallons of water.

Oh no, I thought numbly. Oh dear God.

The carrier was packed to the top with flat plastic packets, each about four inches square. There was again no smell. I pulled one of the packets open, and found the contents were thin four-inch squares of sliced processed cheese.

I counted the packets with a sinking heart, taking them one by one from the carrier and stacking them on the floor. There were sixty of them. All, as far as I could tell, exactly the same.

Wretchedly I counted them from the floor back into the carrier, one by one, and there were still sixty. They had given me enough food and water to last for at least four weeks. There were going to be no twice a day visits: no one to talk to at all.

Sod them, I thought violently. If this was revenge, it was worse than anything I'd ever brought on any crook.

Spurred by anger, I stood without caution to explore the top part of the van, and banged my sore head on the roof. It was very nearly altogether too much. I found myself back on my knees, cursing and holding my head, and trying not to weep. A battered feeble figure, sniffing in the dark.

It wouldn't do, I thought. It was necessary to be sternly unemotional. To ignore the aches and pains. To take a good cold grip of things, and make a plan and routine for survival.

When the fresh waves of headache passed, I got on with it.

The presence of food and drink meant, I thought, that survival was expected. That one day, if I didn't manage a second escape, I would be released. Death, again, was not apparently on the agenda. Well, then, why was I getting into such a fuss?

I had read once of a man who had spent weeks down a pothole in silence and darkness to see how a total lack of external reference would affect the human body. He had survived with his mind intact and his body none the worse for wear, and his sense of time had gone remarkably little astray. What he could do, so could I. It was irrelevant, I thought sternly, that the scientist had volunteered for his incarceration, and had had his heartbeat and other vital signs monitored on the surface, and could have got out again any time he felt he'd had enough.

Feeling a good deal steadier for the one-man pep-talk, I got more slowly to my feet, sliding my spine up the side wall, and feeling for the roof with my hands. It was too low for me to stand upright, by four or six inches. With head and knees bent, I felt my way again right round the van.

Both sides were completely blank. The front wall was broken by the shape of a small panel which must have opened through to the driving cab. It seemed to be intended to slide, but was fastened shut as firmly as if it had been welded. There was no handle or bolt on the inside; only smoothed metal.

The rear doors at first seemed to be promising, as I discovered they were not entirely solid, but had windows. One each side, about twelve inches across, the distance from my wrist to my elbow, and half as high.

There was no glass in the windows. I stretched my hand cautiously through the one on the right, and immediately came to a halt. Something hard was jammed against the doors on the outside, holding them shut.

111

I was concentrating so much on the message from my fingers that I realized that I was crouching there with my eyes shut. Funny, really. I opened them. No light. What good were eyes without light.

Outside each window there was an area of coarse cloth, which felt like heavy canvas. At the outer sides of the window it was possible to push the canvas, to move it three or four inches away from the van. On the inner halves it was held tight against the van by whatever was jamming the doors shut.

I put an arm out of each outer section of window in turn, and felt as much of the outside of the van as I could reach. It was very little, and of no use. The whole of the back of the van was sheeted in canvas.

I slid down again to the floor and tried to visualize what I'd felt. A van covered in canvas with its rear doors jammed shut. Where could one park such a thing so that it wouldn't be immediately discovered. In a garage? A barn? If I banged on the sides, would anyone hear me?

I banged on the sides of the van, but my fists made little noise, and there was nothing else to bang with. I shouted 'Help' a good many times through the windows, but no one came.

There was air perceptibly leaking in through the missing windows: I could feel it when I pushed the canvas outwards. No fear of asphyxiation.

It irritated me that I could do nothing useful with those windows. They were too small to crawl through, even without the canvas and whatever was holding it against the van. I couldn't get my head through the spaces, let alone my shoulders.

I decided to eat some cheese and think things over. The cheese wasn't bad. The thoughts produced the unwelcome reflection that this time I had no mattress, no blanket, no pillow, and no loo. Also no paperback novel, spare socks, or soap. The sail locker had been a Hilton compared with the van.

On the other hand, in an odd sort of way the time in the sail locker had prepared me better for this dourer cell. Instead of feeling more frightened, more hysterical, more despairing, I felt less. I had already been through all the horrors. Also, during the four days of freedom, I had not gone to the South Pole to avoid capture. I'd feared it and done my best to dodge it, but in returning to my usual life, I'd known it might come.

The reason for the first abduction presumably still existed. I had escaped before the intended time, and in someone's eyes this had been a very bad thing. Bad enough to send the squad to retake me, from the cottage, within a day of my return to England. Bad enough to risk carting me off again when this time there would, I hoped, be a police search.

I was pretty sure I must still be in England. I certainly had no memory of being transported from the motel to wherever I was now, but the impression that I'd been unconscious for only an hour or two was convincingly strong.

Sunday morning. No one would miss me. It would be Monday before Debbie and Peter began to wonder. Tuesday, perhaps, before the police took it seriously, if indeed they did, in spite of their assurance. A day or two more before anyone really started looking: and I had no wife or parents to keep the search alive, if I wasn't to be found soon after that.

Jossie might have done, I thought regretfully, if I'd known her for longer. Jossie with her bright eyes and forthright tongue.

At the very least, at the most hopeful assessment, the future still looked a long, hard, weary grind.

Shortening the perspective dramatically, it was becoming imperative to solve immediately the question of liquid waste disposal. I might be having to live in a tin box, but not, if I could help it, in a filthy stinking tin box.

Necessity concentrated the mind wonderfully, as others before me had observed. I took the cheese slices out of one of the thick plastic packets, and used that, and emptied it in relays out of the rear window, pushing the canvas away from the van as far as I could. Not the most sanitary of arrangements, but better than nothing.

After that little excitement, I sat down again. I was still cold, though not now with the through-and-through chill of injury-shock. I could perhaps have done some warming-up arm-swinging exercises, if it hadn't been for protesting bruises. As things were, with every muscle movement a reminder, I simply sat.

Exploration had kept me busy up to that point, but the next few hours revealed the true extent of my isolation.

There was absolutely no external sound. If I suppressed the

faint noise of my own breathing, I could hear literally nothing. No traffic, no hum of aircraft, no wind, no creak, no rustle. Nothing.

There was absolutely no light. Air came steadily in from between the outside of the van and its canvas shroud, but no light came with it. Eyes wide open, or firmly shut, it was all the same.

There was no perceptible change in temperature. It remained just too low for comfort, defying my body's efforts to acclimatize. I had been left trousers, underpants, shirt, sports jacket and socks, though no tie, no belt, no loose belongings of any sort. It was Sunday, April 3rd. It might have been a sunny spring day outside, but wherever I was, it was simply too cold.

People would be reading about the Grand National in their Sunday newspapers, I thought. Lying in bed, warm and comfortable. Getting up and strolling to the pub. Eating hot meals, playing with the kids, deciding not to mow the lawn for another week. Millions of people, living their Sunday.

I served myself a Sunday lunch of cheese slices, and with great care drank some water from the can. It was heavy, being full, and I couldn't afford to tip it over. Enough water went down my neck to make me think of the uses of cheese packets as drinking cups.

After lunch, a snooze, I thought. I made a fairly reasonable pillow by rearranging the cheese packets inside the carrier, and resolutely tried to sleep, but the sum of discomfort kept me awake.

Well, then, I thought, lying on my back and staring at the invisible ceiling, I could sort out what I'd learned during my four free days.

The first of them could be discounted, as I'd spent it in Majorca, organizing my return home. That left two days in the office and one at the races. One night hiding in the cottage, one sleeping soundly in the Gloucester hotel. For all of that period I'd been looking for reasons, which made this present dose of imprisonment a great deal different from the first. Then, I'd been completely bewildered. This time I had at least one or two ideas.

*

Hours passed.

Nothing got any better.

I sat up for a while, and lay down again, and everything hurt, just the same. I cheered myself up with the thought that the stiff ache of bruises always finally got better, never worse. Suppose, for instance, it had been appendicitis. I'd heard that people going off to Everest or other Backs of Beyond had their perfectly healthy appendix removed, just in case. I wished on the whole that I hadn't thought of appendicitis.

Or toothache.

I had a feeling that it was evening, and then that it was night.

There was no change, except in me. I grew slowly even colder, but as if from the inside out. My eyelids stayed heavily shut. I drifted gradually in and out of sleep, a long drowsy twilight punctuated by short groaning awakenings every time I moved. When I woke with a clear mind, it felt like dawn.

If the cycle held, I thought, I could keep a calendar. One empty cheese packet for every day, stacked in the right-hand front corner of the van. If I put one there at every dawn, I would know the days. One for Sunday: a second for Monday. I extracted two wads of cheese slices and shuffled carefully a couple of feet forward to leave the empties.

I ate and drank what I thought of as breakfast: and I had become, I realized, much more at home in the dark. Physically, I was less clumsy. I found it easier to manage the water can, for instance, and no longer tended to put the cap on the floor and feel frustrated when I couldn't at once find it after I'd drunk. I now put my hand back automatically to where I'd parked the cap in the first place.

Mentally, too, it was less of a burden. On the boat I'd loathed it, and of all the rotten prospects of a second term of imprisonment, it had been being thrown back into the dark which I had shrunk from most. I still hated it, but its former heavy oppression was passing. I found that I no longer feared that the darkness on its own would set me climbing the walls.

I spent the morning thinking about reasons for abduction, and in the afternoon made an abacus out of pieces of cheese arranged in rows, and did a string of mathematical computations. I knew that other solitary captives had kept their minds occupied by repeating verses, but I'd always found it easier to think in numbers and symbols, and I'd not learned enough words by heart for them to be of any present use. Goosey goosey gander had its limitations.

Monday night came and went. When I woke I planted another cheese packet in the front right-hand corner, and flexed arms and legs which were no longer too sore to be worth it.

Tuesday morning I spent doing exercises and thinking about reasons for abduction, and Tuesday afternoon I felt my way delicately round the abacus, enlarging its scope as a calculator. Tuesday evening I sat and hugged my knees, and thought disconsolately that it was all very well telling myself to be staunch and resolute, but that staunch and resolute was not really how I felt.

Three days since I'd had dinner with Jossie. Well . . . at least I had her to think about, which I hadn't had on the boat.

The dozing period came round again. I lay down and let it wash over me for hours, and counted it Tuesday night.

Wednesday, for the twentieth time, I felt round the van inch by inch, looking for a possible way out. For the twentieth time, I didn't find one.

There were no bolts to undo. No levers. There was nothing. No way out. I knew it, but I couldn't stop searching.

Wednesday was the day I was supposed to be riding Tapestry at Ascot. Whether because of that, or simply because my body was back approximately to normal, the time passed more slowly than ever.

I whistled and sang, and felt restless, and wished passionately that there was room to stand up straight. The only way to straighten my spine was to lie down flat. I could feel my hard-won calm slipping away round the edges, and it was a considerable effort to give myself something to do with the pieces-of-cheese slide rule.

Wednesday I lost track of whether it was noon or evening, and the idea of days and days more of that existence was demoralizing. Dammit, I thought mordantly. Shut up, shut up with the gloomsville. One day at a time. One day, one hour, one minute at a time.

I ate some cheese and felt sleepy, and that at long last was Wednesday done.

Thursday mid-day, I heard a noise.

I couldn't believe it.

Some distant clicks, and a grinding noise. I was lying on my back doing bicycling exercises with my legs in the air, and I practically disconnected myself getting to my knees and scrambling over to the rear doors.

I pushed the canvas away from one of the windows, and shouted at the top of my lungs.

'Hey . . . hey . . . Come here.'

There were footsteps; more than one set. Soft footsteps, but in that huge dead silence, quite clear.

I swallowed. Whoever it was, there was no point in keeping quiet.

'Hey,' I shouted again. 'Come here.'

The footsteps stopped.

A man's voice, close to the van, spoke very loudly.

'Are you Roland Britten?'

I said weakly, 'Yes . . . who are you?'

'Police, sir,' he said.

12

They took a good long while getting me out, because, as the disembodied voice explained, they would have to take photographs and notes for use in any future prosecution. Also there was the matter of fingerprints, which would mean further delay.

'And we can't get you out without moving the van, you see, sir,' said the voice. 'On account of it's backed hard up against a brick pillar, and we can't open the rear doors. On top of that the driving cab doors are both locked, and the brake's hard on, and there's no key in the ignition. So if you'll be patient, sir, we'll have you out as soon as we can.'

He sounded as if he were reassuring a small child who might scream the place down at any minute, but I found it easy to be patient, if only he knew.

There were several voices outside after a while, and from time to time they asked me if I was all right, and I said yes; and in the end they started the van's engine and drove it forward a few feet, and pulled off the canvas cover.

The return of sight was extraordinary. The two small windows appeared as oblongs of grey, and I had difficulty in focusing. A face looked in, roundly healthy, enquiring and concerned, topped by a uniform cap.

'Have you out in a jiffy now, sir,' he said. 'We're having a bit of difficulty with these doors, see, as the handle's been sabotaged.'

'Fine,' I said vaguely. The light was still pretty dim, but to me a luxury like no other on earth. A half-forgotten joy, newly discovered. Like meeting a dead friend. Familiar, lost, precious, and restored.

I sat on the floor and looked around my prison. It was smaller than I'd imagined: cramped and claustrophobic, now that I could see the grey enclosing walls.

The jerry-can of water was of white plastic, with a red cap. The carrier was brown, as I'd imagined it. The little calendar stack of five empty packets lay in its corner, and the hardening pieces of cheese from my counting machine, in another. There was nothing else, except me and dust.

They opened the doors eventually and helped me out, and then took notes and photographs of where I'd been. I stood a pace or two away and looked curiously at my surroundings.

The van was indeed the white one from Cheltenham, or one exactly like. An old Ford. No tax disc, and no number-plates. The canvas which had covered it was a huge, dirty dark grey tarpaulin, the sort used for sheeting loads on lorries. The van had been wrapped in it like a parcel, and tied with ropes threaded through eyelets in the tarpaulin's edges.

The van, the police and I were all inside a building of about a hundred feet square. All round the walls rose huge lumpy heaps of dust-covered unidentifiable bundles, grey shapes of boxes and things that looked like sandbags. Some of the piles reached the low flat ceiling, which was supported at strategic points by four sturdy brick pillars.

It was against one of these, in the small clear area in the centre, that the van had been jammed.

'What is this place?' I said to the policeman beside me.

'Are you all right, sir?' he said. He shivered slightly. 'It's cold in here.'

'Yes,' I said. 'Where exactly are we?'

'It used to be one of those army surplus stores, selling stuff to the public. Went bust a while back, though, and no one's ever shifted all the muck.'

'Oh. Well . . . whereabouts is it?'

'Down one of those tracks what used to be the railway branch line, before they closed it.'

'Yes,' I said apologetically. 'But what town?'

'Eh?' He looked at me in surprise. 'Newbury, of course, sir.'

The town clocks pointed to five o'clock when the police drove me down to the station. My body's own time had proved remarkably constant, I thought. Much better than on the boat, where noise and tossing and sickness had upset things.

I was given a chair in the office of one of the same policemen as before, who showed no regrets at having earlier thought I was exaggerating.

'How did you find me?' I said.

He tapped his teeth with a pencil, a hard-working Detective-Inspector with an air of suspecting the innocent until they were found guilty.

'Scotland Yard had a call,' he said grudgingly. 'We'll want a statement from you, sir, if you don't mind.'

'A cup of tea first,' I suggested.

His gaze wandered over my face and clothes. I must have looked a wreck. He came somewhere near a smile, and sent a young constable on the errand.

The tea tasted marvellous, though I daresay it wasn't. I drank it slowly and told him fairly briefly what had happened.

'So you didn't see their faces at all, this time?'

'No,' I said.

'Pity.'

'Do you think,' I said tentatively, 'that some one could drive me back to the motel, so I can collect my car?'

'No need, sir,' he said. 'It's parked beside your cottage.'

'What?'

He nodded. 'With a lot of your possessions in it. Suitcase. Wallet. Shoes. Keys. All in the boot. Your assistants notified us on Monday that you were missing again. We sent a man along to your cottage. He reported your car was there, but you weren't. We did what you asked, sir. We did look for you. The whole country's been looking for you, come to that. The motel rang us yesterday to say you'd booked in there last Saturday but hadn't used the room, but apart from that there was nothing to go on. No trace at all. We thought you might have been taken off on another boat, to be frank.'

I finished the tea, and thanked him for it.

'Will you run me back to the cottage, then?'

He thought it could be arranged. He came with me out to the entrance hall, to fix it.

A large man with an over-anxious expression came bustling in from the street, swinging the door wide and assessing rapidly the direction from which he would get most satisfaction. My partner at his most bombastic, his deep voice echoing round the hall as he demanded information.

'Hello, Trevor,' I said. 'Take it easy.'

He stopped in mid-commotion, and stared at me as if I were an intrusive stranger. Then he recognized me, and took in my general appearance, and his face went stiff with shock.

'Ro!' He seemed to have trouble with his voice. 'Ro, my dear fellow. My dear fellow. I've just heard . . . My God, Ro . . .'

I sighed. 'Calm down, Trevor. All I need is a razor.'

'But you're so *thin*.' His eyes were appalled. I reflected that I was probably a good deal thinner than when he'd seen me last, some time in the dim, distant, and safe past.

'Mr King has been bombarding us all day,' said the Detective Inspector with a touch of impatience.

'My dear Ro, you must come back with me. We'll look after you. My *God*, Ro . . .'

I shook my head. 'I'm fine, Trevor. I'm grateful to you, but I'd really rather go home.'

'Alone?' he said anxiously. 'Suppose . . . I mean . . . do you think it's safe?'

'Oh yes,' I nodded. 'Whoever put me in, let me out. It's all over, I think.'

'What's all over?'

'That,' I said soberly, 'is a whole new ball game.'

The cottage embraced me like a balm.

I had a bath, and shaved, and a grey face of gaunt shadows looked at me out of the mirror. No wonder Trevor had been shocked. Just as well, I thought, that he hadn't seen the black and yellow blotches of fading bruises which covered me from head to foot.

I shrugged, and thought the same as before: nothing that a few days' freedom wouldn't fix. I put on jeans and a jersey and went downstairs in search of a large Scotch, and that was the last peaceful moment of the evening.

The telephone rang non-stop. Reporters, to my amazement, arrived at the doorstep. A television camera appeared. When they saw I was astounded, they said hadn't I read the papers.

'What papers?'

They produced them, and spread them out.

The Sporting Life: headline on Tuesday: 'Where is Roland Britten?' followed by an article about my sea trip, as told by me to friends. I had not been seen since Towcester. Friends were worried.

On Wednesday, paragraphs in all the dailies: 'Tapestry's rider again missing' in one of the staider, and 'Fun Jock Twice Removed?' from a tits-and-bums.

Thursday – that day – many front pages carried a broadly smiling picture of me, taken five minutes after the Gold Cup. 'Find Roland Britten' ordered one, and 'Fears for Jockey's

Life' gloomed another. I glanced over them in amazement, remembering ironically that I'd been afraid no one would really look for me at all.

The telephone rang beside my hand. I picked up the receiver and said hello.

'Ro? Is that you?' The voice was fresh and unmistakable.

'Jossie!'

'Where the hell have you been?'

'Have dinner with me tomorrow, and I'll tell you.'

'Pick me up at eight,' she said. 'What's all that noise?'

'I'm pressed by Press,' I said. 'Journalists.'

'Good grief.' She laughed. 'Are you all right?'

'Yes, fine.'

'It was on the news, that you'd been found.'

'I don't believe it.'

'Big stuff, buddy boy.' The mockery was loud and clear.

'Did you start it . . . all this publicity?' I said.

'Not me, no. Moira Longerman. Mrs Tapestry. She tried to get you Sunday, and she tried your office on Monday, and they told her you were missing, and they thought you might have been kidnapped again, so she rang up the editor of *The Sporting Life*, who's a friend of hers, to ask him to help.'

'A determined lady,' I said gratefully.

'She didn't run Tapestry yesterday, you know. There's a sob-stuff bit in *The Sporting Life*. "How can I run my horse while Roland is missing" and all that guff. Fairs turns your stomach.'

'Fair turned Binny Tomkins's, I'll bet.'

She laughed. 'I can hear the wolves howling for you. See you tomorrow. Don't vanish before eight.'

I put the telephone down, but the wolves had to wait a little longer, as the bell immediately rang again.

Moira Longerman, excited and twittering, coming down the wire like an electric current.

'Thank heavens you're free. Isn't it marvellous? Are you all right? Can you ride Tapestry on Saturday? Do tell me all about the horrible place where they found you . . . and Roland, dear, I don't want you listening to a word Binny Tomkins says about you not being fit to ride after all you've been through.'

'Moira,' I said, vainly trying to stop the flow. 'Thank you very much.'

'My dear,' she said, 'it was rather *fun*, getting everyone mobilized. Of course I was truly dreadfully worried that something awful had happened to you, and it was quite clear that somebody had to do *something*, otherwise you might stay kidnapped for *weeks*, and it seemed to me that a jolly good fuss was what was wanted. I thought that if the whole country was looking for you, whoever had taken you might get cold feet and turn you loose, and that's precisely what happened, so I was right and the silly police were all wrong.'

'What silly police?' I said.

'Telling me I might have put you in danger by getting *The Sporting Life* to say you'd vanished again. I ask you! They said if kidnappers get panicky they could kill their victim. Anyway, they were wrong, weren't they?'

'Fortunately,' I agreed.

'So do tell me all about it,' she said. 'Is it true you were shut up in a van? What was it like?'

'Boring,' I said.

'Roland, *really*. Is that all you've got to say?'

'I thought about you all day on Wednesday, imagining you'd be furious when I didn't turn up at Ascot.'

'That's better.' She laughed her tinkly laugh. 'You can make up for it on Saturday. Tapestry's in the Oasthouse Cup at Kempton, though of course he's got top weight there, which was why we wanted to run at Ascot instead. But now we're going to Kempton.'

'I'm afraid . . .' I said, 'that Binny's right. This time, I'm really not fit enough. I'd love to ride him, but . . . well . . . at the moment I couldn't go two rounds with a kitten.'

There was a short silence at the other end.

'Do you mean it?' she demanded doubtfully.

'I hate to say so, but I do.'

The doubt in her voice subsided. 'I'm sure you'll be a hundred per cent after a good night's sleep. After all, you'll have nearly two days to recover, and even Binny admits you're pretty tough as amateurs go . . . so *please*, Roland, *please* ride on

Saturday, because the horse is jumping out of his skin, and the opposition is not so strong as it will be in the Whitbread Gold Cup in two weeks' time, and I feel in my bones that he'll win this race but not the other. And I don't want Binny putting up any other jockey, as to be frank I only trust you, which you know. So *please* say you will. I was so *thrilled* when I heard you were free, so that you could ride on Saturday.'

I rubbed my hand across my eyes. I knew I shouldn't agree, and that I was highly unlikely to be fit enough even to walk the course on my feet, let alone control half a ton of thoroughbred muscle on the rampage. Yet to her, if I refused, it would seem like gross ingratitude after her lively campaign to free me, and I too suspected that if Tapestry started favourite with a different jockey of Binny's choice, he wouldn't win. There was also the insidious old desire to race which raised its head in defiance of common sense. Reason told me I'd fall off from weakness at the first fence, and the irresistible temptation of a go at another of the season's top 'chases kidded me not to believe it.

'Well . . .' I said, hesitating.

'Oh, you *will*,' she said delightedly. 'Oh Roland, I'm so *glad*.'

'I shouldn't.'

'If you don't win,' she said gaily, 'I promise I won't blame you.'

I'd blame myself, I thought, and I'd deserve it.

I went to the office at nine the next morning, and Trevor fussed about a great deal too much.

'You need rest, Ro. You should be in bed.'

'I need people and life and things to do.'

He sat in the clients' armchair in my office and looked worried. The sun-tan of his holiday suited him, increasing his air of distinction. His silvery hair was fluffier than usual, and his comfortable stomach looked rounder.

'Did you have a good time', I said, 'in Spain?'

'What? Oh yes, splendid. Splendid. Until the car broke down, of course. And all the time, while we were enjoying ourselves, you . . .' He stopped and shook his head.

'I'm afraid,' I said wryly, 'that I'm dreadfully behind with the work.'

'For heaven's sake . . .'

'I'll try to catch up,' I said.

'I wish you'd take it easy for a few days.' He looked as if he meant it, his eyes full of troubled concern. 'It won't do either of us any good if you crack up.'

My lips twitched. That was more like the authentic Trevor.

'I'm made of plasticine,' I said; and despite his protests I stayed where I was and once again tried to sort out the trail of broken appointments.

Mr Wells was in a worse mess than ever, having sent a cheque which had promptly bounced. A prosecution for that was in the offing.

'But you knew the bank wouldn't pay it,' I protested when he telephoned with this latest trouble.

'Yes . . . but I thought they *might*.'

His naïvety was frightening: the same stupid hopefulness which had got him enmeshed in the first place. He blanked out reality and believed in fantasies. I'd known others like him, and I'd never known them change.

'Come on Monday afternoon,' I said resignedly.

'Supposing someone kidnaps you again.'

'They won't,' I said. 'Two-thirty, Monday.'

I went through the week's letters with Debbie and sorted out the most urgent. Their complexity made me wilt.

'We'll answer them on Monday morning,' I said.

Debbie fetched some coffee and said at her most pious that I wasn't fit to be at work.

'Did we get those postponements from the Commissioners for Axwood Stables and Coley Young?' I said.

'Yes, they came on Wednesday.'

'And what about Denby Crest's certificate?'

'Mr King said he'd sée about that this morning.'

I rubbed a hand over my face. No use kidding myself. However much I disliked it, I did feel pathetically weak. Agreeing to ride Tapestry had been a selfish folly. The only sensible course was to ring Moira Longerman at once, and cry off: but when it came to race-riding, I'd never been sensible.

'Debbie,' I said, 'please would you go down to the store in the basement, and bring up all the old files on Connaught Powys, and on Glitberg and Ownslow.'

'Who?'

I wrote the names down for her. She glanced at them, nodded, and went away.

Sticks Elroy telephoned, words tumbling out in a rush, incoherent and thick with Oxfordshire accent. A lot more talkative than he'd been at dinner in the pub, when overshadowed by his bull-like dad.

'Stop,' I said. 'I didn't hear a word. Say it slowly.'

'I said I was ever so sorry you got shut up in that van.'

'Well . . . thanks.'

'My old man couldn't have done it, you know.' He sounded anxious, more seeking to convince than convinced.

'Don't you think so?'

'I know he said . . . Look, well, he went on cursing all evening, and I know he's got a van, and all, which is off somewhere getting the gearbox fixed, or something, and I know he was that furious, and he said you should be locked up, but I don't reckon he could have done it, not for real.'

'Did you ask him?' I said curiously.

'Yeah.' He hesitated. 'See . . . we had a bloody big row, him and me.' Another pause. 'He always knocked us about when we were kids. Straps, boots, anything.' A pause. 'I asked him about you . . . he punched me in the face.'

'Mm,' I said. 'What did you decide to do about that cash?'

'Yeah, well, that's what the row was about, see. I reckoned you were right and I didn't want any trouble with the law, and Dad blew his top and said I'd never been grateful for everything he'd done for me. He says if I declare that cash and pay tax on it he'll be in trouble himself, see, and I reckon he was mad enough to do anything.'

I reflected a bit. 'What colour is his van?'

'White, sort of. An old Ford.'

'Um. When did you decide to go to that pub for dinner?'

'Dad drove there straight from the races, for a drink, like, and then he phoned and said they could fix us all in for dinner, and we might as well celebrate my win.'

'Would he be likely,' I said, 'to be able to lay his hands on sixty packets of cheese slices?'

'Whatever are you on about?'

I sighed. 'They were in the van with me.'

'Well, I don't know, do I? I don't live with him any more. I wouldn't reckon on him going to a supermarket, though. Women's work, see?'

'Yes. If you've decided to declare that cash, there are some legitimate expenses to set off against the profit.'

'Bloody tax,' he said. 'Sucks you dry. I'm not going to bother sweating my guts out on any more schemes. Not bloody worth it.'

He made an appointment for the following week and grumbled his way off the phone.

I sat and stared into space, thinking of Sticks Elroy and his violent father. Heavy taxation was always self-defeating, with the country losing progressively more for every tightening of the screw. Overtime and enterprise weren't worth it. Emigration was. The higher the tax rates, the less there was to tax. It was crazy. If I'd been Chancellor, I'd have made Britain a tax-haven, and welcomed back all the rich who had taken their money and left. A fifty per cent tax on millions would be better for the country than a ninety-eight per cent on nothing. As it was, I had to interpret and advise in accordance with what I thought of as bad economics; uphold laws which I thought irra-tional. If the fury the Elroys felt against the system took the form of abuse of the accountant who forced them to face nasty facts, it wasn't unduly surprising. I did doubt though that even Elroy senior would make his abuse physical. Calling me a bas-tard was a long way from imprisonment.

Debbie came in with her arms full of files and her face full of fluster.

'There's a lady outside who insists on seeing you. She hasn't got an appointment and Mr King said you were definitely not to be worried today, but she won't go away. Oh!'

The lady in question was walking into the office in Debbie's wake. Tall, thin, assured, and middle-aged.

I stood up, smiling, and shook hands with Hilary Margaret Pinlock.

'It's all right, Debbie,' I said.

'Oh, very well.' She shrugged, put down the files, and went out.

'How are you?' I said. 'Sit down.'

Margaret Pinlock sat in the clients' chair and crossed her thin legs.

'You,' she said, 'look half-dead.'

.'A half-empty bottle is also half-full.'

'And you're an optimist?'

'Usually,' I said.

She was wearing a brownish-grey flecked tweed coat, to which the sunless April day added nothing in the way of life. Behind the spectacles the eyes looked small and bright, and coral-pink lipstick lent warmth to her mouth.

'I've come to tell you something,' she said. 'Quite a lot of things, I suppose.'

'Good or bad?'

'Facts.'

'You're not pregnant?'

She was amused. 'I don't know yet.'

'Would you like some sherry?'

'Yes, please.'

I stood up and produced a bottle and two glasses from a filing cupboard. Poured. Handed her a generous slug of Harvey's Luncheon Dry.

'I came home yesterday,' she said. 'I read about you being kidnapped again, on the aeroplane coming back. They had newspapers. Then I heard on the news that you were found, and safe. I thought I would come and see you myself, instead of taking my information to the police.'

'What information?' I said. 'And I thought you were due back home last Saturday.'

She sipped her sherry sedately.

'Yes, I was. I stayed on, though. Because of you. It cost me a fortune.' She looked at me over her glass. 'I was sorry to read

128

you had been recaptured after all. I had seen . . . your fear of it.'

'Mm,' I said ruefully.

'I found out about that boat for you,' she said.

I almost spilled the sherry.

She smiled. 'About the man, to be more exact. The man in the dinghy, who was chasing you.'

'How?' I said.

'After you'd gone, I hired a car and drove to all the places on Minorca where they said yachts could be moored. The nearest good harbour to Cala St Galdana was Ciudadela, and I should think that's where the boat went after they lost you, but it had gone by the time I started looking.' She drank some sherry. 'I asked some English people on a yacht there, and they said there had been an English crew on a sixty-footer there the night before, and they'd overheard them talking about wind for a passage to Palma. I asked them to describe the captain, and they said there didn't seem to be a proper captain, only a tall young man who looked furious.' She stopped and considered, and explained further. 'All the yachts at Ciudadela were moored at right angles to the quayside, you see. Stern on. So that they were all close together, side by side, and you walked straight off the back of them on to dry land.'

'Yes,' I said. 'I see.'

'So I just walked along the whole row, asking. There were Spaniards, Germans, French, Swedes . . . all sorts. The English people had noticed the other English crew just because they *were* English, if you see what I mean.'

'I do,' I said.

'And also because it had been the biggest yacht that night in the harbour.' She paused. 'So instead of flying home on Saturday, I went to Palma.'

'It's a big place,' I said.

She nodded. 'It took me three days. But I found out that young man's name, and quite a lot about him.'

'Would you like some lunch?' I said.

13

We walked along to La Riviera at the end of the High Street
and ordered moussaka. The place was full as usual, and Hilary
leaned forward across the table to make herself privately heard.
Her strong plain face was full of the interest and vigour she had
put into her search on my behalf, and it was typical of her self-
confidence that she was concentrating only on the subject in
hand and not the impression she was making as a woman. A
headmistress, I thought: not a lover.

'His name,' she said, 'is Alastair Yardley. He is one of a whole
host of young men who seem to wander around the Mediterranean looking after boats while the owners are home in England, Italy, France, and wherever. They live in the sun, on the
water's edge, picking up jobs where they can, and leading an
odd sort of drop-out existence which supplies a useful service to
boat owners.'

'Sounds attractive.'

'It's bumming around,' she said succinctly.

'I wouldn't mind dropping out, right now,' I said.

'You're made of sterner stuff.'

Plasticine, I thought.

'Go on about Alastair Yardley,' I said.

'I asked around for two days without any success. My description of him seemed to fit half the population, and although
I'd seen the boat, of course, I wasn't sure I would know it again,
as I haven't an educated eye for that sort of thing. There are
two big marinas at Palma, both of them packed with boats.
Some boats are moored stern-on, like at Ciudadela, but dozens
more were anchored away from the quays. I hired a boatman
to take me round the whole harbour in his motorboat, but with
no results. I'm sure he thought I was potty. I was pretty discouraged, actually, and was admitting defeat, when he – the
boatman, that is – said there was another small harbour less
than a day's sail away, and why didn't I look there. So on Wednesday I took a taxi to the port of Andraitx.'

She stopped to eat some moussaka, which had arrived and
smelled magnificent.

'Eat,' she said, scooping up a third generous forkful and waving at my still full plate.

'Yes,' I said. It was the first proper meal I'd approached since the dinner with Jossie, and I should have been ravenous. Instead, the diet of processed cheese seemed to have played havoc with my appetite, and I found difficulty in eating much at all. I hadn't been able to face any supper, the evening before, when the journalists had finally gone, and not much breakfast either.

'Tell me about Andraitx,' I said.

'In a minute,' she said. 'I'm not letting this delicious food get cold.' She ate with enjoyment and disapproved of my unsuccessful efforts to do the same. I had to wait for the next instalment until she had finished the last morsel and lain down her fork.

'That was *good*,' she said. 'A great treat.'

'Andraitx,' I said.

She half laughed. 'All right, then. Andraitx. Small by Palma's standards, but bigger than Ciudadela. The small ports and harbours are the old parts of the islands. The buildings are old . . . there are no new ritzy hotels there, because there are no beaches. Deep water, rocky cliffs, and so on. I found out so much more about the islands this week than if I'd stopped in Cala St Galdana for my week and come home last Saturday. They have such a bloody history of battles and sieges and invasions. A horrible violent history. One may sneer now at the way they've been turned into a tourist paradise, but the brassy modern civilization must be better than the murderous past.'

'Dearest Hilary,' I said. 'Cut the lecture and come to the grit.'

'It was the biggest yacht in Andraitx,' she said. 'I was sure almost at once, and then I saw the young man on the quayside, not far from where I paid off the taxi. He came out of a shop and walked across the big open space that there is there, between the buildings and the water. He was carrying a heavy box of provisions. He dumped it on the edge of the quay, beside that black rubber dinghy which he brought ashore at Cala St Galdana. Then he went off again, up a street leading away from the quay. I didn't exactly follow him, I just watched. He went into a doorway a little way up the street, and soon came out again carrying a bundle wrapped in plastic. He went back to the dinghy, and loaded the box and the bundle and himself, and motored out to the yacht.'

131

The waiter came to take our plates and ask about puddings and coffee.

'Cheese,' Hilary decided.

'Just coffee,' I said. 'And do go on.'

'Well . . . I went into the shop he'd come out of, and asked about him, but they spoke only Spanish, and I don't. So then I walked up the street to the doorway I'd seen him go into, and that was where I hit the jackpot.'

She stopped to cut cheese from a selection on a board. I wondered how long it would be before I liked the stuff again.

'It was a laundry,' she said. 'All white and airy. And run by an English couple who'd gone to Majorca originally for a holiday and fallen in love with the place. A nice couple. Friendly, happy, busy, and very, very helpful. They knew the young man fairly well, they said, because he always took his washing in when he was in Andraitx. They do the boat people's laundry all the time. They reckon to have a bag of dirty clothes washed and ironed in half a day.'

She ate a biscuit and some cheese, and I waited.

'Alastair Yardley,' she said. 'The laundry people said he is a good sailor. Better than most of his kind. He often takes yachts from one place to another, so that they'll be wherever the owner wants. He can handle big boats, and is known for it. He sails into Andraitx four or five times a year, but three years ago he had a flat there, and used it as his base. The laundry people said they don't really know much about him, except that his father worked in a boat-building yard. He told them once that he'd learned to sail as soon as walk, and his first job was as a paid deck-hand in sea-trials for ocean-racing yachts. Apart from that, he hasn't said much about himself or who he's working for now, and the laundry people don't know because they aren't the prying sort, just chatty.'

'You're marvellous,' I said.

'Hm. I took some photographs of the boat, and I've had them processed at an overnight developers.' She opened her handbag, and drew out a yellow packet, which contained, among holiday scenes, three clear colour photographs of my first prison. Three different views, taken as the boat swung round with the tide.

'You can have them, if you like,' she said.

'I could kiss you.'

Her face lit with amusement. 'If you shuffle through that pack, you'll find a rather bad picture of Alastair Yardley. I didn't get the focus right. I was in a bit of a hurry, and he was walking towards me with his laundry, and I didn't want him to think I was taking a picture of him personally. I had to pretend to be taking a general view of the port, you see, and so I'm afraid it isn't very good.'

She had caught him from the waist up, and, as she said, slightly out of focus, but still recognizable to anyone who knew him. Looking ahead, not at the camera, with a white-wrapped bundle under his arm. Even in fuzzy outline, the uncompromising bones gave his face a powerful toughness, a look of aggressive determination. I thought that I might have liked him, if we'd met another way.

'Will you take the photos to the police?' Hilary asked.

'I don't know.' I considered it. 'Could you lend me the negatives, to have more prints made?'

'Sort them out and take them,' she said.

I did that, and we lingered over our coffee.

'I suppose,' she said, 'that you have thought once or twice about . . . the time we spent together?'

'Yes.'

She looked at me with a smile in the spectacled eyes. 'Do you regret it?'

'Of course not. Do you?'

She shook her head. 'It may be too soon to say, but I think it will have changed my entire life.'

'How could it?' I said.

'I think you have released in me an enormous amount of mental energy. I was being held back by feelings of ignorance and even inferiority. These feelings have entirely gone. I feel full of rocket fuel, ready for blast off.'

'Where to?' I said. 'What's higher than a headmistress?'

'Nothing measurable. But my school will be better, and there are such things as power and influence, and the ear of policy makers.'

'Miss Pinlock will be a force in the land?'

'We'll have to see,' she said.

I thought back to the time I'd first slept with a girl, when I was eighteen. It had been a relief to find out what everyone had been going on about, but I couldn't remember any accompanying upsurge of power. Perhaps, for me, the knowledge had come too easily, and too young. More likely that I'd never had the Pinlock potential in the first place.

I paid the bill and went went out into the street. The April air was cold, as it had been for the past entire week, and Hilary shivered slightly inside her coat.

'The trouble with warm rooms . . . life blasts you when you leave.'

'Speaking allegorically?' I said.

'Of course.'

We began to walk back towards the office, up the High Street, beside the shops. People scurried in and out of the doorways like bees at a hive mouth. The familiar street scene, after the last three weeks, seemed superficial and unreal.

We drew level with a bank: not, as it happened, the one where I kept my own money, nor that which we used as a firm, but one which dealt with the affairs of many of our clients.

'Would you wait a sec?' I said. 'I've had a thought or two this week . . . just want to check something.'

Hilary smiled and nodded cheerfully, and waited without comment while I went on my short errand.

'OK?' I said, rejoining her.

'Fine,' she said. 'Where did they keep you, in that van?'

'In a warehouse.' I looked at my watch. 'Do you want to see it? I want to go back for another look.'

'All right.'

'My car's behind the office.'

We walked on, past a small, pleasant-looking dress shop. I glanced idly into the window, and walked two strides past, and then stopped.

'Hilary . . .'

'Yes?'

'I want to give you a present.'

'Don't be ridiculous,' she said.

She protested her way into the shop and was reduced to

134

silence only by the sight of what I wanted her to wear: the garment I'd seen in the window; a long bold scarlet cloak.

'Try it,' I said.

Shaking her head, she removed the dull tweed coat and let the girl assistant lower the bright swirling cape on to her shoulders. She stood immobile while the girl fastened the buttons and arranged the neat collar. Looked at herself in the glass.

Duck into swan, I thought. She looked imposing and magnificent, a plain woman transfigured, her height making dramatic folds in the drop of clear red wool.

'Rockets,' I said, 'are powered by flame.'

'You can't buy me this.'

'Why not?'

I wrote the girl a cheque, and Hilary for once seemed to be speechless.

'Keep it on,' I said. 'It looks marvellous.'

The girl packed the old coat into a carrier, and we continued our walk to the office. People looked at Miss Pinlock as they passed, as they had not done before.

'It takes courage,' she said, raising her chin.

'First flights always do.'

She thought instantly of the night in Cala St Galdana: I saw it in the movement of her eyes. She smiled to herself, and straightened a fraction to her full height. Nothing wrong with the Pinlock nerve, then or ever.

From the front the warehouse looked small and dilapidated, its paint peeling off like white scabs to leave uneven grey scars underneath. A weatherboard screwed to the wall offered 10,500 square feet to let, but judging from the aged dimness of the sign, the customers had hardly queued.

The building stood on its own at the end of a side road which now had no destination, owing to the close-down of the branch railway and the subsequent massive reorganization of the landscape into motorways and roundabouts.

There was a small door let into a large one on rollers at the entrance, neither of them locked. The locks, in fact, appeared to have been smashed, but in time gone by. The splintered wood around them had weathered grey with age.

I pushed open the small door for Hilary, and we stepped in. The gloom as the door swung behind us was as blinding as too much light; I propped the door open with a stone, but even then there were enfolding shadows at every turn. It was clear why vandals had stopped at breaking down the doors. Everything inside was so thick with dust that to kick anything was to start a choking cloud.

Sounds were immediately deadened, as if the high, mouldering piles of junk were soaking up every echo before it could go a yard.

I shouted 'Hey' into the small central space, and it seemed to reach no further than my own throat.

'It's cold in here,' Hilary said. 'Colder than outside.'

'Something to do with ventilation bricks, I expect,' I said. 'A draught, bringing in dust and lowering the temperature.'

Our voices had no resonance. We walked the short distance to where the white van stood, with the dark tarpaulin sprawling in a huge heap beside it.

With eyes adjusting to the dim light, we looked inside. The police had taken the water carrier and the bag of cheese, and the van was empty.

It was a small space. Dirty, and hard.

'You spent nearly a week in there,' Hilary said, disbelievingly.

'Five nights and four and a half days,' I said. 'Let's not exaggerate.'

'Let's not,' she said dryly.

We stood looking at the van for a minute or two, and the deadness and chill of the place began to soak into our brains. I shuddered slightly and walked away, out through the door into the living air.

Hilary followed me, and kicked away the door-stop. The peeling door swung shut.

'Did you sleep well, last night?' she said bleakly.

'No.'

'Nightmares?'

I looked up to the grey sky, and breathed deep luxurious breaths.

'Well . . . dreams,' I said.

She swallowed. 'Why did you want to come back here?'

'To see the name of the estate agent who has this place on his books. It's on the board, on the wall. I wasn't noticing things much when the police took me out of here yesterday.'

She gave a small explosive laugh of escaping tension. 'So practical!'

'Whoever put the van in there knew the place existed,' I said. 'I didn't, and I've lived in Newbury for six years.'

'Leave it to the police,' she said seriously. 'After all, they did find you.'

I shook my head. 'Someone rang Scotland Yard to tell them where I was.'

'Leave it to them,' she urged. 'You're out of it now.'

'I don't know. To coin a cliché, there's a great big iceberg blundering around here, and that van's only the tip.'

We got into my car, and I drove her back to the park in town where she'd left her own. She stood beside it, tall in her scarlet cloak, and fished in her handbag for a pen and notebook.

'Here,' she said, writing. 'This is my address and telephone number. You can come at any time. You might need . . .' She paused an instant, '. . . . a safe place.'

'Can I come for advice?' I said.

'For anything.'

I smiled.

'No,' she said. 'Not for that. I want a memory, not a habit.'

'Take your glasses off,' I said.

'To see you better?' She took them off, humouring me quizzically.

'Why don't you wear contact lenses?' I said. 'Without glasses, your eyes are great.'

On the way back to the office I stopped to buy food, on the premise that if I didn't stock up with things I liked, I wouldn't get back to normal eating. I also left Hilary's negatives for a rush reprint, so that it was nearly five before I went through the door.

Debbie and Peter had both done their usual Friday afternoon bolt, for which dentists and classes were only sample reasons. The variety they had come up with over the years would have been valuable if applied to their work: but I knew from experience that if I forced them both to stay until five I got nothing productive done after a quarter past four. Bess, infected by them, had already covered her typewriter, and was busy applying thick new make-up on top of the old. Bess, eighteen and curvy, thought of work as a boring interruption of her sex life. She gave me a bright smile, ran her tongue round the fresh glistening lipstick, and swung her hips provocatively on her way to the weekend's sport.

There were voices in Trevor's room. Trevor's loud voice in short sentences, and a client's softer tones in long paragraphs.

I tidied my own desk, and carried the Glitberg, Ownslow and Connaught Powys files into the outer office on my way to the car.

The door to Trevor's room opened suddenly, and Trevor and his client were revealed there, warmly shaking hands.

The client was Denby Crest, solicitor, a short plump man with a stiff moustache and a mouth permanently twisted in irritation. Even when he smiled at you personally, he gave an impression of annoyance at the state of things in general. Many of his own clients saw that as sympathy for their troubles, which was their mistake.

'I'll make it worth your while, Trevor,' he was saying. 'I'm eternally grateful.'

Trevor suddenly saw me standing there and stared at me blankly.

'I thought you'd gone, Ro,' he said.

'Came back for some files,' I said, glancing down at them in my arms. 'Good afternoon, Denby.'

'Good afternoon, Roland.'

He gave me a brief nod and made a brisk dive for the outer door; a brusque departure, even by his standards. I watched his fast disappearing back and said to Trevor, 'Did you sign his certificate? He said he would wait until you got back.'

'Yes, I did,' Trevor said. He too showed no inclination for leisurely chat, and turned away from me towards his own desk.

'What was I doing wrong?' I said. 'I kept making him fifty thousand pounds short.'

'Decimal point in the wrong place,' he said shortly.

'Show me,' I said.

'Not now, Ro. It's time to go home.'

I put the files down on Bess's desk and walked into Trevor's office. It was larger than mine, and much tidier, with no wall of waiting cardboard boxes. There were three armchairs for clients, some Stubbs prints on the walls, and a bowl of flowering daffodils on his desk.

'Trevor . . .'

He was busy putting together what I recognized as Denby Crest's papers, and didn't look up. I stood in his room, waiting, until in the end he had to take notice. His face was bland, calm, uninformative, and if there had been any tension there a minute ago, it had now evaporated.

'Trevor,' I said. 'Please show me where I went wrong.'

'Leave it, Ro,' he said pleasantly. 'There's a good chap.'

'If you did sign his certificate, and he really is fifty thousand pounds short, then it concerns me too.'

'You're dead tired, Ro, and you look ill, and this is not a good time to discuss it.' He came round his desk and put his hand gently on my arm. 'My dear chap, you know how horrified and worried I am about what has been happening to you. I am most concerned that you should take things easy and recover your strength.'

It was a long speech for him, and confusing. When he saw me hesitate, he added. 'There's nothing wrong with Denby's affairs. We'll go through them, if you like, on Monday.'

'It had better be now,' I said.

'No.' He was stubbornly positive. 'We have friends coming for the evening, and I promised to be home early. Monday, Ro. It will keep perfectly well until Monday.'

I gave in, partly because I simply didn't want to face what I guessed to be true, that Trevor had signed the certificate knowing the figures were false. I'd done the sums over and over on my cheese abacus, and the answer came monotonously the same, whichever method I used to work them out.

He shepherded me like an uncle to his door, and watched while I picked up the heap of files from Bess's desk.

'What are those?' he said. 'You really mustn't work this weekend.'

'They're not exactly work. They're back files. I just thought I'd take a look.'

He walked over and peered down at the labels, moving the top file to see what was underneath.

'Why these, for heaven's sake?' he said, frowning, coming across Connaught Powys.

'I don't know . . .' I sighed. 'I just thought they might possibly have some connection with my being abducted.'

He looked at me with compassion. 'My dear Ro, why don't you leave it all to the police?'

'I'm not hindering them.' I picked up the armful of files and smiled. 'I don't think I'm high on their urgency list, though. I wasn't robbed, ransomed, or held hostage, and a spot of unlawful imprisonment on its own probably ranks lower than parking on double yellow lines.'

'But,' he said doubtfully, 'don't you think they will ever discover who, or why?'

'It depends on where they look, I should think.' I shrugged a shoulder, walked to the door, and stopped to look back. He was standing by Bess's desk, clearly troubled. 'Trevor,' I said, 'I don't mind one way or the other whether the police come up with answers. I don't madly want public revenge, and I've had my fill of court-case publicity, as a witness. I certainly don't relish it as a victim. But for my own peace of mind, I would like to know. If I find out, I won't necessarily act on the knowledge. The police would have to. So there's the difference. It might be better – you never know – if it's I who did the digging, not the police.'

He shook his head, perturbed and unconvinced.

'See you Monday,' I said.

14

Jossie met me on the doorstep, fizzing with life.

'Dad says please come in for a drink.' She held the door open for me and looked uncertainly at my face. 'Are you all right? I mean . . . I suppose I didn't realize . . .'

I kissed her mouth. Soft and sweet. It made me hungry.

'A drink would be fine,' I said.

William Finch was already pouring Scotch as we walked into his office-sitting-room. He greeted me with a smile and held out the glass.

'You look as if you could do with it,' he said. 'You've been having a rough time, by all accounts.'

'I've a fellow feeling for footballs.' I took the glass, lifted it in a token toast, and sipped the pale fine spirit.

Jossie said 'Kicked around?'

I nodded, smiling. 'Somebody,' I said, 'is playing a strategic game.'

Finch looked at me curiously. 'Do you know who?'

'Not exactly. Not yet.'

Jossie stood beside her father, pouring grapefruit juice out of a small bottle. One could see heredity clearly at work: they both had the same tall, well-proportioned frame, the same high carriage of head on long neck, the same air of bending the world to their ways, instead of being themselves bent. He looked at her fondly, a hint of civilized amusement in his fatherly pride. Even her habitual mockery, it seemed, stemmed from him.

He turned his greying head to me again, and said he expected the police would sort out all the troubles, in time.

'I expect so,' I said neutrally.

'And I hope the villains get shut up in small spaces for years and years,' Jossie said.

'Well,' I said, 'they may.'

Finch buried his nose in a large gin and tonic and surfaced with a return to the subject which interested him most. Kidnappings came a poor second to racing.

'My next ride?' I echoed. 'Tomorrow, as a matter of fact. Tapestry runs in the Oasthouse Cup.'

His astonishment scarcely boosted my non-existent confidence. 'Good heavens,' he said. 'I mean, to be frank, Ro, is it wise?'

'Totally not.'

'Then why?'

'I have awful difficulty in saying no.'

Jossie laughed. 'Spineless,' she said.

The door opened and a dark-haired woman came in, walking beautifully in a long black dress. She seemed to move in a glow of her own; and the joy died out of Jossie like an extinguished fire.

Finch went towards the newcomer with a welcoming smile, took her elbow proprietorially, and steered her in my direction. 'Lida, my dear, this is Roland Britten. Ro, Lida Swann.'

A tapeworm with hooks, Jossie had said. The tapeworm had a broad expanse of unlined forehead, dark blue eyes, and raven hair combed smoothly back. As we shook hands, she pressed my fingers warmly. Her heavy, sweet scent broadcast the same message as full breasts, tiny waist, narrow hips, and challenging smile: the sexual woman in full bloom. Diametrically opposite, I reflected, to my own preference for astringency and humour. Jossie watched our polite social exchanges with a scowl, and I wanted to walk over and hug her.

Why not, I thought. I disengaged myself from the sultry aura of Lida, took the necessary steps, and slid my arm firmly round Jossie's waist.

'We'll be off, then,' I said. 'To feed the starving.'

Jossie's scowl persisted across the hall, into the car, and five miles down the road.

'I hate her,' she said. 'That sexy throaty voice . . . it's all put on.'

'It's gin,' I said.

'What?'

'Too much gin alters the vocal chords.'

'You're having me on.'

'I think I love you,' I said.

'That's a damn silly thing to say.'

'Why?'

'You can't love someone just because she hates her father's girlfriend.'

'A better reason than many.'

She turned her big eyes searchingly my way. I kept my own looking straight ahead, dealing with night on the country road.

'Strong men fall for her like ninepins,' she said.

'But I'm weak.'

'Spineless.' She cheered up a good deal, and finally managed a smile. 'Do you want me to come to Kempton tomorrow and cheer you on?'

'Come and give Moira Longerman a double brandy when I fall off.'

Over dinner she said with some seriousness, 'I suppose it's occurred to you that the last twice you've raced, you've been whipped off into black holes straight after?'

'It has,' I said.

'So are you – uh – at all scared, about tomorrow?'

'I'd be surprised if it happened again.'

'Surprise wouldn't help you much.'

'True.'

'You're absolutely infuriating,' she said explosively. 'If you know why you were abducted, why not tell me?'

'I might be wrong, and I want to ask some questions first.'

'What questions?'

'What are you doing on Sunday?'

'That's not a question.'

'Yes, it is,' I said. 'Would you care for a day on the Isle of Wight?'

With guilty misgivings about riding Tapestry I did my best to eat, and later, after leaving Jossie on her doorstep, to go home and sleep. As my system seemed to be stubbornly resisting my intention that it should return to normal, both enterprises met with only partial success. The Saturday morning face in the shaving mirror would have inspired faith in no one, not even Moira herself.

'You're a bloody fool,' I said aloud, and my reflection agreed.

Coffee, boiled egg and toast to the good, I went down into the town to seek out owners of destitute warehouses. The estate agents, busy with hand-holding couples, told me impatiently that they had already given the information to the police.

'Give it to me, too, then,' I said. 'It's hardly a secret, is it?'

The bearded pale-faced man I'd asked looked harried and went off to consult. He came back with a slip of paper which he handed over as if contact with it had sullied his soul.

'We have ceased to act for these people,' he said earnestly.

'Our board should no longer be affixed to the wall.'

I'd never known anyone actually say the word 'affixed' before. It wasn't all he could say, either. 'We wish to be considered as disassociated from the whole situation.'

I read the words written on the paper. 'I'm sure you do,' I said. 'Could you tell me when you last heard from these people? And has anyone been enquiring recently about hiring or using the warehouse?'

'Those people,' he said disapprovingly, 'appear to have let the warehouse several years ago to some army surplus suppliers, without informing us or paying fees due to us. We have received no instructions from them, then or since, regarding any further letting or sub-letting.'

'Ta ever so,' I said, and went grinning out to the street.

The words on the paper, which had so fussed the agents in retrospect, were 'National Construction (Wessex) Ltd', or in other words the mythical builders invented by Ownslow and Glitberg.

I picked up the rush reprint enlargements of Hilary's photographs, and walked along to the office. All quiet there, as usual on Saturdays, with undone work still sitting reproachfully in heaps.

Averting my eyes, I telephoned to the police.

'Any news?' I said; and they said no there wasn't.

'Did you trace the owner of the van?' I asked. No, they hadn't.

'Did it have an engine number?' I said. Yes, they said, but it was not the original number for that particular vehicle, said vehicle having probably passed through many hands and rebuilding processes on its way to the warehouse.

'And have you asked Mr Glitberg and Mr Ownslow what I was doing in a van inside their warehouse?'

There was silence at the other end.

'Have you?' I repeated.

They wanted to know why I should ask.

'Oh come off it,' I said. 'I've been to the estate agents, same as you.'

Mr Glitberg and Mr Ownslow, it appeared, had been totally mystified as to why their warehouse should have been used in such a way. As far as they were concerned, it was let to an army surplus supply company, and the police should direct their enquiries to them.

'Can you find these army surplus people?' I asked. Not so far, they said. They cleared the police throat and cautiously added that Mr Glitberg and Mr Ownslow had categorically denied that they had imprisoned Mr Britten in a van in their warehouse, or anywhere else, for that matter, as revenge for the said Mr Britten having been instrumental in their custodial sentences for fraud.

'Their actual words?' I asked with interest. Not exactly. I had been given the gist.

I thanked them for the information, and disconnected. I thought they had probably not passed on everything they knew, but then neither had I, which made us quits.

The door of Trevor's private office was locked, as mine had been, but we both had keys for each other's rooms. I knew all the same that he wouldn't have been pleased to see me searching uninvited through the papers in his filing cupboard, but I reckoned that as I'd had access to them anyway while he was on holiday, another peep would be no real invasion. I spent a concentrated hour reading cash books and ledgers; and then with a mind functioning more or less as normal I checked through the Denby Crest figures yet again. I had made no mistake with them, even in a daze. Fifty thousand pounds of clients' trust funds were missing. I stared unseeingly at 'Lady and Gentleman in a Carriage' and thought bleakly about consequences.

There was a photo-copier in the outer office, busily operated every weekday by Debbie and Peter. I spent another hour of that quiet Saturday morning methodically printing private copies for my own use. Then I put all the books and papers back where I'd found them, locked Trevor's office, and went down to the store in the basement.

The files I was looking for there were easy to find but were slim and uninformative, containing only copies of audits and not all the invoices, cash books and paying-in books from which the accounts had been drawn.

There was nothing odd in that. Under the Companies Act 1976, and also under the value added tax system, all such papers had to be kept available for three years and could legally be thrown away only after that, but most accountants returned the books to their clients for keeping, as like us they simply didn't have enough storage space for everyone.

I left the files where they were, locked all the office doors, sealed my folder of photo-copies into a large envelope, and took it with me in some depression to Kempton Park.

The sight of Jossie in her swirly brown skirt brought the sun out considerably, and we despatched grapefruit juice in amicable understanding.

'Dad's brought the detestable Lida,' she said, 'so I came on my own.'

'Does she live with you?' I asked.

'No, thank God.' The idea alarmed her. 'Five miles away, and that's five thousand miles too close.'

'What does the ever-sick secretary have to say about her?'

'Sandy? It makes her even sicker.' She drank the remains of her juice, smiling over the glass. 'Actually Sandy wouldn't be so bad, if she weren't so wet. And you can cast out any slick theories about daughters being possessive of their footloose fathers, because actually I would have liked it rather a lot if he'd fallen for a peach.'

'Does he know you don't like Lida?'

'Oh sure,' she sighed. 'I told him she was a flesh-eating orchid and he said I didn't understand. End of conversation. The funny thing is,' she added, 'that it's only when I'm with you that I can think of her without spitting.'

'Appendicitis diverts the mind from toothache,' I said.

'What?'

'Thoughts from inside little white vans.'

'Half the time,' she said, 'I think you're crazy.'

She met some friends and went off with them, and I repaired to the weighing room to change into breeches, boots, and Moira Longerman's red and white colours. When I came out, with my jacket on over the bright shirt, Binny Tomkins was waiting. On his countenance, the reverse of warmth and light.

'I want to talk to you,' he said.

'Fine. Why not.'

He scowled. 'Not here. Too many people. Walk down this way.' He pointed to the path taken by the horses on their way from parade ring to track: a broad stretch of grass mostly unpopulated by racegoing crowds.

'What is it?' I said, as we emerged from the throng round the weighing room door, and started in the direction he wanted. 'Is there something wrong with Tapestry?'

He shook his head impatiently, as if the idea were silly.

'I want you to give the horse an easy race.'

I stopped walking. An easy race, in those terms, meant trying not to win.

'No,' I said.

'Come on, there's more . . .' He went on a pace or two, looking back and waiting for me to follow. 'I must talk to you. You must listen.'

There was more than usual scowling bad temper in his manner. Something like plain fear. Shaking my head, I went on with him, across the grass.

'How much would you want?' he said.

I stopped again. 'I'm not doing it,' I said.

'I know, but . . . How about two hundred, tax free?'

'You're stupid, Binny.'

'It's all right for you,' he said furiously. 'But if Tapestry wins today I'll lose everything. My yard, my livelihood – everything.'

'Why?'

He was trembling with tension. 'I owe a lot of money.'

'To bookmakers?' I said.

'Of course to bookmakers.'

'You're a fool,' I said flatly.

'Smug bastard,' he said furiously. 'I'd give anything to have you back inside that van, and not here today.'

I looked at him thoughtfully. 'Tapestry may not win anyway,' I said. 'Nothing's a certainty.'

'I've got to know in advance,' he said incautiously.

'And if you assure your bookmaker Tapestry won't win, he'll let you off the hook?'

'He'll let me off a bit,' he said. 'He won't press for the rest.'

'Until next time,' I said. 'Until you're in deeper still.'

Binny's eyes stared inwards to the hopeless future, and I guessed he would never take the first step back to firm ground, which was in his case to stop gambling altogether.

'There are easier ways for trainers to lose races,' I pointed out, 'than trying to bribe the jockey.'

His scowl reached Neanderthal proportions. 'She pays the lad who does her horse to watch him like a hawk and give her a report on everything that happens. I can't sack him or change him to another horse, because she says if I do she'll send Tapestry to another trainer.'

'I'm amazed she hasn't already,' I said: and she would have done, I thought, if she'd been able to hear that conversation.

'You've only got to ride a bad race,' he said. 'Get boxed in down the far side and swing wide coming into the straight.'

'No,' I said. 'Not on purpose.'

I seemed to be remarkably good at inspiring fury. Binny would happily have seen me fall dead at his feet.

'Look,' I said, 'I'm sorry about the fix you're in. I really am, whether you believe it or not. But I'm not going to try to get you out of it by cheating Moira or the horse or the punters or myself, and that's that.'

'You *bastard*,' he said.

Five minutes later, when I was back in the hub of the racecourse outside the weighing room, a hand touched me on the arm and a drawly voice spoke behind my ear.

'My dear Ro, what are your chances?'

I turned, smiling, to the intelligent face of Vivian Iverson. In the daylight on a racecourse, where I'd first met him, he wore his clothes with the same elegance and flair that he had extended to his Vivat Club. Dark green blazer over grey checked trousers; hair shining black in the April sun. Quiet amusement in the observant eyes.

'In love, war, or the three-thirty?' I said.

'Of remaining at liberty, my dear chap.'

I blinked. 'Um,' I said. 'What would you offer?'

'Five to four against?'

'I hope you're wrong,' I said.

Underneath the banter, he was detectably serious. 'It just so happens that last night in the club I heard our friend Connaught Powys talking on the telephone. To be frank, my dear Ro, after I'd heard your name mentioned, I more or less deliberately *listened*.'

'On an extension?'

'Tut tut,' he said reprovingly. 'Unfortunately not. I don't know who he was talking to. But he said – his exact words – "as far as Britten is concerned you must agree that precaution is better than cure", and a bit later he said "if dogs start sniffing around, the best thing to do is chain them up".'

'Charming,' I said blankly.

'Do you need a bodyguard?'

'Are you offering yourself?'

He shook his head, smiling. 'I could hire you one. Karate. Bullet proof glass. All the mod cons.'

'I think,' I said thoughtfully, 'that I'll just increase the insurance policies.'

'Against kidnapping? No one will take you on.'

'Checks and balances,' I said. 'No one'll push me off a springboard if it means a rock falling on their own head.'

'Be sure to let them know the rock exists.'

'Your advice,' I said, smiling, 'is worth its weight in ocean-going sailing boats.'

Moira Longerman twinkled with her bright bird-eyes in the parade ring before Tapestry's race and stroked my arm repeatedly, her small thin hand sliding delicately over the shiny scarlet sleeve.

'Now, Roland, you'll do your best, I know you'll do your best.'

'Yes,' I said guiltily, flexing several flabby muscles and watching Tapestry's highly tuned ones ripple under his coat as he walked round the ring with his lad.

'I saw you talking to Binny just now, Roland.'

'Did you, Moira?' I switched my gaze to her face.

'Yes, I did.' She nodded brightly. 'I was up in the stands, up there in the bar, looking down to the paddock. I saw Binny take you away for a talk.'

She looked at me steadily, shrewdly, asking the vital question in total silence. Her hand went on stroking. She waited intently, expecting an answer.

'I promise you,' I said plainly, 'that if I make a hash of it, it'll be against my will.'

She stopped stroking: patted my arm instead, and smiled. 'That will do nicely, Roland.'

Binny stood ten feet away, unable to make even a show of the civility due from trainer to owner. His face was rigid, his eyes expressionless, and even the usual scowl had frozen into a more general and powerful gloom. I thought I had probably been wrong to think of Binny as a stupid fool. There was something about him at that moment which raised prickles on the skin and images of murder.

The bell rang for jockeys to mount, and it was the lad, not Binny, who gave me a leg-up into the saddle.

'I'm not going to take much more of this,' Moira said pleasantly to the world in general.

Binny ignored her as if he hadn't heard; and maybe he hadn't. He'd also given me no riding instructions, which I didn't mind in the least. He seemed wholly withdrawn and unresponsive, and when Moira waved briefly as I walked away on Tapestry, he did not accompany her across to the stands. Even for him, his behaviour was incredible.

Tapestry himself was in a great mood, tossing his head with excitement and bouncing along in tiny cantering strides as if he had April spring fever in all his veins. I remembered his plunging start in the Gold Cup and realized that this time I'd be lucky if he didn't bolt with me from the post. Far from being last from indecision, this time, in my weakened state, I could be forty lengths in front by the second fence, throwing away all chance of staying-power at the end.

Tapestry bounced gently on his toes in the parade past the stands, while the other runners walked. Bounced playfully back at a canter to the start, which in three mile 'chases at Kempton Park was to the left of the stands and in full view of most of the crowd.

There were eleven other jockeys walking around there, making final adjustments to girths and goggles and answering to the

150

starter's roll call. The starter's assistant, tightening the girths of the horse beside me, looked over his shoulder and asked me if mine were all right, or should he tighten those too.

If I hadn't recently been through so many wringers, I would simply have said yes, and he would have pulled the buckles up a notch or two, and I wouldn't have given it another thought. As it was, in my over-cautious state, I had a sudden sharp vision of Binny's dangerous detachment, and remembered the desperation behind his appeal to me to lose. The prickles returned in force.

I slid off Tapestry's back and looped his reins over my arm.

'Just want to check . . .' I said vaguely to the starter's assistant.

He nodded briefly, glancing at his watch. One minute to race-time, his face said, so hurry up.

It was my own saddle. I intimately knew its every flap, buckle, scratch and stain. I checked it thoroughly inch by inch with fingers and eyes, and could see nothing wrong. Girths, stirrups, leathers, buckles; everything as it should be. I pulled the girths tighter myself, and the starter told me to get mounted.

Looking over my shoulder, I thought, for the rest of my life. Seeing demons in shadows. But the feeling of danger wouldn't go away.

'Hurry up, Britten.'

'Yes, sir.'

I stood on the ground, looking at Tapestry tossing his head.

'*Britten!*'

Reins, I thought. Bridle. Bit. Reins. If the bridle broke, I couldn't control the horse and he wouldn't win the race. Many races had been lost, from broken bridles.

It was not too difficult to see, if one looked really closely. The leather reins were stitched on to the rings at each side of the bit, and the stitches on the off-side rein had nearly all been severed.

Three miles and twenty fences at bucketing speed with just two strands of thread holding my right-hand rein.

'*Britten!*'

I gave a jerking tug, and the remaining stitches came apart in my hand. I pulled the rein off the ring and waved the free end in the air.

'Sorry, sir,' I said. 'I need another bridle.'

'What? Oh very well . . .' He used his telephone to call the weighing room to send a replacement out quickly. Tapestry's lad appeared, looking worried, to help change the headpiece, and I pointed out to him, as I gave him Binny's bridle, the parted stitching.

'I don't know how it could have got like that,' he said anxiously. 'I didn't know it was like that, honest. I cleaned it yesterday, and all.'

'Don't worry,' I said. 'It's not your fault.'

'Yes, but . . .'

'Give me a leg-up,' I said, 'and don't worry.'

He continued all the same to look upset. Good lads took it grievously to heart if anything was proved lacking in the way they turned out their horses, and Tapestry's lad was as good as the horse deserved. Binny, I thought not for the first time, was an all-out, one-man disaster area, a blight to himself and everyone around.

'Line up,' shouted the starter, with his hand on the lever. 'We're five minutes late.'

Tapestry did his best to put that right two seconds later with another arm-wrenching departure, but owing to one or two equally impetuous opponents I thankfully got him anchored in mid-field; and there we stayed for all of the first circuit. The pace, once we'd settled down, was nothing like as fast as the Gold Cup, and I had time to worry about the more usual things, like meeting the fences right, and not running out altogether, which was an added hazard at Kempton where the wings leading to the fences were smaller and lower than on other courses, and tended to give tricky horses bad ideas.

During the second circuit my state of unfitness raised its ugly head in no uncertain way, and it would be fair to say that for the last mile Tapestry's jockey did little except cling on. Tapestry truly was, however, a great performer, and in consequence of the cheers and acclaim in the unsaddling enclosure after the Gold Cup, he seemed, like many much-fêted horses, to have become conscious of his own star status. It was the extra dimension of his new pride which took us in a straight faultless run over the last three fences in the straight, and his own will to win which extended his neck and his stride on the run-in. Tapestry won the Oasthouse Cup by four lengths, and it was all the horse's doing, not mine.

Moira kissed her horse with tears running down her cheeks, and kissed me as well, and everyone else within mouth-shot, indiscriminately. There was nothing uptight or inhibited about the Longerman joy, and the most notable person not there to share it was the horse's trainer. Binny Tomkins was nowhere to be seen.

'Drink,' Moira shrieked at me. 'Owners and trainers bar.'

I nodded, speechless from exertion and back-slapping, and struggled through the throng with my saddle to be weighed in. It was fabulous, I thought dazedly; fantastic, winning another big race. More than I'd ever reckoned possible. A bursting delight like no other on earth. Even knowing how little I'd contributed couldn't dampen the wild inner rejoicing. I'd never be able to give it up, I thought. I'd still be struggling round in the mud and the rain at fifty, chasing the marvellous dream. Addiction wasn't only a matter of needles in the arm.

Moira in the bar was dispensing champagne and bright laughs in copious quantities, and had taken Jossie closely in tow.

'Ro, darling Ro,' Moira said, 'have you seen Binny anywhere?'

'No, I haven't.'

'Wasn't it odd, the bridle breaking like that?' Her innocent-seeming eyes stared up into my own. 'I talked to the lad, you see.'

'These things do happen,' I said.

'You mean, no one can prove anything?'

'Roughly that.'

'But aren't you the teeniest bit angry?'

I smiled from the glowing inner pleasure. 'We won the race. What else matters?'

She shook her head. 'It was a wicked thing to do.'

Desperation, I thought, could spawn deeds the doers wouldn't sanely contemplate. Like cutting loose a rein. Like kidnapping the enemy. Like whatever else lay ahead before we were done. I shut out the shadowy devils and drank to life and the Oasthouse Cup.

Jossie, too, had a go at me when we wandered later out to the car park.

'Is Moira right?' she demanded. 'Did Binny rig it for you to come to grief?'

'I should think so.'

'She says you ought to report it.'

'There's no need.'

'Why not?'

'He's programmed to self-destruct before the end of the season.'

'Do you mean *suicide?*' she said.

'You're too literal. I mean he'll go bust to the bookies with a reverberating bang.'

'You're drunk.'

I shook my head, grinning. 'High. Quite different. Care to join me on my cloud?'

'A puff of wind,' she said, 'and you'd evaporate.'

15

Jossie drove off to some party or other in London, and I, mindful of earlier unscheduled destinations after racing, took myself circumspectly down the road to the nearest public telephone box. No one followed, that I could see.

Hilary Margaret Pinlock answered at the twentieth ring, when I had all but given up, and said breathlessly that she had only that second reached home; she'd been out playing tennis.

'Are you busy this evening?' I said.

'Nothing special.'

'Can I come and see you?'

'Yes.' She hesitated a fraction. 'What do you want? Food? A bed?'

'An ear,' I said. 'And baked beans, perhaps. But no bed.'

'Right,' she said calmly. 'Where are you? Do you need directions?'

She told me clearly how to find her, and I drew up forty

minutes later outside a large Edwardian house in a leafy road on the outskirts of a sprawling Surrey town. Hilary, it transpired, owned the ground floor, a matter of two large, high-ceilinged rooms, modern kitchen, functional bathroom, and a pleasant old fashioned conservatory with plants, cane armchairs, and steps down to an unkempt garden.

Inside, everything was orderly and organized, and comfortable in an uninspired sort of way. Well-built easy chairs in dim covers, heavy curtains in good velvet but of a deadening colour somewhere between brown and green, patterned carpet in olive and fawn. The home of a vigorous academic mind with no inborn response to refracted light. I wondered just how much she would wear the alien scarlet cloak.

The evening sun still shone into the conservatory, and there we sat, in the cane armchairs, drinking sherry, greenly surrounded by palms and rubber plants and monstera deliciosa.

'I don't mind *watering*,' Hilary said. 'But I detest *gardening*. The people upstairs are supposed to do the garden, but they don't.' She waved disgustedly towards the view of straggly bushes, unpruned roses, weedy paths, and dried coffee-coloured stalks of last year's unmown grass.

'It's better than concrete,' I said.

'I'll use you as a parable for the children,' she said, smiling.

'Hm?'

'When things are bad, you endure what you must, and thank God it's not worse.'

I made a protesting sound in my throat, much taken aback. 'Well,' I said helplessly, 'what else is there to do?'

'Go screaming off to the Social Services.'

'For a gardener?'

'You know darned well what I mean.'

'Endurance is like tax,' I said. 'You're silly to pay more than you have to, but you can't always escape it.'

'And you can whine,' she said, nodding, 'or suffer with good grace.'

She drank her sherry collectedly and invited me to say why I'd come.

'To ask you to keep a parcel safe for me,' I said.

'But of course.'

'And to listen to a fairly long tale, so that . . .' I paused. 'I mean, I want someone to know . . .' I stopped once more.

'In case you disappear again?' she said matter-of-factly.

I was grateful for her calmness.

'Yes,' I said. I told her about meeting Vivian Iverson at the races, and our thoughts on insurance, springboards, and rocks. 'So you see,' I ended, 'you'll be the rock, if you will.'

'You can expect,' she said, 'rocklike behaviour.'

'Well,' I said, 'I've brought a sealed package of photo-copied documents. It's in the car.'

'Fetch it,' she said.

I went out to the street and collected the thick envelope from the boot. Habit induced me to look into the back seat floor space, and to scan the harmless street. No one hiding, no one watching, that I could see. No one had followed me from the racecourse, I was sure.

Looking over my shoulder for the rest of my life.

I took the parcel indoors and gave it to Hilary, and also the negatives of her photographs, explaining that I already had the extra prints. She put everything on the table beside her and told me to sit down and get on with the tale.

'I'll tell you a bit about my job,' I said. 'And then you'll understand better.' I stretched out with luxurious weariness in the cane chair and looked at the intent interest on her strong plain face. A pity, I thought, about the glasses.

'An accountant working for a long time in one area, particularly in an area like a country town, tends to get an overall picture of the local life.'

'I follow you,' she said. 'Go on.'

'The transactions of one client tend to turn up in the accounts of others. For instance, a racehorse trainer buys horse food from the forage merchants. I check the invoice through the trainer's accounts, and then, because the forage merchant is also my client, I later check it again through his. I see that the forage merchant has paid a builder for an extension to his house, and later, in the builder's accounts, I see what *he* paid for the bricks and cement. I see that a jockey had paid x pounds on an air-taxi, and later, because the air-taxi firm is also my client, I see the receipt of x pounds from the jockey. I see the

movement of money around the neighbourhood . . . the inter-
locking of interests . . . the pattern of commerce. I learn the
names of suppliers, the size of businesses, and the kinds of services people use. My knowledge increases until I have a sort of
mental map like a wide landscape, in which all the names are
familiar and occur in the proper places.'

'Fascinating,' Hilary said.

'Well,' I said, 'if a totally strange name crops up, and you
can't cross-reference it with anything else, you begin to ask
questions. At first of yourself, and then of others. Discreetly.
And that was how I ran into trouble in the shape of two master
criminals called Glitberg and Ownslow.'

'They sound like a music-hall turn.'

'They're as funny as the Black Death.' I drank some sherry
ruefully. 'They worked for the council, and the council's accounts and audits were done by a large firm in London, who
naturally didn't have any intimate local knowledge. Ownslow
and Glitberg had invented a construction firm called National
Construction (Wessex) Limited, through which they had
syphoned off more than a million pounds each of taxpayers'
money. And I had a client, a builders' merchant, who had received several cheques from National Construction (Wessex).
I'd never heard of National Construction (Wessex) in any other
context, and I asked my client some searching questions, to
which his reply was unmistakable panic. Glitberg and Ownslow
were prosecuted and went to jail swearing to be revenged.'

'On you?'

'On me.'

'Nasty.'

'A few weeks later,' I said, 'much the same thing happened.
I turned up some odd payments made by a director of an electronics firm through the company's computer. His name was
Connaught Powys. He'd taken his firm for over a quarter of a
million, and he too went to jail swearing to get even. He's out
again now, and so are Glitberg and Ownslow. Since then I've
been the basic cause of the downfall of two more big-time embezzlers, both of whom descended to the cells swearing sever-
ally to tear my guts out and cut my throat.' I sighed. 'Luckily,
they're both still inside.'

'And I thought accountants led dull lives! '

'Maybe some do.' I drained my sherry. 'There's another thing that those five embezzlers have in common besides me, and that is that not a penny of what they stole has been recovered.'

'Really?' She seemed not to find it greatly significant. 'I expect it's all sitting around in bank deposits, under different names.'

I shook my head. 'Not unless it is in literally thousands of tiny weeny deposits, which doesn't seem likely.'

'Why thousands?'

'Banks nowadays have to inform the Tax Inspectors of the existence of any deposit account for which the annual interest is £15 or more. That means the Inspectors know of all deposits of over three or four hundred quid.'

'I had no idea,' she said blankly.

'Anyway,' I said, 'I wanted to know if it could be Powys or Glitberg or Ownslow who had kidnapped me for revenge, so I asked them.'

'Good heavens.'

'Yeah. It wasn't a good idea. They wouldn't say yes or no.' I looked back to the night at the Vivat Club. 'They did tell me something else, though . . .' I said, and told Hilary what it was. Her eyes widened behind the glasses and she nodded once or twice.

'I see. Yes,' she said.

'So now,' I said. 'Here we are a few years later, and now I have not only my local area mental map but a broad view of most of the racing world, with uncountable interconnections. I do the accounts for so many racing people, their lives spread out like a carpet, touching, overlapping, each small transaction adding to my understanding of the whole. I'm part of it myself, as a jockey. I feel the fabric around me. I know how much saddles cost, and which saddler does most business, and which owners don't pay their bills, and who bets and who drinks, who saves, who gives to charity, who keeps a mistress. I know how much the woman whose horse I rode today paid to have him photographed for the Christmas cards she sent last year, and how much a bookmaker gave for his Rolls, and thousands and thousands of similar facts. All fitting, all harmless. It's when they don't fit . . . like a jockey suddenly spending more than he's earned, and I find he's running a whole new business and not declaring a penny of it . . . it's when the bits don't fit that I see the monster in the waves. Glimpsed, hidden . . . But definitely there.'

'Like now?' she said, frowning. 'Your iceberg?'

'Mm.' I hesitated. 'Another embezzler.'

'And this one – will he too go to jail swearing to cut your throat?'

I didn't answer at once, and she added dryly, 'Or is he likely to cut your throat before you get him there?'

I gave her half a grin. 'Not with a rock like you, he won't.'

'You be careful, Roland,' she said seriously. 'This doesn't feel to me like a joke.'

She stood up restlessly, towering among the palm fronds, as thin in her way as their stems.

'Come into the kitchen. What do you want to eat? I can do a Spanish omelette, if you like.'

I sat with my elbows on the kitchen table, and while she chopped onions and potatoes and green peppers I told her a good deal more, most of it highly unethical, as an accountant should never disclose the affairs of a client. She listened with increasing dismay, her cooking actions growing slower. Finally she laid down the knife and simply stood.

'Your partner,' she said.

'I don't know how much he's condoned,' I said, 'but on Monday . . . I have to find out.'

'Tell the police,' she said. 'Let them find out.'

'No. I've worked with Trevor for six years. We've always got on well together, and he seems fond of me, in his distant way. I can't shop him, just like that.'

'You'll warn him.'

'Yes,' I said. 'And I'll tell him of the existence of . . . the rock.'

She started cooking again, automatically, her thoughts busy behind her eyes.

'Do you think,' she said, 'that your partner knew about the other embezzlers, and tried to hush them up?'

I shook my head. 'Not Glitberg and Ownslow. Positively not. Not the last two, either. The firms they worked for were both my clients, and Trevor had no contact with them. But Connaught Powys . . .' I sighed. 'I really don't know. Trevor always used to spend about a week at that firm, doing the audit on the spot, as one nearly always does for big concerns, and I went one year only because he had an ulcer. It was Connaught Powys's bad luck that I cottoned on to what he was doing. Trevor might genuinely have missed the warning signs, because he doesn't always work the way I do.'

'How do you mean?'

'Well, a lot of an accountant's work is fairly mechanical. Vouching, for instance. That's checking that cheques written down in the cash book really were issued for the amount stated or, in other words, if the cashier writes down that cheque number 1234 was issued to Joe Bloggs in the sum of eighty pounds to pay for a load of sand, the auditor checks that the bank actually paid eighty pounds to Joe Bloggs on cheque no. 1234. It's routine work and takes a fairly long time on a big account, and it's often, or even usually, done, not by the accountant or auditor himself, but by an assistant. Assistants in our firm tend to come and go, and don't necessarily develop a sense of probability. The present ones wouldn't be likely to query, for instance, whether Joe Bloggs really existed, or sold sand, or sold eighty quid's worth, or delivered only fifty quid's worth, with Joe Bloggs and the cashier conspiring to pocket the thirty pounds profit.'

'Roland!'

I grinned. 'Small fiddles abound. It's the first violins that threaten to cut your throat.'

She broke four eggs into a bowl. 'Do you do all your own . . . er . . . vouching, then?'

'No, not all. It would take too long. But I do all of it for some accounts, and some of it for all accounts. To get the feel of things. To know where I am.'

'To fit into the landscape,' she said.

'Yes.'

'And Trevor doesn't?'

'He does a few himself, but on the whole not. Don't get me wrong. More accountants do as Trevor does, it's absolutely normal practice.'

'You want my advice?' she said.

'Yes, please.'

'Go straight to the police.'

'Thank you. Get on with the omelette.'

She sizzled it in the pan and divided it, succulent and soft in the centre, onto the plates. It tasted like a testimonial to her own efficiency, the best I'd ever had. Over coffee, afterwards, I told her a great deal about Jossie.

She looked into her cup. 'Do you love her?' she said.

'I don't know. It's too soon to say.'

'You sound,' she said dryly, 'bewitched.'

'There have been other girls. But not the same.' I looked at her downturned face. My mouth twitched. 'In case you're wondering about Jossie,' I said, 'no, I haven't.'

She looked up, the spectacles flashing, her eyes suddenly laughing, and a blush starting on her neck. She uttered an unheadmistressly opinion.

'You're a sod,' she said.

It was an hour's drive home from Hilary's house. No one followed me, or took the slightest interest, that I could see.

I rolled quietly down the lane towards the cottage with the car lights switched off, and made a silent reconnoitre on foot for the last hundred yards.

Everything about my home was dark and peaceful. The lights of Mrs Morris's sitting-room, next door, shone dimly through the pattern of her curtains. The night sky was powdered with stars, and the air was cool.

I waited for a while, listening, and was slowly reassured. No horrors in the shadows. No shattering black prisons yawning like mantraps before my feet. No cut-throats with ready steel.

To be afraid, I thought, was no way to live; yet I couldn't help it.

I unlocked the cottage and switched on all the lights; and it was empty, welcoming and sane. I fetched the car from the lane, locked myself into the cottage, pulled shut the curtains, switched on the heaters, and hugged round myself the comforting illusion of being safe in the burrow.

After that I made a pot of coffee, fished out some brandy,

161

and sprawled into an armchair with the ancient records of the misdeeds of Powys, Glitberg and Ownslow.

At one time I'd known every detail in those files with blinding clarity, but the years had blurred my memory. I found notes in my own handwriting about inferences I couldn't remember drawing, and conclusions as startling as acid. I was amazed, actually, at the quality of work I'd done, and it was weird to see it from an objective distance, as with a totally fresh eye. I supposed I could understand the comment there had been then, though at the time what I was doing had seemed a perfectly natural piece of work, done merely as best I could. I smiled to myself in pleased surprise. In that far-off time, I must have been hell to embezzlers. Not like nowadays, when it took me six shots to see Denby Crest.

I came across pages of notes about the workings of computers, details of which I had forgotten as fast as I'd learned them on a crash course in an electronics firm much like Powys's. It had pleased me at the time to be able to dissect and explain just what he'd done, and nothing had made him more furious. It had been vanity on my part, I thought: and I was still vain. Admiring your own work was one of the deadlier intellectual sins.

I sighed. I was never going to be perfect, so why worry.

There was no record anywhere in the Glitberg/Ownslow file of the buying of the warehouse, but it did seem possible, as I dug deeper in the search for clues, that it actually had been built by Glitberg and Ownslow, and was the sole concrete fabrication of National Construction (Wessex). Anyone who could invent whole streets of dwellings could put up a real warehouse without much trouble.

I wondered why they'd needed it, when everything else had been achieved on paper.

A tangible asset, uncashed, gone to seed, in which I had been dumped. The police had been told I was there, and the estate-agent trail had led without difficulty straight to Ownslow and Glitberg.

Why?

I sat and thought about it for a good long time, and then I finished the coffee and brandy and went to bed.

*

I picked Jossie up at ten in the grey morning, and drove to Portsmouth for the hovercraft ferry to the Isle of Wight.

'The nostalgia kick?' Jossie said. 'Back to the boarding house?'

I nodded. 'The sunny isle of childhood.'

'Oh yeah?' She took me literally and looked up meaningfully at the cloudy sky.

'It heads the British sunshine league,' I said.

'Tell that to Torquay.'

A ten-minute zip in the hovercraft took us across the sea at Spithead, and when we stepped ashore at Ryde, the clouds were behind us, hovering like a grey sheet over the mainland.

'It's unfair,' Jossie said, smiling.

'It's often like that.'

The town was bright with new spring paint, the Regency buildings clean and graceful in the sun. Every year, before the holiday-makers came, there was the big brush-up, and every winter, when they'd gone, the comfortable relapse into carpet slippers and salt-caked windows.

'Ryde pier,' I said, 'is two thousand, three hundred and five feet long, and was opened in 1814.'

'I don't want to know that.'

'There are approximately six hundred hotels, motels and boarding houses on this sunny island.'

'Nor that.'

'Nine towns, two castles, a lot of flamingoes and Parkhurst Prison.'

'Nor that, for God's sake.'

'My Uncle Rufus,' I said, 'was chief mucker-out at the local riding school.'

'Good grief.'

'As his assistant mucker-out,' I said, 'I scrambled under horses' bellies from the age of six.'

'That figures.'

'I used to exercise the horses and ponies all winter when the holiday people had gone home. And break in new ones. I can't really remember not being able to ride, but there's no racing here, of course. The first race I ever rode in was the Isle of

Wight Foxhounds point-to-point over on the mainland, and I fell off.'

We walked along the Esplanade with the breeze blowing Jossie's long green scarf out like streamers. She waved an arm at the sparkling water and said, 'Why horses? Why not boats, for heaven's sake, when you had them on your doorstep.'

'They made me seasick.'

She laughed. 'Like going to heaven and being allergic to harps.'

I took her to a hotel I knew, where there was a sunny terrace sheltered from the breeze, with a stunning view of the Solent and the shipping tramping by to Southampton. We drank hot chocolate and read the lunch menu, and talked of this and that and nothing much, and the time slid away like a mill-stream.

After roast beef for both of us, and apple pie, ice-cream and cheese for Jossie, we whistled up a taxi. There weren't many operating on a Sunday afternoon in April, but there was no point in being a native if one didn't know where to find the pearls.

The driver knew me, and didn't approve of my having deserted to become a 'mainlander', but as he also knew I knew the roads backwards, we got a straight run over Blackgang Chine to the wild cliffs on the south-west coast, and no roundabout guff to add mileage. We dawdled along there for about an hour, stopping often to stand out of the car, on the windswept grass. Jossie took in great lungfuls of the soul-filling landscape and said whyever did I live in Newbury.

'Racing,' I said.

'So simple.'

'Do you mind if we call on a friend on the way back?' I said. 'Ten minutes or so?'

'Of course not.'

'Wootton Bridge, then,' I said to the driver. 'Frederick's boatyard.'

'They'll be shut. It's Sunday.'

'We'll try, anyway.'

He shrugged heavily, leaving me to the consequences of my own stupidity, and drove back across the island, through Newport and out on the Ryde road to the deep inlet which formed a natural harbour for hundreds of small yachts.

The white-painted façade of the boatyard showed closed doors and no sign of life.

'There you are,' said the driver. 'I told you so.'

I got out of the car and walked over to the door marked 'Office', and knocked on it. Within a few moments it opened, and I grinned back to Jossie and jerked my head for her to join me.

'I got your message,' Johnny Frederick said. 'And Sunday afternoon, I sleep.'

'At your age?'

His age was the same as mine, almost to the day: we'd shared a desk at school and many a snigger in the lavatories. The round-faced, impish boy had grown into a muscular, salt-tanned man with craftsman's hands and a respectable hatred of paperwork. He occasionally telephoned me to find out if his own local accountant was doing things right, and bombarded the poor man with my advice.

'How's your father?' I said.

'Much the same.'

A balk of timber had fallen on Johnny's father's head in days gone by. There had been a lot of unkind jokes about thick as two planks before, three planks after, but the net result had been that an ailing family business had woken up in the hands of a bright new mind. With Johnny's designs and feeling for materials, Frederick Boats were a growing name.

I introduced Jossie, who got a shrewd once-over for aerodynamic lines and a shake from a hand like a piece of callused teak.

'Pleased to meet you,' he said, which was about the nearest he ever got to social small-talk. He switched his gaze to me. 'You've been in the wars a bit, according to the papers.'

'You might say so.' I grinned. 'What are you building, these days?'

'Come and see.'

He walked across the functional little office and opened the far door, which led straight into the boatyard itself. We went through, and Jossie exclaimed aloud at the unexpected size of the huge shed which sloped away down to the water.

There were several smallish fibreglass hulls supported in building frames, and two large ones, side by side in the centre, with five-foot keels.

'What size are those?' Jossie said.

'Thirty-seven feet overall.'

'They look bigger.'

'They won't on the water. It's the largest size we do, at present.' Johnny walked us round one of them, pointing out subtleties of hull design with pride. 'It handles well in heavy seas. It's stable, and not too difficult to sail, which is what most people want.'

'Not a racer?' I said.

He shook his head. 'Those dinghies are. But the big ocean-racers are specialist jobs. This yard isn't large enough; not geared to that class. And anyway, I like cruisers. A bit of carpet in the saloon and lockers that slide like silk.'

Jossie wandered off down the concrete slope, peering into the half-fitted dinghies and looking contentedly interested. I pulled the envelope of enlarged photographs from my inner pocket and showed them to Johnny. Three views of a sailing boat, one of an out-of-focus man.

'That's the boat I was abducted on. Can you tell anything about it from these photos?'

He peered at them, his head on one side. 'If you leave them with me, maybe. I'll look through the catalogues, and ask the boys over at Cowes. Was there anything special about it, that you remember?'

I explained that I hadn't seen much except the sail locker. 'The boat was pretty new, I think. Or at any rate well maintained. And it sailed from England on Thursday, March 17th, some time in the evening.'

He shuffled the prints to look at the man.

'His name is Alastair Yardley,' I said. 'I've written it on the back. He came from Bristol, and worked from there as a deckhand on sea-trials for ocean-going yachts. He skippered the boat. He's about our age.'

'Are you in a hurry for all this info?'

'Quicker the better.'

166

'OK. I'll ring a few guys. Let you know tomorrow, if I come up with anything.'

'That's great.'

He tucked the prints into their envelope and let his gaze wander to Jossie.

'A racing filly,' he said. 'Good lines.'

'Eyes off.'

'I like earthier ones, mate. Big boobs and not too bright.'

'Boring.'

'When I get home, I want a hot tea, and a cuddle when I feel like it, and no backchat about women's lib.'

When I got home, I thought, I wouldn't mind Jossie.

She walked up the concrete with big strides of her long legs, and came to a stop at our side. 'I had a friend whose boyfriend insisted on taking her sailing,' she said. 'She said she didn't terribly mind being wet, or cold, or hungry, or seasick, or frightened. She just didn't like them all at once.'

Johnny's eyes slid my way. 'With this boyfriend she'd be all right. He gets sick in harbour.'

Jossie nodded. 'Feeble.'

'Thanks,' I said.

'Be my guest.'

We went back through the office and into the taxi, and Johnny waved us goodbye.

'Any more chums?' Jossie said.

'Not this trip. If I start on the aunts, we'll be here for ever. Visit one, visit all, or there's a dust-up.'

We drove, however, at Jossie's request, past the guest house where I'd lived with my mother. There was a new glass sun-lounge across the whole of the front, and a car park where there had been garden. Tubs of flowers, bright sun-awnings, and a swinging sign saying 'Vacancies'.

'Brave,' Jossie said, clearly moved. 'Don't you think?'

I paid off the taxi there and we walked down to the sea, with seagulls squawking overhead and the white little town sleeping to tea-time on its sunny hillside.

'It's pretty,' Jossie said. 'And I see why you left.'

She seemed as content as I to dawdle away the rest of the day.

We crossed again in the hovercraft, and made our way slowly northwards, stopping at a pub at dusk for a drink and rubbery pork pie, and arriving finally outside the sprawling pile of Axwood House more than twelve hours after we'd left.

'That car,' Jossie said, pointing with disfavour at an inoffensive Volvo parked ahead, 'belongs to the detestable Lida.'

The light over the front door shone on her disgruntled face. I smiled, and she transferred the disfavour to me.

'It's all right for you. You aren't threatened with her moving into your home.'

'You could move out,' I said mildly.

'Just like that?'

'To my cottage, perhaps.'

'Good grief!'

'You could inspect it,' I said, 'for cleanliness, dry rot and spiders.'

She gave me her most intolerant stare. 'Butler, cook, and housemaids?'

'Six footmen and a lady's maid.'

'I'll come to tea and cucumber sandwiches. I suppose you do have cucumber sandwiches?'

'Of course.'

'Thin, and without crusts?'

'Naturally.'

I had really surprised her, I saw. She didn't know what to answer. It was quite clear, though, that she was not going to fall swooning into my arms. There was a good deal I would have liked to say, but I didn't know how to. Things about caring, and reassurance, and looking ahead.

'Next Sunday,' she said. 'At half past three. For tea.'

'I'll line up the staff.'

She decided to get out of the car, and I went round to open the door for her. Her eyes looked huge.

'Are you serious?' she said.

'Oh yes. It'll be up to you . . . to decide.'

'After tea?'

I shook my head. 'At any time.'

Her expression slowly softened to unaccustomed gentleness. I kissed her, and then kissed her again with conviction.

'I think I'll go in,' she said waveringly, turning away.

'Jossie . . .'

'What?'

I swallowed. Shook my head. 'Come to tea,' I said helplessly. 'Come to tea.'

16

Monday morning, after another night free of alarms and excursions, I went back to the office with good intentions of actually doing some work. Peter was sulking with Monday morning glooms, Bess had menstrual pains, and Debbie was tearful from a row with the screw-selling fiancé: par for office life as I knew it.

Trevor came into my room looking fatherly and anxious, and seemed reassured to find my appearance less deathly than on Friday.

'You did rest, then, Ro,' he said relievedly.

'I rode in a race and took a girl to the seaside.'

'Good heavens. At any rate, it seems to have done you good. Better than spending your time working.'

'Yes . . .' I said. 'Trevor, I did come into the office on Saturday morning, for a couple of hours.'

His air of worry crept subtly back. He waited for me to go on with the manner of a patient expecting bad news from his doctor: and I felt the most tremendous regret in having to give it to him.

'Denby Crest,' I said.

'Ro . . .' He spread out his hands, palms downwards, in a gesture that spoke of paternal distress at a rebellious son who wouldn't take his senior's word for things.

'I can't help it,' I said. 'I know he's a client, and a friend of yours, but if he's misappropriated fifty thousand pounds and you've condoned it, it concerns us both. It concerns this office, this partnership, and our future. You must see that. We can't just ignore the whole thing and pretend it hasn't happened.'

'Ro, believe me, everything will be all right.'

I shook my head. 'Trevor, you telephone Denby Crest and tell him to come over here today, to discuss what we're going to do.'

'No.'

'Yes,' I said positively. 'I'm not having it, Trevor. I'm half of this firm, and it's not going to do anything illegal.'

'You're uncompromising.' The mixture of sorrow and irritation had intensified. The two emotions, I thought fleetingly, that gave you regrets while you shot the rabbit.

'Get him here at four o'clock,' I said.

'You can't bully him like that.'

'There are worse consequences,' I said. I spoke without emphasis, but he knew quite well that it was a threat.

Irritation won hands down over sorrow. 'Very well, Ro,' he said sourly. 'Very well.'

He went out of my room with none of the sympathetic concern for me with which he had come in, and I felt a lonely sense of loss. I could forgive him anything myself, I thought in depression, but the law wouldn't. I lived by the law, both by inclination and choice. If my friend broke the law, should I abandon it for his sake: or should I abandon my friend for the sake of the law? In the abstract, there was no difficulty in my mind. In the flesh, I shrank. There was nothing frightfully jolly in being the instrument of distress, ruin, and prosecution. How much easier if the miscreant would confess of his own free will, instead of compelling his friend to denounce him: a sentimental solution, I thought sardonically, which happened only in weepy films. I was afraid that for myself there would be no such easy way out.

Those pessimistic musings were interrupted by a telephone call from Hilary, whose voice, when I answered, sounded full of relief.

'What's the matter?' I said.

'Nothing. I just . . .' She stopped.

'Just what?'

'Just wanted to know you were there, as a matter of fact.'

'Hilary!'

'Sounds stupid, I suppose, now that we both know you *are*

there. But I just wanted to be sure. After all, you wouldn't have cast me in the role of rock if you thought you were in no danger at all.'

'Um,' I said, smiling down the telephone. 'Sermons in stones.'

She laughed. 'You just take care of yourself, Ro.'

'Yes, ma'am.'

I put down the receiver, marvelling at her kindness; and almost immediately the bell rang again.

'Roland?'

'Yes, Moira?'

Her sigh came audibly down the wire. 'Thank goodness! I tried all day yesterday to reach you, and there was no reply.'

'I was out all day.'

'Yes, but I didn't know that. I mean, I was imagining all sorts of things, like you being kidnapped again, and all because of me.'

'I'm so sorry.'

'Oh, I don't mind, now that I know you're safe. I've had this terrible picture of you shut up again, and needing someone to rescue you. I've been so worried, because of Binny.'

'What about Binny?'

'I think he's gone really *mad*,' she said. 'Insane. I went over to his stables yesterday morning to see if Tapestry was all right after his race, and he wouldn't let me into the yard. Binny, I mean. All the gates were shut and locked with padlocks and chains. It's insane. He came and stood on the inside of the gate to the yard where Tapestry is, and waved his arms about, and told me to go away. I mean, it's *insane*.'

'It certainly is.'

'I told him he could have caused a terrible accident, tampering with that rein, and he screamed that he hadn't done it, and I couldn't prove it, and anything that happened to you was my fault for insisting that you rode the horse.' She paused for breath. 'He looked so . . . well, so *dangerous*. And I'd never thought of him being dangerous, but just a fool. You'll think I'm silly, but I was quite frightened.'

'I don't think you were silly,' I said truthfully.

'And then it came to me, like a revelation,' she said, 'that it had been Binny who had kidnapped you before, both times, and that he'd done it again, or something even worse . . .'

171

'Moira . . .'

'Yes, but you didn't *see* him. And then there was no answer to your telephone. I know you'll think I'm silly, but I was so worried.'

'I'm very grateful . . .' I started to say.

'You see, Binny never thought you'd win the Gold Cup,' she said, rushing on. 'And the very second you had, I told him you'd ride Tapestry always from then on, and he was *furious*, absolutely furious. You wouldn't believe. So of course he had you kidnapped at once, so that you'd be out of the way, and I'd *have* to have someone else, and then you escaped, and you were going to ride at Ascot, so he kidnapped you *again*, and he went absolutely berserk when I wouldn't let Tapestry go at Ascot with another jockey. And I made such a fuss in the press that he had to let you out, and so he had to try something else, like cutting the rein, and now I think he's so insane that he doesn't really know what he's doing. I mean, I think he thinks that if he kidnaps you, or kills you even, that I'll *have* to get another jockey for the Whitbread Gold Cup a week next Saturday, and honestly I think he's out of his *senses*, and really awfully dangerous because of that *obsession*, and so you see I really was terribly worried.'

'I do see,' I said. 'And I'm incredibly grateful for your concern.'

'But what are you going to *do*?' she wailed.

'About Binny? Listen, Moira, please listen.'

'Yes,' she said, her voice calming down. 'I'm listening.'

'Do absolutely nothing.'

'But *Roland*,' she protested.

'Listen. I'm sure you are quite right that Binny is in a dangerous mental state, but anything you or I could do would make him worse. Let him cool down. Give him several days. Then send a horsebox with if possible a police escort – and you can get policemen for private jobs like that, you just apply to the local nick, and offer to pay for their time – collect Tapestry, and send him to another trainer.'

'Roland!'

'You can carry loyalty too far,' I said. 'Binny's done marvels with training the horse, I agree, but you owe him nothing. If it

172

weren't for your own strength of mind he'd have manipulated the horse to make money only for himself, as well you know, and your enjoyment would have come nowhere.'

'But about kidnapping you . . .' she began.

'No, Moira,' I said. 'He didn't; it wasn't Binny. I don't doubt he was delighted it was done, but he didn't do it.'

She was astonished. 'He must have.'

'No.'

'But why not?'

'Lots of complicated reasons. But for the one thing, he wouldn't have kidnapped me straight after the Gold Cup. He wouldn't have had any need to. If he'd wanted to abduct me to stop me riding Tapestry, he wouldn't have done it until just before the horse's next race, nearly three weeks later.'

'Oh,' she said doubtfully.

'The first abduction was quite elaborate,' I said. 'Binny couldn't possibly have had time to organize it between the Gold Cup and the time I was taken, which was only an hour or so later.'

'Are you sure?'

'Yes, Moira, quite sure. And when he really did try to stop me winning, he did very direct and simple things, not difficult like kidnapping. He offered me a bribe, and cut the rein. Much more in character. He always was a fool, and now he's a dangerous fool, but he isn't a kidnapper.'

'Oh dear,' she said, sounding disappointed. 'And I was so *sure*.'

She cheered up a bit and asked me to ride Tapestry in the Whitbread. I said I'd be delighted, and she deflated my ego by passing on the opinion of a press friend of hers to the effect that Tapestry was one of those horses who liked to be in charge, and an amateur who just sat there doing nothing very much was exactly what suited him best.

Grinning to myself I put down the receiver. The press friend was right; but who cared.

For the rest of the morning I tried to make inroads into the backlog of correspondence, but found it impossible to concentrate. The final fruit of two hours of reading letters and shuffling them around, was three heaps marked 'overdue', 'urgent', and 'if you don't get these off today there will be trouble'.

Debbie looked down her pious nose at my inability to apply myself, and primly remarked that I was under-utilizing her capability. Under-utilizing . . . Ye Gods! Where did the gobbledegook jargon come from?

'You mean I'm not giving you enough to do.'

'That's what I said.'

At luncheon I stayed alone in the office and stared into space: and my telephone rang again.

Johnny Frederick, full of news.

'Do you mind if I send you a bill for 'phone calls?' he said. 'I must have spent thirty quid. I've been talking all morning.'

'I'll send you a cheque.'

'OK. Well, mate, pin back your lugholes. That boat you were on was built at Lymington, and she sailed from there after dark on March 17th. She was brand spanking new, and she hadn't completed her trials, and she wasn't registered or named. She was built by a top-notch shipyard called Goldenwave Marine, for a client called Arthur Robinson.'

'Who?'

'Arthur Robinson. That's what he said his name was, anyway. And there was only one slightly unusual thing about Mr Robinson, and that was that he paid for the boat in cash.'

He waited expectantly.

'How much cash?' I said.

'Two hundred thousand pounds.'

'Crikey.'

'Mind you,' Johnny said, 'that's bargain basement stuff for Goldenwave. They do a nice job in mini-liners at upwards of a million, with gold taps, for Arabs.'

'In cash?'

'Near enough, I dare say. Anyway, Arthur Robinson always paid on the nail, in instalments as they came due during the boat-building, but always in your actual folding. Goldenwave Marine wouldn't be interested in knowing whether the cash had had tax paid on it. None of their business.'

'Quite,' I said. 'Go on.'

'That Thursday – March 17th – in the morning, some time, Arthur Robinson rang Goldenwave and said he wanted to take some friends aboard for a party that evening, and would they please see that the water and fuel tanks were topped up, and everything ship-shape. Which Goldenwave did.'

'Without question.'

'Of course. You don't argue with two hundred thousand quid. Anyway, the boat was out on a mooring in the deep water passage, so they left her fit for the owner's visit and brought her tender ashore, for him to use when he got there.'

'A black rubber dinghy?'

'I didn't ask. The nightwatchman had been told to expect the party, so he let them in, and helped generally, and saw them off. I got him out of bed this morning to talk to him, and he was none too pleased, but he remembers the evening quite well, because of course the boat sailed off that night and never came back.

'What did he say?'

'There were two lots of people, he said. One lot came in an old white van, which he didn't think much of for an owner of such a boat. You'd expect a Rolls, he said.' Johnny chuckled. 'The first arrivals, three people, were the crew. They unloaded stores from an estate car and made two trips out to the boat. Then the white van arrived with several more men, and one of those was lying down. They told the nightwatchman he was dead drunk, and that was you, I reckon. Then the first three men and the drunk man went out to the boat, and the other men drove away in the old van and the estate car, and that was that. The nightwatchman thought it a very boring sort of party, and noted the embarkation in his log, and paid no more attention. Next morning, no boat.'

'And no report to the police?'

'The owner had taken his own property, which he'd fully paid for. Goldenwave had expected him to take command of her a week later, anyway, so they made no fuss.'

'You've done absolute marvels,' I said.

'Do you want to hear about Alastair Yardley?'

'There's more?'

'There sure is. He seems to be quite well-known. Several of the bigger shipyards have recommended him to people who want their boats sailed from England, say, to Bermuda, or the

Caribbean, and so on, and don't have a regular crew, and also don't want to cross oceans themselves. He signs on his own crew, and pays them himself. He's no crook. Got a good reputation. Tough, though. And he's not cheap. If he agreed to help shanghai you, you can bet Mr Arthur Robinson paid through the nose for the service. But you can ask him yourself, if you like.'

'What do you mean?'

Johnny was justifiably triumphant. 'I struck dead lucky, mate. Mind you, I chased him round six shipyards, but he's in England now to fetch another yacht, and he'll talk to you if you ring him more or less at once.'

'I don't believe it!'

'Here's the number.' He read out the numbers, and I wrote them down. 'Ring him before two o'clock. You can also talk to the chap in charge of Goldenwave, if you like. This is his number. He said he'd help in any way he could.'

'You're fantastic,' I said, stunned to breathlessness by his success.

'We got a real lucky break, mate, because when I took those photographs to Cowes first thing this morning, I asked around everybody, and there was a feller in the third yard I tried who'd worked at Goldenwave last year, and he said it looked like their Golden Sixty Five, so I rang them, and it was the departure date that clinched it.'

'I can't begin to thank you.'

'To tell you the truth, mate, it's been a bit of excitement, and there isn't all that much about, these days. I've enjoyed this morning, and that's a fact.'

'I'll give you a ring. Tell you how things turn out.'

'Great. Can't wait. And see you.'

He disconnected, and with an odd sinking feeling in my stomach I rang the first of the numbers he'd given me. A shipyard. Could I speak to Alastair Yardley? Hang on, said the switchboard. I hung.

'Hullo?'

The familiar voice. Bold, self-assertive, challenging the world.

'It's Roland Britten,' I said.

There was a silence, then he said, 'Yeah,' slowly.

'You said you'd talk to me.'

'Yeah.' He paused. 'Your friend this morning, John Frederick, the boat-builder, he tells me I was sold a pup about you.'

'How do you mean?'

'I was told you were a blackmailer.'

'A *what?*'

'Yeah.' He sighed. 'Well, this guy Arthur Robinson, he said you'd set up his wife in some compromising photographs and were trying to blackmail her, and he wanted you taught a lesson.'

'Oh,' I said blankly. It explained a great deal, I thought.

'Your friend Frederick told me that was all crap. He said I'd been conned. I reckon I was. All the other guys in the yard here know all about you winning that race and going missing. They just told me. Seems it was in all the papers. But I didn't see them, of course.'

'How long,' I said, 'were you supposed to keep me on board?'

'He said to ring him Monday evening, April 4th, and he'd tell me when and where and how to set you loose. But of course, you jumped ship the Tuesday before, and how you got that lever off is a bloody mystery . . . I rang him that night, and he was so bloody angry he couldn't get the words out. So then he said he wouldn't pay me for the job on you, and I said if he didn't he could whistle for his boat, I'd just sail it into some port somewhere and walk away, and he'd have God's own job finding it. So I said he could send me the money to Palma, where I bank, and when I got it I'd do what he wanted, which was to take his boat to Antibes and deliver it to the ship brokers there.'

'Brokers?'

'Yeah. Funny, that. He'd only just bought it. What did he want to sell it for?'

'Well . . .' I said. 'Do you remember his telephone number?'

'No. Threw it away, didn't I, as soon as I was shot of his boat.'

'At Antibes?'

'That's right.'

'Did you meet him?' I asked.

177

'Yeah. That night at Lymington. He told me not to talk to you, and not to listen, because you'd tell me lies, and not to let you know where we were, and not to leave a mark on you, and to watch out because you were as slippery as an eel.' He paused a second. 'He was right about that, come to think.'

'Do you remember what he looked like?'

'Yeah,' he said, 'what I saw of him; but it was mostly in the dark, out on the quay.' He described Arthur Robinson as I'd expected, and well enough to be conclusive.

'I wasn't intending to go for another week,' he said. 'The weather forecasts were all bad for Biscay, and I'd only been out in her once, in light air, not enough to know how she'd handle in a gale, but he rang Goldenwave that morning and spoke to me, and told me about you, and said gale or no gale he'd make it worth my while if I'd go that evening and take you with me.'

'I hope it was worth it,' I said.

'Yeah,' he said frankly. 'I got paid double.'

I laughed in my throat. 'Er . . .' I said, 'is it possible for a boat just to sail off from England and wander round Mediterranean ports, when it hasn't even got a name? I mean, do you have to pass Customs, and things like that?'

'You can pass Customs if you want to waste a bloody lot of time. Otherwise, unless you tell them, a port doesn't know whether you've come from two miles down the coast, or two thousand. The big ports collect mooring fees, that's all they're interested in. If you drop anchor at somewhere like Formentor, which we did one night with you, no one takes a blind bit of notice. Easy come, easy go, that's what it's like on the sea. Best way to live, I reckon.'

'It sounds marvellous,' I sighed enviously.

'Yeah. Look . . .' he paused a second, 'are you going to set the police on me, or anything? Because I'm off today, on the afternoon tide, and I'm not telling where.'

'No,' I said. 'No police.'

He let his breath out audibly in relief. 'I reckon . . .' He paused. 'Thanks, then. And well, sorry, like.'

I remembered the paperback, and the socks, and the soap, and I had no quarrel with him.

*

From Goldenwave Marine, ten minutes later, I learned a good many background facts about big boats in general and Arthur Robinson in particular.

Goldenwave had four more Golden Sixty Fives on the stocks at the moment, all commissioned by private customers, and Arthur Robinson had been one of a stream. Their Golden Sixty Five had been a successful design, they were pleased and proud to say, and their standard of ship-building was respected the world over.

End of commercial.

I replaced the receiver gratefully. Sat, thinking, chewing bits off my fingernails. Decided, without joy, to take a slightly imprudent course.

Debbie, Peter, Bess and Trevor came back, and the place filled up with tap-tap and bustle. Mr Wells arrived for his appointment twenty minutes before the due time, reminding me of the psychiatrists'-eye-view of patients: if they're early, they're anxious, if they're late, they're aggressive, and if they're on time, they're pathological. I often thought the psychiatrists didn't understand about trains, buses and traffic flow, but in this case there wasn't much doubt about the anxiety. Mr Wells' hair, manner and eyes were all out of control.

'I rang the people you sent the rubber cheque to,' I said. 'They were a bit sticky, but they've agreed not to prosecute if you take care of them after the inevitable Receiving Order.'

'I what?'

'Pay them later,' I said. Jargon . . . I did it myself.

'Oh.'

'The order of paying,' I said, 'will be first the Inland Revenue, who will collect tax in full, and will also charge interest for every day overdue.'

'But I haven't anything to pay them with.'

'Did you sell your car, as we agreed you should?'

He nodded, but wouldn't meet my eyes.

'What have you done with the money?' I said.

'Nothing.'

'Pay it to the Revenue, then, on account.'

He looked away evasively, and I sighed at his folly. 'What have you done with the money?' I repeated.

He wouldn't tell me, and I concluded that he had been following the illegal path of many an imminent bankrupt, selling off his goods and banking the proceeds distantly under a false name, so that when the bailiffs came there wouldn't be much left. I gave him some good advice which I knew he wouldn't take. The suicidal hysterics of his earlier visit had settled into resentment against everyone pressing him, including me. He listened with a mulish stubbornness which I'd seen often enough before, and all he would positively agree to was not to write any more cheques.

By three-thirty I'd had enough of Mr Wells, and he of me.

'You need a good solicitor,' I said. 'He'll tell you the same as me, but maybe you'll listen.'

'It was a solicitor who gave me your name,' he said glumly.

'Who's your solicitor?'

'Fellow called Denby Crest.'

It was a small community, I thought. Touching, overlapping, a patchwork fabric. When the familiar names kept turning up, things were normal.

As it happened, Trevor was in the outer office when I showed Mr Wells to the door. I introduced them, explaining that Denby had sent him to see us. Trevor cast a benign eye, which would have been jaundiced had he known the Wells state of dickiness, and made affable small talk. Mr Wells took in Trevor's substantial air, seniority, and general impression of worldliness, and I practically saw the thought cross his mind that perhaps he had consulted the wrong partner.

And perhaps, I thought cynically, he had.

When he'd gone, Trevor looked at me sombrely.

'Come into my office,' he sighed.

17

I sat in one of the clients' chairs, with Trevor magisterially behind his desk. His manner was somewhere between unease and cajoling, as if he were not quite sure of his ground.

'Denby said he'd be here by four.'

'Good.'

'But Ro . . . he'll explain. He'll satisfy you, I'm sure. I think I'll leave it to him to explain, and then you'll see . . . that there's nothing for us to worry about.'

He raised an unconvincing smile and rippled his fingertips on his blotter. I looked at the familiar, friendly figure, and wished with all my heart that things were not as they were.

Denby came ten minutes early, which would have gratified the psychiatrists, and he was wound up like a tight spring, as well he might be. His backbone was ramrod stiff inside the short plump frame, the moustache bristling on the forward jutting mouth, the irritated air plainer than ever.

He didn't shake hands with me: merely nodded. Trevor came round his desk to offer a chair, a politeness I thought excessive.

'Well, Ro,' Denby said crossly. 'I hear you have reservations about my certificate.'

'That's so.'

'What, exactly?'

'Well,' I said. 'To be exact . . . fifty thousand pounds missing from the clients' deposit account.'

'Rubbish.'

I sighed. 'You transferred money belonging to three separate clients from the clients' deposit to the clients' current account,' I said. 'You then drew five cheques from the current account, made out to yourself, in varying sums, over a period of six weeks, three to four months ago. Those cheques add up to fifty thousand pounds exactly.'

'But I've repaid the money. If you'd've looked more carefully you'd have seen the counter credits on the bank statement.' He was irritated. Impatient.

'I couldn't make out where those credits had come from,' I

said, 'so I asked the bank to send a duplicate statement. It came this morning.'

Denby sat as if turned to stone.

'The duplicate statement,' I said regretfully, 'shows no record of the money having been repaid. The bank statement you gave us was . . . well . . . a forgery.'

Time ticked by.

Trevor looked unhappy. Denby revised his position.

'I've only *borrowed* the money,' he said. There was still no regret, and no real fear. 'It's perfectly safe. It will be repaid very shortly. You have my word for it.'

'Um . . .' I said. 'Your word isn't enough.'

'Really, Ro, this is ridiculous. If I say it will be repaid, it will be repaid. Surely you know me well enough for that?'

'If you mean,' I said, 'would I have thought you a thief, then no, I wouldn't.'

'I'm not a thief,' he said angrily. 'I told you, I borrowed the money. A temporary expediency. It's unfortunate that . . . as things turned out . . . I was not able to repay it before the certificate became due. But as I explained to Trevor, it is only a matter of a few weeks, at the most.'

'The clients' money,' I said reasonably, 'is not entrusted to you so that you can use it for a private loan to yourself.'

'We all know that,' Denby said snappily, in a teaching-grand-mother-to-suck-eggs manner. My grandmother, I reflected fleetingly, had never sucked an egg in her life.

'You're fifty thousand short,' I said, 'and Trevor's condoned it, and neither of you seems to realize you'll be out of business if it comes to light.'

They both looked at me as if I were a child.

'But there's no need for it to come to light, Ro,' Trevor said. 'Denby will repay the money soon, and all will be well. Like I told you.'

'It isn't ethical,' I said.

'Don't be so pompous, Ro,' Trevor said, at his most fatherly, shaking his head with sorrow.

'Why did you take the money?' I asked Denby. 'What for?'

Denby looked across enquiringly at Trevor, who nodded.

'You'll have to tell him everything, Denby. He's very persistent. Better tell him, then he'll understand, and we can clear the whole thing up.'

Denby complied with bad grace. 'I had a chance,' he said, 'of buying a small block of flats. Brand new. Not finished. Builder in difficulties, wanted a quick sale, that sort of thing. Flats were going cheap, of course. So I bought them. Too good to miss. Done that sort of deal before, of course. Not a fool, you know. Knew what I was doing, and all that.'

'Your own conveyancer?' I said.

'What? Oh yes.' He nodded. 'Well, then, I needed a bit more extra capital to finance the deal. Perfectly safe. Good flats. Nothing wrong with them.'

'But they haven't sold?' I said.

'Takes time. Market's sluggish in the winter. But they're all sold now, subject to contracts. Formalities, mortgages, all that. Takes time.'

'Mm.' I said. 'How many flats in the block, and where is it?'

'Eight flats, small, of course. At Newquay, Cornwall.'

'Have you seen them?' I said.

'Of course.'

'Do you mind if I do?' I said. 'And will you give me the addresses of all the people who are buying the flats, and tell me how much each is paying?'

Denby bristled. 'Are you saying you don't believe me?'

'I'm an auditor,' I said. 'I don't believe. I check.'

'You can take my word for it.'

I shook my head. 'You sent us a forged bank statement. I can't take your word for anything.'

There was a silence.

'If those flats exist, and if you repay that money this week, I'll keep quiet,' I said. 'I'll want confirmation by letter from the bank. The money must be there by Friday, and the letter here by Saturday. Otherwise, no deal.'

'I can't get the money this week,' Denby said peevishly.

'Borrow it from a loan shark.'

'But that's ridiculous. The interest I would have to pay would wipe out all my profit.'

Serve you right, I thought unfeelingly. I said, 'Unless the clients' money is back in the bank by Friday, the Law Society will have to be told.'

'Ro!' Trevor protested.

'However much you try to wrap it up as "unfortunate" and "expedient",' I said, 'the fact remains that all three of us know that what Denby has done is a criminal offence. I'm not putting my name to it as a partner of this firm. If the money is not repaid by Friday, I'll write a letter explaining that in the light of fresh knowledge we wish to cancel the certificate just issued.'

'But Denby would be struck off!' Trevor said.

They both looked as if the stark realities of life were something that only happened to other people.

'Unfriendly,' Denby said angrily. 'Unnecessarily aggressive, that's what you are, Ro. Righteous. Unbending.'

'All those, I dare say,' I said.

'It's no good, I suppose, suggesting I . . . er . . . cut you in?'

Trevor made a quick horrified gesture, trying to stop him.

'Denby, Denby,' he said, distressed. 'You'll never bribe him. For God's sake have some sense. If you really want to antagonize Ro, you offer him a bribe.'

Denby scowled at me and got explosively to his feet.

'All *right*,' he said bitterly. 'I'll get the money by Friday. And don't ever expect any favours from me for the rest of your life.'

He strode furiously out of the office leaving eddies of disturbed air and longer trails of disturbed friendship. Turbulent wake, I thought. Churning and destructive, overturning everything it touched.

'Are you satisfied, Ro?' Trevor said gently, in sorrow.

I sat without answering.

I felt like a man on a high diving board, awaiting the moment of strength. Ahead, the plunge. Behind, the quiet way down. The choice, within me.

I could walk away, I thought. Pretend I didn't know what I knew. Settle for silence, friendship and peace. Refrain from bringing distress and disgrace and dreary unhappiness.

My friend or the law. To which did I belong? To the law or my own pleasure . . .

O great God almighty.

I swallowed with a dry mouth.

'Trevor,' I said, 'do you know Arthur Robinson?'

*

There was no fun, no fun at all, in looking into the face of ultimate disaster.

The blood slowly drained from Trevor's skin, leaving his eyes like great dark smudges.

'I'll get you some brandy,' I said.

'Ro . . .'

'Wait.'

I fetched him a tumbler, from his entertaining cupboard, heavy with alcohol, light on soda.

'Drink it,' I said with compassion. 'I'm afraid I've given you a shock.'

'How . . .' His mouth quivered suddenly, and he put the glass to his lips to hide it. He drank slowly, and took the glass a few inches away: a present help in trouble. 'How much . . . do you know?' he said.

'Why I was abducted. Who did it. Who owns the boat. Who sailed her. Where she is now. How much she cost. And where the money comes from.'

'My God . . . My God . . .' His hands shook.

'I want to talk to him,' I said. 'To Arthur Robinson.'

A faint flash of something like hope shone in his eyes.

'Do you know . . . his other name?'

I told him what it was. The spark of light died to a pebble-like dullness. He clattered the glass against his teeth.

'I want you to telephone,' I said. 'Tell him I know. Tell him I want to talk. Tell him, if he has any ideas of doing anything but what I ask, I'll go straight from this office to the police. I want to talk to him tonight.'

'But Ro, knowing you . . .' He sounded despairing. 'You'll go to the police anyway.'

'Tomorrow morning,' I said.

He stared at me for a long, long time. Then with a heavy half-groaning sigh, he stretched out his hand to the telephone.

We went to Trevor's house. Better for talking, he suggested, than the office.

'Your wife?' I said.

'She's staying with her sister, tonight. She often does.'

We drove in two cars, and judging by the daze of his expression Trevor saw nothing consciously of the road for the whole four miles.

His big house sat opulently in the late afternoon sunshine, nineteen-twenties respectability in every brick. Acres of diamond-shaped leaded window panes, black paint, a wide portico with corkscrew pillars, wisteria creeping here and there, lots of gables with beams stuck on for effect.

Trevor unlocked the front door and led the way into dead inside air which smelled of old coffee and furniture polish. Parquet flooring in the roomy hall, and rugs.

'Come into the snug,' he said, walking ahead.

The snug was a longish room which lay between the more formal sitting and dining rooms, looking outwards to the pillared loggia, with the lawn beyond it. To Trevor the snug was psychologically as well as geographically the heart of the house, the place where he most felt a host to his businessmen friends.

There was the bar, built in, where he liked to stand, genially pouring drinks. Several dark red leather armchairs. A small, sturdy dining table, with four leather-seated dining chairs. A large television. Bookshelves. An open brick fireplace, with a leather screen. A palm in a brass pot. More Stubbs prints. Several small chair-side tables. A leaf-patterned carpet. Heavy red velvet curtains. Red lampshades. On winter evenings, with the fire lit, curtains drawn, and lights glowing warmly, snug, in spite of its size, described it.

Trevor switched on the lights, and although it was full daylight, drew the curtains. Then he made straight for the bar.

'Do you want a drink?' he said.

I shook my head. He fixed himself a brandy of twice the size I'd given him in the office.

'I can't believe any of this is happening,' he said.

He took his filled glass and slumped down in one of the red leather armchairs, staring into space. I hitched a hip on to the table, which like so much in that house was protected by a sheet of plate glass. We both waited, neither of us enjoying our thoughts. We waited nearly an hour.

Nothing violent, I told myself numbly, would happen in that genteel house. Violence occurred in back alleys and dark corners. Not in a well-to-do sitting-room on a Monday evening. I felt the flutter of apprehension in every nerve and thought about eyes black with the lust for revenge.

A car drew up outside. A door slammed. There were footsteps outside on the gravel. Footsteps crossing the threshold, coming through the open front door, treading across the parquet, coming to the door of the snug. Stopping there.

'Trevor?' he said.

Trevor looked up dully. He waved a hand towards me, where I sat to one side, masked by the open door.

He pushed the door wider. Stepped into the room.

He held a shotgun; balanced over his forearm, butt under the armpit, twin barrels pointing to the floor.

I took a deep steadying breath, and looked into his firm, familiar face.

Jossie's father. William Finch.

'Shooting me,' I said, 'won't solve anything. I've left photostats and all facts with a friend.'

'If I shoot your foot off, you'll ride no more races.'

His voice already vibrated with the smashing hate: and this time I saw it not from across a courtroom thick with policemen, but from ten feet at the wrong end of a gun.

Trevor made jerky calming gestures with his hands.

'William . . . surely you see. Shooting Ro would be disastrous. Irretrievably disastrous.'

'The situation is already irretrievable.' His voice was thick, roughened and deepened by the tension in throat and neck. 'This little creep has seen to that.'

'Well,' I said, and heard the tension in my own voice, 'I didn't make you steal.'

It wasn't the best of remarks. Did nothing to reduce the critical mass: and William Finch was like a nuclear reactor with the rods too far out already. The barrels of the gun swung up into his hands and pointed at my loins.

'William, for God's sake,' Trevor said urgently, climbing ponderously out of his armchair. 'Use your reason. If he says killing him would do no good, you must believe him. He'd never have risked coming here if it wasn't true.'

Finch vibrated with fury through all his elegant height. The conflict between hatred and commonsense was plain in the bunching muscles along his jaw and the claw-like curve of his fingers. There was a fearful moment when I was certain that the blood-lust urge to avenge himself would blot out all fear of consequences, and I thought disconnectedly that I wouldn't feel it . . . you never felt the worst of wounds in the first few seconds. It was only after, if you lived, that the tide came in. I wouldn't know . . . I wouldn't feel it, and I might not even know . . .

He swung violently away from me and thrust the shotgun into Trevor's arms.

'Take it. Take it,' he said through his teeth. 'I don't trust myself.'

I could feel the tremors down my legs, and the prickling of sweat over half my body. He hadn't killed me at the very start, when it would have been effective, and it was all very well risking he wouldn't do it now when he'd nothing to gain. It had come a good deal too close.

I leaned my behind weakly against the table, and worked some saliva into my mouth. Tried to set things out in a dry-as-dust manner, as if we were discussing a small point of policy.

'Look . . .' It came out half-strangled. I cleared my throat and tried again. 'Tomorrow I will have to telephone to New York, to talk to the Nantucket family. Specifically, to talk to one of the directors on the board of their family empire; the director to whom Trevor sends the annual Axwood audited accounts.'

Trevor took the shotgun and stowed it away out of sight behind the ornate bar. William Finch stood in the centre of the room with unreleased energy quivering through all his frame. I watched his hands clench and unclench, and his legs move inside his trousers, as if wanting to stride about.

'What will you tell them, then?' he said fiercely. 'What?'

'That you've been . . . er . . . defrauding the Nantucket family business during the past financial year.'

For the first time some of the heat went out of him.

'During the past . . .' He stopped.

'I can't tell,' I said, 'about earlier years. I didn't do the audits. I've never seen the books, and they are not in our office. They

188

have to be kept for three years, of course, so I expect you have them.'

There was a lengthy silence.

'I'm afraid,' I said, 'that the Nantucket director will tell me to go at once to the police. If it was old Naylor Nantucket who was involved, it might be different. He might just have hushed everything up, for your sake. But this new generation, they don't know you. They're hard-nosed businessmen who disapprove of the stable anyway. They never come near the place. They do look upon it as a business proposition, though, and they pay you a good salary to manage it, and they undoubtedly regard any profits as being theirs. However mildly I put it, and I'm not looking forward to it at all, they are going to have to know that for this financial year their profits have gone to you.'

My deadpan approach began to have its results. Trevor poured two drinks and thrust one into William Finch's hand. He looked at it unseeingly and after a few moments put it down on the bar.

'And Trevor?' he said.

'I'll have to tell the Nantucket director,' I said regretfully, 'that the auditor they appointed has helped to rip them off.'

'Ro,' Trevor said, protesting, I gathered, at the slang expression more than the truth of it.

'Those Axwood books are a work of fiction,' I said to him. 'Cash books, ledgers, invoices . . . all ingenious lies. William would never have got away with such a wholesale fraud without your help. Without, anyway . . .' I said, modifying it slightly, 'without you knowing, and turning a blind eye.'

'And raking off a bloody big cut,' Finch said violently, making sure he took his friend down with him.

Trevor made a gesture of distaste, but it had to be right. Trevor had a hearty appetite for money, and would never have taken such a risk without the gain.

'These books look all right at first sight,' I said. 'They would have satisfied an outside auditor, if the Nantuckets had wanted a check from a London firm, or one in New York. But as for Trevor, and as for me, living here . . .' I shook my head. 'Axwood Stables have paid thousands to forage merchants who didn't receive the money, to saddlers who don't exist, to maintenance men, electricians and plumbers who did no work. The invoices are there, all nicely printed, but the transactions they refer to are thin air. The cash went straight to William Finch.'

Some of the slowly evaporating heat returned fast to Finch's manner, and I thought it wiser not to catalogue aloud all the rest of the list of frauds.

He'd charged the Nantuckets wages for several more lads than he'd employed: a dodge hard to pin down, as the stable-lad population floated from yard to yard.

He'd charged the Nantucket company more than nine thousand pounds for the rent of extra loose boxes and keep for horses by a local farmer, when I knew he had paid only a fraction of that, as the farmer was one of my clients.

He'd charged much more for shares in jockeys' retainers than the jockeys had received; and had invented travelling expenses to the races for horses which according to the form books had never left the yard.

He had pocketed staggering sums from a bloodstock agent in the form of commission on the sales of Nantucket horses to outside owners: fifty thousand or so in the past year, the agent had confirmed casually on the telephone, not knowing that Finch had no right to it.

I imagined Finch had also been sending enlarged bills to all the non-Nantucket owners, getting them to make out their cheques to him personally rather than to the company, and then diverting a slice to himself before paying a reasonable sum into the business.

The Nantuckets were far away, and uninterested. All I guessed they'd wanted had been a profit on the bottom line, and he'd given them just enough to keep them quiet.

As a final irony, he'd charged the Nantuckets six thousand pounds for auditors' fees, and nowhere in our books was there a trace of six thousand pounds from Axwood Stables. Trevor might have had his half, though, on the quiet: it was enough to make you laugh.

A long list of varied frauds. Much harder to detect than one large one. Adding up, though, to an average rake-off for Finch of over two thousand pounds a week. Untaxed.

Year in, year out.

Assisted by his auditor.

Assisted also, it was certain, by the ever-sick secretary, Sandy, though with or without her knowledge I didn't know. If she was ill as often as all that, and away from her post, maybe she didn't know. Or maybe the knowledge made her ill. But as in most big frauds, the paperwork had to be done well, and in the Axwood Stables case, there had been a great deal of it done well.

Ninety to a hundred horses. Well trained, well raced. A big stable with a huge weekly turnover. A top trainer. A trainer, I thought, who didn't own his own stable, who was paid only a salary, and a highly taxed one at that, and who faced having no capital to live on in old age, in a time of inflation. A man in his fifties, an employee, seeing into a future without enough money. An enforced retirement. No house of his own. No power. A man with money at present passing daily through his hands like a river in flood.

All racehorse trainers were entrepreneurs, with organizing minds. Most were in business on their own account, and had no absent company to defraud. If William Finch had been his own master, I doubted that he would ever have thought of embezzlement. With his abilities, in the normal course of things, he would have had no need.

Need. Ability. Opportunity. I wondered how big a step it had been to dishonesty. To crime.

Probably not very big. A pay-packet for a non-existent stable lad, for a little extra regular cash. The cost of an unordered ton of hay.

Small steps, ingenious swindles, multiplying and swelling, leading to a huge swathing highway.

'Trevor,' I said mildly, 'how long ago did you spot William's . . . irregularities?'

Trevor looked at me sorrowfully, and I half-smiled.

'You saw them . . . some of the first ones . . . in the books,' I said, 'and you told him it wouldn't do.'

'Of course.'

'You suggested,' I said, 'that if he really put his mind to it you would both be a great deal better off.'

Finch reacted strongly with a violent gesture of his whole arm, but Trevor's air of sorrow merely intensified.

'Just like Connaught Powys,' I said. 'I tried hard to believe that you genuinely hadn't seen how he was rigging that computer, but I reckon . . . I have to face it that you were doing it together.'

'Ro . . .' he said sadly.

'Anyway,' I said to Finch, 'you sent the books in for the annual audit, and after all this time neither you nor Trevor are particularly nervous. Trevor and I have been chronically behind with our work for ages, so I guess he just locked them in his cupboard, to see to as soon as he could. He would know I wouldn't look at your books. I never had, in six years; and I had too many clients of my own. And then, when Trevor was away on his holidays, the unforeseen happened. On Gold Cup day, through your letterbox, and mine, came the summons for you to appear before the Tax Commissioners a fortnight later.'

He stared at me with furious dark eyes, his strong, elegant figure tall and straight like a great stag at bay against an impudent hound. Round the edges of the curtains the daylight was fading to dark. Inside, electric lights shone smoothly on civilized man.

I smiled twistedly. 'I sent you a message. Don't worry, I said, Trevor's on holiday, but I'll apply for a postponement, and make a start on the books myself. I went straight off to ride in the Gold Cup and never gave it another thought. But you, to you, that message meant ruin. Degradation, prosecution, probably prison.'

A quiver ran through him. Muscles moved along his jaw.

'I imagine,' I said, 'that you thought the simplest thing would be to get the books back; but they were locked in Trevor's cupboard, and only he and I have keys. And in any case I would have thought it very suspicious, if, with the Commissioners breathing down our necks, you refused to let me see the books. Especially suspicious if the office had been broken into and those papers stolen. Anything along those lines would have led to investigation, and disaster. So as you couldn't keep the books from *me*, you decided to keep *me* from the books. You had the means to hand. A new boat, nearly ready to sail. You simply arranged for it to go early, and take me with it. If you could keep me away from the office until Trevor returned, all would be well.'

'This is all nonsense,' he said stiffly.

'Don't be silly. It's past denying. Trevor was due back in the office on Monday, April 4th, which would give him three days to apply for a postponement to the Commissioners. A perfectly safe margin. Trevor would then do the Axwood books as usual, and I would be set free, never knowing why I'd been abducted.'

Trevor buried his face in his brandy, which made me thirsty.

'If you've any mineral water, or tonic, Trevor, I'd like some,' I said.

'Give him nothing,' Finch said, the pent-up violence still thick in his voice.

Trevor made fluttery motions with his hands, but after a moment, with apologetic glances at Finch's tightened mouth, he fetched a tumbler and poured into it a bottle of tonic water.

'Ro . . .' he said, giving me the glass. 'My dear chap . . .'

'My dear *shit*,' Finch said.

I drank the fizzy quinine water gratefully.

'I bust things up by getting home a few days early,' I said. 'I suppose you were frantic. Enough, anyway, to send the kidnapping squads to my cottage to pick me up again. And when they didn't manage it, you sent someone else.' I drank bubbles and tasted gall. 'Next day, you sent your daughter Jossie.'

'She knows nothing, Ro,' Trevor said.

'Shut up,' Finch said. 'She strung him along by the nose.'

'Maybe she did,' I said. 'It was supposed to be only for a day or two. Trevor was due back that Sunday. But I told you, while you were busy filling my time by showing me round your yard, that Trevor's car had broken down in France, and he wouldn't be back until Wednesday or Thursday. And I assured you again that you didn't have to worry, I had already applied for the postponement, and I would start the audit myself. The whole situation was back to square one, and the outlook was as deadly as ever.'

Finch glared, denying nothing.

'You offered me a day at the races with Jossie,' I said. 'And a ride in the novice hurdle. I'm a fool about accepting rides.

Never know when to say no. You must have known that Notebook was unable to jump properly. You must have hoped when you flew off to the Grand National, that I'd fall with him and break a leg.'

'Your neck,' he said vindictively, with no vestige of a joke.

Trevor glanced at his face and away again, as if embarrassed by so much raw emotion.

'Your men must have been standing by in case I survived undamaged, which of course I did,' I said. 'They followed us to the pub where I had dinner with Jossie, and then to the motel where I planned to stay. Your second attempt at abduction was more successful, in that I couldn't get out. And when Trevor was safely back, you rang Scotland Yard, and the police set me free. From one point of view all your efforts had produced precisely the desired result, because I had not in fact by then seen one page or one entry of the Axwood books.'

I thought back, and amended that statement. 'I hadn't seen any except the petty cash book, which you gave me yourself. And that, I imagine, was your own private accurate record, and not the one re-written and padded for the sake of the audit. It was left in my car with all my other belongings, and I took it to the office when I went back last Friday. It was still there on Saturday. It was Saturday morning that I got out the Axwood books and studied them, and made the photocopies.'

'But why, Ro?' Trevor asked frustratedly. 'What made you think . . . Why did you think of William?'

'The urgency,' I said. 'The ruthless haste, and the time factors. I believed, you see, when I was on the boat, that I'd been kidnapped for revenge. Any auditor who's been the downfall of embezzlers would think that, if he'd found himself in such a position. Especially if he's been directly threatened, face to face, as I had, by Connaught Powys, and earlier by Ownslow and Glitberg, and later also by others. But when I escaped and came home, there was hardly any interval before I was in danger again. Hunted, really. And caught. So the second time, last week, in the van, I began to think . . . that perhaps it wasn't revenge, but *prevention*, and after that, it was a matter of deduction, elimination, boring things, on the whole. But I had hours . . .' I swallowed involuntarily, remembering. 'I had hours in which to think of all the possible people, and work it out. So then, on Saturday morning, I went to the office, when I had the place to myself, and checked.'

Finch turned on Trevor, looking for a whipping boy. 'Why the hell did you keep those books where he could see them? Why didn't you lock them in the bloody safe?'

'I've a key to the safe,' I said dryly.

'Christ!' He raised his hands in a violent, exploding, useless gesture. 'Why didn't you take them home?'

'I never take books home,' Trevor said. 'And you told me that Ro was going to the races Saturday, and out with Jossie Sunday, so we'd nothing to worry about. And anyway, neither of us dreamt that he knew . . . or guessed.'

Finch swung his desperate face in my direction.

'What's your price?' he said. 'How much?'

I didn't answer. Trevor said protestingly, 'William . . .'

'He must want something,' Finch said. 'Why is he telling us all this instead of going straight to the police? Because he wants a deal, that's why.'

'Not money,' I said.

Finch continued to look like a bolt of lightning trapped in bones and flesh, but he didn't pursue the subject. He knew, as he'd always known, that it wasn't a question of money.

'Where did you get the men who abducted me?' I said.

'You know so much. You can bloody well find out.'

Rent-a-thug, I thought cynically. Someone, somewhere, knew how to hire some bully boys. The police could find out, I thought, if they wanted to. I wouldn't bother.

'The second time,' I said. 'Did you tell them not to leave a mark on me?'

'So what?'

'Did you?' I said.

'I didn't want the police taking any serious interest,' he said. 'No marks. No stealing. Made you a minor case.'

So the fists and boots, I thought, had been a spot of private enterprise. Payment for the general run-around I'd given the troops. Not orders from above. I supposed I was glad, in a sour sort of way.

He'd chosen the warehouse, I guessed, because it couldn't

have been easy to find a safer place in a hurry: and because he thought it would divert my attention even more strongly towards Ownslow and Glitberg, and away from any thought of himself.

Trevor said, 'Well . . . What . . . what are we going to do now?' but no one answered, because there were wheels outside on the gravel. Car doors slammed.

'Did you leave the front door open?' Trevor said.

Finch didn't need to answer. He had. Several feet tramped straight in, crossed the hall, and made unerringly for the snug.

'Here we are then,' said a powerful voice. 'Let's get on with it.'

The light of triumph shone in Finch's face, and he smiled with grateful welcome at the newcomers crowding into the room.

Glitberg. Ownslow. Connaught Powys.

'Got the rat cornered, then?' Powys said.

18

I had an everlasting picture of the five of them, in that freezing moment. I straightened to my feet, and my heart thumped, and I looked at them one by one.

Connaught Powys in his city suit, as Establishment as a pillar of the government. Coffee-coloured tan on his fleshy face. Smooth hair; pale hands. A large man aiming to throw his weight about, and enjoying it.

Glitberg with his mean eyes and the repulsive four-inch frill of white whiskers, which stood out sideways from his cheeks like a ruff. Little pink lips, and a smirk.

Ownslow the bull, with his bald crown and long straggling blond hair. He'd shut the door of the snug and leaned against it, and folded his arms with massive satisfaction.

William Finch, tall and distinguished, vibrating in the centre of the room in a tangle of fear, and anger, and unpleasant pleasure.

196

Trevor, silver-haired, worldly, come to dust. Sitting apprehensively in his armchair, facing his future with more sorrow than horror. The only one of them who showed the slightest sign of realizing that it was they who had got themselves into trouble, not I.

Embezzlers were not normally men of violence. They robbed on paper, not with their fists. They might hate and threaten, but actual physical assault wasn't natural to them. I looked bleakly at the five faces and thought again of the nuclear effect of critical mass. Small separate amounts of radio-active matter could release harnessable energy. If small amounts got together into a larger mass, they exploded.

'Why did you come?' Trevor said.

'Finchy rang and told us he'd be here,' Powys said, jerking his head in my direction. 'Never get another opportunity like it, will we? Seeing as you and Finchy will be out of circulation, for a bit.'

Finch shook his head fiercely: but I reckoned there were different sorts of circulation, and it would be a very long time before he was back on a racetrack. I wouldn't have wanted to face the ruin before him: the crash from such a height.

Glitberg said, 'Four years locked in a cell. Four sodding years, because of him.'

'Don't bellyache,' I said. 'Four years in jail for a million pounds is a damned good bargain. You offer it around, you'd get a lot of takers.'

'Prison is dehumanizing,' Powys said. 'They treat you worse than animals.'

'Don't make me cry,' I said. 'You chose the way that led there. And all of you have got what you wanted. Money, money, money. So run away and play with it.' Maybe I spoke with too much heat, but nothing was going to defuse the developing bomb.

Anger that I'd let myself in for such a mess was a stab in the mind. I simply hadn't thought of Finch summoning reinforcements. He'd had no need of it: it had been merely spite. I'd believed I could manage Finch and Trevor with reasonable safety, and here all of a sudden was a whole new battle.

'Trevor,' I said, flatly, 'don't forget the photostats I left with a friend.'

197

'What friend?' Finch said, gaining belligerence from his supporters.

'Barclays Bank,' I said.

Finch was furious, but he couldn't prove it wasn't true, and even he must have seen that any serious attempt at wringing out a different answer might cost them more time in the clink.

I had hoped originally to make a bargain with Finch, but it was no longer possible. I thought merely, at that point, of getting through whatever was going to happen with some semblance of grace. A doubtful proposition, it seemed to me.

'How much does he know?' Ownslow demanded of Trevor.

'Enough . . .' Trevor said. 'Everything.'

'Bloody hell.'

'How did he find out?' Glitberg demanded.

'Because William took him on his boat,' Trevor said.

'A mistake,' Powys said. 'That was a mistake, Finchy. He came sniffing round us in London, asking about boats. Like I told you.'

'You chain dogs up,' Finch said.

'But not in a floating kennel, Finchy. Not this bastard here with his bloody quick eyes. You should have kept him away from your boat.'

'I don't see that it matters,' Trevor said. 'Like he said, we've all got our money.'

'And what if he tells?' Ownslow demanded.

'Oh, he'll tell,' Trevor said with certainty. 'And of course there will be trouble. Questions and enquiries and a lot of fuss. But in the end, if we're careful, we should keep the cash.'

'Should isn't enough,' Powys said fiercely.

'Nothing's certain,' Trevor said.

'One thing's certain,' Ownslow said. 'This creep's going to get his come-uppance.'

All five of the faces turned my way together, and in each one, even in Trevor's, I read the same intent.

'That's what we came for,' Powys said.

'Four bloody years,' Ownslow said. 'And the sneers my kids suffered.' He pushed off the door and uncrossed his arms.

Glitberg said, 'Judges looking down their bloody noses.'

198

They all, quite slowly, came nearer.

It was uncanny, and frightening. The forming of a pack.

Behind me there was the table, and behind that, solid wall. They were between me and the windows, and between me and the door.

'Don't leave any marks,' Powys said. 'If he goes to the police it'll be his word against ours, and if he's nothing to show that can't do much.' To me, directly, he said, 'We'll have a bloody good alibi, I'll tell you that.'

The odds looked appalling. I made a sudden thrusting jump to one side, to dodge the menacing advance, outflank the cohorts, scramble for the door.

I got precisely nowhere. Two strides, no more. Their hands clutched me from every direction, dragging me back, their bodies pushing against me with their collective weight. It was as if my attempt to escape had triggered them off. They were determined, heavy, and grunting. I struggled with flooding fury to disentangle myself, and I might as well have wrestled with an octopus.

They lifted me up bodily and sat me on the end of the table. Three of them held me there with hands like clamps.

Finch pulled open a drawer in the side of the table, and threw out a checked red and white table cloth, which floated across the room and fell on a chair. Under the cloth, several big square napkins. Red and white checks. Tapestry's racing colours. Ridiculous thought at such a moment.

Finch and Connaught Powys each rolled a napkin into a shape like a bandage and knotted it round one of my ankles. They tied my ankles to the legs of the table. They pulled my jacket off. They rolled and tied a red and white napkin round each of my wrists, pulling the knots tight and leaving cheerful bright loose ends like streamers.

They did it fast.

All of the faces were flushed, and the eyes fuzzy, in the fulfilment of lust. Glitberg and Ownslow, one on each side, pushed me down flat on my back. Finch and Connaught Powys pulled my arms over my head and tied the napkins on my wrists to the other two legs of the table. My resistance made them rougher.

The table was, I supposed, about two feet by four. Long enough to reach from my knees to the top of my head. Hard, covered with glass, uncomfortable.

They stood back to admire their handiwork. All breathing heavily from my useless fight. All overweight, out of condition, ripe to drop dead from coronaries at any moment. They went on living.

'Now what?' said Ownslow, considering. He went down on his knees and took off my shoes.

'Nothing,' Trevor said. 'That's enough.'

The pack instinct had died out of him fastest. He turned away, refusing to meet my eyes.

'Enough!' Glitberg said. 'We've done nothing yet.'

Powys eyed me assessingly from head to foot, and maybe he saw just what they had done.

'Yes,' he said slowly. 'That's enough.'

Ownslow said 'Here!' furiously, and Glitberg said, 'Not on your life.' Powys ignored them and turned to Finch.

'He's yours,' he said. 'But if I were you I'd just leave him here.'

'*Leave* him?'

'You've got better things to do than fool around with him. You don't want to leave marks on him, and I'm telling you, the way we've tied him will be enough.'

William Finch thought about it, and nodded, and came half way back to cold sense. He stepped closer until he stood near my ribs. He stared down, eyes full of the familiar hate.

'I hope you're satisfied,' he said.

He spat in my face.

Powys, Glitberg and Ownslow thought it a marvellous idea. They did it in turn, as disgustingly as they could.

Not Trevor. He looked on uncomfortably and made small useless gestures of protest with his hands.

I could hardly see for slime. It felt horrible, and I couldn't get it off.

'All right,' Powys said. 'That's it, then. You push off now, Finchy, and you get packed, Trevor, and then we'll all leave.'

'Here!' Ownslow said again, protestingly.

'Do you want an alibi, or don't you?' Powys said. 'You got to make some effort. Be seen by a few squares. Help the lies along.'

Ownslow gave in with a bad grace, and contented himself with making sure that none of the table napkins had worked loose. Which they hadn't.

Finch had gone from my diminished sight and also, it appeared, from my life. A car started in the drive, crunched on the gravel, and faded away.

Trevor went out of the room and presently returned carrying a suitcase. In the interval Ownslow sniggered, Glitberg jeered, and Powys tested the amount that I could move my arms. Half an inch, at the most.

'You won't get out of that,' he said. He shook my elbow and watched the results. 'I reckon this'll make us even.' He turned as Trevor came back. 'Are all doors locked?'

'All except the front one,' Trevor said.

'Right. Then let's be off.'

'But what about *him*?' Trevor said. 'We can't just leave him like that.'

'Can't we? Why not?'

'But . . .' Trevor said: and fell silent.

'Someone will find him tomorrow,' Powys said. 'A cleaner, or something. Do you have a cleaner?'

'Yes,' Trevor said doubtfully. 'But she doesn't come in on Tuesdays. My wife will be back though.'

'There you are, then.'

'All right.' He hesitated. 'My wife keeps some money in the kitchen. I'll just fetch it.'

'Right.'

Trevor went on his errand and came back. He stood near me, looking worried.

'Ro . . .'

'Come on,' said Powys impatiently. 'He's ruined you, like he ruined us. You owe him bloody nothing.'

He shepherded them out of the door; Trevor unhappy, Glitberg sneering, Ownslow unassuaged. Powys looked back from the doorway, his own face, what I could see of it, full of smug satisfaction.

'I'll think of you,' he said. 'All night.'

He pulled the door towards him, to shut it, and switched off the light.

Human bodies were not designed to remain for hours in one position. Even in sleep, they regularly shifted. Joints bent and unbent, muscles contracted and relaxed.

No human body was designed to lie as I was lying, with constant strain already running up through legs, stomach, chest, shoulders and arms. Within five minutes, while they were still there, it had become in any normal way intolerable. One would not have stayed in that attitude from choice.

When they had gone, I simply could not visualize the time ahead. My imagination short-circuited. Blanked out. What did one do if one couldn't bear something, and had to?

The worst of the spit slid slowly off my face, but the rest remained, sticky and itching. I blinked my eyes wide open in the dark and thought of being at home in my own quiet bed, as I'd hoped to be that night.

I realized that I was having a surprising amount of difficulty in breathing. One took breathing so much for granted; but the mechanics weren't all that simple. The muscles between the ribs pulled the ribcage out and upwards, allowing air to rush down to the lungs. It wasn't, so to speak, the air going in which expanded the chest, but the expansion of the chest which drew in the air. With the ribcage pulled continuously up, the normal amount of muscle movement was much curtailed.

I still wore a collar and tie. I would choke, I thought.

The other bit that breathed for you was the diaphragm, a nice hefty floor of muscle between the heart-lung cavity and the lower lot of guts. Thank God for diaphragms, I thought. Long may they reign. Mine chugged away, doing its best.

If I passed the night in delirium, I thought, it would be a good idea. If I'd studied Yoga . . . mind out of body. Too late for that. I was always too late. Never prepared.

Stabs of strain afflicted both my shoulders. Needles. Swords. Think of something else.

Boats. Think of boats. Big expensive boats, built to high standards in top British boat yards, sailing away out of Britain to ship-brokers in Antibes and Antigua.

Huge floating assets in negotiable form. None of the usual bureaucratic trouble about transferring money abroad in huge amounts. No dollar premiums to worry about, or other such hurdles set up by grasping governments. Just put your money in fibreglass and ropes and sails, and float away on it on the tide.

The man at Goldenwave had told me they never lacked for orders. Boats, he said, didn't deteriorate like aeroplanes or cars. Put a quarter of a million into a boat, and it would most likely increase in value, as years went by. Sell the boat, bank the money, and hey presto, all nicely, tidily, and legally done.

There were frightful protests from my arms and legs. I couldn't move them in any way more than an inch: could give them no respite. It really was, I thought, an absolutely bloody revenge.

No use reflecting that it was I who had stirred up Powys and Ownslow and Glitberg. Poke a rattlesnake with a stick, don't be surprised if he bites you. I'd gone to find out if it was they who'd abducted me, and found out instead what they'd done with all the missing money.

Paid for boats. The mention of boats had produced the menace, not the mention of abduction. Boats paid for by the taxpayers, the electronics firm, and the Nantuckets of New York. Gone with the four winds. Exchanged for a pile of nice strong currency, lying somewhere in a foreign bank, waiting for the owners to stroll along and collect.

Trevor linked them all. Maybe the boats had originally been his idea. I hadn't thought of William Finch knowing Connaught Powys: certainly not as well as he clearly did. But through Trevor, along the track from embezzlement to ship building . . . along the way, they had met.

The pains in my arms and legs intensified, and there was a great shaft of soreness up my chest.

I thought: I don't know how to face this. I don't know how. It isn't possible.

Trevor, I thought. Surely Trevor wouldn't have left me like this . . . not like this . . . if he had realized. Trevor, who had been so distressed at my dishevelled appearance in the police station, who as far as I could see had really cared about my health.

Ye Gods, I thought, I'd go gladly back to the sail locker . . . to the van . . . to almost anywhere one could think of.

Some of my muscles were trembling. Would the fibres simply collapse, I wondered. Would the muscles just tear apart; the ligaments disconnect from the bones? Oh for God's sake, I told myself, you've got enough to worry about, without that. Think of something cheerful.

I couldn't, off-hand. Even cheerful subjects like Tapestry were no good. I couldn't see me being able to ride in the Whitbread Gold Cup.

Minutes dragged and telescoped, stretching to hours. The various separate pains gradually coalesced into an all pervading fire. Thought became fragmentary, and then, I reckon, more or less stopped.

The unbearable was there, inside, savage and consuming. Unbearable . . . there was no such word.

By morning I'd gone a long way into an extreme land I hadn't known existed. A different dimension, where the memory of ordinary pain was a laugh.

An internal place; a heavy core. The external world had retreated. I no longer felt as if I were any particular shape: had no picture of hands or feet, or where they were. Everything was crimson and dark.

I existed as a mass. Unified. A single lump of matter, of a weight and fire like the centre of the earth.

There was nothing else. No thought. Just feeling, and eternity.

A noise dragged me back.

People talking. Voices in the house.

I saw that daylight had returned and was trickling in round the edge of the curtains. I tried to call out, and could not.

Footsteps crossed and recrossed the hall, and at last, at last, someone opened the door, and switched on the light.

Two women came in. I stared at them, and they stared at me: on both sides with disbelief.

They were Hilary Pinlock, and Jossie.

Hilary cut through the red checked table napkins with a small pair of scissors from her handbag.

I tried to sit up and behave with sangfroid, but my stretched muscles wouldn't respond to directions. I ended somehow with my face against her chest and my throat heaving with unstoppable half-stifled groans.

'It's all right, Ro. It's all right, my dear, my dear.'

Her thin arms held me close and tight, rocking me gently, taking into herself the impossible pain, suffering for me like a mother. Mother, sister, lover, child . . . a woman who crossed the categories and left them blurred.

I had a mouthful of blouse button and was comforted to my soul.

She put an arm round my waist and more or less carried me to the nearest chair. Jossie stood looking on, her face filled with a greater shock than finding me there.

'Do you realize,' she said, 'that Dad's gone?'

I didn't feel like saying much.

'Did you hear?' Jossie said. Her voice was tight, unfriendly. 'Dad's gone. Walked out. Left all the horses. Do you hear? He's cleared half the papers out of the office and burned them in the incinerator, and this lady says it is because my father is an embezzler, and you . . . you are going to give him away to the Nantuckets, and the police.'

The big eyes were hard. 'And Trevor, too. Trevor. I've known him all my life. How could you? And you *knew* . . . you knew on Sunday . . . all day . . . what you were going to do. You took me out, and you knew you were going to ruin all our lives. I think you're hateful.'

Hilary took two strides, gripped her by the shoulders, and positively shook her.

'Stop it, you silly girl. Open your silly eyes. He did all this for you.'

Jossie tore herself free. 'What do you mean?' she demanded.

'He didn't want your father to go to prison. Because he's your father. He's sent others there, but he didn't want it to happen to your father, or to Trevor King. So he warned them, and gave them time to destroy things. Evidence. Paper and records.' She glanced back at me. 'He told me on Saturday what he planned . . . to tell your father how much he knew, and to offer him a bargain. Time, enough time, if he would destroy his tracks and

205

go, in a way which would cause you least pain. Time to go before the police arrived to confiscate his passport. Time to arrange his life as best he could. And they made him pay for the time he gave them. He paid for every second of it . . .' She gestured in frustrated disgust towards the table and the cut pieces of cloth, '. . . in *agony*.'

'Hilary,' I protested.

There never had been any stopping Hilary Pinlock in full flight. She said fiercely to Jossie, 'He can put up with a lot, but I reckon it's too much to have you reviling him for what he's suffered for your sake. So you just get some sense into your little bird-brain, and beg his pardon.'

I helplessly shook my head. Jossie stood with her mouth open in shattered shock, and then she looked at the table, and discarded the thought.

'Dad would never have done that,' she said.

'There were five of them,' I said wearily. 'People do things in gangs which they would never have done on their own.'

She looked at me with shadowed eyes. Then she turned abruptly on her heel and walked out of the room.

'She's terribly upset,' Hilary said, making allowances.

'Yes.'

'Are you all right?'

'No.'

She made a face. 'I'll get you something. They must at least have aspirins in this house.'

'Tell me first,' I said, 'how you got here.'

'Oh. I was worried. I rang your cottage all evening. Late into the night. And again this morning, early. I had a feeling . . . I didn't think it would hurt if I came over to check, so I drove to your cottage . . . but of course you weren't there. I saw your neighbour, Mrs Morris, and she said you hadn't been home all night. So then I went to your office. They were in a tizzy because sometime between last night and this morning your partner had taken away a great many papers, and neither of you had turned up for work.'

'What time . . .' I said.

'About half past nine, when I went to the office.' She looked at her watch. 'It's a quarter to eleven, now.'

Fourteen hours, I thought numbly. It must have been at least fourteen hours, that I'd been lying there.

'Well, I drove to Finch's house,' she said. 'I had a bit of trouble finding the way, and when I got there, everything was in a shambles. There was a girl secretary weeping all over the place. People asking what was going on . . . and your girl Jossie in a dumbstruck state. I asked her if she'd seen you. I said I thought you could be in real trouble. I asked her where Trevor King lived. I made her come with me, to show me the way. I tried to tell her what her father had been doing, and how he'd abducted you, but she didn't want to believe it.'

'No.'

'So then we arrived here, and found you.'

'How did you get in?'

'The back door was wide open.'

'Wide . . . ?'

I had a sudden picture of Trevor going out to the kitchen, saying it was to fetch some money. To open the door. To give me a tiny chance. Poor Trevor.

'That package I gave you,' I said. 'With all the photostats. When you get home, will you burn it?'

'If that's what you want.'

'Mm.'

Jossie came back and sprawled in a red armchair, all angular legs.

'Sorry,' she said abruptly.

'So am I.'

'You did help him,' she said.

Hilary said, 'Do good to those who despitefully use you.'

I slid my eyes her way. 'That's enough of that.'

'What are you talking about?' Jossie demanded.

Hilary shook her head with a smile and went on an aspirin hunt. Butazolidin, I imagined, would do more good. Things were better now I was sitting in a chair, but a long old way from right.

'He left me a letter,' Jossie said. 'More or less the same as yours.'

'How do you mean?'

'Dear Jossie, Sorry, Love, Dad.'

'Oh.'

'He said he was going to France . . .' She broke off, and stared ahead of her, her face full of misery. 'Life's going to be unutterably bloody, isn't it,' she said, 'for a long time to come?'

'Mm.'

'What am I going to do?' The question was a rhetorical wail, but I answered it.

'I did want to warn you,' I said. 'But I couldn't . . . before I'd talked to your father. I meant it, though, about you coming to live in the cottage. If you thought . . . that you could.'

'Ro . . .' Her voice was little more than a breath.

I sat and ached, and thought in depression about telephoning the Nantuckets, and the chaos I'd have to deal with in the office.

Jossie turned her head towards me and gave me a long inspection.

'You look spineless,' she said. Her voice was half way back in spirit to the old healthy mockery; shaky, but doing its best. 'And I'll tell you something else.' She paused and swallowed.

'When Dad went, he left *me* behind, but he took the detestable Lida with him.'

There was enough, in that, for the future.

ENQUIRY

Part One

FEBRUARY

CHAPTER ONE

Yesterday I lost my licence.

To a professional steeplechase jockey, losing his licence and being warned off Newmarket Heath is like being chucked off the medical register, only more so.

Barred from race riding, barred from racecourses. Barred, moreover, from racing stables. Which poses me quite a problem, as I live in one.

No livelihood and maybe no home.

Last night was a right so-and-so, and I prefer to forget those grisly sleepless hours. Shock and bewilderment, the feeling that it couldn't have happened, it was all a mistake ... this lasted until after midnight. And at least the disbelieving stage had had some built-in comfort. The full thudding realization which followed had none at all. My life was lying around like the untidy bits of a smashed teacup, and I was altogether out of glue and rivets.

This morning I got up and percolated some coffee and looked out of the window at the lads bustling around in the yard and mounting and cloppeting away up the road to the Downs, and I got my first real taste of being an outcast.

Fred didn't bellow up at my window as he usually did, 'Going to stay there all day, then?'

This time, I was.

None of the lads looked up ... they more or less kept their eyes studiously right down. They were quiet, too. Dead quiet. I watched Bouncing Bernie heave his ten stone seven on to the gelding I'd been riding lately, and there was something apologetic about the way he lowered his fat bum into the saddle.

And he, too, kept his eyes down.

Tomorrow, I guessed, they'd be themselves again. Tomorrow they'd be curious and ask questions. I understood that they weren't despising me. They were sympathetic. Probably too sympathetic for their own comfort. And embarrassed: that too. And instinctively delicate about looking too soon at the face of total disaster.

When they'd gone I drank my coffee slowly and wondered what to do next. A nasty, very nasty, feeling of emptiness and loss.

The papers had been stuck as usual through my letterbox. I wondered what the boy had thought, knowing what he was delivering. I shrugged. Might as well read what they'd said, the Goddamned pressmen, God bless them.

The *Sporting Life*, short on news, had given us the headlines and the full treatment.

'Cranfield and Hughes Disqualified.'

There was a picture of Cranfield at the top of the page, and halfway down one of me, all smiles, taken the day I won the Hennessy Gold Cup. Some little sub-editor letting his irony loose, I thought sourly, and printing the most cheerful picture he could dig out of the files.

The close-printed inches north and south of my happy face were unrelieved gloom.

'"The Stewards said they were not satisfied with my explanation," Cranfield said. "They have withdrawn my licence. I have no further comment to make."'

Hughes, it was reported, had said almost exactly the same. Hughes, if I remembered correctly, had in fact said nothing whatsoever. Hughes had been too stunned to put one word collectedly after another, and if he had said anything at all it would have been unprintable.

I didn't read all of it. I'd read it all before, about the other people. For 'Cranfield and Hughes' one could substitute any other trainer and jockey who had been warned off. The newspaper reports on these occasions were always the same; totally uninformed. As a racing Enquiry was a private trial the ruling authorities were not obliged to open the proceedings to the public or the Press, and as they were

7

not obliged to, they never did. In fact like many another inward-looking concern they seemed to be permanently engaged in trying to stop too many people from finding out what was really going on.

The *Daily Witness* was equally fog-bound, except that Daddy Leeman had suffered his usual rush of purple prose to the head. According to him:

'Kelly Hughes, until now a leading contender for this season's jump-jockeys' crown, and fifth on the list last year, was sentenced to an indefinite suspension of his licence. Hughes, thirty, left the hearing ten minutes after Cranfield. Looking pale and grim, he confirmed that he had lost his licence, and added "I have no further comment."'

They had remarkable ears, those pressmen.

I put down the paper with a sigh and went into the bedroom to exchange my dressing-gown for trousers and a jersey, and after that I made my bed, and after that I sat on it, staring into space. I had nothing else to do. I had nothing to do for as far ahead as the eye could see. Unfortunately I also had nothing to think about except the Enquiry.

Put baldly, I had lost my licence for losing a race. More precisely, I had ridden a red-hot favourite into second place in the Lemonfizz Crystal Cup at Oxford in the last week of January, and the winner had been an unconsidered outsider. This would have been merely unfortunate, had it not been that both horses were trained by Dexter Cranfield.

The finishing order at the winning post had been greeted with roars of disgust from the stands, and I had been booed all the way to the unsaddling enclosure. Dexter Cranfield had looked worried more than delighted to have taken first and second places in one of the season's big sponsored steeplechases, and the Stewards of the meeting had called us both in to explain. They were not, they announced, satisfied with the explanations. They would refer the matter to the Disciplinary Committee of the Jockey Club.

The Disciplinary Committee, two week later, were equally

8

sceptical that the freak result had been an accident. Deliberate fraud on the betting public, they said. Disgraceful, dishonest, disgusting, they said. Racing must keep its good name clean. Not the first time that either of you have been suspected. Severe penalties must be inflicted, as a deterrent to others.

Off, they said. Warned off. And good riddance.

It wouldn't have happened in America, I thought in depression. There, all runners from one stable, or one owner, for that matter, were covered by a bet on any of them. So if the stable's outsider won instead of its favourite, the backers still collected their money. High time the same system crossed the Atlantic. Correction, more than high time; long, long overdue.

The truth of the matter was that Squelch, my red-hot favourite, had been dying under me all the way up the straight, and it was in the miracle class that I'd finished as close as second, and not fifth or sixth. If he hadn't carried so many people's shirts, in fact, I wouldn't have exhausted him as I had. That it had been Cranfield's other runner Cherry Pie who had passed me ten yards from the finish was just the worst sort of luck.

Armed by innocence, and with reason to believe that even if the Oxford Stewards had been swayed by the crowd's hostile reception, the Disciplinary Committee were going to consider the matter in an atmosphere of cool commonsense, I had gone to the Enquiry without a twinge of apprehension.

The atmosphere was cool, all right. Glacial. Their own common-sense was taken for granted by the Stewards. They didn't appear to think that either Cranfield or I had any.

The first faint indication that the sky was about to fall came when they read out a list of nine previous races in which I had ridden a beaten favourite for Cranfield. In six of them, another of Cranfield's runners had won. Cranfield had also had other runners in the other three.

'That means,' said Lord Gowery, 'that this case before us is by no means the first. It has happened again and again. These results seem to have been unnoticed in the past, but this time you have clearly overstepped the mark.'

I must have stood there looking stupid with my mouth falling open in astonishment, and the trouble was that they obviously thought I was astonished at how much they had dug up to prove my guilt.

'Some of those races were years ago,' I protested. 'Six or seven, some of them.'

'What difference does that make?' asked Lord Gowery. 'They happened.'

'That sort of thing happens to every trainer now and then,' Cranfield said hotly. 'You must know it does.'

Lord Gowery gave him an emotionless stare. It stirred some primeval reaction in my glands, and I could feel the ripple of goose pimples up my spine. He really believes, I thought wildly, he really believes us guilty. It was only then that I realized we had to make a fight of it; and it was already far too late.

I said to Cranfield, 'We should have had that lawyer,' and he gave me an almost frightened glance of agreement.

Shortly before the Lemonfizz the Jockey Club had finally thrown an old autocratic tradition out of the twentieth century and agreed that people in danger of losing their livelihood could be legally represented at their trials, if they wished. The concession was so new that there was no accepted custom to be guided by. One or two people had been acquitted with lawyers' help who would presumably have been acquitted anyway; and if an accused person engaged a lawyer to defend him, he had in all cases to pay the fees himself. The Jockey Club did not award costs to anyone they accused, whether or not they managed to prove themselves innocent.

At first Cranfield had agreed with me that we should find a lawyer, though both of us had been annoyed at having to shell out. Then Cranfield had by chance met at a party the newly elected Disciplinary Steward who was a friend of his, and had reported to me afterwards, 'There's no need for us to go to the expense of a lawyer. Monty Midgely told me in confidence that the Disciplinary Committee think the Oxford Stewards were off their heads reporting us, that he knows the Lemonfizz result was just one of those things, and not to worry, the Enquiry will only be a formality. Ten minutes or so, and it will be over.'

That assurance had been good enough for both of us. We hadn't even seen any cause for alarm when three or four days later Colonel Sir Montague Midgely had turned yellow with jaundice and taken to his bed, and it had been announced that one of the Committee, Lord Gowery, would deputize for him in any Enquiries which might be held in the next few weeks.

Monty Midgely's liver had a lot to answer for. Whatever he had intended, it now seemed all to appallingly clear that Gowery didn't agree.

The Enquiry was held in a large lavishly furnished room in the Portman Square headquarters of the Jockey Club. Four Stewards sat in comfortable armchairs along one side of a polished table with a pile of papers in front of each of them, and a shorthand writer was stationed at a smaller table a little to their right. When Cranfield and I went into the room the shorthand writer was fussing with a tape-recorder, unwinding a lead from the machine which stood on his own table and trailing it across the floor towards the Stewards. He set up a microphone on a stand in front of Lord Gowery, switched it on, blew into it a couple of times, went back to his machine, flicked a few switches, and announced that everything was in order.

Behind the Stewards, across a few yards of plushy dark red carpet, were several more armchairs. Their occupants included the three Stewards who had been unconvinced at Oxford, the Clerk of the Course, the Handicapper who had allotted the Lemonfizz weights, and a pair of Stipendiary Stewards, officials paid by the Jockey Club and acting at meetings as an odd mixture of messenger boys for the Stewards and the industry's private police. It was they who, if they thought there had been an infringement of the rules, brought it to the notice of the Stewards of the meeting concerned, and advised them to hold an Enquiry.

As in any other job, some Stipendiaries were reasonable

men and some were not. The Stipe who had been acting at Oxford on Lemonfizz day was notoriously the most difficult of them all.

Cranfield and I were to sit facing the Stewards' table, but several feet from it. For us, too, there were the same luxurious armchairs. Very civilized. Not a hatchet in sight. We sat down, and Cranfield casually crossed his legs, looking confident and relaxed.

We were far from soul-mates, Cranfield and I. He had inherited a fortune from his father, an ex-soap manufacturer who had somehow failed to acquire a coveted peerage in spite of donating madly to every fashionable cause in sight, and the combination of wealth and disappointed social ambition had turned Cranfield *fils* into a roaring snob. To him, since he employed me, I was a servant; and he didn't know how to treat servants.

He was, however, a pretty good trainer. Better still, he had rich friends who could afford good horses. I had ridden for him semi-regularly for nearly eight years, and although at first I had resented his snobbish little ways, I had eventually grown up enough to find them amusing. We operated strictly as a business team, even after all that time. Not a flicker of friendship. He would have been outraged at the very idea, and I didn't like him enough to think it a pity.

He was twenty years older than me, a tallish, thin Anglo-Saxon type with thin fine mousy hair, greyish-blue eyes with short fair lashes, a well-developed straight nose, and aggressively perfect teeth. His bone structure was of the type acceptable to the social circle in which he tried to move, but the lines his outlook on life had etched in his skin were a warning to anyone looking for tolerance or generosity. Cranfield was mean-minded by habit and open handed only to those who could lug him upwards. In all his dealings with those he considered his inferiors he left behind a turbulent wake of dislike and resentment. He was charming to his friends, polite in public to his wife, and his three teenage children echoed his delusions of superiority with pitiful faithfulness.

Cranfield had remarked to me some days before the Enquiry that the Oxford Stewards were all good chaps and that two of them had personally apologized to him for having to send the case on to the Disciplinary Committee. I nodded without answering. Cranfield must have known as well as I did that all three of the Oxford Stewards had been elected for social reasons only; that one of them couldn't read a number board at five paces, that another had inherited his late uncle's string of racehorses but not his expert knowledge, and that the third had been heard to ask his trainer which his own horse was, during the course of a race. Not one of the three could read a race at anything approaching the standard of a racecourse commentator. Good chaps they might well be, but as judges, frightening.

'We will show the film of the race,' Lord Gowery said.

They showed it, projecting from the back of the room on to a screen on the wall behind Cranfield and me. We turned our armchairs round to watch it. The Stipendiary Steward from Oxford, a fat pompous bully, stood by the screen, pointing out Squelch with a long baton.

'This is the horse in question,' he said, as the horses lined up for the start. I reflected mildly that if the Stewards knew their job they would have seen the film several times already, and would know which was Squelch without needing to have him pointed out.

The Stipe more or less indicated Squelch all the way round. It was an unremarkable race, run to a well-tried pattern : hold back at the start, letting someone else make the pace; ease forwards to fourth place and settle there for two miles or more; move smoothly to the front coming towards the second last fence, and press on home regardless. If the horse liked that sort of race, and if he were good enough, he would win.

Squelch hated to be ridden any other way. Squelch was, on his day, good enough. It just hadn't been his day.

The film showed Squelch taking the lead coming into the second last fence. He rolled a bit on landing, a sure sign of tiredness. I'd had to pick him up and urge him into the last, and it was obvious on the film. Away from the last, towards

13

the winning post, he'd floundered about beneath me, and if I hadn't been ruthless he'd have slowed to a trot. Cherry Pie, at the finish, came up surprisingly fast and passed him as if he'd been standing still.

The film flicked off abruptly and someone put the lights on again. I thought that the film was conclusive and that that would be the end of it.

'You didn't use your whip,' Lord Gowery said accusingly.

'No, sir,' I agreed. 'Squelch shies away from the whip. He has to be ridden with the hands.'

'You were making no effort to ride him out.'

'Indeed I was, sir. He was dead tired, you can see on the film.'

'All I can see on the film is that you were making absolutely no effort to win. You were sitting there with your arms still, making no effort whatsoever.'

I stared at him. 'Squelch isn't an easy horse to ride, sir. He'll always do his best but only if he isn't upset. He has to be ridden quietly. He stops if he's hit. He'll only respond to being squeezed, and to small flicks on the reins, and to his jockey's voice.'

'That's quite right,' said Cranfield piously. 'I always give Hughes orders not to treat the horse roughly.'

As if he hadn't heard a word, Lord Gowery said, 'Hughes didn't pick up his whip.'

He looked enquiringly at the two Stewards flanking him, as if to collect their opinions. The one on his left, a young-ish man who had ridden as an amateur, nodded non-committally. The other one was asleep.

I suspected Gowery kicked him under the table. He woke up with a jerk, said 'Eh? Yes, definitely,' and eyed me suspiciously.

It's a farce, I thought incredulously. The whole thing's a bloody farce.

Gowery nodded, satisfied. 'Hughes never picked up his whip.'

The fat bullying Stipe was oozing smugness. 'I am sure you will find this next film relevant, sir.'

'Quite,' agreed Gowery. 'Show it now.'

14

'Which film is this?' Cranfield enquired.

Gowery said, 'This film shows Squelch winning at Reading on January 3rd.'

Cranfield reflected. 'I was not at Reading on that day.'

'No,' agreed Gowery. 'We understand you went to the Worcester meeting instead.' He made it sound suspicious instead of perfectly normal. Cranfield had run a hot young hurdler at Worcester and had wanted to see how he shaped. Squelch, the established star, needed no supervision.

The lights went out again. The Stipe used his baton to point out Kelly Hughes riding a race in Squelch's distinctive colours of black and white chevrons and a black cap. Not at all the same sort of race as the Lemonfizz Crystal Cup. I'd gone to the front early to give myself a clear view of the fences, pulled back to about third place for a breather at midway, and forced to the front again only after the last fence, swinging my whip energetically down the horse's shoulder and urging him vigorously with my arms.

The film stopped, the lights went on, and there was a heavy accusing silence. Cranfield turned towards me, frowning.

'You will agree,' said Gowery ironically, 'that you used your whip, Hughes.'

'Yes, sir,' I said. 'Which race did you say that was?'

'The last race at Reading,' he said irritably. 'Don't pretend you don't know.'

'I agree that the film you've just shown was the last race at Reading, sir. But Squelch didn't run in the last race at Reading. The horse in that film was Wanderlust. He belongs to Mr Kessel, like Squelch does, so the colours are the same, and both horses are by the same sire, which accounts for them looking similar, but the horse you've just shown is Wanderlust. Who does, as you saw, respond well if you wave a whip at him.'

There was dead silence. It was Cranfield who broke it, clearing his throat.

'Hughes is quite right. That is Wanderlust.'

He hadn't realized it, I thought in amusement, until I'd

pointed it out. It's all too easy for people to believe what they're told.

There was a certain amount of hurried whispering going on. I didn't help them. They could sort it out for themselves.

Eventually Lord Gowery said, 'Has anyone got a form book?' and an official near the door went out to fetch one. Gowery opened it and took a long look at the Reading results.

'It seems,' he said heavily, 'that we have the wrong film. Squelch ran in the sixth race at Reading, which is of course usually the last. However, it now appears that on that day there were seven races, the Novice Chase having been divided and run in two halves, at the beginning and end of the day. Wanderlust won the *seventh* race. A perfectly understandable mix-up, I am afraid.'

I didn't think I would help my cause by saying that I thought it a disgraceful mix-up, if not criminal.

'Could we now, sir,' I asked politely, 'see the right film? The one that Squelch won.'

Lord Gowery cleared his throat. 'I don't, er, think we have it here. However,' he recovered fast, 'we don't need it. It is immaterial. We are not considering the Reading result, but that at Oxford.'

I gasped. I was truly astounded. 'But sir, if you watch Squelch's race, you will see that I rode him at Reading exactly as I did at Oxford, without using the whip.'

'That is beside the point, Hughes, because Squelch may not have needed the whip at Reading, but at Oxford he did.'

'Sir, it *is* the point,' I protested. 'I rode Squelch at Oxford in exactly the same manner as when he won at Reading, only at Oxford he tired.'

Lord Gowery absolutely ignored this. Instead he looked left and right to his Stewards alongside and remarked, 'We must waste no more time. We have three or four witnesses to call before lunch.'

The sleepy eldest Steward nodded and looked at his watch. The younger one nodded and avoided meeting my

16

eyes. I knew him quite well from his amateur jockey days, and had often ridden against him. We had all been pleased when he had been made a Steward, because he knew at first-hand the sort of odd circumstances which cropped up in racing to make a fool of the brightest, and we had thought that he would always put forward or explain our point of view. From his downcast semi-apologetic face I now gathered that we had hoped too much. He had not so far contributed one single word to the proceedings, and he looked, though it seemed extraordinary, intimidated.

As plain Andrew Tring he had been lighthearted, amusing, and almost reckless over fences. His recently inherited baronetcy and his even more recently acquired Stewardship seemed on the present showing to have hammered him into the ground.

Of Lord Plimborne, the elderly sleepyhead, I knew very little except his name. He seemed to be in his seventies and there was a faint tremble about many of his movements as if old age were shaking at his foundations and would soon have him down. He had not, I thought, clearly heard or understood more than a quarter of what had been said.

An Enquiry was usually conducted by three Stewards, but on this day there were four. The fourth, who sat on the left of Andrew Tring, was not, as far as I knew, even on the Disciplinary Committee, let alone a Disciplinary Steward. But he had in front of him a pile of notes as large if not larger than the others, and he was following every word with sharp hot eyes. Exactly where his involvement lay I couldn't work out, but there was no doubt that Wykeham, second Baron Ferth, cared about the outcome.

He alone of the four seemed really disturbed that they should have shown the wrong film, and he said quietly but forcefully enough for it to carry across to Cranfield and me, 'I did advise against showing the Reading race, if you remember.'

Gowery gave him an icelance of a look which would have slaughtered thinner-skinned men, but against Ferth's inner furnace it melted impotently.

'You agreed to say nothing,' Gowery said in the same

piercing undertone. 'I would be obliged if you would keep to that.'

Cranfield had stirred beside me in astonishment, and now, thinking about it on the following day, the venomous little exchange seemed even more incredible. What, I now wondered, had Ferth been doing there, where he didn't really belong and was clearly not appreciated.

The telephone bell broke up my thoughts. I went into the sitting-room to answer it and found it was a jockey colleague ringing up to commiserate. He himself, he reminded me, had had his licence suspended for a while three or four years back, and he knew how I must be feeling.

'It's good of you, Jim, to take the trouble.'

'No trouble, mate. Stick together, and all that. How did it go?'

'Lousy,' I said. 'They didn't listen to a word either Cranfield or I said. They'd made up their minds we were guilty before we ever went there.'

Jim Enders laughed. 'I'm not surprised. You know what happened to me?'

'No. What?'

'Well, when they gave me my licence back, they'd called the Enquiry for the Tuesday, see, and then for some reason they had to postpone it until the Thursday afternoon. So along I went on Thursday afternoon and they hummed and hahed and warned me as to my future conduct and kept me in suspense for a bit before they said I could have my licence back. Well, I thought I might as well collect a Racing Calendar and take it home with me, to keep abreast of the times and all that, so, anyway, I collected my Racing Calendar which is published at twelve o'clock on Thursdays, twelve o'clock mind you, and I opened it, and what is the first thing I see but the notice saying my licence has been restored. So how about *that*? They'd published the result of that meeting two hours before it had even begun.'

'I don't believe it,' I said.

'Quite true,' he said. 'Mind you, that time they were giving my licence back, not taking it away. But even so, it shows they'd made up their minds. I've always wondered why they bothered to hold that second Enquiry at all. Waste of everyone's time, mate.'

'It's incredible,' I said. But I did believe him: which before my own Enquiry I would not have done.

'When are they giving you your licence back?' Jim asked.

'They didn't say.'

'Didn't they tell you when you could apply?'

'No.'

Jim shoved one very rude word down the wires. 'And that's another thing, mate, you want to pick your moment right when you *do* apply.'

'How do you mean?'

'When I applied for mine, on the dot of when they told me I could, they said the only Steward who had authority to give it back had gone on a cruise to Madeira and I would have to wait until he turned up again.'

CHAPTER TWO

When the horses came back from second exercise at mid-day my cousin Tony stomped up the stairs and trod muck and straw into my carpet. It was his stable, not Cranfield's, that I lived in. He had thirty boxes, thirty-two horses, one house, one wife, four children, and an overdraft. Ten more boxes were being built, the fifth child was four months off, and the overdraft was turning puce. I lived alone in the flat over the yard and rode everything which came along.

All very normal. And, in the three years since we had moved in, increasingly successful. My suspension meant that Tony and the owners were going to have to find another jockey.

He flopped down gloomily in a green velvet armchair.

'You all right?'

'Yes,' I said.

'Give me a drink, for God's sake.'

I poured half a cupful of J and B in to a chunky tumbler.
'Ice?'
'As it is.'
I handed him the glass and he made inroads. Restoration began to take place.

Our mothers had been Welsh girls, sisters. Mine had married a local boy, so that I had come out wholly Celt, shortish, dark, compact. My aunt had hightailed off with a six-foot-four languid blond giant from Wyoming who had endowed Tony with most of his physique and double his brain. Out of USAAF uniform, Tony's father had reverted to ranch-hand, not ranch owner, as he had led his in-laws to believe, and he'd considered it more important for his only child to get to ride well than to acquire any of that there fancy book learning.

Tony therefore played truant for years with enthusiasm, and had never regretted it. I met him for the first time when he was twenty-five, when his Pa's heart had packed up and he had escorted his sincerely weeping Mum back to Wales. In the seven years since then he had acquired with some speed an English wife, a semi-English accent, an unimpassioned knowledge of English racing, a job as assistant trainer, and a stable of his own. And also, somewhere along the way, an unquenchable English thirst. For Scotch.

He said, looking down at the diminished drink, 'What are you going to do?'
'I don't know, exactly.'
'Will you go back home?'
'Not to live,' I said. 'I've come too far.'

He raised his head a little and looked round the room, smiling. Plain white walls, thick brown carpet, velvet chairs in two or three greens, antique furniture, pink and orange striped curtains, heavy and rich. 'I'll say you have,' he agreed. 'A big long way from Coedlant Farm, boyo.'
'No farther than your prairie.'
He shook his head. 'I still have grass roots. You've pulled yours up.'

Penetrating fellow, Tony. An extraordinary mixture of raw intelligence and straws in the hair. He was right; I'd shaken the straws out of mine. We got on very well.

'I want to talk to someone who has been to a recent Enquiry,' I said, abruptly.

'You want to just put it behind you and forget it,' he advised. 'No percentage in comparing hysterectomies.'

I laughed, which was truly something in the circumstances. 'Not on a pain for pain basis,' I explained. 'It's just that I want to know if what happened yesterday was ... well, unusual. The procedure, that is. The form of the thing. Quite apart from the fact that most of the evidence was rigged.'

'Is that what you were mumbling about on the way home? Those few words you uttered in a wilderness of silence?'

'Those,' I said, 'were mostly "they didn't believe a word we said".'

'So who rigged what?'

'That's the question.'

He held out his empty glass and I poured some more into it.

'Are you serious?'

'Yes. Starting from point A, which is that I rode Squelch to win, we arrive at point B, which is that the Stewards are convinced I didn't. Along the way were three or four little birdies all twittering their heads off and lying in their bloody teeth.'

'I detect,' he said, 'that something is stirring in yesterday's ruins.'

'What ruins?'

'You.'

'Oh.'

'You should drink more,' he said. 'Make an effort. Start now.'

'I'll think about it.'

'Do that.' He wallowed to his feet. 'Time for lunch. Time to go back to the little nestlings with their mouths wide open for worms.'

'Is it worms, today?'

'God knows. Poppy said to come, if you want.'

21

I shook my head.

'You must eat,' he protested.

'Yes.'

He looked at me consideringly. 'I guess,' he said, 'that you'll manage.' He put down his empty glass. 'We're here, you know, if you want anything. Company. Food. Dancing girls. Trifles like that.'

I nodded my thanks, and he clomped away down the stairs. He hadn't mentioned his horses, their races, or the other jockeys he would have to engage. He hadn't said that my staying in the flat would be an embarrassment to him.

I didn't know what to do about that. The flat was my home. My only home. Designed, converted, furnished by me. I liked it, and didn't want to leave.

I wandered into the bedroom.

A double bed, but pillows for one.

On the dressing chest, in a silver frame, a photograph of Rosalind. We had been married for two years when she went to spend a routine weekend with her parents. I'd been busy riding five races at Market Rasen on the Saturday, and a policeman had come into the weighing-room at the end of the afternoon and told me unemotionally that my father-in-law had set off with his wife and mine to visit friends and had misjudged his overtaking distance in heavy rain and had driven head on into a lorry and killed all three of them instantly.

It was four years since it had happened. Quite often I could no longer remember her voice. Other times she seemed to be in the next room. I had loved her passionately, but she no longer hurt. Four years was a long time.

I wished she had been there, with her tempestuous nature and fierce loyalty, so that I could have told her about the Enquiry, and shared the wretchedness, and been comforted.

That Enquiry...

Gowery's first witness had been the jockey who had finished third in the Lemonfizz, two or three lengths behind Squelch. About twenty, round faced and immature, Master Charlie West was a boy with a lot of natural talent but too little self-discipline. He had a great opinion of himself, and was in danger of throwing away his future through an apparent belief that rules only applied to everyone else.

The grandeur of Portman Square and the trappings of the Enquiry seemed to have subdued him. He came into the room nervously and stood where he was told, at one end of the Stewards' table: on their left, and to our right. He looked down at the table and raised his eyes only once or twice during his whole testimony. He didn't look across to Cranfield and me at all.

Gowery asked him if he remembered the race.

'Yes, sir.' it was a low mumble, barely audible.

'Speak up,' said Gowery irritably.

The shorthand writer came across from his table and moved the microphone so that it was nearer Charlie West. Charlie West cleared his throat.

'What happened during the race?'

'Well, sir ... Shall I start from the beginning, sir?'

'There's no need for unnecessary detail, West,' Gowery said impatiently. 'Just tell us what happened on the far side of the course on the second circuit.'

'I see, sir. Well ... Kelly, that is, I mean, Hughes, sir ... Hughes ... Well ... Like ...'

'West, come to the point.' Gowery's voice would have left a lazer standing. A heavy flush showed in patches on Charlie West's neck. He swallowed.

'Round the far side, sir, where the stands go out of sight, like, for a few seconds, well, there, sir ... Hughes gives this hefty pull back on the reins, sir ...'

'And what did he say, West?'

'He said, sir, "OK. Brakes on, chaps." Sir.'

Gowery said meaningfully, though everyone had heard the first time and a pin would have crashed on the Wilton, 'Repeat that, please, West.'

'Hughes, sir, said, "OK. Brakes on, chaps."'

'And what did you take him to mean by that, West?'

'Well sir, that he wasn't trying, like. He always says that when he's pulling one back and not trying.'

'*Always?*'

'Well, something like that, sir.'

23

There was a considerable silence.

Gowery said formally, 'Mr Cranfield ... Hughes ... You may ask this witness questions, if you wish.'

I got slowly to my feet.

'Are you seriously saying,' I asked bitterly, 'that at any time during the Lemonfizz Cup I pulled Squelch back and said "OK, brakes on, chaps?"'

He nodded. He had begun to sweat.

'Please answer aloud,' I said.

'Yes. You said it.'

'I did not.'

'I heard you.'

'You couldn't have done.'

'I heard you.'

I was silent. I simply had no idea what to say next. It was too like a playground exchange: you did, I didn't, you did, I didn't ...

I sat down. All the Stewards and all the officials ranked behind them were looking at me. I could see that all, to a man, believed West.

'Hughes, are you in the habit of using this phrase?' Gowery's voice was dry acid.

'No, sir.'

'Have you *ever* used it?'

'Not in the Lemonfizz Cup, sir.'

'I said, Hughes, have you *ever* used it?'

To lie or not to lie ... 'Yes, sir, I have used it, once or twice. But not on Squelch in the Lemonfizz Cup.'

'It is sufficient that you said it at all, Hughes. We will draw our own conclusions as to *when* you said it.'

He shuffled one paper to the bottom of his pack and picked up another. Consulting it with the unseeing token glance of those who know their subject by heart, he continued, 'And now, West, tell us what Hughes did after he had said these words.'

'Sir, he pulled his horse back, sir.'

'How do you know this?' The question was a formality. He asked with the tone of one already aware of the answer.

'I was just beside Hughes, sir, when he said that about

brakes. Then he sort of hunched his shoulders, sir, and give a pull, sir, and, well, then he was behind me, having dropped out, like.'

Cranfield said angrily, 'But he finished in front of you.'

'Yes, sir.' Charlie West flicked his eyes upwards to Lord Gowery, and spoke only to him. 'My old horse couldn't act on the going, sir, and Hughes came past me again going into the second last, like.'

'And how did Squelch jump that fence?'

'Easy, sir. Met it just right. Stood back proper, sir.'

'Hughes maintains that Squelch was extremely tired at that point.'

Charlie West left a small pause. Finally he said, 'I don't know about that, sir. I thought as how Squelch would win, myself, sir. I still think as how he ought to have won, sir, being the horse he is, sir.'

Gowery glanced left and right, to make sure that his colleagues had taken the point. 'From your position during the last stages of the race, West, could you see whether or not Hughes was making every effort to win?'

'Well he didn't look like it, sir, which was surprising, like.'

'Surprising?'

'Yes, sir. See, Hughes is such an artist at it, sir.'

'An artist at what?'

'Well, at riding what looks from the stands one hell of a finish, sir, while all the time he's smothering it like mad.'

'Hughes is in the habit of not riding to win?'

Charlie West worked it out. 'Yes, sir.'

'Thank you, West,' Lord Gowery said with insincere politeness. 'You may go and sit over there at the back of the room.'

Charlie West made a rabbit's scurry towards the row of chairs reserved for those who had finished giving evidence. Cranfield turned fiercely to me and said, 'Why didn't you deny it more vehemently, for God's sake? Why the Hell didn't you insist he was making the whole thing up?'

'Do you think they'd believe me?'

He looked uneasily at the accusing ranks opposite, and

found his answer in their inplacable stares. All the same, he stood up and did his best.

'Lord Gowery, the film of the Lemonfizz Cup does not bear out West's accusation. At no point does Hughes pull back his horse.'

I lifted my hand too late to stop him. Gowery's and Lord Ferth's intent faces both registered satisfaction. They knew as well as I did that what West had said was borne out on the film. Sensing that Squelch was going to run out of steam, I'd give him a short breather a mile from home, and this normal everyday little act was now wide open to mis-interpretation.

Cranfield looked down at me, surprised by my reaction.

'I gave him a breather,' I said apologetically. 'It shows.'

He sat down heavily, frowning in worry.

Gowery was saying to an official, 'Show in Mr Newton-nards' as if Cranfield hadn't spoken. There was a pause before Mr Newtonnards, whoever he was, materialized. Lord Gowery was looking slightly over his left shoulder, towards the door, giving me the benefit of his patrician profile. I realized with almost a sense of shock that I knew nothing about him as a person, and that he most probably knew nothing about me. He had been, to me, a figure of author-ity with a capital A. I hadn't questioned his right to rule over me. I had assumed naïvely that he would do so with integrity, wisdom, and justice.

So much for illusions. He was leading his witnesses in a way that would make the Old Bailey reel. He heard truth in Charlie West's lies and lies in my truth. He was prosecutor as well as judge, and was only admitting evidence if it fitted his case.

He was dispersing the accepting awe I had held him in like candyfloss in a thunderstorm, and I could feel an un-forgiving cynicism growing in its stead. Also I was ashamed of my former state of trust. With the sort of education I'd had, I ought to have known better.

Mr Newtonnards emerged from the waiting-room and made his way to the witnesses' end of the Stewards' table, sporting a red rosebud in his lapel and carrying a large blue ledger. Unlike Charlie West he was confident, not nervous. Seeing that everyone else was seated he looked around for a chair for himself, and not finding one, asked.

After a fractional pause Gowery nodded, and the official-of-all-work near the door pushed one forwards. Mr Newtonnards deposited into it his well-cared-for pearl-grey-suited bulk.

'Who is he?' I said to Cranfield. Cranfield shook his head and didn't answer, but he knew, because his air of worry had if anything deepened.

Andrew Tring flipped through his pile of papers, found what he was looking for, and drew it out. Lord Plimborne had his eyes shut again. I was beginning to expect that: and in any case I could see that it didn't matter, since the power lay somewhere between Gowery and Ferth, and Andy Tring and Plimborne were so much window-dressing.

Lord Gowery too picked up a paper, and again I had the impression that he knew its contents by heart.

'Mr Newtonnards?'

'Yes, my lord.' He had a faint cockney accent overlaid by years of cigars and champagne. Mid-fifties, I guessed; no fool, knew the world, and had friends in show business. Not too far out: Mr Newtonnards, it transpired, was a book-maker.

Gowery said, 'Mr Newtonnards, will you be so good as to tell about a certain bet you struck on the afternoon of the Lemonfizz Cup?'

'Yes, my lord. I was standing on my pitch in Tattersall's when this customer come up and asked me for five tenners on Cherry Pie.' He stopped there, as if that was all he thought necessary.

Gowery did some prompting. 'Please describe this man, and also tell us what you did about his request.'

'Describe him? Let's see, then. He was nothing special. A biggish man in a fawn coat, wearing a brown trilby and carrying race glasses over his shoulder. Middle-aged, I suppose. Perhaps he had a moustache. Can't remember, really.'

The description fitted half the men on the racecourse.

'He asked me what price I'd give him about Cherry Pie,'

27

Newtonnards went on. 'I didn't have any price chalked on my board, seeing Cherry Pie was such an outsider. I offered him tens, but he said it wasn't enough, and he looked like moving off down the line. Well...' Newtonnards waved an expressive pudgy hand '...business wasn't too brisk, so I offered him a hundred to six. Couldn't say fairer than that now, could I, seeing as there were only eight runners in the race? Worse decision I made in a long time.' Gloom mixed with stoicism settled on his well-covered features.

'So when Cherry Pie won, you paid out?'

'That's right. He put down fifty smackers I paid him nine hundred.'

'Nine hundred pounds?'

'That's right, my lord.' Newtonnards confirmed easily, 'nine hundred pounds.'

'And we may see the record of this bet?'

'Certainly.' He opened the big blue ledger at a marked page. 'On the left, my lord, just over halfway down. Marked with a red cross. Nine hundred and fifty, ticket number nine seven two.'

The ledger was passed along the Stewards' table. Plimborne woke up for the occasion and all four of them peered at the page. The ledger returned to Newtonnards, who shut it and let it lie in front of him.

'Wasn't that a very large bet on an outsider?' Gowery asked.

'Yes it was, my lord. But then, there are a lot of mugs about. Except, of course, that once in a while they go and win.'

'So you had no qualms about risking such a large amount?'

'Not really, my lord. Not with Squelch in the race. And anyway, I laid a bit of it off. A quarter of it, in fact, at thirty-threes. So my actual losses were in the region of four hundred and eighty-seven pounds ten. Then I took three hundred and two-ten on Squelch and the others, which left a net loss on the race of one eight five.'

Cranfield and I received a glare in which every unit of the one eight five rankled.

Gowery said, 'We are not enquiring into how much you lost Mr Newtonnards, but into the identity of the client who won nine hundred pounds on Cherry Pie.'

I shivered. If West could lie, so could others.

'As I said in my statement, my lord, I don't know his name. When he came up to me I thought I knew him from somewhere, but you see a lot of folks in my game, so I didn't think much of it. You know. So it wasn't until after I paid him off. After the last race, in fact. Not until I was driving home. Then it came to me, and I went spare, I can tell you.'

'Please explain more clearly,' Gowery said patiently. The patience of a cat at a mousehole. Anticipation making the waiting sweet.

'It wasn't him, so much, as who I saw him talking to. Standing by the parade ring rails before the first race. Don't know why I should remember it, but I do.'

'And who did you see this client talking to?'

'Him.' He jerked his head in our direction. 'Mr Cranfield.'

Cranfield was immediately on his feet.

'Are you suggesting that I advised this client of yours to back Cherry Pie?' His voice shook with indignation.

'No, Mr Cranfield,' said Gowery like the North Wind, 'the suggestion is that the client was acting on your behalf and that it was you yourself that backed Cherry Pie.'

'That's an absolute lie.'

His hot denial fell on a lot of cold ears.

'Where is this mysterious man?' he demanded. 'This unidentified, unidentifiable nobody? How can you possibly trump up such a story and present is as serious evidence? It is ridiculous. Utterly, utterly ridiculous.'

'The bet was struck,' Gowery said plonkingly, pointing to the ledger.

'And I saw you talking to the client,' confirmed Newton-nards.,

Cranfield's fury left him gasping for words, and in the end he too sat down again, finding like me nothing to say that could dent the preconceptions ranged against us.

'Mr Newtonnards.' I said, 'would you know this client again?'

He hesitated only a fraction. 'Yes, I would.'

'Have you seen him at the races since Lemonfizz day?'

'No. I haven't.'

'If you see him again, will you point him out to Lord Gowery?'

'If Lord Gowery's at the races.' Several of the back ranks of officials smiled at this, but Newtonnards, to give him his due, did not.

I couldn't think of anything else to ask him, and I knew I had made no headway at all. It was infuriating. By our own choice we had thrust ourselves back into the bad old days when people accused at racing trials were not allowed a legal defendant. If they didn't know how to defend themselves: if they didn't know what sort of questions to ask or in what form to ask them, that was just too bad. Just their hard luck. But this wasn't hard luck. This was our own stupid fault. A lawyer would have been able to rip Newtonnards' testimony to bits, but neither Cranfield nor I knew how.

Cranfield tried. He was back on his feet.

'Far from backing Cherry Pie, I backed Squelch. You can check up with my own bookmaker.'

Gowery simply didn't reply. Cranfield repeated it.

Gowery said, 'Yes, yes. No doubt you did. It is quite beside the point.'

Cranfield sat down again with his mouth hanging open. I knew exactly how he felt. Not so much banging the head against a brick wall as being actively attacked by a cliff.

They waved Newtonnards away and he ambled easily off to take his place beside Charlie West. What he had said stayed behind him, stuck fast in the officials' minds. Not one of them had asked for corroboration. Not one had suggested that there might have been a loophole in identity. The belief was written plain on their faces: if someone had backed Cherry Pie to win nine hundred pounds, it must have been Cranfield.

Gowery hadn't finished. With a calm satisfaction he

picked up another paper and said, 'Mr Cranfield, I have here an affidavit from a Mrs Joan Jones, who handled the five-pound selling window on the Totalizator in the paddock on Lemonfizz Cup day, that she sold ten win-only tickets for horse number eight to a man in a fawn raincoat, middle-aged, wearing a trilby. I also have here a similar testimony from a Mr Leonard Roberts, who was paying out at the five-pound window in the same building, on the same occasion. Both of these Tote employees remember the client well, as these were almost the only five-pound tickets sold on Cherry Pie, and certainly the only large block. The Tote paid out to this man more than eleven hundred pounds in cash. Mr Roberts advised him not to carry so much on his person, but the man declined to take his advice.'

There was another accusing silence. Cranfield looked totally nonplussed and came up with nothing to say. This time, I tried for him. 'Sir, did this man back any other horses in the race, on the Tote? Did he back all, or two or three or four, and just hit the jackpot by accident?'

'There was no accident about this, Hughes.'

'But did he, in fact, back any other horses?'

Dead silence.

'Surely you asked?' I said reasonably.

Whether anyone had asked or not, Gowery didn't know. All he knew was what was on the affidavit. He gave me a stony stare, and said, 'No one puts fifty pounds on an outsider without good grounds for believing it will win.'

'But sir...'

'However,' he said, 'we will find out.' He wrote a note on the bottom of one of the affidavits. 'It seems to me extremely unlikely. But we will have the question asked.'

There was no suggestion that he would wait for the answer before giving his judgement. And in fact he did not.

CHAPTER THREE

I wandered aimlessly round the flat, lost and restless. Re-heated the coffee. Drank it. Tried to write to my parents, and gave it up after half a page. Tried to make some sort of decision about my future, and couldn't.

Felt too battered. Too pulped. Too crushed.

Yet I had done nothing.

Nothing.

Late afternoon. The lads were bustling round the yard setting the horses fair for the night, and whistling and calling to each other as usual. I kept away from the windows and eventually went back to the bedroom and lay down on the bed. The day began to fade. The dusk closed in.

After Newtonnards they had called Tommy Timpson, who had ridden Cherry Pie.

Tommy Timpson 'did his two' for Cranfield and rode such of the stable's second strings as Cranfield cared to give him. Cranfield rang the changes on three jockeys: me, Chris Smith (at present taking his time over a fractured skull) and Tommy. Tommy got the crumbs and deserved better. Like many trainers, Cranfield couldn't spot talent when it was under his nose, and it wasn't until several small local trainers had asked for his services that Cranfield woke up to the fact that he had a useful emerging rider in his own yard.

Raw, nineteen years old, a stutterer, Tommy was at his worst at the Enquiry. He looked as scared as a two-year-old colt at his first starting gate, and although he couldn't help being jittery it was worse than useless for Cranfield and me.

Lord Gowery made no attempt to put him at ease but simply asked questions and let him get on with the answers as best he could.

'What orders did Mr Cranfield give you before the race? How did he tell you to ride Cherry Pie? Did he instruct you to ride to win?'

Tommy stuttered and stumbled and said Mr Cranfield had told him to keep just behind Squelch all the way round and try to pass him after the last fence.

Cranfield said indignantly, 'That's what he *did*. Not what I told him to do.'

Gowery listened, turned his head to Tommy, and said again, 'Will you tell us what instructions Mr Cranfield gave you *before* the race? Please think carefully.

Tommy swallowed, gave Cranfield an agonized glance, and tried again. 'M ... M ... M ... Mr Cranfield s ... s ... said to take my p ... p ... pace from S ... S ... Squelch and s ... s ... stay with him as long as I c ... c ... could.'

'And did he tell you to win?'

'He s ... s .. said of course g ... go ... go on and w ... w ... win if you c ... c ... can, sir.'

These were impeccable instructions. Only the most suspicious or biased mind could have read any villainy into them. If these Stewards' minds were not suspicious and biased, snow would fall in the Sahara.

'Did you hear Mr Cranfield giving Hughes instructions as to how he should ride Squelch?'

'N ... No, sir. M ... Mr Cranfield did ... didn't g ... give Hughes any orders at all, sir.'

'Why not?'

Tommy ducked it and said he didn't know. Cranfield remarked furiously that Hughes had ridden the horse twenty times and knew what was needed.

'Or you had discussed it with him privately, beforehand?'

Cranfield had no explosive answer to that because of course we *had* discussed it beforehand. In general terms. In an assessment of the opposition. As a matter of general strategy.

'I discussed the race with him, yes. But I gave him no specific orders.'

'So according to you,' Lord Gowery said, 'you intended both of your jockeys to try to win?'

'Yes. I did. My horses are always doing their best.'

Gowery shook his head. 'Your statement is not borne out by the facts.'

'Are you calling me a liar?' Cranfield demanded.

Gowery didn't answer. But yes, he was.

They shooed a willing Tommy Timpson away and Cranfield went on simmering at boiling point beside me. For myself, I was growing cold, and no amount of central heating could stop it. I thought we must now have heard everything, but I was wrong. They had saved the worst until last, building up the pyramid of damning statements until they could put the final cap on it and stand back and admire their four-square structure, their solid, unanswerable edifice of guilt.

The worst, at first, had looked so harmless. A quiet slender man in his early thirties, endowed with an utterly forgettable face. After twenty-four hours I couldn't recall his features or remember his voice, and yet I couldn't think about him without shaking with sick impotent fury.

His name was David Oakley. His business, enquiry agent. His address, Birmingham.

He stood without fidgeting at the end of the Stewards' table holding a spiral-bound notebook which he consulted continually, and from beginning to end not a shade of emotion affected his face or his behaviour or even his eyes.

'Acting upon instructions, I paid a visit to the flat of Kelly Hughes, jockey, of Corrie House training stables, Corrie, Berkshire, two days after the Lemonfizz Crystal Cup.'

I sat up with a jerk and opened my mouth to deny it, but before I could say a word he went smoothly on.

'Mr Hughes was not there, but the door was open, so I went in to wait for him. While I was there I made certain observations.' He paused.

Cranfield said to me, 'What is all this about?'

'I don't know. I've never seen him before.'

Gowery steamrollered on. 'You found certain objects.'

'Yes, my lord.'

Gowery sorted out three large envelopes, and passed one each to Tring and Plimborne. Ferth was before them. He had removed the contents from a similar envelope as soon

34

as Oakley had appeared, and was now, I saw, watching me with what I took to be contempt.

The envelopes each held a photograph.

Oakley said, 'The photograph is of objects I found on a chest of drawers in Hughes' bedroom.'

Andy Tring looked, looked again, and raised a horrified face, meeting my eyes accidentally and for the first and only time. He glanced away hurriedly, embarrassed and disgusted.

'I want to see that photograph,' I said hoarsely.

'Certainly.' Lord Gowery turned his copy round and pushed it across the table. I got up, walked the three dividing steps, and looked down at it.

For several seconds I couldn't take it in, and when I did, I was breathless with disbelief. The photograph had been taken from above the dressing chest, and was sparkling clear. There was the edge of the silver frame and half of Rosalind's face, and from under the frame, as if it had been used as a paperweight, protruded a sheet of paper dated the day after the Lemonfizz Cup. There were three words written on it, and two initials.

As agreed. Thanks. D.C.

Slanted across the bottom of the paper, and spread out like a pack of cards, were a large number of ten-pound notes.

I looked up, and met Lord Gowery's eyes, and almost flinched away from the utter certainty I read there.

'It's a fake,' I said. My voice sounded odd. 'It's a complete fake.'

'What is it?' Cranfield said from behind me, and in his voice too everyone could hear the awareness of disaster.

I picked up the photograph and took it across to him, and I couldn't feel my feet on the carpet. When he had grasped what it meant he stood up slowly and in a low biting voice said formally, 'My lords, if you believe this, you will believe anything.'

It had not the slightest effect.

Gowery said merely, 'That is your handwriting, I believe.'

35

Cranfield shook his head. 'I didn't write it.'

'Please be so good as to write those exact words on this sheet of paper.' Gowery pushed a plain piece of paper across the table, and after a second Cranfield went across and wrote on it. Everyone knew that the two samples would look the same, and they did. Gowery passed the sheet of paper significantly to the other Stewards, and they all compared and nodded.

'It's a fake,' I said again. 'I never had a letter like that.'

Gowery ignored me. To Oakley he said, 'Please tell us where you found the money.'

Oakley unnecessarily consulted his notebook. 'The money was folded inside this note, fastened with a rubber band, and both were tucked behind the photo of Hughes's girlfriend, which you see in the picture.'

'It's not true,' I said. I might as well not have bothered. No one listened.

'You counted the money, I believe?'

'Yes, my lord. There was five hundred pounds.'

'There was no money,' I protested. Useless. 'And anyway,' I added desperately, 'why would I take five hundred for losing the race when I would get about as much as that for winning?'

I thought for a moment that I might have scored a hit. Might have made them pause. A pipe dream. There was an answer to that, too.

'We understand from Mr Kessel, Squelch's owner,' Gowery said flatly, 'that he pays you ten per cent of the winning stake money through official channels by cheque. This means that all presents received by you from Mr Kessel are taxed; and we understand that as you pay a high rate of tax your ten per cent from Mr Kessel would have in effect amounted to half, or less than half, of five hundred pounds.'

They seemed to have enquired into my affairs down to the last penny. Dug around in all directions. Certainly I had never tried to hide anything, but this behind-my-back tin-opening made me feel naked. Also, revolted. Also, finally, hopeless. And it wasn't until then that I realized I had been

36

subconsciously clinging to a fairytale faith that it would all finally come all right, that because I was telling the truth I was bound to be believed in the end.

I stared across at Lord Gowery, and he looked briefly back. His face was expressionless, his manner entirely calm. He had reached his conclusions and nothing could over-throw them.

Lord Ferth, beside him, was less bolted down, but a great deal of his earlier heat seemed to have evaporated. The power he had generated no longer troubled Gowery at all, and all I could interpret from his expression was some kind of resigned acceptance.

There was little left to be said. Lord Gowery briefly summed up the evidence against us. The list of former races. The non-use of the whip. The testimony of Charlie West. The bets struck on Cherry Pie. The riding orders given in private. The photographic proof of a pay off from Cranfield to Hughes.

'There can be no doubt that this was a most flagrant fraud on the racing public ... No alternative but to suspend your licences ... And you, Dexter Cranfield, and you, Kelly Hughes, will be warned off Newmarket Heath until further notice.'

Cranfield, pale and shaking, said, 'I protest that this has not been a fair hearing. Neither Hughes nor I are guilty. The sentence is outrageous.'

No response from Lord Gowery. Lord Ferth, however, spoke for the second time in the proceedings.

'Hughes?'

'I rode Squelch to win,' I said. 'The witnesses were lying.'

Gowery shook his head impatiently. 'The Enquiry is closed. You may go.'

Cranfield and I both hesitated, still unable to accept that that was all. But the official near the door opened it, and all the ranks opposite began to talk quietly to each other and ignore us, and in the end we walked out. Stiff legged. Feel-ing as if my head were a floating football and my body a chunk of ice. Unreal.

There were several people in the waiting-room outside,

but I didn't see them clearly. Cranfield, tight lipped, strode away from me, straight across the room and out of the far door. shaking off a hand or two laid on his sleeve. Dazed, I started to follow him, but was less purposeful, and was effectively stopped by a large man who planted himself in my way.

I looked at him vaguely. Mr Kessel. The owner of Squelch.

'Well?' he said challengingly.

'They didn't believe us. We've both been warned off.'

He hissed a sharp breath out between his teeth. 'After what I've been hearing, I'm not surprised. And I'll tell you this, Hughes, even if you get your licence back, you won't be riding for me again.'

I looked at him blankly and didn't answer. It seemed a small thing after what had already happened. He had been talking to the witnesses, in the waiting-room. They would convince anyone, it seemed. Some owners were unpredictable anyway, even in normal times. One day they had all the faith in the world in their jockey, and the next day, none at all. Faith with slender foundations. Mr Kessel had forgotten all the races I had won for him because of the one I had lost.

I turned blindly away from his hostility and found a more welcome hand on my arm. Tony, who had driven up with me instead of seeing his horses work.

'Come on,' he said. Let's get out of here.'

I nodded and went down with him in the lift, out into the hall, and towards the front door. Outside there we could see a bunch of newspaper reporters waylaying Cranfield with their notebooks at the ready, and I stopped dead at the sight.

'Let's wait till they've gone,' I said.

'They won't go. Not before they've chewed you up too.'

We waited, hesitating, and a voice called behind me, 'Hughes.'

I didn't turn round. I felt I owed no one the slightest politeness. The footsteps came up behind me and he finally came to a halt in front.

Lord Ferth. Looking tired.

'Hughes. Tell me. Why in God's name did you do it?'

I looked at him stonily.

'I didn't.'

He shook his head. 'All the evidence...'

'You tell me,' I said, rudely, 'why decent men like Stewards so easily believe a lot of lies.'

I turned away from him, too. Twitched my head at Tony and made for the front door. To hell with the Press. To hell with the Stewards and Mr Kessel. And to everything to do with racing. The upsurge of fury took me out of the building and fifty yards along the pavement in Portman Square and only evaporated into grinding misery when we had climbed into the taxi Tony whistled for.

Tony thumped up the stairs to the darkened flat. I heard him calling.

'Are you there, Kelly?'

I unrolled myself from the bed, stood up, stretched, went out into the sitting-room and switched on the lights. He was standing in the far doorway, blinking, his hands full of tray.

'Poppy insisted,' he explained.

He put the tray down on the table and lifted off the covering cloth. She'd sent hot chicken pie, a tomato, and about half a pound of Brie.

'She says you haven't eaten for two days.'

'I suppose not.'

'Get on with it, then.' He made an instinctive line for the whisky bottle and poured generously into two tumblers.

'And here. For once, drink this.'

I took the glass and a mouthful and felt the fire trickle down inside my chest. The first taste was always the best. Tony tossed his off and ordered himself a refill.

I ate the pie, the tomato, and the cheese. Hunger, I hadn't consciously felt, rolled contentedly over and slept.

'Can you stay a bit?' I asked.

'Natch.'

'I'd like to tell you about the Enquiry.'

'Shoot,' he said with satisfaction. 'I've been waiting.'

I told him all that had happened, almost word for word. Every detail had been cut razor sharp into my memory in the way that only happens in disasters.

Tony's astonishment was plain. 'You were framed!'

'That's right.'

'But surely no one can get away with that?'

'Someone seems to be doing all right.'

'But was there *nothing* you could say to prove...'

'I couldn't think of anything yesterday, which is all that matters. It's always easy to think of all the smart clever things one *could* have said, afterwards, when it's too late.'

'What would you have said, then?'

'I suppose for a start I should have asked who had given that so-called enquiry agent instructions to search my flat. Acting on instructions, he said. Well, *whose* instructions? I didn't think of asking, yesterday. Now I can see that it could be the whole answer.'

'You assumed the Stewards had instructed him?'

'I suppose so. I didn't really think. Most of the time I was so shattered that I couldn't think clearly at all.'

'Maybe it *was* the Stewards.'

'Well, no. I suppose it's barely possible they might have sent an investigator, though when you look at it in cold blood it wouldn't really seem likely, but it's a tear drop to the Atlantic that they wouldn't have supplied him with five hundred quid and a forged note and told him to photograph them somewhere distinctive in my flat. But that's what he did. Who instructed him?'

'Even if you'd asked, he wouldn't have said.'

'I guess not. But at least it might have made the Stewards think a bit too.'

Tony shook his head. 'He would still have said he found the money behind Rosalind's picture. His word against yours. Nothing different.'

He looked gloomily into his glass. I looked gloomily into mine.

'That bloody little Charlie West,' I said. 'Someone got at him, too.'

'I presume you didn't in fact say "Brakes on, chaps?"'

'I did say it, you see. Not in the Lemonfizz, of course, but a couple of weeks before, in that frightful novice 'chase at Oxford, the day they abandoned the last two races because it was snowing. I was hitting every fence on that deadly bad jumper that old Almond hadn't bothered to school properly, and half the other runners were just as green, and a whole bunch of us had got left about twenty lengths behind the four who were any use, and sleet was falling, and I didn't relish ending up with a broken bone at nought degrees centigrade, so as we were handily out of sight of the stands at that point I shouted "OK, brakes on, chaps," and a whole lot of us eased up thankfully and finished the race a good deal slower than we could have done. It didn't affect the result, of course. But there you are. I did say it. What's more, Charlie West heard me. He just shifted it from one race to another.'

'The bastard.'

'I agree.'

'Maybe no one got at him. Maybe he just thought he'd get a few more rides if you were out of the way.'

I considered it and shook my head. 'I wouldn't have thought he was *that* much of a bastard.'

'You never know.' Tony finished his drink and absent-mindedly replaced it. 'What about the bookmaker?'

'Newtonnards? I don't know. Same thing, I suppose. Someone has it in for Cranfield too. Both of us, it was. The Stewards couldn't possibly have warned off one of us without the other. We were knitted together so neatly.'

'It makes me livid,' Tony said violently. 'It's wicked.'

I nodded. 'There was something else, too, about that Enquiry. Some undercurrent, running strong. At least, it was strong at the beginning. Something between Lord Gowery and Lord Ferth. And then Andy Tring, he was sitting there looking like a wilted lettuce.' I shook my head in puzzlement. 'It was like a couple of heavy animals lurking in the undergrowth, shaping up to fight each other.

You couldn't see them, but there was a sort of quiver in the air. At least, that's how it seemed at one point . . .'

'Stewards are men,' Tony said with bubble-bursting matter-of-factness. 'Show me any organization which doesn't have some sort of power struggle going on under its gentlemanly surface. All you caught was a whiff of the old brimstone. State of nature. Nothing to do with whether you and Cranfield were guilty or not.'

He half convinced me. He polished off the rest of the whisky and told me not to forget to get some more.

Money. That was another thing. As from yesterday I had no income. The Welfare State didn't pay unemployment benefits to the self-employed, as all jockeys remembered every snow-bound winter.

'I'm going to find out,' I said abruptly.

'Find out what?'

'Who framed us.'

'Up the Marines,' Tony said unsteadily. 'Over the top, boys, Up and at 'em.' He picked up the empty bottle and looked at it regretfully. 'Time for bed, I guess. If you need any help with the campaign, count on my Welsh blood to the last clot.'

He made an unswerving line to the door, turned, and gave me a grimace of friendship worth having.

'Don't fall down the stairs,' I said.

Part Two

MARCH

CHAPTER FOUR

Roberta Cranfield looked magnificent in my sitting-room. I came back from buying whisky in the village and found her gracefully draped all over my restored Chippendale. The green velvet supported a lot of leg and a deep purple size-ten wool dress, and her thick long hair the colour of dead beech leaves clashed dramatically with the curtains. Under the hair she had white skin, incredible eyebrows, amber eyes, photogenic cheekbones and a petulant mouth.

She was nineteen, and I didn't like her.

'Good morning,' I said.

'Your door was open.'

'It's a habit I'll have to break.'

I peeled the tissue wrapping off the bottle and put it with the two chunky glasses on the small silver tray I had once won in a race sponsored by some sweet manufacturers. Troy weight, twenty-four ounces: but ruined by the inscription, K. HUGHES, WINNING JOCKEY, STARCHOCS SILVER STEEPLECHASE. Starchocs indeed. And I never ate chocolates. Couldn't afford to, from the weight point of view.

She flapped her hand from a relaxed wrist, indicating the room.

'This is all pretty lush.'

I wondered what she had come for. I said, 'Would you like some coffee?'

'Coffee and cannabis.'

'You'll have to go somewhere else.'

'You're very prickly.'

'As a cactus,' I agreed.

She gave me a half-minute unblinking stare with her liquid eyes. Then she said, 'I only said cannabis to jolt you.'

'I'm not jolted.'

'No. I can see that. Waste of effort.'

44

'Coffee, then?'

'Yes.'

I went into the kitchen and fixed up the percolator. The kitchen was white and brown and copper and yellow. The colours pleased me. Colours gave me the sort of mental food I imagined others got from music. I disliked too much music, loathed the type of stuff you couldn't escape in restaurants and airliners, didn't own a record-player, and much preferred silence.

She followed me in from the sitting-room and looked around her with mild surprise.

'Do all jockeys live like this?'

'Naturally.'

'I don't believe it.'

She peered into the pine-fronted cupboard I'd taken the coffee from.

'Do you cook for yourself?'

'Mostly.'

'*Recherché* things like *shashlik*?' An undercurrent of mockery.

'Steaks'

I poured the bubbling coffee into two mugs and offered her cream and sugar. She took the cream, generously, but not the sugar, and perched on a yellow-topped stool. Her copper hair fitted the kitchen, too.

'You seem to be taking it all right,' she said.

'What?'

'Being warned off.'

I didn't answer.

'A cactus,' she said, 'isn't in the same class.'

She drank the coffee slowly, in separate mouthfuls, watching me thoughtfully over the mug's rim. I watched her back. Nearly my height, utterly self-possessed, as cool as the stratosphere. I had seen her grow from a demanding child into a selfish fourteen-year-old, and from there into a difficult-to-please debutante and from there to a glossy imitation model girl heavily tinged with boredom. Over the eight years I had ridden for her father we had met briefly and spoken seldom, usually in parade rings and outside the weighing-room, and on the occasions when she did speak to me she seemed to be aiming just over the top of my head.

'You're making it difficult,' she said.

'For you to say why you came?'

She nodded. 'I thought I knew you. Now it seems I don't.'

'What did you expect?'

'Well ... Father said you came from a farm cottage with pigs running in and out of the door.'

'Father exaggerates.'

She lifted her chin to ward off the familiarity, a gesture I'd seen a hundred times in her and her brothers. A gesture copied from her parents.

'Hens,' I said, 'not pigs.'

She gave me an up-stage stare. I smiled at her faintly and refused to be reduced to the ranks. I watched the wheels tick over while she worked out how to approach a cactus, and gradually the chin came down.

'Actual hens?'

Not bad at all. I could feel my own smile grow genuine.

'Now and then.'

'You don't look like ... I mean ...'

'I know exactly what you mean,' I agreed. 'And it's high time you got rid of those chains.'

'Chains? What are you talking about?'

'The fetters in your mind. The iron bars in your soul.'

'My mind is all right.

'You must be joking. It's chock-a-block with ideas half a century out of date.'

'I didn't come here to ...' she began explosively, and then stopped.

'You didn't come here to be insulted,' I said ironically.

'Well, as you put it in that well-worn hackneyed phrase, no, I didn't. But I wasn't going to say that.'

'What did you come for?'

She hesitated. 'I wanted you to help me.'

'To do what?'

'To ... to *cope* with Father.'

I was surprised, first that Father needed coping with, and second that she needed help to do it.

'What sort of help?'

'He's ... he's so *shattered*.' Unexpectedly there were tears standing in her eyes. They embarrassed and angered her, and she blinked furiously so that I shouldn't see. I admired the tears but not her reason for trying to hide them.

'Here are you,' she said in a rush, 'walking about as cool as you please and buying whisky and making coffee as if no screaming avalanche had poured out on you and smothered your life and made every thought an absolute bloody Hell, and maybe you don't understand how anyone in that state needs help, and come to that I don't understand why *you* don't need help, but anyway, Father *does*.'

'Not from me,' I said mildly. 'He doesn't think enough of me to give it any value.'

She opened her mouth angrily and shut it again and took two deep controlling breaths. 'And it looks as though he's right.'

'Ouch,' I said ruefully. 'What sort of help, then?'

'I want you to come and talk to him.'

My talking to Cranfield seemed likely to be as therapeutic as applying itching powder to a baby. However she hadn't left me much room for kidding myself that fruitlessness was a good reason for not trying.

'When?'

'Now ... Unless you have anything else to do.'

'No,' I said carefully. 'I haven't.'

She made a face and an odd little gesture with her hands. 'Will you come now, then ... please?'

She herself seemed surprised about the real supplication in that 'please'. I imagined that she had come expecting to instruct, not to ask.

'All right.'

'Great.' She was suddenly very cool, very employer's daughter again. She put her coffee mug on the draining board and started towards the door. 'You had better follow me, in your car. It's no good me taking you, you'll need your own car to come back in.'

'That is so,' I agreed.

47

She looked at me suspiciously, but decided not to pursue it. 'My coat is in your bedroom.'

'I'll fetch it for you.'

'Thank you.'.

I walked across the sitting-room and into the bedroom. Her coat was lying on my bed in a heap. Black and white fur, in stripes going round. I picked it up and turned, and found she had followed me.

'Thank you so much.' She presented her back to me and put her arms in the coat-putting-on position. On went the coat. She swivelled slowly, buttoning up the front with shiny black saucers. 'This flat really is fantastic. Who is your decorator?'

'Chap called Kelly Hughes.'

She raised her eyebrows. 'I know the professional touch when I see it.'

'Thank you.'

She raised the chin. 'Oh well, if you won't say...'

'I would say. I did say. I did the flat myself. I've been whitewashing pigsties since I was six.'

She wasn't quite sure whether to be amused or offended, and evaded it by changing the subject.

'That picture ... that's your wife, isn't it?'

I nodded.

'I remember her,' she said. 'She was always so sweet to me. She seemed to know what I was feeling. I was really awfully sorry when she was killed.'

I looked at her in surprise. The people Rosalind had been sweetest to had invariably been unhappy. She had had a knack of sensing it, and of giving succour without being asked. I would not have thought of Roberta Cranfield as being unhappy, though I supposed from twelve to fifteen, when she had known Rosalind, she could have had her troubles.

'She wasn't bad, as wives go,' I said flippantly, and Miss Cranfield disapproved of that, too.

We left the flat and this time I locked the door, though such horses as I'd had had already bolted. Roberta had parked her Sunbeam Alpine behind the stables and across the doors of the garage where I kept my Lotus. She backed and turned her car with aggressive poise, and I left a leisurely interval before I followed her through the gates, to avoid a competition all the eighteen miles to her home.

Cranfield lived in an early Victorian house in a hamlet four miles out of Lambourn. A country gentleman's residence, estate agents would have called it: built before the Industrial Revolution had invaded Berkshire and equally impervious to the social revolution a hundred years later. Elegant, charming, timeless, it was a house I liked very much. Pity about the occupants.

I drove up the back drive as usual and parked alongside the stable yard. A horsebox was standing there with its ramp down, and one of the lads was leading a horse into it. Archie, the head lad, who had been helping, came across as soon as I climbed out of the car.

'This is a God awful bloody business,' he said. 'It's wicked, that's what it is. Downright bloody wicked.'

'The horses are going?'

'Some owners have sent boxes already. All of them will be gone by the day after tomorrow.' His weather-beaten face was a mixture of fury, frustration, and anxiety. 'All the lads have got the sack. Even me. And the missus and I have just taken a mortgage on one of the new houses up the road. Chalet bungalow, just what she'd always set her heart on. Worked for years, she has, saving for it. Now she won't stop crying. We moved in only a month ago, see? How do you think we're going to keep up the payments? Took every pound we had, what with the deposit and the solicitors, and curtains and all. Nice little place, too, she's got it looking real nice. And it isn't as if the Guvnor really fiddled the blasted race. That Cherry Pie, anyone could see with half an eye he was going to be good some day. I mean, if the Guvnor had done it, like, somehow all this wouldn't be so bad. I mean, if he deserved it, well serve him right, and I'd try and get a bit of compensation from him because we're going to have a right job selling the house again, I'll tell you, because there's still two of them empty, they weren't so easy to sell in the first place, being so far out of Lambourn ... I'll tell you straight, I wish to God we'd never moved out of the Guvnor's cottage, dark and damp though it may be ... George,' he suddenly shouted at a lad swearing and tugging at a reluctant animal, 'don't take it out on the horse, it isn't *his* fault...' He bustled across the yard and took the horse himself, immediately quietening it and leading it without trouble into the horsebox.

He was an excellent head lad, better than most, and a lot of Cranfield's success was his doing. If he sold his house and got settled in another job, Cranfield wouldn't get him back. The training licence might not be lost for ever, but the stable's main prop would be.

I watched another lad lead a horse round to the waiting box. He too looked worried. His wife, I knew, was on the point of producing their first child.

Some of the lads wouldn't care, of course. There were plenty of jobs going in racing stables, and one lot of digs was much the same as another. But they too would not come back. Nor would most of the horses, nor many of the owners. The stable wasn't being suspended for a few months. It was being smashed.

Sick and seething with other people's fury as well as my own, I walked down the short stretch of drive to the house. Roberta's Alpine was parked outside the front door and she was standing beside it looking cross.

'So there you are. I thought you'd ratted.'

'I parked down by the yard.'

'I can't bear to go down there. Nor can Father. In fact, he won't move out of his dressing-room. You'll have to come upstairs to see him.'

She led the way through the front door and across thirty square yards of Persian rug. When we had reached the foot of the stairs the door of the library was flung open and Mrs Cranfield came through it. Mrs Cranfield always flung doors open, rather as if she suspected something reprehensible was going on behind them and she was intent on catching the sinners in the act. She was a plain woman who wore no make-up and dressed in droopy woollies. To me she had never talked about anything except horses, and I didn't know whether she could. Her father was an Irish baron, which may have accounted for the marriage.

'My father-in-law, Lord Coolihan . . .' Cranfield was wont to say: and he was wont to say it far too often. I wondered whether, after Gowery, he was the tiniest bit discontented with the aristocracy.

'Ah, there you are, Hughes,' Mrs Cranfield said. 'Roberta told me she was going to fetch you. Though what good you can do I cannot understand. After all, it was you who got us into the mess.'

'I what?'

'If you'd ridden a better race on Squelch, none of this would have happened.'

I bit back six answers and said nothing. If you were hurt enough you lashed out at the nearest object. Mrs Cranfield continued to lash.

'Dexter was thoroughly shocked to hear that you had been in the habit of deliberately losing races.'

'So was I,' I said dryly.

Roberta moved impatiently. 'Mother, do stop it. Come along, Hughes. This way.'

I didn't move. She went up three steps, paused, and looked back. 'Come on, what are you waiting for?'

I shrugged. Whatever I was waiting for, I wouldn't get it in that house. I followed her up the stairs, along a wide passage, and into her father's dressing-room.

There was too much heavy mahogany furniture of a later period than the house, a faded plum-coloured carpet, faded plum plush curtains, and a bed with an Indian cover.

On one side of the bed sat Dexter Cranfield, his back bent into a bow and his shoulders hunched round his ears. His hands rolled loosely on his knees, fingers curling, and he was staring immovably at the floor.

'He sits like that for hours,' Roberta said on a breath beside me. And, looking at him, I understood why she had needed help.

'Father,' she said, going over and touching his shoulder. 'Kelly Hughes is here.'

Cranfield said, 'Tell him to go and shoot himself.'

She saw the twitch in my face, and from her expression thought that I minded, that I believed Cranfield too thought me the cause of all his troubles. On the whole I decided not to crystallize her fears by saying I thought Cranfield had said shoot because shoot was in his mind.

'Hop it,' I said, and jerked my head towards the door. The chin went up like a reflex. Then she looked at the husk of her father, and back to me, whom she'd been to some trouble to bring, and most of the starch dissolved.

'All right. I'll be down in the library. Don't go without ... telling me.'

I shook my head, and she went collectedly out of the room, shutting the door behind her.

I walked to the window and looked at the view. Small fields trickling down into the valley. Trees all bent one way by the wind off the Downs. A row of pylons, a cluster of council-house roofs. Not a horse in sight. The dressing-room was on the opposite side of the house to the stables.

'Have you a gun?' I asked.

No answer from the bed. I went over and sat down beside him. 'Where is it?'

His eyes slid a fraction in my direction and then back. He had been looking past me. I got up and went to the table beside his bed, but there was nothing lethal on it, and nothing in the drawer.

I found it behind the high mahogany bedhead. A finely wrought Purdey more suitable for pheasants. Both barrels were loaded. I unloaded them.

'Very messy,' I remarked. 'Very inconsiderate. And anyway, you didn't mean to do it.'

I wasn't at all sure about that, but there was no harm in trying to convince him.

'What are you doing here?' he said indifferently.

'Telling you to snap out of it. There's work to be done.'

'Don't speak to me like that.'

'How, then?'

His head came up a little, just like Roberta's. If I made him angry, he'd be halfway back to his normal self. And I could go home.

'It's useless sitting up here sulking. It won't achieve anything at all.'

'*Sulking?*' He was annoyed, but not enough.

'Someone took our toys away. Very unfair. But nothing to be gained by grizzling in corners.'

'*Toys*... You're talking nonsense.'

'Toys, licences, what's the difference. The things we prized most. Someone's snatched them away. Tricked us out of them. And nobody except us can get them back. Nobody else will bother.'

'We can apply,' he said without conviction.

'Oh, we can apply. In six months' time, I suppose. But there's no guarantee we'd get them. The only sensible thing to do is to start fighting back right now and find out who fixed us. Who, and why. And after that I'll wring his bloody neck.'

He was still staring at the floor, still hunched. He couldn't even look me in the face yet, let alone the world. If he hadn't been such a climbing snob, I thought uncharitably, his present troubles wouldn't have produced such a complete cave-in. He was on the verge of literally not being able to bear the public disgrace of being warned off.

Well, I wasn't so sure I much cared for it myself. It was all very well knowing that one was not guilty, and even having one's closest friends believe it, but one could hardly walk around everywhere wearing a notice proclaiming 'I am innocent. I never done it. It were all a stinking frame-up.'

'It's not so bad for you,' he said.

'That's perfectly true.' I paused. 'I came in through the yard.'

He made a low sound of protest.

'Archie seems to be seeing to everything himself. And he's worried about his house.'

Cranfield made a waving movement of his hand as much as to ask how did I think he could be bothered with Archie's problems on top of his own.

'It wouldn't hurt you to pay Archie's mortgage for a bit.'

'*What?*' That finally reached him. His head came up at least six inches.

'It's only a few pounds a week. Peanuts to you. Life or death to him. And if you lose him, you'll never get so many winners again.'

'You ... you ...' He spluttered. But he still didn't look up.

'A trainer is as good as his lads.'

'That's stupid.'

'You've got good lads just now. You've chucked out the duds, the rough and lazy ones. It takes time to weed out and build up a good team, but you can't get a high ratio of winners without one. You might get your licence back but you won't get these lads back and it'll take years for the stable to recover. If it ever does. And I hear you have already given them all the sack.'

'What else was there to do?'

'You could try keeping them on for a month.'

His head came up a little more. 'You haven't the slightest idea what that would cost me. The wages come to more than four hundred pounds a week.'

'There must still be quite a lot to come in in training fees. Owners seldom pay in advance. You won't have to dig very deep into your own pocket. Not for a month, anyway, and it might not take as long as that.'

'What might not?'

'Getting our licences back.'

'Don't be so bloody ridiculous.'

'I mean it. What is it worth to you? Four weeks' wages for your lads? Would you pay that much if there was a chance you'd be back in racing in a month? The owners would send their horses back, if it was as quick as that. Particularly if you tell them you confidently expect to be back in business almost immediately.'

'They wouldn't believe it.'

'They'd be uncertain. That should be enough.'

'There isn't a chance of getting back.'

'Oh yes there damn well is,' I said forcefully. 'But only if you're willing to take it. Tell the lads you're keeping them on for a bit. Especially Archie. Go down to the yard and tell them now.'

'Now.'

'Of course,' I said impatiently. 'Probably half of them have already read the Situations Vacant columns and written to other trainers.'

'There isn't any point.' He seemed sunk in fresh gloom. 'It's all hopeless. And it couldn't have happened, it simply could *not* have happened at a worse time. Edwin Byler was going to send me his horses. It was all fixed up. Now of course he's telephoned to say it's all off, his horses are staying where they are, at Jack Roxford's.'

To train Edwin Byler's horses was to be presented with a pot of gold. He was a North country businessman who had made a million or two out of mail order, and had used a little of it to fulfil a long held ambition to own the best string of steeplechasers in Britain. Four of his present horses had in turn cost more than anyone had paid before. When he wanted, he bid. He only wanted the best, and he had bought enough of them to put him for the two previous seasons at the top of the Winning Owners' list. To have been going to train Edwin Byler's horses, and now not to be going to, was a refined cruelty to pile on top of everything else.

To have been going to *ride* Edwin Byler's horses ... as I would no doubt have done ... that too was a thrust where it hurt.

'There's all the more point, then,' I said. 'What more do you want in the way of incentive? You're throwing away without a struggle not only what you've got but what you might have ... Why in the Hell don't you get off your bed and behave like a gentleman and show some spirit?'

'Hughes!' He was outraged. But he still sat. He still wouldn't look at me.

I paused, considering him. Then, slowly, I said, 'All right, then. I'll tell you why you won't. You won't because ... to some degree ... you are in fact guilty. You made sure Squelch wouldn't win. And you backed Cherry Pie.'

That got him. Not just his head up, but up, trembling, on to his feet.

CHAPTER FIVE

'How dare you?'

'Frankly, just now I'd dare practically anything.'

'You said we were framed.'

'So we were.'

Some of his alarm subsided. I stoked it up again.

'You handed us away on a plate.'

He swallowed, his eyes flicking from side to side, looking everywhere except at me.

'I don't know what you mean.'

'Don't be so weak,' I said impatiently. 'I rode Squelch, remember? Was he his usual self? He was not.'

'If you're suggesting,' he began explosively, 'that I doped...'

'Oh of course not. Anyway, they tested him, didn't they? Negative result. Naturally. No trainer needs to dope a horse he doesn't want to win. It's like swatting a fly with a bull-dozer. There are much more subtle methods. Undetectable. Even innocent. Maybe you should be kinder to yourself and admit that you quite innocently stopped Squelch. Maybe you even did it subconsciously, wanting Cherry Pie to win.'

'Bull,' he said.

'The mind plays tricks,' I said. 'People often believe they are doing something for one good reason, while they are subconsciously doing it for another.'

'Twaddle.'

'The trouble comes sometimes when the real reason rears its ugly head and slaps you in the kisser.'

'Shut up.' His teeth and jaw were clenched tight.

I drew a deep breath. I'd been guessing, partly. And I'd guessed right.

I said, 'You gave Squelch too much work too soon before the race. He lost the Lemonfizz on the gallops at home.'

He looked at me at last. His eyes were dark, as if the

pupils had expanded to take up all the iris. There was a desperate sort of hopelessness in his expression.

'It wouldn't have been so bad,' I said, 'if you had admitted it to yourself. Because then you would never have risked not engaging a lawyer to defend us.'

'I didn't mean to over-train Squelch,' he said wretchedly. 'I didn't realize it until afterwards. I did back him, just as I said at the Enquiry.'

I nodded. 'I imagined you must have done. But you backed Cherry Pie as well.'

He explained quite simply, without any of his usual superiority, 'Trainers are often caught out, as you know, when one of their horses suddenly develops his true form. Well, I thought Cherry Pie might just be one of those. So I backed him, on the off chance.'

Some off chance. Fifty pounds with Newtonnards and fifty pounds on the Tote. Gross profit, two thousand.

'How much did you have on Squelch?'

'Two hundred and fifty.'

'Whew.' I said. 'Was that your usual sort of bet?'

'He was odds on ... I suppose a hundred is my most usual bet.'

I had come to the key question, and I wasn't sure I wanted to ask it, let alone have to judge whether the answer was true. However ...

'Why,' I said matter-of-factly, 'didn't you back Cherry Pie with your own usual bookmaker?'

He answered without effort, 'Because I didn't want Kessel knowing I'd backed Cherry Pie, if he won instead of Squelch. Kessel's a funny man, he takes everything personally, he'd as like as not have whisked Squelch away ...' He trailed off, remembering afresh that Squelch was indeed being whisked.

'Why should Kessel have known?'

'Eh? Oh, because he bets with my bookmaker too, and the pair of them are as thick as thieves.'

Fair enough.

'Well, who was the middle-aged man who put the bets on for you?'

'Just a friend. There's no need to involve him. I want to keep him out of it.'

'Could Newtonnards have seen you talking to him by the parade ring before the first race?'

'Yes,' he said with depression. 'I did talk to him. I gave him the money to bet with.'

And he still hadn't seen any danger signals. Had taken Monty Midgley's assurance at its face value. Hadn't revealed the danger to me. I could have throttled him.

'What did you do with the winnings?'

'They're in the safe downstairs.'

'And you haven't been able to admit to anyone that you've got them.'

'No.'

I thought back. 'You lied about it at the Enquiry.'

'What else was there to do?'

By then, what indeed. Telling the truth hadn't done much for me.

'Let's see, then.' I moved over to the window again, sorting things out. 'Cherry Pie won on his merits. You backed him because he looked like coming into form rather suddenly. Squelch had had four hard races in two months, and a possibly over-zealous training gallop. These are the straight facts.'

'Yes . . . I suppose so.'

'No trainer should lose his licence because he didn't tell the world he might just possibly have a flier. I never see why the people who put in all the work shouldn't have the first dip into the well.'

Owners, too, were entitled. Cherry Pie's owner, however, had died three weeks before the Lemonfizz, and Cherry Pie had run for the executors. Someone was going to have a fine time deciding his precise value at the moment of his owner's death.

'It means, anyway, that you do have a fighting fund,' I pointed out.

'There's no point in fighting.'

'You,' I said exasperatedly, 'are so soft that you'd make a marshmallow look like granite.'

His mouth slowly opened. Before that morning I had never given him anything but politeness. He was looking at me as if he'd really noticed me, and it occurred to me that if we did indeed get our licences back he would remember that I'd seen him in pieces, and maybe find me uncomfortable to have around. He paid me a retainer, but only on an annual contract. Easy enough to chuck me out, and retain someone else. Expediently, and not too pleased with myself for it, I took the worst crags out of my tone.

'I presume,' I said, 'that you do want your licence back?'

'There isn't a chance.'

'If you'll keep the lads for a month, I'll get it back for you.'

Defeatism still showed in every sagging muscle, and he didn't answer.

I shrugged. 'Well, I'm going to try. And if I give you your licence back on a plate it will be just too bad if Archie and the lads have gone.' I walked towards the door and put my hand on the knob. 'I'll let you know how I get on.'

Twisted the job. Opened the door.

'Wait,' he said.

I turned round. A vestige of starch had returned, mostly in the shape of the reappearance of the mean lines round his mouth. Not so good.

'I don't believe you can do it. But as you're so cocksure, I'll make a bargain with you. I'll pay the lads for two weeks. If you want me to keep them on for another two weeks after that, you can pay them yourself.'

Charming. He'd made two thousand pounds out of Cherry Pie and had over-trained Squelch and was the direct cause of my being warned off. I stamped on a violent inner tremble of anger and gave him a cold answer.

'Very well. I agree to that. But you must make a bargain with me too. A bargain that you'll keep your mouth tight shut about your guilt feelings. I don't want to be sabotaged by you hairshirting it all over the place and confessing your theoretical sins at awkward moments.'

'I am unlikely to do that,' he said stiffly.

I wasn't so sure. 'I want your word on it,' I said.

He drew himself up, offended. It at least had the effect of straightenening his backbone.

'You have it.'

'Fine.' I held the door open for him. 'Let's go down to the yard, then.'

He still hesitated, but finally made up his mind to it, and went before me through the door and down the stairs.

Roberta and her mother were standing in the hall, looking as if they were waiting for news at a pithead after a disaster. They watched the reappearance of the head of the family in mixture of relief and apprehension, and Mrs Cranfield said tentatively, 'Dexter? . . .'

He answered irritably, as if he saw no cause for anxiety in his having shut himself away with a shotgun for thirty-six hours, 'We're going down to the yard.'

'Great,' said Roberta practically smothering any tendency to emotion from her mother, 'I'll come too.'

Archie hurried to meet us and launched into a detailed account of which horses had gone and which were about to go next. Cranfield hardly listened and certainly didn't take it in. He waited for a gap in the flow, and when he'd waited long enough, impatiently interrupted.

'Yes, yes, Archie, I'm sure you have everything in hand. That is not what I've come down for, however. I want you to tell the lads at once that their notice to leave is withrawn for one month.'

Archie looked at me, not entirely understanding.

'The sack,' I said, 'is postponed. Pending attempts to get wrongs righted.'

'Mine too?'

'Absolutely,' I agreed. 'Especially, in fact.'

'Hughes thinks there is a chance we can prove ourselves innocent and recover our licences,' Cranfield said formally, his own disbelief showing like two heads. 'In order to help me keep the stable together while he makes enquiries, Hughes has agreed to contribute one half towards your wages for one month.' I looked at him sharply. That was not at all what I had agreed. He showed no sign of acknowledging his reinterpretation (to put it charitably) of the offer

I had accepted, and went authoritatively on. 'Therefore, as your present week's notice still has five days to run, none of you will be required to leave here for five weeks. In fact,' he added grudgingly, 'I would be obliged if you would all stay.'

Archie said to me, 'You really mean it?' and I watched the hope suddenly spring up in his face and thought that maybe it wasn't only my own chance of a future that was worth eight hundred quid.

'That's right,' I agreed. 'As long as you don't all spend the month busily fixing up to go somewhere else at the end of it.'

'What do you take us for?' Archie protested.

'Cynics,' I said, and Archie actually laughed.

I left Cranfield and Archie talking together with most of the desperation evaporating from both of them, and walked away to my aerodynamic burnt-orange car. I didn't hear Roberta following me until she spoke in my ear as I opened the door.

'Can you really do it?' she said.

'Do what?'

'Get your licences back.'

'It's going to cost me too much not to. So I guess I'll have to or . . .'

'Or what?'

I smiled. 'Or die in the attempt.'

It took me an hour to cross into Gloucestershire and almost half as long to sort out the geography of the village of Downfield, which mostly seemed to consist of cul-de sacs.

The cottage I eventually found after six misdirections from local inhabitants was old but not beautiful, well painted but in dreary colours, and a good deal more trustworthy than its owner.

When Mrs Charlie West saw who it was, she tried to shut the front door in my face. I put out a hand that was used to dealing with strong horses and pulled her by the wrist, so that if she slammed the door she would be squashing her own arm.

61

She screeched loudly. An inner door at the back of the hall opened all of six inches, and Charlie's round face appeared through the crack. A distinct lack of confidence was discernible in that area.

'He's hurting me,' Mrs West shouted.

'I want to talk to you,' I said to Charlie over her shoulder.

Charlie West was less than willing. Abandoning his teen-age wife, long straight hair, Dusty Springfield eyelashes, beige lipstick and all, he retreated a pace and quite firmly shut his door. Mrs West put up a loud and energetic defence to my attempt to establish further contact with Master Charlie, and I went through the hall fending off her toes and fists.

Charlie had wedged a chair under the door handle.

I shouted through the wood. 'Much as you deserve it, I haven't come here to beat you up. Come out and talk.'

No response of any sort. I rattled the door. Repeated my request. No results. With Mrs West still stabbing around like an agitated hornet I went out of the front door and round the outside to try to talk to him through the window. The window was open, and the sitting-room inside was empty.

I turned round in time to see Charlie's distant backview disappearing across a field and into the next parish. Mrs West saw him too, and gave a nasty smile.

'So there,' she said triumphantly.

'Yes,' I said. 'I'm sure you must be very proud of him.'

The smile wobbled. I walked back down their garden path, climbed into the car, and drove away.

Round one slightly farcically to the opposition.

Two miles away from the village I stopped the car in a farm gateway and thought it over. Charlie West had been a great deal more scared of me than I would have supposed, even allowing for the fact that I was a couple of sizes bigger and a fair amount stronger. Maybe Charlie was as much afraid of my fury as of my fists. He almost seemed to have been expecting that I would attempt some sort of retaliation, and certainly after what he had done, he had a right to. All the same, he still represented my quickest and easiest route to who, if not to why.

After a while I started up again and drove on into the nearest town. Remembered I hadn't eaten all day, put away some rather good cold beef at three-thirty in a home-made café geared more to cake and scones, dozed in the car, waited until dark, and finally drove back again to Charlie's village.

There were lights on in several rooms of his cottage. The Wests were at home. I turned the car and re-tracked about a hundred yards, stopping half on and half off a grassy verge. Climbed out. Stood up.

Plan of attack: vague. I had had some idea of ringing the front-door bell, disappearing and waiting for either Charlie or his dolly wife to take one incautious step outside to investigate. Instead, unexpected allies materialized in the shape of one small boy and one large dog.

The boy had a torch, and was talking to his dog, who paused to dirty up the roadside five yards ahead.

'What the hell d'you think you were at, you bloody great nit, scoffing our Mum's stewing steak? Gor blimey mate, don't you ever learn nothing? Tomorrow's dinner gone down your useless big gullet and our Dad will give us both a belting this time I shouldn't wonder, not just you, you senseless rotten idiot. Time you knew the bloody difference between me Mum's stewink steak and dog meat, it is straight, though come to think of it there isn't all that difference, 'specially as maybe your eyes don't look at things the same. Do they? I damn well wish you could talk, mate.'

I clicked shut the door of the car and startled him, and he swung round with the torch searching wildly. The beam caught me and steadied on my face.

The boy said, 'You come near me and I'll set my dog on you.' The dog, however, was still squatting and showed no enthusiasm.

'I'll stay right here, then,' I said amicably, leaning back against the car. 'I only want to know who lives in that cottage over there, where the lights are.'

'How do I know? We only come to live here the day before yesterday.'

'Great . . . I mean, that must be great for you, moving.'

'Yeah. Sure. You stay there, then. I'm going now.' He beckoned to the dog. The dog was still busy.

'How would it be if you could offer your Mum the price of the stewing steak? Maybe she wouldn't tell your Dad, then, and neither you nor the dog would get a belting.'

'Our Mum says we mustn't talk to strange men.'

'Hm. Well, never mind then. Off you go.'

'I'll go when I'm ready,' he said belligerently. A natural born rebel. About nine years old, I guessed.

'What would I have to do for it?' he said, after a pause.

'Nothing much. Just ring the front-door bell of that cottage and tell whoever answers that you can't stop your dog eating the crocuses they've got growing all along the front there. Then when they come out to see, just nip off home as fast as your dog can stagger.'

It appealed to him. 'Steak probably cost a good bit,' he said.

'Probably.' I dug into my pocket and came up with a small fistful of pennies and silver. 'This should leave a bit over.'

'He doesn't really have to eat the crocuses, does he?'

'No.'

'OK then.' Once his mind was made up he was jaunty and efficient. He shovelled my small change into his pocket, marched up to Charlie's front door, and told Mrs West, who cautiously answered it, that she was losing her crocuses. She scolded him all the way down the path, and while she was bending down to search for the damage, my accomplice quietly vanished. Before Mrs West exactly realized she had been misled I had stepped briskly through her front door and shut her out of her own house.

When I opened the sitting-room door Charlie said, without lifting his eyes from a racing paper, 'It wasn't him again, then.'

'Yes,' I said, 'it was.'

Charlie's immature face crumpled into a revolting state

of fear and Mrs West leaned on the door bell. I shut the sitting-room door behind me to cut out some of the din.

'What are you so afraid of?' I said loudly.

'Well ... you ...'

'And so you damn well ought to be,' I agreed. I took a step towards him and he shrank back into his armchair. He was brave enough on a horse, which made this abject cringing all the more unexpected, and all the more unpleasant. I took another step. He fought his way into the upholstery.

Mrs West gave the door bell a rest.

'Why did you do it?' I said.

He shook his head dumbly, and pulled his feet up on to the chair seat in the classic womb position. Wishful regression to the first and only place where the world couldn't reach him.

'Charlie, I came here for some answers, and you're going to give them to me.'

Mrs West's furious face appeared at the window and she started rapping hard enough to break the glass. With one eye on her husband to prevent him making another bolt for it, I stepped over and undid the latch.

'Get out of here,' she shouted. 'Go on, get out.'

'You get in. Through here, I'm not opening the door.'

'I'll fetch the police.'

'Do what you like. I only want to talk to your worm of a husband. Get in or stay out, but shut up.'

She did anything but. Once she was in the room it took another twenty minutes of fruitless slanging before I could ask Charlie a single question without her loud voice obliterating any chance of an answer.

Charlie himself tired of it first and told her to stop, but at least her belligerence had given him a breathing space. He put his feet down on the floor again and said it was no use asking those questions, he didn't know the answers.

'You must do. Unless you told those lies about me out of sheer personal spite.'

'No.'

'Then why?'

'I'm not telling you.'

'Then I'll tell you something, you little louse. I'm going to find out who put you up to it. I'm going to stir everything up until I find out, and then I'm going to raise such a stink about being framed that sulphur will smell like sweet peas by comparison, and you, Master Charlie West, *you* will find yourself without a licence, not me, and even if you get it back you'll never live down the contempt everyone will feel for you.'

'Don't you talk to my Charlie like that!'

'Your Charlie is a vicious little liar who would sell you too for fifty pounds.'

'It wasn't fifty,' she snapped triumphantly. 'It was five hundred.'

Charlie yelled at her and I came as near to hitting him as the distance between my clenched teeth. Five hundred pounds. He'd lied my licence away for a handout that would have insulted a tout.

'That does it,' I said. 'And now you tell me who paid you.'

The girl wife started to look as frightened as Charlie, and it didn't occur to me then that my anger had flooded through that little room like a tidal wave.

Charlie stuttered, 'I d ... d ... don't know.'

I took a pace towards him and he scrambled out of his chair and took refuge behind it.

'K ... k ... keep away from me. I don't know. I don't know.'

'That isn't good enough.'

'He really doesn't know,' the girl wailed. 'He really doesn't.'

'He does,' I repeated furiously.

The girl began to cry. Charlie seemed to be on the verge of copying her.

'I never saw ... never saw the bloke. He telephoned.'

'And how did he pay you?'

'In two ... in two packages. In one-pound notes. A hundred of them came the day before the Enquiry, and I was to get...' His voice trailed away.

'You were to get the other four hundred if I was warned off?'

He nodded, a fractional jerk. His head was tucked into his shoulders, as if to avoid a blow.

'And have you?'

'What?'

'Have you had it yet? The other four hundred?'

His eyes widened, and he spoke in jerks. 'No ... but ... of course ... it ... will ... come.'

'Of course it won't,' I said brutally. 'You stupid treacherous little ninny.' My voice sounded thick, and each word came out separately and loaded with fury.

Both of the Wests were trembling, and the girl's eye make-up was beginning to run down her cheeks.

'What did he sound like, this man on the telephone?'

'Just ... just a man,' Charlie said.

'And did it occur to you to ask *why* he wanted me warned off?'

'I said ... you hadn't done anything to harm me ... and he said ... you never know ... supposing one day he does ...'

Charlie shrank still farther under my astounded glare.

'Anyway ... five hundred quid ... I don't earn as much as you, you know.' For the first time there was a tinge of spite in his voice, and I knew that in truth jealousy had been a factor, that he hadn't in fact done it entirely for the money. He'd got his kicks, too.

'You're only twenty,' I said. 'What exactly do you expect?'

But Charlie expected everything, always, to be run entirely for the best interests of Charlie West.

I said, 'And you'll be wise to spend that money carefully, because, believe me, it's going to be the most expensive hundred quid you've ever earned.'

'Kelly ...' He was halfway to entreaty. Jealous, greedy, dishonest, and afraid. I felt not the remotest flicker of compassion for him only a widening anger that the motives behind his lies were so small.

'And when you lose your licence for this, and I'll see that you do, you'll have plenty of time to understand that it *serves you right*.'

The raw revenge in my voice made a desert of their little home. They both stood there dumbly with wide miserable eyes, too broken up to raise another word. The girl's beige mouth hung slackly open, mascara halfway to her chin, long hair straggling in wisps across her face and round her shoulders. She looked sixteen. A child. So did Charlie. The worst vandals are always childish.

I turned away from them and walked out of their cottage, and my anger changed into immense depression on the drive home.

CHAPTER SIX

At two o'clock in the morning the rage I'd unleashed on the Wests looked worse and worse.

To start with, it had achieved nothing helpful. I'd known before I went there that Charlie must have had a reason for lying about me at the Enquiry. I now knew the reason to be five hundred pounds. Marvellous. A useless scrap of information out of a blizzard of emotion.

Lash out when you're hurt ... I'd done that, all right. Poured out on them the roaring bitterness I'd smothered under a civilized front ever since Monday.

Nor had I given Charlie any reason to do me any good in future. Very much the reverse. He wasn't going to be contrite and eager to make amends. When he'd recovered himself he'd be sullen and vindictive.

I'd been taught the pattern over and over. Country A plays an isolated shabby trick. Country B is outraged and exacts revenge. Country A is forced to express apologies and meekly back down, but thoroughly resents it. Country A now holds a permanent grudge, and harms Country B whenever possible. One of the classic variations in the history of politics and aggression. Also applicable to individuals.

To have known about the pitfalls and jumped in regardless was a mite galling. It just showed how easily good sense lost out to anger. It also showed me that I wasn't going to get results that way. A crash course in detection would have been handy. Failing that, I'd have to start taking stock of things coolly, instead of charging straight off again towards the easiest looking target, and making another mess of it.

Cool stock-taking...

Charlie West hadn't wanted to see me because he had a guilty conscience. It followed that everyone else who had a guilty conscience wouldn't want to see me. Even if they didn't actually spring off across the fields, they would all do their best to avoid my reaching them. I was going to have to become adept – and fast – at entering their lives when their backs were turned.

If Charlie West didn't know who had paid him, and I believed that he didn't, it followed that perhaps no one else who had lied knew who had persuaded them to. Perhaps it had all been done on the telephone. Long-distance leverage. Impersonal and undiscoverable.

Perhaps I had set myself an impossible task and I should give up the whole idea and emigrate to Australia.

Except that they had racing in Australia, and I wouldn't be able to go. The banishment covered the world. Warned off. Warned off.

Oh God.

All right, so maybe I did let the self-pity catch up with me for a while. But I was privately alone in my bed in the dark, and I'd jeered myself out of it by morning.

Looking about as ragged as I felt, I got up at six and pointed the Lotus's smooth nose towards London, NW7, Mill Hill.

Since I could see no one at the races I had to catch them at home, and in the case of George Newtonnards, book-maker, home proved to be a sprawling pink-washed ranch-type bungalow in a prosperous suburban road. At eight-thirty AM I hoped to find him at breakfast, but in fact he was opening his garage door when I arrived. I parked squarely across the entrance to his drive, which was hardly likely to make me popular, and he came striding down towards me to tell me to move.

I climbed out of the car. When he saw who it was, he stopped dead. I walked up the drive to meet him, shivering a little in the raw east wind and regretting I wasn't snug inside a fur-collared jacket like his.

'What are you doing here?' he said sharply.

'I would be very grateful if you would just tell me one or two things...'

'I haven't time.' He was easy, self-assured, dealing with a small-sized nuisance. 'And nothing I can say will help you. Move your car, please.'

'Certainly ... Could you tell me how it was that you came to be asked to give evidence against Mr Cranfield?'

'How it was? ... He looked slightly surprised. 'I received an official letter, requiring me to attend.'

'Well, why? I mean, how did the Stewards know about Mr Cranfield's bet on Cherry Pie? Did you write and tell them?'

He gave me a cool stare. 'I hear, he said, 'that you are maintaining you were framed.'

'News travels.'

A faint smile. 'News always travels – towards me. An accurate information service is the basis of good bookmaking.'

'How did the Stewards know about Mr Cranfield's bet?'

'Mm. Well, yes, that I don't know.'

'Who, besides you, knew that you believed that Cranfield had backed Cherry Pie?'

'He did back him.'

'Well, who besides you knew that he had?'

'I haven't time for this.'

'I'll be happy to move my car ... in a minute or two.'

His annoyed glare gradually softened round the edges into a half-amused acceptance. A very smooth civilized man, George Newtonnards.

'Very well. I told a few of the lads ... other bookmakers,

that is. I was angry about it, see? Letting myself be taken to the cleaners like that. Me, at my age, I should know better. So maybe one of them passed on the word to the Stewards, knowing the Enquiry was coming up. But no, I didn't do it myself.'

'Could you guess which one might have done? I mean, do you know of anyone who has a grudge against Cranfield?'

'Can't think of one.' He shrugged. 'No more than against any other trainer who tries it on.'

'Tries it on?' I echoed, surprised. 'But he doesn't.'

'Oh yeah?'

'I ride them,' I protested. 'I should know.'

'Yes,' he said sarcastically. 'You should. Don't come the naïve bit with me, chum. Your friend Chris Smith, him with the cracked skull, he's a proper artist at strangulation, wouldn't you say? Same as you are. A fine pair, the two of you.'

'You believe I pulled Squelch, then?'

'Stands to reason.'

'All the same, I didn't.'

'Tell it to the Marines.' A thought struck him. 'I don't know any bookmakers who have a grudge against Cranfield, but I sure know one who has a grudge against *you*. A whopping great life-sized grudge. One time, he was almost coming after you with a chopper. You got in his way proper, mate, you did indeed.'

'How? And who?'

'You and Chris Smith, you were riding two for Cranfield ... about six months ago. It was ... right at the beginning of the season anyway ... in a novice 'chase at Fontwell. Remember? There was a big holiday crowd in from the South Coast because it was a bit chilly that day for lying on the beach ... anyway, there was a big crowd all primed with holiday money ... and there were you and Chris Smith on these two horses, and the public fancying both of them, and Pelican Jobberson asked you which was off, and you said you hadn't an earthly on yours, so he rakes in the cash on you and doesn't bother to balance his book, and then you go and ride a hell of a finish and win by a neck, when you

71

could have lost instead without the slightest trouble. Pelican went spare and swore he'd be even with you when he got the chance.'

'I believed what I told him,' I said. 'It was that horse's first attempt over fences. No one could have predicted he'd have been good enough to win.'

'Then why did you?'

'The owner wanted to, if possible.'

'Did he bet on it?'

'The owner? No. It was a woman. She never bets much. She just likes to see her horses win.'

'Pelican swore you'd backed it yourself, and put him off so that you could get a better price.'

'You bookmakers are too suspicious for your own good.'

'Hard experience proves us right.'

'Well, he's wrong this time,' I insisted. 'This bird friend of yours. If he asked me ... and I don't remember him asking ... then I told him the truth. And anyway, any bookmaker who asks jockeys questions like that is asking for trouble. Jockeys are the worst tipsters in the world.'

'Some aren't,' he said flatly. 'Some are good at it.'

I skipped that. 'Is he still angry after all these months? And if so, would he be angry enough not just to tell the Stewards that Cranfield backed Cherry Pie, but to bribe other people to invent lies about us?'

His eyes narrowed while he thought about it. He pursed his mouth, undecided. 'You'd better ask him yourself.'

'Thanks.' Hardly an easy question.

'Move your car now?' he suggested.

'Yes.' I walked two steps towards it, then stopped and turned back. 'Mr Newtonnards, if you see the man who put the money on for Mr Cranfield, will you find out who he is ... and let me know?'

'Why don't you ask Cranfield?'

'He said he didn't want to involve him.'

'But you do?'

'I suppose I'm grasping at anything,' I said. 'But yes, I think I do.'

'Why don't you just quieten down and take it?' he said

reasonably. 'All this thrashing about . . . you got copped. So, you got copped. Fair enough. Sit it out, then. You'll get your licence back, eventually.'

'Thank you for your advice,' I said politely, and went and moved my car out of his gateway.

It was Thursday. I should have been going to Warwick to ride in four races. Instead, I drove aimlessly back round the North Circular Road wondering whether or not to pay a call on David Oakley, enquiry agent and imaginative photographer. If Charlie West didn't know who had framed me, it seemed possible that Oakley might be the only one who did. But even if he did, he was highly unlikely to tell me. There seemed no point in confronting him, and yet nothing could be gained if I made no attempt.

In the end I stopped at a telephone box and found his number via enquiries.

A girl answered. 'Mr Oakley isn't in yet.'

'Can I make an appointment?'

She asked me what about.

'A divorce.'

She said Mr Oakley could see me at 11.30, and asked me my name.'

'Charles Crisp.'

'Very well, Mr Crisp. Mr Oakley will be expecting you.'

I doubted it. On the other hand, he, like Charlie West, might in general be expecting some form of protest.

From the North Circular Road I drove ninety miles up the M1 Motorway to Birmingham and found Oakley's office above a bicycle and radio shop half a mile from the town centre.

His street door, shabby black, bore a neat small name-plate stating, simply, 'Oakley'. There were two keyholes, Yale and Chubb, and a discreetly situated peephole. I tried the handle of this apparent fortress, and the door opened easily under my touch. Inside, there was a narrow passage with pale blue walls leading to an uncarpeted staircase stretching upwards.

I walked up, my feet sounding loud on the boards. At the top there was a small landing with another shabby black door, again and similarly fortified. On this door, another neat notice said, 'Please ring'. There was a bell push I gave it three seconds' work.

The door was opened by a tall strong-looking girl dressed in a dark coloured leather trouser-suit. Under the jacket she wore a black sweater, and under the trouser legs, black leather boots. Black eyes returned my scrutiny, black hair held back by a tortoiseshell band fell straight to her shoulders before curving inwards. She seemed at first sight to be about twenty-four, but there were already wrinkle lines round her eyes, and the deadness in their expression indicated too much familiarity with dirty washing.

'I have an appointment,' I said. 'Crisp.'

'Come in.' She opened the door wider and left it for me to close.

I followed her into the room, a small square office furnished with a desk, typewriter, telephone, and four tall filing cabinets. On the far side of the room there was another door. Not black; modern flat hardboard, painted grey. More keyholes. I eyed them thoughtfully.

The girl opened the door, said through it, 'It's Mr Crisp,' and stood back for me to pass her.

'Thank you,' I said. Took three steps forwards, and shut myself in with David Oakley.

His office was not a great deal larger than the anteroom, and no thrift had been spared with the furniture. There was dim brown linoleum, a bentwood coat stand, a small cheap armchair facing a grey metal desk, and over the grimy window, in place of curtains, a tough-looking fixed frame covered with chicken wire. Outside the window there were the heavy bars and supports of a fire escape. The Birmingham sun, doing its best against odds, struggled through and fell in wrinkled honeycomb shadows on the surface of an ancient safe. In the wall on my right, another door, firmly closed. With yet more keyholes.

Behind the desk in a swivel chair sat the proprietor of all this glory, the totally unmemorable Mr Oakley. Youngish.

74

Slender. Mouse-coloured hair. And this time, sunglasses.

'Sit down, Mr Crisp,' he said. Accentless voice, entirely emotionless, as before. 'Divorce, I believe? Give me the details of your requirements, and we can arrive at a fee.' He looked at his watch. 'I can give you just ten minutes, I'm afraid. Shall we get on?'

He hadn't recognized me. I thought I might as well take advantage of it.

'I understand you would be prepared to fake some evidence for me . . . photographs?'

He began to nod, and then grew exceptionally still. The unrevealing dark glasses were motionless. The pale straight mouth didn't twitch. The hand lying on the desk remained loose and relaxed.

Finally he said, without any change of inflection, 'Get out.'

'How much do you charge for faking evidence?'

'Get out.'

I smiled. 'I'd like to know how much I was worth.'

'Dust,' he said. His foot moved under the desk.

'I'll pay you in gold dust, if you'll tell me who gave you the job.'

He considered it. Then he said, 'No.'

The door to the outer office opened quietly behind me.

Oakley said calmly, 'this is not a Mr Crisp, Didi. This is a Mr Kelly Hughes. Mr Hughes will be leaving.'

'Mr Hughes is not ready,' I said.

'I think Mr Hughes will find he is,' she said.

I looked at her over my shoulder. She was carrying a large black-looking pistol with a very large black-looking silencer. The whole works were pointing steadily my way.

'How dramatic,' I said. 'Can you readily dispose of bodies in the centre of Birmingham?'

'Yes,' Oakley said.

'For a fee, of course, usually,' Didi added.

I struggled not to believe them, and lost. All the same . . .

'Should you decide after all to sell the information I need, you know where to find me.' I relaxed against the back of the chair.

'I may have a liking for gold dust,' he said calmly. 'But I am not a fool.'

'Opinions differ,' I remarked lightly.

There was no reaction. 'It is not in my interest that you should prove you were ... shall we say ... set up.'

'I understand that. Eventually, however, you will wish that you hadn't helped to do it.'

He said smoothly, 'A number of other people have said much the same, though few, I must confess, as quietly as you.'

It occurred to me suddenly that he must be quite used to the sort of enraged onslaught I'd thrown at the Wests, and that perhaps that was why his office ... Didi caught my wandering glance and cynically nodded.

'That's right. Too many people tried to smash the place up. So we keep the damage to a minimum.'

'How wise.'

'I'm afraid I really do have another appointment now,' Oakley said. 'So if you'll excuse me? ...'

I stood up. There was nothing to stay for.

'It surprises me,' I remarked, 'that you're not in jail.'

'I am clever,' he said matter-of-factly. 'My clients are satisfied, and people like you, ... impotent.'

'Someone will kill you, one day.'

'Will you?'

I shook my head. 'Not worth it.'

'Exactly,' he said calmly. 'The jobs I accept are never what the victims would actually kill me for. I really am not a fool.'

'No,' I said.

I walked across to the door and Didi made room for me to pass. She put the pistol down on her desk in the outer office and switched off a red bulb which glowed brightly in a small switchboard.

'Emergency signal?' I enquired. 'Under his desk.'

'You could say so.'

'Is that gun loaded?'

Her eyebrows rose. 'Naturally.'

'I see.' I opened the outer door. She walked over to close it behind me as I went towards the stairs.

'Nice to have met you, Mr Hughes,' she said unemotionally. 'Don't come back.'

I walked along to my car in some depression. From none of the three damaging witnesses at the Enquiry had I got any change at all, and what David Oakley had said about me being impotent looked all too true.

There seemed to be no way of proving that he had simply brought with him the money he had photographed in my flat. No one at Corrie had seen him come or go: Tony had asked all the lads, and none of them had seen him. And Oakley would have found it easy enough to be unobserved. He had only had to arrive early, while everyone was out riding on the Downs at morning exercise. From seven-thirty to eight-thirty the stable yard would be deserted. Letting himself in through my unlocked door, setting up his props, loosing off a flash or two, and quietly retreating ... The whole process would have taken him no more than ten minutes.

It was possible he had kept a record of his shady transactions. Possible, not probable. He might need to keep some hold over his clients, to prevent their later denouncing him in fits of resurgent civil conscience. If he did keep such records, it might account for the multiplicity of locks. Or maybe the locks were simply to discourage people from breaking in to search for records, as they were certainly discouraging me.

Would Oakley, I wondered, have done what Charlie West had done, and produced his lying testimony for a voice on the telephone? On the whole, I decided not. Oakley had brains where Charlie had vanity, and Oakley would not involve himself without his clients up tight too. Oakley had to know who had done the engineering.

But stealing that information ... or beating it out of him ... or tricking him into giving it ... as well as buying it from him ... every course looked as hopeless as the next. I could only ride horses. I couldn't pick locks, fights, or pockets. Certainly not Oakley's.

Oakley and Didi. They were old at the game. They'd invented the rules. Oakley and Didi were senior league.

How did anyone get in touch with Oakley, if they needed his brand of service?

He could scarcely advertise.

Someone had to know about him.

I thought it over for a while, sitting in my car in the car park wondering what to do next. There was only one person I knew who could put his finger on the pulse of Birmingham if he wanted to, and the likelihood was that in my present circumstances he wouldn't want to.

However...

I started the car, threaded away through the one-way streets, and found a slot in the crowded park behind the Great Stag Hotel. Inside, the ritual of Business Lunch was warming up, the atmosphere thickening nicely with the smell of alcohol, the resonance of fruity voices, the haze of cigars. The Great Stag Hotel attracted almost exclusively a certain grade of wary, prosperous, level-headed business-men needing a soft background for hard options, and it attracted them because the landlord, Teddy Dewar, was the sort of man himself.

I found him in the bar, talking to two others almost indistinguishable from him in their dark grey suits, white shirts, neat maroon ties, seventeen-inch necks, and thirty-eight-inch waists.

A faint glaze came over his professionally noncommittal expression when he caught sight of me over their shoulders. A warned-off jockey didn't rate too high with him. Lowered the tone of the place, no doubt.

I edged through to the bar on one side of him and ordered whisky.

'I'd be grateful for a word with you,' I said.

He turned his head a fraction in my direction, and without looking at me directly answered. 'Very well. In a few minutes.'

No warmth in the words. No ducking of the unwelcome situation, either. He went on talking to the two men about the dicky state of oil shares, and eventually smoothly disengaged himself and turned to me.

'Well, Kelly . . .' His eyes were cool and distant, waiting to see what I wanted before showing any real feeling.

'Will you lunch with me?' I made it casual.

His surprise was controlled. 'I thought . . .'

'I may be banned,' I said, 'but I still eat.'

He studied my face. 'You mind.'

'What do you expect . . .? I'm sorry it shows.'

He said neutrally, 'There's a muscle in your jaw . . . Very well: if you don't mind going in straight-away.'

We sat against the wall at an inconspicuous table and chose beef cut from a roast on a trolley. While he ate his eyes checked the running of the dining-room, missing nothing. I waited until he was satisfied that all was well and then came briefly to the point.

'Do you know anything about a man called David Oakley? He's an enquiry agent. Operates from an office about half a mile from here.'

'David Oakley? I can't say I've ever heard of him.'

'He manufactured some evidence which swung things against me at the Stewards' Enquiry on Monday.'

'Manufactured?' There was delicate doubt in his voice.

'Oh yes,' I sighed. 'I suppose it sounds corny, but I really was not guilty as charged. But someone made sure it looked like it.' I told him about the photograph of money in my bedroom.

'And you never had this money?'

'I did not. And the note supposed to be from Cranfield was a forgery. But how could we prove it?'

He thought it over.

'You can't.'

'Exactly,' I agreed.

'This David Oakley who took the photograph . . . I suppose you got no joy from him.'

'No joy is right.'

'I don't understand precisely why you've come to me.' He finished his beef and laid his knife and fork tidily together. Waiters appeard like genii to clear the table and bring coffee. He waited still noncommittally while I paid the bill.

'I expect it is too much to ask,' I said finally. 'After all, I've only stayed here three or four times, I have no claim on you personally for friendship or help ... and yet, there's no one else I know who could even begin to do what you could ... if you will.'

'What?' he said succinctly.

'I want to know how people are steered towards David Oakley, if they want some evidence faked. He as good as told me he is quite accustomed to do it. Well ... how does he get his clients? Who recommends him? I thought that among all the people you know, you might think of someone who could perhaps pretend he wanted a job done ... or pretend he had a friend who wanted a job done ... and throw out feelers, and see if anyone finally recommended Oakley. And if so, who.'

He considered it. 'Because if you found one contact you might work back from there to another ... and eventually perhaps to a name which meant something to you? ...'

'I suppose it sounds feeble,' I said resignedly.

'It's a very outside chance,' he agreed. There was a long pause. Then he added, 'All the same, I do know of someone who might agree to try.' He smiled briefly, for the first time.

'That's ...' I swallowed. 'That's marvellous.'

'Can't promise results.'

CHAPTER SEVEN

Tony came clomping up my stairs on Friday morning after first exercise and poured half an inch of Scotch into the coffee I gave him. He drank the scalding mixture and shuddered as the liquor bit.

'God,' he said. 'It's cold on the Downs.'

'Rather you than me,' I said.

'Liar,' he said amicably. 'It must feel odd to you, not riding.'

'Yes.'

He sprawled in the green armchair. 'Poppy's got the morning ickies again. I'll be glad when this lousy pregnancy is over. She's been ill half the time.'

'Poor Poppy.'

'Yeah ... Anyway, what it means is that we ain't going to that dance tonight. She says she can't face it.'

'Dance? ...'

'The Jockey's Fund dance. You know. You've got the tickets on your mantel over there.'

'Oh ... yes. I'd forgotten about it. We were going together.'

'That's right. But now, as I was saying, you'll have to go without us.'

'I'm not going at all.'

'I thought you might not.' He sighed and drank deeply. 'Where did you get to yesterday?'

'I called on people who didn't want to see me.'

'Any results?'

'Not many.' I told him briefly about Newtonnards and David Oakley, and about the hour I'd spent with Andrew Tring.

It was because the road home from Birmingham led near his village that I'd thought of Andrew Tring, and my first instinct anyway was to shy away from even the thought of him. Certainly visiting one of the Stewards who had helped to warn him off was not regulation behaviour for a disbarred jockey. If I hadn't been fairly strongly annoyed with him I would have driven straight on.

He was disgusted with me for calling. He opened the door of his prosperous sprawling old manor house himself and had no chance of saying he was out.

'Kelly! What are you doing here?'

'Asking you for some explanation.'

'I've nothing to say to you.'

'You have indeed.'

He frowned. Natural good manners were only just preventing him from retreating and shutting the door in my face. 'Come in then. Just for a few minutes.'

'Thank you,' I said without irony, and followed him into a nearby small room lined with books and containing a vast desk, three deep armchairs and a colour television set.

'Now,' he said, shutting the door and not offering the armchairs, 'why have you come?'

He was four years older than me, and about the same size. Still as trim as when he rode races, still outwardly the same man. Only the casual, long-established changing-room friendliness seemed to have withered somewhere along the upward path from amateurship to Authority.

'Andy,' I said, 'do you really and honestly believe that that Squelch race was rigged?'

'You were warned off,' he said coldly.

'That's far from being the same thing as guilty.'

'I don't agree.'

'Then you're stupid,' I said bluntly. 'As well as scared out of your tiny wits.'

'That's enough, Kelly. I don't have to listen to this.' He opened the door again and waited for me to leave. I didn't. Short of throwing me out bodily he was going to have to put up with me a little longer. He gave me a furious stare and shut the door again.

I said more reasonably, 'I'm sorry, Really, I'm sorry. It's just that you rode against me for at least five years ... I'd have thought you wouldn't so easily believe I'd deliberately lose a race. I've never yet lost a race I could win.'

He was silent. He knew that I didn't throw races. Anyone who rode regularly knew who would and who wouldn't, and in spite of what Charlie West had said at the Enquiry, I was not an artist at stopping one because I hadn't given it the practice.

'There was that money,' he said at last. He sounded disillusioned and discouraged.

'I never had it. Oakley took it with him into my flat and photographed it there. All that so-called evidence, the whole bloody Enquiry in fact, was as genuine as a lead sixpence.'

He gave me a long doubtful look. Then he said, 'There's nothing I can do about it.'

'What are you afraid of?'

'Stop saying I'm afraid,' he said irritably. 'I'm not afraid. I just can't do anything about it, even if what you say is true.'

'It is true ... and maybe you don't think you are afraid, but that's definitely the impression you give. Or maybe ... are you simply overawed? The new boy among the old powerful prefects. Is that it? Afraid of putting a foot wrong with them?'

'Kelly!' he protested; but it was the protest of a touched nerve.

I said unkindly, 'You're a gutless disappointment,' and took a step towards his door. He didn't move to open it for me. Instead he put up a hand to stop me, looking as angry as he had every right to.

'That's not fair. Just because I can't help you ...'

'You could have done. At the Enquiry.'

'You don't understand.'

'I do indeed. You found it easier to believe me guilty than to tell Gowery you had any doubts.'

'It wasn't as easy as you think.'

'Thanks,' I said ironically.

'I don't mean ...' he shook his head impatiently. 'I mean, it wasn't all as simple as you make out. When Gowery asked me to sit with him at the Enquiry I believed it was only going to be a formality, that both you and Cranfield had run the Lemonfizz genuinely and were surprised yourselves by the result. Colonel Midgley told me it was ridiculous having to hold the Enquiry at all, really. I never expected to be caught up in having to warn you off.'

'Did you say,' I said, 'that Lord Gowery asked you to sit with him?'

'Of course. That's the normal procedure. The Stewards sitting at an Enquiry aren't picked out of a hat ...'

'There isn't any sort of rota?'

'No. The Disciplinary Steward asks two colleagues to officiate with him ... and that's what put me on the spot, if you must know, because I didn't want to say no to Lord Gowery...' He stopped.

'Go on,' I urged without heat. 'Why not?'

'Well because...' He hesitated, then said slowly, 'I suppose in a way I owe it to you ... I'm sorry Kelly, desperately sorry, I do know you don't usually rig races ... I'm in an odd position with Gowery and it's vitally important I keep in with him.'

I stifled my indignation. Andrew Tring's eyes were looking inward and from his expression he didn't very much like what he could see.

'He owns the freehold of the land just north of Manchester where our main pottery is.' Andrew Tring's family fortunes were based not on fine porcelain but on smashable teacups for institutions. His products were dropped by washers-up in schools and hospitals from Waterloo to Hong Kong, and the pieces in the world's dustbins were his perennial licence to print money.

He said, 'There's been some redevelopment round there and that land is suddenly worth about a quarter of a million. And our lease runs out in three years ... We have been negotiating a new one, but the old one was for ninety-nine years and no one is keen to renew for that long ... The ground rent is in any case going to be raised considerably, but if Gowery changes his mind and wants to sell that land for development, there's nothing we can do about it. We only own the buildings ... We'd lose the entire factory if he didn't renew the lease ... And we can only make cups and saucers so cheaply because our overheads are small ... If we have to build or rent a new factory our prices will be less competitive and our world trade figures will slump. Gowery himself has the final say as to whether our lease will be renewed or not, and on what terms ... so you see, Kelly, it's not that I'm afraid of him ... there's so much more at stake ... and he's always a man to hold it against you if you argue with him.'

He stopped and looked at me gloomily. I looked gloomily back. The facts of life stared us stonily in the face.

'So that's that,' I agreed. 'You are quite right. You can't

help me. You couldn't, right from the start. I'm glad you explained . . .' I smiled at him twistedly, facing another dead end, the last of a profitless day.

'I'm sorry, Kelly . . .'

'Sure,' I said.

Tony finished his fortified breakfast and said, 'So there wasn't anything sinister in Andy Tring's lily-livered bit on Monday.'

'It depends what you call sinister. But no, I suppose not.'

'What's left, then?'

'Damn all. I said in depression.

'You can't give up, he protested.

'Oh no. But I've learned one thing in learning nothing, and that is that I'm getting nowhere because I'm me. First thing Monday morning I'm going to hire me my own David Oakley.'

'Attaboy,' he said. He stood up. 'Time for second lot, I hear.' Down in the yard the lads were bringing out the horses, their hooves scrunching hollowly on the packed gravel.

'How are they doing?' I asked.

'Oh . . . so so. I sure hate having to put up other jocks. Given me a bellyful of the whole game, this business has.'

When he'd gone down to ride I cleaned up my already clean flat and made some more coffee. The day stretched emptily ahead. So did the next day and the one after that, and every day for an indefinite age.

Ten minutes of this prospect was enough. I searched around and found another straw to cling to: telephoned to a man I knew slightly at the BBC. A cool secretary said he was out, and to try again at eleven.

I tried again at eleven. Still out. I tried at twelve. He was in then, but sounded as if he wished he weren't.

'Not Kelly Hughes, the . . .' His voice trailed off while he failed to find a tactful way of putting it.

'That's right.'

'Well . . . er . . . I don't think . . .'

'I don't want anything much,' I assured him resignedly. 'I just want to know the name of the outfit who make the films of races. The camera patrol people.'

'Oh.' He sounded relieved. 'That's the Racecourse Technical Services. Run by the Levy Board. They've a virtual monopoly, though there's one other small firm operating sometimes under licence. Then there are the television companies, of course. Did you want any particular race? Oh . . . the Lemonfizz Crystal Cup, I suppose.'

'No,' I said. 'The meeting at Reading two weeks earlier.'

'Reading . . . Reading . . . Let's see, then. Which lot would that be?' He hummed a few out-of-tune bars while he thought it over. 'I should think . . . yes, definitely the small firm, the Cannot Lie people. Cannot Lie, Ltd. Offices at Woking, Surrey. Do you want their number?'

'Yes please.'

He read it to me.

'Thank you very much,' I said.

'Any time . . . er . . . well . . . I mean . . .'

'I know what you mean,' I agreed. 'But thanks anyway.'

I put down the receiver with a grimace. It was still no fun being everyone's idea of a villain.

The BBC man's reaction made me decide that the telephone might get me nil results from the Cannot Lie brigade. Maybe they couldn't lie, but they would certainly evade. And anyway, I had the whole day to waste.

The Cannot Lie office was a rung or two up the luxury ladder from David Oakley's, which wasn't saying a great deal. A large rather bare room on the second floor of an Edwardian house in a side street. A rickety lift large enough for one slim man or two starving children. A well-worn desk with a well-worn blonde painting her toenails on top of it.

'Yes?' she said, when I walked in.

She had lilac panties on, with lace. She made no move to prevent me seeing a lot of them.

'No one in?' I asked.

'Only us chickens,' she agreed. She had a South London accent and the smart back-chatting intelligence that often

86

goes with it. 'Which do you want, the old man or our Alfie?'

'You'll do nicely,' I said.

'Ta.' She took it as her due, with a practised come-on-so-far-but-no-further smile. One foot was finished. She stretched out her leg and wiggled it up and down to help with the drying.

'Going to a dance tonight,' she explained. 'In me peep-toes.'

I didn't think anyone would concentrate on the toes. Apart from the legs she had a sharp pointed little bosom under a white cotton sweater and a bright pink patent leather belt clasping a bikini-sized waist. Her body looked about twenty years old. Her face looked as if she'd spent the last six of them hopping.

'Paint the other one,' I suggested.

'You're not in a hurrry?'

'I'm enjoying the scenery.'

She gave a knowing giggle and started on the other foot. The view was even more hair-raising than before. She watched me watching, and enjoyed it.

'What's your name?' I asked.

'Carol. What's yours?'

'Kelly.'

'From the Isle of Man?'

'No. The land of our fathers.'

She gave me a bright glance. 'You catch on quick, don't you?'

I wished I did. I said regretfully, 'How long do you keep ordinary routine race films?'

'Huh? For ever, I suppose.' She changed mental gear effortlessly, carrying straight on with her uninhibited painting. 'We haven't destroyed any so far, that's to say. 'Course, we've only been in the racing business eighteen months. No telling what they'll do when the big storeroom's full. We're up to the eyebrows in all the others with films of motor races, golf matches, three-day events, any old things like that.'

'Where's the big storeroom?'

'Through there.' She waved the small pink enamelling brush in the general direction of a scratched once-cream door. 'Want to see?'

'If you don't mind.'

'Go right ahead.'

She had finished the second foot. The show was over. With a sigh I removed my gaze and walked over to the door in question. There was only a round hole where most doors have a handle. I pushed against the wood and the door swung inwards into another large high room, furnished this time with rows of free standing bookshelves, like a public library. The shelves, however, were of bare functional wood, and there was no covering on the planked floor.

Well over half the shelves were empty. On the others were rows of short wide box files, their backs labelled with neat typed strips explaining what was to be found within. Each box proved to contain all the films from one day's racing, and they were all efficiently arranged in chronological order. I pulled out the box for the day I rode Squelch and Wanderlust at Reading, and looked inside. There were six round cans of sixteen-millimetre film, numbered one to six, and space enough for another one, number seven.

I took the box out to Carol. She was still sitting on top of the desk, dangling the drying toes and reading through a woman's magazine.

'What have you found then?'

'Do you lend these films to anyone who wants them?'

'Hire, not lend. Sure.'

'Who to?'

'Anyone who asks. Usually it's the owners of the horses. Often they want prints made to keep, so we make them.'

'Do the Stewards often want them?'

'Stewards? Well, see, if there's any doubt about a race the Stewards see the film on the racecourse. That van the old man and our Alfie's got develops it on the spot as soon as it's collected from the cameras.'

'But sometimes they send for them afterwards?'

'Sometimes, yeah. When they want to compare the running of some horse or other.' Her legs suddenly stopped swinging. She put down the magazine and gave me a straight stare.

'Kelly ... Kelly *Hughes*?'

I didn't answer.

'Hey, you're not a bit like I thought.' She put her blonde head on one side, assessing me. 'None of those sports writers ever said anything about you being smashing looking and dead sexy.'

I laughed. I had a crooked nose and a scar down one cheek from where a horse's hoof had cut my face open, and among jockeys I was an also-ran as a bird-attracter.

'It's your eyes,' she said. 'Dark and sort of smiley and sad and a bit withdrawn. Give me the happy shivers, your eyes do.'

'You read all that in a magazine,' I said.

'I never!' but she laughed.

'Who asked for the film that's missing from the box?' I said. 'And what exactly did they ask for?'

She sighed exaggeratedly and edged herself off the desk into a pair of bright pink sandals.

'Which film is that?' She looked at the box and its reference number, and did a Marilyn Monroe sway over to a filing cabinet against the wall. 'Here we are. One official letter from the Stewards' secretary saying please send film of last race at Reading ...'

I took the letter from her and read it myself. The words were quite clear: 'the last race at Reading'. Not the sixth race. The last race. And there had been seven races. It hadn't been Carol or the Cannot Lie Co who had made the mistake.

'So you sent it?'

'Of course. Off to the authorities, as per instructions.' She put the letter back in the files. 'Did you in, did it?'

'Not that film, no.'

'Alfie and the old man say you must have made a packet out of the Lemonfizz, to lose your licence over it.'

'Do you think so too?'

'Stands to reason. Everyone thinks so.'

'Man in the street?'

'Him too.'

'Not a cent.'

'You're a nit, then,' she said frankly. 'Whatever did you do it for?'

'I didn't.'

'Oh yeah?' She gave me a knowing wink. 'I suppose you have to say that, don't you?'

'Well,' I said, handing her the Reading box to put back in the storeroom. 'Thanks anyway.' I gave her half a smile and went away across the expanse of mottled linoleum to the door out.

I drove home slowly, trying to think. Not a very profitable exercise. Brains seemed to have deteriorated into a mushy blankness.

There were several letters for me in the mailbox on my front door, including one from my parents. I unfolded it walking up the stairs, feeling as usual a million miles away from them on every level.

My mother had written the first half in her round regular handwriting on one side of a large piece of lined paper. As usual there wasn't a full stop to be seen. She punctuated entirely with commas.

Dear Kelly,

Thanks for your note, we got it yesterday, we don't like reading about you in the papers, I know you said you hadn't done it, son, but no smoke without fire is what Mrs Jones the post office says, and it is not nice for us what people are saying about you round here, all the airs and graces they say you are and pride goes before a fall and all that, well the pullets have started laying at last, we are painting your old room for Auntie Myfanwy who is coming to live here her arthritis is too bad for those stairs she has, well Kelly, I wish I could say we want you to come home but your Da is that angry and now Auntie Myfanwy needs the room anyway, well son, we never wanted you to go for a jockey, there was that nice job at the Townhall in Tenby you could have had, I don't like to say it but you have disgraced us, son, there's horrid it is going into the village now, everyone whispering, your loving Mother.

I took a deep breath and turned the page over to receive the blast from my father. His writing was much like my mother's as they had learned from the same teacher, but he had pressed so hard with his ballpoint that he had almost dug through the paper.

Kelly,

You're a damned disgrace boy. It's soft saying you didn't do it. They wouldn't of warned you off if you didn't do it. Not lords and such. They know what's right. You're lucky you're not here I would give you a proper belting. After all that scrimping your Ma did to let you go off to the University. And people said you would get too ladidah to speak to us, they were right. Still, this is worse, being a cheat. Don't you come back here, your Ma's that upset, what with that cat Mrs Jones saying things. It would be best to say don't send us any more money into the bank. I asked the manager but he said only you can cancel a banker's order so you'd better do it. Your Ma says it's as bad as you being in prison, the disgrace and all.

He hadn't signed it. He wouldn't know how to, we had so little affection for each other. He had despised me from childhood for my liking school, and had mocked me unmercifully all the way to college. He showed his jolly side only to my two older brothers, who had had what he considered a healthy contempt for education: one of them had gone into the Merchant Navy and the other lived next door and worked alongside my father for the farmer who owned the cottages.

When in the end I had turned my back on all the years of learning and taken to racing my family had again all disapproved of me, though I guessed they would have been pleased enough if I'd chosen it all along. I'd wasted the country's money, my father said; I wouldn't have been given all those grants if they'd known that as soon as I was out I'd go racing. That was probably true. It was also true that since I'd been racing I'd paid enough in taxes to send several other farm boys through college on grants.

I put my parents' letter under Rosalind's photograph. Even she had been unable to reach their approval, because they thought I should have married a nice girl from my own sort of background, not the student daughter of a colonel.

They had rigid minds. It was doubtful now if they would ever be pleased with me, whatever I did. And if I got my licence back, as like as not they would think I had somehow cheated again.

You couldn't take aspirins for that sort of pain. It stayed there, sticking in knives. Trying to escape it I went into the kitchen, to see if there was anything to eat. A tin of sardines, one egg, the dried-up remains of some port salut.

Wrinkling my nose at that lot I transferred to the sitting-room and looked at the television programmes.

Nothing I wanted to see.

I slouched in the green velvet armchair and watched the evening slowly fade the colours into subtle greys. A certain amount of pace edged its way past the dragging gloom of the last four days. I wondered almost academically whether I would get my licence back before or after I stopped wincing at the way people looked at me, or spoke to me, or wrote about me. Probably the easiest course would be to stay out of sight, hiding myself away.

Like I was hiding away at that minute, by not going to the Jockeys' Fund dance.

The tickets were on the mantel. Tickets for Tony and Poppy, and for me and the partner I hadn't got around to inviting. Tickets which were not going to be used, which I had paid twelve fund-raising guineas for.

I sat in the dark for half an hour thinking about the people who would be at the Jockeys' Fund dance.

Then I put on my black tie and went to it.

CHAPTER EIGHT

I went prepared to be stared at.

I was stared at.

Also pointed out and commented on. Discreetly, however, for the most part. And only two people decisively turned their backs.

The Jockeys' Fund dance glittered as usual with titles, diamonds, champagne, and talent. Later it might curl round the edges into spilled drinks, glassy eyes, raddled make-up, and slurring voices, but the gloss wouldn't entirely disappear. It never did. The Jockeys' Fund dance was one of the great social events of the steeplechasing year.

I handed over my ticket and walked along the wide passage to where the lights were low, the music hot, and the air thick with smoke and scent. The opulent ballroom of the Royal Country Hotel, along the road from Ascot racecourse.

Around the dancing area there were numbers of large circular tables with chairs for ten or twelve round each, most of them occupied already. According to the chart in the hall, at table number thirty-two I would find the places reserved for Tony and me, if in fact they were still reserved. I gave up looking for table thirty-two less than halfway down the room because whenever I moved a new battery of curious eyes swivelled my way. A lot of people raised a hello but none of them could hide their slightly shocked surprise. It was every bit as bad as I'd feared.

A voice behind me said incredulously, 'Hughes!'

I knew the voice. I turned round with an equal sense of the unexpected. Roberta Cranfield. Wearing a honey-coloured silk dress with the top smothered in pearls and gold thread and her copper hair drawn high with a trickle of ringlets down the back of her neck.

'You look beautiful,' I said.

Her mouth opened. 'Hughes!'

'Is your father here?'

93

'No,' she said disgustedly. 'He wouldn't face it. Nor would Mother. I came with a party of neighbours but I can't say I was enjoying it much until you turned up.'

'Why not?'

'You must be joking. Just look around. At a rough guess fifty people are rubber-necking at you. Doesn't it make you cringe inside? Anyway, I've had quite enough of it myself this evening, and I didn't even *see* the damned race, let alone get myself warned off.' She stopped. 'Come and dance with me. If we're hoisting the flag we may as well do it thoroughly.'

'On one condition,' I said.

'What's that?'

'You stop calling me Hughes.'

'What?'

'Cranfield, I'm tired of being called Hughes.'

'Oh!' It had obviously never occurred to her. 'Then . . . Kelly . . . how about dancing?'

'Enchanted, Roberta.'

She gave me an uncertain look. 'I still feel I don't know you.'

'You never bothered.'

'Nor have you.'

That jolted me. It was true. I'd disliked the idea of her. And I didn't really know her at all.

'How do you do?' I said politely. 'Come and dance.'

We shuffled around in one of those affairs which look like formalized jungle rituals, swaying in rhythm but never touching. Her face was quite calm, remotely smiling. From her composure one would have guessed her to be entirely at ease, not the target of turned heads, assessing glances, half-hidden whispers.

'I don't know how you do it,' she said.

'Do what?'

'Look so . . . so matter of fact.'

'I was thinking exactly the same about you.'

She smiled, eyes crinkling and teeth gleaming, and incredibly in the circumstances she looked happy.

We stuck it for a good ten minutes. Then she said we

94

would go back to her table, and made straight off to it without waiting for me to agree. I didn't think her party would be pleased to have me join them, and half of them weren't.

'Sit down and have a drink, my dear fellow,' drawled her host, reaching for a champagne bottle with a languid hand. 'And tell me all about the bring-back-Cranfield campaign. Roberta tells me you are working on a spot of reinstatement.'

'I haven't managed it yet,' I said deprecatingly.

'My dear chap . . .' He gave me an inspecting stare down his nose. He'd been in the Guards, I thought. So many ex-Guards' officers looked at the world down the sides of their noses: it came of wearing those blinding hats. He was blond, in his forties, not unfriendly. Roberta called him Bobbie.

The woman the other side of him leaned over and drooped a heavy pink satin bosom perilously near her brimming glass.

'Do tell me,' she said, giving me a thorough gaze from heavily made-up eyes, 'what made you come?'

'Natural cussedness,' I said pleasantly.

'Oh.' She looked taken aback. 'How extraordinary.'

'Joined to the fact that there was no reason why I shouldn't.'

'And are you enjoying it?' Bobbie said. 'I mean to say, my dear chap, you are somewhat in the position of a rather messily struck-off doctor turning up four days later at the British Medical Association's grandest function.'

I smiled. 'Quite a parallel.'

'Don't needle him Bobbie,' Roberta protested.

Bobbie removed his stare from me and gave it to her instead. 'My dear Roberta, this cookie needs no little girls rushing to his defence. He's as tough as old oak.'

A disapproving elderly man on the far side of the pink bosom said under his breath. 'Thick skinned, you mean.'

Bobbie heard, and shook his head. 'Vertebral,' he said. 'Different altogether.' He stood up. 'Roberta, my dear girl, would you care to dance?'

I stood up with him.

'No need to go, my dear chap. Stay. Finish your drink.'

'You are most kind,' I said truthfully. 'But I really came tonight to have a word with one or two people ... If you'll excuse me, I'll try to find them.'

He gave me an odd formal little inclination of the head, halfway to a bow. 'Come back later, if you'd care to.'

'Thank you,' I said, 'very much.'

He took Roberta away to dance and I went up the stairs to the balcony which encircled the room. There were tables all round up there too, but in places one could get a good clear view of most people below. I spent some length of time identifying them from the tops of their heads.

There must have been about six hundred there, of whom I knew personally about a quarter. Owners, trainers, jockeys, Stewards, pressmen, two or three of the bigger bookmakers, starters, judges, Clerks of Courses, and all the others, all with their wives and friends and chattering guests.

Kessel was there, hosting a party of twelve almost exactly beneath where I stood. I wondered if his anger had cooled since Monday, and decided if possible not to put it to the test. He had reputedly sent Squelch off to Pat Nikita, a trainer who was a bitter rival of Cranfield's, which had been rubbing it in a bit. The report looked likely to be true, as Pat Nikita was among the party below me.

Cranfield and Nikita regularly claimed each other's horses in selling races and were apt to bid each other up spitefully at auctions. It was a public joke. So in choosing Nikita as his trainer, Kessel was unmistakably announcing worldwise that he believed Cranfield and I had stopped his horse. Hardly likely to help convince that we hadn't.

At one of the most prominent tables, near the dancing space, sat Lord Ferth, talking earnestly to a large lady in pale blue ostrich feathers. All the other chairs round the table were askew and unoccupied, but while I watched the music changed to a latin rhythm, and most of the party drifted back. I knew one or two of them slightly, but not well. The man I was chiefly looking for was not among them.

Two tables away from Lord Ferth sat Edwin Byler,

gravely beckoning to the waiter to fill his guests' glasses, too proud of his home-made wealth to lift the bottle himself. His cuddly little wife on the far side of the table was loaded with half the stock of Hatton Garden and was rather touchingly revelling in it.

Not to be going to ride Edwin Byler's string of super horses ... The wry thrust of regret went deeper than I liked.

There was a rustle behind me and the smell of Roberta's fresh flower scent. I turned towards her.

'Kelly? ...'

She really looked extraordinarily beautiful.

'Kelly ... Bobbie suggested that you should take me in to supper.'

'That's generous of him.'

'He seems to approve of you. He said ...' She stopped abruptly. 'Well, never mind what he said.'

We went down the stairs and through an archway to the supper room. The light there was of a heartier wattage. It didn't do any damage to Roberta.

Along one wall stretched a buffet table laden with aspic-shining cold meats and oozing cream gateaux. Roberta said she had dined at Bobbie's before coming on to the dance and wasn't hungry, but we both collected some salmon and sat down at one of the twenty or so small tables clustered into half of the room.

Six feet away sat three fellow jockeys resting their elbows among a debris of empty plates and coffee cups.

'Kelly!' One of them exclaimed in a broad northern voice. 'My God. Kelly. Come over here, you old so and so. Bring the talent with you.'

The talent's chin began its familiar upward tilt.

'Concentrate on the character, not the accent,' I said.

She gave me a raw look of surprise, but when I stood up and picked up her plate, she came with me. They made room for us, admired Roberta's appearance, and didn't refer to anyone being warned off. Their girls, they explained, were powdering their noses, and when the noses reappeared, immaculate, they all smiled goodbye and went back to the ballroom.

'They were kind.' She sounded surprised.

'They would be.'

She fiddled with her fork, not looking at me. 'You said the other day that my mind was in chains. Was that what you meant ... that I'm inclined to judge people by their voices ... and that it's wrong?'

'Eton's bred its rogues,' I said. 'Yes.'

'Cactus. You're all prickles.'

'Original sin exists,' I said mildly. 'So does original virtue. They both crop up regardless. No respecters of birth.'

'Where did you go to school?'

'In Wales.'

'You haven't a Welsh accent. You haven't any accent at all. And that's odd really, considering you are only...' Her voice trailed away and she looked aghast at her self-betrayal. 'Oh dear ... I'm sorry.'

'It's not surprising,' I pointed out. 'Considering your father. And anyway, in my own way I'm just as bad. I smothered my Welsh accent quite deliberately. I used to practise in secret, while I was still at school, copying the BBC news' announcers. I wanted to be a Civil Servant, and I was ambitious, and I knew I wouldn't get far if I sounded like the son of a Welsh farm labourer. So in time this became my natural way of talking. And my parents despise me for it.'

'Parents!' She said despairingly. 'Why can we never escape them? Whatever we are, it is because of *them*. I want to be *me*.' She looked astonished at herself. 'I've never felt like this before. I don't understand...'

'Well I do,' I said, smiling. 'Only it happens to most people around fifteen or sixteen. Rebellion, it's called.

'You're mocking me.' But the chin stayed down.

'No.'

We finished the salmon and drank coffee. A large loudly chattering party collected food from the buffet and pushed the two tables next to us together so that they could all sit at one. They were well away on a tide of alcohol and bonhomie, loosened and expansive. I watched them idly. I knew four of them, two trainers, one wife, one owner.

One of the trainers caught sight of me and literally dropped his knife.

'That's Kelly Hughes,' he said disbelievingly. The whole party turned round and stared. Roberta drew a breath in distress. I sat without moving.

'What are you doing here?'

'Drinking coffee,' I said politely.

His eyes narrowed. Trevor Norse was not amused. I sighed inwardly. It was never good to antagonize trainers, it simply meant one less possible source of income: but I'd ridden for Trevor Norse several times already, and knew that it was practically impossible to please him anyway.

A heavy man, six feet plus, labouring under the misapprehension that size could substitute for ability. He was much better with owners than with horses, tireless at cultivating the one and lazy with the other.

His brainless wife said brightly, 'I hear you're paying Dexter's lads' wages, because you're sure you'll get your licence back in a day or two.'

'What's all that?' Norse said sharply. 'Where did you hear all that nonsense?'

'Everyone's talking about it, darling,' she said protestingly.

'Who's everyone?'

She giggled weakly. 'I heard it in the ladies, if you must know. But it's quite true, I'm sure it is. Dexter's lads told Daphne's lads in the local pub, and Daphne told Miriam, and Miriam was telling us in the ladies...'

'Is it true?' Norse demanded.

'Well, more or less,' I agreed.

'Good Lord.'

'Miriam said Kelly Hughes says he and Dexter were framed, and that he's finding out who did it.' Mrs Norse giggled at me. 'My *dear*, isn't it all such fun.'

'Great,' I said dryly. I stood up, and Roberta also.

'Do you know Roberta Cranfield?' I said formally, and they all exclaimed over her, and she scattered on them a bright artificial smile, and we went back and tried another dance.

It wasn't altogether a great idea because we were stopped halfway round by Daddy Leeman of the *Daily Witness* who raked me over with avid eyes and yelled above music was it true I was claiming I'd been framed. He had a piercing voice. All the nearby couples turned and stared. Some of them raised sceptical eyebrows at each other.

'I really can't stand a great deal more of this,' Roberta said in my ear. 'How can you? Why don't you go home now?'

'I'm sorry,' I said contritely. 'You've been splendid. I'll take you back to Bobbie.'

'But you? . . .'

'I haven't done what I came for. I'll stay a bit longer.'

She compressed her mouth and started to dance again. 'All right. So will I.'

We danced without smiling.

'Do you want a tombola ticket?' I asked.

'No.' She was astonished.

'You might as well. I want to go down that end of the room.'

'Whatever for?'

'Looking for someone. Haven't been down that end at all.'

'Oh. All right, then.'

She stepped off the polished wood on to the thick dark carpet, and threaded her way to the clear aisle which led down to the gaily decorated tombola stall at the far end of the ballroom.

I looked for the man I wanted, but I didn't see him. I met too many other eyes, most of which hastily looked away.

'I hate them.' Roberta said fiercely. 'I hate people.'

I bought her four tickets. Three of them were blanks. The fourth had a number which fitted a bottle of vodka.

'I don't like it much,' she said, holding it dubiously.

'Nor do I.'

'I'll give it to the first person who's nice to you.'

'You might have to drink it yourself.'

We went slowly back down the aisle, not talking.

A thin woman sprang up from her chair as we approached her table and in spite of the embarrassed holding-back clutches of her party managed to force her way out into our path. We couldn't pass her without pushing. We stopped.

'You're Roberta Cranfield, aren't you?' she said. She had a strong-boned face, no lipstick, angry eyes, and stiffly-regimented greying hair. She looked as if she'd had far too much to drink.

'Excuse us,' I said gently, trying to go past.

'Oh no you don't,' she said. 'Not until I've had my say.'

'Grace!' wailed a man across the table. I looked at him more closely. Edwin Byler's trainer, Jack Roxford. 'Grace, dear, leave it. Sit down, dear,' he said.

Grace dear had no such intentions. Grace dear's feelings were far too strong.

'Your father's got exactly what he deserves, my lass, and I can tell you I'm glad about it. Glad.' She thrust her face towards Roberta's, glaring like a mad woman. Roberta looked down her nose at her, which I would have found as infuriating as Grace did.

'I'd dance on his grave,' she said furiously. 'That I would.'

'Why?' I said flatly.

She didn't look at me. She said to Roberta, 'He's a bloody snob, your father. A bloody snob. And he's got what he deserved. So there. You tell him that.'

'Excuse me,' Roberta said coldly, and tried to go forwards.

'Oh no you don't.' Grace clutched at her arm. Roberta shook her hand off angrily. 'Your bloody snob of a father was trying to get Edwin Byler's horses away from us. Did you know that? Did you know that? All those grand ways of his. Thought Edwin would do better in a bigger stable, did he? Oh, I heard what he said. Trying to persuade Edwin he needed a grand top-drawer trainer now, not poor little folk like us, who've won just rows of races for him. Well, I could have laughed my head off when I heard he'd been had up. I'll tell you. Serves him right, I said. What a laugh.'

'Grace,' said Jack Roxford despairingly. 'I'm sorry, Miss Cranfield. She isn't really like this.'

He looked acutely embarrassed. I thought that probably Grace Roxford was all too often like this. He had the haunted expression of the for-ever apologizing husband.

'Cheer up then, Mrs Roxford,' I said loudly. 'You've got what you want. You're laughing. So why the fury?'

'Eh?' She twisted her head round at me, staggering a fraction. 'As for you, Kelly Hughes, you just asked for what you got, and don't give me any of that crap we've been hearing this evening that you were framed, because you know bloody well you weren't. People like you and Cranfield, you think you can get away with murder, people like you. But there's justice somewhere in this world sometimes and you won't forget that in a hurry, will you now, Mr Clever Dick.'

One of the women of the party stood up and tried to persuade her to quieten down, as every ear for six tables around was stretched in her direction. She was oblivious to them. I wasn't.

Roberta said under her breath, 'Oh God.'

'So you go home and tell your bloody snob of a father,' Grace said to her, 'that it's a great big laugh him being found out. That's what it is, a great big laugh.'

The acutely embarrassed woman friend pulled her arm, and Grace swung angrily round from us to her. We took the brief opportunity and edged away round her back, and as we retreated we could hear her shouting after us, her words indistinct above the music except for 'laugh' and 'bloody snob'.

'She's *awful*,' Roberta said.

'Not much help to poor old Jack,' I agreed.

'I do hate scenes. They're so messy.'

'Do you think all strong emotions are messy?'

'That's not the same thing,' she said. 'You can have strong emotions without making scenes. Scenes are disgusting.'

I sighed. 'That one was.'

'Yes.'

She was walking, I noticed, with her neck stretched very tall, the classic signal to anyone watching that she was not responsible or bowed down or amused at being involved in noise and nastiness. Rosalind, I reflected nostalgically, would probably have sympathetically agreed with dear disturbed Grace, led her off to some quiet mollifying corner, and reappeared with her eating out of her hand. Rosalind had been tempestuous herself and understood uncontrollable feelings.

Unfortunately at the end of the aisle we almost literally bumped into Kessel, who came in for the murderous glance from Roberta which had been earned by dear Grace. Kessel naturally misinterpreted her expression and spat first.

'You can tell your father that I had been thinking for some time of sending my horses to Pat Nikita, and that this business has made me regret that I didn't do it a long time ago. Pat has always wanted to train for me. I stayed with your father out of a mistaken sense of loyalty, and just look how he repaid me.'

'Father has won a great many races for you,' Roberta said coldly. 'And if Squelch had been good enough to win the Lemonfizz Cup, he would have done.'

Kessel's mouth sneered. It didn't suit him.

'As for you, Hughes, it's a disgrace you being here tonight and I cannot think why you were allowed in. And don't think you can fool me by spreading rumours that you are innocent and on the point of proving it. That's all piffle, and you know it, and if you have any ideas you can reinstate yourself with me that way, you are very much mistaken.'

He turned his back on us and bristled off, pausing triumphantly to pat Nikita on the shoulder, and looking back to make sure we had noticed. Very small of him.

'There goes Squelch,' I said resignedly.

'He'll soon be apologizing and sending him back,' she said, with certainty.

'Not a hope. Kessel's not the humble-pie kind. And Pat Nikita will never let go of that horse. Not to see him go back to your father. He'd break him down first.'

'Why are people so jealous of each other,' she exclaimed.

'Born in them,' I said. 'And almost universal.'

'You have a very poor opinion of human nature.' She disapproved.

'An objective opinion. There's as much good as bad.'

'You can't be objective about being warned off,' she protested.

'Er ... no,' I conceded. 'How about a drink?'

She looked instinctively towards Bobbie's table, and I shook my head. 'In the bar.'

'Oh ... still looking for someone?'

'That's right. We haven't tried the bar yet.'

'Is there going to be another scene?'

'I shouldn't think so.'

'All right, then.'

We made our way slowly through the crowd. By then the fact that we were there must have been known to almost everyone in the place. Certainly the heads no longer turned in open surprise, but the eyes did, sliding into corners, giving us a surreptitious once-over, probing and hurtful. Roberta held herself almost defiantly straight.

The bar was heavily populated, with cigar smoke lying in a haze over the well-groomed heads and the noise level doing justice to a discotheque. Almost at once through a narrow gap in the cluster I saw him, standing against the far wall, talking vehemently. He turned his head suddenly and looked straight at me, meeting my eyes briefly before the groups between us shifted and closed the line of sight. In those two seconds, however, I had seen his mouth tighten and his whole face compress into annoyance; and he had known I was at the dance, because there was no surprise.

'You've seen him,' Roberta said.

'Yes.'

'Well ... who is it?'

'Lord Gowery.'

She gasped. 'Oh no, Kelly.'

'I want to talk to him.'

'It can't do any good.'

'You never know.'

'Annoying Lord Gowery is the last, positively the last way of getting your licence back. Surely you can see that?'

'Yes ... he's not going to be kind, I don't think. So would you mind very much if I took you back to Bobbie first?'

She looked troubled. 'You won't say anything silly? It's Father's licence as well, remember.'

'I'll bear it in mind,' I said flippantly. She gave me a sharp suspicious glance, but turned easily enough to go back to Bobbie.

Almost immediately outside the bar we were stopped by Jack Roxford, who was hurrying towards us through the throng.

'Kelly,' he said, half panting with the exertion. 'I just wanted to catch you ... to say how sorry I am that Grace went off the deep end like that. She's not herself, poor girl ... Miss Cranfield, I do apologize.'

Roberta unbent a little. 'That's all right, Mr Roxford.'

'I wouldn't like you to believe that what Grace said ... all those things about your father ... is what I think too.' He looked from her to me, and back again, the hesitant worry furrowing his forehead. A slight, unaggressive man of about forty-five; bald crown, nervous eyes, permanently worried expression. He was a reasonably good trainer but not enough of a man of the world to have achieved much personal stature. To me, though I had never ridden for him, he had always been friendly, but his restless anxiety-state made him tiring to be with.

'Kelly,' he said, 'if it's really true that you were both framed, I do sincerely hope that you get your licences back. I mean, I know there's a risk that Edwin will take his horses to your father, Miss Cranfield, but he did tell me this evening that he won't do so now, even if he could ... But please believe me, I hold no dreadful grudge against either of you, like poor Grace ... I do hope you'll forgive her.'

'Of course, Mr Roxford,' said Roberta, entirely placated. 'Please don't give it another thought. And oh!' she added impulsively, 'I think you've earned this!' and into his astonished hands she thrust the bottle of vodka.

CHAPTER NINE

When I went back towards the bar I found Lord Gowery had come out of it. He was standing shoulder to shoulder with Lord Ferth, both of them watching me walk towards them with faces like thunder.

I stopped four feet away, and waited.

'Hughes,' said Lord Gowery for openers, 'you shouldn't be here.'

'My lord,' I said politely. 'This isn't Newmarket Heath.'

It went down badly. They were both affronted. They closed their ranks.

'Insolence will get you nowhere,' Lord Ferth said, and Lord Gowery added, 'You'll never get your licence back, if you behave like this.'

I said without heat, 'Does justice depend on good manners?'

They looked as if they couldn't believe their ears. From their point of view I was cutting my own throat, though I had always myself doubted that excessive meekness got licences restored any quicker than they would have been without it. Meekness in the accused brought out leniency in some judges, but severity in others. To achieve a minimum sentence, the guilty should always bone up on the character of their judge, a sound maxim which I hadn't had the sense to see applied even more to the innocent.

'I would have thought some sense of shame would have kept you away,' Lord Ferth said.

'It took a bit of an effort to come,' I agreed.

His eyes narrowed and opened again quickly.

Gowery said, 'As to spreading these rumours ... I say categorically that you are not only not on the point of being given your licence back, but that your suspension will be all the longer in consequence of your present behaviour.'

I gave him a level stare and Lord Ferth opened his mouth and shut it again.

'It is no rumour that Mr Cranfield and I are not guilty,' I said at length. 'It is no rumour that two at least of the witnesses were lying. These are facts.'

'Nonsense,' Gowery said vehemently.

'What you believe, sir,' I said, 'doesn't alter the truth.'

'You are doing yourself no good, Hughes.' Under his heavy authoritative exterior he was exceedingly angry. All I needed was a bore hole and I'd get a gusher.

I said, 'Would you be good enough to tell me who suggested to you or the other Stewards that you should seek out and question Mr Newtonnards?'

There was the tiniest shift in his eyes. Enough for me to be certain.

'Certainly not.'

'Then will you tell me upon whose instructions the enquiry agent David Oakley visited my flat?'

'I will not.' His voice was loud, and for the first time, alarmed.

Ferth looked in growing doubt from one of us to the other.

'What is all this about?' he said.

'Mr Cranfield and I were indeed wrongly warned off,' I said. 'Someone sent David Oakley to my flat to fake that photograph. And I believe Lord Gowery knows who it was.'

'I most certainly do not,' he said furiously. 'Do you want to be sued for slander?'

'I have not slandered you, sir.'

'You said . . .'

'I said you knew who sent David Oakley. I did not say that you knew the photograph was a fake.'

'And it wasn't,' he insisted fiercely.

'Well,' I said. 'It was.'

There was a loaded, glaring silence. Then Lord Gowery said heavily, 'I'm not going to listen to this,' and turned on his heel and dived back into the bar.

Lord Ferth, looking troubled, took a step after him.

I said, 'My lord, may I talk to you?' And he stopped and turned back to me and said, 'Yes, I think you'd better.'

He gestured towards the supper room next door and we

went through the archway into the brighter light. Nearly everyone had eaten and gone. The buffet table bore shambled remains and all but two of the small tables were unoccupied. He sat down at one of these and pointed to the chair opposite. I took it, facing him.

'Now,' he said. 'Explain.'

I spoke in a flat calm voice, because emotion was going to repel him where reason might get through. 'My lord, if you could look at the Enquiry from my point of view for a minute, it is quite simple. I know that I never had any five hundred pounds or any note from Mr Cranfield, therefore I am obviously aware that David Oakley was lying. It's unbelievable that the Stewards should have sent him, since the evidence he produced was faked. So someone else did. I thought Lord Gowery might know who. So I asked him.'

'He said he didn't know.'

'I don't altogether believe him.'

'Hughes, that's preposterous.'

'Are you intending to say, sir, that men in power positions are infallibly truthful?'

He looked at me without expression in a lengthening silence. Finally he said, as Roberta had done, 'Where did you go to school?'

In the usual course of things I kept dead quiet about the type of education I'd had because it was not likely to endear me to either owners or trainers. Still, there was a time for everything, so I told him.

'Coedlant Primary, Tenby Grammar, and LSE.'

'LSE ... you don't mean ... the London School of Economics?' He looked astonished.

'Yes.'

'My God ...'

I watched while he thought it over. 'What did you read there?'

'Politics, philosophy, and economics.'

'Then what on earth made you become a jockey?'

'It was almost an accident,' I said. 'I didn't plan it. When I'd finished my final exams I was mentally tired, so I thought I'd take a sort of paid holiday working on the land

... I knew how to do that, my father's a farm-hand. I worked at harvesting for a farmer in Devon and every morning I used to ride his 'chasers out at exercise, because I'd ridden most of my life, you see. He had a permit, and he was dead keen. And then his brother, who raced them for him, broke his shoulder at one of the early Devon meetings, and he put me up instead, and almost at once I started winning ... and then it took hold of me ... so I didn't get around to being a Civil Servant, as I'd always vaguely intended, and ... well ... I've never regretted it.'

'Not even now?' he said with irony.

I shook my head. 'Not even now.'

'Hughes...' His face crinkled dubiously. 'I don't know what to think. At first I was sure you were not the type to have stopped Squelch deliberately ... and then there was all that damning evidence. Charlie West saying you had definitely pulled back...'

I looked down at the table. I didn't after all want an eye for an eye, when it came to the point.

'Charlie was mistaken,' I said. 'He got two races muddled up. I did pull back in another race at about that time ... riding a novice 'chaser with no chance, well back in the field. I wanted to give it a good schooling race. That was what Charlie remembered.'

He said doubtfully, 'It didn't sound like it.'

'No,' I agreed. 'I've had it out with Charlie since. He might be prepared to admit now that he was talking about the wrong race. If you will ask the Oxford Stewards, you'll find that Charlie said nothing to them directly after the Lemonfizz, when they made their first enquiries, about me not trying. He only said it later, at the Enquiry in Portman Square.' Because in between some beguiling seducer had offered him five hundred pounds for the service.

'I see.' He frowned. 'And what was it that you asked Lord Gowery about Newtonnards?'

'Newtonnards didn't volunteer the information to the Stewards about Mr Cranfield backing Cherry Pie, but he did tell several bookmaker colleagues. Someone told the Stewards. I wanted to know who.'

'Are you suggesting that it was the same person who sent Oakley to your flat?'

'It might be. But not necessarily.' I hesitated, looking at him doubtfully.

'What is it?' he said.

'Sir, I don't want to offend you, but would you mind telling me why you sat in at the Enquiry? Why there were four of you instead of three, when Lord Gowery, if you'll forgive me saying so, was obviously not too pleased at the arrangement.'

His lips tightened. 'You're being uncommonly tactful all of a sudden.'

'Yes, sir.'

He looked at me steadily. A tall thin man with high cheekbones, strong black hair, hot fiery eyes. A man whose force of character reached out and hit you, so that you'd never forget meeting him. The best ally in the whole 'chasing set up, if I could only reach him.

'I cannot give you my reasons for attending,' he said with some reproof.

'Then you had some ... reservations ... about how the Enquiry would be conducted?'

'I didn't say that,' he protested. But he had meant it.

'Lord Gowery chose Andrew Tring to sit with him at the hearing, and Andrew Tring wants a very big concession from him just now. And he chose Lord Plimborne as the third Steward, and Lord Plimborne continually fell asleep.'

'Do you realize what you're saying?' He was truly shocked.

'I want to know how Lord Gowery acquired all that evidence against us. I want to know why the Stewards' Secretaries sent for the wrong film. I want to know why Lord Gowery was so biased, so deaf to our denials, so determined to warn us off.'

'That's slanderous ...'

'I want you to ask him,' I finished flatly.

He simply stared.

I said, 'He might tell you. He might just possibly tell you. But he'd never in a million years tell *me*.'

'Hughes ... You surely don't expect ...'

'That wasn't a straight trial, and he knows it. I'm just asking you to tackle him with it, to see if he will explain.'

'You are talking about a much respected man,' he said coldly.

'Yes, sir. He's a baron, a rich man, a Steward of long standing. I know all that.'

'And you *still* maintain? . . .'

'Yes.'

His hot eyes brooded. 'He'll have you in Court for this.'

'Only if I'm wrong.'

'I can't possibly do it,' he said, with decision.

'And please, if you have one, use a tape-recorder.'

'I told you . . .'

'Yes, sir, I know you did.'

He got up from the table, paused as if about to say something, changed his mind, and as I stood up also, turned abruptly and walked sharply away. When he had gone I found that my hands were trembling, and I followed him slowly out of the supper room feeling a battered wreck.

I had either resurrected our licences or driven the nails into them, and only time would tell which.

Bobbie said, 'Have a drink, my dear fellow. You look as though you've been clobbered by a steamroller.'

I took a mouthful of champagne and thanked him, and watched Roberta swing her body to a compelling rhythm with someone else. The ringlets bounced against her neck. I wondered without disparagement how long it had taken her to pin them on.

'Not the best of evenings for you, old pal,' Bobbie observed.

'You never know.'

He raised his eyebrows, drawling down his nose, 'Mission accomplished?'

'A fuse lit, rather.'

He lifted his glass. 'To a successful detonation.'

'You are most kind,' I said formally.

The music changed gear and Roberta's partner brought her back to the table.

I stood up. 'I came to say goodbye,' I said. 'I'll be going now.'

'Oh not yet,' she exclaimed. 'The worst is over. No one's staring any more. Have some fun.'

'Dance with the dear girl,' Bobbie said, and Roberta put out a long arm and pulled mine, and so I went and danced with her.

'Lord Gowery didn't eat you then?'

'He's scrunching the bones at this minute.'

'Kelly! If you've done any damage . . .'

'No omelettes without smashing eggs, love.'

The chin went up. I grinned. She brought it down again. Getting quite human, Miss Cranfield.

After a while the hot rhythm changed to a slow smooch, and couples around us went into clinches. Bodies to bodies, heads to heads, eyes shut, swaying in the dimming light. Roberta eyed them coolly and prickled when I put my arms up to gather her in. She danced very straight, with four inches of air between us. Not human enough.

We ambled around in that frigid fashion through three separate wodges of glutinous music. She didn't come any closer, and I did nothing to persuade her, but equally she seemed to be in no hurry to break it up. Composed, cool, off-puttingly gracious, she looked as flawless in the small hours as she had when I'd arrived.

'I'm glad you were here,' I said.

She moved her head in surprise. 'It hasn't been exactly the best Jockeys' Fund dance of my life . . . but I'm glad I came.'

'Next year this will be all over, and everyone will have forgotten.'

'I'll dance with you again next year,' she said.

'It's a pact.'

She smiled, and just for a second a stray beam of light shimmered on some expression in her eyes which I didn't understand.

She was aware of it. She turned her head away, and then detached herself altogether, and gestured that she wanted to go back to the table. I delivered her to Bobbie, and she sat down immediately and began powdering a non-shiny nose.

'Goodnight,' I said to Bobbie. 'And thank you.'

'My dear fellow. Any time.'

'Goodnight, Roberta.'

She looked up. Nothing in the eyes. Her voice was collected. 'Goodnight, Kelly.'

I lowered myself into the low-slung burnt-orange car in the park and drove away thinking about her. Roberta Cranfield. Not my idea of a cuddly bed mate. Too cold, too controlled, too proud. And it didn't go with that copper hair, all that rigidity. Or maybe she was only rigid to me because I was a farm labourer's son. Only that, and only a jockey ... and her father had taught her that jockeys were the lower classes dear and don't get your fingers dirty ...

Kelly, I said to myself, you've a fair-sized chip on your shoulder, old son. Maybe she does think like that, but why should it bother you? And even if she does, she spent most of the evening with you ... although she was really quite careful not to touch you too much. Well ... maybe that was because so many people were watching ... and maybe it was simply that she didn't like the thought of it.

I was on the short cut home that led round the south of Reading, streaking down deserted back roads, going fast for no reason except that speed had become a habit. This car was easily the best I'd ever had, the only one I had felt proud of. Mechanically a masterpiece and with looks to match. Even thirty thousand miles in the past year hadn't dulled the pleasure I got from driving it. Its only fault was that like so many other sports cars it had a totally inefficient heater, which in spite of coaxing and overhauls stubbornly refused to do more than demist the windscreen and raise my toes one degree above frostbite. If kicked, it retaliated with a smell of exhaust.

I had gone to the dance without a coat, and the night was frosty. I shivered and switched on the heater to maximum. As usual, damn all.

There was a radio in the car, which I seldom listened to,

and a spare crash helmet, and my five-pound racing saddle which I'd been going to take to Wetherby races.

Depression flooded back. Fierce though the evening had been, in many ways I had forgotten for a while the dreariness of being banned. It could be a long slog now, after what I had said to the Lords Gowery and Ferth. A very long slog indeed. Cranfield wouldn't like the gamble. I wasn't too sure that I could face telliing him, if it didn't come off.

Lord Ferth ... would he or wouldn't he? He'd be torn between loyalty to an equal and a concept of justice. I didn't know him well, enough to be sure which would win. And maybe anyway he would shut everything I'd said clean out of his mind, as too far-fetched and preposterous to bother about.

Bobbie had been great, I thought. I wondered who he was. Maybe one day I'd ask Roberta.

Mrs Roxford ... poor dear Grace. What a life Jack must lead ... Hope he liked vodka ...

I took an unexpectedly sharp bend far too fast. The wheels screeched when I wrenched the nose round and the car went weaving and skidding for a hundred yards before I had it in control again. I put my foot gingerly back on the accelerator and still had in my mind's eye the solid trunks of the row of trees I had just missed by centimetres.

God, I thought, how could I be so careless. It rocked me. I was a careful driver, even if fast, and I'd never had an accident. I could feel myself sweating. It was something to sweat about.

How stupid I was, thinking about the dance, not concentrating on driving, and going too fast for these small roads. I rubbed my forehead, which felt tense and tight, and kept my speed down to forty.

Roberta had looked beautiful ... keep your mind on the road Kelly, for God's sake ... Usually I drove semi-automatically without having to concentrate every yard of the way. I found myself going slower still, because both my reactions and my thoughts were growing sluggish. I'd drunk a total of about half a glass of champagne all evening, so it couldn't be that.

I was simply going to sleep.

I stopped the car, got out, and stamped about to wake myself up. People who went to sleep at the wheels of sports cars on the way home from dances were not a good risk.

Too many sleepless nights, grinding over my sorry state. Insulting the lions seemed to have released the worst of that. I felt I could now fall unconscious for a month.

I considered sleeping there and then, in the car. But the car was cold and couldn't be heated. I would drive on, I decided, and stop for good if I felt really dozy again. The fresh air had done the trick; I was wide awake and irritated with myself.

The beam of my headlights on the cats' eyes down the empty road was soon hypnotic. I switched on the radio to see if that would hold my attention, but it was all soft and sweet late-night music. Lullaby. I switched it off.

Pity I didn't smoke. That would have helped.

It was a star-clear night with a bright full moon. Ice crystals sparkled like diamond dust on the grass verges, now that I'd left the wooded part behind. Beautiful but unwelcome, because a hard frost would mean no racing tomorrow at Sandown ... With a jerk I realized that that didn't matter to me any more.

I glanced at the speedometer. Forty. It seemed very fast. I slowed down still further to thirty-five, and nodded owlishly to myself. Anyone would be safe at thirty-five.

The tightness across my forehead slowly developed into a headache. Never mind, only an hour to home, then sleep ... sleep ... sleep ...

It's no good, I thought fuzzily. I'll have to stop and black out for a bit, even if I do wake up freezing, or I'll black out without stopping first, and that will be that.

The next layby, or something like that ...

I began looking, forgot what I was looking for, took my foot still farther off the accelerator and reckoned that thirty miles an hour was quite safe. Maybe twenty five ... would be better.

A little farther on there were some sudden bumps in the road surface and my foot slipped off the accelerator altogether. The engine stalled. Car stopped.

Oh well, I thought. That settles it. Ought to move over to the side though. Couldn't see the side. Very odd.

The headache was pressing on my temples, and now that the engine had stopped I could hear a faint ringing in my ears.

Never mind. Never mind. Best to go to sleep. Leave the lights on ... no one came along that road much ... not at two in the morning ... but have to leave the lights on just in case.

Ought to pull in to the side.

Ought to ...

Too much trouble. Couldn't move my arms properly, anyway, so couldn't possibly do it.

Deep deep in my head a tiny instinct switched itself to emergency.

Something was wrong. Something was indistinctly but appallingly wrong.

Sleep. Must sleep.

Get out, the flickering instinct said. Get out of the car.

Ridiculous.

Get out of the car.

Unwillingly, because it was such an effort, I struggled weakly with the handle. The door swung open. I put one leg out and tried to pull myself up, and was swept by a wave of dizziness. My head was throbbing. This wasn't ... it couldn't be ... just ordinary sleep.

Get out of the car ...

My arms and legs belonged to someone else. They had me on my feet ... I was standing up ... didn't remember how I got there. But I was out.

Out.

Now what?

I took three tottering steps towards the back of the car and leant against the rear wing. Funny, I thought, the moonlight wasn't so bright any more.

The earth was trembling.

Stupid. Quite stupid. The earth didn't tremble.

Trembling. And the air was wailing. And the moon was

falling on me. Come down from the sky and rushing towards me ...

Not the moon. A great roaring wailing monster with a blinding moon eye. A monster making the earth tremble. A monster racing to gobble me up, huge and dark and faster than the wind and unimaginably terrifying ...

I didn't move. Couldn't.

The one-thirty mail express from Paddington to Plymouth ploughed into my sturdy little car and carried its crumpled remains half a mile down the track.

CHAPTER TEN

I didn't know what had happened. Didn't understand. There was a tremendous noise of tearing metal and a hundred-mile-an-hour whirl of nincty-ton diesel engine one inch away from me, and a thudding catapulting scrunch which lifted me up like a rag doll and toppled me somersaulting through the air in a kaleidoscopic black arc.

My head crashed against a concrete post. The rest of my body felt mangled beyond repair. There were rainbows in my brain, blue, purple, flaming pink, with diamond-bright pin stars. Interesting while it lasted. Didn't last very long. Dissolved into an embracing inferno in which colours got lost in pain.

Up the line the train had screeched to a stop. Lights and voices were coming back that way.

The earth was cold, hard, and damp. A warm stream ran down my face. I knew it was blood. Didn't care much. Couldn't think properly, either. And didn't really want to.

More lights. Lots of lights Lots of people. Voices.

A voice I knew.

'Roberta, my dear girl, don't look.'

'It's Kelly!' she said. Shock. Wicked, unforgettable shock. 'It's Kelly.' The second time, despair.

'Come away, my dear girl.'

She didn't go. She was kneeling beside me. I could smell her scent, and feel her hand on my hair. I was lying on my side, face down. After a while I could see a segment of honey silk dress. There was blood on it.

I said, 'You're ruining ... your dress.'

'It doesn't matter.'

It helped somehow to have her there. I was grateful that she had stayed. I wanted to tell her that. I tried ... and meant ... to say 'Roberta'. What in fact I said was ... 'Rosalind'.

'Oh Kelly ...' Her voice held a mixture of pity and distress.

I thought groggily that she would go away, now that I'd made such a silly mistake, but she stayed, saying small things like, 'You'll be all right soon,' and sometimes not talking at all, but just being there. I didn't know why I wanted her to stay. I remembered that I didn't even like the girl.

All the people who arrive after accidents duly arrived. Police with blue flashing lights. Ambulance waking the neighbourhood with its siren. Bobbie took Roberta away, telling her there was no more she could do. The ambulance men scooped me unceremoniously on to a stretcher and if I thought them rough it was only because every movement brought a scream up as far as my teeth and heaven knows whether any of them got any farther.

By the time I reached the hospital the mists had cleared. I knew what had happened to my car. I knew that I wasn't dying. I knew that Bobbie and Roberta had taken the backroads detour like I had, and had reached the level crossing not long after me.

What I didn't understand was how I had come to stop on the railway. That crossing had drop-down-fringe gates, and they hadn't been shut.

A young dark-haired doctor with tired dark-ringed eyes came to look at me, talking to the ambulance men.

'He'd just come from a dance,' they said. 'The police want a blood test.'

'Drunk?' said the doctor.

The ambulance men shrugged. They thought it possible. 'No,' I said. 'It wasn't drink. At least...'

They didn't pay much attention. The young doctor stooped over my lower half, feeling the damage with slender gentle fingers. 'That hurts? Yes.' He parted my hair, looking at my head. 'Nothing much up there. More blood than damage.' He stood back. 'We'll get your pelvis X-rayed. And that leg. Can't tell what's what until after that.'

A nurse tried to take my shoes off. I said very loudly, 'Don't.'

She jumped. The doctor signed to her to stop. 'We'll do it under an anaesthetic. Just leave him for now.'

She came instead and wiped my forehead.

'Sorry,' she said.

The doctor took my pulse. 'Why ever did you stop on a level crossing?' he said conversationally. 'Silly thing to do.'

'I felt ... sleepy. Had a headache.' It didn't sound very sensible.

'Had a bit to drink?'

'Almost nothing.'

'At a dance?' He sounded sceptical.

'Really,' I said weakly. 'I didn't.'

He put my hand down. I was still wearing my dinner jacket, though someone had taken off my tie. There were bright scarlet blotches down my white shirt and an unmendable tear down the right side of my black trousers.

I shut my eyes. Didn't do much good. The screaming pain showed no signs of giving up. It had localized into my right side from armpit to toes, with repercussions up and down my spine. I'd broken a good many bones racing, but this was much worse. Much. It was impossible.

'It won't be long now, the doctor said comfortingly. 'We'll have you under.'

'The train didn't hit me,' I said. 'I got out of the car ... I was leaning against the back of it ... the train hit the car ... not me.'

I felt sick. How long? ...

'If it had hit you, you wouldn't be here.'

'I suppose not ... I had this thumping headache ...

needed air...' Why couldn't I pass out, I thought. People always passed out, when it became unbearable. Or so I'd always believed.

'Have you still got the headache?' he asked clinically.

'It's gone off a bit. Just sore now.' My mouth was dry. Always like that, after injuries. The least of my troubles.

Two porters came to wheel me away, and I protested more than was stoical about the jolts. I felt grey. Looked at my hands. They were quite surprisingly red.

X-ray department. Very smooth, very quick. Didn't try to move me except for cutting the zip out of my trousers. Quite enough.

'Sorry,' they said.

'Do you work all night?' I asked.

They smiled. On duty, if called.

'Thanks,' I said.

Another journey. People in green overalls and white masks, making soothing remarks. Could I face taking my coat off? No? Never mind then. Needle into vein in back of hand. Marvellous. Oblivion rolled through me in grey and black and I greeted it with a sob of welcome.

The world shuffled back in the usual way, bit by uncomfortable bit, with a middle-aged nurse patting my hand and telling me to wake up dear, it was all over.

I had to admit that my wildest fears were not realized. I still had two legs. One I could move. The other had plaster on. Inside the plaster it gently ached. The scream had died to a whisper. I sighed with relief.

What was the time? Five o'clock, dear.

Where was I? In the recovery ward, dear. Now go to sleep again and when you wake up you'll be feeling much better, you'll see.

I did as she said, and she was quite right.

Mid-morning, a doctor came. Not the same one as the night before. Older, heavier, but just as tired looking.

'You had a lucky escape,' he said.

'Yes, I did.'

'Luckier than you imagine. We took a blood test. Actually

we took two blood tests. The first one for alcohol. With practically negative results. Now this interested us, because who except a drunk would stop a car on a level crossing and get out and lean against it? The casualty doctor told us you swore you hadn't been drinking and that anyway you seemed sober enough to him ... but that you'd had a bad headache which was now better ... We gave you a bit of thought, and we looked at those very bright scarlet stains on your shirt ... and tested your blood again ... and there it was!' He paused triumphantly.

'What?'

'Carboxyhaemoglobin.'

'*What?*'

'Carbon monoxide, my dear chap. Carbon-monoxide poisoning. Explains everything, don't you see?'

'Oh ... but I thought ... with carbon monoxide ... one simply blacked out.'

'It depends. If you got a large dose all at once that would happen, like it does to people who get stuck in snow drifts and leave their engines running. But a trickle, that would affect you more slowly. But it would all be the same in the end, of course. The haemoglobin in the red corpuscles has a greater affinity for carbon monoxide than for oxygen, so it mops up any carbon monoxide you breathe in, and oxygen is disregarded. If the level of carbon monoxide in your blood builds up gradually ... you get gradual symptoms. Very insidious they are too. The trouble is that it seems that when people feel sleepy they light a cigarette to keep themselves awake, and tobacco smoke itself introduces significant quantities of carbon monoxide into the body, so the cigarette may be the final knock out. Er ... do you smoke?'

'No.' And to think I'd regretted it.

'Just as well. You obviously had quite a dangerous concentration of CO in any case.'

'I must have been driving for half an hour ... maybe forty minutes. I don't really know.'

'It's a wonder you stopped safely at all. Much more likely to have crashed into something.'

'I nearly did ... on a corner.'

He nodded. 'Didn't you smell exhaust fumes?'

'I didn't notice. I had too much on my mind. And the heater burps out exhaust smells sometimes. So I wouldn't take much heed, if it wasn't strong.' I looked down at myself under the sheets. 'What's the damage?'

'Not much now,' he said cheerfully. 'You were lucky there too. You had multiple dislocations ... hip, knee, and ankle. Never seen all three before. Very interesting. We reduced them all successfully. No crushing or fractures, no severed tendons. We don't even think there will be a recurring tendency to dislocate. One or two frayed ligaments round your knee, that's all.'

'It's a miracle.'

'Interesting case, yes. Unique sort of accident, of course. No direct force involved. We think it might have been air impact ... that it sort of blew or stretched you apart. Like being on the rack, eh?' He chuckled. 'We put plaster on your knee and ankle, to give them a chance to settle, but it can come off in three or four weeks. We don't want you to put weight on your hip yet, either. You can have some physiotherapy. But take it easy for a while when you leave here. There was a lot of spasm in the muscles, and all your ligaments and so on were badly stretched. Give everything time to subside properly before you run a mile.' He smiled, which turned halfway through into a yawn. He smothered it apologetically. 'It's been a long night ...'

'Yes,' I said.

I went home on Tuesday afternoon in an ambulance with a pair of crutches and instructions to spend most of my time horizontal.

Poppy was still sick. Tony followed my slow progress up the stairs apologizing that she couldn't manage to have me stay, the kids were exhausting her to distraction.

'I'm fine on my own.'

He saw me into the bedroom, where I lay down in my clothes on top of the bedspread, as per instructions. Then he made for the whisky and refreshed himself after my labours.

'Do you want anything? I'll fetch you some food, later.'

'Thanks,' I said. 'Could you bring the telephone in here?'

He brought it in and plugged the lead into the socket beside my bed.

'OK?'

'Fine,' I said.

'That's it, then.' He tossed off his drink quickly and made for the door, showing far more haste than usual and edging away from me as though embarrassed.

'Is anything wrong?' I said.

He jumped. 'No. Absolutely nothing. Got to get the kids their tea before evening stables. See you later, pal. With the odd crust.' He smiled sketchily and disappeared.

I shrugged. Whatever it was that was wrong, he would tell me in time, if he wanted to.

I picked up the telephone and dialled the number of the local garage. Its best mechanic answered.

'Mr Hughes ... I heard ... Your beautiful car.' He commiserated genuinely for half a minute.

'Yes,' I said. 'Look, Derek, is there any way that exhaust gas could get into the car through the heater?'

He was affronted. 'Not the way I looked after it. Certainly not.'

'I apparently breathed in great dollops of carbon monoxide,' I said.

'Not through the heater ... I can't understand it.' He paused, thinking. 'They take special care not to let that happen, see? At the design stage. You could only get exhaust gas through the heater if there was a loose or worn gasket on the exhaust manifold *and* a crack or break in the heater tubing *and* a tube connecting the two together, and you can take it from me, Mr Hughes, there was nothing at all like that on your car. Maintained perfect, it is.'

'The heater does sometimes smell of exhaust. If you remember, I did mention it, some time ago.'

'I give the whole system a thorough check then, too. There wasn't a thing wrong. Only thing I could think of was the exhaust might have eddied forwards from the back of the car when you slowed down, sort of, and got whirled in through the fresh-air intake, the one down beside the heater.'

'Could you possibly go and look at my car? At what's left of it? . . .'

'There's a good bit to do here,' he said dubiously.

'The police have given me the name of the garage where it is now. Apparently all the bits have to stay there until the insurance people have seen them. But you know the car . . . it would be easier for you to spot anything different with it from when you last serviced it. Could you go?'

'D'you mean,' he paused. 'You don't mean . . . there might be something . . . well . . . *wrong* with it?'

'I don't know,' I said. 'But I'd like to find out.'

'It would cost you,' he said warningly. 'It would be working hours.'

'Never mind. If you can go, it will be worth it.'

'Hang on, then.' He departed to consult. Came back. 'Yes, all right. The Guvnor says I can go first thing in the morning.

'That's great,' I said. 'Call me when you get back.'

'It couldn't have been a gasket,' he said suddenly.

'Why not?'

'You'd have heard it. Very noisy. Unless you had the radio on?'

'No.'

'You'd have heard a blown gasket,' he said positively. 'But there again, if the exhaust was being somehow fed straight into the heater . . . perhaps not. The heater would damp the noise, same as a silencer . . . but I don't see how it could have happened. Well . . . all I can do is take a look.'

I would have liked to have gone with him. I put down the receiver and looked gloomily at my right leg. The neat plaster casing stretched from well up my thigh down to the base of my toes, which were currently invisible inside a white hospital theatre sock. A pair of Tony's slacks, though too long by six inches, had slid up easily enough over the plaster, decently hiding it, and as far as looks went, things were passable.

I sighed. The plaster was a bore. They'd designed it somehow so that I found sitting in a chair uncomfortable. Standing and lying down were both better. It wasn't going to stay on a minute longer than I could help, either. The muscles inside it were doing themselves no good in immobility. They would be getting flabby, unfit, wasting away. It would be just too ironic if I got my licence back and was too feeble to ride.

Tony came back at eight with half a chicken. He didn't want to stay, not even for a drink.

'Can you manage?' he said.

'Sure. No trouble.'

'Your leg doesn't hurt, does it?'

'Not a flicker,' I said. 'Can't feel a thing.'

'That's all right then.' He was relieved: wouldn't look at me squarely: went away.

Next morning, Roberta Cranfield came.

'Kelly?' she called. 'Are you in?'

'In the bedroom.'

She walked across the sitting-room and stopped in the doorway. Wearing the black-and-white striped fur coat, hanging open. Underneath it, black pants and a stagnant pond-coloured sweater.

'Hullo,' she said. 'I've brought you some food. Shall I put it in the kitchen?'

'That's pretty good of you.'

She looked me over. I was lying, dressed, on top of the bedspread, reading the morning paper. 'You look comfortable enough.'

'I am. Just bored. Er ... not now you've come, of course.'

'Of course,' she agreed. 'Shall I make some coffee?'

'Yes, do.'

She brought it back in mugs, shed her fur, and sat loose limbed in my bedroom armchair.

'You look a bit better today,' she observed.

'Can you get that blood off your dress?'

She shrugged. 'I chucked it at the cleaners. They're trying.'

'I'm sorry about that ...'

'Think nothing of it.' She sipped her coffee. 'I rang the hospital on Saturday. They said you were OK.'

'Thanks.'

'Why on earth did you stop on the railway?'

'I didn't know it was the railway, until too late.'

'But how did you get there, anyway, with the gates down?'

'The gates weren't down.'

'They were when we came along,' she said. 'There were all those lights and people shouting and screaming and we got out of the car to see what it was all about, and someone said the train had hit a car ... and then I saw you, lying spark out with your face all covered in blood, about ten feet up the line. Nasty. Very nasty. It was, really.'

'I'm sorry ... I'd had a couple of lungfuls of carbon monoxide. What you might call diminished responsibility.'

She grinned. 'You're some moron.'

The gates must have shut after I'd stopped on the line. I hadn't heard them or seen them. I must, I supposed, have been more affected by the gas than I remembered.

'I called you Rosalind,' I said apologetically.

'I know.' She made a face. 'Did you think I was her?'

'No ... It just came out. I meant to say Roberta.'

She unrolled herself from the chair, took a few steps, and stood looking at Rosalind's picture. 'She'd have been glad ... knowing she still came first with you after all this time.'

The telephone rang sharply beside me and interrupted my surprise. I picked up the receiver.

'Is that Kelly Hughes?' The voice was cultivated, authoritative, loaded indefinably with power. 'This is Wykeham Ferth speaking. I read about your accident in the papers ... a report this morning says you are now home. I hope ... you are well?'

'Yes, thank you, my lord.'

It was ridiculous, the way my heart had bumped. Sweating palms, too.

'Are you in any shape to come to London?'

'I'm ... I've got plaster on my leg ... I can't sit in a car very easily, I'm afraid.'

'Hm.' A pause. 'Very well. I will drive down to Corrie instead. It's Harringay's old place, isn't it?'

'That's right. I live in a flat over the yard. If you walk into the yard from the drive, you'll see a green door with a brass letter box in the far corner. It won't be locked. There are some stairs inside. I live up there.'

'Right,' he said briskly. 'This afternoon? Good. Expect me at . . . er . . . four o'clock. Right?'

'Sir . . .' I began.

'Not now, Hughes. This afternoon.'

I put the receiver down slowly. Six hours' suspense. Damn him.

'What an absolutely heartless letter,' Roberta exclaimed.

I looked at her. She was holding the letter from my parents, which had been under Rosalind's photograph.

'I dare say I shouldn't have been so nosey as to read it,' she said unrepentantly.

'I dare say not.'

'How *can* they be so beastly?'

'They're not really.'

'This sort of thing always happens when you get one bright son in a family of twits,' she said disgustedly.

'Not always. Some bright sons handle things better than others.'

'Stop clobbering yourself.'

'Yes, ma'am.'

'Are you going to stop sending them money?'

'No. All they can do about that is not spend it . . . or give it to the local cats' and dogs' home.'

'At least they had the decency to see they couldn't take your money *and* call you names.'

'Rigidly moral man, my father,' I said. 'Honest to the last farthing. Honest for its own sake. He taught me a lot that I'm grateful for.'

'And that's why this business hurts him so much?'

'Yes.'

'I've never . . . Well, I know you'll despise me for saying it . . . but I've never thought about people like your father before as . . . well . . . *people*.'

'If you're not careful,' I said, 'those chains will drop right off.'

She turned away and put the letter back under Rosalind's picture.

'Which university did you go to?'

'London. Starved in a garret on a grant. Great stuff.'

'I wish ... how odd ... I wish I'd trained for something. Learned a job.'

'It's hardly too late,' I said, smiling.

'I'm nearly twenty. I didn't bother much at school with exams ... no one made us. Then I went to Switzerland for a year, to a finishing school ... and since then I've just lived at home ... What a waste!'

'The daughters of the rich are always at a disadvantage,' I said solemnly.

'Sarcastic beast.'

She sat down again in the armchair and told me that her father really seemed to have snapped out of it at last, and had finally accepted a dinner invitation the night before. All the lads had stayed on. They spent most of their time playing cards and football, as the only horses left in the yard were four half-broken two-year-olds and three old 'chasers recovering from injuries. Most of the owners had promised to bring their horses back at once, if Cranfield had his licence restored in the next few weeks.

'What's really upsetting Father now is hope. With the big Cheltenham meeting only a fortnight away, he's biting his nails about whether he'll get Breadwinner back in time for him to run in his name in the Gold Cup.'

'Pity Breadwinner isn't entered in the Grand National. That would give us a bit more leeway.'

'Would your leg be right in time for the Gold Cup?'

'If I had my licence, I'd saw the plaster off myself.'

'Are you any nearer ... with the licences?'

'Don't know.'

She sighed. 'It was a great dream while it lasted. And you won't be able to do much about it now.'

She stood up and came over and picked up the crutches which were lying beside the bed. They were black tubular

128

metal with elbow supports and hand grips.

'These are much better than those old fashioned under-the-shoulder affairs,' she said. She fitted the crutches round her arms and swung around the room a bit with one foot off the floor. 'Pretty hard on your hands, though.'

She looked unselfconscious and intent. I watched her. I remembered the revelation it had been in my childhood when I first wondered what it was like to be someone else.

Into this calm sea Tony appeared with a wretched face and a folded paper in his hand.

'Hi,' he said, seeing Roberta. A very gloomy greeting.

He sat down in the armchair and looked at Roberta standing balanced on the crutches with one knee bent. His thoughts were not where his eyes were.

'What is it, then?' I said. 'Out with it.'

'This letter ... came yesterday,' he said heavily.

'It was obvious last night that something was the matter.'

'I couldn't show it to you then, not straight out of hospital. And I don't know what to do, Kelly pal, sure enough I don't.'

'Let's see, then.'

He handed me the paper worriedly. I opened it up. A brief letter from the racing authorities. Bang bang, both barrels.

'Dear Sir,
    It has been brought to our attention that a person warned off Newmarket Heath is living as a tenant in your stable yard. This is contrary to the regulations, and you should remedy the situation as soon as possible. It is perhaps not necessary to warn you that your own training licence might have to be reviewed if you should fail to take the steps suggested.'

'Sods,' Tony said forcefully. 'Bloody sods.'

CHAPTER ELEVEN

Derek from the garage came while Roberta was clearing away the lunch she had stayed to cook. When he rang the door bell she went downstairs to let him in.

He walked hesitatingly across the sitting-room looking behind him to see if his shoes were leaving dirty marks and out of habit wiped his hands down his trousers before taking the one I held out to him.

'Sit down,' I suggested. He looked doubtfully at the khaki velvet armchair, but in the end lowered himself gingerly into it. He looked perfectly clean. No grease, no filthy overalls, just ordinary slacks and sports jacket. He wasn't used to it.

'You all right?' he said.

'Absolutely.'

'If you'd been in that car...' He looked sick at what he was thinking, and his vivid imagination was one of the things which made him a reliable mechanic. He didn't want death on his conscience. Young, fair haired, diffident, he kept most of his brains in his fingertips and outside of cars used the upstairs lot sparingly.

'You've never seen nothing like it,' he said. 'You wouldn't know it was a car, you wouldn't straight. It's all in little bits ... I mean, like, bits of metal that don't look as if they were ever part of anything. Honestly. It's like twisted shreds of stuff.' He swallowed. 'They've got it collected up in tin baths.'

'The engine too?'

'Yeah. Smashed into fragments. Still, I had a look. Took me a long time, though, because everything is all jumbled up, and honest you can't tell what anything used to be. I mean, I didn't think it was a bit of exhaust manifold that I'd picked up, not at first, because it wasn't any shape that you'd think of.'

'You found something?'

'Here.' He fished in his trouser pocket. 'This is what it was all like. This is a bit of the exhaust manifold. Cast iron, that is, you see, so of course it was brittle, sort of, and it had shattered into bits. I mean, it wasn't sort of crumpled up like all the aluminium and so on. It wasn't bent, see, it was just in bits.'

'Yes, I do see,' I said. The anxious lines on his forehead dissolved when he saw that he had managed to tell me what he meant. He came over and put the small black jagged edged lump into my hands. Heavy for its size. About three inches long. Asymmetrically curved. Part of the side wall of a huge tube.

'As far as I can make out, see,' Derek said, pointing, 'it came from about where the manifold narrows down to the exhaust pipe, but really it might be anywhere. There were quite a few bits of manifold, when I looked, but I couldn't see the bit that fits into this, and I dare say it's still rusting away somewhere along the railway line. Anyway, see this bit here...' He pointed a stubby finger at a round dent in part of one edge. 'That's one side of a hole that was bored in the manifold wall. Now don't get me wrong, there's quite a few holes might have been drilled through the wall. I mean, some people have exhaust-gas temperature gauges stuck into the manifold... and other gauges too. Things like that. Only, see, there weren't no gauges in your manifold, now, were there?'

'You tell me,' I said.

'There weren't, then. Now you couldn't really say what the hole was for, not for certain you couldn't. But as far as I know, there weren't any holes in your manifold last time I did the service.'

I fingered the little semi-circular dent. No more than a quarter of an inch across.

'However did you spot something so small?' I asked.

'Dunno, really. Mind you, I was there a good couple of hours, picking through those tubs. Did it methodical, like. Since you were paying for it and all.'

'Is it a big job ... drilling a hole this size through an exhaust manifold. Would it take long?'

'Half a minute, I should think.'

'With an electric drill?' I asked.

'Oh yeah, sure. If you did it with a hand drill, then it would take five minutes. Say nearer eight or ten, to be on the safe side.'

'How many people carry drills around in their tool kits?'

'That, see, it depends on the chap. Now some of them carry all sorts of stuff in their cars. Proper work benches, some of them. And then others, the tool kit stays strapped up fresh from the factory until the car's dropping to bits.'

'People do carry drills, then?'

'Oh yeah, sure. Quite a lot do. Hand drills, of course. You wouldn't have much call for an electric drill, not in a tool kit, not unless you did a lot of repairs, like, say on racing cars.'

He went and sat down again. Carefully, as before.

'If someone drilled a hole this size through the manifold, what would happen?'

'Well, honestly, nothing much. You'd get exhaust gas out through the engine, and you'd hear a good lot of noise, and you might smell it in the car, but it would sort of blow away, see, it wouldn't come in through the heater. To do that, like I said before, you'd have to put some tubing into the hole there and then stick the other end of the tubing into the heater. Mind you that would be pretty easy, you wouldn't need a drill. Some heater tubes are really only cardboard.'

'Rubber tubing from one end to the other?' I suggested.

He shook his head. 'No. Have to be metal. Exhaust gas, that's very hot. It'd melt anything but metal.'

'Do you think anyone could do all that on the spur of the moment?'

He put his head on one side, considering. 'Oh sure, yeah. If he'd got a drill. Like, say the first other thing he needs is some tubing. Well, he's only got to look around for that. Lots lying about, if you look. The other day, I used a bit of a kiddy's old cycle frame, just the job it was. Right, you get the tube ready first and then you fit a drill nearest the right size, to match. And Bob's your uncle.'

'How long, from start to finish?'

'Fixing the manifold to the heater? Say, from scratch, including maybe having to cast around for a bit of tube, well, at the outside half an hour. A quarter, if you had something all ready handy. Only the drilling would take any time, see? The rest would be like stealing candy from a baby.'

Roberta appeared in the doorway shrugging herself into the stripy coat. Derek stood up awkwardly and didn't know where to put his hands. She smiled at him sweetly and unseeingly and said to me, 'Is there anything else you want, Kelly?'

'No. Thank you very much.'

'Think nothing of it. I'll see ... I might come over again tomorrow.'

'Fine,' I said.

'Right.'

She nodded, smiled temperately, and made her usual poised exit. Derek's comment approached, 'Cor.'

'I suppose you didn't see any likely pieces of tube in the wreckage?' I asked.

'Huh?' He tore his eyes away with an effort from the direction Roberta had gone. 'No, like it was real bad. Lots of bits, you couldn't have told what they were. I never seen anything like it. Sure, I seen crashes, stands to reason. Different, this was.' He shivered.

'Did you have any difficulty with being allowed to search?'

'No, none. They didn't seem all that interested in what I did. Just said to help myself. 'Course, I told them it was my car, like. I mean, that I looked after it. Mind you, they were right casual about it, anyway, because when I came away they were letting this other chap have a good look too.'

'Which other chap?'

'Some fellow. Said he was an insurance man, but he didn't have a notebook.'

I felt like saying Huh? too. I said, 'Notebook?'

'Yeah, sure, insurance men, they're always crawling round our place looking at wrecks and never one without a notebook. Write down every blessed detail, they do. But this other chap, looking at your car, he didn't have any notebook.'

'What did he look like?'

He thought.

'That's difficult, see. He didn't look like anything, really. Medium, sort of. Not young and not old really either. A nobody sort of person, really.'

'Did he wear sunglasses?'

'No. He had a hat on, but I don't know if he had ordinary glasses. I can't actually remember. I didn't notice that much.'

'Was he looking through the wreckage as if he knew what he wanted?'

'Uh ... don't know, really. Strikes me he was a bit flummoxed, like, finding it was all in such small bits.'

'He didn't have a girl with him?'

'Nope.' He brightened. 'He came in a Volkswagen, an oldish grey one.'

'Thousands of those about,' I said.

'Oh yeah, sure. Er ... was this chap important?'

'Only if he was looking for what you found.'

He worked it out.

'Cripes,' he said.

Lord Ferth arrived twenty minutes after he'd said, which meant that I'd been hopping round the flat on my crutches for half an hour, unable to keep still.

He stood in the doorway into the sitting-room holding a briefcase and bowler hat in one hand and unbuttoning his short fawn overcoat with the other.

'Well, Hughes,' he said. 'Good afternoon.'

'Good afternoon, my lord.'

He came right in, shut the door behind him, and put his hat and case on the oak chest beside him.

'How's the leg?'

'Stagnating,' I said. 'Can I get you some tea ... coffee ... or a drink?'

'Nothing just now...' He laid his coat on the chest and

picked up the briefcase again, looking round him with the air of surprise I was used to in visitors. I offered him the green armchair with a small table beside it. He asked where I was going to sit.

'I'll stand,' I said. 'Sitting's difficult.'

'But you don't stand all day!'

'No. Lie on my bed, mostly.'

'Then we'll talk in your bedroom.'

We went through the door at the end of the sitting-room and this time he murmured aloud.

'Whose flat is this?' he asked.

'Mine.'

He glanced at my face, hearing the dryness in my voice. 'You resent surprise?'

'It amuses me.'

'Hughes ... it's a pity you didn't join the Civil Service. You'd have gone all the way.'

I laughed. 'There's still time ... Do they take in warned-off jockeys at the Administrative Grade?'

'So you can joke about it?'

'It's taken nine days. But yes, just about.'

He gave me a long straight assessing look, and there was subtle shift somewhere in both his manner to me and in basic approach, and when I shortly understood what it was I was shaken, because he was taking me on level terms, level in power and understanding and experience: and I wasn't level.

Few men in his position would have thought that this course was viable, let alone chosen it. I understood the compliment. He saw, too, that I did, and I knew later that had there not been this fundamental change of ground, this cancellation of the Steward–jockey relationship, he would not have said to me all that he did. It wouldn't have happened if he hadn't been in my flat.

He sat down in the khaki velvet armchair, putting the briefcase carefully on the floor beside him. I took the weight off my crutches and let the bed springs have a go.

'I went to see Lord Gowery,' he said neutrally. 'And I can see no reason not to tell you straight away that you and

Dexter Cranfield will have your warning off rescinded within the next few days.'

'Do you mean it?' I exclaimed. I tried to sit up. The plaster intervened.

Lord Ferth smiled. 'As I see it, there is no alternative. There will be a quiet notice to that effect in next week's Calendar.'

'That is, of course,' I said, 'all you need to tell me.'

He looked at me levelly. 'True. But not all you want to know.'

'No.'

'No one has a better right ... and yet you will have to use your discretion about whether you tell Dexter Cranfield.'

'All right.'

He sighed, reached down to open the briefcase, and pulled out a neat little tape-recorder.

'I did try to ignore your suggestion. Succeeded, too, for a while. However...' He paused, his fingers hovering over the controls. 'This conversation took place late on Monday afternoon, in the sitting-room of Lord Gowery's flat near Sloane Square. We were alone ... you will see that we were alone. He knew, though, that I was making a recording.' He still hesitated. 'Compassion. That's what you need. I believe you have it.'

'Don't con me,' I said.

He grimaced. 'Very well.'

The recording began with the selfconscious platitudes customary in front of microphones, especially when no one wants to take the first dive into the deep end. Lord Ferth had leapt, eventually.

'Norman, I explained why we must take a good look at this Enquiry.'

'Hughes is being ridiculous. Not only ridiculous, but downright slanderous. I don't understand why you should take him seriously.' Gowery sounded impatient.

'We have to, even if only to shut him up.' Lord Ferth looked across the room, his hot eyes gleaming ironically. The recording ploughed on, his voice like honey. 'You know perfectly well, Norman, that it will be better all round if we can show there is nothing whatever in these allegations he is spreading around. Then we can emphatically confirm the suspension and squash all the rumours.'

Subtle stuff. Lord Gowery's voice grew easier, assured now that Ferth was still an ally. As perhaps he was. 'I do assure you Wykeham, that if I had not sincerely believed that Hughes and Dexter Cranfield were guilty, I would not have warned them off.'

There was something odd about that. Both Ferth and Gowery had thought so too, as there were several seconds of silence on the tape.

'But you do still believe it?' Ferth said eventually.

'Of course.' He was emphatic. 'Of course I do.' Much too emphatic.

'Then ... er ... taking one of Hughes' questions first ... How did it come about that Newtonnards was called to the Enquiry?'

'I was informed that Cranfield had backed Cherry Pie with him.'

'Yes ... but who informed you?'

Gowery didn't reply.

Ferth's voice came next, with absolutely no pressure in it.

'Um ... Have you any idea how we managed to show the wrong film of Hughes racing at Reading?'

Gowery was on much surer ground. 'My fault, I'm afraid. I asked the Secretaries to write off for the film of the last race. Didn't realize there were seven races. Careless of me, I'll admit. But of course, as it was the wrong film, it was irrelevant to the case.'

'Er ...' said Lord Ferth. But he hadn't yet been ready to argue. He cleared his throat and said, 'I suppose you thought it would be relevant to see how Hughes had ridden Squelch last time out.'

After another long pause Gowery said, 'Yes.'

'But in the event we didn't show it.'

'No.'

'Would we have shown it if, after having sent for it, we found that the Reading race bore out entirely Hughes' assertion that he rode Squelch in the Lemonfizz in exactly the same way as he always did?'

More silence. Then he said quietly, 'Yes,' and he sounded very troubled.

'Hughes asked at the Enquiry that we should show the right film,' Ferth said.

'I'm sure he didn't.'

'I've been reading the transcript. Norman, I've been reading and re-reading that transcript all weekend and frankly, that is why I'm here. Hughes did in fact suggest that we should show the right film, presumably because he knew it would support his case...'

'Hughes was guilty!' Gowery broke in vehemently. 'Hughes was guilty. I had no option but to warn him off.'

Lord Ferth pressed the stop button on the tape-recorder.

'Tell me,' he said, 'what you think of that last statement?'

'I think,' I said slowly, 'that he did believe it. Both from that statement and from what I remember of the Enquiry. His certainty that day shook me. He believed me guilty so strongly that he was stone deaf to anything which looked even remotely likely to assault his opinion.'

'That was your impression?'

'Overpowering,' I said.

Lord Ferth took his lower lip between his teeth and shook his head, but I gathered it was at the general situation, not at me. He pressed the start button again. His voice came through, precise, carefully without emotion, gentle as vaseline.

'Norman, about the composition of the Enquiry ... the members of the Disciplinary Committee who sat with you ... What guided you to choose Andrew Tring and old Plimborne?'

'What guided me?' He sounded astonished at the question. 'I haven't any idea.'

'I wish you'd cast back.'

'I can't see that it has any relevance ... but let's see ... I suppose I had Tring in my mind anyway, as I'm in the middle of some business negotiations with him. And Plimborne ... well, I just saw him snoozing away in the Club. I was talking to him later in the lobby, and I asked him just on the spur of the moment to sit with me. I don't see the point of your asking.'

'Never mind. It doesn't matter. Now ... about Charlie West. I can see that of course you would call the rider of the third horse to give evidence. And it is clear from the transcript that you knew what the evidence would be. However, at the preliminary enquiry at Oxford West said nothing at all about Hughes having pulled his horse back. I've consulted all three of the Oxford Stewards this morning. They confirm that West did not suggest it at the time. He asserted it, however, at the Enquiry, and you knew what he was going to say, so ... er ... how did you know?'

More silence.

Ferth's voice went on a shade anxiously. 'Norman, if you instructed a Stipendiary Steward to interview West privately and question him further, for heaven's sake say so. These jockeys stick together. It is perfectly reasonable to believe that West wouldn't speak up against Hughes to begin with, but might do so if pressed with questions. Did you send a Stipendiary?'

Gowery said faintly, 'No.'

'Then how did you know what West was going to say?'

Gowery didn't answer. He said instead, 'I did instruct a Stipendiary to look up all the races in which Cranfield had run two horses and compile me a list of all the occasions when the lesser-backed had won. And as you know, it is the accepted practice to bring up everything in a jockey's past history at an Enquiry. It was a perfectly normal procedure.'

'I'm not saying it wasn't,' Ferth's voice said, puzzled.

Ferth stopped the recorder and raised his eyebrows at me. 'What d'you make of *that*?'

'He's grabbing for a rock in a quicksand.'

He sighed, pressed the starter again and Gowery's voice came back.

'It was all there in black and white ... It was quite true ... they'd been doing it again and again.'

'What do you mean, it was quite true? Did someone *tell* you they'd been doing it again and again?'

More silence. Gowery's rock was crumbling.

Again Ferth didn't press him. Instead he said in the same unaccusing way, 'How about David Oakley?'

'Who?'

'David Oakley. The enquiry agent who photographed the money in Hughes' flat. Who suggested that he should go there?'

No answer.

Ferth said with the first faint note of insistence, 'Norman, you really must give some explanation. Can't you see that all this silence just won't do? We *have* to have some answers if we are going to squash Hughes' rumours.'

Gowery reacted with defence in his voice. 'The evidence against Cranfield and Hughes was collected. What does it matter who collected it?'

'It matters because Hughes asserts that much of it was false.'

'No,' he said fiercely. 'It was not false.'

'Norman,' Ferth said, 'is that what you believe ... or what you *want* to believe?'

'Oh ...' Gowery's exclamation was more of anguish than surprise. I looked sharply across at Ferth. His dark eyes were steady on my face. His voice went on, softer again. Persuasive.

'Norman, was there any reason why you *wanted* Cranfield and Hughes warned off?'

'No.' Half a shout. Definitely a lie.

'Any reason why you should go so far as to manufacture evidence against them, if none existed?'

'Wykeham!' He was outraged. 'How can you say that! You are suggesting ... You are suggesting ... something so dishonourable ...'

Ferth pressed the stop button. 'Well?' he said challengingly.

'That was genuine,' I said. 'He didn't manufacture it himself. But then I never thought he did. I just wanted to know where he got it from.'

Ferth nodded. Pressed the start again.

His voice. 'My dear Norman, you lay yourself open to

140

such suggestions if you will not say how you came by all the evidence. Do you not see? If you will not explain how you came by it, you cannot be too surprised if you are thought to have procured it yourself.'

'The evidence was genuine!' he asserted. A rearguard action.

'You are still trying to convince yourself that it was.'

'No! It was.'

'Then where did it come from?'

Gowery's back was against the wall. I could see from the remembered emotion twisting Ferth's face that this had been a saddening and perhaps embarrassing moment.

'I was sent,' said Gowery with difficulty, 'a package. It contained ... various statements ... and six copies of the photograph taken in Hughes' flat.'

'Who sent it to you?'

Gowery's voice was very low. 'I don't know.'

'You don't know?' Ferth was incredulous. 'You warned two men off on the strength of it, and you don't know where it came from?'

A miserable assenting silence.

'You just accepted all that so-called evidence on its face value?'

'It was all true.' He clung to it.

'Have you still got that package?'

'Yes.'

'I'd like to see it.' A touch of iron in Ferth's voice.

Gowery hadn't argued. There were sounds of moving about, a drawer opening and closing, a rustling of papers.

'I see,' Ferth said slowly. 'These papers do, in fact, look very convincing.'

'Then you see why I acted on them,' Gowery said eagerly, with a little too much relief.

'I can see why you should consider doing so ... after making a careful check.'

'I did check.'

'To what extent?'

'Well ... the package only came four days before the Enquiry. On the Thursday before. I had the Secretaries send out the summonses to Newtonnards, Oakley, and West immediately. They were asked to confirm by telegram that they would be attending, and they all did so. Newtonnards was asked to bring his records for the Lemonfizz Cup. And then of course I asked a Stipendiary to ask the Totalizator people if anyone had backed Cherry Pie substantially, and he collected those affidavits ... the ones we produced at the Enquiry. There was absolutely no doubt whatsoever that Cranfield had backed Cherry Pie. He lied about it at the Enquiry. That made it quite conclusive. He was entirely guilty, and there was no reason why I should not warn him off.'

Ferth stopped the recorder. 'What do you say to that?' he asked.

I shrugged. 'Cranfield did back Cherry Pie. He was stupid to deny it, but admitting it was, as he saw it, cutting his own throat. He told me that he backed him – through this unidentified friend – with Newtonnards and on the Tote, and not with his normal bookmaker, because he didn't want Kessel to know, as Kessel and the bookmaker are tattle-swapping buddies. He in fact put a hundred pounds on Cherry Pie because he thought the horse might be warming up to give everyone a surprise. He also put two hundred and fifty pounds on Squelch, because reason suggested that *he* would win. And where is the villainy in that?'

Ferth looked at me levelly. 'You didn't know he had backed Cherry Pie, not at the Enquiry.'

'I tackled him with it afterwards. It had struck me by then that that had to be true, however hard he had denied it. Newtonnards might have lied or altered his books, but no one can argue against Tote tickets.'

'That was one of the things which convinced me too,' he admitted.

He started the recorder. He himself was speaking and now there was a distinct flavour in his voice of cross examination. The whole interview moved suddenly into the shape of an Enqiry of its own. 'This photograph ... didn't it seem at all odd to you?'

'Why should it?' Gowery said sharply.

'Didn't you ask yourself how it came to be taken?'

'No.'

'Hughes says Oakley took the money and the note with him and simply photographed them in his flat.'

'No.'

'How can you be sure?' Ferth pounced on him.

'No!' Gowery said again. There was a rising note in his voice, the sound of pressure approaching blow-up.

'Who sent Oakley to Hughes' flat?'

'I've told you, I don't know.'

'But you're sure that is a genuine photograph?'

'Yes. Yes it is.'

'You are sure beyond doubt?' Ferth insisted.

'Yes!' The voice was high, the anxiety plain, the panic growing. Into this screwed up moment Ferth dropped one intense word, like a bomb.

'*Why?*'

CHAPTER TWELVE

The tape ran on for nearly a minute. When Gowery finally answered his voice was quite different. Low, broken up, distressed to the soul.

'It had ... to be true. I said at first ... I couldn't warn them off if they weren't guilty ... and then the package came ... and it was such a relief ... they really were guilty ... I could warn them off ... and everything would be all right.'

My mouth opened. Ferth watched me steadily, his eyes narrowed with the pity of it.

Gowery went on compulsively. Once started, he needed to confess.

'If I tell you ... from the beginning ... perhaps you will understand. It began the day after I was appointed to substitute for the Disciplinary Steward at the Cranfield–

Hughes Enquiry. It's ironic to think of it now, but I was quite pleased to be going to do it ... and then ... and then ...' He paused and took an effortful control of his voice. 'Then, I had a telephone call.' Another pause. 'This man said ... said ... I must warn Cranfield off.' He cleared his throat. 'I told him I would do no such thing, unless Cranfield was guilty. Then he said ... then he said ... that he knew things about me ... and he would tell everyone ... if I didn't warn Cranfield off. I told him I couldn't warn him off if he wasn't guilty ... and you see I didn't think he *was* guilty. I mean, racehorses are so unpredictable, and I saw the Lemonfizz myself and although after that crowd demonstration it was obvious the Stewards would have Cranfield and Hughes in, I was surprised when they referred it to the Disciplinary Committee ... I thought that there must have been circumstances that I didn't know of ... and then I was asked to take the Enquiry ... and I had an open mind ... I told the man on the telephone that no threats could move me from giving Cranfield a fair judgement.'

Less jelly in his voice while he remembered that first strength. It didn't last.

'He said ... in that case ... I could expect ... after the Enquiry ... if Cranfield got off ... that my life wouldn't be worth living ... I would have to resign from the Jockey Club ... and everyone would know ... And I said again that I would not warn Cranfield off unless I was convinced of his guilt, and that I would not be blackmailed, and I put down the receiver and cut him off.'

'And then,' Ferth suggested, 'you began to worry?'

'Yes.' Little more than a whisper.

'What exactly did he threaten to publish?'

'I can't ... can't tell you. Not criminal ... not a matter for the police ... but ...'

'But enough to ruin you socially?'

'Yes ... I'm afraid so ... yes, completely.'

'But you stuck to your guns?'

'I was desperately worried ... I couldn't ... how could I? ... take away Cranfield's livelihood just to save myself ... It would have been dishonourable ... and I couldn't see myself living with it ... and in any case I couldn't just warn him off, just like that, if there was no proof he was guilty ... So I did worry ... couldn't sleep ... or eat ...'

'Why didn't you ask to be relieved of the Enquiry?'

'Because he told me ... if I backed out ... it would count the same with him as letting Cranfield off ... so I had to go on, just in case some proof turned up.'

'Which it did,' Ferth said drily. 'Conveniently.'

'Oh ...' Again the anguish. 'I didn't realize ... I didn't indeed ... that it might have been the blackmailer who had sent the package. I didn't wonder very much who had sent it. It was release ... that's all I could see ... it was a heaven-sent release from the most unbearable ... I didn't question ... I just believed it ... believed it absolutely ... and I was so grateful ... so grateful ...'

Four days before the Enquiry, that package had come. He must have been sweating for a whole week, taking a long bleak look at the wilderness. Send a St Bernard to a dying mountaineer and he's unlikely to ask for the dog licence.

'When did you begin to doubt?' Ferth said calmly.

'Not until afterwards. Not for days. It was Hughes ... at the dance. You told me he was insisting he'd been framed and was going to find out who ... and then he asked me directly who had sent Oakley to his flat ... and it ... Wyke-ham it was *terrible*. I realized ... what I'd done. Inside, I did know ... but I couldn't admit to it myself ... I shut it away ... they *had* to be guilty ...'

There was another long silence. Then Gowery said, 'You'll see to it ... that they get their licences back?'

'Yes,' Ferth said.

'I'll resign ...' He sounded desolate.

'From the Disciplinary Committee, I agree,' Ferth said reasonably. 'As to the rest ... we will see.'

'Do you think the ... the blackmailer ... will tell ... everyone ... anyway, when Cranfield has his licence back?'

'He would have nothing to gain.'

'No, but ...'

'There are laws to protect you.'

'They couldn't.'

'What does he in fact have over you?'

'I ... I ... oh God.' The tape stopped abruptly, cutting off words that were disintegrating into gulps.

Ferth said, 'I switched it off. He was breaking down. One couldn't record that.'

'No.'

'He told me what it was he was being blackmailed about. I think I am prepared to tell you also, although he would hate it if he knew. But you only.'

'Only,' I said. 'I won't repeat it.'

'He told me ...' His nose wrinkled in distaste. 'He told me that he has ... he suffers from ... unacceptable sexual appetites. Not homosexual. Perhaps that would have been better ... simpler ... he wouldn't nowadays have been much reviled for that. No. He says he belongs to a sort of club where people like him can gratify themselves fairly harmlessly, as they are all there because they enjoy ... in varying forms ... the same thing.' He stopped. He was embarrassed.

'Which is what?' I said matter-of-factly.

He said, as if putting a good yard of clean air between himself and the world, 'Flagellation.'

'That old thing!' I said.

'What?'

'The English disease. Shades of Fanny Hill. Sex tangled up with self-inflicted pain, like nuns with their little disciplines and sober citizens paying a pound a lash to be whipped.'

'Kelly!'

'You must have read their coy little advertisements? "Correction given". That's what it's all about. More widespread than most people imagine. Starts with husbands spanking their wives regularly before they bed them, and carries right on up to the parties where they all dress up in leather and have a right old orgy I don't actually understand why anyone should get fixated on leather or rubber or hair, or on those instead of anything else. Why not coal, for instance ... or silk? But they do, apparently.'

'In this case ... leather.'

'Boots and whips and naked bosoms?'

146

Ferth shook his head in disbelief. 'You take it so coolly.'

'Live and let live,' I said. 'If that's what they feel compelled to do ... why stop them? As he said, they're not harming anyone, if they're in a club where everyone else is the same.'

'But for a Steward,' he protested. 'A member of the Disciplinary Committee!'

'Gives you pause,' I agreed.

He looked horrified. 'But there would be nothing sexual in his judgement on racing matters.'

'Of course not. Nothing on earth as unsexual as racing.'

'But one can see ... he would be finished in the racing world, if this got out. Even I ... I cannot think of him now without this ... this perversion ... coming into my mind. It would be the same with everyone. One can't respect him any more. One can't like him.'

'Difficult,' I agreed.

'It's ... horrible.' In his voice, all the revulsion of the normal for the deviation. Most racing men were normal. The deviation would be cast out. Ferth felt it. Gowery knew it. And so did someone else ...

'Don't they wear masks, at this club?' I asked.

Ferth looked surprised. 'Why, yes, they do. I asked him who could know about him ... in order to blackmail him ... and he said he didn't know, they all wore masks. Hoods, actually, was the word he used. Hoods ... and aprons ...' He was revolted.

'All leather?'

He nodded. 'How can they?'

'They do less harm than the ones who go out and rape small children.'

'I'm glad I ...' he said passionately.

'Me too,' I said. 'But it's just luck.' Gowery had been unlucky, in more ways than one. 'Someone may have seen him going in, or leaving afterwards.'

'That's what he thinks. But he says he doesn't know the real names of any of his fellow members. They all call each other by fanciful made-up names, apparently.'

'There must be a secretary ... with a list of members?'

Ferth shook his head. 'I asked him that. He said he'd never given his own name to anyone there. It wasn't expected. There's no annual subscription, just ten pounds in cash every time he attends. He says he goes about once a month, on average.'

'How many other members are there?'

'He didn't know the total number. He says there are never fewer than ten, and sometimes thirty or thirty-five. More men than women, usually. The club isn't open every day; only Mondays and Thursdays.'

'Where is it?'

'In London. He wouldn't tell me exactly where.'

'He wants ... needs ... to keep on going,' I said.

'You don't think he will!'

'After a while. Yes.'

'Oh no ...'

'Who introduced him to the club, do you know?'

'He said it couldn't be the person who introduced him to the club. She was a prostitute ... he'd never told her his real name.'

'But she understood his needs.'

He sighed. 'It would seem so.'

'Some of those girls make more money out of whipping men than sleeping with them.'

'How on earth do you know?'

'I had digs once in the next room to one. She told me.'

'Good Lord.' He looked as if he'd turned over a stone and found creepy-crawlies underneath. He had plainly no inkling of what it was like to *be* a creepy-crawly. His loss.

'Anyway,' he said slowly, 'you will understand why he accepted that package at its face value.'

'And why he chose Lord Plimborne and Andy Tring.'

Lord Ferth nodded. 'At the end, when he'd recovered a little, he understood that he'd chosen them for the reasons you said, but he believed at the time that they were impulsive choices. And he is now, as you would expect, a very worried and troubled man.'

'Was he,' I asked, 'responsible for this?'

I held out to him the letter Tony had received from the

Stewards' Secretaries. He stood up, came to take it, and read its brief contents with exasperation.

'I don't know,' he said explosively. 'I really don't know. When did this arrive?'

'Tuesday. Postmarked noon on Monday.'

'Before I saw him ... He didn't mention it.'

'Could you find out if it was his doing?'

'Do you mean ... it will be all the more impossible to forgive him?'

'No. Nothing like that. I was just wondering if it was our little framer-blackmailer at work again. See those words "It has been brought to our attention"? ... What I'd like to know is who brought it.'

'I'll find out,' he agreed positively. 'That shouldn't be difficult. And of course, disregard the letter. There won't be any question now of your having to move.'

'How are you going to work it? Giving our licences back. How are you going to explain it?'

He raised his eyebrows. 'We never have to give reasons for our decisions.'

I smothered a laugh. The system had its uses.

Lord Ferth sat down in the chair again and put the letter in his briefcase. Then he packed up the tape-recorder and tucked that away too. Then with an air of delicately choosing his words he said, 'A scandal of this sort would do racing a great deal of harm.'

'So you want me to take my licence back and shut up?'

'Er ... yes.'

'And not chase after the blackmailer, in case he blows the gaffe?'

'Exactly.' He was relieved that I understood.

'No.' I said.

'Why not?' Persuasion in his voice.

'Because he tried to kill me.'

'*What?*'

I showed him the chunk of exhaust manifold, and explained. 'Someone at the dance,' I said. 'That means that our blackmailer is one of about six hundred people, and from there it shouldn't be too hard. You can more or less rule out the women, because few of them would drill through cast iron wearing an evening dress. Much too conspicuous, if anyone saw them. That leaves three hundred men.'

'Someone who knew your car,' he said. 'Surely that would narrow it down considerably.'

'It might not. Anyone could have seen me getting out of it at the races. It was a noticeable car, I'm afraid. But I arrived late at the dance. The car was parked right at the back.'

'Have you...' he cleared his throat. 'Are the police involved in this?'

'If you mean are they at present investigating an attempted murder, then no, they are not. If you mean, am I going to ask them to investigate, etc, then I haven't decided.'

'Once you start the police on something, you can't stop them.'

'On the other hand if I don't start them the blackmailer might have another go at me, with just a fraction of an inch more success. Which would be quite enough.'

'Um.' He thought it over. 'But if you made it clear to everyone now that you are not any longer trying to find out who framed you ... he might not try again.'

I said curiously, 'Do you really think it would be best for racing if we just leave this blackmailing murderer romping around free?'

'Better than a full-blown scandal.'

The voice of Establishment diplomacy.

'And if he doesn't follow your line of reasoning ... and he does kill me ... how would that do for a scandal?'

He didn't answer. Just looked at me levelly with the hot eyes.

'All right, then,' I said. 'No police.'

'Thank you.'

'Us, though. We'll have to do it ourselves. Find him and deal with him.'

'How do you mean?'

'I'll find him. You deal with him.'

'To your satisfaction, I suppose,' he said ironically.

'Absolutely.'

'And Lord Gowery?'

'He's yours entirely. I shan't tell Dexter Cranfield anything at all.'

'Very well.' He stood up, and I struggled off the bed on to the crutches.

'Just one thing,' I said. 'Could you arrange to have that package of Lord Gowery's sent to me here?'

'I have it with me.' Without hesitation he took a large Manila envelope out of the briefcase and put it on the bed. 'You'll understand how he fell on it with relief.'

'Things being as they were,' I agreed. He walked across the sitting-room to the way out, stopping by the chest to put on his coat.

'Can Cranfield tell his owners to shovel their horses back?' I said. 'The sooner the better, you see, if they're to come back in time for Cheltenham.'

'Give me until tomorrow morning. There are several other people who must know first.'

'All right.'

He held out his hand. I transferred the right crutch to the left, and shook it.

He said, 'Perhaps one day soon ... when this is over ... you will dine with me?'

'I'd like to,' I said.

'Good.' He picked up his bowler and his briefcase, swept a last considering glance round my flat, nodded to me as if finalizing a decision, and quietly went away.

I telephoned to the orthopod who regularly patched me up after falls.

'I want this plaster off.'

He went into a long spiel of which the gist was two or three more weeks.

'Monday,' I said.

'I'll give you up.'

'Tuesday I start getting it off with a chisel.'

I always slept in shirt-and-shorts pyjamas, which had come in very handy in the present circs. Bedtime that day I struggled into a lime-green and white checked lot I had bought in an off moment at Liverpool the year before with my mind more on the imminent Grand National than on what they would do to my yellow complexion at six on a winter's morning.

Tony had gloomily brought me some casseroled beef and had stayed to celebrate when I told him I wouldn't have to leave. I was out of whisky again in consequence.

When he'd gone I went to bed and read the pages which had sent me to limbo. And they were, indeed, convincing. Neatly typed, well set out, written in authoritative language. Not at first, second, or even third sight the product of malevolence. Emotionless. Cool. Damaging.

'Charles Richard West is prepared to testify that during the course of the race, and in particular at a spot six furlongs from the winning post on the second circuit, he heard Hughes say that he (Hughes) was about to ease his horse so that it should be in no subsequent position to win. Hughes' precise words were, 'OK. Brakes on chaps'.'

The four other sheets were equally brief, equally to the point. One said that through an intermediary Dexter Cranfield had backed Cherry Pie with Newtonnards. The second pointed out that an investigation of the past form would show that on several other occasions Cranfield's second string had beaten his favourite. The third suggested watching the discrepancies in Hughes' riding in the Lemonfizz and in the last race at Reading ... and there it was in black and white, 'the last race at Reading.' Gowery hadn't questioned it or checked; had simply sent for the last race at Reading. If he had shown it privately to Plimborne and Tring only, and not to me as well, no one might ever have realized it was the wrong race. This deliberate piece of misleading had in fact gone astray, but only just. And the rest hadn't. Page four stated categorically that Cranfield had bribed Hughes not to win, and photographic evidence to prove it was hereby attached.

There was also a short covering note of explanation.

'These few facts have come to my notice. They should clearly be laid before the appropriate authorities, and I am therefore sending them to you, sir, as Steward in command of the forthcoming Enquiry.'

The typewriting itself was unremarkable, the paper medium-quality quarto. The paper clip holding the sheets together was sold by the hundred million, and the buff envelope in which they'd been sent cost a penny or two in any stationer's in the country.

There were two copies only of the photograph. On the back, no identifications.

I slid them all back into the envelope, and put it in the drawer of the table beside my bed. Switched out the light. Lay thinking of riding races again with a swelling feeling of relief and excitement. Wondered how poor old Gowery was making out, going fifteen rounds with his conscience. Thought of Archie and his mortgage ... Kessel having to admit he'd been wrong ... Roberta stepping off her dignity ... the blackmailer biting his nails in apprehension ... sweet dreams every one ... slid into the first easy sleep since the Enquiry.

I woke with a jolt, knowing I'd heard a sound which had no business to be there.

A pen-sized flashlight was flickering round the inside of one of the top drawers of the dressing chest. A dark shape blocked off half of its beam as an arm went into the drawer to feel around. Cautious. Very quiet, now.

I lay watching through slit-shut eyes, wondering how close I was this time to the pearly gates. Inconveniently my pulse started bashing against my eardrums as fear stirred up the adrenals, and inside the plaster all the hairs on my leg fought to stand on end.

Trying to keep my breathing even and make no rustle with the sheets I very cautiously slid one arm over the side of the bed and reached down to the floor for a crutch. Any weapon handy was better than none.

No crutches.

I felt around, knowing exactly where I'd laid them beside me, feeling nothing but carpet under my fingers.

The flashlight moved out of the drawer and swung in a

small arc while the second top drawer was opened, making the same tiny crack as it loosened which had woken me with the other. The scrap of light shone fractionally on my two crutches propped up against the wall by the door.

I drew the arm very slowly back into bed and lay still. If he'd meant just to kill me, he would have done it by now: and whatever he intended I had little chance of avoiding. The plaster felt like a ton, chaining me immobile.

A clammy crawling feeling all over my skin. Jaw tight clenched with tension. Dryness in the mouth. Head feeling as if it were swelling. I lay and tried to beat the physical sensations, tried to will them away.

No noticeable success.

He finished with the drawers. The flashlight swung over the khaki chair and steadied on the polished oak chest behind it, against the wall. He moved over there soundlessly and lifted the lid. I almost cried out to him not to, it would wake me. The lid always creaked loudly. I really didn't want him to wake me, it was much too dangerous.

The lid creaked sharply. He stopped dead with it six inches up. Lowered it back into place. It creaked even louder.

He stood there, considering. Then there were quick soft steps on the carpet, a hand fastening in my hair and yanking my head back, and the flashlight beam full in my eyes.

'Right, mate. You're awake. So you'll answer some questions.'

I knew the voice. I shut my eyes against the light and spoke in as bored a drawl as I could manage.

'Mr Oakley, I presume?'

'Clever Mr Hughes.'

He let go of my hair and stripped the bedclothes off with one flick. The flashlight swung away and fell on top of them. I felt his grip on my neck and the front of my shirt as he wrenched me off the bed and on to the floor. I fell with a crash.

'That's for starters,' he said.

CHAPTER THIRTEEN

He was fast, to give him his due. Also strong and ruthless and used to this sort of thing.

'Where is it?' he said.

'What?'

'A chunk of metal with a hole in it.'

'I don't know what you're talking about.'

He swung his arm and hit me with something hard and knobbly. When it followed through to the tiny light I could see what it was. One of my own crutches. Delightful.

I tried to disentangle my legs and roll over and stand up. He shone the light on me to watch. When I was half up he knocked me down again.

'Where is it?'

'I told you . . .'

'We both know, chum, that you have this chunk of metal. I want it. I have a customer for it. And you're going to hand it over like a good little warned-off crook.'

'Go scratch yourself.'

I rolled fast and almost missed the next swipe. It landed on the plaster. Some flakes came off. Less work for Tuesday.

'You haven't a hope,' he said. 'Face facts.'

The facts were that if I yelled for help only the horses would hear.

Pity.

I considered giving him the chunk of metal with the hole in it. Correction, half a hole. He didn't know it was only half a hole. I wondered whether I should tell him. Perhaps he'd be only half as savage.

'Who wants it?' I said.

'Be your age.' He swung the crutch.

Contact.

I cursed.

'Save yourself, chum. Don't be stupid.'

'What is this chunk of metal?'

'Just hand it over.'

'I don't know what you're looking for?'

'Chunk of metal with a hole in it.'

'What chunk of metal?'

'Look, chum, what does it matter what chunk of metal? The one you've got.'

'I haven't.'

'Stop playing games.' He swung the crutch. I grunted. 'Hand it over.'

'I haven't ... got ... any chunk of metal.'

'Look chum, my instructions are as clear as glass. You've got some lump of metal and I've come to fetch it. Understand? Simple. So save yourself, you stupid crumb.'

'What is he paying for it?'

'You still offering more?'

'Worth a try.'

'So you said before. But nothing doing.'

'Pity.'

'Where's the chunk? ...'

I didn't answer, heard the crutch coming, rolled at the right instant, and heard it thud on the carpet, roughly where my nose had been.

The little flashlight sought me out. He didn't miss the second time, but it was only my arm, not my face.

'Didn't you ask what it was?' I said.

'None of your bloody business. You just tell me' ... bash ... 'where' ... bash ... 'it is.'

I'd had about enough. Too much, in fact. And I'd found out all I was likely to, except how far he was prepared to go, which was information I could do without.

I'd been trying to roll towards the door. Finally made it near enough. Stretched backwards over my head and felt my fingers curl round the bottom of the other crutch still propped against the wall.

The rubber knob came into my hand, and with one scything movement I swept the business end round viciously at knee level.

It caught him square and unexpected on the back of the legs just as he himself was in mid swing, and he overbal-

156

anced and crashed down half on top of me. I reached out
and caught something, part of his coat, and gripped and
pulled, and tried to swing my plaster leg over his body to
hold him down.

He wasn't having any. We scrambled around on the floor,
him trying to get up and me trying to stop him, both of us
scratching and punching and gouging in a thoroughly un-
sportsmanlike manner. The flashlight had fallen away
across the far side of the room and shone only on the wall.
Not enough light to be much good. Too much for total
evasion of his efficient fists.

The bedside table fell over with a crash and the lamp
smashed. Oakley somehow reached into the ruins and
picked up a piece of glass, and I just saw the light shimmer
on it as he slashed it towards my eyes. I dodged it by a
millimetre in the last half-second.

'You bugger,' I said bitterly.

We were both gasping for breath. I loosed the grip I had
on his coat in order to have both hands free to deal with
the glass, and as soon as he felt me leave go he was heaving
himself back on to his feet.

'Now,' he said, panting heavily, 'where bloody is it?'

I didn't answer. He'd got hold of a crutch again. Back to
square one. On the thigh, that time.

I was lying on the other crutch. The elbow supports were
digging into my back. I twisted my arm underneath me and
pulled out the crutch, hand-swung it at him just as he was
having a second go. The crutches met and crashed together
in the air. I held on to mine for dear life and rolled towards
the bed.

'Give ... up ...' he said.

'Get ... stuffed.'

I made it to the bed and lay in the angle between it and
the floor. He couldn't get a good swing at me there. I
turned the crutch round, and held it by the elbow and hand
grips with both of my own. To hit me where I was lying he
had to come nearer.

He came. His dark shadow was above me, exaggerated by
the dim torchlight. He leant over, swinging. I shoved the

stick end of the crutch hard upwards. It went into him solidly and he screeched sharply. The crutch he had been swinging dropped harmlessly on top of me as he reeled away, clutching at his groin.

'I'll ... kill you ... for that...' His voice was high with pain. He groaned, hugging himself.

'Serves ... you ... right,' I said breathlessly.

I pulled myself across the floor, dragging the plaster, aiming for the telephone which had crashed on to the floor with the little table. Found the receiver. Pulled the cord. The telephone bumped over the carpet into my hand.

Put my finger on the button. Small ting. Dialling tone. Found the numbers. Three ... nine ... one ...

'Yeah?' Tony's voice, thick with sleep.

Dead careless, I was. Didn't hear a thing. The crutch swung wickedly down on the back of my head and I fell over the telephone and never told him to gallop to the rescue.

I woke where Oakley had left me, still lying on the floor over the telephone, the receiver half in and half out of my hand.

It was daylight, just. Grey and raw and raining. I was stiff. Cold. Had a headache.

Remembered bit by bit what had happened. Set about scraping myself off the carpet.

First stop, back on to the bed, accompanied by bed-clothes. Lay there feeling terrible and looking at the mess he had made of my room.

After he'd knocked me out, he had nothing to be quiet about. Everything had been pulled out of the closet and drawers and flung on the floor. Everything smashable was smashed. The sleeves of some of my suits were ripped and lying in tatters. Rosalind's picture had been torn into four pieces and the silver frame twisted and snapped. It had been revenge more than a search. A bad loser, David Oakley.

What I could see of the sitting-room through the open door seemed to have received the same treatment.

I lay and ached in most places you could think of.

Didn't look to see if Oakley had found the piece of manifold because I knew he wouldn't have. Thought about him coming, and about what he'd said.

Thought about Cranfield.

Thought about Gowery.

Once I got the plaster off and could move about again, it shouldn't take me too long now to dig out the enemy. A bit of leg work. Needed two legs.

Oakley would shortly be reporting no success from the night's work. I wondered if he would be sent to try again. Didn't like that idea particularly.

I shifted on the bed, trying to get comfortable. I'd been concussed twice in five days once before, and got over it. I'd been kicked along the ground by a large field of hurdlers, which had been a lot worse than the crutches. I'd broken enough bones to stock a cemetery and this time they were all whole. But all the same I felt sicker than after racing falls, and in the end realized my unease was revulsion against being hurt by another man. Horses, hard ground, even express trains, were impersonal. Oakley had been a different type of invasion. The amount you were mentally affected by a pain always depended on how you got it.

I felt terrible. Had no energy at all to get up and tidy the mess.

Shut my eyes to blot it out. Blotted myself out, too. Went to sleep.

A voice said above my head, 'Won't you ever learn to keep your door shut?'

I smiled feebly. 'Not if you're coming through it.'

'Finding you flat out is becoming a habit.'

'Try to break it.'

I opened my eyes. Broad daylight. Still raining.

Roberta was standing a foot from the bed wearing a blinding yellow raincoat covered in trickling drops. The copper hair was tied up in a pony tail and she was looking around her with disgust.

'Do you realize it's half past ten?' she said.

'No.'

'Do you always drop your clothes all over the place when you go to bed?'

'Only on Wednesdays.'

'Coffee?' she said abruptly, looking down at me.

'Yes, please.'

She picked her way through the mess to the door, and then across the sitting-room until she was out of sight. I rubbed my hand over my chin. Bristly. And there was a tender lump on the back of my skull and a sore patch all down one side of my jaw, where I hadn't dodged fast enough. Bruises in other places set up a morning chorus. I didn't listen.

She came back minus the raincoat and carrying two steaming mugs which she put carefully on the floor. Then she picked up the bedside table and transferred the mugs to its top.

The drawer had fallen out of the table, and the envelope had fallen out of the drawer. But Oakley hadn't apparently looked into it: hadn't known it was there to find.

Roberta picked up the scattered crutches and brought them over to the bed.

'Thanks,' I said.

'You take it very calmly.'

'I've seen it before,' I pointed out.

'And you just went to sleep?'

'Opted out,' I agreed.

She looked more closely at my face and rolled my head over on the pillow. I winced. She took her hand away.

'Did you get the same treatment as the flat?'

'More or less.'

'What for?'

'For being stubborn.'

'Do you mean,' she said incredulously, 'that you could have avoided all this ... and didn't?'

'If there's a good reason for backing down, you back down. If there isn't, you don't.'

'And all this ... isn't a good enough reason?'

'No.'

'You're crazy,' she said.

'You're so right,' I sighed, pushed myself up a bit, and reached for the coffee.

'Have you called the police?' she asked.

I shook my head. 'Not their quarrel.'

'Who did it, then?'

I smiled at her. 'Your father and I have got our licences back.'

'*What?*'

'It'll be official some time today.'

'Does Father know? How did it happen? Did you do it?'

'No, he doesn't know yet. Ring him up. Tell him to get on to all the owners. It'll be confirmed in the papers soon, either today's evening editions, or tomorrow's dailies.'

She picked the telephone off the floor and sat on the edge of my bed, and telephoned to her father with real joy and sparkling eyes. He wouldn't believe it at first.

'Kelly says it's true,' she said.

He argued again, and she handed the telephone to me.

'You tell him.'

Cranfield said, 'Who told you?'

'Lord Ferth.'

'Did he say why?'

'No,' I lied. 'Just that the sentences had been reviewed ... and reversed. We're back, as from today. The official notice will be in next week's Calendar.'

'No explanation at all?' he insisted.

'They don't have to give one,' I pointed out.

'All the same ...'

'Who cares why?' I said. 'The fact that we're back ... that's all that matters.'

'Did you find out who framed us?'

'No.'

'Will you go on trying?'

'I might do,' I said. 'We'll see.'

He had lost interest in that. He bounded into a stream of plans for the horses, once they were back. 'And it will give me great pleasure to tell Henry Kessel ...'

'I'd like to see his face,' I agreed. But Pat Nikita would

never part with Squelch, nor with Kessel, now. If Cranfield thought Kessel would come crawling apologetically back, he didn't know his man. 'Concentrate on getting Bread-winner back,' I suggested. 'I'll be fit to ride in the Gold Cup.'

'Old Strepson promised Breadwinner would come back at once ... and Pound Postage of his ... that's entered in the National, don't forget.'

'I haven't,' I assured him, 'forgotten.'

He ran down eventually and disconnected, and I could imagine him sitting at the other end still wondering whether to trust me.

Roberta stood up with a spring, as if the news had filled her with energy.

'Shall I tidy up for you?'

'I'd love some help.'

She bent down and picked up Rosalind's torn picture.

'They didn't have to do that,' she said in disgust.

'I'll get the bits stuck together and re-photographed.'

'You'd hate to lose her ...'

I didn't answer at once. She looked at me curiously, her eyes dark with some unreadable expression.

'I lost her,' I said slowly. 'Rosalind ... Roberta ... you are so unalike.'

She turned away abruptly and put the pieces on the chest of drawers where they had always stood.

'Who wants to be a carbon copy?' she said, and her voice was high and cracking. 'Get dressed ... while I start on the sitting-room.' She disappeared fast and shut the door behind her.

I lay there looking at it.

Roberta Cranfield. I'd never liked her.

Roberta Cranfield. I couldn't bear it ... I was beginning to love her.

She stayed most of the day, helping me clear up the mess.

Oakley had left little to chance: the bathroom and kit-chen both looked as if they'd been gutted by a whirlwind. He'd searched everywhere a good enquiry agent could think of, including in the lavatory cistern and the refrigerator; and everywhere he'd searched he'd left his trail of damage.

After midday, which was punctuated by some scrambled eggs, the telephone started ringing. Was it true, asked the *Daily Witness* in the shape of Daddy Leeman, that Cranfield and I? ... 'Check with the Jockey Club,' I said.

The other papers had checked first. 'May we have your comments?' they asked.

'Thrilled to bits,' I said gravely. 'You can quote me.'

A lot of real chums rang to congratulate, and a lot of pseudo chums rang to say they'd never believed me guilty anyway.

For most of the afternoon I lay flat on the sitting-room floor with my head on a cushion talking down the telephone while Roberta stepped around and over me nonchalantly, putting everything back into place.

Finally she dusted her hands off on the seat of her black pants, and said she thought that that would do. The flat looked almost as good as ever. I agreed gratefully that it would do very well.

'Would you consider coming down to my level?' I asked.

She said calmly, 'Are you speaking literally, metaphorically, intellectually, financial, or socially?'

'I was suggesting you might sit on the floor.'

'In that case,' she said collectedly, 'yes.' And she sank gracefully into a cross-legged sprawl.

I couldn't help grinning. She grinned companionably back.

'I was scared stiff of you when I came here last week,' she said.

'You were *what*?'

'You always seemed so aloof. Unapproachable.'

'Are we talking about me ... or you?'

'You, of course,' she said in surprise. 'You always made me nervous. I always get sort of ... strung up ... when I'm nervous. Put on a bit of an act, to hide it, I suppose.'

'I see,' I said slowly.

'You're still a pretty good cactus, if you want to know ...

but ... well, you see people differently when they've been bleeding all over your best dress and looking pretty vulnerable ...'

I began to say that in that case I would be prepared to bleed on her any time she liked, but the telephone interrupted me at halfway. And it was old Strepson, settling down for a long cosy chat about Breadwinner and Pound Postage.

Roberta wrinkled her nose and got to her feet.

'Don't go,' I said, with my hand over the mouthpiece.

'Must. I'm late already.'

'Wait.' I said. But she shook her head, fetched the yellow raincoat from the bath, where she'd put it, and edged herself into it.

' 'Bye,' she said.

'Wait ...'

She waved briefly and let herself out of the door. I struggled up on to my feet, and said, 'Sir ... could you hold on a minute ...' into the telephone, and hopped without the crutches over to the window. She looked up when I opened it. She was standing in the yard, tying on a headscarf. The rain had eased to drizzle.

'Will you come tomorrow?' I shouted down.

'Can't tomorrow. Got to go to London.'

'Saturday?'

'Do you want me to?'

'Yes.'

'I'll try, then.'

'Please come.'

'Oh ...' She suddenly smiled in a way I'd never seen before. 'All right.'

Careless I might be about locking my front door, but in truth I left little about worth stealing. Five hundred pounds would never have been lying around on my chest of drawers for enquiry agents to photograph.

When I'd converted the flat from an old hay loft I'd built in more than mod cons. Behind the cabinet in the kitchen which housed things like fly killer and soap powder, and

164

tucked into a crafty piece of brickwork, lay a maximum security safe. It was operated not by keys or combinations, but by electronics. The manufacturers had handed over the safe itself and also the tiny ultrasonic transmitter which sent out the special series of radio waves which alone would release the lock mechanism, and I'd installed them myself: the safe in the wall and the transmitter in a false bottom to the cabinet. Even if anyone found the transmitter, they had still to find the safe and to know the sequence of frequencies which unlocked it.

A right touch of the Open Sesame. I'd always liked gadgets.

Inside the safe there were, besides money and some racing trophies, several pieces of antique silver, three paintings by Houthuesen, two Chelsea figures, a Meissen cup and saucer, a Louis XIV snuff box, and four uncut diamonds totalling twenty-eight carats. My retirement pension, all wrapped in green baize and appreciating nicely. Retirement for a steeplechase jockey could lurk in the very next fall: and the ripe age of forty, if one lasted that long, was about the limit.

There was also a valueless lump of cast iron, with a semicircular dent in it. To these various treasures I added the envelope which Ferth had given me, because it wouldn't help if I lost that either.

Bolting my front door meant a hazardous trip down the stairs, and another in the morning to open it. I decided it could stay unlocked as usual. Wedged a chair under the door into my sitting-room instead.

During the evening I telephoned to Newtonnards in his pink washed house in Mill Hill.

'Hallo,' he said. 'You've got your licence back then. Talk of the meeting it was at Wincanton today, soon as the Press Association chaps heard about it.'

'Yes, it's great news.'

'What made their lordships change their minds?'

'I've no idea ... Look, I wondered if you'd seen that man again yet, the one who backed Cherry Pie with you.'

'Funny thing,' he said, 'but I saw him today. Just after I'd heard you were back in favour, though, so I didn't think you'd be interested any more.'

'Did you by any chance find out who he is?'

'I did, as a matter of fact. More to satisfy my own curiosity, really. He's the Honourable Peter Foxcroft. Mean anything to you?'

'He's a brother of Lord Middleburg.'

'Yeah. So I'm told.'

I laughed inwardly. Nothing sinister about Cranfield refusing to name his mysterious pal. Just another bit of ladder climbing. He might be one rung up being in a position to use the Hon P. Foxcroft as a runner: but he would certainly be five rungs down involving him in a messy Enquiry.

'There's one other thing...' I hesitated. 'Would you ... could you ... do me a considerable favour?'

'Depends what it is.' He sounded cautious but not truculent. A smooth, experienced character.

'I can't offer much in return.'

He chuckled. 'Warning me not to expect tip offs when you're on a hot number?'

'Something like that,' I admitted.

'OK then. You want something for strictly nothing. Just as well to know where we are. So shoot.'

'Can you remember who you told about Cranfield backing Cherry Pie?'

'Before the Enquiry, you mean?'

'Yes. Those bookmaker colleagues you mentioned.'

'Well...' he sounded doubtful.

'If you can,' I said, 'could you ask *them* who *they* told?'

'Phew.' He half breathed, half whistled down the receiver. 'That's some favour.'

'I'm sorry. Just forget it.'

'Hang on, hang on, I didn't say I wouldn't do it. It's a bit of a tall order, though, expecting them to remember.'

'I know. Very long shot. But I still want to know who told the Stewards about the bet with you.'

'You've got your licence back. Why don't you let it rest?'

'Would you?'

He sighed. 'I don't know. All right then, I'll see what I can do. No promises, mind. Oh, and by the way, it can be just as useful to know when one of your mounts is *not* fit or likely to win. If you take my meaning.'

'I take it,' I said smiling. 'It's a deal.'

I put down the receiver reflecting that only a minority of bookmakers were villains, and that most of them were more generous than they got credit for. The whole tribe were reviled for the image of the few. Like students.

CHAPTER FOURTEEN

Oakley didn't come. No one came. I took the chair from under the door knob to let the world in with the morning. Not much of the world accepted the invitation.

Made some coffee. Tony came while I was standing in the kitchen drinking it and put whisky into a mug of it for himself by way of breakfast. He'd been out with one lot of horses at exercise and was waiting to go out with the other, and spent the interval discussing their prospects as if nothing had ever happened. For him the warning off was past history, forgotten. His creed was that of newspapers; today is important, tomorrow more so, but yesterday is nothing.

He finished the coffee and left, clapping me cheerfully on the shoulder and setting up a protest from an Oakley bruise. I spent most of the rest of the day lying flat on my bed, answering the telephone, staring at the ceiling, letting Nature get on with repairing a few ravages, and thinking.

Another quiet night. I had two names in my mind, juggling them. Two to work on. Better than three hundred. But both could be wrong.

Saturday morning the postman brought the letters right upstairs, as he'd been doing since the era of plaster. I thanked him, sorted through them, dropped a crutch, and had the usual awkward fumble picking it up. When I opened one of the letters I dropped both the crutches again in surprise.

Left the crutches on the floor. Leant against the wall and read.

Dear Kelly Hughes,

I have seen in the papers that you have had your licence restored, so perhaps this information will be too late to be of any use to you. I am sending it anyway because the friend who collected it is considerably out of pocket over it, and would be glad if you could reimburse him. I append also his list of expenses.

As you will see he went to a good deal of trouble over this, though to be fair he also told me that he had enjoyed doing it. I hope it is what you wanted.

Sincerely,
Teddy Dewar.
Great Stag Hotel, Birmingham.

Clipped behind the letter were several other sheets of varying sizes. The top one was a schematic presentation of names which looked at first glance like an inverted family tree. There were clumps of three or four names inside two-inch circles. The circles led via arrows to other circles below and sometimes beside them, but the eye was led downwards continually until all the arrows had converged to three circles, and then to two, and finally to one. And the single name in the bottom circle was David Oakley.

Behind the page was an explanatory note.

I knew one contact, the J. L. Jones underlined in the third row of circles. From him I worked in all directions, checking people who knew of David Oakley. Each clump of people heard about him from one of the people in the next clump. Everyone on the page, I guarantee, has heard either directly or indirectly that Oakley is the man to go to if one is in trouble. I posed as a man in trouble, as you suggested, and nearly all that I talked to either mentioned him of their own accord, or agreed when I brought him up as a possibility.

I only hope that one at least of these names has some significance for you, as I'm afraid the expenses were rather high. Most of the investigation was conducted in pubs or hotels, and it was sometimes necessary to get the contact tight before he would divulge.

Faithfully,

B. R. S. Timieson.

The expense list was high enough to make me whistle. I turned back to the circled names, and read them carefully through.

Looking for one of two.

One was there.

Perhaps I should have rejoiced. Perhaps I should have been angry. Instead, I felt sad.

I doubled the expenses and wrote out a cheque with an accompanying note:

'This is really magnificent. Cannot thank you enough. One of the names has great significance, well worth all your perseverance. My eternal thanks.'

I wrote also a grateful letter to Teddy Dewar saying the information couldn't have been better timed, and enclosing the envelope for his friend Timieson.

As I was sticking on the stamp the telephone rang. I hopped over to it and lifted the receiver.

George Newtonnards.

'Spent all last evening on the blower. Astronomical phone bill, I'm going to have.'

'Send me the account,' I said resignedly.

'Better wait to see if I've got results,' he suggested. 'Got a pencil handy?'

'Just a sec.' I fetched a writing pad and ballpoint. 'OK. Go ahead.'

'Right then. First, here are the chaps *I* told.' He dictated five names. 'The last one, Pelican Jobberson, is the one who holds a fierce grudge against you for that bum steer you gave him, but as it happens he didn't tell the Stewards or anyone else because he went off to Casablanca the next day for a holiday. Well ... here are the people Harry Ingram told ...' He read out three names. 'And these are the people Herbie Subbing told ...' Four names. 'These are the people Dimmie Ovens told ...' Five names. 'And Clobber Mackintosh, he really spread it around ...' Eight names. 'That's all they can remember. They wouldn't swear there was no one else. And of course, all those people they've mentioned could have passed the info on to someone else ... I mean, things like this spread out in ripples.'

'Thanks anyway,' I said sincerely. 'Thank you very much indeed for taking so much trouble.'

'Has it been any help?'

'Oh yes, I think so. I'll let you know, some time.'

'And don't forget. The obvious non-winner ... give me the wink.'

'I'll do that,' I promised. 'If you'll risk it, after Pelican Jobberson's experience.'

'He's got no sense,' he said. 'But I have.'

He rang off, and I studied his list of names. Several were familiar and belonged to well-known racing people: the bookmakers' clients, I supposed. None of the names were the same as those on Timieson's list of Oakley contacts, but there was something ...

For ten minutes I stood looking at the paper wondering what was hovering around the edge of consciousness, and finally, with a thud, the association clicked.

One of the men Herbie Subbing had told was the brother-in-law of the person I had found among the Oakley contacts.

I thought for a while, and then opened the newspaper and studied the programme for the day's racing, which was at Reading. Then I telephoned to Lord Ferth at his London house, and reached him via a plummy-voiced manservant.

'Well, Kelly? ...' There was something left of Wednesday's relationship. Not all, but something.

'Sir,' I said, 'are you going to Reading races?'

'Yes, I am.'

'I haven't yet had any official notice of my licence being

restored ... Will it be all right for me to turn up there? I would particularly like to talk to you.'

'I'll make sure you have no difficulty, if it's important.' There was a faint question in his tone, which I answered.

'I know,' I said, 'who engineered things.'

'Ah ... Yes. Then come. Unless the journey would be too uncomfortable for you? I could, you know, come on to Corrie after the races. I have no engagements tonight.'

'You're very thoughtful. But I think our engineer will be at the races too ... or at least there's a very good chance of it.'

'As you like,' he agreed. 'I'll look out for you.'

Tony had two runners at the meeting and I could ask him to take me. But there was also Roberta ... she was coming over, probably, and she too might take me. I smiled wryly to myself. She might take me anywhere. Roberta Cranfield. Of all people.

As if by telepathy the telephone rang, and it was Roberta herself on the other end. She sounded breathless and worried.

'Kelly! I can't come just yet. In fact ...' The words came in a rush. 'Can you come over here?'

'What's the matter?'

'Well ... I don't really know if *anything's* the matter ... seriously, that is. But Grace Roxford has turned up here.'

'Dear Grace?'

'Yes ... look, Kelly, she's just sitting in her car outside the house sort of glaring at it. Honestly, she looks a bit mad. We don't know quite what to do. Mother wants to call the police, but, I mean, one *can't* ... Supposing the poor woman has come to apologize or something, and is just screwing herself up?'

'She's still sitting in the car?'

'Yes. I can see her from here. Can you come? I mean ... Mother's useless and you know how dear Grace feels about *me* ... She looks pretty odd, Kelly.' Definite alarm in her voice.

'Where's your father?'

171

'Out on the gallops with Breadwinner. He won't be back for about an hour.'

'All right then. I'll get Tony or someone to drive me over. As soon as I can.'

'That's great,' she said with relief. 'I'll try and stall her till you come.'

It would take half an hour to get there. More, probably. By then dear Grace might not still be sitting in her car . . .

I dialled three nine one.

'Tony,' I said urgently. 'Can you drop everything instantly and drive me to Cranfield's? Grace Roxford has turned up there and I don't like the sound of it.'

'I've got to go to Reading,' he protested.

'You can go on from Cranfield's when we've sorted Grace out . . . and anyway, I want to go to Reading too, to talk to Lord Ferth. So be a pal, Tony. Please.'

'Oh all right. If you want it that much. Give me five minutes.'

He took ten. I spent some of them telephoning to Jack Roxford. He was surprised I should be calling him.

'Look, Jack,' I said, 'I'm sorry to be upsetting you like this, but have you any idea where your wife has gone?'

'Grace?' More surprise, but also anxiety. 'Down to the village, she said.'

The village in question was roughly forty miles from Cranfield's house.

'She must have gone some time ago,' I said.

'I suppose so . . . what's all this about?' The worry was sharp in his voice.

'Roberta Cranfield has just telephoned to say that your wife is outside their house, just sitting in her car.'

'Oh God,' he said. 'She can't be.'

'I'm afraid she is.'

'Oh *no* . . .' he wailed. 'She seemed better this morning . . . quite her old self . . . it seemed safe to let her go and do the shopping . . . she's been so upset, you see . . . and then you and Dexter got your licences back . . . it's affected her . . . it's all been so awful for her.'

'I'm just going over there to see if I can help,' I said. 'But ... can you come down and collect her?'

'Oh *yes*,' he said. 'I'll start at once. Oh poor dear Grace ... Take care of her, till I come.'

'Yes,' I said reassuringly, and disconnected.

I made it without mishap down the stairs and found Tony had commandeered Poppy's estate car for the journey. The back seat lay flat so that I could lie instead of sit, and there were even cushions for my shoulders and head.

'Poppy's idea,' Tony said briefly, helping me climb in through the rear door. 'Great girl.'

'She sure is,' I said gratefully, hauling in the crutches behind me. 'Lose no time, now, friend.'

'You sound worried.' He shut the doors, switched on and drove away with minimum waste of time.

'I am, rather. Grace Roxford is unbalanced.'

'But surely not dangerous?'

'I hope not.'

I must have sounded doubtful because Tony's foot went heavily down on the accelerator. 'Hold on to something,' he said. We rocked round corners. I couldn't find any good anchorage: had to wedge my useful foot against the rear door and push myself off the swaying walls with my hands.

'OK?' he shouted.

'Uh ... yes,' I said breathlessly.

'Good bit of road just coming up.' We left all the other traffic at a standstill. 'Tell me if you see any cops.'

We saw no cops. Tony covered the eighteen miles through Berkshire in twenty-three minutes. We jerked to a stop outside Cranfield's house, and the first thing I saw was that there was no one in the small grey Volkswagen standing near the front door.

Tony opened the back of the car with a crash and unceremoniously tugged me out.

'She's probably sitting down cosily having a quiet cup of tea,' he said.

She wasn't.

Tony rang the front-door bell and after a lengthy interval Mrs Cranfield herself opened it.

Not her usual swift wide-opening fling. She looked at us through a nervous six inches.

'Hughes. What are you doing here? Go away.'

'Roberta asked me to come. To see Grace Roxford.'

'Mrs Roxford is no longer here.' Mrs Cranfield's voice was as strung up as her behaviour.

'Isn't that her car?' I pointed to the Volkswagen.

'No,' she said sharply.

'Whose is it, then?'

'The gardener's. Now Hughes, go away at once. Go away.'

'Very well,' I said, shrugging. And she instantly shut the door.

'Help me back into the car,' I said to Tony.

'Surely you're not just *going*?'

'Don't argue,' I said. 'Get me into the car, drive away out through the gates, then go round and come back in through the stable entrance.'

'That's better.' He shuffled me in, threw in the crutches, slammed the door and hustled round to the driving seat.

'Don't rush so,' I said. 'Scratch your head a bit. Look disgusted.'

'You think she's watching?' He didn't start the car: looked at me over his shoulder.

'I think Mrs Cranfield would never this side of doomsday allow her gardener to park outside her front door. Mrs Cranfield was doing her best to ask for help.'

'Which means,' he added slowly, 'that Grace Roxford is very dangerous indeed.'

I nodded with a dry mouth. 'Drive away, now.'

He went slowly. Rolled round into the back drive, accelerated along that, and stopped with a jerk beside the stables. Yet again he helped me out.

'There's a telephone in the small office in the yard,' I said. 'Next to the tackroom. Look up in the classified directory and find a local doctor. Tell him to come smartish. Then wait here until Dexter Cranfield comes back with the horses, and stop him going into the house.'

'Kelly, couldn't you be exaggerating? ...'

'I'll never be able to stop Cranfield.'

'Tell him no one ever believes anything tragic will happen until it has.'

He looked at me for two seconds, then wheeled away into the yard.

I peg-legged up the back drive and tried the back door. Open. It would be. For Cranfield to walk easily through it. And to what?

I went silently along into the main hall, and listened. There was no sound in the house.

Tried the library first, juggling the crutches to get a good grip on the door handle, sweating lest I should drop one with a crash. Turned the handle, pressed the door quietly inwards.

The library was uninhabited. A large clock on the mantel ticked loudly. Out of time with my heart.

I left the door open. Went slowly, silently towards the small sitting-room beside the front door. Again the meticulously careful drill with the handle. If they'd seen me come, they would most probably be in this room.

The door swung inwards. Well oiled. No creaks. I saw the worn chintz covers on the armchairs, the elderly rugs, the debris of living, scattered newspapers, a pair of spectacles on some letters, a headscarf and a flower basket. No people.

On the other side of the hall there were the double doors into the large formal drawing-room, and at the back, beyond the staircase, the doors to the dining-room and to Dexter Cranfield's own study, where he kept his racing books and did all his paper work.

I swung across to the study, and opened the door. It was quiet in there. Dust slowly gravitated. Nothing else moved.

That left only the two large rooms downstairs, and the whole of upstairs. I looked at the long broad flight uneasily. Wished it were an escalator.

The dining-room was empty. I shifted back through the hall to the double doors of the drawing-room. Went through the crutch routine with more difficulty, because if I were going in there I would need both doors open, and to open both doors took both hands. I managed it in the end by hooking both crutches over my left arm like walking sticks, and standing on one leg.

The doors parted and I pushed them wide. The quarter-acre of drawing-room contained chairs of gold brocade upholstery, a pale cream Chinese carpet and long soft blue curtains. A delicate, elegant, class-conscious room designed for Cranfield's glossiest aspirations.

Everything in there was motionless. A tableau.

I hitched the crutches into place, and walked forwards. Stopped after a very few paces. Stopped because I had to.

Mrs Cranfield was there. And Roberta. And Grace Roxford. Mrs Cranfield was standing by the fireplace, hanging on to the shoulder-high mantel as if needing support. Roberta sat upright in an armless wooden chair set out of its usual place in a large clear area of carpet. Behind her and slightly to one side, and with one hand firmly grasping Roberta's shoulder, stood Grace Roxford.

Grace Roxford held the sort of knife used by fishmongers. Nearly a foot long, razor sharp, with a point like a needle. She was resting the lethal end of it against Roberta's neck.

'Kelly!' Roberta said. Her voice was high and a trifle wavery, but the relief in it was overwhelming. I feared it might be misplaced.

Grace Roxford had a bright colour over her taut cheekbones and a piercing glitter in her eyes. Her body was rigid with tension. The hand holding the knife trembled in uneven spasms. She was as unstable as wet gelignite; but she still knew what she was doing.

'You went away, Kelly Hughes,' she said. 'You went away.'

'Yes, Grace,' I agreed. 'But I came back to talk to Roberta.'

'You come another step,' she said, 'and I'll cut her throat.'

Mrs Cranfield drew a breath like a sob, but Roberta's expression didn't change. Grace had made that threat already. Several times, probably. Especially when Tony and I had arrived at the front door.

She was desperately determined. Neither I nor the Cranfields had room to doubt that she wouldn't do as she said.

And I was twenty feet away from her and a cripple besides.

'What do you want, Grace?' I said, as calmly as possible.

'Want? Want?' Her eyes flickered. She seemed to be trying to remember what she wanted. Then her rage sharpened on me like twin darts, and her purpose came flooding back.

'Dexter Cranfield . . . bloody snob . . . I'll see he doesn't get those horses . . . I'm going to kill him, see, kill him . . . then he can't get them, can he? No . . . he can't.'

Again there was no surprise either in Roberta or her mother. Grace had told them already what she'd come for.

'Grace, killing Mr Cranfield won't help your husband.'

'Yes. Yes. Yes. Yes.' She nodded sharply between each yes, and the knife jumped against Roberta's neck. Roberta shut her eyes for a while and swayed on the chair.

I said, 'How do you hope to kill him, Grace?'

She laughed. It got out of control at halfway and ended in a maniacal high-pitched giggle. 'He'll come here, won't he? He'll come here and stand beside me, because he'll do just what I say, won't he? Won't he?'

I looked at the steel blade beside Roberta's pearly skin and knew that he would indeed do as she said. As I would.

'And then, see,' she said, 'I'll just stick the knife into *him*, not into her. See? See?'

'I see,' I said.

She nodded extravagantly and her hand shook.

'And then what?' I asked.

'Then what?' She looked puzzled. She hadn't got any further than killing Cranfield. Beyond that lay only darkness and confusion. Her vision didn't extend to consequences.

'Edwin Byler could send his horses away to someone else,' I said.

'No. No. Only Dexter Cranfield. Only him. Telling him he ought to have a more snobbish trainer. Taking him away from us. I'm going to kill him. Then he can't have those horses.' The words tumbled out in a vehement monotone, all the more frightening for being clearly automatic. These were thoughts she'd had in her head for a very long time.

'It would have been all right, of course,' I said slowly. 'If Mr Cranfield hadn't got his licence back.'

'Yes!' It was a bitterly angry shriek.

'I got it back for him,' I said.

'They just gave it back. They just gave it back. They shouldn't have done that. They shouldn't.'

'They didn't just give it back,' I said. 'They gave it back because I made them.'

'You couldn't...'

'I told everyone I was going to. And I did.'

'No. No. No.'

'Yes.' I said flatly.

Her expression slowly changed, and highly frightening it was too. I waited while it sank into her disorganized brain that if Byler sent his horses to Cranfield after all it was me alone she had to thank for it. I watched the intention to kill widen to embrace me too. The semi-cautious restraint in her manner towards me was transforming itself into a vicious glare of hate.

I swallowed. I said again, 'If I hadn't made the Stewards give Mr Cranfield's licence back, he would still be warned off.'

Roberta said in horror, 'No, Kelly. Don't. Don't do it.'

'Shut up,' I said. 'Me or your father ... which has more chance? And run, when you can.'

Grace wasn't listening. Grace was grasping the essentials and deciding on a course of action.

There was a lot of white showing round her eyes.

'I'll kill you,' she said. 'I'll kill you.'

I stood still. I waited. The seconds stretched like centuries.

'Come here' she said. 'Come here, or I'll cut her throat.'

CHAPTER FIFTEEN

I took myself crutch by crutch towards her. When I was halfway there Mrs Cranfield gave a moaning sigh and fainted, falling awkwardly on the rug and scattering the brass fire irons with a nerve-shattering crash.

Grace jumped. The knife snicked into Roberta's skin and she cried out. I stood half unbalanced, freezing into immobility, trying to will Grace not to disintegrate into panic, not to go over the edge, not to lose the last tiny grip she had on her reason. she wasn't far off stabbing everything in sight.

'Sit still,' I said to Roberta with dreadful urgency and she gave me a terrified look and did her best not to move. She was trembling violently. I had never thought I could pray. I prayed.

Grace was moving her head in sharp birdlike jerks. The knife was still against Roberta's neck. Grace's other hand still grasped Roberta's shoulder. A thread of blood trickled down Roberta's skin and was blotted up in a scarlet patch by her white jersey.

No one went to help Roberta's mother I didn't even dare to look at her, because it meant turning my eyes away from Grace.

'Come here,' Grace said. 'Come here.'

Her voice was husky, little more than a loud whisper. And although she was watching me come with unswerving murder in her eyes, I was inexpressibly thankful that she could still speak at all, still think, still hold a purpose.

During the last few steps I wondered how I was going to dodge, since I couldn't jump, couldn't bend my knees, and hadn't even my hands free. A bit late to start worrying. I took the last step short so that she would have to move to reach me and at the same time eased my elbow out of the right-hand crutch.

She was almost too fast. She struck at me instantly, in a

flashing thrust directed at my throat. and although I managed to twist the two inches needed to avoid it, the hissing knife came close enough, through the collar of my coat. I brought my right arm up and across, crashing crutch against her as she prepared to try again.

Out of the corner of my eye I saw Roberta wrench herself out of Grace's clutching grasp, and half stumble, half fall as she got away from the chair.

'Kill you,' Grace said. The words were distorted. The meaning clear. She had no thought of self-defence. No thought at all, as far as I could see. Just one single burning obsessive intention.

I brought up the left-hand crutch like a pole to push her away. She dived round it and tried to plunge her knife through my ribs, and in throwing myself away from that I over-balanced and half fell down, and she was standing over me with her arm raised like a priest at a human sacrifice.

I dropped one crutch altogether. Useless warding off a knife with a bare hand. I tried to shove the other crutch round into her face, but got it tangled up against an armchair.

Grace brought her arm down. I fell right to the floor as soon as I saw her move and the knife followed me harmlessly, all the impetus gone by the time it reached me. Another tear in my coat.

She came down on her knees beside me, her arm going up again.

From nowhere my lost crutch whistled through the air and smashed into the hand which held the knife. Grace hissed like a snake and dropped it, and it fell point down in to my plaster. She twisted round to see who had hit her and spread out her hands towards the crutch that Roberta was aiming at her again.

She caught hold of it and tugged. I wriggled round on the floor, stretched until I had my fingers round the handle of the knife, and threw it as hard as I could towards the open door into the hall.

Grace was too much for Roberta. Too much for me. She was appallingly, insanely, strong. I heaved myself up on to my left knee and clasped my arms tight round her chest from behind, trying to pin her arms down to her sides. She shook me around like a sack of feathers, struggling to get to her feet.

She managed it, lifting me with her, plaster and all. She knew where I'd thrown the knife. She started to go that way, dragging me with her still fastened to her back like a leech.

'Get that knife and run to the stables,' I gasped to Roberta. A girl in a million. She simply ran and picked up the knife and went on running, out into the hall and out of the house.

Grace started yelling unintelligibly and began trying to unclamp the fingers I had laced together over her thin breastbone. I hung on for everyone's dear life, and when she couldn't dislodge them she began pinching wherever she could reach with fierce hurting spite.

The hair which she usually wore screwed into a fold up the back of her neck had come undone and was falling into my face. I could see less and less of what was going on. I knew only that she was still headed towards the doorway, still unimaginably violent, and mumbling now in a continuous flow of senseless words interspersed with sudden shrieks.

She reached the doorway and started trying to get free of me by crashing me against the jamb. She had a hard job of it, but she managed it in the end, and then she felt my weight fall off her she turned in a flash, sticking out her hands with rigid fingers towards my neck.

Her face was a dark congested crimson. Her eyes were stretched wide in a stark screaming stare. Her lips were drawn back in a tight line from her teeth.

I had never in all my life seen anything so terrifying. Hadn't imagined a human could look like that, had never visualized homicidal madness.

She would certainly have killed me if it hadn't been for Tony, because her strength made a joke of mine. He came tearing into the hall from the kitchen and brought her down with a rugger tackle about the knees, and I fell too, on top of her, because she was trying to tear my throat out in handfuls, and she didn't leave go.

It took all Tony could do, all Archie could do, all three other lads could do to unlatch her from me and hold her down on the floor. They sat on her arms and legs and chest and head, and she threshed about convulsively underneath them.

Roberta had tears streaming down her face and I hadn't any breath left to tell her to cheer up, there was no more danger, no more ... no more ... I leant weakly against the wall and thought it would be too damned silly to pass out now. Took three deep breaths instead. Everything steadied again, reluctantly.

Tony said, 'There's a doctor on his way. Don't think he's expecting this, though.'

'He'll know what to do.'

'Mother!' Exclaimed Roberta suddenly. 'I'd forgotten about her.' She hurried past me into the drawing-room and I heard her mother's voice rising in a disturbed, disorientated question.

Grace was crying out, but her voice sounded like seagulls and nothing she said made sense. One of the lads said sympathetically, 'Poor thing, oughtn't we to let her get up?' and Tony answered fiercely, 'Only under a tiger net.'

'She doesn't know what's happening,' I said wearily. 'She can't control what she does. So don't for God's sake let go of her.'

Except for Tony's resolute six foot they all sat on her gingerly and twice she nearly had them off. Finally and at long last the front door bell rang, and I hopped across the hall to answer it.

It was the local doctor, looking tentative, wondering no doubt if it were a hoax. But he took one look at Grace and was opening his case while he came across the hall. Into her arm he pushed a hypodermic needle and soon the convulsive threshing slackened, and the high-pitched crying dulled to murmurs and in the end to silence.

The five men slowly stood up and stepped away from her, and she lay there looking shrunk and crumpled, her greying hair falling in streaks away from her flacidly relaxing face. It seemed incredible that such thin limbs, such a meagre body, could have put out such strength. We all stood looking down at her with more awe than pity, watching while the last twitches shook her and she sank into unconscious peace.

Half an hour later Grace still lay on the floor in the hall, but with a pillow under her head and a rug keeping her warm.

Dexter Cranfield had come back from watching the horses work and walked unprepared into the aftermath of drama. His wife's semi-hysterical explanations hadn't helped him much.

Roberta told him that Grace had come to kill him because he had his licence back and that she was the cause of his losing it in the first place, and he stamped around in a fury which I gathered was mostly because the source of our troubles was a woman. He basically didn't like women. She should have been locked up years ago, he said. Spiteful, petty minded, scheming, interfering ... just like a woman, he said. I listened to him gravely and concluded he had suffered from a bossy nanny.

The doctor had done some intensive telephoning, and presently an ambulance arrived with two compassionate-looking men and a good deal of special equipment. The front door stood wide open and the prospect of Grace's imminent departure was a relief to everyone.

Into this active bustling scene drove Jack Roxford.

He scrambled out of his car, took a horrified look at the ambulance, and ploughed in through the front door. When he saw Grace lying there with the ambulance men preparing to lift her on to a stretcher, he went down on his knees beside her.

'Grace dear ...' He looked at her more closely. She was still unconscious, very pale now, looking wizened and sixty. 'Grace dear!' There was anguish in his voice. 'What's the matter with her?'

The doctor started to break it to him. Cranfield interrupted the gentle words and said brutally. 'She's raving mad. She came here trying to kill me and she could have killed my wife and daughter. It's absolutely disgraceful that she should have been running around free in that state. I'm going to see my solicitors about it.'

Jack Roxford only heard the first part. His eyes went to the cut on Roberta's neck and the blood-stain on her jersey, and he put his hand over his mouth and looked sick.

'Grace,' he said. 'Oh Grace...'

There was no doubt he loved her. He leant over her, stroking the hair away from her forehead, murmuring to her, and when he finally looked up there were tears in his eyes and on his cheeks.

'She'll be all right, won't she?'

The doctor shifted uncomfortably and said one would have to see, only time would tell, there were marvellous treatments nowadays...

The ambulance men loaded her gently on to the stretcher and picked it up.

'Let me go with her,' Jack Roxford said. 'Where are you taking her? Let me go with her.'

One of the ambulance men told him the name of the hospital and advised him not to come.

'Better try this evening, sir. No use you waiting all day, now, is it?' And the doctor added that Grace would be unconscious for some time yet and under heavy sedation after that, and it was true, it would be better if Roxford didn't go with her.

The uniformed men carried Grace out into the sunshine and loaded her into the ambulance, and we all followed them out into the drive. Jack Roxford stood there looking utterly forlorn as they shut the doors, consulted finally with the doctor, and with the minimum of fuss, drove away.

Roberta touched his arm. 'Can't I get you a drink, Mr Roxford?'

He looked at her vaguely, and then his whole face crumpled and he couldn't speak.

'Don't, Mr Roxford,' Roberta said with pity. 'She isn't in any pain, or anything.'

184

He shook his head. Roberta put her arm across his shoulders and steered him back into the house.

'Now what?' Tony said. 'I've really got to get to Reading, pal. Those runners of mine have to be declared for the second race.'

I looked at my watch. 'You could spare another quarter of an hour. I think we should take Jack Roxford with us. He's got a runner too, incidentally, though I imagine he doesn't much care about that ... Except that it's one of Edwin Byler's. But he's not fit to drive anywhere himself, and the races would help to keep him from brooding too much about Grace.'

'Yeah. A possible idea,' Tony grinned.

'Go into the house and see if you can persuade him to let you take him.'

'OK.' He went off amiably, and I passed the time swinging around the drive on my crutches and peering into the cars parked there. I'd be needing a new one ... probably choose the same again, though.

I leant against Tony's car and thought about Grace. She'd left on me a fair legacy of bruises from her pinches to add to the crop grown by Oakley. Also my coat would cost a fortune at the invisible menders, and my throat felt like a well-developed case of septic tonsils. I looked gloomily down at my plastered leg. The dangers of detection seemed to be twice as high as steeplechasing. With luck, I thought with a sigh, I could now go back to the usual but less frequent form of battery.

Tony came out of the house with Roberta and Jack Roxford. Jack looked dazed, and let Tony help him into the front of the estate car as if his thoughts were miles away. As indeed they probably were.

I scrunched across the gravel towards Roberta.

'Is your neck all right?' I asked.

'Is yours?'

I investigated her cut more closely. It wasn't deep. Little more than an inch long.

'There won't be much of a scar,' I said.

'No,' she agreed.

Her face was close to mine. Her eyes were amber with dark flecks.

'Stay here,' she said abruptly. 'You don't have to go to the races.'

'I've an appointment with Lord Ferth ... Best to get this business thoroughly wrapped up.'

'I suppose so.' She looked suddenly very tired. She'd had a wearing Saturday morning.

'If you've nothing better to do,' I suggested, 'would you come over tomorrow ... and cook me some lunch?'

A small smile tugged at her mouth and wrinkled her eyes.

'I fell hopelessly in love with you,' she said, 'when I was twelve.'

'And then it wore off?'

'Yes.'

'Pity,' I said.

Her smile broadened.

'Who is Bobbie?' I asked.

'Bobbie? Oh ... he's Lord Iceland's son.'

'He would be.'

She laughed. 'Father wants me to marry him.'

'That figures.'

'But Father is going to be disappointed.'

'Good,' I said.

'Kelly,' yelled Tony. 'Come on, for Hell's sakes, or I'll be late.'

'Goodbye,' she said calmly. 'See you tomorrow.'

Tony drove to Reading races with due care and attention and Jack Roxford sat sunk in gloomy silence from start to finish. When we stopped in the car park he stepped out of the car and walked dazedly away towards the entrance without a word of thanks or explanation.

Tony watched him go and clicked his tongue. 'That woman isn't worth it.'

'She is, to him,' I said.

Tony hurried off to declare his horses, and I went more slowly through the gate looking out for Lord Ferth.

It felt extraordinary being back on a racecourse. Like being let out of prison. The same people who had looked sideways at me at the Jockey's Fund dance now slapped me familiarly on the back and said they were delighted to see me. Oh yeah, I thought ungratefully. Never kick a man once he's up.

Lord Ferth was standing outside the weighing-room in a knot of people from which he detached himself when he saw me coming.

'Come along to the Steward's dining-room,' he said. 'We can find a quiet corner there.'

'Can we postpone it until after the third race?' I asked. 'I want my cousin Tony to be there as well, and he has some runners...'

'Of course,' he agreed. 'Later would be best for me too, as it happens. After the third, then.'

I watched the first three races with the hunger of an exile returned. Tony's horse, my sometime mount, finished a fast fourth, which augured well for next time out, and Byler's horse won the third. As I hurried round to see how Jack Roxford would make out in the winner's enclosure I almost crashed into Kessel. He looked me over, took in the plaster and crutches, and said nothing at all. I watched his cold expressionless face with one to match. After ramming home the point that he had no intention of apologizing he turned brusquely on his heel and walked away.

'Get that,' Tony said in my ear. 'You could sue him for defamation.'

'He's not worth the effort.'

From Charlie West, too, I'd had much the same reaction. Defiance, slightly sullen variety. I shrugged resignedly. That was my own fault, and only time would tell.

Tony walked with me to the winner's enclosure. Byler was there, beaming. Jack Roxford still looked lost. We watched Byler suggest a celebration drink, and Jack shake his head vaguely as if he hadn't understood.

'Go and fish Jack out,' I said to Tony. 'Tell him you're still looking after him.'

'If you say so, pal.' He obligingly edged through the

187

crowd, took Jack by the elbow, said a few explanatory words to Byler, and steered Jack out.

I joined them and said neutrally, 'This way,' and led them along towards the Stewards' dining-room. They both went through the door taking off their hats and hanging them on the pegs inside.

The long tables in the Stewards' dining-room had been cleared from lunch and laid for tea, but there was no one in there except Lord Ferth. He shook hands with Tony and Jack and invited them to sit down around one end of a table.

'Kelly? ...' he suggested.

'I'll stand,' I said. 'Easier.'

'Well now,' Ferth said, glancing curiously at Tony and Jack, 'you told me, Kelly, that you knew who had framed you and Dexter Cranfield.'

I nodded.

Tony said regretfully, 'Grace Roxford. Jack's wife.'

Jack looked vaguely down at the tablecloth and said nothing at all.

Tony explained to Lord Ferth just what had happened at Cranfield's and he looked more and more upset.

'My dear Roxford,' he said uncomfortably, 'I'm so sorry. So very sorry.' He looked up at me. 'One could never have imagined that she ... that Grace Roxford of all people ... could have framed you.'

'That's right,' I said mildly. 'She didn't.'

CHAPTER SIXTEEN

Both Tony and Jack sat up as if electrified.

Lord Ferth said, 'But you said ...' And Tony answered, 'I thought there was no doubt ... She tried to kill Kelly ... she was going to kill Cranfield too.'

'She tried to kill me this time,' I agreed. 'But not the time before. It wasn't she who fiddled with my car.'

'Then *who*?' Lord Ferth demanded.

'Her husband.'

Jack stood up. He looked a lot less lost.

I poked Tony on the shoulder with my crutch, and he took the hint and stood up too. He was sitting between Jack and the door.

'Sit down, Mr Roxford,' Ferth said authoritatively, and after a pause, slowly, he obeyed.

'That's nonsense,' he said protestingly. 'I didn't touch Kelly's car. No one could have arranged that accident.'

'You couldn't have imagined I would be hit by a train,' I agreed. 'But some sort of smash, yes, definitely.'

'But Grace ...' began Tony, still bewildered.

'Grace,' I said prosaically, 'has in most respects displayed exactly opposite qualities to the person who engineered Cranfield's and my suspension. Grace has been wild, accusing, uncontrolled, and emotional. The planning which went into getting us warned off was cool, careful, efficient, and brutal.'

'Mad people are very cunning,' Tony said doubtfully.

'It wasn't Grace,' I said positively. 'It was Jack.'

There was a pause. Then Jack said in a rising wail, 'Why ever did she have to go to Cranfield's this morning? Why ever couldn't she leave things alone?'

'It wouldn't have done any good,' I said, 'I already knew it was you.'

'That's impossible.'

Ferth cleared his throat. 'I think ... er ... you'd better tell us, Kelly, what your grounds are for making this very serious accusation.'

'It began,' I said, 'when Dexter Cranfield persuaded Edwin Byler to take his horses away from Roxford and send them to him. Cranfield did no doubt persuade Byler, as Grace maintained, that he was a more highly regarded trainer socially than Roxford. Social standing means a great deal to Mr Cranfield, and he is apt to expect that it does to everyone else. And in Edwin Byler's case, he was very likely right. But Jack had trained Byler's horses from the day he bought his first, and as Byler's fortune and string grew, so did Jack's prosperity and prestige. To lose Byler was to him a total disaster. A return to obscurity. The end of everything. Jack isn't a bad trainer, but he hasn't the personality to make the top ranks. Not without an accident ... a gift from Heaven ... like Byler. And you don't find two Bylers in your yard in one lifetime. So almost from the start I wondered about Jack; from as soon as Cranfield told me, two days after the Enquiry, that Byler had been going to transfer his horses. Because I felt such a wrench of regret, you see, that I was not going to ride them ... and I realized that that was nothing compared to what Jack would have felt if he'd lost them.'

'I didn't feel so bad as that,' said Jack dully.

'I had an open mind,' I said, 'because Pat Nikita had much the same motive, only the other way round. He and Cranfield detest each other. He had been trying to coax Kessel away from Cranfield for years, and getting Cranfield warned off was one way of clinching things. Then there were various people with smaller motives, like Charlie West, who might have hoped to ride Squelch for Nikita if I were out of the way. And there was a big possibility that it was someone else altogether, someone I hadn't come across, whose motive I couldn't even suspect.'

'So why must it be Mr Roxford?' Ferth said.

I took the paper Teddy Dewar had sent me out of my pocket and handed it to him, explaining what it meant.

'That shows a direct link between Oakley and the people in the circles. One of those people is Jack Roxford. He did, you see, know of Oakley's existence. He knew Oakley would agree to provide faked evidence.'

'But...' Lord Ferth began.

'Yes, I know,' I said. 'Circumstantial. Then there's this list of people from George Newtonnards.' I gave him the list, and pointed. 'These are the people who definitely knew that Cranfield had backed Cherry Pie with Newtonnards. Again this is not conclusive, because other people might have known, who are not on this list. But that man,' I pointed to the name in Herbie Subbings' list of contacts, 'that man is

Grace Roxford's brother. Jack's brother-in-law.'

Ferth looked at me levelly. 'You've taken a lot of trouble.'

'It was taken for me,' I said. 'by Teddy Dewar and his friend, and by George Newtonnards.'

'They acted on your suggestions, though.'

'Yes.'

'Anything else?'

'Well,' I said. 'There are those neatly typed sheets of accusations which were sent to Lord Gowery. So untypical, by the way, of Grace. We could compare the typewriter with Jack's ... Typewriters are about as distinctive as finger prints. I haven't had an opportunity to do that yet.'

Jack looked up wildly. The typewriter made sense to him. He hadn't followed the significance of the lists.

Ferth said slowly, 'I obtained from the Stewards' Secretaries the letter which pointed out to them that a disqualified person was living in a racing stable. As far as I remember, the typing is the same as in the original accusations.'

'Very catty, that,' I said. 'More like Grace. Revengeful, and without much point.

'I never wrote to the Stewards' Secretaries,' Jack said.

'Did Grace?'

He shook his head. I thought perhaps he didn't know. It didn't seem to be of any great importance. I said instead: 'I looked inside the boot of Jack's car this morning, while he was in Mr Cranfield's house. He carries a great big tool kit, including a hand drill.'

'No,' Jack said.

'Yes, indeed. Also you have an old grey Volkswagen, the one Grace drove today. That car was seen by the mechanic from my garage when you went to pick over the remains of my car. I imagine you were hoping to remove any tell-tale drill holes which might have led the insurance company to suspect attempted murder, but Derek was there before you. And you either followed him or asked the garage whether he'd taken anything from the wreckage, because you sent David Oakley to my flat to get it back. Oakley didn't know the significance of what he was looking for. A chunk of metal with a hole in it. That was all he knew. He was there to earn a fee.'

'Did he find it?' Ferth asked.

'No. I still have it. Can one prove that a certain drill made a certain hole?'

Ferth didn't know. Jack didn't speak.

'When you heard, at the dance,' I said, 'that I was trying to find out who had framed Cranfield and me, you thought you would get rid of me, in case I managed it. Because if I managed it, you'd lose far more than Byler's horses ... so while I was talking to Lord Ferth and dancing with Roberta, you were out at the back of the car park rigging up your booby trap. Which,' I added calmly, remembering the blazing hell of the dislocations, 'I find hard to forgive.'

'I'll strangle him,' Tony said forcefully.

'What happens to him,' I shook my head, 'depends on Lord Ferth.'

Ferth regarded me squarely. 'You find him. I deal with him.'

'That was the agreement.'

'To your satisfaction.'

'Yes.'

'And what *is* your satisfaction?'

I didn't know.

Tony moved restlessly, looking at his watch. 'Lord Ferth, Kelly, look, I'm sorry, but I've got a horse to saddle for the last race ... I'll have to go now.'

'Yes, of course,' said Lord Ferth. 'But we'd all be obliged if you wouldn't talk about what you've learned in here.'

Tony looked startled. 'Sure. If you say so. Not a word.' He stood up and went over to the door. 'See you after,' he said to me. 'You secretive so-and-so.'

As he went out a bunch of Stewards and their wives came in chattering for their tea. Lord Ferth went over to them and exerted the flashing eyes, and they all went into reverse. A waiter who had materialized behind them was stationed outside the door with instructions to send all customers along to the members' tea room.

While this was going on Jack looked steadfastly down at

the tablecloth and said not a word. I didn't feel like chatting to him idly either. He'd cost me too much.

Lord Ferth came briskly back and sat down.

'Now then, Roxford,' he said in his most businesslike way, 'we've heard Kelly's accusations. It's your turn now to speak up in your defence.'

Jack slowly lifted his head. The deep habitual lines of worry were running with sweat.

'It was someone else.' His voice was dead.

'It certainly wasn't Grace,' I said, 'because Lord Gowery was quite clear that the person who tried to blackmail him on the telephone was a man.' So was the person who had got at Charlie West a man, or so he'd said.

Jack Roxford jerked.

'Yes, Roxford, we know about Lord Gowery,' Ferth said.

'You *can't*...'

'You belong to the same club,' I said assertively, as if I knew.

For Jack Roxford, too, the thought of that club was the lever which opened the floodgates. Like Gowery before him he broke into wretched pieces.

'You don't understand...'

'Tell us then,' Ferth said. 'And we'll try.'

'Grace ... we ... I ... Grace didn't like...' He petered out.

I gave him a shove. 'Grace liked her sex natural and wouldn't stand for what you wanted.'

He gulped. 'Soon after we were married we were having rows all the time, and I hated that. I loved her, really I did. I've always loved her. And I felt ... all tangled up ... she didn't understand that when I beat her it was because of love ... she said she'd leave me and divorce me for cruelty ... so I asked a girl I'd known ... a street girl, who didn't mind ... I mean ... she let you, if you paid well enough ... if I could go on seeing her ... but she said she'd given that up now ... but there was a club in London ... and I went there ... and it was a terrific relief ... and then I was all right with Grace ... but of course we didn't ... well, hardly ever ... but somehow ... we could go on being married.'

Lord Ferth looked revolted.

'I couldn't believe it at first,' Jack said more coherently, 'when I saw Lord Gowery there. I saw him in the street, just outside. I thought it was just a coincidence. But then, one night, inside the club, I was sure it was him, and I saw him again in the street another time ... but I didn't say anything. I mean, how could I? And anyway, I knew how he felt ... you don't go there unless you must ... and you can't keep away.'

'How long have you known that Lord Gowery went to the same club?' I asked.

'Oh ... two or three years. A long time. I don't know exactly.'

'Did he know you were a member?'

'No. He hadn't a clue. I spoke to him once or twice on the racecourse about official things ... He didn't have any idea.'

'And then,' Ferth said thoughtfully, 'you read that he had been appointed in Colonel Midgley's place to officiate at the Cranfield–Hughes Enquiry, and you saw what you thought was a good chance of getting Cranfield out of racing, and keeping Byler's horses yourself.'

Jack sat huddled in his chair, not denying it.

'And when Lord Gowery declined to be blackmailed, you couldn't bear to give up the idea, and you set about faking evidence that would achieve your ends.'

A long silence. Then Jack said in a thick disjointed voice. 'Grace minded so much ... about Cranfield taking our horses. She went on and on about it ... morning, noon, and night. Couldn't stop. Talk, talk, talk. All the time. Saying she'd like to kill Cranfield ... and things like that. I mean ... she's always been a bit nervy ... a bit strung up ... but Cranfield was upsetting her ... I got a bit frightened for her sometimes, she was that violent about him ... Well, it was really because of that that I tried to get Cranfield warned off ... I mean, he was better warned off than Grace trying to kill him.'

'Did you truly believe she would?' I asked.

'She was ranting about it all the time ... I didn't know if she really would ... but I was so afraid ... I didn't want her to get into trouble ... dear dear Grace ... I wanted to help her ... and make things right again ... so I set about it ... and it wasn't too difficult really, not once I'd set my mind to it.'

Ferth gave me a twisted smile. I gave him a similar one back and reflected that marriage could be a deadly institution. Grace's strung-up state would have been aggravated by the strain of living with a sexually odd man, and Jack would have felt guilty about it and wanted to make it up to her. Neither of them had been rationally inclined, and the whole situation had boiled up claustrophobically inside their agonized private world. Having dear Grace harping on endlessly would have driven many a stronger man to explosive action: but Jack couldn't desert her, because he had to stay with his horses, and he couldn't drive her away because he loved her. The only way he'd seen of silencing his wife had been to ruin Cranfield.

'Why me?' I said, trying to keep out the bitterness. 'Why me too?'

'Eh?' He squinted at me, half focussing. 'You ... well ... I haven't anything against you personally ... But I thought it was the only way to make it a certainty ... Cranfield couldn't have swindled that race without Squelch's jockey being in the know.'

'That race was no swindle,' I said.

'Oh ... I know that. Those stupid Oxford Stewards ... still, they gave me such an opportunity ... when I heard about Lord Gowery being in charge. And then, when I'd fixed up with Charlie West and Oakley ... Grace's brother told me, just told me casually, mind you, that his bookmaker had told him that Cranfield had backed Cherry Pie, and do you know what, I couldn't stop laughing. Just like Grace, I felt ... dead funny, it was, that he really had backed Cherry Pie ...'

'What was that about Charlie West?' Ferth said sharply.

'I paid him ... to say Kelly pulled Squelch back. I telephoned and asked him ... if Kelly ever did anything like that ... and he said once, in a novice 'chase, Kelly had said, "OK. Brakes on, chaps," and I told him to say Kelly had said that in the Lemonfizz Cup, because it sounded so convincing, didn't it, saying something Kelly really had said . . .'

Ferth looked at me accusingly. 'You shielded West.'

I shrugged ruefully. Jack paid no attention: didn't hear.

He went on miserably: 'Grace was all right before the dance. She was wonderfully calm again, after Cranfield was warned off. And then Edwin Byler said that we would be keeping his horses for always . . . and we were happy . . . in our way . . . and then we heard . . . that Kelly was at the dance . . . saying he'd been framed . . . and was just on the point of finding out who . . . and Grace saw Cranfield's daughter and just boiled over all over again, nearly as bad as before . . . and I thought . . . if Kelly was dead . . . it would be all right again . . .'

Ferth slowly shook his head. The reasoning which had led Jack Roxford step by step from misfortune to crime defeated him.

'I thought he wouldn't feel anything,' Jack said. 'I thought that you just blacked out suddenly from carbon monoxide. I thought it would be like going to sleep . . . he wouldn't know about it. Just wouldn't wake up.'

'You didn't drill a big enough hole,' I said without irony. 'Not enough gas came through at once to knock me out.'

'I couldn't find a large enough tube,' he said with macabre sense. 'Had to use a piece I had. It was a bit narrow. That was why.'

'I see,' I said gravely. So close. Not a few inches from the express train. One eighth of an inch extra in the tube's diameter would have done it.

'And you went to look for the pieces of manifold, afterwards?'

'Yes . . . but you know about that. I was furious with Oakley for not finding it . . . he said he tried to make you tell, but you wouldn't . . . and I said it didn't surprise me . . .'

'Why didn't you ask *him* to kill me?' I said matter-of-factly.

'Oh, I did. He said he didn't kill. He said he would dispose of the body if I did it, but he never did the job himself. Not worth it, he said.'

That sounded like the authentic Oakley. Straight from the agent's mouth.

'But you couldn't risk it?' I suggested.

'I didn't have any chance. I mean ... I didn't like to leave Grace alone much ... she was so upset ... and then, you were in hospital ... and then you went back to your flat ... and I did try to shift you out into the open somewhere ...'

'You did write to the Stewards' Secretaries,' Ferth exclaimed. 'After all.'

'Yes ... but it was too late ... wasn't it ... She really meant it ... poor Grace, poor Grace ... why did I let her go out ... But she seemed so much better this morning ... and now ... and now ...' His face screwed up and turned red as he tried not to cry. The thought of Grace as he'd last seen her was too much for him. The tears rolled. He sniffed into a handkerchief.

I wondered how he would have felt if he'd seen Grace as I'd seen her. But probably the uncritical love he had would have survived even that.

'Just sit here quietly a moment, Roxford,' Lord Ferth directed, and he himself stood up and signed for me to walk with him over to the door.

'So what do we do with him?' he said.

'It's gone too far now,' I said reluctantly, 'to be entirely hushed up. And he's if anything more dangerous than Grace ... She will live, and he will very likely see everything for ever in terms of her happiness. Anyone who treats her badly in any way could end up as a victim of his scheming. End up ruined ... or dead. People like nurses ... or relations ... or even people like me, who did her no harm at all. Anybody ...'

Ferth said, 'You seem to understand his mind. I must say that I don't. But what you say makes sense. We cannot just take away his licence and leave it at that ... It isn't a racing matter any more. But Lord Gowery ...'

'Lord Gowery will have to take his chance,' I said without satisfaction. 'Very likely you can avoid busting open his reputation ... but it's much more important to stop Jack Roxford doing the same sort of thing again.'

'Yes,' he said. 'It is.' He spread out his hands sideways in a pushing gesture as if wanting to step away from the decision. 'All this is so *distressing*.'

I looked down the room at Jack, a huddled defeated figure with nervous eyes and an anxious forehead. He was picking at the tablecloth with his fingers. folding it into senseless little pleats. He didn't look like a villain. No hardened criminal. Just a tenacious little man with a fixed idea, to make up to dear Grace for being what he was.

Nothing was more useless than sending him to prison, and nothing could do him more harm: yet that, I imagined, was where he would go. Putting his body in a little cage wouldn't straighten the kinks in his mind. The system, for men like him, was screwy.

He stood up slowly and walked unsteadily towards us.

'I suppose,' he said without much emotion, 'that you are going to get the police. I was wondering ... please ... don't tell them about the club ... I won't say Lord Gowery goes there ... I won't tell anybody ever ... I never really wanted to ... it wouldn't have done any good, would it? I mean, it wouldn't have kept those horses in my yard ... wouldn't have made a scrap of difference ... So do you think anyone need know about ... the club?'

'No,' said Ferth with well-disguised relief. 'They need not.'

A faint smile set up a rival set of creases to the lines of anxiety. 'Thank you.' The smile faded away. The lost look deepened. 'How long ... do you think I'll get?'

Ferth moved uncomfortably. 'No point in worrying about that until you have to.'

'You could probably halve it,' I said.

'How?' He was pathetically hopeful. I flung him the rope.

'By giving evidence at another trial I have in mind, and taking David Oakley down with you.'

Part Three

MARCH EPILOGUE

Yesterday I rode Breadwinner in the Cheltenham Gold Cup.

A horse of raw talent with more future than past. A shambling washy chestnut carrying his head low. No one's idea of equine beauty.

Old Strepson watched him slop around the parade ring and said with a sigh, 'He looks half asleep.'

'Hughes will wake him up,' Cranfield said condescendingly.

Cranfield stood in the chill March sunshine making his usual good stab at arrogance. The mean calculating lines round his mouth seemed to have deepened during the past month, and his manner to me was if anything more distant, more master–servant, than ever before. Roberta said she had told him that I had in some way managed to get our licences back, but he saw no reason to believe her and preferred the thought of divine intervention.

Old Strepson said conversationally, 'Kelly says Breadwinner was a late foal and a late developer, and won't reach his true strength until about this time next year.'

Cranfield gave me a mouth-tightening mind-your-own-business glare, and didn't seem to realize that I'd given him an alibi if the horse didn't win and built him up into one heck of a good trainer if it did. Whatever low opinion Cranfield held of me, I reciprocated it in full.

Farther along the parade ring stood a silent little group of Kessel, Pat Nikita, and their stable jockey, Al Roach. They were engaged in running poor old Squelch, and their interest lay not so fiercely in winning as in finishing at all costs in front of Breadwinner. Kessel himself radiated so much hatred that I thought it was probably giving him a headache. Hating did that. The day I found it out, I gave up hating.

Grace's hatred-headache must have been unbearable . . .

Grace's recovery was still uncertain. Ferth had somehow wangled the best available psychiatrist on to her case, and had also arranged for him to see Jack. Outside the weighing-room when I had arrived, he had jerked his head for me to join him, and told me what the psychiatrist had reported.

'He says Jack is sane according to legal standards, and will have to stand trial. He wouldn't commit himself about Grace's chances. He did say, though, that from all points of view their enforced separation was a godsend. He said he thought their only chance of leading fairly normal lives in the future was to make the separation total and permanent. He said a return to the same circumstances could mean a repeat of the whole cycle.'

I looked at Ferth gloomily. 'What a cold, sad, depressing solution.'

'You never know,' he said optimistically, 'once they get over it, they might both feel . . . well . . . released.'

I smiled at him. He said abruptly, 'Your outlook is catching, dammit . . . How about that dinner?'

'Any time,' I said.

'Tomorrow, then? Eight o'clock. The Caprice, round the corner from the Ritz . . . The food's better there than at my club.'

'Fine,' I said.

'And you can tell me how the police are getting on with David Oakley . . .'

I'd had the Birmingham police on my telephone and doorstep for much of the past week. They had almost fallen on my neck and sobbed when I first went to them with enough to make an accusation stick, and had later promised to deliver to me, framed, one of the first fruits of their search warrant: a note from Cranfield to Jack Roxford dated two years earlier, thanking him for not bidding him up at an auction after a selling race and enclosing a cheque for fifty pounds. Across the bottom of the page Cranfield had written:

As agreed. Thanks. D.C.

It was the note Oakley had photographed in my flat.

Supplied by Roxford, who had suggested the photograph.

Kept by Oakley, as a hold over Roxford.

The police also told me that Jack Roxford had drawn six hundred pounds in new notes out of his bank during the two weeks before the Enquiry, and David Oakley had paid three hundred of the same notes into his own account five days later.

Clever, slippery Mr Oakley had been heard to remark that he regretted not having slaughtered Kelly Hughes.

The bell rang for the jockeys to mount, and Cranfield and old Strepson and I walked over to where Breadwinner waited.

The one jockey missing from the day's proceedings was Charlie West, whose licence had been suspended for the rest of the season. And it was only thanks to Hughes' intervention, Ferth had told him forcefully, that he hadn't got his deserts and been warned off for life. Whether Charlie West would feel an atom of gratitude was another matter.

I swung up easily on to Breadwinner and fitted my right foot carefully into the stirrup. A compromise between me and the orthopod had seen the plaster off seven days previously, but the great surgeon's kind parting words had been, 'You haven't given that leg enough time and if it dislocates again it's your own bloody fault.'

I had told him that I couldn't afford to have Cranfield engage another jockey for Breadwinner with all the horse's future races at stake. Old Strepson was the grateful type who didn't dislodge a jockey who had won for him, and if some other jockey won the Gold Cup on Breadwinner I would lose the mount for life: and it was only this argument which had grudgingly brought out the saw.

I gathered up the reins and walked the horse quietly round the ring while everyone sorted themselves out into the right order for the parade down the course. Apart from the Grand National, the Cheltenham Gold Cup was the biggest steeplechase of the year. In prestige, probably the greatest of all. All the stars turned out for it, meeting each other in level terms. Bad horses hadn't a hope.

There were nine runners. Breadwinner was the youngest, Squelch the most experienced, and a bad-tempered grey called Ironclad, the favourite.

Al Roach, uninfected by Kessel, lined up beside me at the start and gave me his usual wide friendly Irish grin. 'Now Kelly my bhoy,' he said, 'tell me how you ride this little fellow, now.'

'You want to be warned off?' I said.

He chuckled. 'What's the owner got against you, Kelly me bhoy?'

'I was right and he was wrong, and he can't forgive that.'

'Peculiar fellow, he is, that Kessel...'

The tapes went up and we were away. Three and a quarter miles, twenty-one jumps, two whole circuits of the course.

Nothing much happened on the first circuit. No horses fell and no jockeys got excited, and going past the stands and outward bound for the second time a fair-sized sheet would have covered the lot. The next mile sorted the men from the boys, and the bunch flattened out into a relentless, thundering, muscle-straining procession in which hope and sweat and tactics merged into a rushing private world of conflict. Speed ... jumping at near-disaster rate ... gambling on the horse's coordination ... stretching your own ... a race like the Gold Cup showed you what you were made of...

Coming to the second last fence, Ironclad was leading Squelch by three lengths which could have been ten, and he set himself right with all the time in the world. Squelch followed him over, and four lengths behind Breadwinner strained forwards to be third.

Between the last two fences the status quo was unchanged, Breadwinner making no impression on Squelch, nor Squelch on Ironclad. Oh well, I thought resignedly. Third. That wasn't really too bad for such a young horse. One couldn't have everything. And there was always Pound Postage in the Grand National, two weeks on Saturday...

Ironclad set himself right for the last fence, launched himself muscularly into the air, crossed the birch with a good foot of air beneath him ... and pitched forwards on to his nose on landing.

I couldn't believe it. Shook up Breadwinner with a bang of renewed hope and drove him into the last fence for the jump of his young life.

Squelch was over it first, of course. Squelch the sure-footed trained-to-the-minute familiar old rascal ... Irony of ironies, to be beaten to the Gold Cup by Squelch.

Breadwinner did the best he could to catch him, and I saw that as in the Lemonfizz, Squelch was dying from tiredness. Length by length my gangling chestnut pegged back the gap, straining, stretching, quivering to get past ... but the winning post was too near ... it was no good ... there wasn't time ...

Al Roach looked round to see who was pressing him. Saw me. Knew that Breadwinner was of all others the one he had to beat. Was seized with panic. If he had sat still, he would have won by two lengths. Instead, he picked up his whip and hit Squelch twice down the flank.

You stupid ass, I thought breathlessly. He hates that. He'll stop. He always stops if you hit him ...

Squelch's tail swished in fury. His rhythmic stride broke up into bumps. He shook his head violently from side to side.

I saw Al's desperate face as Breadwinner caught him ... and the winning post was there and gone in a flash ... and neither of us knew even then which had won.

The photograph gave it to Breadwinner by a nostril. And if I got booed by the crowd after the Lemonfizz they made up for it after the Gold Cup.

Kessel, predictably, was purple with fury, and he seemed on the brink of explosion when someone remarked loudly that Squelch would have won if Hughes had been riding him. I laughed. Kessel looked almost as murderous as Grace.

Old Strepson was pale with emotion but even the Gold Cup did not raise much observable joy in Cranfield; and I found out later that Edwin Byler had just told him he wouldn't be sending him his horses after all. Grace's psychiatrist had written to say that Grace's ultimate sanity might depend on Cranfield not having the horses, and Byler said he felt he owed the Roxfords something ... sorry and all that, but there it was.

Roberta with her mother had been there patting Breadwinner in the winner's enclosure, and when I came out of the weighing-room twenty minutes later after changing into street clothes, she was leaning against the rails there, waiting.

'You're limping,' she said calmly.

'Unfit, that's all.'

'Coffee?' she suggested.

'Yes,' I said.

She walked sedately ahead of me into the coffee room. Her copper hair still shone after she'd stepped out of the sunshine, and I liked the simple string-coloured coat which went underneath it.

I bought her some coffee and sat at a little plastic-topped table and looked at the litter left by the last occupants; empty coffee cups, plates with crumbs, cigarette butts, and a froth-lined beer glass. Roberta packed them coolly to one side and ignored them.

'Winning and losing,' she said. 'That's what it's all about.'

'Racing?'

'Life.'

I looked at her.

She said, 'Today is marvellous, and being warned off was terrible. I suppose everything goes on like that ... up and down ... always.'

'I suppose so,' I agreed.

'I've learned a lot, since the Enquiry.'

'So have I ... about you.'

'Father says I must remember your background...'

'That's true,' I said. 'You must.'

'Father's mind has chains on. Iron bars in his soul. His head's chock-a-block with ideas half a century out of date.' She mimicked my own words with pompous mischief.

I laughed. 'Roberta...'

'Please tell me...' She hesitated. '...At the level crossing
...when you called me Rosalind... was it her you wanted?'

'No,' I said slowly, 'it was you... In her place.'

She sighed contentedly.

'That's all right, then,' she said. 'Isn't it?'

THE DANGER

Liberty Market Ltd is fictional, though similar organisations exist. No one who has helped me with the background of this book wants to be mentioned, but my thanks to them just the same.

I acknowledge my debt also to *Kidnap and Ransom: The Response* by Richard Clutterbuck

Kidnapping is a fact of life. Always has been, always will be. Extorting a ransom is an age-old pastime, less risky and more lucrative than robbing banks.

Kidnapping, twentieth-century style, has meant train loads and 'plane loads of hostages, athletes killed in company at Munich, men of substance dying lonely deaths. All kidnappers are unstable, but the political variety, hungry for power and publicity as much as money, make quicksand look like rock.

Give me the straightforward criminal any day, the villain who seizes and says pay up or else. One does more or less know where one is, with those.

Kidnapping, you see, is my business.

My job, that is to say, as a partner in the firm of Liberty Market Ltd, is both to advise people at risk how best not to be kidnapped, and also to help negotiate with the kidnappers once a grab has taken place: to get the victim back alive for the least possible cost.

Every form of crime generates an opposing force, and to fraud, drugs and murder one could add the Kidnap Squad, except that the kidnap squad is unofficial and highly discreet . . . and is often *us*.

Italy

one

There was a God-awful cock-up in Bologna.

I stood as still as possible while waves of cold rage and fiery anxiety jerked at my limbs and would have had me pacing.

Stood still . . . while a life which might depend on me was recklessly risked by others. Stood still among the ruins of a success nearly achieved, a freedom nearly won, safety within grasp.

The most dangerous, delicate stage of any kidnap is the actual handing over of the ransom, because it is then, at the moment of collection, that someone, somehow, must step out of the shadows . . . and a kidnapper comes to his waterhole with more caution than any beast in the jungle.

One suspicion, one sight or glint of a watcher, is enough to send him scuttling away; and it is afterwards, seething with fright and in a turmoil of vengeful anger, that he can most easily kill. To bungle the drop is to escalate the threat to the victim a hundredfold.

Alessia Cenci, twenty-three years old, had by that time been in the hands of kidnappers for five weeks, three days, ten hours, and her life had never been closer to forfeit.

Enrico Pucinelli climbed grim-faced through the rear door of the ambulance in which I stood: a van, more accurately, which looked like an ambulance from the outside but whose darkly tinted windows concealed a bench, a chair, and a mass of electronic equipment within.

'I was off duty,' he said. 'I did not give those orders.'

He spoke in Italian, but slowly, for my sake. As men, we got on very well. As linguists, speaking a little of each other's language but understanding more, we had to take time. We spoke to each other carefully, each in our own tongue, and listened with attention, asking for repetition whenever necessary.

He was the carabinieri officer who had been leading the official investigations. He had agreed throughout on the need for extreme care and for the minimum of visible involvement. No emblazoned cars with busily flashing lights had driven to or from the Villa Francese, where Paola Cenci waited with white face for news of his daughter. No uniformed men had been in evidence in any place where hostile eyes could watch. Not while Pucinelli himself had been able to prevent it.

He had agreed with me that the first priority was the girl's safety, and only the second priority the catching of the kidnappers. Not every policeman by any means saw things that way round, the hunting instincts of law enforcers everywhere being satisfied solely by the capture of their prey.

Pucinelli's colleague-on-duty on that devastating evening, suddenly learning that he could pounce with fair ease on the kidnappers at the moment they picked up the ransom, had seen no reason to hold back. Into the pregnant summer darkness, into the carefully negotiated, patiently damped-down moment of maximum quiet, he had sent a burst of men with batons waving, lights blazing, guns rising ominously against the night sky, voices shouting, cars racing, sirens wailing, uniforms running . . . all the moral aggression of a righteous army in full pursuit.

From the dark stationary ambulance a long way down the street I had watched it happen with sick disbelief and impotent fury. My driver, cursing steadily, had started the engine and crawled forward towards the mêlée, and we had both quite clearly heard the shots.

'It is regretted,' Pucinelli said with formality, watching me.

I could bet it was. There had been so many carabinieri on the move in the poorly-lit back street that, unsure where to look precisely, they had missed their target altogether. Two dark-clad men, carrying the suitcase which contained the

10

equivalent of six hundred and fifty thousand pounds, had succeeded in reaching a hidden car, in starting it and driving off before the lawmen noticed; and certainly their attention had been more clearly focused, as was my own, on the sight of the young man spilling head-first from the car which all along had been plainly in everyone's view, the car in which the ransom had been carried to this blown-open rendezvous.

The young man, son of a lawyer, had been shot. I could see the crimson flash on his shirt and the weak flutter of his hand, and I thought of him, alert and confident, as we'd talked before he set off. Yes, he'd said, he understood the risk, and yes, he would follow their instructions absolutely, and yes, he would keep me informed by radio direct from the car to the ambulance. Together we had activated the tiny transmitter sewn into the handle of the suitcase containing the ransom money and had checked that it was working properly as a homer, sending messages back to the radar in the ambulance.

Inside the ambulance that same radar tracker was showing unmistakably that the suitcase was on the move and going rapidly away. I would without doubt have let the kidnappers escape, because that was safest for Alessia, but one of the carabinieri, passing and catching sight of the blip, ran urgently towards the bull-like man who with blowing whistle appeared to be chiefly in charge, shouting to him above the clamour and pointing a stabbing finger towards the van.

With wild and fearful doubt the officer looked agonisedly around him and then shambled towards me at a run. With his big head through the window of the cab he stared mutely at the radar screen, where he read the bad news unerringly with a pallid outbreak of sweat.

'Follow,' he said hoarsely to my driver, and brushed away my attempt at telling him in Italian why he should do no such thing.

The driver shrugged resignedly and we were on our way with a jerk, accompanied, it seemed to me, by a veritable posse of wailing cars screaming through the empty streets of the industrial quarter, the factory workers long ago gone home.

'Since midnight,' Pucinelli said, 'I am on duty. I am again in charge.'

I looked at him bleakly. The ambulance stood now in a wider street, its engine stilled, the tracker showing a steady trace, locating the suitcase inside a modern lower-income block of flats. In front of the building, at an angle to the kerb, stood a nondescript black car, its overheated engine slowly cooling. Around it, like a haphazard barrier, the police cars were parked at random angles, their doors open, headlights blazing, occupants in their fawn uniforms ducking into cover with ready pistols.

'As you see, the kidnappers are in the front apartment on the third floor,' Pucinelli said. 'They say they have taken hostage the people who live there and will kill them, and also they say Alessia Cenci will surely die, if we do not give them safe passage.'

I had heard them shouting from the open window, and had hardly needed the repetition.

'In a short time the listening bug will be in position,' Pucinelli said, glancing uneasily at my rigid face. 'And soon we will have a tap on the telephone. We have men on the staircase outside. They are fixing them.'

I said nothing.

'My men say you would have let the kidnappers get away . . . taking the money with them.'

'Of course.'

We looked at each other unsmilingly, almost foes where recently we'd been allies. He was thin and about forty, give or take. Dark and intense and energetic. A communist in a communist city, disapproving of the capitalist whose daughter was at risk.

'They had shot the boy who drove the car,' he said. 'We could not possibly let them escape.'

'The boy took his chances. The girl must still be saved.'

'You English,' he said. 'So cold.'

The anger inside me would have scorched asbestos. If his men hadn't tried their abortive ambush, the boy would not

12

have been shot. He would have walked away unharmed and left the ransom in the car, as he'd been instructed.

Pucinelli turned his attention to the benchful of bolted-down radio receivers, turning a few knobs and pressing switches. 'I am sending a man in here to receive messages,' he said. 'I will be here also. You can stay, if you wish.'

I nodded. It was too late to do anything else.

It had been absolutely against my instincts and my training to be anywhere near the dropping point of the ransom, yet Pucinelli had demanded my presence there in return for a promise of his force's absence.

'You can go in our van,' he said. 'Our radio van. Like an ambulance. Very discreet. You go. I'll send you a driver. When the kidnappers take the suitcase, you follow it. You can tell us where they're hiding. Then, when the girl is free, we'll arrest them. OK?'

'When the girl is free, I will tell you where they took the money.'

He had narrowed his eyes slightly, but had clapped me on the shoulder and agreed to it, nodding. 'The girl first.'

Not knowing, as one never does, precisely when the kidnappers would set the handing-over procedure rolling, Pucinelli had stationed the van permanently in the garage at the Villa Francese, with the driver living in the house. Four days after we'd signalled to the kidnappers that the agreed money had been collected and was ready for them, they had sent their delivery instructions: and as promised between Pucinelli and myself, I had telephoned his office to tell him the drop was about to start.

Pucinelli had not been there, but we had planned for that contingency.

In basic Italian I had said, 'I am Andrew Douglas. Tell Enrico Pucinelli immediately that the ambulance is moving.'

The voice at the other end had said it understood.

I now wished with all my heart that I had not kept my promise to give Pucinelli that message; but cooperation with the local police was one of the firm's most basic policies.

Pucinelli's own trust in me, it now turned out, had not been so very great. Perhaps he had known I would rather have lost track of the suitcase then give away my presence near the drop. In any case, both the suitcase's homer, and a further homer in the van, had been trackable from Pucinelli's own official car. The colleague-on-duty, receiving my message, had not consulted Pucinelli but had simply set out with a maximum task force, taking Pucinelli's staff car and chasing personal glory. Stupid, swollen-headed, lethal human failing.

How in God's name was I going to tell Paolo Cenci? And who was going to break it to the lawyer that his bright student son had been shot?

'The boy who was driving,' I said to Pucinelli. 'Is the boy alive?'

'He's gone to hospital. He was alive when they took him. Beyond that, I don't know.'

'His father must be told.'

Pucinelli said grimly, 'It's being done. I've sent a man.'

This mess, I thought, was going to do nothing at all for the firm's reputation. It was positively my job to help to resolve a kidnap in the quietest way possible, with the lowest of profiles and minimum action. My job to calm, to plan, to judge how little one could get a kidnapper to accept, to see that negotiations were kept on the coolest, most businesslike footing, to bargain without angering, to get the timing right. My brief, above all, to bring the victim home.

I had by that time been the advisor-on-the-spot in fifteen kidnaps, some lasting days, some weeks, some several months. Chiefly because kidnappers usually do release their victims unharmed once the ransom is in their hands, I hadn't so far been part of a disaster; but Alessia Cenci, reportedly one of the best girl jockeys in the world, looked set to be my first.

'Enrico,' I said, 'don't talk to these kidnappers yourself. Get someone else, who has to refer to you for decisions.'

'Why?' he said.

'It calms things down. Takes time. The longer they go on talking the less likely they are to kill those people in the flat.'

He considered me briefly. 'Very well. Advise me. It's your job.'

We were alone in the van and I guessed he was sorely ashamed of his force's calamity, otherwise he would never have admitted such a tacit loss of face. I had realised from shortly after my first arrival at the villa that as officer-in-charge he had never before had to deal with a real kidnap, though he had carefully informed me that all carabinieri were instructed in the theory of kidnap response, owing to the regrettable frequency of that crime in Italy. Between us, until that night, his theory and my experience had done well enough, and it seemed that he did still want the entente to go on.

I said, 'Telephone that flat direct from here. Tell the kidnappers you are arranging negotiations. Tell them they must wait for a while. Tell them that if they tire of the waiting they may telephone you. Give them a number . . . you have a line in this van?'

He nodded. 'It's being connected.'

'Once their pulses settle it will be safer, but if they are pressed too hard to start with they may shoot again.'

'And my men would fire. . . .' He blinked rapidly and went outside, and I could hear him speaking to his forces through a megaphone. 'Do not return fire. I repeat, do not shoot. Await orders before firing.'

He returned shortly, accompanied by a man unrolling a wire, and said briefly, 'Engineer.'

The engineer attached the wire to one of the switch boxes and passed Pucinelli an instrument which looked a cross between a microphone and a handset. It appeared to lead a direct line to the flat's telephone because after a pause Pucinelli was clearly conversing with one of the kidnappers. The engineer, as a matter of course, was recording every word.

The Italian was too idiomatic for my ears, but I understood at least the tone. The near-hysterical shouting from the kidnapper slowly abated in response to Pucinelli's determined calmness and ended in a more manageable agitation. To a final forceful question Pucinelli, after a pause, answered slowly and

15

distinctly, 'I don't have the authority. I have to consult my superiors. Please wait for their reply.'

The result was a menacing, grumbling agreement and a disconnecting click.

Pucinelli wiped his hand over his face and gave me the tiniest flicker of a smile. Sieges, as I supposed he knew, could go on for days, but at least he had established communications, taking the first vital step.

He glanced at the engineer and I guessed he was wanting to ask me what next, but couldn't because of the engineer and his recordings.

I said, 'Of course you will be aiming searchlights at those windows soon so that the kidnappers will feel exposed.'

'Of course.'

'And if they don't surrender in an hour or two, naturally you'd bring someone here who's used to bargaining, to talk to them. Someone from a trades union, perhaps. And after that a psychiatrist to judge the kidnappers' state of mind and tell you when he thinks is the best time to apply most pressure, to make them come out.' I shrugged deprecatingly. 'Naturally you know that these methods have produced good results in other hostage situations.'

'Naturally.'

'And of course you could tell them that if Alessia Cenci dies, they will never get out of prison.'

'The driver . . . they'll know they hit him. . . .'

'If they ask, I am sure you would tell them he is alive. Even if he dies, you would of course tell them he is still alive. One wouldn't want them to think they had nothing to lose.'

A voice spluttered suddenly from one of the so far silent receivers, making both the engineer and Pucinelli whirl to listen. It was a woman's voice, gabbling, weeping, to me mostly unintelligible but, in gist, again plain enough.

The kidnapper's rough voice sliced in over hers, far too angry for safety, and then, in a rising wail, came a child's voice, crying, then another, calling 'Mama! Papa! Mama!'

'God,' Pucinelli said, 'children! There are children, too, in that flat.' The thought appalled him. In one instant he cared more for them than he had in five weeks for the girl, and for the first time I saw real concern in his olive face. He listened intently to the now-jumbled loud voices crowding through from the bug on the flat, a jumble finally resolving into a kidnapper yelling at the woman to give the children some biscuits to shut them up, or he personally would throw them out of the window.

The threat worked. Comparative quietness fell. Pucinelli took the opportunity to begin issuing rapid orders by radio to his own base, mentioning searchlights, negotiator, psychiatrist. Half the time he looked upward to the third floor windows, half down to the cluttered street outside: both, from our side of the van's darkly tinted glass, unrealistically dim. Not dark enough, however, for him not to catch sight of something which displeased him mightily and sent him speeding out of the van with a shout. I followed the direction of his agitation and felt the same dismay: a photographer with flashlight had arrived, first contingent of the press.

For the next hour I listened to the voices from the flat, sorting them gradually into father, mother, two children, a baby, and two kidnappers, one, the one who had talked on the telephone, a growling bass, the other a more anxious tenor.

It was the tenor, I thought, who would more easily surrender: the bass the more likely killer. Both, it appeared, were holding guns. The engineer spoke rapidly with Pucinelli, who then repeated everything more slowly for my benefit: the kidnappers had locked the mother and three children in one of the bedrooms, and had mentioned ropes tying the father. The father moaned occasionally and was told violently to stop.

In the street the crowd multiplied by the minute, every apartment block in the neighbourhood, it seemed, emptying its inhabitants to the free show on the doorstep. Even at two in the morning there were hordes of children oozing round every attempt of the carabinieri to keep them back, and every-

17

where, increasingly, sprouted the cameras, busy lenses pointing at the windows, now shut, where drama was the tenor
kidnapper agreeing to warm the baby's bottle in the kitchen.

I ground my teeth and watched a television van pull up,
its occupants leaping out with lights, cameras, microphones,
setting up instant interviews, excitedly telling the world.

The kidnapping of Alessia Cenci had until that time been a
piano affair, the first shock news of her disappearance having
made the papers, but only briefly, for most editors all over the
world acknowledged that reporters glued to such stories could
be deadly. A siege in a public street, though, was everyone's
fair game; and I wondered cynically how long it would be
before one of the fawn-uniformed law-enforcers accepted a
paper gift in exchange for the fact of just whose ransom was
barricaded there, three flights up.

I found myself automatically taking what one might call a
memory snapshot, a clear frozen picture of the moving scene
outside. It was a habit from boyhood, then consciously cultivated, a game to while away the boring times I'd been left in
the car while my mother went into shops. Across the road
from the bank I used to memorise the whole scene so that if
any bank robbers had rushed out I would have been able to
tell the police about all the cars which had been parked nearby,
make, colour, and numbers, and describe all the people in the
street at the time. Get-away cars and drivers would never have
got away unspotted by eagle-eyed ten-year-old Andrew D.

No bank robbers ever obliged me, nor smash-and-grabbers
outside the jewellers, nor baby snatchers from prams outside
the bakers, nor muggers of the elderly collecting their
pensions, nor even car thieves trying for unlocked doors. A
great many innocent people had come under my sternly suspicious eye – and though I'd grown out of the hope of actually
observing a crime, I'd never lost the ability of freeze-frame
recall.

Thus it was that from behind the darkened glass, after a
few moments' concentration, I had such a sharp mind's-eye
picture that I could have described with certainty the numbers

of windows in the block of flats facing, the position of each of the carabinieri cars, the clothes of the television crew, the whereabouts of each civilian inside the police circle, even the profile of the nearest press photographer, who was hung with two cameras but not at that moment taking pictures. He had a roundish head with smooth black hair, and a brown leather jacket with gold buckles at the cuffs.

A buzzer sounded sharply inside the van and Pucinelli lifted the handset which was connected with the flat's telephone. The bass-voiced kidnapper, edgy with waiting, demanded action; demanded specifically a safe passage to the airport and a light aircraft to fly him, and his colleage and the ransom, out.

Pucinelli told him to wait again, as only his superiors could arrange that. Tell them to bloody hurry, said the bass. Otherwise they'd find Alessia Cenci's dead body in the morning.

Pucinelli replaced the handset, tight-lipped.

'There will be no aeroplane,' he said to me flatly. 'It's impossible.'

'Do what they want,' I urged. 'You can catch them again later, when the girl is free.'

He shook his head. 'I cannot make that decision. Only the highest authority . . .'

'Get it, then.'

The engineer looked up curiously at the fierceness in my voice. Pucinelli, however, with calculation was seeing that shuffling off the decision had seductive advantages, so that if the girl did die it couldn't be held to be his fault. The thoughts ticked visibly behind his eyes, coming to clarity, growing to a nod.

I didn't know whether or not his superiors would let the kidnappers out; I only knew that Enrico couldn't. It was indeed a matter for the top brass.

'I think I'll go back to the Villa Francese,' I said.

'But why?'

'I'm not needed here, but there . . . I might be.' I paused fractionally. 'But I came from there in this van. How, at this time of night, can I get a car to take me back there quietly?'

He looked vaguely at the official cars outside, and I shook my head. 'Not one of those.'

'Still the anonymity . . . ?'

'Yes,' I said.

He wrote a card for me and gave me directions.

'All-night taxi, mostly for late drunks and unfaithful husbands. If he is not there, just wait.'

I let myself out through the cab, through the door on the dark side, away from the noisy, brightly-lit embroilment in the street, edging round behind the gawpers, disentangling myself from the public scene, heading for the unremarked shadows, my most normal sphere of work.

With one corner behind me the visible nightmare faded, and I walked fast through the sleeping summer streets, even my shoes, from long custom, making no clatter in the quiet. The taxi address lay beyond the far side of the old main square, and I found myself slowing briefly there, awed by the atmosphere of the place.

Somewhere in or near that aged city a helpless young woman faced her most dangerous night, and it seemed to me that the towering walls, with their smooth closed faces, embodied all the secrecy, the inimity and the implacability of those who held her.

The two kidnappers, now besieged, had been simply the collectors. There would be others. At the very least there would be guards still with her; but also, I thought, there was the man whose voice over five long weeks had delivered instructions, the man I thought of as HIM.

I wondered if he knew what had happened at the drop. I wondered if he knew yet about the siege, and where the ransom was.

Above all, I wondered if he would panic.

Alessia had no future, if he did.

two

Paolo Cenci was doing the pacing I had stifled in myself: up and down his tiled and pillared central hall, driven by intolerable tension. He broke from his eyes-down automatic-looking measured stride and came hurrying across as soon as he saw me walking through from the kitchen passage.

'Andrew!' His face was grey in the electric light. 'What in God's name has happened? Giorgio Traventi has telephoned me to say his son has been shot. He telephoned from the hospital. They are operating on Lorenzo at this minute.'

'Haven't the carabinieri told you . . .?'

'No one has told me anything. I am going mad with anxiety. It is five hours since you and Lorenzo set out. For five hours I've been waiting.' His hoarse voice shook over the gracefully accented English, the emotion raw and unashamed. At fifty-six he was a strong man at the height of his business ability, but the past weeks had made appalling demands on his mental stamina, and even his hands now trembled often. I saw so much of this distress in my job; and no matter how rich, no matter how powerful, the victim's family suffered in direct simple ratio to the depth of their love. Alessia's mother was dead: Alessia's father felt anguish enough for two.

With compassion I drew him into the library, where he sat most evenings, and with my own anger, I suppose, apparent, told him the details of the disaster. He sat with his head in his hands when I'd finished, as near to weeping as I'd seen him.

'They'll kill her . . .'

'No,' I said.

'They are animals.'

There had been enough bestial threats during the past weeks for me not to argue. The assaults on her body the kidnappers had promised should Cenci not obey their instructions had been brutally calculated to break any father's nerve, and my

21

assurances that threats were more common than performance hadn't comforted him to any extent. His imagination was too active, his fear too relentlessly acute.

My relationship with victims' families was something like that of a doctor's: called in in an emergency, consulted in a frightening and unsettling situation, looked to for miracles, leant on for succour. I'd set off on my first solo advisory job without any clear idea of the iron I would need to grow in my own core, and still after four years could quake before the demands made on my strength. Never get emotionally involved, I'd been told over and over during my training, you'll crack up if you do.

I was thirty. I felt, at times, a hundred.

Paolo Cenci's numbness at the nature and extent of the disaster began turning before my eyes to anger and, not surprisingly, to resentment against myself.

'If you hadn't told the carabinieri we were about to hand over the ransom, this wouldn't have happened. It's your fault. Yours. It's disgraceful. I should never have called you in. I shouldn't have listened to you. Those people warned me all along that if I brought in the carabinieri they would do unspeakable things to Alessia, and I let you persuade me, and I should not have done, I should have paid the ransom at once when they first demanded it, and Alessia would have been free weeks ago.'

I didn't argue with him. He knew, but in his grief was choosing not to remember, that to raise the ransom at first demanded had been impossible. Rich though he was, the equivalent of six million pounds sterling represented the worth not only of his whole estate but in addition of a large part of his business. Nor, as I'd forcefully told him, had the kidnappers ever expected him to pay that much: they were simply bludgeoning him with a huge amount so that anything less would seem a relief.

'Everything that Alessia has suffered has been your fault.'

Barring, presumably, the kidnap itself.

'Without you, I would have got her back. I would have paid. I would have paid anything. . . .'

To pay too much too soon was to make kidnappers think they had underestimated the family's resources, and sometimes resulted in the extortion of a second ransom for the same victim. I had warned him of that, and he had understood.

'Alessia is worth more to me than everything I possess. I wanted to pay . . . you wouldn't let me. I should have done what I thought best. I would have given everything . . .'

His fury bubbled on, and I couldn't blame him. It often seemed to those who loved that literally no price was too great to pay for the safe return of the loved one, but I'd learned a great deal about the unexpected faces of stress over the past four years, and I'd seen that for the future health of the family's relationships it was essential that one member had not in fact cost the rest everything. After the first euphoria, and when the financial loss had begun to bite, the burden of guilt on the paid-for victim became too great, and the resentment of the payers too intense, and they too began to feel guilt for their resentment, and could eventually hate the victim for love of whom they had beggared themselves.

To save the victims' future equilibrium had gradually become to me as important as their actual physical freedom, but it was an aim I didn't expect Paolo Cenci at that moment to appreciate.

The telephone at his elbow started ringing, making him jump. He put out his hand towards it and then hesitated, and with a visible screwing-up of courage lifted the receiver to his ear.

'Ricardo! . . . Yes . . . yes . . . I understand. I will do that now, at once.' He put down the receiver and rose galvanically to his feet.

'Ricardo Traventi?' I asked, standing also. 'Lorenzo's brother?'

'I must go alone,' he said, but without fire.

'You certainly must not. I will drive you.'

I had been acting as his chauffeur since I had arrived,

wearing his real chauffeur's cap and navy suit, while that grateful man took a holiday. It gave me the sort of invisibility that the firm had found worked best: kidnappers always knew everything about a household they had attacked, and a newcomer too officiously visiting alarmed them. A kidnapper was as nervous as a stalking fox and tended to see dangers when they didn't exist, let alone when they did. I came and went to the villa through the servants' entrance, taking it for granted that everything else would be noted.

Cenci's fury had evaporated as quickly as it had grown, and I saw that we were back to some sort of trust. I was grateful both for my sake and his that he would still accept my presence, but it was with some diffidence that I asked, 'What did Ricardo say?'

'They telephoned . . .' No need to ask who 'they' were. 'They' had been telephoning Traventi's house with messages all along, taking it for granted that there was an official tap on the telephones to the Villa Francese. That the Traventis' telephone was tapped also, with that family's reluctant permission, seemed to be something 'they' didn't know for certain.

'Ricardo says he must meet us at the usual place. He says he took the message because his parents are both at the hospital. He doesn't want to worry them. He says he will come on his scooter.'

Cenci was already heading towards the door, sure that I would follow.

Ricardo, Lorenzo's younger brother, was only eighteen, and no one originally had intended the two boys to be involved. Giorgio Traventi had agreed, as a lawyer, to act as a negotiator between Paolo Cenci and the kidnappers. It was he who took messages, passed them on, and in due course delivered the replies. The kidnappers themselves had a negotiator . . . HIM . . . with whom Giorgio Traventi spoke.

At times Traventi had been required to pick up packages at a certain spot, usually but not always the same place, and it was to that place that we were now headed. It had become not just the post-box for proof of Alessia's still being alive, or for appeals from her, or demands from HIM, or finally, earlier that evening, for the instructions about where to take the ransom, but also the place where Giorgio Traventi met Paolo Cenci, so that they could consult together in private. Neither had been too happy about the carabinieri overhearing their every word on the telephone and I had to admit that their instincts had been right.

It was ironic that at the beginning Giorgio Traventi had been approached by Cenci and his own lawyer simply because Traventi did not know the Cenci family well, and could act calmly on their behalf. Since then the whole Traventi family had become determined on Alessia's release, until finally nothing could have dissuaded Lorenzo from carrying the ransom himself. I hadn't approved of their growing emotional involvement – exactly what I had been warned against myself – but had been unable to stop it, as all of the Traventis had proved strong-willed and resolute, staunch allies when Cenci needed them most.

Indeed, until the carabinieri's ambush, the progress of negotiations had been, as far as was possible in any kidnap, smooth. The demand for six million had been cooled to about a tenth of that, and Alessia, on that afternoon at least, had been alive, unmolested and sane, reading aloud from that day's newspaper onto tape, and saying she was well.

The only comfort now, I thought, driving Cenci in his Mercedes to meet Ricardo, was that the kidnappers were still talking. Any message at all was better than an immediate dead body in a ditch.

The meeting place had been carefully chosen – by HIM – so that even if the carabinieri had had enough plain-clothes men to watch there day and night for weeks on end, they could have missed the actual delivery of the message: and indeed it was pretty clear that this had happened at least once. To confuse things during the period of closest continual watch, the messages had been delivered somewhere else.

We were heading for a motorway restaurant several miles outside Bologna, where even at night people came and went anonymously, travellers unremembered, different every hour of every day. Carabinieri who sat for too long over a coffee could be easily picked out.

Messages from HIM were left in a pocket in a cheap, grey, thin plastic waterproof, to be found hanging from a coat-rack inside the restaurant. The row of pegs was passed by everyone who went in or out of the cafeteria-style dining-room, and we guessed that the nondescript garment was in its place each time before the collect-the-message telephone call was made.

Traventi had taken the whole raincoat each time, but they had never been useful as clues. They were of a make sold throughout the region in flat, pocket-sized envelopes as a handy insurance against sudden rainstorms. The carabinieri had been given the four raincoats so far collected from the restaurant, and the one from the airport and the one from the bus station. All had been new, straight out of the packet, wrinkled from being folded, and smelling of the chemicals they were made from.

The messages had all been on tape. Regular-issue cassettes, sold everywhere. No fingerprints on anything. Everything exceedingly careful; everything, I had come to think, professional.

Each tape had contained proof of Alessia's being alive. Each tape contained threats. Each tape carried a response to Traventi's latest offer. I had advised him to offer only two hundred thousand at first, a figure received by HIM with fury, faked or real. Slowly, with hard bargaining, the gap between demand and credibility had been closed, until the ransom was big enough to be worth HIS trouble, and manageable enough not to cripple Cenci entirely. At the point where each felt comfortable if not content, the amount had been agreed.

The money had been collected: Italian currency in used everyday notes, fastened in bundles with rubber bands and packed in a suitcase. Upon its safe delivery, Alessia Cenci would be released.

Safe delivery . . . ye gods.

The motorway restaurant lay about equidistant from

Bologna and the Villa Francese, which stood in turreted idyllic splendour on a small country hillside, facing south. By day the road was busy with traffic, but at four in the morning only a few solitary pairs of headlights flooded briefly into our car. Cenci sat silent beside me, his eyes on the road and his mind heaven knew where.

Ricardo on his scooter arrived before us in the car park, though if anything he had had further to travel. Like his brother he was assertively intelligent, his eyes full now of the aggression brought on by the shooting, the narrow jaw jutting, the lips tight, the will to fight shouting from every muscle. He came across to the car as we arrived and climbed into the back seat.

'The bastards,' he said intensely. 'Lorenzo's state is critical, Papa says.' He spoke Italian, but distinctly, like all his family, so that I could nearly always understand them.

Paolo Cenci made a distressed gesture with his hands, sparing a thought for someone else's child. 'What is the message?' he said.

'To stand here by the telephones. He said I was to bring you, to speak to him yourself. No negotiator, he said. He sounded angry, very angry.'

'Was it the same man?' I asked.

'I think so. I've heard his voice on the tapes, but I've never spoken to him before. Always Papa speaks to him. Before tonight he wouldn't speak to anyone but Papa, but I told him Papa was at the hospital with Lorenzo and would be there until morning. Too late, he said. I must take the message myself. He said that you, Signor Cenci, must be alone. If there were any more carabinieri, he said, you wouldn't see Alessia again. They wouldn't return even her body.'

Cenci trembled beside me. 'I'll stay in the car,' I said. 'In my cap. They'll accept that. Don't be afraid.'

'I'll go with you,' Ricardo said.

'No.' I shook my head. 'Ricardo too might be taken for carabinieri. Better stay here with me.' I turned to Cenci. 'We'll wait. Have you any *gettoni* if he asks you to call him back?'

He fished vaguely through his pockets, and Ricardo and I gave him some of the necessary tokens; then he fumbled with the door handle and stood up, as if disoriented, in the car park.

'The telephones are near the restaurant,' Ricardo said. 'In the hall just outside. I have telephoned from there often.'

Cenci nodded, took a grip on the horrors, and walked with fair steadiness to the entrance.

'Do you think there will be someone watching?' Ricardo said.

'I don't know. We cannot take the risk.' I used the Italian word for danger, not risk, but he nodded comprehension. It was the third time I'd worked in Italy: time I spoke the language better than I did.

We waited a long time, not speaking much. We waited so long that I began to fear either that no call would come to Cenci at all, that the message had been a retributive piece of cruelty, or even worse, that it had been a ruse to lure him away from his house while something dreadful took place in it. My heart thumped uncomfortably. Alessia's elder sister, Ilaria, and Paolo Cenci's sister, Luisa, were both upstairs in the villa, asleep.

Perhaps I should have stayed there . . . but Cenci had been in no state to drive. Perhaps I should have awoken his gardener in the village, who drove sometimes on the chauffeur's days off. . . . Perhaps, perhaps.

The sky was already lightening to dawn when he returned, the shakiness showing in his walk, his face rigid as he reached the car. I stretched over and opened the door for him from the inside, and he subsided heavily into the passenger seat.

'He rang twice.' He spoke in Italian, automatically. 'The first time, he said wait. I waited . . .' He stopped and swallowed. Cleared his throat. Started again with a better attempt at firmness. 'I waited a long time. An hour. More. Finally, he telephoned. He says Alessia is still alive but the price has gone up. He says I must pay two thousand million lire in two days.'

His voice stopped, the despair sounding in it clearly. Two thousand million lire was approaching a million pounds.

'What else did he say?' I asked.

'He said that if anyone told the carabinieri of the new demand, Alessia would die at once.' He seemed suddenly to remember that Ricardo was in the car, and turned to him in alarm. 'Don't speak of this meeting, not to anyone. Promise me, Ricardo. On your soul.'

Ricardo, looking serious, promised. He also said he would go now to the hospital, to join his parents and get news of Lorenzo, and with a further passionate assurance of discretion he went over to his scooter and put-putted away.

I started the car and drove out of the car park.

Cenci said dully, 'I can't raise that much. Not again.'

'Well,' I said, 'you should eventually get back the money in the suitcase. With luck. That means that the real extra is . . . um . . . seven hundred million lire.'

Three hundred thousand pounds. Said quickly, it sounded less.

'But in two days . . .'

'The banks will lend it. You have the assets.'

He didn't answer. So close on the other collection of random used notes, this would be technically more difficult. More money, much faster. The banks, however, would read the morning papers – and raising a ransom was hardly a process unknown to them.

'What are you to do, when you've collected it?' I asked.

Cenci shook his head. 'He told me . . . But this time I can't tell you. This time I take the money myself . . . alone.'

'It's unwise.'

'I must do it.'

He sounded both despairing and determined, and I didn't argue. I said merely, 'Will we have time to photograph the notes and put tracers on them?'

He shook his head impatiently. 'What does it matter now? It is Alessia only that is important. I've been given a second chance. . . .This time I do what he says. This time I act alone.'

Once Alessia was safe – if she were so lucky – he would regret he'd passed up the best chance of recovering at least part of the ransom and of catching the kidnappers. Emotion, as so often in kidnap situations, was stampeding common sense. But one couldn't, I supposed, blame him.

Pictures of Alessia Cenci, the girl I had never seen, adorned most rooms in the Villa Francese.

Alessia Cenci on horses, riding in races round the world. Alessia the rich girl with the hands of silk and a temperament like the sun (a fanciful newspaper report had said), bright, warm, and occasionally scorching.

I knew little about racing, but I'd heard of her, the glamour girl of the European tracks who nevertheless could really ride: one would have to have averted one's eyes from newspapers pretty thoroughly not to. There seemed to be something about her that captivated the daily scribblers, particularly in England, where she raced often; and in Italy I heard genuine affection in every voice that spoke of her. In every voice, that is to say, except for that of her sister Ilaria, whose reaction to the kidnap had been complex and revealing.

Alessia in close-up photographs wasn't particularly beautiful: thin, small-featured, dark-eyed, with short head-hugging curls. It was her sister, by her side in silver frames, who looked more feminine, more friendly, and more pretty. Ilaria in life however was not particularly any of those things, at least not in the present horrific family circumstances. One couldn't tell what happiness might do.

She and her aunt Luisa still slept when Cenci and I returned to the villa. All was quiet there, all safe. Cenci walked straight into the library and poured a large amount of brandy into a tumbler, indicating that I should help myself to the same. I joined him, reflecting that seven in the morning was as good a time as any to get drunk.

'I'm sorry,' he said. 'I know it's not your fault. The carabinieri . . . do what they want.'

I gathered he was referring back to the anger he'd poured

on me the last time we'd sat in those same two chairs. I made a vague don't-think-about-it gesture and let the brandy sear a path to my stomach, a shaft of vivid feeling going down through my chest. It might not have been wise, but the oldest tranquilliser was still the most effective.

'Do you think we'll get her back?' Cenci asked. 'Do you really think so?'

'Yes.' I nodded. 'They wouldn't be starting again more or less from scratch if they meant to kill her. They don't want to harm her, as I've told you all along. They only want you to believe they will . . . and yes, I do think it's a good sign they still have the nerve to bargain, with two of their number besieged by the carabinieri.'

Cenci looked blank. 'I'd forgotten about those.'

I hadn't; but then the ambush and the siege were imprinted in my mind as memories, not reports. I had wondered, through most of the night, whether the two collectors had been carrying walkie-talkie radios, and whether HE had known of the debacle at almost the moment it happened, not simply when neither his colleagues nor the money turned up.

I thought that if I were HIM I'd be highly worried about those two men, not necessarily for their own sakes, but for what they knew. They might know where Alessia was. They might know who had planned the operation. They had to know where they'd been expected to take the money. They might be hired hands . . . but trusted enough to be collectors. They might be full equal partners, but I doubted it. Kidnap gangs tended to have hierarchies, like every other organisation.

One way or another those two were going to fall into the grasp of the carabinieri, either talking or shot. They themselves had promised that if they didn't go free, Alessia would die, but apparently HE had said nothing like that to Cenci. Did that mean that HIS priority was money, that he was set on extorting only what he almost certainly could – money from Cenci – and not what he almost as certainly couldn't – the return of his friends? Or did it mean that he didn't have radio contact with his colleagues, who had made the threat in faith more than promise . . . or did it mean that by radio he had persuaded the colleagues to barricade themselves in and make the fiercest threats continually, staying out of the carabinieri's clutches long enough for HIM to spirit Alessia away to a new hide-out, so that it wouldn't matter if the colleagues finally did talk, they wouldn't know the one thing worth telling?

'What are you thinking?' Cenci asked.

'Of hope,' I said; and thought that the kidnappers in the flat probably didn't have contact by radio after all, because they hadn't made any reference to it during the hour I'd listened to them via the bug. But then HE might guess about bugs . . . if HE was that clever . . . and have told them to switch off after his first burst of instructions.

If I'd been HIM, I'd have been in touch with those collectors from the moment they set out . . . but then there weren't so many radio frequencies as all that, and the possibility of being overheard was high. But there were codes and pre-arranged phrases. . . . And how did you pre-arrange a message which said the carabinieri have swarmed all over us and we've shot the man who brought the ransom?

If they hadn't taken the ransom with its homing transmitter, they would probably have escaped. If they hadn't been fanatical about taking the ransom, they wouldn't have shot the driver to get it.

If the carabinieri had acted stupidly, so had the kidnappers, and only as long as HE didn't decide after all to cut his losses was there any positive hope. I still thought that hope to be frail. One didn't however admit it to the victim's dad.

Cenci anyway had tears at last running down his cheeks, released, I guessed, by the brandy. He made no sound, nor tried to brush them away or hide them. Many a man would have come to that stage sooner, and in my own experience, most victims' parents did. Through outrage, anger, anxiety and grief, through guilt and hope and pain, the steps they trod were the same. I'd seen so many people in despair that sometimes a laughing face would jolt me.

The Paolo Cenci I knew was the man sitting opposite, who

hadn't smiled once in my sight. He had attempted at first to put up a civilised front, but the mask had soon crumbled as he got used to my presence, and it was the raw man whose feelings and strengths and blindnesses I knew. The urban successful man-of-the-world looking out with genial wisdom from the portrait in the drawing-room, he was the stranger.

For his part, after his first blink at my not being in his own age group, he had seemed to find me compatible on all counts. His cry for help had reached our office within a day of Alessia's disappearance, and I had been on his back-doorstep the next; but forty-eight hours could seem a lifetime in that sort of nightmare and his relief at my arrival had been undemanding. He would very likely have accepted a four-armed dwarf with blue skin, not just a five-ten thin frame with ordinary dark hair and washed-out grey eyes: but he was, after all, paying for my help, and if he really hadn't liked me he had an easy way out.

His original call to our office had been brief and direct. 'My daughter has been kidnapped. I telephoned Tomasso Linardi, of the Milan Fine Leather Company, for advice. He gave me your name . . . he says it was your firm which got him safely home and helped the police trace the kidnappers. I need your help now myself. Please come.'

Tomasso Linardi, owner of the Milan Fine Leather Company, had himself been held to ransom two years earlier, and it wasn't surprising that Paolo Cenci should have known him, as Cenci too was in the leather business, heading a corporation with world-wide trade. Half the Italian shoes imported into England, he had told me, had passed in the uncut leather stage through his firm.

The two men incidentally had proved to have a second and more tenuous factor in common, an interest in horses; Cenci of course because of Alessia's jockeyship, and Linardi because he had owned a majority share in a racetrack. This holding in a fashionable, profit-making piece of flat land had been one of the things sold to raise his ransom, much to his sorrow when on his release he found out. In his case, although some of his kidnappers had been arrested a month later, only a small part of the million-pound ransom had been recovered. The seven million which had at first been strongly demanded would have meant losing his business as well, so on the whole he had been relieved, resigned, and obviously content enough with Liberty Market to recommend us to the next guy in trouble.

I had shared the Linardi assignment with another partner. We'd found Linardi's wife less than distraught about her husband and furious about the cost of getting him back. His mistress had wept buckets, his son had usurped his office chair, his cook had had hysterics, his sisters had squabbled and his dog had pined. The whole thing had been conducted with operatic histrionics fortissimo, leaving me finally feeling I'd been swamped by a tidal wave.

In the Villa Francese, a much quieter house, Paolo Cenci and I sat for a further half-hour, letting the brandy settle and thinking of this and that. At length, his tears long dried, he sighed deeply and said that as the day had to be faced he would change his clothes, have breakfast and go to his office. I would drive him no doubt as usual. And I could photograph the new ransom money, as before. He had been thinking, and of course I was right, it was the best chance of getting any of it back.

Breakfast in that formal household was eaten in the dining-room: coffee, fruit and hot breads against murals of shepher-desses à la Marie Antoinette.

Ilaria joined us there, silently as usual, assembling her own preferences onto her plate. Her silences were a form of aggression; a positive refusal, for instance, to say good-morning to her father even out of good manners. He seemed to be used to it, but I found it extraordinary, especially in the circum-stances, and especially as it seemed there was no animosity or discord between them. Ilaria lived a privileged life which included no gainful occupation: mostly travel, tennis, singing lessons, shopping and lunches, thanks to her father's money. He gave, she received. I wondered sometimes if it was resent-ment at this dependency that made her so insistently refuse to acknowledge it even to the extent of behaving sweetly, but she had apparently never wanted or sought a job. Her Aunt Luisa had told me so, with approval.

Ilaria was a fresh-looking twenty-four, curved, not skinny, with brown wavy hair superbly cut and frequently shampooed. She had a habit of raising her eyebrows and looking down her nose, as she was now doing at her coffee cup, which probably reflected her whole view of life and would undoubtedly set into creases before forty.

She didn't ask if there was any news of Alessia: she never did. She seemed if anything to be angry with her sister for being kidnapped, though she hadn't exactly said so. Her reaction however to my suggestion that she should not go so predictably at set times to the tennis court and in fact should go away altogether and stay with friends, because kidnappers if feeling frustrated by delays had been known to take a second speeding-up bite at the same family, had been not only negative but acid. 'There wouldn't be the same agonised fuss over me.'

Her father had looked aghast at her bitterness, but both she and I saw in his face that what she'd said was true, even if he had never admitted it to himself. It would in fact have been very much easier to abduct Ilaria, but even as a victim she had been passed over in favour of her famous little sister, her father's favourite. She had continued, with the same defiance as in her silences, to go at the same time to the same places, an open invitation to trouble. Cenci had begged her not to, to no avail.

I wondered if she even positively wanted to be taken, so that her father would have to prove his love for her, as for Alessia, by selling precious things to get her back.

Because she hadn't asked, we hadn't told her the evening before that that was the night for paying the ransom. Let her sleep, Cenci had said, contemplating his own wakeful ordeal and wishing to spare her. 'Perhaps Alessia will be home for breakfast,' he'd said.

He looked at Ilaria now and with great weariness told her

35

that the hand-over had gone wrong, and that another and bigger ransom had to be collected for Alessia.

'Another . . .' She stared at him in disbelief, cup stopping halfway to her mouth.

'Andrew thinks we may get the first one back again, but meanwhile . . .' he made an almost beseeching gesture with his hand. 'My dear, we are going to be poorer. Not just temporarily, but always. This extra demand is a grave setback. . . . I have decided to sell the house on Mikonos, but even that will not be enough. Your mother's jewels must go, also the collection of snuff boxes. The rest I must raise on the worth of this house and this estate, and if we do not recover the first ransom I will be paying interest on the loan out of the receipts from the olives, which will leave nothing over. The land I sold in Bologna to raise the first ransom will not now be providing us with any revenue, and we have to live on what I make in the business.' He shrugged slightly. 'We'll not starve. We'll continue to live here. But there are the pensions for our retired servants, and the allowances for my uncles' widows, which they live on. . . . It is going to be a struggle, my dear, and I think you should know, and be prepared.'

She looked at him with absolute shock, and I thought that until that moment she hadn't realised that paying a ransom was a very cruel business.

three

I drove Cenci to his office and left him there to his telephone and his grim task with the banks. Then, changing from chauffeur's uniform into nondescript trousers and sweater, I went by bus and foot to the street where the siege might still be taking place.

Nothing, it seemed, had changed there. The dark-windowed ambulance still stood against the kerb on the far side of the road from the flats, the carabinieri's cars were still parked helter-skelter in the same positions with fawn uniforms crouching around them, the television van still sprouted wires and aerials, and a commentator was still talking into camera.

Daylight had subtracted drama. Familiarity had done the same to urgency. The scene now looked not frightening but peaceful, with figures moving at walking pace, not in scurrying little runs. A watching crowd stood and stared bovinely, growing bored.

The windows on the third floor were shut.

I hovered at the edge of things, hands in pockets, hair tousled, local paper under arm, looking, I hoped, not too English. Some of the partners in Liberty Market were stunning at disguises, but I'd always found a slouch and vacant expression my best bet for not being noticed.

After a while during which nothing much happened I wandered off in search of a telephone, and rang the number of the switchboard inside the ambulance.

'Is Enrico Pucinelli there?' I asked.

'Wait.' Some mumbling went on in the background, and then Pucinelli himself spoke, sounding exhausted.

'Andrew? Is it you?'

'Yes. How's it going?'

'Nothing has altered. I am off duty at ten o'clock for an hour.'

I looked at my watch. Nine thirty-eight. 'Where are you eating?' I said.

'Gino's.'

'OK,' I said, and disconnected.

I waited for him in the brightly-lit glass-and-tile-lined restaurant that to my knowledge served fresh pasta at three in the morning with good grace. At eleven it was already busy with early lunchers, and I held a table for two by ordering loads of fettucine that I didn't want. Pucinelli, when he arrived, pushed away his cooling plateful with horror and ordered eggs.

He had come, as I knew he would, in civilian clothes, and the tiredness showed in black smudges under his eyes and in the droop of his shoulders.

'I hope you slept well,' he said sarcastically.

I moved my head slightly, meaning neither yes nor no.

'I have had two of the top brass on my neck in the van all night,' he said. 'They can't make up their fat minds about the aeroplane. They are talking to Rome. Someone in the government must decide, they say, and no one in the government wanted to disturb his sleep to think about it. You would have gone quite crazy, my friend. Talk, talk, talk, and not enough action to shit.'

I put on a sympathetic face and thought that the longer the siege lasted, the safer now for Alessia. Let it last, I thought, until she was free. Let HIM be a realist to the end.

'What are the kidnappers saying?' I asked.

'The same threats. The girl will die if they and the ransom money don't get away safely.'

'Nothing new?'

He shook his head. His eggs came with rolls and coffee, and he ate without hurry. 'The baby cried half the night,' he said with his mouth full. 'The deep-voiced kidnapper keeps telling the mother he'll strangle it if it doesn't shut up. It gets on his nerves.' He lifted his eyes to my face. 'You always tell me they threaten more than they do. I hope you're right.'

I hoped so to. A crying baby could drive even a temperate man to fury. 'Can't they feed it?' I said.

'It has colic.'

He spoke with familiarity of experience, and I wondered vaguely about his private life. All our dealings had been essentially impersonal, and it was only in flashes, as now, that I heard the man behind the policeman.

'You have children?' I asked.

He smiled briefly, a glimmer in the eyes. 'Three sons, two daughters, one . . . expected.' He paused. 'And you?'

I shook my head. 'Not yet. Not married.'

'Your loss. Your gain.'

I laughed. He breathed deprecatingly down his nose as if to disclaim the disparagement of his lady. 'Girls grow into mamas,' he said. He shrugged. 'It happens.'

Wisdom, I thought, showed up in the most unexpected places. He finished his eggs as one at peace with himself, and drank his coffee. 'Cigarette?' he asked, edging a packet out of his shirt pocket. 'No. I forgot. You don't.' He flicked his lighter and inhaled the first lungful with the deep relief of a dedicated smoker. Each to his own release: Cenci and I had found the same thing in brandy.

'During the night,' I said, 'did the kidnappers talk to anyone else?'

'How do you mean?'

'By radio.'

He lifted his thin face sharply, the family man retreating. 'No. They spoke only to each other, to the hostage family, and to us. Do you think they have a radio? Why do you think that?'

'I wondered if they were in touch with their colleagues guarding Alessia.'

He considered it with concentration and indecisively shook his head. 'The two kidnappers spoke of what was happening, from time to time, but only as if they were talking to each other. If they were also transmitting on a radio and didn't want us to know, they are very clever. They would have to guess we are already listening to every word they say.' He thought it over a bit longer and finally shook his head with more certainty. 'They are not clever. I've listened to them all night. They are violent, frightened, and . . .' he searched for a word I would understand ' . . . ordinary.'

'Average intelligence?'

'Yes. Average.'

'All the same, when you finally get them out, will you look around for a radio?'

'You personally want to know?'

39

'Yes.'

He looked at me assessingly with a good deal of professional dispassion. 'What are you not telling me?' he said.

I was not telling him what Cenci passionately wished to keep private, and it was Cenci who was paying me. I might advise full consultation with the local law, but only that. Going expressly against the customer's wishes was at the very least bad for future business.

'I simply wonder,' I said mildly, 'if the people guarding Alessia know exactly what's going on.'

He looked as if some sixth sense was busy doubting me, so to take his mind off it I said, 'I dare say you've thought of stun grenades as a last resort?'

'Stun?' He didn't know the word. 'What's stun?'

'Grenades which more or less knock people out for a short while. They produce noise and shock waves, but do no permanent damage. While everyone is semi-conscious, you walk into the flat and apply handcuffs where they're needed.'

'The army has them, I think.'

I nodded. 'You are part of the army.'

'Special units have them. We don't.' He considered. 'Would they hurt the children?'

I didn't know. I could see him discarding stun grenades rapidly. 'We'll wait,' he said. 'The kidnappers cannot live there for ever. In the end, they must come out.'

Cenci stared morosely at a large cardboard carton standing on the desk in his office. The carton bore stick-on labels saying FRAGILE in white letters on red, but the contents would have survived any drop. Any drop, that is, except one to kidnappers.

'Fifteen hundred million lire,' he said. 'The banks arranged for it to come from Milan. They brought it straight to this office, with security guards.'

'In that box?' I asked, surprised.

'No. They wanted their cases back . . . and this box was here.' His voice sounded deathly tired. 'The rest comes tomorrow. They've been understanding and quick, but the interest they're demanding will cripple me.'

I made a mute gesture of sympathy, as no words seemed appropriate. Then I changed into my chauffeur's uniform, carried the heavy carton to the car, stowed it in the boot, and presently drove Cenci home.

We ate dinner late at the villa, though meals were often left unfinished according to the anxiety level of the day. Cenci would push his plate away in revulsion, and I sometimes thought my thinness resulted from never being able to eat heartily in the face of grief. My suggestions that Cenci might prefer my not living as family had been met with emphatic negatives. He needed company, he said, if he were to stay sane. I would please be with him as much as possible.

On that evening, however, he understood that I couldn't be. I carried the FRAGILE box upstairs to my room, closed the curtains, and started the lengthy task of photographing every note, flattening them in a frame of non-reflecting glass, four at a time of the same denomination. Even with the camera on a tripod, with bulk film, cable release and motor drive, the job always took ages. It was one that I did actually prefer not to leave to banks or the police, but even after all the practice I'd had I could shift only about fifteen hundred notes an hour. Large ransoms had me shuffling banknotes in my dreams.

It was Liberty Market routine to send the undeveloped films by express courier to the London office, where we had simple developing and printing equipment in the basement. The numbers of the notes were then typed into a computer, which sorted them into numerical order for each denomination and then printed out the lists. The lists returned, again by courier, to the advisor in the field, who, after the victim had been freed, gave them to the police to circulate to all the country's banks, with a promise that any teller spotting one of the ransom notes would be rewarded.

It was a system which seemed to us best, principally because photography left no trace on the notes. The problem with physically marking them was that anything the banks could detect, so could the kidnappers. Banks had no monopoly, for instance, in scans to reveal fluorescence. Geiger counters for radioactive pin dots weren't hard to come by. Minute perforations could be seen as easily by any eyes against a bright light, and extra lines and marks could be spotted by anyone's magnification. The banks, through simple pressure of time, had to be able to spot tracers easily, which put chemical invisible inks out of court. Kidnappers, far more thorough and with fear always at their elbows, could test obsessively for everything.

Kidnappers who found tracers on the ransom had to be considered lethal. In Liberty Market, therefore, the markings we put on notes were so difficult to find that we sometimes lost them ourselves, and they were certainly unspottable by banks. They consisted of transparent microdots (the size of the full stops to which we applied them) which when separated and put under a microscope revealed a shadowy black logo of L and M, but through ordinary magnifying glasses appeared simply black. We used them only on larger denomination notes, and then only as a back-up in case there should be any argument about the photographed numbers. To date we had never had to reveal their existence, a state of affairs we hoped to maintain.

By morning, fairly dropping from fatigue, I'd photographed barely half, the banks having taken the 'small denomination' instruction all too literally. Locking all the money into a wardrobe cupboard I showered and thought of bed, but after breakfast drove Cenci to the office as usual. Three nights I could go without sleep. After that, zonk.

'If the kidnappers get in touch with you,' I said, on the way, 'you might tell them you can't drive. Say you need your chauffeur. Say . . . um . . . you've a bad heart, something like that. Then at least you'd have help, if you needed it.'

There was such an intense silence from the back seat that at first I thought he hadn't heard, but eventually he said, 'I suppose you don't know, then.'

'Know what?'

'Why I have a chauffeur.'

'General wealth, and all that,' I said.

'No. I have no licence.'

I had seen him driving round the private roads on his estate in a jeep on one or two occasions, though not, I recalled, with much fervour. After a while he said, 'I choose not to have a licence, because I have epilepsy. I've had it most of my life. It is of course kept completely under control with pills, but I prefer not to drive on public roads.'

'I'm sorry,' I said.

'Forget it. I do. It's an inconvenience merely.' He sounded as if the subject bored him, and I thought that regarding irregular brain patterns as no more than a nuisance was typical of what I'd gleaned of his normal business methods: routine fast and first, planning slow and thorough. I'd gathered from things his secretary had said in my hearing that he'd made few decisions lately, and trade was beginning to suffer.

When we reached the outskirts of Bologna he said, 'I have to go back to those telephones at the motorway restaurant tomorrow morning at eight. I have to take the money in my car. I have to wait for him . . . for his instructions. He'll be angry if I have a chauffeur.'

'Explain. He'll know you always have a chauffeur. Tell him why.'

'I can't risk it.' His voice shook.

'Signor Cenci, he wants the money. Make him believe you can't drive safely. The last thing he wants is you crashing the ransom into a lamppost.'

'Well . . . I'll try.'

'And remember to ask for proof that Alessia is alive and unharmed.'

'Yes.'

I dropped him at the office and drove back to the Villa Francese, and because it was what the Cenci chauffeur always did when he wasn't needed during the morning, I washed the car. I'd washed the damn car so often I knew every inch intimately, but one couldn't trust kidnappers not to be watching; and the villa and its hillside, with its glorious views, could be observed closely by telescope from a mile away in most directions. Changes of routine from before to after a kidnap were of powerful significance to kidnappers, who were often better detectives than detectives, and better spies than spies. The people who'd taught me my job had been detectives and spies and more besides, so when I was a chauffeur, I washed cars.

That done I went upstairs and slept for a couple of hours and then set to again on the photography, stopping only to go and fetch Cenci at the usual hour. Reporting to his office I found another box on the desk, this time announcing it had been passed by customs at Genoa.

'Shall I carry it out?' I asked.

He nodded dully. 'It is all there. Five hundred million lire.'

We drove home more or less in silence, and I spent the evening and night as before, methodically clicking until I felt like a zombie. By morning it was done, with the microdots applied to a few of the fifty-thousand lire notes, but not many, through lack of time. I packed all the rubber-banded bundles into the FRAGILE box and humped it down to the hall to find Cenci already pacing up and down in the dining-room, white with strain.

'There you are!' he exclaimed. 'I was just coming to wake you. It's getting late. Seven o'clock.'

'Have you had breakfast?' I asked.

'I can't eat.' He looked at his watch compulsively, something I guessed he'd been doing for hours. 'We'd better go. Suppose we were held up on the way? Suppose there was an accident blocking the road?'

His breathing was shallow and agitated, and I said diffidently, 'Signor Cenci, forgive me for asking, but in the anxiety of this morning . . . have you remembered your pills?'

He looked at me blankly. 'Yes. Yes, of course. Always with me.'

'I'm sorry . . .'

44

He brushed it away. 'Let's go. We must go.'

The traffic on the road was normal: no accidents. We reached the rendezvous half an hour early, but Cenci sprang out of the car as soon as I switched off the engine. From where I'd parked I had a view of the entrance across a double row of cars, the doorway like the mouth of a beehive with people going in and out continually.

Cenci walked with stiff legs to be lost among them, and in the way of chauffeurs I slouched down in my seat and tipped my cap forward over my nose. If I wasn't careful, I thought, I'd go to sleep. . . .

Someone rapped on the window beside me. I opened my eyes, squinted sideways, and saw a youngish man in a white open-necked shirt with a gold chain round his neck making gestures for me to open the window.

The car, rather irritatingly, had electric windows: I switched on the ignition and pressed the relevant button, sitting up slightly while I did it.

'Who are you waiting for?' he said.

'Signor Cenci.'

'Not Count Rieti?'

'No. Sorry.'

'Have you seen another chauffeur here?'

'Sorry, no.'

He was carrying a magazine rolled into a cylinder and fastened by a rubber band. I thought fleetingly of one of the partners in Liberty Market who believed one should never trust a stranger carrying a paper cylinder because it was such a handy place to stow a knife . . . and I wondered, but not much.

'You're not Italian?' the man said.

'No. From Spain.'

'Oh.' His gaze wandered, as if seeking Count Rieti's chauffeur. Then he said absently in Spanish, 'You're a long way from home.'

'Yes,' I said.

'Where do you come from?'

'Andalucía.'

'Very hot, at this time of year.'

'Yes.'

I had spent countless school holidays in Andalucia, staying with my divorced half-Spanish father who ran a hotel there. Spanish was my second tongue, learned on all levels from kitchen to penthouse: any time I didn't want to appear English, I became a Spaniard.

'Is your employer having breakfast?' he asked.

'I don't know.' I shrugged. 'He said to wait, so I wait.'

His Spanish had a clumsy accent and his sentences were grammatically simple, as careful as mine in Italian.

I yawned.

He could be a coincidence, I thought. Kidnappers were normally much too shy for such a direct approach, keeping their faces hidden at all costs. This man could be just what he seemed, a well-meaning citizen carrying a magazine, looking for Count Rieti's chauffeur and with time to spare for talking.

Could be. If not, I would tell him what he wanted to know: if he asked.

'Do you drive always for Signor . . . Cenci?' he said casually.

'Sure,' I said. 'It's a good job. Good pay. He's considerate. Never drives himself, of course.'

'Why not?'

I shrugged. 'Don't know. He hasn't a licence. He has to have someone to drive him always.'

I wasn't quite sure he had followed that, though I'd spoken pretty slowly and with a hint of drowsiness. I yawned again and thought that one way or another he'd had his ration of chat. I would memorise his face, just in case, but it was unlikely . . .

He turned away as if he too had found the conversation finished, and I looked at the shape of his round smooth head from the side, and felt most unwelcome tingles ripple all down my spine. I'd seen him before. . . . I'd seen him outside the ambulance, through the tinted glass, with cameras slung from his neck and gold buckles on the cuffs of his jacket. I could

46

remember him clearly. He'd appeared at the siege . . . and he was here at the drop, asking questions.

No coincidence.

It was the first time I'd ever knowingly been physically near one of the shadowy brotherhood, those foes I opposed by proxy, whose trials I never attended, whose ears never heard of my existence. I slouched down again in my seat and tipped my cap over my nose and thought that my partners in London would emphatically disapprove of my being in that place at that time. The low profile was down the drain.

If I'd seen him, he'd seen me.

It might not matter: not if he believed in the Spanish chauffeur who was bored with waiting. If he believed in the bored Spanish chauffeur, he'd forget me. If he hadn't believed in the bored Spanish chauffeur I would quite likely be sitting there now with a knife through my ribs, growing cold.

In retrospect I felt distinctly shivery. I had not remotely expected such an encounter, and at first it had only been habit and instinct, reinforced by true tiredness, that had made me answer him as I had. I found it definitely scary to think that Alessia's life might have hung on a yawn.

Time passed. Eight o'clock came and went. I waited as if asleep. No one else came to my still open window to ask me anything at all.

It was after nine before Cenci came back, half-running, stumbling, sweating. I was out of the car as soon as I saw him, politely opening a rear door and helping him in as a chauffeur should.

'Oh my God,' he said. 'I thought he wouldn't telephone. . . . It's been so long.'

'Is Alessia all right?'

'Yes . . . yes. . . .'

'Where to, then?'

'Oh . . .' He drew in some calming breaths while I got back behind the wheel and started the engine. 'We have to go to Mazara, about twenty kilometres south. Another restaurant . . . another telephone. In twenty minutes.'

'Um . . .' I said. 'Which way from here?'

He said vaguely, 'Umberto knows,' which wasn't especially helpful, as Umberto was his real chauffeur, away on holiday. I grabbed the road map from the glove compartment and spread it on the passenger seat beside me, trying unsuccessfully to find Mazara while pulling in a normal fashion out of the car park.

The road we were on ran west to east. I took the first major-looking turn towards the south, and as soon as we were out of sight of the motorway drew into the side and paused for an update on geography. One more turn, I thought, and there would be signposts: and in fact we made it to Mazara, which proved to be little more than a crossroads, with breathing time to spare.

On the way Cenci said, 'Alessia was reading from today's paper . . . on tape, it must have been, because she just went on reading when I spoke to her . . . but to hear her voice . . .'

'You're sure it was her?'

'Oh yes. She started as usual with one of those memories of her childhood that you suggested. It was Alessia herself, my darling, darling daughter.'

Well, I thought. So far, so good.

'He said . . .' Cenci gulped audibly. 'He said if there are homers this time in the ransom he'll kill her. He says if there are marks on the notes, he'll kill her. He says if we are followed . . . if we don't do exactly as he says . . . if anything . . . *anything* goes wrong, he'll kill her.'

I nodded. I believed it. A second chance was a partial miracle. We'd never get a third.

'You promise,' he said, 'that he'll find nothing on the notes?'

'I promise,' I said.

At Mazara Cenci ran to the telephone, but again he was agonisingly kept waiting. I sat as before in the car, stolidly patient, as if the antics of my employer were of little interest, and surreptitiously read the map.

The restaurant at this place was simply a café next to a garage, a stop for coffee and petrol. People came and went, but not many. The day warmed up under the summer sun, and as a good chauffeur should I started the purring engine and switched on the air-conditioning.

He returned with his jacket over his arm and flopped gratefully into the cool.

'Casteloro,' he said. 'Why is he doing this?'

'Standard procedure, to make sure we're not followed. He'll be doubly careful because of last time. We might be chasing about all morning.'

'I can't stand it,' he said; but he could, of course, after the last six weeks.

I found the way to Casteloro and drove there: thirty-two kilometres, mostly of narrow, straight, exposed country roads. Open fields on both sides. Any car following us would have shown up like a rash.

'He made no trouble about you,' Cenci said. 'I said straight away that I'd brought my chauffeur because I have epilepsy, that it was impossible for me to drive, to come alone. He just said to give you instructions and not explain anything.'

'Good,' I said, and thought that if HE were me he'd check up with Alessia about the epilepsy, and be reassured.

At Casteloro, a small old town with a cobbled central square full of pigeons, the telephone Cenci sought was in a café, and this time there was no delay.

'Return to Mazara,' Cenci said with exhaustion.

I reversed the car and headed back the way we had come, and Cenci said, 'He asked me what I had brought the money in. I described the box.'

'What did he say?'

'Nothing. Just to follow instructions or Alessia would be killed. He said they would kill her . . . horribly.' His voice choked and came out as a sob.

'Listen,' I said, 'they don't want to kill her. Not now, not when they're so close. And did they say what "horribly" meant? Were they . . . specific?'

On another sob he said, 'No.'

'They're frightening you,' I said. 'Using threats to make

49

sure you'd elude the carabinieri, even if up to now you'd been letting them follow you.'

'But I haven't!' he protested.

'They have to be convinced. Kidnappers are very nervous.'

It was reassuring though, I thought, that they were still making threats, because it indicated they were serious about dealing. This was no cruel dummy run: this was the actual drop.

Back at the Mazara crossroads there was another lengthy wait. Cenci sat in the café, visible through the window, trembling over an undrunk cup of coffee. I got out of the car, stretched, ambled up and down a bit, got back in, and yawned. Three unexceptional cars filled with petrol and the garage attendant scratched his armpits.

The sun was high, blazing out of the blue sky. An old woman in black cycled up to the crossroads, turned left, cycled away. Summer dust stirred and settled in the wake of passing vans, and I thought of Lorenzo Traventi, who had driven the last lot of ransom and now clung to life on machines.

Inside the café Cenci sprang to his feet, and after a while came back to the car in no better state than before. I opened the rear door for him as usual and helped him inside.

'He says . . .' He took a deep breath. 'He says there is a sort of shrine by the roadside between here and Casteloro. He says we've passed it twice already . . . but I didn't notice . . .'

I nodded. 'I saw it.' I closed his door and resumed my own seat.

'Well, there,' Cenci said. 'He says to put the box behind the shrine, and drive away.'

'Good,' I said with relief. 'That's it, then.'

'But Alessia . . .' he wailed. 'I asked him, when will Alessia be free, and he didn't answer, he just put the telephone down . . .'

I started the car and drove again towards Casteloro.

'Be patient,' I said gently. 'They'll have to count the money. To examine it for tracers. Maybe, after last time, to leave it for a while in a place they can observe, to make sure no one is tracking it by homer. They won't free Alessia until they're certain they're safe, so I'm afraid it means waiting. It means patience.'

He groaned on a long breath. 'But they'll let her go . . . when I've paid . . . they'll let her go, won't they?'

He was asking desperately for reassurance, and I said, 'Yes,' robustly: and they would let her go, I thought, if they were satisfied, if they were sane, if something unforeseen didn't happen and if Alessia hadn't seen their faces.

About ten miles from the crossroads, by a cornfield, stood a simple stone wayside shrine, a single piece of wall about five feet high by three across, with a weatherbeaten foot-high stone madonna offering blessings from a niche in front. Rain had washed away most of the blue paint of her mantle, and time or vandals had relieved her of the tip of her nose, but posies of wilting flowers lay on the ground before her, and someone had left some sweets beside her feet.

The road we were on seemed deserted, running straight in each direction. There were no woods, no cover, no obstructions. We could probably be seen for miles.

Cenci stood watching while I opened the boot, lugged out the box, and carried it to the back of the shrine. The box had just about been big enough to contain the whole ransom, and there it stood on the dusty earth, four-square, brown and ordinary, tied about with thick string to make carrying easier and cheerfully labelled with red. Almost a million pounds. The house on Mikonos, the snuff box collection, his dead wife's jewellery, the revenue forever from the olives.

Cenci stared at it blindly for a few moments, then we both returned to the car and I reversed and drove away.

four

For the rest of that day, Saturday, and all Sunday, Cenci walked slowly round his estate, came heavily home, drank too much brandy and lost visible weight.

Ilaria, silently defiant, went to the tennis club as usual. Luisa, her aunt, drifted about in her usual wispy fashion, touching things as if to make sure they were still there.

I drove to Bologna, sent off the films, washed the car. Lorenzo still breathed precariously on his machines and in the meagre suburban street the two kidnappers remained barricaded in the third-floor flat, with talk going on from both sides, but no action, except a delivery of milk for the baby and bread and sausage for the others.

On the Sunday evening Ilaria came into the library where I was watching the news on television. The scene in the street looked almost exactly the same, except that there was no crowd, long discouraged from lack of excitement, and perhaps fewer fawn uniforms. The television coverage had become perfunctory: repetitive as-you-were sentences only.

'Do you think they'll release her?' Ilaria said, as the screen switched away to politicians.

'Yes, I think so.'

'When?'

'Can't tell.'

'Suppose they've told the carabinieri they'll keep her until those men in the flat go free? Suppose the ransom isn't enough?'

I glanced at her. She'd spoken not with dread but as if the question didn't concern her beyond a certain morbid interest. Her face was unstudiedly calm. She appeared really not to care.

'I talked to Enrico Pucinelli this morning,' I said. 'By then they hadn't said anything like that.'

She made a small, noncommittal puffing noise through her

nose and changed the television channel to a tennis match, settling to watch with concentration.

'I'm not a bitch, you know,' she said suddenly. 'I can't help it if I don't fall down and kiss the ground she walks on, like everyone else.'

'And six weeks is a long time to keep up the hair-tearing?'

'God,' she said, 'you're on the ball. And don't think I'm not glad you're here. Otherwise he would have leant on me for everything he gets from you, and I'd have ended up despising him.'

'No,' I said.

'Yes.'

Her eyes had been on the tennis throughout.

'How would you behave,' I said, 'if you had a son, and he was kidnapped?'

The eyes came round to my face. 'You're a righteous sod,' she said.

I smiled faintly. She went resolutely back to the tennis, but where her thoughts were, I couldn't tell.

Ilaria spoke perfect idiomatic English, as I'd been told Alessia did also, thanks to the British widow who had managed the Cenci household for many years after the mother's death. Luisa, Ilaria and Alessia ran things between them nowadays, and the cook in exasperation had complained to me that nothing got done properly since dear Mrs Blackett had retired to live with her brother in Eastbourne.

The next morning, during the drive to the office, Cenci said, 'Turn round, Andrew. Take me home. It's no good, I can't work. I'll sit there staring at the walls. I hear people talk but I don't listen to what they say. Take me home.'

I said neutrally. 'It might be worse at home.'

'No. Turn round. I can't face a new week in the office. Not today.'

I turned the car and drove back to the villa, where he telephoned to his secretary not to expect him.

'I can't think,' he said to me, 'except of Alessia. I think of her as she was as a little girl, and at school, and learning to ride. She was always so neat, so small, so full of life . . .' He swallowed, turned away and walked into the library, and in a few seconds I heard bottle clink against glass.

After a while I went after him.

'Let's play backgammon,' I said.

'I can't concentrate.'

'Try.' I got out the board and set up the pieces, but the moves he made were mechanical and without heart. He did nothing to capitalise on my shortcomings, and after a while simply fell to staring into space, as he'd done for hour after hour since we'd left the money.

At about eleven the telephone at his elbow brought him out of it, but sluggishly.

'Hello? . . . Yes, Cenci speaking . . .' He listened briefly and then looked at the receiver with an apathetic frown before putting it back in its cradle.

'What was it?' I said.

'I don't know. Nothing much. Something about my goods being ready, and to collect them. I don't know what goods . . . he rang off before I could ask.'

I breathed deeply. 'Your telephone's still tapped,' I said.

'Yes, but what's that . . .' His voice died as his eyes widened. 'Do you think . . . ? Do you really?'

'We could see,' I said. 'Don't bank on anything yet. What did he sound like?'

'A gruff voice.' He was uncertain. 'Not the usual one.'

'Well . . . let's try, anyway. Better than sitting here.'

'But where? He didn't say where.'

'Perhaps . . . where we left the ransom. Logical place.'

Hope began swelling fast in his expression and I said hastily, 'Don't expect anything. Don't believe. You'll never be able to stand it, if she isn't there. He may mean somewhere else . . . but I think we should try there first.'

He tried to take a grip on things but was still hectically optimistic. He ran through the house to where the car stood waiting near the back door, where I'd parked it. Putting on my cap I followed him at a walk, to find him beckoning frantically and telling me to hurry. I climbed behind the wheel stolidly and thought that someone had known Cenci was at home when he was normally in the office. Perhaps his office had said so . . . or perhaps there was still a watcher. In any case, I reckoned that until Alessia was safely home, a chauffeur in all things was what I needed to be.

'Do hurry,' Cenci said. I drove out of the gates without rush. 'For God's sake, man . . .'

'We'll get there. Don't hope . . .'

'I can't help it.'

I drove faster than usual, but it seemed an eternity to him; and when we pulled up by the shrine there was no sign of his daughter.

'Oh no . . . oh no.' His voice was cracking. 'I can't . . . I can't . . .'

I looked at him anxiously, but it was normal crushing grief, not a heart attack, not a fit.

'Wait,' I said, getting out of the car. 'I'll make sure.'

I walked round to the back of the shrine, to the spot where we'd left the ransom, and found her there, unconscious, curled like a foetus, wrapped in a grey plastic raincoat.

Fathers are odd. The paramount emotion filling Paolo Cenci's mind for the rest of that day was not joy that his beloved daughter was alive, safe, and emerging unharmed from a drugged sleep, but fear that the press would find out she had been more or less naked.

'Promise you won't say, Andrew. Not to anyone. Not at all.'

'I promise.'

He made me promise at least seven separate times, though in any case it wasn't necessary. If anyone told, it would be Alessia herself.

Her lack of clothes had disturbed him greatly, especially as he and I had discovered when we tried to pick her up that her arms weren't through the sleeves of the raincoat, and the buttons weren't buttoned. The thin grey covering had slid right off.

She had the body of a child, I thought. Smooth skin, slender limbs, breasts like buds. Cenci had strangely been too embarrassed to touch her, and it had been I, the all-purpose advisor, who'd steered her arms through the plastic and fastened her more discreetly inside the folds. She had been light to carry to the car, and I'd lain her on her side on the rear seat, her knees bent, her curly head resting on my rolled-up jacket.

Cenci sat beside me in front: and it was then that he'd started exacting the promise. When we reached the villa he hurried inside to reappear with a blanket, and I carried her up to her half-acre bedroom in woolly decency.

Ilaria and Luisa were nowhere to be found. Cenci discarded the cook as too talkative and finally asked in a stutter if I would mind very much substituting clothes for the raincoat while he called the doctor. As I'd seen her already once, he said. As I was sensible. Astonished but obliging I unearthed a shift-like dress and made the exchange, Alessia sleeping peacefully throughout.

She was more awkward than anything else. I pulled the blue knitted fabric over her head, fed her hands through the armholes, tugged the hem down to her knees and concentrated moderately successfully on my own non-arousal. Then I laid her on top of the bedclothes and covered her from the waist down with the blanket. Her pulse remained strong and regular, her skin cool, her breathing easy: sleeping pills, probably, I thought; nothing worse.

Her thin face was calm, without strain, long lashes lying in half-moon fringes on taut cheeks. Strong eyebrows, pale lips, hollows along the jaw. Hair tousled, clearly dirty. Let her sleep, I thought: she'd have little peace when she woke up.

I went downstairs and found Cenci again drinking brandy, standing up.

'Is she all right?' he said.

'Fine. Just fine.'

'It's a miracle.'

'Mm.'

He put down the glass and began to weep. 'Sorry. Can't help it,' he said.

'It's natural.'

He took out a handkerchief and blew his nose. 'Do all parents weep?'

'Yes.'

He put in some more work with the handkerchief, sniffed a bit, and said, 'You lead a very odd life, don't you?'

'Not really.'

'Don't say she had no clothes on. Promise me, Andrew.'

'I promise.'

I said I'd have to tell Pucinelli she was safe, and, immediately alarmed, he begged for the promise again. I gave it without impatience, because stress could come out in weird ways and the return of the victim was never the end of it.

Pucinelli was fortunately on duty in the ambulance, though presumably I could have spread the news directly via the wire-tappers.

'She's home,' I said laconically. 'I'm in the villa. She's upstairs.'

'Alessia?' Disbelief, relief, a shading of suspicion.

'Herself. Drugged but unharmed. Don't hurry, she'll probably sleep for hours. How's the siege going?'

'Andrew!' The beginnings of exasperation. 'What's been going on?'

'Will you be coming here yourself?'

A short pause came down the line. He'd told me once that I always put suggestions into the form of questions, and I supposed that it was true that I did. Implant the thought, seek the decision. He knew the tap was on the telephone, he'd ordered it himself, with every word recorded. He would guess there were things I might tell him privately.

'Yes,' he said. 'I'll be coming.'

'And of course you'll have a great lever now with those two kidnappers in the flat, won't you? And – um – will you bring the ransom money straight here when you lay your hands on it? It does, of course, belong to Signor Cenci.'

'Of course,' he said dryly. 'But it may not be my decision.'

'Mm. Well . . . I photographed all the notes, of course.'

A pause. 'You're wicked, you know that?'

'Things have disappeared out of police custody before now.'

'You insult the carabinieri!' He sounded truly affronted, loyally angry.

'Certainly not. Police stations are not banks. I am sure the carabinieri would be pleased to be relieved of the responsibility of guarding so much money.'

'It is evidence.'

'The rest of the kidnappers, of course, are still free, and no doubt still greedy. The money could be held safe from them under an official seal in a bank of Signor Cenci's choosing.'

A pause. 'It's possible that I may arrange it,' he said stiffly, not quite forgiving. 'No doubt I will see you at the villa.'

I put the telephone down with a rueful smile. Pucinelli himself I trusted, but not all law-enforcers automatically. In South American countries particularly, where I had worked several times, kidnappers regularly bribed or threatened policemen to look the wrong way, a custom scarcely unknown elsewhere. Kidnappers had no scruples and seldom any mercy, and many a policeman had had to choose between his duty and the safety of wife and children.

Within ten minutes Pucinelli was back on the line.

'Just to tell you . . . things are moving here. Come if you want. Come into the street from the west, on this side. I'll make sure you get through.'

'Thanks.'

The partners wouldn't have approved, but I went. I'd studied many case-histories of sieges and been to lectures by people involved in some of them, but I'd never been on the spot before at first hand: too good a chance to miss. I changed from Spanish chauffeur to nondescript onlooker, borrowed the family's runabout, and was walking along the Bologna street in record time.

Pucinelli had been as good as his word: a pass awaiting me at the first barrier saw me easily through to the still-parked ambulance. I went into it as I'd left, through the nearside passenger door, and found Pucinelli there with his engineer and three men in city suits.

'You came,' he said.

'You're kind.'

He gave me a small smile and briefly introduced me to the civilians: negotiator, psychiatrist, psychiatrist.

'These two medical gentlemen have been advising us about the changing mental state of the kidnappers.' Pucinelli spoke formally; they nodded gravely back.

'Mostly their mental state has been concerned with the baby,' Pucinelli said. 'The baby has cried a lot. Apparently the milk we sent in upset its stomach even worse.'

As if on cue the bug on the flat produced the accelerating wail of the infant getting newly into its stride, and from the faces of the five men in front of me it wasn't only the kidnappers who were finding the sound a frazzle.

'Forty minutes ago,' Pucinelli said, turning down the baby's volume, 'the deep-voiced kidnapper telephoned here and said they would come out if certain conditions were met. No aeroplane – they've abandoned that. They want only to be sure they aren't shot. In about twenty minutes . . . that's one hour from when they telephoned . . . they say the mother will leave with the baby. Then one of the kidnappers will come out. There are to be no carabinieri anywhere in the flats. The stairs must be clear, also the front door and the pavement outside. The mother and baby will come out into the road, followed by the first kidnapper. He will have no gun. If he is taken peacefully, one of the children will leave, and after an interval, the father. If the second kidnapper is then sure he will be safe, he will come out with the second child in his arms. No gun. We are to arrest him quietly.'

I looked at him. 'Did they discuss all this between themselves? Did you hear them plan it, on the bug?'

He shook his head. 'Nothing.'

'They telephoned you very soon after Alessia was home.'

'Suspiciously soon.'

'You'll look for the radio?' I said.

'Yes.' He sighed. 'We have been monitoring radio frequencies these past few days. We've had no results, but I have thought once or twice before this that the kidnappers were being instructed.'

Instructed, I thought, by a very cool and bold intelligence. A pity such a brain was criminal.

'What do they plan to do with the money?' I asked.

'Leave it in the flat.'

I glanced at the screen which had shown the whereabouts of the homer in the ransom suitcase, but it was dark. I leant over and flicked the on-off switch, and the trace obligingly appeared, efficient and steady. The suitcase, at least, was still there.

I said, 'I'd like to go up there, as Signor Cenci's representative, to see that it's safely taken care of.'

With suppressed irritation he said, 'Very well.'

'It's a great deal of money,' I said reasonably.

'Yes . . . yes, I suppose it is.' He spoke grudgingly, partly, I guessed, because he was himself honest, partly because he was a communist. So much wealth in one man's hands offended him, and he wouldn't care if Cenci lost it.

Across the street the flat's windows were still closed. All the windows of all the flats were closed, although the day was hot.

'Don't they ever open them?' I asked.

Pucinelli glanced across at the building. 'The kidnappers open the windows sometimes for a short while when we switch off the searchlights at dawn. The blinds are always drawn, even then. There are no people now in any of the other flats. We moved them for their own safety.'

Down on the road there was little movement. Most of the official cars had been withdrawn, leaving a good deal of empty space. Four carabinieri crouched with guns behind the pair still parked, their bodies tense. Metal barriers down the street kept a few onlookers at bay, and the television van looked closed. One or two photographers sat on the ground in its shade, drinking beer from cans. On the bug the colicky crying had stopped, but no one seemed to be saying very much. It was siesta, after all.

Without any warning a young woman walked from the flats carrying a baby and shielding her eyes against the brilliance of the sunlight. She was very dishevelled and also heavily pregnant.

Pucinelli glanced as if stung at his wristwatch, said 'They're early,' and jumped out of the van. I watched him through the dark glass as he strode without hesitation towards her, taking her arm. Her head turned towards him and she began to fall, Pucinelli catching the baby and signalling furiously with his head to his men behind the cars.

One scurried forward, hauled the fainting woman unceremoniously to her feet and hustled her into one of the cars. Pucinelli gave the baby a sick look, carried it at arm's length in the wake of its mother, and, having delivered it, wiped his hands disgustedly on a handkerchief.

The photographers and the television van came to life as if electrified, and a young plump man walked three steps out of the flats and slowly raised both hands.

Pucinelli, now sheltering behind the second car, stretched an arm through the window, removed a loudhailer, and spoke through it.

'Lie face down on the road. Legs apart. Arms outstretched.'

The plump young man wavered a second, looked as if he would retreat, and finally did as he was bid.

Pucinelli spoke again. 'Stay where you are. You will not be shot.'

There was a long breath-holding hush. Then a boy came out; about six, in shorts, shirt and bright blue and white training shoes. His mother frantically waved to him through the car window, and he ran across to her, looking back over his shoulder at the man on the ground.

I switched up the volume to full on the bug on the flat, but there was still no talking, simply a few grunts and unidentifiable movements. After a while these ended, and shortly afterwards another man walked out into the street, a youngish man this time, with his hands tied behind his back. He looked gaunt and tottery, with stubbled chin, and he stopped dead at the sight of the spreadeagled kidnapper.

'Come to the cars,' Pucinelli said through the loudhailer. 'You are safe.'

The man seemed unable to move. Pucinelli, again exposing his whole body to the still-present threat of the guns in the flat, walked calmly across the road, took him by the arm, and led him behind the car holding his wife.

The psychiatrists watching beside me shook their heads over Pucinelli, not approving such straightforward courage. I picked up a pair of binoculars which were lying on the bench and focused them on the opposite windows, but nothing stirred. Then I scanned the onlookers at the barriers down the street, and took in a close-up of the photographers, but there was no sign of the man from the motorway car park.

I put down the glasses, and time gradually stretched out, hot and silent, making me wonder, making everyone wonder if by some desperate mischance at the last minute the surrender had gone wrong. There was no sound from the bug. There was stillness in the street. Forty-six minutes had passed since the mother and baby had emerged.

Pucinelli spoke through the loudhailer with firmness but not aggression. 'Bring out the child. You will not be hurt.'

Nothing happened.

Pucinelli repeated his instructions.

Nothing.

I thought of guns, of desperation, of suicide, murder and spite.

Pucinelli's voice rang out. 'Your only hope of ever being released from prison is to come out now as arranged.'

No result.

Pucinelli's hand put the loudhailer through the car's window and reappeared holding a pistol. He pushed the pistol through his belt in the small of his back, and without more ado walked straight across the street and in through the door of the flats.

The psychiatrists gasped and made agitated motions with their hands and I wondered if I would ever have had the nerve, in those circumstances, to do what Pucinelli was doing.

There were no shots: none that we could hear. No sounds at all, just more long-drawn-out quiet.

The carabinieri behind the cars began to grow dangerously restive for lack of their leader and to look at each other for guidance, waving their guns conspicuously. The engineer in the van was muttering ominously under his breath, and there was still silence from the bug. If nothing happened soon, I thought, there could be another excited, destructive, half-cocked raid.

Then, suddenly there was a figure in the doorway: a strong burly man carrying a little girl like a feather on one arm.

Behind him came Pucinelli, gun nowhere in sight. He pointed to the first kidnapper, still spreadeagled, and the big man with a sort of furious resignation walked over to him and put the small child on the ground. Then he lowered his bulk into the same outstretched attitude, and the little girl, only a toddler, stood looking at him for a moment and then lay down and copied him, as if it were a game.

The carabinieri burst like uncorked furies from behind the cars and bristling with guns and handcuffs descended on the prone figures with no signs of loving-kindness. Pucinelli watched while the kidnappers were marched to the empty car and the child returned to her parents, then came casually back to the open door of the ambulance as if he'd been out for a stroll.

He thanked the negotiator and the psychiatrists from there, and jerked his head to me to come out and follow him. I did: across the road, in through the door of the flats and up the stone staircase beyond.

'The big man,' Pucinelli said, 'was up there,' he pointed, 'right at the top, sixth floor, where the stairs lead to the roof.

It took me some time to find him. But we had barricaded that door, of course. He couldn't get out.'

'Was he violent?' I asked.

Pucinelli laughed. 'He was sitting on the stairs with the little girl on his knee, telling her a story.'

'What?'

'When I went up the stairs with my pistol ready he said to put it away, the show was over, he knew it. I told him to go down into the street. He said he wanted to stay where he was for a while. He said he had a child of his own of that age and he'd never be able to hold her on his knee again.'

Sob stuff, I thought. 'What did you do?' I asked.

'Told him to go down at once.'

The 'at once' however had taken quite a long time. Pucinelli like all Italians liked children, and even carabinieri, I supposed, could be sentimental.

'That poor deprived father,' I said, 'abducted someone else's daughter and shot someone else's son.'

'Your head,' Pucinelli said, 'is like ice.'

He led the way into the flat that had been besieged for four and a half days, and the heat and stink of it were indescribable. Squalor took on a new meaning. Apart from the stench of sweat and the decomposing remains of meals there were unmentionable heaps of cloth and rags and newspaper in two of the three small rooms: the baby, incontinent at both ends, had done more than cry.

'How did they stand it?' I wondered. 'Why didn't they wash anything?'

'The mother wanted to. I heard her asking. They wouldn't let her.'

We searched our way through the mess, finding the ransom suitcase almost immediately under a bed. As far as I could tell, the contents were untouched: good news for Cenci. Pucinelli gave the packets of notes a sour look and poked around for the radio.

The owners of the flat had one themselves, standing openly on top of a television set, but Pucinelli shook his head over it, saying it was too elementary. He started a methodical search, coming across it eventually inside a box of Buttoni in a kitchen cupboard.

'Here we are,' he said, brushing off pasta shells. 'Complete with earplug for private listening.' A smallish but elaborate walkie-talkie, aerial retracted.

'Don't disturb the frequency,' I said.

'I wasn't born yesterday. And nor was the man giving the instructions, I shouldn't think.'

'He might not have thought of everything.'

'Maybe not. All criminals are fools sometimes, otherwise we'd never catch them.' He wound the cord with its earpiece carefully around the radio and put it by the door.

'What range do you think that has?' I asked.

'Not more than a few miles. I'll find out. But too far, I would think, to help us.'

There remained the pistols, and these were easy: Pucinelli found them on a windowsill when he let up one of the blinds to give us more light.

We both looked down from the window. The ambulance and the barriers were still there, though the drama had gone. I thought that the earlier host of official cars and of highly armed men crouching behind them must have been a fearsome sight. What with that threat ever present and the heat, the baby, the searchlights and the stench, their nerves must have been near exploding point the whole time.

'He could have shot you any time,' I said, 'when you walked out across the street.'

'I reckoned he wouldn't.' He spoke unemotionally. 'But when I was creeping up the stairs . . .' he smiled fractionally, ' . . . I did begin to wonder.'

He gave me a cool and comradely nod and departed, saying he would arrange transit for the ransom and send his men to collect and label the pistols and radio.

'You'll stay here?' he asked.

I pinched my nose. 'On the stairs outside.'

He smiled and went away, and in due course people arrived.

65

I accompanied the ransom to the bank of Pucinelli's choosing, followed it to the vaults and accepted bank and carabinieri receipts. Then, on my way back to collect the Cenci runabout, I made a routine collect call to my firm in London. Reports from advisors-in-the-field were expected regularly, with wisdom from the collective office mind flowing helpfully back.

'The girl's home,' I said. 'The siege is over, the first ransom's safe, and how are my snaps doing on the second?'

'Lists with you tomorrow morning.'

'Right.'

They wanted to know how soon I'd be back.

'Two or three days,' I said. 'Depends on the girl.'

five

Alessia woke in the evening, feeling sick. Cenci rushed upstairs to embrace her, came down damp-eyed, said she was still sleepy and couldn't believe she was home.

I didn't see her. Ilaria slept all night on an extra bed in Alessia's room at her aunt Luisa's suggestion, and did seem genuinely pleased at her sister's return. In the morning she came down with composure to breakfast and said that Alessia felt ill and wouldn't get out of the bath.

'Why not?' Cenci said, bewildered.

'She says she's filthy. She's washed her hair twice. She says she smells.'

'But she doesn't,' he protested.

'No. I've told her that. It makes no difference.'

'Take her some brandy and a bottle of scent,' I said.

Cenci looked at me blankly but Ilaria said, 'Well, why not?' and went off on the errand. She had talked more easily that morning than at any breakfast before, almost as if her sister's release had been also her own.

Pucinelli arrived mid-morning with a note-taking aide, and Alessia came downstairs to meet him. Standing there beside him in the hall I watched the tentative figure on the stairs and could clearly read her strong desire to retreat. She stopped four steps from the bottom and looked behind her, but Ilaria, who had gone up to fetch her, was nowhere to be seen.

Cenci went forward and put his arm round her shoulders, explaining briefly who I was, and saying Pucinelli wanted to know everything that happened to her, hoping for clues to lead him to arrests.

She nodded slightly, looking pale.

I'd seen victims return with hectic jollity, with hysteria, with apathy; all with shock. Alessia's state looked fairly par for the circumstances: a mixture of shyness, strangeness, weakness, relief and fear.

Her hair was still damp. She wore a T-shirt, jeans and no lipstick. She looked a defenceless sixteen, recently ill; the girl I'd seen undressed. What she did not look was the glossy darling of the European racetracks.

Cenci led her to the library, and we scattered around on chairs.

'Tell us,' Pucinelli said. 'Please tell us what happened, from the beginning.'

'I . . . it seems so long ago.' She spoke mostly to her father, looking seldom at Pucinelli and not at all at me; and she used Italian throughout, though as she spoke slowly with many pauses, I could follow her with ease. Indeed it occurred to me fleetingly that I'd soaked in a good deal more of the language than I'd arrived with, and more than I'd noticed until then.

'I'd been racing here on our local track . . . but you know that.'

Her father nodded.

'I won the six o'clock race, and there was an objection . . .'

More nods, both from Cenci and Pucinelli. The note-taking aide, eyes down to the task, kept his shorthand busily flowing.

'I drove home. I was thinking of England. Of riding Brunelleschi in the Derby . . .' She broke off. 'Did he win?'

Her father looked blank. At the time, shortly after her disappearance, he'd have been unlikely to notice an invasion of Martians in the back yard.

'No,' I said. 'Fourth.'

She said 'Oh,' vaguely, and I didn't bother to explain that I knew where the horse had finished simply because it was she who had been going to ride it. Ordinary curiosity, nothing more.

'I was here . . . in sight of the house. Not far from the gate. I slowed down, to turn in . . .'

The classic spot for kidnaps; right outside the victim's house. She had a red sports car, besides, and had been driving it that day with the roof down, as she always did in fine weather. Some people, I'd thought when I'd heard it, made abduction too simple for words.

'There was a car coming towards me . . . I waited for it to pass, so that I could turn . . . but it didn't pass, it stopped suddenly between me and the gate . . . blocking the way.' She paused and looked anxiously at her father. 'I couldn't help it, Papa. I really couldn't.'

'My dear, my dear . . .' He looked surprised at the very thought. He didn't see, as I did, the iceberg tip of the burden of guilt, but then he hadn't seen it so often.

'I couldn't think what they were doing,' she said. 'Then all the car doors opened at once, and there were four men . . . all wearing horrid masks . . . truly horrible . . . devils and monsters. I thought they wanted to rob me. I threw my purse at them and tried to reverse to get away backwards . . . and they sort of leapt into my car . . . just jumped right in . . .' She stopped with the beginnings of agitation and Pucinelli made small damping-down motions with his hands to settle her.

'They were so fast,' she said, her voice full of apology. 'I couldn't do anything . . .'

'Signorina,' Pucinelli said calmly, 'there is nothing to be ashamed of. If kidnappers wish to kidnap, they kidnap. Even all Aldo Moro's guards couldn't prevent it. And one girl alone, in an open car . . .' He shrugged expressively, finishing the sentence without words, and for the moment at least she seemed comforted.

A month earlier, to me in private, he had said that any rich girl who drove around in an open sports car was inviting everything from mugging to rape. 'I'm not saying they wouldn't have taken her anyway, but she was stupid. She made it easy.'

'There's not much fun in life if you're twenty-three and successful and can't enjoy it by driving an open sports car on a sunny day. What would you advise her to do, go round in a middle-aged saloon with the doors locked?'

'Yes,' he had said. 'So would you, if your firm was asked. That's the sort of advice you'd be paid for.'

'True enough.'

Alessia continued, 'They put a hood of cloth right over my head . . . and then it smelled sweet . . .'

'Sweet?' Pucinelli said.

'You know. Ether. Chloroform. Something like that. I simply went to sleep. I tried to struggle. . . . They had their hands on my arms . . . sort of lifting me . . . nothing else.'

'They lifted you out of the car?'

'I think so. I suppose so. They must have done.'

Pucinelli nodded. Her car had been found a bare mile away, parked on a farm track.

'I woke up in a tent,' Alessia said.

'A tent?' echoed Cenci, bewildered.

'Yes . . . well . . . it was inside a room, but I didn't realise that at first.'

'What sort of tent?' Pucinelli asked. 'Please describe it.'

'Oh . . .' she moved a hand weakly, 'I can describe every stitch of it. Green canvas. About two and a half metres square . . . a bit less. It had walls . . . I could stand up.'

A frame tent.

'It had a floor. Very tough fabric. Grey. Waterproof, I suppose, though of course that didn't matter . . .'

'When you woke up,' Pucinelli asked, 'what happened?'

'One of the men was kneeling on the floor beside me, slapping my face. Quite hard. Hurry up, he was saying. Hurry up. When I opened my eyes he grunted and said I must just repeat a few words and I could go back to sleep.'

'Was he wearing a mask?'

'Yes . . . a devil face . . . orange . . . all warts.'

We all knew what the few words had been. We'd all listened to them, over and over, on the first of the tapes.

'This is Alessia. Please do as they say. They will kill me if you don't.' A voice slurred with drugs, but alarmingly her own.

'I knew what I said,' she said. 'I knew when I woke up properly . . . but when I said them, everything was fuzzy. I couldn't see the mask half the time. . . . I kept switching off, then coming back.'

'Did you ever see any of them without masks?' Pucinelli asked.

A flicker of a smile reached the pale mouth. 'I didn't see any of them again, even in masks. Not at all. No one. The first person I saw since that first day was Aunt Luisa . . . sitting by my own bed . . . sewing her tapestry, and I thought . . . I was dreaming.' Tears unexpectedly appeared in her eyes and she blinked them slowly away. 'They said . . . if I saw their faces, they would kill me. They told me not to try to see them . . .' She swallowed. 'So . . . I didn't . . . try.'

'You believed them?'

A pause. Then she said 'Yes' with a conviction that brought understanding of what she'd been through vividly to life. Cenci, although he had believed the threats himself, looked shattered. Pucinelli gravely assured her that he was sure she had been right: and so, though I didn't mention it, was I.

'They said . . . I would go home safely . . . if I was quiet . . . and if you would pay for my release.' She was still trying not to cry. 'Papa . . .'

'My dearest . . . I would pay anything.' He was himself close to tears.

'Yes,' Pucinelli said matter-of-factly. 'Your father paid.'

I glanced at him. 'He paid,' he repeated, looking steadily at Cenci. 'How much, and where he paid it, only he knows. In no other way would you be free.'

Cenci said defensively, 'I was lucky to get the chance, after your men . . .'

Pucinelli cleared his throat hurriedly and said, 'Let's get on. Signorina, please describe how you have lived for the past six weeks.'

'I didn't know how long it was, until Aunt Luisa told me. I lost count . . . there were so many days, I had no way of counting . . . and then it didn't seem to matter much. I asked why it was so long, but they didn't answer. They never answered any questions. It wasn't worth asking . . . but sometimes I did, just to hear my own voice.' She paused. 'It's odd to talk as much as this. I went days without saying anything at all.'

'They talked to you, though, Signorina?'

'They gave me orders.'

'What orders?'

'To take in the food. To put out the bucket . . .' She stopped, then said, 'It sounds so awful, here in this room.'

She looked round at the noble bookcases stretching to the high ceiling, at the silk brocaded chairs, at the pale chinese carpet on the marble-tiled floor. Every room in the house had the same unselfconscious atmosphere of wealth, of antique things having stood in the same places for decades, of treasures taken for granted. She must have been in many a meagre room in her racing career, but she was seeing her roots, I guessed, with fresh eyes.

'In the tent,' she said resignedly, 'there was a piece of foam for me to lie on, and another small piece for a pillow. There was a bucket . . . an ordinary bucket, like out of a stable. There was nothing else.' She paused. 'There was a zip to open one side of the tent. It would open only about fifty centimetres

71

. . . it was jammed above that. They told me to unzip it, and I would find food . . .'

'Could you see anything of the room outside the tent?' Pucinelli asked.

She shook her head. 'Beyond the zip there was just more tent . . . but folded a bit, I think . . . I mean, not properly put up like another room . . .' She paused. 'They told me not to try to get into it.' Another pause. 'The food was always where I could reach it easily, just by the zip.'

'What was the food?' Cenci asked, deeply concerned.

'Pasta.' A pause. 'Sometimes warm, sometimes cold. Mixed with sauce. Tinned, I think. Anyway . . .' she said tiredly, 'it came twice a day . . . and the second lot usually had sleeping pills in it.'

Cenci exclaimed in protest, but Alessia said, 'I didn't mind . . . I just ate it . . . it was better really than staying awake.'

There was a silence, then Pucinelli said, 'Was there anything you could hear, which might help us to find where you were held?'

'Hear?' She glanced at him vaguely. 'Only the music.'

'What music?'

'Oh . . . tapes. Taped music. Over and over, always the same.'

'What sort of music?'

'Verdi. Orchestral, no singing. Three-quarters of that, then one-quarter of pop music. Still no singing.'

'Could you write down the tunes in order?'

She looked mildly surprised but said, 'Yes, I should think so. All that I know the names of.'

'If you do that today, I'll send a man for the list.'

'All right.'

'Is there anything else at all you can think of?'

She looked dully at the floor, her thin face tired with the mental efforts of freedom. Then she said, 'About four times they gave me a few sentences to read aloud, and they told me each time to mention something that had happened in my

72

childhood, which only my father would know about, so that he could be sure I was still . . . all right.'

Pucinelli nodded. 'You were reading from daily papers.'

She shook her head. 'They weren't newspapers. Just sentences typed on ordinary paper.'

'Did you keep those papers?'

'No . . . they told me to put them out through the zip.' She paused. 'The only times they turned the music off was when I made the recordings.'

'Did you see a microphone?'

'No . . . but I could hear them talk clearly through the tent, so I suppose they recorded me from outside.'

'Would you remember their voices?'

An involuntary shudder shook her. 'Two of them, yes. They spoke most – but there were others. The one who made the recordings . . . I'd remember him. He was just . . . cold. The other one was beastly . . . He seemed to enjoy it . . . but he was worse at the beginning . . . or at least perhaps I got used to him and didn't care. Then there was one sometimes who kept apologising . . . "Sorry Signorina" . . . when he told me the food was there. And another who just grunted. . . . None of them ever answered, if I spoke.'

'Signorina,' Pucinelli said, 'if we play you one of the tapes your father received, will you tell us if you recognise the man's voice?'

'Oh . . .' She swallowed. 'Yes, of course.'

He had brought a small recorder and copies of the tapes with him, and she watched apprehensively while he inserted a cassette and pressed a button. Cenci put out a hand to grasp one of Alessia's, almost as if he could shield her from what she would hear.

'Cenci,' HIS voice said. 'We have your daughter Alessia. We will return her on payment of one hundred and fifty thousand million lire. Listen to your daughter's voice.' There was a click, followed by Alessia's slurred words. Then, 'Believe her. If you do not pay, we will kill her. Do not delay. Do not inform the carabinieri, or your daughter will be beaten. She will be beaten every day you delay, and also . . .' Pucinelli pressed the stop button decisively, abruptly and mercifully shutting off the worse, the bestial threats. Alessia anyway was shaking and could hardly speak. Her nods were small and emphatic. 'Mm . . . yes . . .'

'You could swear to it?'

' . . . Yes . . .'

Pucinelli methodically put away the recorder. 'It is the same male voice on all the tapes. We have had a voice print made, to be sure.'

Alessia worked saliva into her mouth. 'They didn't beat me,' she said. 'They didn't even threaten it. They said nothing like that.'

Pucinelli nodded. 'The threats were for your father.'

She said with intense anxiety. 'Papa, you didn't pay that much? That's everything . . . you couldn't.'

He shook his head reassuringly. 'No, no, nothing like that. Don't fret . . . don't worry.'

'Excuse me,' I said in English.

All the heads turned in surprise, as if the wallpaper had spoken.

'Signorina,' I said, 'were you moved from place to place at all? Were you in particular moved four or five days ago?'

She shook her head. 'No.' Her certainty however began to waver, and with a frown she said, 'I was in that tent all the time. But . . .'

'But what?'

'The last few days, there was a sort of smell of bread baking, sometimes, and the light seemed brighter . . . but I thought they had drawn a curtain perhaps . . . though I didn't think much at all. I mean, I slept so much . . . it was better . . .'

'The light,' I said, 'it was daylight?'

She nodded. 'It was quite dim in the tent, but my eyes were so used to it . . . They never switched on any electric lights. At night it was dark, I suppose, but I slept all night, every night.'

'Do you think you could have slept through a move, if they'd taken the tent from one room in one place and driven it to another place and set it up again?'

The frown returned while she thought it over. 'There was one day not long ago I hardly woke up at all. When I did wake it was already getting dark and I felt sick . . . like I did when I woke here yesterday . . . and oh,' she exclaimed intensely, 'I'm so glad to be here, so desperately grateful . . . I can't tell you. . . .' She buried her face on her father's shoulder and he stroked her hair with reddening eyes.

Pucinelli rose to his feet and took a formal leave of father and daughter, removing himself, his note-taker and myself to the hall.

'I may have to come back, but that seems enough for now.' He sighed. 'She knows so little. Not much help. The kidnappers were too careful. If you learn any more, Andrew, you'll tell me?'

I nodded.

'How much was the ransom?' he said.

I smiled. 'The list of the notes' numbers will come here today. I'll let you have them. Also, do you have the Identikit system, like in England?'

'Something like it, yes.'

'I could build a picture of one of the other kidnappers, I think. Not the ones in the siege. If you like.'

'If I like! Where did you see him. How do you know?'

'I've seen him twice. I'll tell you about it when I come in with the lists.'

'How soon?' he demanded.

'When the messenger comes. Any time now.'

The messenger obligingly arrived while Pucinelli was climbing into his car, so I borrowed the Fiat runabout again and followed him to his headquarters.

Fitting together pieces of head with eyes and mouth, chin and hairline, I related the two sightings. 'You probably saw him yourself, outside the ambulance, the night the siege started,' I said.

'I had too much to think of.'

I nodded and added ears. 'This man is young. Difficult to tell . . . not less than twenty-five, though. Lower thirties, probably.'

I built a full face and a profile, but wasn't satisfied, and Pucinelli said he would get an artist in to draw what I wanted.

'He works in the courts. Very fast.'

A telephone call produced the artist within half an hour. He came, fat, grumbling, smelling of garlic and scratching, and saying that it was siesta, how could any sane man be expected to work at two in the afternoon? He stared with disillusion at my composite efforts, fished out a thin charcoal stick, and began performing rapid miracles on a sketch pad. Every few seconds he stopped to raise his eyebrows at me, inviting comment.

'Rounder head,' I said, describing it with my hands. 'A smooth round head.'

The round head appeared. 'What next?'

'The mouth . . . a fraction too thin. A slightly fuller lower lip.'

He stopped when I could think of no more improvements and showed the results to Pucinelli. 'This is the man as your English friend remembers him,' he said, sniffing. 'Memories are usually wrong, don't forget.'

'Thanks,' Pucinelli said. 'Go back to sleep.'

The artist grumbled and departed, and I said, 'What's the latest on Lorenzo Traventi?'

'Today they say he'll live.'

'Good,' I said with relief. It was the first time anyone had been positive.

'We've charged the two kidnappers with intent to kill. They are protesting.' He shrugged. 'So far they are refusing to say anything about the kidnap, though naturally we are pointing out that if they lead us to other arrests their sentences will be shorter.' He picked up the artist's drawings. 'I'll show them these. It will shock them.' A fleeting look of savage pleasure crossed his face: the look of a born policeman poised for a kill.

I'd seen it on other faces above other uniforms, and never despised it. He deserved his satisfaction, after the strains of the past week.

'The radio,' Pucinelli said, pausing as he turned away.

'Yes?'

'It could transmit and receive on aircraft frequencies.'

I blinked. 'That's not usual, is it?'

'Not very. And it was tuned to the international emergency frequency . . . which is monitored all the time, and which certainly did not pick up any messages between kidnappers. We checked at the airport this morning.'

I shook my head in frustration. Pucinelli went off with eagerness to his interrogations, and I returned to the villa.

Alessia said, 'Do you mind if I ask you something?'

'Fire away.'

'I asked Papa but he won't answer, which I suppose anyway is an answer of sorts.' She paused. 'Did I have any clothes on, when you found me?'

'A plastic raincoat,' I said matter-of-factly.

'Oh.'

I couldn't tell whether the answer pleased her or not. She remained thoughtful for a while, and then said, 'I woke up here in a dress I haven't worn for years. Aunt Luisa and Ilaria say they don't know how it happened. Did Papa dress me? Is that why he's so embarrassed?'

'Didn't you expect to have clothes on?' I asked curiously.

'Well . . .' She hesitated.

I lifted my head. 'Were you naked . . . all the time?'

She moved her thin body restlessly in the armchair as if she would sink into it, out of sight. 'I don't want . . .' she said; and broke off, swallowing, while in my mind I finished the sentence. Don't want everyone to know.

'It's all right,' I said. 'I won't say.'

We were sitting in the library, the evening fading to dark, the heat of the day diminishing; freshly showered, casually dressed, waiting in the Cenci household routine to be joined

77

by everyone for a drink or two before dinner. Alessia's hair was again damp, but she had progressed as far as lipstick.

She gave me short glances of inspection, not sure of me.

'Why are you here?' she said. 'Papa says he couldn't have got through these weeks without you, but . . . I don't really understand.'

I explained my job.

'An advisor?'

'That's right.'

She thought for a while, her gaze wandering over my face and down to my hands and up again to my eyes. Her opinions were unreadable, but finally she sighed, as if making up her mind.

'Well . . . advise me too,' she said. 'I feel very odd. Like jet lag, only much worse. Time lag. I feel as if I'm walking on tissue paper. As if nothing's real. I keep wanting to cry. I should be deliriously happy . . . why aren't I?'

'Reaction,' I said.

'You don't know . . . you can't imagine . . . what it was like.'

'I've heard from many people what it's like. From people like you, straight back from kidnap. They've told me. The first bludgeoning shock, the not being able to believe it's happening. The humiliations, forced on you precisely to make you afraid and defenceless. No bathrooms. Sometimes no clothes. Certainly no respect. No kindness or gentleness of any sort. Imprisonment, no one to talk to, nothing to fill the mind, just uncertainty and fear . . . and guilt. . . . Guilt that you didn't escape at the beginning, guilt at the distress brought on your family, guilt at what a ransom will cost . . . and fear for your life . . . if the money can't be raised . . . or if something goes wrong . . . if the kidnappers panic.'

She listened intently, at first with surprise and then with relief. 'You do know. You do understand. I haven't been able to say. . . . I don't want to upset them . . . and also . . . also . . .'

'Also you feel ashamed,' I said.

78

'Oh.' Her eyes widened. 'I . . . Why do I?'

'I don't know, but nearly everyone does.'

'Do they?'

'Yes.'

She sat quiet for a while, then she said, 'How long will it take . . . for me to get over it?'

To that there was no answer. 'Some people shake it off almost at once,' I said. 'But it's like illness, or a death . . . you have to grow scar tissue.'

Some managed it in days, some in weeks, some in years; some bled for ever. Some of the apparently strong disintegrated most. One couldn't tell, not on the day after liberation.

Ilaria came into the room in a stunning scarlet and gold toga and began switching on the lamps.

'It was on the radio news that you're free,' she said to Alessia. 'I heard it upstairs. Make the most of the peace, the paparazzi will be storming up the drive before you can blink.'

Alessia shrank again into her chair and looked distressed. Ilaria, it occurred to me uncharitably, had dressed for such an event: another statement about not wanting to be eclipsed.

'Does your advice stretch to paparazzi?' Alessia asked weakly, and I nodded, 'If you like.'

Ilaria patted the top of my head as she passed behind my chair. 'Our Mr Fixit. Never at a loss.'

Paolo Cenci himself arrived with Luisa, the one looking anxious, the other fluttery, as usual.

'Someone telephoned from the television company,' Cenci said. 'They say a crew is on the way here. Alessia, you'd better stay in your room until they've gone.'

I shook my head. 'They'll just camp on your doorstep. Better, really, to get it over.' I looked at Alessia. 'If you could possibly . . . and I know it's hard . . . make some sort of joke, they'll go away quicker.'

She said in bewilderment, 'Why?'

'Because good news is brief news. If they think you had a really bad time, they'll keep on probing. Tell them the kidnappers treated you well, say you're glad to be home, say you'll be back on the racecourse very soon. If they ask you anything which it would really distress you to answer, blank the thoughts out and make a joke.'

'I don't know . . . if I can.'

'The world wants to hear that you're all right,' I said. 'They want to be reassured, to see you smile. If you can manage it now it will make your return to normal life much easier. The people you know will greet you with delight . . . they won't find meeting you uncomfortable, which they could if they'd seen you in hysterics.'

Cenci said crossly, 'She's not in hysterics.'

'I know what he means,' Alessia said. She smiled wanly at her father. 'I hear you're paying for the advice, so we'd better take it.'

Once mobilised, the family put on a remarkable show, like actors on stage. For Ilaria and Luisa it was least difficult, but for Cenci the affable host role must have seemed bizarre, as he admitted the television people with courtesy and was helpful about electric plugs and moving furniture. A second television crew arrived while the first was still setting up, and after that several cars full of reporters, some from international news agencies, and a clatter of photographers. Ilaria moved like a scarlet bird among them, gaily chatting, and even Luisa was appearing gracious, in her unfocused way.

I watched the circus assemble from behind the almost closed library door, while Alessia sat silent in her armchair, developing shadows under her eyes.

'I can't do it,' she said.

'They won't expect a song and dance act. Just be . . . normal.'

'And make a joke.'

'Yes.'

'I feel sick,' she said.

'You're used to crowds,' I said. 'Used to people staring at you. Think of being . . .' I groped, ' . . . in the winner's circle. Lots of fuss. You're used to it, which gives you a shield.'

She merely swallowed, but when her father came for her she walked out and faced the barrage of flashlights and questions without cracking. I watched from the library door, listening to her slow, clear Italian.

'I'm delighted to be home with my family. Yes, I'm fine. Yes, I hope to be racing again very soon.'

The brilliant lighting for the television cameras made her look extra pale, especially near the glowing Ilaria, but the calm half-smile on her face never wavered.

'No, I never saw the kidnappers' faces. They were very . . . discreet.'

The newsgatherers reacted to the word with a low growing rumble of appreciation.

'Yes, the food was excellent . . . if you liked tinned pasta.'

Her timing was marvellous: this time she reaped a full laugh.

'I've been living in the sort of tent people take on holiday. Size? A single bedroom . . . about that size. Yes . . . quite comfortable . . . I listened to music, most of the time.'

Her voice was quiet, but rock-steady. The warmth of the newsmen towards her came over clearly now in their questions, and she told them an open sports car had proved a liability and she regretted having caused everyone so much trouble.

'How much ransom? I don't know. My father says it wasn't too much.'

'What was the worst thing about being kidnapped?' She repeated the question as if herself wondering, and then, after a pause, said, 'Missing the English Derby, I guess. Missing the ride on Brunelleschi.'

It was the climax. To the next question she smiled and said she had a lot of things to catch up with, and she was a bit tired, and would they please excuse her?

They clapped her. I listened in amazement to the tribute from the most cynical bunch in the world, and she came into the library with a real laugh in her eyes. I saw in a flash what her fame was all about: not just talent, not just courage, but style.

England

six

I spent two more days at the Villa Francese and then flew back to London; and Alessia came with me.

Cenci, crestfallen, wanted her to stay. He hadn't yet returned to his office, and her deliverance had not restored him to the man-of-the-world in the picture. He still wore a look of ingrained anxiety and was still making his way to the brandy at unusual hours. The front he had raised for the media had evaporated before their cars were out through the gate, and he seemed on the following day incapably lethargic.

'I can't understand him,' Ilaria said impatiently· 'You'd think he'd be striding about, booming away, taking charge You'd think he'd be his bossy self again Why isn't he?'

'He's had six terrible weeks.'

'So what? They're over. Time for dancing, you'd think·' She sketched a graceful ballet gesture with her arm, gold bracelets jangling. 'Tell you the truth, I was goddam glad she's back, but the way Papa goes on, she might just as well not be.'

'Give him time,' I said mildly.

'I want him the way he was,' she said. 'To be a man.'

When Alessia said at dinner that she was going to England in a day or two, everyone, including myself, was astonished.

'Why?' Ilaria said forthrightly.

'To stay with Popsy.'

Everyone except myself knew who Popsy was, and why Alessia should stay with her, and I too learned afterwards. Popsy was a woman racehorse trainer, widowed, with whom Alessia usually lodged when in England.

'I'm unfit,' Alessia said. 'Muscles like jelly.'

'There are horses here,' Cenci protested.

'Yes, but . . . Papa, I want to go away. It's fantastic to be home, but . . . I tried to drive my car out of the gate today and I was shaking. . . It was stupid. I meant to go to the hairdressers. My hair needs cutting so badly. But I just couldn't. I came back to the house, and look at me, still curling onto my shoulders.' She tried to laugh, but no one found it funny.

'If that's what you want,' her father said worriedly.

'Yes . . . I'll go with Andrew, if he doesn't mind.'

I minded very little. She seemed relieved by her decisions, and the next day Ilaria drove her in the Fiat to the hairdresser, and bought things for her because she couldn't face shops, and brought her cheerfully home. Alessia returned with short casual curls and a slight case of the trembles, and Ilaria helped her pack.

On that evening I tried to persuade Cenci that his family should still take precautions.

'The first ransom is still physically in one suitcase, and until the carabinieri or the courts, or whatever, free it and allow you to use it to replace some of the money you borrowed from Milan, I reckon it's still at risk. What if the kidnappers took you . . . or Ilaria? They don't often hit the same family twice, but this time . . . they might.'

The horror was too much. He had crumbled almost too far.

'Just get Ilaria to be careful,' I said hastily, having failed to do that myself. 'Tell her to vary her life a bit. Get her to stay with friends, invite friends here. You yourself are much safer because of your chauffeur, but it wouldn't hurt to take the gardener along too for a while, he has the shoulders of an ox and he'd make a splendid bodyguard.'

After a long pause, and in a low voice, he said, 'I can't face things, you know.'

'Yes, I do know,' I agreed gently. 'Best to start, though, as soon as you can.'

A faint smile. 'Professional advice?'

'Absolutely.'

He sighed. 'I can't bear to sell the house on Mikonos. My wife loved it.'

'She loved Alessia too. She'd think it a fair swap.'

He looked at me for a while. 'You're a strange young man,' he said. 'You make things so clear.' He paused. 'Don't you ever get muddled by emotion?'

'Yes, sometimes,' I said. 'But when it happens . . . I try to sort myself out. To see some logic.'

'And once you see some logic, you act on it?'

'Try to.' I paused. 'Yes.'

'It sounds . . . cold.'

I shook my head. 'Logic doesn't stop you feeling. You can behave logically, and it can hurt like hell. Or it can comfort you. Or release you. Or all at the same time.'

After a while, he said, stating a fact, 'Most people don't behave logically.'

'No,' I said.

'You seem to think everyone could, if they wanted to?'

I shook my head. 'No.' He waited, so I went on diffidently, 'There's genetic memory against it, for one thing. And to be logical you have to dig up and face your own hidden motives and emotions, and of course they're hidden principally because you don't want to face them. So . . . um . . . it's easier to let your basement feelings run the upper storeys, so to speak, and the result is rage, quarrels, love, jobs, opinions, anorexia, philanthropy . . . almost anything you can think of. I just like to know what's going on down there, to pick out why I truly want to do things, that's all. Then I can do them or not. Whichever.'

He looked at me consideringly. 'Self-analysis . . . did you study it?'

'No. Lived it. Like everyone does.'

He smiled faintly. 'At what age?'

'Well . . . from the beginning. I mean, I can't remember not doing it. Digging into my own true motives. Knowing in one's heart of hearts. Facing the shameful things . . . the discreditable impulses . . . Awful, really.'

He picked up his glass and drank some brandy. 'Did it result in sainthood?' he said, smiling.

'Er . . . no. In sin, of course, from doing what I knew I shouldn't.'

The smile grew on his lips and stayed there. He began to describe to me the house on the Greek island that his wife had loved so, and for the first time since I'd met him I saw the uncertain beginnings of peace.

On the aeroplane Alessia said, 'Where do you live?'

'In Kensington. Near the office.'

'Popsy trains in Lambourn.' She imparted it as if it were a casual piece of information. I waited, though, and after a while she said, 'I want to keep on seeing you.'

I nodded. 'Any time.' I gave her one of my business cards, which had both office and home telephone numbers, scribbling my home address on the back.

'You don't mind?'

'Of course not. Delighted.'

'I need . . . just for now . . . I need a crutch.'

'De luxe model at your service.'

Her lips curved. She was pretty, I thought, under all the strain, her face a mingling of small delicate bones and firm positive muscles, smooth on the surface, taut below, finely shaped under all. I had always been attracted by taller, softer, curvier girls, and there was nothing about Alessia to trigger the usual easy urge to the chase. All the same I liked her increasingly, and would have sought her out if she hadn't asked me first.

In bits and pieces over the past two days she had told me many more details of her captivity, gradually unburdening herself of what she'd suffered and felt and worried over; and I'd encouraged her, not only because sometimes in such accounts one got a helpful lead towards catching the kidnappers, but also very much for her own sake. Victim therapy, paragraph one: let her talk it all out and get rid of it.

At Heathrow we went through immigration, baggage claims

and customs in close proximity, Alessia keeping near to me nervously and trying to make it look natural.

'I won't leave you,' I assured her, 'until you meet Popsy. Don't worry.'

Popsy was late. We stood and waited, with Alessia apologising twice every five minutes and me telling her not to and, finally, like a gust of wind, a large lady arrived with outstretched arms.

'My darling,' she said, enveloping Alessia, 'a bloody crunch on the motorway. Traffic crawling past like snails. Thought I'd never get here.' She held Alessia away from her for an inspection. 'You look marvellous. What an utterly drear thing to happen. When I heard you were safe I bawled, absolutely bawled.'

Popsy was forty-fiveish and wore trousers, shirt and padded sleeveless waistcoat in navy, white and olive green. She had disconcertingly green eyes, a mass of fluffy greying hair, and a personality as large as her frame.

'Popsy . . .' Alessia began.

'My darling, what you need is a large steak. Look at your arms . . . matchsticks. The car's just outside, probably got some traffic cop writing a ticket, I left it on double yellows, so come on, let's go.'

'Popsy, this is Andrew Douglas.'

'Who?' She seemed to see me for the first time. 'How do you do.' She thrust out a hand, which I shook. 'Popsy Teddington. Glad to know you.'

'Andrew travelled with me . . .'

'Great,' Popsy said. 'Well done.' She had her eyes on the exit, searching for trouble.

'Can we ask him to lunch on Sunday?' Alessia said.

'What?' The eyes swivelled my way, gave me a quick assessment, came up with assent. 'OK darling, anything you like.' To me she said, 'Go to Lambourn, ask anybody, they'll tell you where I live.'

'All right,' I said.

Alessia said 'Thank you,' half under her breath, and allowed herself to be swept away, and I reflected bemusedly about irresistible forces in female form.

From Heathrow I went straight to the office, where Friday afternoon was dawdling along as usual.

The office, a nondescript collection of ground floor rooms along either side of a central corridor, had been designed decades before the era of open-plan, half-acre windows and Kew Gardens rampant. We stuck to the rabbit hutches with their strip lighting because they were comparatively cheap; and as most of us were partners, not employees, we each had a sharp interest in low overheads. Besides, the office was not where we mostly worked. The war went on on distant fronts: headquarters was for discussing strategy and writing up reports.

I dumped my suitcase in the hutch I sometimes called my own and wandered along the row, both to announce my return and to see who was in.

Gerry Clayton was there, making a complicated construction in folded paper.

'Hello,' he said. 'Bad boy, Tut tut.'

Gerry Clayton, tubby, asthmatic, fifty-three and bald, had appointed himself father-figure to many wayward sons. His speciality was insurance, and it was he who had recruited me from a firm at Lloyds, where I'd been a water-treading clerk looking for more purpose in life.

'Where's Twinkletoes?' I said. 'I may as well get the lecture over.'

'Twinkletoes, as you so disrespectfully call him, went to Venezuela this morning. The manager of Luca Oil got sucked.'

'Luca Oil?' My eyebrows rose. 'After all the work we did for them, setting up defences?'

Gerry shrugged, carefully knifing a sharp crease in stiff white paper with his thumbnail. 'That work was more than a year ago. You know what people are. Dead keen on precautions to start with, then perfunctory, then dead sloppy. Human nature. All any self-respecting dedicated kidnapper has to do is wait.

He was unconcerned about the personal fate of the abducted manager. He frequently said that if everyone took fortress-like precautions and never got themselves – in his word – sucked, we'd all be out of a job. One good kidnapping in a corporation encouraged twenty others to call us in to advise them how to avoid a similar embarrassment; and as he regularly pointed out, the how-not-to-get-sucked business was our bread and butter and also some of the jam.

Gerry inverted his apparently wrinkled heap of white paper and it fell miraculously into the shape of a cockatoo. When not advising anti-kidnap insurance policies to Liberty Market clients he sold origami patterns to a magazine, but no one grudged his paper-folding in the office. His mind seemed to coast along while he creased and tucked, and would come up often as if from nowhere with highly productive business ideas.

Liberty Market as a firm consisted at that time of thirty-one partners and five secretarial employees. Of the partners, all but Gerry and myself were ex-S.A.S., ex-police, or ex-something-ultra-secret in government departments. There were no particular rules about who did which job, though if possible everyone was allowed their preferences. Some opted for the lecture tour full-time, giving seminars, pointing out dangers; all the how-to-stay-free bit. Some sank their teeth gratefully into the terrorist circuit, others, like myself, felt more useful against the simply criminal. Everyone in between times wrote their own reports, studied everyone else's, manned the office switchboard year round and polished up their techniques of coercive bargaining.

We had a Chairman (the firm's founder) for our Monday morning state-of-the-nation meetings, a Co-ordinator who kept track of everyone's whereabouts, and an Adjuster – Twinkle-toes – to whom partners addressed all complaints. If their complaints covered the behaviour of any other partner, Twinkletoes passed the comments on. If enough partners disapproved of one partner's actions, Twinkletoes delivered the censure. I wasn't all that sorry he'd gone to Venezuela.

This apparently shapeless company scheme worked in a highly organised way, thanks mostly to the ingrained discipline of the ex-soldiers. They were lean, hard, proud and quite amazingly cunning, most of them preferring to deal with the action of the after-kidnap affairs. They were, in addition, almost paranoid about secrecy, as also the ex-spies were, which to begin with I'd found oppressive but had soon grown to respect.

It was the ex-policemen who did most of the lecturing, not only advising on defences but telling potential kidnap targets what to do and look for if they were taken, so that their captors could be in turn captured.

Many of us knew an extra like photography, languages, weaponry and electronics, and everyone could use a wordprocessor, because no one liked the rattle of typewriters all day long. No one was around the office long enough for serious feuds to develop, and the Co-ordinator had a knack of keeping incompatibles apart. All in all it was a contented ship which everyone worked in from personal commitment, and, thanks to the kidnappers, business was healthy.

I finished my journey along the row of hutches, said a few hellos, saw I was pencilled in with a question mark for Sunday midnight on the switchboard roster, and came at length to the big room across the far end, the only room with windows to the street. It just about seated the whole strength if we were ever there together, but on that afternoon the only person in it was Tony Vine.

"Lo,' he said. 'Hear you made an effing balls of it in Bologna.'

'Yeah.'

'Letting the effing carabinieri eff up the R.V.'

'Have you tried giving orders to the Italian army?'

He sniffed as a reply. He himself was an ex-S.A.S. sergeant, now nearing forty, who would never in his service days have dreamed of obeying a civilian. He could move across any terrain in a way that made a chameleon look flamboyant, and he had three times tracked and liberated a victim before the ransom had been paid, though no one, not even the victim, was quite sure how. Tony Vine was the most secretive of the whole tight-lipped bunch, and anything he didn't want to tell didn't get told.

It was he who had warned me about knives inside rolled up magazines, and I'd guessed he'd known because he'd carried one that way himself.

His humour consisted mostly of sarcasm, and he could hardly get a sentence out without an oiling of fuck, shit and piss. He worked nearly always on political kidnaps because he, like Pucinelli, tended to despise personal and company wealth.

'If you're effing poor,' he'd said to me once, 'and you see some capitalist shitting around in a Roller, it's not so effing surprising you think of ways of levelling things up. If you're down to your last bit of goat cheese in Sardinia, maybe, or short of beans in Mexico, a little kidnap makes effing sense.'

'You're romantic,' I'd answered. 'What about the poor Sardinians who steal a child from a poor Sardinian village, and grind all the poor people there into poorer dust, forcing them all to pay out their pitiful savings for a ransom?'

'No one's effing perfect.'

For all that he'd been against me joining the firm in the first place, and in spite of his feeling superior in every way, whenever we'd worked together it had been without friction. He could feel his way through the psyches of kidnappers as through a minefield, but preferred to have me deal with the families of the victims.

'When you're with them, they stay in one effing piece. If I tell them what to do, they fall to effing bits.'

He was at his happiest cooperating with men in uniform, among whom he seemed to command instant recognition and respect. Good sergeants ran the army, it was said, and when he wanted to he had the air about him still.

No one was allowed to serve in the S.A.S. for an extended

period, and once he'd been bounced out because of age, he'd been bored. Then someone had murmured in his ear about fighting terrorists a different way, and Liberty Market had never regretted taking him.

'I put you in for Sunday midnight on the blower, did you see, instead of me?' he said.

I nodded.

'The wife's got this effing anniversary party organised, and like as not by midnight I'll be pissed.'

'All right,' I said.

He was short for a soldier: useful for passing as a woman, he'd told me once. Sandy-haired, blue-eyed, and light on his feet, he was a fanatic about fitness, and it was he who had persuaded everyone to furnish (and use) the iron-pumping room in the basement. He never said much about his origins: the tougher parts of London, from his accent.

'When did you get back?' I asked. 'Last I heard you were in Columbia.'

'End of the week.'

'How was it?' I said.

He scowled. 'We winkled the effing hostages out safe, and then the local strength got excited and shot the shit out of the terrorists, though they'd got their effing hands up and were coming out peaceful.' He shook his head. 'Never keep their bullets to themselves, those savages. Effing stupid, the whole shitting lot of them.'

Shooting terrorists who'd surrendered was, as he'd said, effing stupid. The news would get around, and the next bunch of terrorists, knowing they'd be shot if they did and also shot if they didn't, would be more likely to kill their victims.

I had missed the Monday meeting where that debacle would have been discussed, but meanwhile there was my own report to write for the picking over of Bologna. I spent all Saturday on it and some of Sunday morning, and then drove seventy-five miles westward to Lambourn.

Popsy Teddington proved to live in a tall white house near the centre of the village, a house seeming almost suburban but surprisingly fronting a great amount of stabling. I hadn't until that day realised that racing stables could occur actually inside villages, but when I remarked on it Popsy said with a smile that I should see Newmarket, they had horses where people in other towns had garages, greenhouses and sheds.

She was standing outside when I arrived, looming over a five-foot man who seemed glad of the interruption.

'Just see to that, Sammy. Tell them I won't stand for it,' she was saying forcefully as I opened the car door. Her head turned my way and a momentary 'who-are-you?' frown crossed her forehead. 'Oh yes, Alessia's friend. She's around the back, somewhere. Come along.' She led me past the house and behind a block of stabling, and we arrived suddenly in view of a small railed paddock, where a girl on a horse was slowly cantering, watched by another girl on foot.

The little paddock seemed to be surrounded by the backs of other stables and other houses, and the grass within it had seen better days.

'I hope you can help her,' Popsy said straightly, as we approached. 'I've never known her like this. Very worrying.'

'How do you mean?' I asked.

'So insecure. She wouldn't ride out yesterday with the string, which she always does when she's here, and now look at her, she's supposed to be up on that horse, not watching my stable girl riding.'

'Has she said much about what happened to her?' I asked.

'Not a thing. She just smiles cheerfully and says it's all over.'

Alessia half turned as we drew near, and looked very relieved when she saw me.

'I was afraid you wouldn't come,' she said.

'You shouldn't have been.'

She was wearing jeans and a checked shirt and lipstick, and was still unnaturally pale from six weeks in dim light. Popsy shouted to the girl riding the horse to put it back in its stable. 'Unless, darling, you'd like . . .' she said to Alessia. 'After all?'

Alessia shook her head. 'Tomorrow, I guess.' She sounded as if she meant it, but I could see that Popsy doubted. She put a motherly arm round Alessia's shoulders and gave her a small hug. 'Darling, do just what you like. How about a drink for your thirsty traveller?' To me she said, 'Coffee? Whisky? Methylated spirits?'

'Wine,' Alessia said. 'I know he likes that.'

We went into the house: dark antique furniture, worn Indian rugs, faded chintz, a vista of horses through every window.

Popsy poured Italian wine into cut crystal glasses with a casual hand and said she would cook steaks if we were patient. Alessia watched her disappear kitchenwards and said uncomfortably, 'I'm a nuisance to her. I shouldn't have come.'

'You're quite wrong on both counts,' I said. 'It's obvious she's glad to have you.'

'I thought I'd be all right here. . . . That I'd feel different. I mean, that I'd feel all right.'

'You're sure to, in a while.'

She glanced at me. 'It bothers me that I just can't . . . shake it off.'

'Like you could shake off double septic pneumonia?'

'That's different,' she protested.

'Six weeks of no sunlight, no exercise, no decent food and a steady diet of heavy sleeping pills is hardly a recipe for physical health.'

'But . . . it's not just . . . physical.'

'Still less can you just shake off the non-physical.' I drank some wine. 'How are your dreams?'

She shuddered. 'Half the time I can't sleep. Ilaria said I should keep on with the sleeping pills for a while, but I don't want to, it revolts me to think of it. . . . But when I do sleep . . . I have nightmares . . . and wake up sweating.'

'Would you like me,' I said neutrally, 'to introduce you to a psychiatrist? I know quite a good one.'

'No.' The answer was instinctive. 'I'm not mad, I'm just . . . not right.'

'You don't need to be dying to go to a doctor.'

She shook her head. 'I don't want to.'

She sat on a large sofa with her feet on a coffee table, looking worried.

'It's you that I want to talk to, not some shrink. You understand what happened, and to some strange doctor it would sound exaggerated. You know I'm telling the truth, but he'd be worrying half the time if I wasn't fantasising or dramatising or something and be looking for ways of putting me in the wrong. I had a friend who went to one . . . She told me it was weird, when she said she wanted to give up smoking he kept suggesting she was unhappy because she had repressed incestuous longings for her father.' She ended with an attempt at a laugh, but I could see what she meant. Psychiatrists were accustomed to distortion and evasion, and looked for them in the simplest remark.

'I do think all the same that you'd be better off with expert help,' I said.

'You're an expert.'

'No.'

'But it's you I want . . . Oh dear,' she broke off suddenly, looking most confused. 'I'm sorry. . . . You don't want to. . . . How stupid of me.'

'I didn't say that. I said . . .' I too stopped. I stood up, walked over, and sat next to her on the sofa, not touching. 'I'll untie any knots I can for you, and for as long as you want me to. That's a promise. Also a pleasure, not a chore. But you must promise me something too.'

She said 'What?' glancing at me and away.

'That if I'm doing you no good, you will try someone else.'

'A shrink?'

'Yes.'

She looked at her shoes. 'All right,' she said; and like any psychiatrist I wondered if she were lying.

Popsy's steaks came tender and juicy, and Alessia ate half of hers.

'You must build up your strength, my darling,' Popsy said without censure. 'You've worked so hard to get where you are. You don't want all those ambitious little jockey-boys elbowing you out, which they will if they've half a chance.'

'I telephoned Mike,' she said. 'I said . . . I'd need time.'

'Now my darling,' Popsy protested. 'You get straight back on the telephone and tell him you'll be fit a week today. Say you'll be ready to race tomorrow week, without fail.'

Alessia looked at her in horror. 'I'm too weak to stay in the saddle . . . let alone race.'

'My darling, you've all the guts in the world. If you want to, you'll do it.'

Alessia's face said plainly that she didn't know whether she wanted to or not.

'Who's Mike?' I asked.

'Mike Noland,' Popsy said. 'The trainer she often rides for in England. He lives here, in Lambourn, up the road.'

'He said he understood,' Alessia said weakly.

'Well of course he understands. Who wouldn't? But all the same, my darling, if you want those horses back, it's you that will have to get them.'

She spoke with brisk, affectionate commonsense, hallmark of the kind and healthy who had never been at cracking point. There was a sort of quiver from where Alessia sat, and I rose unhurriedly to my feet and asked if I could help carry the empty dishes to the kitchen.

'Of course you can,' Popsy said, rising also, 'and there's cheese, if you'd like some.'

Alessia said horses slept on Sunday afternoons like everyone else, but after coffee we walked slowly round the yard anyway, patting one or two heads.

'I can't possibly get fit in a week,' Alessia said. 'Do you think I should?'

'I think you should try sitting on a horse.'

'Suppose I've lost my nerve.'

'You'd find out.'

'That's not much comfort.' She rubbed the nose of one of the horses absentmindedly, showing at least no fear of its teeth. 'Do you ride?' she asked.

'No,' I said. 'And . . . er . . . I've never been to the races.'

She was astonished. 'Never?'

'I've watched them often on television.'

'Not the same at all.' She laid her own cheek briefly against the horse's. 'Would you like to go?'

'With you, yes, very much.'

Her eyes filled with sudden tears, which she blinked away impatiently. 'You see,' she said. 'That's always happening. A kind word . . . and something inside me melts. I do try . . . I honestly do try to behave decently, but I know I'm putting on an act . . . and underneath there's an abyss . . . with things coming up from it, like crying for nothing, for no reason, like now.'

'The act,' I said, 'is Oscar class.'

She swallowed and sniffed and brushed the unspilt tears away with her fingers. 'Popsy is so generous,' she said. 'I've stayed with her so often.' She paused. 'She doesn't exactly say "Snap out of it" or "Pull yourself together", but I can see her thinking it. And I expect if I were someone looking at me, I'd think it too. I mean, she must be thinking that here I am, free and undamaged, and I should be grateful and getting on with life, and that far from moping I should be full of joy and bounce.'

We wandered slowly along and peered into the shadowy interior of a box where the inmate dozed, its weight on one hip, its ears occasionally twitching.

'After Vietnam,' I said, 'when the prisoners came home, there were very many divorces. It wasn't just the sort of thing that happened after the war in Europe, when the wives grew apart from the husbands just by living, while for the men time stood still. After Vietnam it was different. Those prisoners had suffered dreadfully, and they came home to families who expected them to be joyful at their release.'

Alessia leant her arms on the half-door, and watched the unmoving horse.

'The wives tried to make allowances, but a lot of the men were impotent, and would burst into tears in public, and many of them took offence easily . . . and showed permanent symptoms of mental breakdown. Hamburgers and coke couldn't cure them, nor going to the office nine to five.' I fiddled with the bolt on the door. 'Most of them recovered in time and lead normal lives, but even those will admit they had bad dreams for years and will never forget clear details of their imprisonment.'

After a while she said, 'I wasn't a prisoner of war.'

'Oh yes, just the same. Captured by an enemy through no fault of your own. Not knowing when – or whether – you would be free. Humiliated . . . deprived of free will . . . dependent on your enemy for food. All the same, but made worse by isolation . . . by being the only one.'

She put the curly head down momentarily on the folded arms. 'All they ever gave me, when I asked, were some tissues, and I begged . . . I begged . . . for those.' She swallowed. 'One's body doesn't stop counting the days, just because one's in a tent.'

I put my arm silently round her shoulders. There were things no male prisoner ever had to face. She cried quietly, with gulps and small compulsive sniffs, and after a while simply said, 'Thank you,' and I said, 'Any time,' and we moved on down the line of boxes knowing there was a long way still to go.

seven

Manning the office switchboard day and night was essential because kidnappers kept anti-social hours; and it was always a partner on duty, not an employee, for reasons both of reliability and secrecy. The ex-spies feared 'moles' under every secretarial desk and positive-vetted the cleaner.

That particular Sunday night was quiet, with two calls only: one from a partner in Equador saying he'd discovered the local police were due to share in the ransom he was negotiating and asking for the firm's reactions, and the second from Twinkletoes, who wanted a copy of the set of precautions we'd drawn up for Luca Oil.

I made a note of it, saying 'Surely Luca Oil have one?'

'The kidnappers stole it,' Twinkletoes said tersely. 'Or bribed a secretary to steal it. Anyway, it's missing, and the manager was abducted at the weakest point of his daily schedule, which I reckon was no coincidence.'

'I'll send it by courier straight away.'

'And see who's free to join me out here. This will be a long one. It was very carefully planned. Send me Derek, if you can. And oh . . . consider yourself lucky I'm not there to blast you for Bologna.'

'I do,' I said, smiling.

'I'll be back,' he said darkly. 'Goodnight.'

I took one more call, at nine in the morning, this time from the head of a syndicate at Lloyds which insured people and firms against kidnap. Much of our business came direct from him, as he was accustomed to make it a condition of insurance that his clients should call on our help before agreeing to pay a ransom. He reckoned we could bring the price down, which made his own liability less; and we in return recommended him to the firms asking our advice on defences.

'Two English girls have been snatched in Sardinia,' he said. 'The husband of one of them insured her against kidnap for her two weeks holiday as he wasn't going to be with her, and he's been on to us. It seems to have been a fairly unplanned affair – the girls just happened to be in the wrong place, and were ambushed. Anyway, the husband is distraught and wants to pay what they're asking, straight away, so can you send someone immediately?'

'Yes,' I said. 'Er . . . what was the insurance?'

'I took a thousand pounds against two hundred thousand. For two weeks.' He sighed. 'Win some, lose some.'

I took down names and details and checked on flights to Sardinia, where in many regions bandits took, ransomed and released more or less as they pleased.

'Very hush-hush,' the Lloyds man had said. 'Don't let it get to the papers. The husband has pressing reasons. If all goes well she'll be home in a week, won't she, and no one the wiser?'

'With a bit of luck,' I agreed.

Bandits had nowhere to keep long-term prisoners and had been known to march their victims miles over mountainsides daily, simply abandoning them once they'd been paid. Alessia, I thought, would have preferred that to her tent.

The partners began arriving for the Monday conference and it was easy to find one with itchy feet ready to go instantly to Sardinia, and easy also to persuade Derek to join Twinkletoes at Luca Oil. The Co-ordinator wrote them in on the new week's chart and I gave the request from the partner in Equador to the Chairman.

After about an hour of coffee, gossip and reading reports the meeting began, the bulk of it as usual being a review of work in progress.

'This business in Equador,' the Chairman said. 'The victim's an American national, isn't he?'

A few heads nodded.

The Chairman pursed his lips. 'I think we'll have to advise that corporation to use local men and not send any more from the States. They've had three men captured in the last ten years, all Americans . . . you'd think they'd learn.'

'It's an American-owned corporation,' someone murmured.

'They've tried paying the police themselves,' another said. 'I was out there myself last time. The police took the money saying they would guard all the managers with their lives, but I reckon they also took a cut of the ransom then, too. And don't forget, the corporation paid a ransom of something like ten million dollars . . . plenty to spread around.'

There was a small gloomy silence.

'Right,' the Chairman said. 'Future advice, no Americans. Present advice?' He looked around. 'Opinions, anyone?'

'The kidnappers know the corporation will pay in the end,' Tony Vine said. 'The corporation can't afford not to.'

All corporations had to ransom their captured employees if they wanted anyone ever to work overseas for them in future. All corporations also had irate shareholders, whose dividends diminished as ransoms rose. Corporations tended to keep abductions out of the news, and to write the ransoms down as a 'trading loss' in the annual accounts.

'We've got the demand down to ten million again,' Tony Vine said. 'The kidnappers won't take less, they'd be losing face against last time, even if – especially if – they're a different gang.'

The Chairman nodded. 'We'll advise the corporation to settle?'

Everyone agreed, and the meeting moved on.

The Chairman, around sixty, had once been a soldier himself, and like Tony felt comfortable with other men whose lives had been structured, disciplined and official. He had founded the firm because he'd seen the need for it; the action in his case of a practical man, not a visionary. It had been a friend of his, now dead, who had suggested partnerships rather than a hierarchy, advising the sweeping away of all former ranks in favour of one new one: equal.

The Chairman was exceptionally good-looking, a distinctly marketable plus, and had an air of quiet confidence to go with it. He could maintain that manner in the face of total disaster, so that one always felt he would at any moment devise a brilliant victory-snatching solution, even if he didn't. It had taken me a while, when I was new there, to see that it was Gerry Clayton who had that sort of mind.

The Chairman came finally to my report, photocopies of which most people had already read, and asked if any partners would like to ask questions. We gained always from what others had learned during a case, and I usually found question time very fruitful – though better when not doing the answering.

'This carabinieri officer . . . er . . . Pucinelli, what sort of a personal relationship could you have with him? What is your estimate of his capabilities?' It was a notoriously pompous partner asking; Tony would have said, 'How did you get on with the sod? What's he like?'

'Pucinelli's a good policeman,' I said. 'Intelligent, bags of courage. He was helpful. More helpful, I found, than most, though never stepping out of the official line. He hasn't yet . . .' I paused. 'He hasn't the clout to get any higher, I don't think. He's second-in-command in his region, and I'd say that's as far as he'll go. But as far as his chances of catching the kidnappers are concerned, he'll be competent and thorough.'

'What was the latest, when you left?' someone asked. 'I haven't yet had time to finish your last two pages.'

'Pucinelli said that when he showed the drawings of the man I'd seen to the two kidnappers from the siege, they were both struck dumb. He showed them to them separately, of course, but in each case he said you could clearly see the shock. Neither of them would say anything at all and they both seemed scared. Pucinelli said he was going to circulate copies of the drawings and see if he could identify the man. He was very hopeful, when I left.'

'Sooner the better,' Tony said. 'That million quid will be laundered within a week.'

'They were a pretty cool lot,' I said, not arguing. 'They might hold it for a while.'

'And they might have whisked it over a border and changed it into francs or schillings before they released the girl.'

I nodded. 'They could have set up something like that for the first ransom, and been ready.'

Gerry Clayton's fingers as usual were busy with any sheet of paper within reach, this time the last page of my report. 'You say Alessia Cenci came to England with you. Any chance she'll remember any more?' he asked.

'You cannot rule it out, but Pucinelli and I both went

102

through it with her pretty thoroughly in Italy. She knows so little. There were no church bells, no trains, no close aeroplanes, no dogs . . . she couldn't tell whether she was in city or country. She thought the faint smell she was conscious of during the last few days might have been someone baking bread. Apart from that . . . nothing.'

A pause.

'Did you show the drawings to the girl?' someone asked. 'Had she ever seen the man, before the kidnap?'

I turned to him. 'I took a photostat to the villa, but she hadn't ever seen him that she could remember. There was absolutely no reaction. I asked if he could have been one of the four who abducted her, but she said she couldn't tell. None of her family or anyone in the household knew him. I asked them all.'

'His voice . . . when he spoke to you outside the motorway restaurant . . . was it the voice on the tapes?'

'I don't know,' I admitted. 'I'm not good enough at Italian. It wasn't totally different, that's all I could say.'

'You brought copies of the drawings and the tapes back with you?' the Chairman asked.

'Yes. If anyone would like . . . ?'

A few heads nodded.

'Anything you didn't put in the report?' the Chairman asked. 'Insignificant details?'

'Well. . . . I didn't include the lists of the music. Alessia wrote what she knew, and Pucinelli said he would try to find out if they were tapes one could buy in shops, ready recorded. Very long shot, even if they were.'

'Do you have the lists?'

'No, afraid not. I could ask Alessia to write them again, if you like.'

One of the ex-policemen said you never knew. The other ex-policemen nodded.

'All right,' I said. 'I'll ask her.'

'How is she?' Gerry asked.

'Just about coping.'

There were a good many nods of understanding. We'd all seen the devastation, the hurricane's path across the spirit. All of us, some oftener than others, had listened to the experiences of the recently returned: the de-briefing, as the firm called it, in its military way.

The Chairman looked around for more questions but none were ready. 'All finished? Well, Andrew, we can't exactly sack you for coming up with pictures of an active kidnapper, but driving a car to the drop is not on the cards. Whether or not it turns out well this time, don't do it again. Right?'

'Right,' I said neutrally; and that, to my surprise, was the full extent of the ticking-off.

A couple of days later the partner manning the switchboard called to me down the corridor, where I was wandering with a cup of coffee in search of anything new.

'Andrew? Call for you from Bologna. I'll put it through to your room.'

I dumped the coffee and picked up the receiver, and a voice said 'Andrew? This is Enrico Pucinelli.'

We exchanged hellos, and he began talking excitedly, the words running together in my ear.

'Enrico,' I shouted. 'Stop. Speak slowly. I can't understand you.'

'Hah.' He sighed audibly and began to speak clearly and distinctly, as to a child. 'The young one of the kidnappers has been talking. He is afraid of being sent to prison for life, so he is trying to make bargains. He has told us where Signorina Cenci was taken after the kidnap.'

'Terrific,' I said warmly. 'Well done.'

Pucinelli coughed modestly, but I guessed it had been a triumph of interrogation.

'We have been to the house. It is in a suburb of Bologna, middle-class, very quiet. We have found it was rented by a father with three grown sons.' He clicked his tongue disgustedly. 'All of the neighbours saw men going in and out, but so far no one would know them again.'

I smiled to myself. Putting the finger on a kidnapper was apt to be unhealthy anywhere.

'The house has furniture belonging to the owner, but we have looked carefully, and in one room on the upper floor all the marks where the furniture has stood on the carpet for a long time are in slightly different places.' He stopped and said anxiously, 'Do you understand, Andrew?'

'Yes,' I said. 'All the furniture had been moved.'

'Correct.' He was relieved. 'The bed, a heavy chest, a wardrobe, a bookcase. All moved. The room is big, more than big enough for the tent, and there is nothing to see from the window except a garden and trees. No one could see into the room from outside.'

'And have you found anything useful . . . any clues in the rest of the house?'

'We are looking. We went to the house for the first time yesterday. I thought you would like to know.'

'You're quite right. Great news.'

'Signorina Cenci,' he said, 'has she thought of anything else?'

'Not yet.'

'Give her my respects.'

'Yes,' I said. 'I will indeed.'

'I will telephone again,' he said. 'I will reverse the charges again, shall I, like you said? As this is private, between you and me, and I am telephoning from my own house?'

'Every time,' I said.

He said goodbye with deserved satisfaction, and I added a note of what he'd said to my report.

By Thursday morning I was back in Lambourn, chiefly for the lists of music, and I found I had arrived just as a string of Popsy's horses were setting out for exercise. Over her jeans and shirt Popsy wore another padded waistcoat, bright pink this time, seeming not to notice that it was a warm day in July; and her fluffy grey-white hair haloed her big head like a private cumulus cloud.

She was on her feet in the stable-yard surrounded by scrunching skittering quadrupeds, and she beckoned when she saw me, with a huge sweep of her arm. Trying not to look nervous and obviously not succeeding, I dodged a few all-too-mobile half-tons of muscle and made it to her side.

The green eyes looked at me slantwise, smiling. 'Not used to them, are you?'

'Er . . .' I said. 'No.'

'Want to see them on the gallops?'

'Yes, please.' I looked round at the riders, hoping to see Alessia among them, but without result.

The apparently disorganised throng suddenly moved off towards the road in one orderly line, and Popsy jerked her head for me to follow her into the kitchen; and at the table in there, coffee cup in hand, sat Alessia.

She still looked pale, but perhaps now only in contrast to the outdoor health of Popsy, and she still looked thin, without strength. Her smile when she saw me started in the eyes and then curved to the pink lipstick; an uncomplicated welcome of friendship.

'Andrew's coming up on the Downs to see the schooling,' Popsy said.

'Great.'

'You're not riding?' I asked Alessia.

'No . . . I . . . anyway, Popsy's horses are jumpers.'

Popsy made a face as if to say that wasn't a satisfactory reason for not riding them, but passed no other comment. She and I talked for a while about things in general and Alessia said not much.

We all three sat on the front seat of a dusty Land Rover while Popsy drove with more verve than caution out of Lambourn and along a side road and finally up a bumpy track to open stretches of grassland.

Away on the horizon the rolling terrain melted into blue haze, and under our feet, as we stepped from the Land Rover, the close turf had been mown to two inches. Except for a bird call or two in the distance there was a gentle enveloping silence, which was in itself extraordinary. No drone of aeroplanes, no clamour of voices, no hum of faraway traffic. Just wide air and warm sunlight and the faint rustle from one's own clothes.

'You like it, don't you?' observed Popsy, watching my face.

I nodded.

'You should be up here in January with the wind howling across. Though mind you, it's beautiful even when you're freezing.'

She scanned a nearby valley with a hand shading her eyes. 'The horses will be coming up from there at half-speed canter,' she said. 'They'll pass us here. Then we'll follow them up in the Land Rover to the schooling fences.'

I nodded again, not reckoning I'd know a half-speed canter from a slow waltz, but in fact when the row of horses appeared like black dots from the valley I soon saw what speed she meant. She watched with concentration through large binoculars as the dots became shapes and the shapes flying horses, lowering the glasses only when the string of ten went past, still one behind the other so that she had a clear view of each. She pursed her mouth but seemed otherwise not too displeased, and we were soon careering along in their wake, jerking to a stop over the brow of the hill and disembarking to find the horses circling with tossing heads and puffing breath.

'See those fences over there?' said Popsy, pointing to isolated timber and brushwood obstacles looking like refugees from a racecourse. 'Those are schooling fences. To teach the horses how to jump.' She peered into my face, and I nodded. 'The set on this side, they're hurdles. The far ones are . . . er . . . fences. For steeplechasers.' I nodded again. 'From the start of the schooling ground up to here there are six hurdles – and six fences – so you can give a horse a good work-out if you want to, but today I'm sending my lot over these top four only, as they're not fully fit.'

She left us abruptly and strode over to her excited four-legged family, and Alessia with affection said, 'She's a good trainer. She can see when a horse isn't feeling right, even if there's nothing obviously wrong. When she walks into the yard all the horses instantly know she's there. You see all the heads come out, like a chorus.'

Popsy was despatching three of the horses towards the lower end of the schooling ground. 'Those three will come up over the hurdles,' Alessia said. 'Then those riders will change onto three more horses and start again.'

I was surprised. 'Don't all of the riders jump?' I asked.

'Most of them don't ride well enough to teach. Of those three doing the schooling, two are professional jockeys and the third is Popsy's best lad.'

Popsy stood beside us, binoculars ready, as the three horses came up over the hurdles. Except for a ratatatat at the hurdles themselves it was all very quiet, mostly, I realised, because there was no broadcast commentary as on television, but partly also because of the Doppler effect. The horses seemed to be making far more noise once they were past and going away.

Popsy muttered unintelligibly under her breath and Alessia said 'Borodino jumped well,' in the sort of encouraging voice which meant the other two hadn't.

We all waited while the three schooling riders changed horses and set off again down the incline to the starting point – and I felt Alessia suddenly stir beside me and take a bottomless breath – moving from there into a small, restless, aimless circle. Popsy glanced at her but said nothing, and after a while Alessia stopped her circling and said, 'Tomorrow . . .'

'Today, here and now,' Popsy interrupted firmly, and yelled to a certain Bob to come over to her at once.

Bob proved to be a middle-aged lad riding a chestnut which peeled off from the group and ambled over in what looked to me a sloppy walk.

'Hop off, will you?' Popsy said, and when Bob complied she said to Alessia, 'OK, just walk round a bit. You've no helmet so I don't want you breaking the speed limit, and besides old Paperbag here isn't as fit as the others.'

She made a cradle for Alessia's knee and threw her casually up into the saddle, where the lady jockey landed with all the thump of a feather. Her feet slid into the stirrups and her hands gathered the reins, and she looked down at me for a second as if bemused at the speed with which things were happening. Then as if impelled she wheeled her mount and trotted away, following the other three horses down the schooling ground.

'At last,' Popsy said. 'And I'd begun to think she never would.'

'She's a brave girl.'

'Oh yes.' She nodded. 'One of the best.'

'She had an appalling time.'

Popsy gave me five seconds of the direct green eyes. 'So I gather,' she said, 'from her refusal to talk about it. Let it all hang out, I told her, but she just shook her head and blinked a couple of tears away, so these past few days I've stopped trying to jolly her along, it was obviously doing no good.' She raised the binoculars to watch her three horses coming up over the hurdles and then swung them back down the hill, focusing on Alessia.

'Hands like silk,' Popsy said. 'God knows where she got it from, no one else in the family knows a spavin from a splint.'

'She'll be better now,' I said, smiling. 'But don't expect . . .'

'Instant full recovery?' she asked, as I paused.

I nodded. 'It's like a convalescence. Gradual.'

Popsy lowered the glasses and glanced at me briefly. 'She told me about your job. What you've done for her father. She says she feels safe with you.' She paused. 'I've never heard of a job like yours. I didn't know people like you existed.'

'There are quite a few of us . . . round the world.'

'What do you call yourself, if people ask?'

'Safety consultant, usually. Or insurance consultant. Depends how I feel.'

She smiled. 'They both sound dull and worthy.'

'Yes . . . er . . . that's the aim.'

We watched Alessia come back up the hill, cantering now, but slowly, and standing in the stirrups. Though of course I'd seen them do it, I'd never consciously noted before then that that was how jockeys rode, not sitting in the saddle but tipped right forward so their weight could be carried over the horse's shoulder, not on the lower spine. Alessia stopped beside Bob, who took hold of the horse's reins, and she dismounted by lifting her right leg forward over the horse's neck and dropping lightly, feet together, to the ground: a movement as graceful and springy as ballet.

A different dimension, I thought. The expertise of the professional. Amazing to the non-able, like seeing an artist drawing.

She patted the horse's neck, thanked Bob and came over to us, slight in shirt and jeans, smiling.

'Thanks,' she said to Popsy.

'Tomorrow?' Popsy said. 'With the string?'

Alessia nodded, rubbing the backs of her thighs. 'I'm as unfit as marshmallow.'

With calmness she watched the final trio of horses school, and then Popsy drove us again erratically back to her house, while the horses walked, to cool down.

Over coffee in the kitchen Alessia rewrote the lists of the music she listened to so often, a job she repeated out of generosity, and disliked.

'I could hum all the other tunes that I don't know the titles of,' she said. 'But frankly I don't want to hear them ever again.' She pushed the list across: Verdi, as before, and modern gentle songs like 'Yesterday' and 'Bring in the Clowns', more British and American in origin than Italian.

'I did think of something else,' she said hesitantly. 'I dreamed it, the night before last. You know how muddled things are in dreams . . . I was dreaming I was walking out to race. I had silks on, pink and green checks, and I know I was supposed to be going to ride, but I couldn't find the parade ring, and I asked people, but they didn't know, they were all catching trains or something and then someone said, "At least an hour to Viralto," and I woke up. I was sweating and my heart was thumping, but it hadn't been a nightmare, not a bad one anyway. Then I thought that I'd actually heard someone say "at least an hour to Viralto" at that minute, and I was afraid there was someone in the room. . . . It was horrible, really.' She put a hand on her forehead, as if the clamminess still stood there. 'But of course, when I woke up properly, there I was in Popsy's spare bedroom, perfectly safe. But my heart was still thumping.' She paused, then said, 'I think I must have heard one of them say that, when I was almost asleep.'

'This dream,' I asked slowly, considering, 'was it in English . . . or Italian?'

'Oh.' Her eyes widened. 'I was riding in England. Pink and green checks . . . one of Mike Noland's horses. I asked the way to the parade ring in English . . . they were English people, but that voice saying "at least an hour to Viralto", that was Italian.' She frowned. 'How awfully odd. I translated it into English in my mind, when I woke up.'

'Do you often go to Viralto?' I asked.

'No. I don't even know where it is.'

'I'll tell Pucinelli,' I said, and she nodded consent.

'He found the house you were kept in most of the time,' I said neutrally.

'Did he?' It troubled her. 'I . . . I don't want . . .'

'You don't want to hear about it?'

'No.'

'All right.'

She sighed with relief. 'You never make me face things. I'm very grateful. I feel . . . I still feel I could be pushed over a cliff . . . break down, I suppose . . . if too much is forced on me. And it's absolutely ridiculous – I didn't cry at all, not once, when I was . . . in that tent.'

'That's thoroughly normal, and you're doing fine,' I said. 'And you look fabulous on a horse.'

She laughed. 'God knows why it took me so long. But up on the Downs . . . such a gorgeous morning . . . I just felt . . .' She paused. 'I love horses, you know. Most of them, anyway. They're like friends . . . but they live internal lives,

111

secret, with amazing instincts. They're telepathic . . . I suppose I'm boring you.'

'No,' I said truthfully, and thought that it was horses, not I, who would lead her finally back to firm ground.

She came out to the car with me when I left and kissed me goodbye, cheek to cheek, as if I'd known her for years.

eight

'Viralto?' Pucinelli said doubtfully. 'It's a village off one of the roads into the mountains. Very small. No roads in the village, just alleyways between houses. Are you sure she said Viralto?'

'Yes,' I said. 'Is it one of those hill-top villages with houses all stuck together with red tiled roofs and blinding white walls without windows? All on slopes, shut in and secret?'

'Like that, yes.'

'Would it be an hour's drive from Bologna? From the house where Alessia was kept?'

'I suppose so . . . If you knew the way. It is not on a main road.'

'And . . . er . . . would it have a bakery?'

After the faintest of pauses he said smoothly, 'My men will be up there at once, searching thoroughly. But Andrew, it would not be usual to take a kidnapped person there. In these villages everyone knows everyone. There is no room to hide a stranger.'

'Try Viralto on the kidnapper who told you about the first house,' I said.

'You can be sure I will,' he said happily. 'He has now confessed that he was one of the four in masks who abducted Alessia. He also sometimes sat in the house at night to guard her, but he says he never spoke to her, she was always asleep.'

112

He paused. 'I have asked him several times every day for the name of the man in the drawings. He says the man's name is Giuseppe. He says that's what he called him and he doesn't know any other name for him. This may be true. Maybe not. I keep asking. Perhaps one day he will tell me different.'

'Enrico,' I said diffidently, 'you are an expert investigator. I hesitate to make a suggestion . . .'

A small laugh travelled by wire from Bologna, 'You don't hesitate very often.'

'Then . . . before you go to Viralto, shall we get Paolo Cenci to offer a reward for the recovery of any of the ransom money? Then you could take that promise and also the drawings of "Giuseppe" with you . . . perhaps?'

'I will also take photographs of our kidnappers and of Alessia,' he said. 'Signor Cenci will surely agree to the reward. But . . .' he paused, 'Viralto . . . was only a word in a dream.'

'A word which caused sweating and an accelerated heartbeat,' I said. 'It frightened her.'

'Did it? Hmm. Then don't worry, we'll sweep through the village like the sirocco.'

'Ask the children,' I said.

He laughed. 'Andrew Machiavelli Douglas . . . every child's mother would prevent us.'

'Pity.'

When we'd finished talking I telephoned to Paolo Cenci, who said 'willingly' to the reward, and then again to Pucinelli to confirm it.

'I am making a leaflet for photocopying,' he said. 'The reward offer and all the pictures. I'll call you if there are any results.'

'Call me anyway.'

'Yes, all right.'

He called me again on the following day, Friday, in the evening, while I happened to be on duty at the switchboard.

'I've been up in that damned village all day,' he said exhaustedly. 'Those people . . . they shut their doors and their faces and their minds.'

'Nothing?' I asked with disappointment.

'There's something,' he said, 'but I don't know what. The name of Viralto was a shock to the kidnapper who talks, but he swears it means nothing to him. He swears it on his dead mother's soul, but he sweats while he swears. He is lying.' He paused. 'But in Viralto . . . we found nothing. We went into the bakery. We threatened the baker, who also keeps the very small grocery store. There is nowhere near his bakehouse that Alessia could have been hidden, and we searched everywhere. He gave us permission. He said he had nothing to hide. He said he would have known if Alessia had been brought to the village; he says he knows everything. He says she was never there.'

'Did you believe him?' I asked.

'I'm afraid so. We asked at every single house. We did even ask one or two children. We found nothing; we heard nothing. But . . .'

'But . . . ?' I prompted.

'I have looked at a map,' he said, yawning. 'Viralto is up a side road which goes nowhere else. But if when one gets to the turn to Viralto one drives past it, straight on, that road goes on up into the mountains, and although it is not a good road it crosses the Apennines altogether and then descends towards Firenze. Above Viralto there is a place which used to be a castle but is now a hotel. People go there to walk and enjoy the mountains. Perhaps the Signorina didn't hear enough . . . perhaps it was at least an hour to Viralto, and longer still to wherever they planned to go? Tomorrow,' he paused, sighing, 'tomorrow I am off duty. Tomorrow I expect I will however be on duty after all. I'll go up to the hotel and blow the sirocco through that.'

'Send some of your men,' I suggested.

After a definite pause he said levelly, 'I have given instructions that no one is to act again in this case in any way without my being there in person.'

'Ah.'

'So I will telephone again tomorrow, if you like.'

'Tomorrow I'll be here from four until midnight,' I said gratefully. 'After that, at home.'

In the morning, Saturday, Popsy telephoned while I was pottering round my flat trying to shut my eyes to undone chores.

'Something the matter?' I asked, interpreting the tone of her hello.

'Sort of. I want your help. Can you come?'

'This instant, or will tomorrow do? I have to be in the office, really, by four.'

'On Saturday afternoon?' she sounded surprised.

'"Fraid so.'

She hesitated, 'Alessia didn't ride out with the string yesterday because of a headache.'

'Oh . . . and today?'

'Today she didn't feel like it. Look,' she said abruptly, 'I'd say the idea scared her, but how can it, you saw how she rode?' The faint exasperation in her voice came over clearly, accompanying the genuine concern. When I didn't answer immediately she demanded, 'Are you there?'

'Yes. Just thinking.' I paused. 'She wasn't scared of the horses or of riding, that's for sure. So perhaps she's scared . . . and I don't think that's the right word, but it'll do for now . . . of being closed in, of being unable to escape . . . of being in the string. Like a sort of claustrophobia, even though it's out in the open air. Perhaps that's why she wouldn't go in the string before, but felt all right on her own, up on the Downs.'

She thought it over, then said, 'Perhaps you're right. She certainly wasn't happy yesterday . . . she spent most of the day in her room, avoiding me.'

'Popsy . . . don't press her. She needs you very badly, but just as someone there . . . and undemanding. Tell her not to try to go out with the string until she can't bear not to. Say it's fine with you, you're glad to have her, she can do what

115

she likes. Would that be OK? Could you say that? And I'll come down tomorrow morning.'

'Yes, yes, and yes,' she said sighing. 'I'm very fond of her. Come to lunch and wave your wand.'

Pucinelli telephoned late in the evening with the news: good, bad and inconclusive.

'The Signorina was right,' he said first, sounding satisfied. 'She was taken past Viralto, up to the hotel. We consulted the manager. He said he knew nothing, but we could search all the outbuildings, of which there are very many, most used for storage, but once living quarters for servants and carriage horses and farm animals. In one of the old animal feed lofts we found a tent!' He broke off for dramatic effect, and I congratulated him.

'It was folded,' he said. 'But when we opened it, it was the right size. Green canvas walls, grey floor-covering, just as she said. The floor of the loft itself was of wood, with hooks screwed into it, for the tent ropes.' He paused. 'In the house in the suburbs, we think they tied the tent ropes to the furniture.'

'Mm,' I said encouragingly.

'The loft is in a disused stable yard which is a small distance behind the hotel kitchens. It is perhaps possible she could smell baking . . . the hotel bakes its own bread.'

'Terrific,' I said.

'No, not terrific. No one there saw her. No one is saying anything. The stores of the hotel are kept in the outbuildings and there are great stocks of household items there, also cold stores for vegetables and meat, and a huge freezer room . . . vans make deliveries to these storerooms every day. I think the Signorina could have been taken to the hotel in a van, and no one would have paid much attention. There are so many outbuildings and courtyards at the back . . . garages, garden equipment stores, furniture stores for things not in use, barns full of useless objects which used to be in the old castle, ancient cooking stoves, old baths, enough rubbish to fill a town dump. You could hide for a month there. No one would find you.'

'No luck, then, with the pictures of the kidnapper?' I said.

'No. No one knew him. No one knew the two we have in jail. No one knew anything.' He sounded tired and discouraged.

'All the same,' I said, 'you do have the tent. And it's pretty certain that one of the kidnappers knew the hotel fairly well, because that loft doesn't sound like a place you'd find by accident.'

'No.' He paused. 'Unfortunately the Vistaclara has many people staying there and working there. One of the kidnappers might have stayed there, or worked there, in the past.'

'Vistaclara . . . is that the name of the hotel?' I asked.

'Yes. In the past there were horses in the stable yard, but the manager says they no longer have them, not enough people want to ride in the hills, they prefer now to play tennis.'

Horses, I thought vaguely.

'How long ago did they have horses?' I asked.

'Before the manager came. I could ask him, if you like. He said the stable yard was empty when he started, about five years ago. It has been empty ever since. Nothing has been stored there in case one day it would again be profitable to offer riding for holidays.'

'Pony trekking,' I said.

'What?'

'Riding over hills on ponies. Very popular in some parts of Britain.'

'Oh,' he said without enthusiasm. 'Anyway, there were grooms once and a riding instructor, but now they have a tennis pro instead . . . and he didn't know any of the kidnappers in our pictures.'

'It's a big hotel, then?' I said.

'Yes, quite. People go there in the summer, it is cooler than on the plains or on the coast. Just now there are thirty-eight on the staff besides the manager, and there are rooms for a hundred guests. Also a restaurant with views of the mountains.'

'Expensive?' I suggested.

'Not for the poor,' he said. 'But also not for princes. For people who have money, but not for the jet-set. A few of the guests live there always . . . old people, mostly.' He sighed. 'I asked a great many questions, as you see. No one at all, however long they had lived there, or been employed there, showed any interest in our pictures.'

We talked it over for a while longer but without reaching any conclusion except that he would try 'Vistaclara' on the talkative kidnapper the next day: and on that next day, Sunday, I drove down again to Lambourn.

Alessia had by that time been free for nearly two weeks and had progressed to pink varnish on her nails. A lifting of the spirits, I thought.

'Did you buy the varnish?' I asked.

'No . . . Popsy did.'

'Have you been shopping yet on your own?'

She shook her head. I made no comment, but she said, 'I suppose you think I ought to.'

'No. Just wondered.'

'Don't press me.'

'No.'

'You're as bad as Popsy.' She was looking at me almost with antagonism, something wholly new.

'I thought the varnish looked pretty,' I said equably.

She turned her head away with a frown, and I drank the coffee Popsy had poured before she'd walked out round her yard.

'Did Popsy ask you to come?' Alessia said sharply.

'She asked me to lunch, yes.'

'Did she complain that I've been acting like a cow?'

'No,' I said. 'Have you?'

'I don't know. I expect so. All I know is that I want to scream. To throw things. To hit someone.' She spoke indeed as if a head of steam was being held in by slightly precarious will-power.

'I'll drive you up to the Downs.'

'Why?'

'To scream. Kick the tyres. So on.'

She stood up restlessly, walked aimlessly round the kitchen and then went out of the door. I followed in a moment and found her standing halfway to the Land Rover, irresolute.

'Go on, then,' I said. 'Get in.' I made a questioning gesture to where Popsy stood, pointing to the Land Rover, and from the distance collected a nod.

The keys were in the ignition. I sat in the driver's seat and waited, and Alessia presently climbed in beside me.

'This is stupid,' she said.

I shook my head, started the engine, and drove the way we'd gone three days earlier, up to the silence and the wide sky and the calling birds.

When I braked to a stop and switched off, Alessia said defensively, 'Now what? I can't just . . . scream.'

'If you care to walk off along there on your own and see if you want to, I'll wait here.'

Without looking at me directly she did exactly as I'd said, sliding down from the Land Rover and walking away. Her narrow figure diminished in the distance but stayed in sight, and after a fair while she came slowly back. She stopped with dry eyes at the open window beside me and said calmly, 'I can't scream. It's pointless.'

I got out of the Land Rover and stood on the grass near her. I said, 'What is it about riding in the string which makes you feel trapped?'

'Did Popsy say that?'

'No, she just said you didn't want to.'

She leaned against the front wing of the Land Rover, not looking at me.

'It's nonsense,' she said. 'I don't know why. On Friday I got dressed to go. I wanted to go . . . but I felt all churned up. Breathless. Worse than before my first big race . . . but the same sort of feeling. I went downstairs, and it got much worse. Stifling. So I told Popsy I had a headache . . . which was nearly true . . . and yesterday it was just the same. I didn't even go downstairs . . . I felt so wretched, but I just couldn't . . .'

I pondered, then said, 'Start from getting up. Think of riding clothes. Think of the horses. Think of riding through the streets. Think of everything separately, one by one, and then say at what thought you begin to feel . . . churned up.'

She looked at me dubiously, but blinked a few times as she went through the process and then shook her head. 'I don't feel churned now. I don't know what it is . . . I've thought of everything. *It's the boys.*' The last three words came out as if impelled; as if unpremeditated and from the depths.

'The boys?'

'The lads.'

'What about them?'

'Their eyes.' The same erupting force.

'If you rode at the back they wouldn't see you,' I said.

'I'd think of their eyes.'

I glanced at her very troubled face. She was taking me out of my depth, I thought. She needed professional help, not my amateur common sense.

'Why their eyes?' I said.

'Eyes . . .' She spoke loudly, as if the words themselves demanded violence. 'They watched me. I knew they did. When I was asleep. They came in and watched.'

She turned suddenly towards the Land Rover and did actually kick the tyre.

'They came in. I know they did. I hate . . . I hate . . . I can't bear . . . their eyes.'

I stretched out, put my arms round her and pulled her against my chest. 'Alessia . . . Alessia . . . It doesn't matter. What if they did?'

'I feel . . . filthy . . . dirty.'

'A kind of rape?' I said.

'Yes.'

'But not . . . ?'

She shook her head silently and conclusively.

120

'How do you know they came in?' I said.

'The zip,' she said. 'I told you I knew every stitch of the tent . . . I knew how many teeth in the zip. And some days, it would open higher than others. They undid the zip . . . and came in . . . and fastened it at a different level . . . six or seven teeth higher, ten lower . . . I dreaded it.'

I stood holding her, not knowing what to say.

'I try not to care,' she said. 'But I dream . . .' She stopped for a while, then said, 'I dream about eyes.'

I rubbed one of my hands over her back, trying to comfort. 'Tell me what else,' I said. 'What else is unbearable?'

She stood quiet for so long with her nose against my chest that I thought there might be nothing, but finally, with a hard sort of coldness, she said, 'I wanted him to like me. I wanted to please him. I told Papa and Pucinelli that his voice was cold . . . but that was . . . at the beginning. When he came each time with the microphone, to make the tapes, I was . . . ingratiating.' She paused. 'I . . . loathe . . . myself. I am . . . hateful . . . and dreadfully . . . *unbearably* . . . ashamed.'

She stopped talking and simply stood there, and after a while I said, 'Very often people who are kidnapped grow to like their kidnappers. It isn't even unusual. It's as if a normal human being can't live without some sort of friendly contact. In ordinary criminal prisons, the prisoners and warders grow into definitely friendly relationships. When a lot of hostages are taken, some of them always make friends with one or more of the terrorists holding them. Hostages sometimes beg the police who are rescuing them not to harm their kidnappers. You mustn't, you shouldn't, blame yourself for trying to make the man with the microphone like you. It's normal. Usual. And . . . how did he respond?'

She swallowed. 'He called me . . . dear girl.'

'Dear girl,' I said myself, meaning it. 'Don't feel guilty. You are normal. Everyone tries to befriend their kidnappers to some extent, and it's better that they should.'

'Why?' The word was muffled, but passionate.

'Because antagonism begets antagonism. A kidnapped

person who can make the kidnappers like her is much safer. They'll be less likely to harm her . . . and more careful, for her own sake, not to let her see their faces. They wouldn't want to kill someone they'd grown to like.'

She shivered.

'And as for coming in to see you when you were asleep . . . maybe they looked on you with friendship . . . Maybe they wanted to be sure you were all right, as they couldn't see you when you were awake.'

I wasn't sure whether I believed that last bit myself, but it was at least possible: and the rest was all true.

'The lads are not the kidnappers,' I said.

'No, of course not.'

'Just other men.'

She nodded her smothered head.

'It's not the lads' eyes you dream about.'

'No.' She sighed deeply.

'Don't ride with the string until you feel OK about it. Popsy will arrange a horse for you up on the Downs.' I paused. 'Don't worry if tomorrow you still feel churned up. Knowing the reason for feelings doesn't necessarily stop them coming back.'

She stood quiet for a while and then disconnected herself slowly from my embrace, and without looking at my face said, 'I don't know where I'd be without you. In the nut-house, for sure.'

'One day,' I said mildly, 'I'll come to the Derby and cheer you home.'

She smiled and climbed into the Land Rover, but instead of pointing its nose homewards I drove on over the hill to the schooling ground.

'Where are you going?' she said.

'Nowhere. Just here.' I stopped the engine and put on the brakes. The flights of hurdles and fences lay neat and deserted on the grassy slope, and I made no move to get out of the car.

'I've been talking to Pucinelli,' I said.

'Oh.'

'He's found the second place, where you were kept those last few days.'

'Oh.' A small voice, but not panic-stricken.

'Does the Hotel Vistaclara mean anything to you?'

She frowned, thought, and shook her head.

'It's up in the mountains,' I said, 'above the place called Viralto, that you told me about. Pucinelli found the green tent there, folded, not set up, in a loft over a disused stable yard.'

'Stables?' She was surprised.

'Mm.'

She wrinkled her nose. 'There was no smell of horses.'

'They've been gone five years,' I said. 'But you said you could smell bread. The hotel makes its own, in the kitchens. The only thing is . . .' I paused, ' . . . why just bread? Why not all cooking smells?'

She looked forward through the windscreen to the peaceful rolling terrain and breathed deeply of the sweet fresh air, and calmly, without strain or tears, explained.

'At night when I had eaten the meal one of them would come and tell me to put the dish and the bucket out through the zip. I could never hear them coming because of the music. I only knew they were there when they spoke.' She paused. 'Anyway, in the morning when I woke they would come and tell me to take the bucket in again . . . and at that point it would be clean and empty.' She stopped again. 'It was then that I could smell the bread, those last few days. Early . . . when the bucket was empty.' She fell silent and then turned her head to look at me, seeking my reaction.

'Pretty miserable for you,' I said.

'Mm.' She half smiled. 'It's incredible . . . but I got used to it. One wouldn't think one could. But it was one's own smell, after all . . . and after the first few days I hardly noticed it.' She paused again. 'Those first days I thought I'd go mad. Not just from anxiety and guilt and fury . . . but from boredom. Hour after hour of nothing but that damned music . . . no one to talk to, nothing to see . . . I tried exercises, but day after day I grew less fit and more dopey, and after maybe two or three weeks I just stopped. The days seemed to run into each other, then. I just lay on the foam mattress and let the music wash in and out, and I thought about things that had happened in my life, but they seemed far away and hardly real. Reality was the bucket and pasta and a polystyrene cup of water twice a day . . . and hoping that the man with the microphone would think I was behaving well . . . and like me.'

'Mm,' I said. 'He liked you.'

'Why do you think so?' she asked, and I saw that curiously she seemed glad at the idea, that she still wanted her kidnapper to approve of her, even though she was free.

'I think,' I said, 'that if you and he had felt hate for each other he wouldn't have risked the second ransom. He would have been very much inclined to cut his losses. I'd guess he couldn't face the thought of killing you . . . because he liked you.' I saw the deep smile in her eyes and decided to straighten things up in her perspective. No good would come of her falling in love with her captor in fantasy or in retrospect. 'Mind you,' I said, 'he gave your father an appalling time and stole nearly a million pounds from your family. We may thank God he liked you, but it doesn't make him an angel.'

'Oh . . .' She made a frustrated, very Italian gesture with her hands. 'Why are you always so . . . so sensible?'

'Scottish ancestors,' I said. 'The dour sort, not the firebrands. They seem to take over and spoil the fun when the quarter of me that's Spanish aches for flamenco.'

She put her head on one side, half laughing. 'That's the most I've ever heard you say about yourself.'

'Stick around,' I said.

'I don't suppose you'll believe it,' she said, sighing deeply and stretching her limbs to relax them, 'but I am after all beginning to feel fairly sane.'

nine

July crept out in a drizzle and August swept in with a storm in a week of little activity in the London office but a good deal in Italy.

Pucinelli telephoned twice to report no progress and a third time, ecstatically, to say that Cenci's offer of a reward had borne results. The offer, along with the kidnappers' pictures, had been posted in every possible public place throughout Bologna and the whole province around; and an anonymous woman had telephoned to Paolo Cenci himself to say she knew where a part of the ransom could be found.

'Signor Cenci said she sounded spiteful. A woman scorned. She told him it would serve "him" right to lose his money. She wouldn't say who "he" was. In any case, tomorrow Signor Cenci and I go to where she says the money can be found, and if she is right, Signor Cenci will post a reward to her. The address to send the reward is a small hotel, not high class. Perhaps we will be able to find the woman and question her.'

On the following evening he sounded more moderately elated.

'It was true we found some of the money,' he said. 'But unfortunately not very much, when you think of the whole amount.'

'How much?' I asked.

'Fifty million lire.'

'That's . . . er . . .' I did rapid sums, 'nearly twenty-five thousand pounds. Hm . . . The loot of a gang member, not a principal, wouldn't you say?'

'I agree.'

'Where did you find it?' I asked.

'In a luggage locker at the railway station. The woman told Signor Cenci the number of the locker, but we had no key. We had a specialist to open the lock for us.'

'So whoever left the money thinks it's still there?'

'Yes. It is indeed still there, but we have had the lock altered. If anyone tries to open it, he will have to ask for another key. Then we catch him. We've set a good trap. The money is in a soft travel bag, with a zip. The numbers on the notes match the photographs. There is no doubt it is part of the ransom. Signor Cenci has sent a reward of five million lire and we will try to catch the woman when she collects it. He is disappointed, though, as I am, that we didn't find more.'

'Better than nothing,' I said. 'Tell me how you get on.'

There were two usual ways to deal with 'hot' money, of which the simplest was to park the loot somewhere safe until the fiercest phase of investigation was over. Crooks estimated the safety margin variously from a month to several years, and were then fairly careful to spend the money far from home, usually on something which could instantly be resold.

The second, more sophisticated method, most used for large amounts, was to sell the hot money to a sort of fence, a professional who would buy it for about two-thirds of its face value, making his profit by floating it in batches onto the unsuspecting public via the operators of casinos, markets, fairgrounds, racecourses or anywhere else where large amounts of cash changed hands quickly. By the time the hot money percolated back to far-flung banks the source of it couldn't be traced.

Some of Paolo Cenci's million quid could have been lopped by a third in such laundering, some could have been split between an unknown number of gang members, and some could have been spent in advance on outgoings, such as renting the suburban house. The expenses of a successful kidnapping were high, the ransom never wholly profit. All the same, despite its risks, it was the fastest way to a fortune yet devised, and in Italy particularly the chances of being detected and caught were approximately five per cent. In a country where no woman could walk in the streets of Rome with a handbag over her arm for fear of having it razored off by thieves on motorcycles, kidnapping was regarded as a fact of life, like ulcers.

Pucinelli telephoned two days later in a good mood to report that the woman who had collected the reward had been followed home without challenge and had proved to be the wife of a man who had served two terms in jail for raids on liquor stores. Neighbours said the man was known for chasing girls, his wife hot-bloodedly jealous. Pucinelli thought that an arrest and search of the man on suspicion would present no problems, and the next evening reported that the search had revealed the luggage locker ticket in the man's wallet. The man, identified as Giovanni Santo, was now in a cell and pouring out information like lava from a volcano.

'He is stupid,' Pucinelli said disparagingly. 'We've told him he will spend his whole life in jail if he doesn't co-operate, and he's shit scared. He has told us the names of all the kidnappers. There were seven of them altogether. Two we already have, of course, and now Santo. At this minute we have men picking up three others.'

'And Giuseppe?' I asked, as he stopped.

'Giuseppe,' he said reluctantly 'is not one of them. Giuseppe is the seventh. He was the leader. He recruited the others, who were all criminals before. Santo doesn't know Giuseppe's real name, nor where he came from, nor where he's gone. I'm afraid in this instance Santo speaks the truth.'

'You've done marvels,' I said.

He coughed modestly. 'I've been lucky. And Andrew . . . between us privately I will admit it . . . it has been most helpful to talk to you. It clears things in my mind to tell them to you. Very odd.'

'Carry right on,' I said.

'Yes. It's a pleasure,' he said; and he telephoned three days later to say they now had all six gang members in custody and had recovered a further hundred million lire of Cenci's money.

'We have also taken recordings of all six men and had voice prints made and analysed, but none of them is the voice on the tapes. And none of them is the man you saw, of whom we have the picture.'

'Giuseppe,' I said. 'On the tapes.'

'Yes,' he agreed gloomily. 'None of them knew him before. He recruited one as a stranger in a bar, and that one recruited the other five. We will convict the six, there's no doubt, but it's hollow without Giuseppe.'

'Mm.' I hesitated. 'Enrico, isn't it true that some of the students who joined the Red Brigades in their hot-headed youth grew out of it and became ordinary blameless citizens?'

'I've heard so, but of course they keep the past secret.'

'Well . . . it just struck me a day or two ago that Giuseppe might have learned the techniques of kidnapping from the Red Brigades, when he was a student, perhaps, or even as a member.'

Pucinelli said doubtfully, 'Your Identikit pictures don't match anyone with a criminal record.'

'I just wondered if it might be worthwhile to show those pictures to ex-students of about the same age, say twenty-five to forty, at perhaps some sort of students' reunion? It's a faint chance, anyway.'

'I'll try,' he said. 'But the Red Brigades, as I'm sure you know, are organised in small cells. People in one cell can't identify people in other cells because they never meet them.'

'I know it's a long shot and involves a lot of probably fruitless work,' I agreed.

'I'll think about it.'

'OK.'

'All the universities are closed for summer vacations.'

'So they are,' I said. 'But in the autumn . . .'

'I will think about it,' he said again. 'Goodnight, friend. Sleep well.'

Alessia heard from her father about the recovery of some of the ransom and from me of the capture of six of the kidnappers.

'Oh,' she said blankly.

'Your man with the microphone isn't among them.'

'Oh.' She looked at me guiltily, hearing, as I did, the faint relief in her voice. We were sitting in Popsy's minute tree-shaded garden where four lounging chairs squeezed onto a square of grass and low stone surrounding walls failed to obscure views of stableyard on three sides. We were drinking iced coffee in the heat wave which had followed the storms, clinking the cubes and being watched politely by equine heads peering in rows over half-doors.

I had invited myself down on my day off, a move neither Alessia nor Popsy had objected to, and I'd found Popsy alone when I arrived, as usual out in her yard.

'Hello,' she said, as I drew up. 'Sorry about the wet.' She was standing in green gumboots, hose in hand, watering the lower hind leg of a large chestnut horse. Bob held its head. Its eyes blinked at me as if bored. The water ran in a stream across the yard to a drain. 'It's got a leg,' Popsy said, as if that explained things.

I stifled a desire to say that as far as I could see it had four.

'Alessia walked along to the shops,' she said. 'She won't be long.' She squelched away and turned off a tap, flinging the hose in loose coils beside it. 'That'll do for now, Bob,' she said. 'Get Jamie to roll up that hose.' She dried her hands on the seat of her trousers and gave me a bright blaze from the green eyes.

'She rides, you know,' she said as Bob led the watered horse off to an empty box, 'but only up on the Downs. She goes up and down with me in the Land Rover. We don't discuss it. It's routine.'

'How is she otherwise?'

'Much happier, I'd say.' She grinned hugely and clapped me lightly on the shoulder. 'Don't know how anyone so cold can bring someone else to life.'

'I'm not cold,' I protested.

'No?' She considered me quizzically. 'There's a feeling of iron about you. Like a rod. You don't smile much. You're not intimidating . . . but I'm sure you could be, if you tried.'

I shook my head.

'Do you ever get drunk?' she said.

'Not often.'

'Never, more like.' She waved a hand towards the kitchen. 'Like a drink? It's so bloody hot.'

We went into a cool interior with her shaking off her gumboots on the doorstep, and she brought white wine from the refrigerator in the kitchen in fawn socks.

'I'll bet for instance,' she said, pouring, 'that you never get helpless giggles or sing vulgar songs or generally make an ass of yourself.'

'Often.'

She gave me an 'oh yeah' look and settled her large self comfortably onto a kitchen chair, putting her heels up on the table.

'Well, sometimes,' I said.

She drank some wine cheerfully. 'What makes you giggle, then?' she asked.

'Oh . . . one time I was with an Italian family during kidnap and they all behaved like a comic soap opera at the top of their voices, and it was painful. I had to go upstairs sometimes to stop myself laughing . . . awful giggles over and over, when really the whole thing was deadly dangerous. I had terrible trouble. My face was aching with the effort of keeping it straight.'

'Like wanting to explode in church,' Popsy said, nodding.

'Just like that.'

We sipped the cold wine and regarded each other with friendliness, and in a moment or two Alessia appeared with a bag of groceries and a welcoming smile. There was colour in her cheeks at last, and a sort of rebirth taking place of the girl she must have been before. I could see a great difference in even the carriage of her head; self respect returning to straighten the spine.

I got up at the sight of her and kissed her cheek in greeting and she put the groceries on the table and gave me a positive hug.

'Hi,' she said. 'Please note, I've been shopping. That's the third time. We are now back in business . . . no nerves, not to speak of.'

130

'Terrific.'

She poured herself some wine and the three of us amicably ate lunch, and it was afterwards, when Popsy had gone off to her office to do paperwork, that I told Alessia in the garden about the new arrests.

'Do you think they'll catch him . . . the man with the microphone?' she asked.

'He called himself Giuseppe,' I said, 'though that's almost certainly not his name. The six kidnappers knew him just as Giuseppe, and none of them knows anything else. I think he's cool and intelligent, and I'm afraid Pucinelli won't find him, or the bulk of your ransom.'

She was quiet for a while and then said, 'Poor Papa. Poor all of us. I love the house on Mikonos . . . so full of brilliant light, right by the sapphire sea . . . Papa says the money so far recovered won't be enough to save it. He says he keeps postponing putting it up for sale, just hoping . . . but it's not just its value, there's the upkeep, and the fares there two or three times a year. It was always a luxury, even before.' She paused. 'Part of my childhood. Part of my life.'

'Giuseppe took it,' I said.

She stirred slightly and finally nodded. 'Yes, you are right.'

We drank the iced coffee. Time passed tranquilly.

'I thought of going to the races next week,' she said. 'To Brighton. Mike Noland runs a lot of horses there, because he used to train in Sussex, and many of his owners still live there. I may as well go and talk to them . . . show them I'm still alive.'

'If I went,' I said, 'would I be in your way?'

She smiled at the still-watching horses. 'No, you wouldn't.'

'Which day?'

'Wednesday.'

I thought of switchboard schedules. 'I'll fix it,' I said.

Gerry Clayton having agreed with a thoroughly false martyred expression to sit in for me from four to midnight, I drove early to Lambourn to collect Alessia, pausing only for coffee and encouragement from Popsy before setting off on the three-hour trek to Brighton.

'I could have got a lift,' Alessia said. 'You didn't have to come all this huge way round.'

'Sure,' I said.

She sighed, but not apparently with regret. 'Half a dozen trainers or jockeys will be driving from here to Brighton.'

'Bully for them.'

'So I could always get a lift back.'

I looked at her sideways. 'I'll drive you unless you definitely prefer not.'

She didn't answer; just smiled. We drove to Brighton and talked of many things for which there had never been peace enough before; of likes and dislikes, places, books, people; cabbages and kings.

It was the first time, I thought, that I had seen her in a skirt: if one excepted, of course, the dress I had pulled over her unconscious head. A vision of her lean nakedness rose unbidden; an agreeable memory, to be honest. For Brighton she had covered the basics with a neat pale-coffee-coloured dress, and wore big gold earrings under the short curls.

Her reappearance on a racecourse was greeted with a warmth that almost overwhelmed her, with everyone who saw her seemingly intent on hugging her until her bones cracked. She introduced me vaguely many times but no one took any notice. The eyes were only for her, devouring her with curiosity, but also with love.

'Alessia! How super!'

'Alessia! Fantastic!'

'Alessia! Marvellous . . . smashing . . . delirious . . . terrific . . .'

She need not have doubted that Mike Noland's owners would notice her re-emergence. At least four widely-grinning couples assured her that as soon as she was fit they would be thrilled to have her back in their saddles. Mike Noland himself, big and fifty, told her it was time to leave Popsy's jumpers and come to ride work on the two-year-olds; and

132

passing bright-silked jockeys, I was interested to see, greeted
her with genuine pleasure under more casual greetings.

'Hello Alessia, how's it going?'

'How ya doing?'

'Well done; glad you're back.'

'Get your boots on, Cenci.'

Their direct camaraderie meant a lot to her. I could see the
faint apprehension of the outward journey vanishing minute
by minute, replaced by the confidence of being at home. She
kept me beside her all the same, glancing at me frequently to
check I was still there and never moving a step without being
sure I followed. One might have thought of it as courtesy
except for what had gone before.

I saw little enough of the races themselves, and nor did she,
from the press of people wanting to talk; and the afternoon
was cut short, as far as I was concerned, by a message broadcast over the loudspeakers after the fourth event.

'Would Mr Andrew Douglas please go to the Clerk of the
Course's office. Mr Andrew Douglas, please, go to the Clerk
of the Course's office.'

Alessia, looking worried, said she'd show me where the
office was, and told me that messages of that sort nearly always
meant bad news. 'I hope it's not . . . Papa,' she said. 'Popsy
would ask for you . . . so as not to frighten me.'

We went quickly to the Clerk's office, brushing away the
non-stop clutching greetings with quick smiles. Alessia's
anxiety deepened with every step, but when we arrived at the
office the Clerk of the Course himself put her fears to rest.

'I'm so sorry, Mr Douglas,' he said to me, 'but we have a
distressing message for you. Please would you ring this number
. . . ?' he handed me a slip of paper. 'Your sister has had a
bad accident. I'm so sorry.'

Alessia said 'Oh!' faintly, as if not sure whether to be glad
or horrified, and I put a hand comfortingly on her arm.

'There's a more private telephone just over there,' the Clerk
said, pointing to a small alcove at the rear. 'Do use it. How
splendid, Miss Cenci, to see you back.'

She nodded vaguely and followed me across the room. 'I'm so sorry . . .' she said.

I shook my head. I had no sister. The number on the slip of paper was that of the office. I dialled the number and was answered by Gerry Clayton.

'It's Andrew,' I said.

'Thank God. I had to tell all sorts of lies before they'd put out a call for you.'

'What happened?' I said with an amount of agitation appropriate to the circumstances.

He paused, then said, 'Can you be overheard?'

'Yes.'

The Clerk himself was listening with half an ear and Alessia with both. Two or three other people were looking my way.

'Right. I won't expect comments. There's been a boy kidnapped from the beach at West Wittering. That's about an hour's drive along the coast from Brighton, I'd guess. Go over there pronto and talk to the mother, will you?'

'Where is she?' I said.

'In the Breakwater Hotel, Beach Road, climbing the walls. I promised her we'd have someone with her in two hours, and to hang on. She's incoherent, most unhelpful. We had a telephone call from Hoppy at Lloyds, the father got in touch with his insurers and got passed along a chain to us. The father's had instructions to stay by his home telephone. Tony Vine's on his way to him now. Can you take down the number?'

'Yes, hang on.' I fumbled for pen and paper. 'Fire away.'

He read out the father's number. 'His name is John Nerrity.' He spelled it. 'The child's name is Dominic. Mother's, Miranda. Mother and son were alone in the hotel on holiday, father busy at home. Got all that?'

'Yes.'

'Get her to agree to the police.'

'Yes.'

'Hear from you later? Sorry about your day at the races.'

'I'll go at once,' I said.

'Break a leg.'

I thanked the Clerk of the Course and left his office with Alessia still looking distressed on my behalf.

'I'll have to go,' I said apologetically. 'Can you possibly get a lift back to Lambourn? With Mike Noland, perhaps?'

Even though she had herself earlier suggested it, she looked appalled at the idea and vigorously shook her head. Panic stood quite clear in her eyes.

'No,' she said. 'Can't I come with you? Please . . . I won't be a nuisance. I promise. I could help . . . with your sister.'

'You're never a nuisance, but I can't take you.' I looked down at her beseeching face, at the insecurity still so close to the surface. 'Come out to the car with me, away from these crowds, and I'll explain.'

We walked through the gates and along to the car park, and I said, 'I haven't any sisters. There was no crash. I have to go on a job . . . a child's been kidnapped, and I have to go to his mother . . . so dearest Alessia, we must find Mike Noland. You'll be safe with him. You know him well.'

She was horrified and apologetic and also shaking. 'Couldn't I comfort the mother?' she said. 'I could tell her . . . her child will come back . . . as I did?'

I hesitated, knowing the suggestion stemmed from her not wanting to go home with Mike Noland but also thinking that perhaps it made sense. Perhaps Alessia would indeed be good for Miranda Nerrity.

I looked at my watch. 'Mrs Nerrity's expecting me,' I said indecisively, and she interrupted sharply, 'Who? Who did you say?'

'Nerrity. Miranda Nerrity. But . . .'

Her mouth had literally fallen open. 'But I know her,' she said. 'Or at least, I've met her . . . Her husband is John Nerrity, isn't he?'

I nodded, nonplussed.

'Their horse won the Derby,' Alessia said.

I lifted my head.

Horses.

So many horses.

'What is it,' Alessia said. 'Why do you look so . . . bleak?'

'Right,' I said, not directly answering. 'Get in the car. I'd be glad for you to come, if you really mean it. But there's a good chance we won't be going back to Lambourn tonight. Would you mind that?'

For answer she slid into the front passenger seat and closed the door, and I walked round to climb in beside her.

As I started the engine and drove out of the gate she said, 'The Nerritys' horse won the Derby last year. Ordinand. Don't you remember?'

'Um . . .' No, actually, I didn't.

'It wasn't one of the really greats,' she said assessingly, 'or at least no one thought so. He was an outsider. Thirty-three to one. But he's been winning this year quite well.' She stopped. 'I can't bear to think of that child.'

'His name's Dominic,' I said. 'Haul the map out of the glove compartment and find the fastest route to Chichester.'

She reached for the map. 'How old is he?'

'Don't know.'

We sped westwards through Sussex in the golden afternoon and came eventually to the Breakwater Hotel, right on the pebbly beach at West Wittering.

'Look,' I said, putting on brakes and pulling off my tie. 'Behave like a holidaymaker. Walk into the hotel slowly. Smile. Talk to me. Don't seem worried. OK?'

She looked at me with puzzlement turning to comprehension. 'Do you think . . . someone's watching?'

'Someone usually is,' I said astringently. 'Always take it for granted that someone is. Kidnappers post watchers to make sure the police don't arrive in huge numbers.'

'Oh.'

'So we're on holiday.'

'Yes,' she said.

'Let's go in.'

We climbed, stretching, out of the car, and Alessia wand-

136

ered a few steps away from the hotel to look out to the English Channel, shading her eyes and speaking to me over her shoulder. 'I'm going in for a swim.'

I put my arm round her shoulders and stood beside her for a few seconds, then with me saying teasingly 'Mind the jellyfish' we walked through the hotel's glass entrance doors into a wide armchair-scattered lounge. A few people sat around drinking tea, and a girl in a black dress was moving to and fro behind a polished brown counter labelled 'Reception'.

'Hello,' I said, smiling. 'We think a friend of ours is staying here. A Mrs Nerrity?'

'And Dominic,' Alessia said.

'That's right,' the girl said calmly. She looked at a guest list. 'Room sixty-three . . . but they're probably still on the beach. Lovely day, isn't it?'

'Gorgeous,' Alessia agreed.

'Could you give their room a ring?' I asked. 'Just in case.'

The girl obligingly turned to the switchboard and was surprised at receiving an answer. 'Pick up the 'phone,' she said, pointing to a handset on the counter, and I lifted the receiver with an appropriate smile.

'Miranda?' I said. 'This is Andrew Douglas.'

'Where are you?' a small voice said tearfully.

'Downstairs, here in the hotel.'

'Oh . . . Come up . . . I can't bear . . .'

'On my way,' I said.

The girl gave us directions which we followed to a room with twin beds, private bathroom, view of the sea. Miranda Nerrity opened her door to us with swollen eyes and a clutched, soaking handkerchief and said between gulps, 'They said . . . the man in London said . . . you would get Dominic back . . . he promised me . . . Andrew Douglas will get him back . . . he always does, he said . . . don't worry . . . but how can I not worry? Oh my God . . . my baby . . . Get him back for me. Get him back.'

'Yes,' I said gently. 'Come and sit down,' I put my arm round her shoulders this time, not Alessia's, and guided her over to one of the armchairs. 'Tell us what happened. Then we'll make a plan to get him back.'

Miranda took a very small grip on things, recognising Alessia with surprise and pointing to a piece of paper which lay on one of the beds.

'A little girl gave it to me,' she said, the tears rolling. 'She said a man had asked her. Oh dear . . . oh dear . . .'

'How old was the little girl?' I asked.

'What? Oh . . . eight . . . something like that . . . I don't know.'

Alessia knelt beside Miranda to comfort her, her own face pale again and taut with strain, and I picked up the sheet of paper and unfolded it, and read its brutal block-lettered message.

WE'VE TAKEN YOUR KID. GIVE YOUR OLD MAN A BELL. TELL HIM TO GO HOME. WE'LL TELL YOUR HUBBY WHAT WE WANT. DON'T GO SQUAWKING AROUND. TELL NO ONE AT ALL, SEE. IF YOU WANT TO SEE YOUR KID AGAIN DON'T GO TO THE POLICE. WE'LL TIE A PLASTIC BAG OVER HIS HEAD IF YOU GET THE POLICE. SAVVY?

I lowered the page. 'How old is Dominic?' I asked.

'Three and a half,' Miranda said.

ten

Miranda, twenty-six, had long blond hair falling from a centre parting and on other occasions might have been pretty. She still wore a bathing suit with a towelling robe over, and there was still sand on her legs from the beach. Her eyes were glazed behind the puffed eyelids as if too much devastated emotion had put a film over them to repel reality, and she made vague

138

pointless movements with her hands as if total inactivity was impossible.

Out of habit I carried with me a flat container like a cigarette case, which contained among other things a small collection of pills. I took out the case, opened it, and sorted out a strip of white tablets in foil.

'Take one of these,' I said, fetching water in a toothmug and sliding a pill from its wrapper.

Miranda simply swallowed as instructed. It was Alessia who said, 'What are you giving her?'

'Tranquilliser.'

'Do you carry those round with you always?' she asked incredulously.

'Mostly,' I nodded. 'Tranquillisers, sleeping pills, aspirins, things for heart attacks. First aid, that's all.'

Miranda drank all the water.

'Do they have room service in this hotel?' I asked.

'What?' she said vaguely. 'Yes, I suppose so . . . They'll be bringing Dominic's supper soon. . . .' The idea of it reduced her to fresh deep sobs, and Alessia put her arm round her and looked shattered.

I telephoned to room service for tea, strong, as soon as possible, for three. Biscuits? Certainly biscuits. Coming right away, they said: and with very little delay the tray arrived, with me meeting the maid at the door and thanking her for her trouble.

'Mrs Nerrity, drink this,' I said, putting down the tray and pouring tea for her. 'And eat the biscuits.' I poured another cup for Alessia. 'You too,' I said.

The girls each drank and ate like automatons, and slowly in Miranda the combined simple remedies of tranquilliser, caffeine and carbohydrate took the worst edge off the pain so that she could bear to describe what happened.

'We were on the sand . . . with his bucket and spade . . . making a sandcastle. He loves making sandcastles . . .' She stopped and swallowed, tears trickling down her cheeks. 'A lot of the sand was wet, and I'd left our things up on the

shingle . . . towels, a beach chair, our lunch box, packed by
the hotel, Dominic's toys. . . . It was a lovely hot day, not
windy like usual . . . I went up to sit on the chair . . . I was
watching him all the time, he was only thirty yards away . . .
less, less . . . squatting, playing with his bucket and spade,
patting the sandcastle. . .. I was watching him all the time,
I really was.' Her voice tapered off into a wail, the dreadful
searing guilt sounding jagged and raw.

'Were there a lot of people on the beach?' I asked.

'Yes, yes there were . . . it was so warm. . . . But I was
watching him, I could see him all the time. . . .'

'And what happened?' I said.

'It was the boat. . . .'

'What boat?'

'The boat on fire. I was watching it. Everyone was watching
it. And then . . . when I looked back . . . he wasn't there. I
wasn't scared. It was less than a minute . . . I thought he'd
be going over to look at the boat. . . . I was looking for him
. . . and then the little girl gave me the note . . . and I read
it. . . .'

The awfulness of that moment swept over her again like a
tidal wave. The cup and saucer rattled and Alessia took them
from her.

'I shouted for him everywhere . . . I ran up and down. . . .
I couldn't believe it . . . I couldn't . . . I'd seen him such a
short time ago, just a minute . . . and then I came up here
. . . I don't know how I got up here . . . I telephoned John
. . . and I've left all our things . . . on the beach.'

'When is high tide?' I said.

She looked at me vaguely. 'This morning. . . . The tide had
just gone out . . . the sand was all wet. . . .'

'And the boat? Where was the boat?'

'On the sand.'

'What sort of boat?' I asked.

She looked bewildered. 'A sailing dinghy. What does it
matter? There are millions of sailing dinghies round here.'

But millions of sailing dinghies didn't go on fire at the

exact moment that a small child was kidnapped. A highly untrustworthy coincidence of timing.

'Both of you drink more tea,' I said. 'I'll go down and fetch the things from the beach. Then I'll ring Mr Nerrity . . .'

'No,' Miranda interrupted compulsively. 'Don't. Don't.'

'But we must.'

'He's so angry,' she said piteously. 'He's . . . livid. He says it's my fault. . . . He's so angry . . . you don't know what he's like . . . I don't want to talk to him. . . . I can't.'

'Well,' I said. 'I'll telephone from another place. Not this room. I'll be as quick as I can. Will you both be all right?'

Alessia nodded, although she was herself shaking, and I went downstairs and found a public telephone tucked into a private corner of the entrance hall.

Tony Vine answered from John Nerrity's number.

'Are you alone?' I asked.

'No. Are you?'

'Yes. What's the score?'

'The pinchers have told him he'll get his boy safe . . . on conditions.'

'Such as?'

'Five million.'

'For God's sake,' I said, 'has he got five million?' The Breakwater Hotel, nice enough, wasn't a millionaire's playground.

'He's got a horse,' Tony said baldly.

A horse.

Ordinand, winner of the Derby.

'Ordinand?' I said.

'No slouch, are you? Yeah, Ordinand. The pinchers want him to sell it at once.'

'How did they tell him?' I asked.

'On the telephone. No tap, of course, at that point. He says it was a rough voice full of slang. Aggressive. A lot of threats.'

I told Tony about the block-lettered note. 'Same level of language?'

'Yeah.' Tony's occasional restraint in the matter of eff this

141

and eff that was always a source of wonder, but in fact he seldom let rip in front of clients. 'Mr Nerrity's chief, not to say sole, asset, as I understand it, is the horse. He is . . . er . . .'

'Spitting mad?' I suggested.

'Yeah.'

I half smiled. 'Mrs Nerrity is faintly scared of him.'

'Not in the least surprising.'

I told Tony how the kidnap had been worked and said I thought the police ought to investigate the dinghy very fast.

'Have you told the local fuzz anything yet?'

'No. Miranda will take a bit of persuading. I'll do it next. What have you told them from your end?'

'Nothing so far. I tell Mr Nerrity we can't help him without the police, but you know what it's like.'

'Mm. I'll call you again, shortly.'

'Yeah.' He put his receiver down and I strolled out of the hotel and rolled my trouser legs up to the knees on the edge of the shingle, sliding down the banks of pebbles in great strides towards the sand. Once there I took off shoes and socks and ambled along carrying them, enjoying the evening sun.

There were a few breakwaters at intervals along the beach, black fingers stretching stumpily seawards, rotten in places and overgrown with molluscs and seaweed. Miranda's chair, towels and paraphernalia were alone on the shingle, most other people having packed up for the day; and not far away there was still a red plastic bucket and a blue plastic spade on the ground beside a half-trampled sandcastle. The British seaside public, I reflected, were still remarkably honest.

The burnt remains of the dinghy were the focal point for the few people still on the sand, the returning tide already swirling an inch deep around the hull. I walked over there as if drawn like everyone else, and took the closest possible look, paddling, like others, to see inside the shell.

The boat had been fibreglass and had melted as it burned. There were no discernible registration numbers on what was left of the exterior, and although the mast, which was aluminium, had survived the blaze and still pointed heavenward like an exclamation mark, the sail, which would have born identification, lay in ashes round its foot. Something in the scorched mess might tell a tale – but the tide was inexorable.

'Shouldn't we try to haul it up to the shingle?' I suggested to a man paddling like myself.

He shrugged. 'Not our business.'

'Has anyone told the police?' I said.

He shrugged again. 'Search me.'

I paddled round to the other side of the remains and tried another more responsible-looking citizen but he too shook his head and muttered about being late already, and it was two fourteen-sized boys, overhearing, who said they would give me a hand, if I liked.

They were strong and cheerful. They lifted, strained, staggered willingly. The keel slid up the sand leaving a deep single track and between us we manhandled it up the shingle to where the boys said the tide wouldn't reach it to whisk it away.

'Thanks,' I said.

They beamed. We all stood hands on hips admiring the result of our labours and then they too said they had to be off home to supper. They loped away, vaulting a breakwater, and I collected the bucket and spade and all Miranda's belongings and carried them up to her room.

Neither she nor Alessia was in good shape, and Alessia, if anything, seemed the more relieved at my return. I gave her a reassuring hug, and to Miranda I said, 'We're going to have to get the police.'

'No.' She was terrified. 'No . . . no . . .

'Mm.' I nodded. 'Believe me, it's best. The people who've taken Dominic don't want to kill him, they want to sell him back to you safe and sound. Hold on to that. The police will be very helpful and we can arrange things so that the kidnappers won't know we've told them. I'll do that. The police will want to know what Dominic was wearing on the beach, and if you have a photograph, that would be great.'

She wavered helplessly. 'John said . . . keep quiet, I'd done enough damage. . . .'

I picked up the telephone casually and got through again to her husband's number. Tony again answered.

'Andrew,' I said.

'Oh.' His voice lost its tension; he'd been expecting the kidnappers.

'Mrs Nerrity will agree to informing the police on her husband's say-so.'

'Go ahead then. He understands we can't act for him without. He . . . er . . . doesn't want us to leave him. He's just this minute decided, when he heard the 'phone ring.'

'Good. Hang on . . .' I turned to Miranda. 'Your husband says we can tell the police. Do you want to talk to him?'

She shook her head violently. 'OK.' I said to Tony. 'Let's get started and I'll call you later.'

'What was the kid wearing?' he asked.

I repeated the question to Miranda and between new sobs she said red bathing trunks. Tiny towelling trunks. No shoes, no shirt . . . it had been hot.

Tony grunted and rang off, and as unhurriedly as I could I asked Miranda to put some clothes on and come out driving with me in my car. Questioning, hesitant and fearful she nevertheless did what was needed, and presently, having walked out of the hotel in scarf and sunglasses between Alessia and myself, sat with Alessia in the rear seats as I drove all three of us in the direction of Chichester.

Checks on our tail and an unnecessary detour showed no one following, and with one pause to ask directions I stopped the car near the main police station but out of sight of it, round a corner. Inside the station I asked for the senior officers on duty, and presently explained to a chief inspector and a CID man how things stood.

I showed them my own identification and credentials, and one of them, fortunately, knew something of Liberty Market's work. They looked at the kidnappers' threatening note with the blankness of shock, and rapidly paid attention to the account of the death of the dinghy.

'We'll be on to that straight away,' said the Chief Inspector, stretching a hand to the telephone. 'No one's reported it yet, as far as I know.'

'Er. . . .' I said. 'Send someone dressed as a seaman. Gumboots. Seaman's sweater. Don't let them behave like policemen, it would be very dangerous for the child.'

The Chief Inspector drew back from the telephone, frowning. Kidnapping in England was so comparatively rare that very few local forces had any experience of it. I repeated that the death threat to Dominic was real and should be a prime consideration in all procedure.

'Kidnappers are full of adrenalin and easily frightened,' I said. 'It's when they think they're in danger of being caught that they kill . . . and bury . . . the victim. Dominic really is in deadly danger, but we'll get him back safe if we're careful.'

After a silence the CID officer, who was roughly my own age, said they would have to call in his super.

'How long will that take?' I asked. 'Mrs Nerrity is outside in my car with a woman friend, and I don't think she can stand very much waiting. She's highly distressed.'

They nodded. Telephoned. Guardedly explained. The super, it transpired to their relief, would speed back to his office within ten minutes.

Detective Superintendent Eagler could have been born to be a plain-clothes cop. Even though I was expecting him I gave the thin, harmless-looking creature who came into the room no more than a first cursory glance. He had wispy balding hair and a scrawny neck rising from an ill-fitting shirt. His suit looked old and saggy and his manner seemed faintly apologetic. It was only when the other two men straightened at his arrival that with surprise I realised who he was.

He shook my hand, not very firmly, perched a thin rump on one corner of the large official desk, and asked me to ıdentify myself. I gave him one of the firm's business cards with my name on. With neither haste nor comment he dialled the office number and spoke, I supposed, to Gerry Clayton. He made no remark about whatever answers Gerry gave him, but merely said 'Thanks' and put down the receiver.

'I've studied other cases,' he said directly to me and without more preamble. 'Lesley Whittle . . . and others that went wrong. I want no such disasters on my patch. I'll listen to your advice, and if it seems good to me, I'll act on it. Can't say more than that.'

I nodded and again suggested seamen-lookalikes to collect the dinghy, to which he instantly agreed, telling his junior to doll himself up and take a partner, without delay.

'Next?' he asked.

I said, 'Would you talk to Mrs Nerrity in my car, not in here? I don't think she should be seen in a police station. I don't think even that I should walk with you directly to her. I could meet you somewhere. One may be taking precautions quite unnecessarily, but some kidnappers are very thorough and suspicious, and one's never quite sure.'

He agreed and left before me, warning his two colleagues to say nothing whatever yet to anyone else.

'Especially not before the press blackout has been arranged,' I added. 'You could kill the child. Seriously; I mean it.'

They gave earnest assurances, and I walked back to the car to find both girls near to collapse. 'We're going to pick someone up,' I said. 'He's a policeman, but he doesn't look like it. He'll help to get Dominic back safely and to arrest the kidnappers.' I sighed inwardly at my positive voice, but if I couldn't give Miranda even a shred of confidence, I could give her nothing. We stopped for Eagler at a crossroads near the cathedral, and he slid without comment into the front passenger seat.

Again I drove a while on the look-out for company, but as far as I could see no kidnappers had risked it. After a few miles I stopped in a parking place on the side of a rural road, and Eagler got Miranda again to describe her dreadful day.

'What time was it?' he said.

'I'm not sure. . . . After lunch. We'd eaten out lunch.'

'Where was your husband, when you telephoned him?'

'In his office. He's always there by two.'

Miranda was exhausted as well as tearful. Eagler, who was having to ask his questions over the clumsy barrier of the front seats, made a sketchy stab at patting her hand in a fatherly way. She interpreted the intention behind the gesture and wept the harder, choking over the details of red swimming trunks, no shoes, brown eyes, fair hair, no scars, suntanned skin . . . they'd been at the seaside for nearly two weeks . . . they were going home on Saturday.

'She ought to go home to her husband tonight,' I said to Eagler, and although he nodded, Miranda vehemently protested.

'He's so angry with me. . . .' she wailed.

'You couldn't help it,' I said. 'The kidnappers have probably been waiting their chance for a week or more. Once your husband realises. . . .'

But Miranda shook her head and said I didn't understand.

'That dinghy,' Eagler said thoughtfully, 'the one which burnt . . . had you seen it on the beach on any other day?'

Miranda glanced at him vaguely as if the question were unimportant. 'The last few days have been so windy . . . we haven't sat on the beach much. Not since the weekend, until today. We've mostly been by the pool, but Dominic doesn't like that so much because there's no sand.'

'The hotel has a pool?' Eagler asked.

'Yes, but last week we were always on the beach . . . Everything was so simple, just Dominic and me.' She spoke between sobs, her whole body shaking.

Eagler glanced at me briefly, 'Mr Douglas, here,' he said to Miranda, 'he says you'll get him back safe. We all have to act calmly, Mrs Nerrity. Calm and patience, that's the thing. You've had a terrible shock, I'm not trying to minimise it, but what we have to think of now is the boy. To think calmly for the boy's sake.'

Alessia looked from Eagler to me and back again. 'You're both the same,' she said blankly. 'You've both seen so much suffering . . . so much distress. You both know how to make it so that people can hold on. . . . It makes the unbearable . . . possible.'

Eagler gave her a look of mild surprise, and in a totally unconnected thought I concluded that his clothes hung loosely about him because he'd recently lost weight.

'Alessia herself was kidnapped,' I explained to him. 'She knows too much about it.' I outlined briefly what had happened in Italy, and mentioned the coincidence of the horses.

His attention focused in a thoroughly Sherlockian manner.

'Are you saying there's a positive significance?'

I said, 'Before Alessia I worked on another case in Italy in which the family sold their shares in a racecourse to raise the ransom.'

He stared. 'You do, then, see a . . . a thread?'

'I fear there's one, yes.'

'Why fear?' Alessia asked.

'He means,' Eagler said, 'that the three kidnaps have been organised by the same perpetrator. Someone normally operating within the racing world and consequently knowing which targets to hit. Am I right?'

'On the button,' I agreed, talking chiefly to Alessia. 'The choice of target is often a prime clue to the identity of the kidnappers. I mean . . . to make the risks worthwhile, most kidnappers make sure in advance that the family or business actually can pay a hefty ransom. Of course every family will pay what they can, but the risks are just as high for a small ransom as a large, so it makes more sense to aim for the large. To know, for instance, that your father is much richer than the father of most other jockeys, girls or not.'

Alessia's gaze seemed glued to my face. 'To know . . . that the man who owns Ordinand has a son . . . ?' She stopped, the sentence unfinished, the thought trotting on.

'Yes,' I said.

She swallowed. 'It costs just as much to keep a bad horse in training as a good one. I mean, I do clearly understand what you're saying.'

Miranda seemed not to have been listening but the tears had begun to dry up, like a storm passing.

'I don't want to go home tonight,' she said in a small voice. But if I go . . . Alessia, will you come with me?'

Alessia looked as if it were the last thing she could face and I answered on her behalf, 'No, Mrs Nerrity, it wouldn't be a good idea. Have you a mother, or a sister . . . someone you like? Someone your husband likes?'

Her mordant look said as much as words about the current state of her marriage, but after a moment or two she said faintly, 'I suppose . . . my mother.'

'That's right,' Eagler said paternally. 'Now would you two ladies just wait a few minutes while I walk a little way with Mr Douglas?'

'We won't be out of sight,' I said.

All the same they both looked as insecure as ever as we opened the front doors and climbed out. I looked back as we walked away and waggled a reassuring hand at their two anxious heads showing together from the rear seat.

'Very upsetting,' Eagler observed as we strolled away. 'But she'll get her kid back, with a bit of luck, not like some I've dealt with. Little kids snatched at random by psychos and murdered . . . sexual, often. Those mothers. . . . Heartbreaking. Rotten. And quite often we know the psychos. Know they'll probably do something violent one day. Kill someone. We can often arrest them within a day of the body being found. But we can't prevent them. We can't keep them locked up for ever, just in case. Nightmare, those people. We've got one round here now. Time bomb waiting to go off. And some poor kid, somewhere, will be cycling along, or walking, at just the wrong time, just the wrong place. Some woman's kid. Something triggers the psycho. You never know what it is. Something small. Tips them over. After, they don't know why they've done it, like as not.'

'Mm,' I said. 'Worse than kidnappers. With them there's always hope.'

During his dissertation he'd given me several sideways glances: reinforcing his impressions, I thought. And I too had been doing the same, getting to know what to expect of him, good or bad. Occasionally someone from Liberty Market came across a policeman who thought of us as an unnecessary nuisance encroaching on their jealously-guarded preserves, but on the whole they accepted us along the lines of if you want to understand a wreck, consult a diver.

'What can you tell me that you wouldn't want those two girls to hear?' he asked.

I gave him a small smile; got reserved judgement back.

'The man who kidnapped Alessia,' I said, 'recruited local talent. He recruited one, who roped in another five. The carabinieri have arrested those six, but the leader vanished. He called himself Giuseppe, which will do for now. We produced a drawing of him and flooded the province with it, with no results. I'll let you have a copy of it, if you like,' I paused. 'I know it's a long shot. This horse thing may be truly and simply a coincidence.'

Eagler put his head on one side. 'File it under fifty-fifty, then.'

'Right. And there's today's note. . . .'

'Nothing Italian about that, eh?' Eagler looked genial. 'But local talent? Just the right style for local talent, wouldn't you say?'

'Yes, I would.'

'Just right for an Italian leaning over the local talent's shoulder saying in broken English "tell her to telephone her husband, tell her not to inform the police".' He smiled fleetingly. 'But that's all conjecture, as they say.'

We turned as of one accord and began to stroll back to the car.

'The girl jockey's a bit jumpy still,' he said.

'It does that to them. Some are jumpy with strangers for ever.'

'Poor girl,' he said, as if he hadn't thought of freedom having problems; victims naturally being vastly less interesting than villains to the strong arm of the law.

I explained about Tony Vine being at that moment with John Nerrity, and said that Nerrity's local force would also by now know about Dominic. Eagler noted the address and said he would 'liaise'.

'I expect Tony Vine will be in charge from our point of view,' I said. 'He's very bright, if you have any dealings with him.'

'All right.'

We arranged that I would send the photostats of Giuseppe and a report on Alessia's kidnapping down to him on the first morning train; and at that point we were back at the car.

'Right then, Mr Douglas.' He shook my hand limply as if sealing a bargain, as different from Pucinelli as a tortoise from a hare; one wily, one sharp, one wrinkled in his carapace, one leanly taut in his uniform, one always on the edge of his nerves, one avuncularly relaxed.

I thought that I would rather be hunted by Pucinelli, any day.

eleven

John Nerrity was a heavily-built man of medium height with greying hair cut neat and short; clipped moustache to match. On good days I could imagine him generating a fair amount of charm, but on that evening I saw only a man accustomed to power who had married a girl less than half his age and looked like regretting it.

They lived in a large detached house on the edge of a golf course near Sutton, south of London, only about three miles distant from where their four-legged wonder had made a fortune on Epsom Downs.

The exterior of the house, in the dusk of our arrival, had revealed itself as thirties-developed Tudor, but on a restrained and successful scale. Inside, the carpets wall-to-wall looked untrodden, the brocade chairs un-sat-on, the silk cushions unwrinkled, the paper and paint unscuffed. Unfaded velvet curtains hung in stiff regular folds from beneath elaborate pelmets, and upon several glass and chromium coffee tables lay large glossy books, unthumbed. There were no photographs and no flowers, and the pictures had been chosen to occupy wall-space, not the mind; the whole thing more like a shop-window than the home of a little boy.

John Nerrity was holding a gin and tonic with ice clinking and lemon slice floating, a statement in itself of his resistance to crisis. I couldn't imagine Paolo Cenci organising ice and lemon six hours after the first ransom demand: it had been almost beyond him to pour without spilling.

With Nerrity were Tony Vine, wearing his most enigmatic expression, and another man, sour of mouth and bitter of eye, who spoke with Tony's accent and looked vaguely, in his flannels and casual sweater, as if he'd been out for a stroll with his dog.

'Detective Superintendent Rightsworth,' Tony said, introducing him deadpan. 'Waiting to talk to Mrs Nerrity.'

Rightsworth gave me barely a nod, and that more of repression than of acknowledgement. One of those, I thought. A civilian-hater. One who thought of the police as 'us' and the public as 'them', the 'them' being naturally inferior. It always surprised me that policemen of that kind got promoted, but Rightsworth was proof enough that they did. The old ridiculous joke of 'Where do the police live? In Letsby Avenue,' crossed my mind; and Popsy would have appreciated my struggle to keep a straight face.

Alessia and Miranda had come into the sitting room close together and a step behind me, as if using me as a riot shield: and it was clear from John Nerrity's face that the first sight of his wife prompted few loving, comforting or supportive feelings.

He gave her no kiss. No greeting. He merely said, as if in a continuing conversation, 'Do you realise that Ordinand isn't mine to sell? Do you realise we're in hock to the limit? No, you don't. You can't do anything. Not even something simple like looking after a kid.'

Miranda crumpled behind me and sank to the floor. Alessia and I bent to help her up, and I said to Miranda's ear, 'People who are frightened are often angry and say things that hurt. He's as frightened as you are. Hang on to that.'

'What are you mumbling about?' Nerrity demanded. 'Miranda, for Christ's sake get up, you look a wreck.' He stared with disfavour at the ravaged face and untidy hair of his son's mother, and with only the faintest flicker of overdue compassion said impatiently, 'Get up, get up, they say it wasn't your fault.'

She would always think it had been, though; and so would he. Few people understood how persistent, patient, ingenious and fast committed kidnappers could be. Whomever they planned to take, they took.

Rightsworth said he wanted to ask Mrs Nerrity some questions and guided her off to a distant sofa, followed by her bullish husband with his tinkling glass.

Alessia sat in an armchair as if her legs were giving way, and Tony and I retreated to a window seat to exchange quiet notes.

'He . . .' Tony jerked his head towards Nerrity, 'has been striding up and down here wearing holes in the effing carpet and calling his wife an effing cow. All sorts of names. Didn't know some of them myself.' He grinned wolfishly. 'Takes them like that, sometimes, of course.'

'Pour the anger on someone that won't kick back?'

'Poor little bitch.'

'Any more demands?' I asked.

'Zilch. All pianissimo. That ray of sunshine Rightsworth brought a suitcase full of bugging gear with him from the telephone blokes but he didn't know how to use half of it, I ask you. I fixed the tap on the 'phone myself. Can't bear to see effing amateurs mucking about.'

'I gather he doesn't like us,' I said.

'Rightsworth? Despises the ground we walk on.'

'Is it true John Nerrity can't raise anything on the horse?'

I'd asked very quietly, but Tony looked round to make sure neither the Nerritys nor Rightsworth could hear the answer. 'He was blurting it all out, when I got here. Seems his effing business is dicky and he's pledged bits of that horse to bail him out. Borrowed on it, you might say. All this bluster, I reckon it's because he hasn't a hope of raising the wherewithal to get his nipper back, he's in a blue funk and sending his effing underpants to the laundry.'

'What did he say about our fee?'

'Yeah.' Tony looked at me sideways. 'Took him in the gut. He says he can't afford us. Then he begs me not to go. He's not getting on too effing well with Rightsworth, who would? So there he is, knackered every which way and taking it out on the lady wife.' He glanced over at Miranda who was again in tears. 'Seems she was his secretary. That's her photo, here on this table. She was a knockout, right enough.'

I looked at the glamorous studio-lit portrait; a divinely pretty face with fine bones, wide eyes and the hint of a smile. A likeness taken just before marriage, I guessed, at the point of her maximum attraction: before life rolled on and trampled over the heady dreams.

'Did you tell him we'd help him for nothing?' I asked.

'No, I effing didn't. I don't like him, to be honest.'

We sometimes did, as a firm, work for no pay: it depended on circumstances. All the partners agreed that a family in need should get help regardless, and none of us begrudged it. We never charged enough anyway to make ourselves rich, being in existence on the whole to defeat extortion, not to practise it. A flat fee, plus expenses: no percentages. Our clients knew for sure that the size of the ransom in no way affected our own reward.

154

The telephone rang suddenly, making everyone in the room jump. Both Tony and Rightsworth gestured to Nerrity to answer it and he walked towards it as if it were hot. I noticed that he pulled his stomach in as the muscles tightened and saw his breath become shallow. If the room had been silent I guessed we would actually have heard his heart thump. By the time he stretched out an unsteady hand to pick up the receiver Tony had the recorder running and the amplifier set so that everyone in the room could hear the caller's words.

'Hello,' Nerrity said hoarsely.

'Is that you, John?' It was a woman's voice, high and anxious. 'Are you expecting me?'

'Oh.' Miranda jumped to her feet in confusion. 'It's Mother. I asked her . . .' Her voice tailed off as her husband held out the receiver with the murderous glare of a too-suddenly released tension, and she managed to take it from him without touching him skin to skin.

'Mother?' she said, waveringly, 'Yes, please do come. I thought you were coming . . .'

'My dear girl, you sounded so flustered when you telephoned earlier. Saying you wouldn't tell me what was wrong! I was worried. I don't like to interfere between you and John, you know that.'

'Mother, just come.'

'No, I . . .'

John Nerrity snatched the telephone out of his wife's grasp and practically shouted, 'Rosemary, just come. Miranda needs you. Don't argue. Get here as fast as you can. Right?' He crashed the receiver down in annoyance, and I wondered whether or not the masterfully bossy tone would indeed fetch the parent. The telephone rang again almost immediately and Nerrity snatched it up in fury, saying 'Rosemary, I told you . . .'

'John Nerrity, is it?' a voice said. Male, loud, aggressive, threatening. Not Rosemary. My own spine tingled. Tony hovered over the recording equipment, checking the quivering needles.

'Yes,' Nerrity said breathlessly, his lungs deflating.

'Listen once. Listen good. You'll find a tape in a box by your front gate. Do what it says.' There was a sharp click followed by the dialling tone, and then Tony, pressing buttons, was speaking to people who were evidently telephone engineers.

'Did you get the origin of the second call?' he asked. We read the answer on his face. 'OK,' he said resignedly. 'Thanks.' To Nerrity he said, 'They need fifteen seconds. Better than the old days. Trouble is, the crooks know it too.'

Nerrity was on his way to the front door and could presently be heard crunching across his gravel.

Alessia was looking very frail indeed. I went down on my knees by her chair and put my arms protectively around her.

'You could wait in another room,' I said. 'Watch television. Read a book.'

'You know I can't.'

'I'm sorry about all this.'

She gave me a rapid glance. 'You tried to get me to go home to Popsy. It's my own fault I'm here. I'm all right. I won't be a nuisance, I promise.' She swallowed. 'It's all so odd . . . to see it from the other side.'

'You're a great girl,' I said. 'Popsy told me so, and she's right.'

She looked a small shade less fraught and rested her head briefly on my shoulder. 'You're my foundations, you know,' she said. 'Without you the whole thing would collapse.'

'I'll be here,' I said. 'But seriously it would be best if you and Miranda went into the kitchen and found some food. Get her to eat. Eat something yourself. Carbohydrate. Biscuits, cake – something like that.'

'Fattening,' she said automatically: the jockey talking.

'Best for your bodies just now, though. Carbohydrates are a natural tranquilliser. It's why unhappy people eat and eat.'

'You do know the most extraordinary things.'

'And also,' I said, 'I don't want Miranda to hear what's on the tape.'

156

'Oh.' Her eyes widened as she remembered. 'Pucinelli switched off that tape . . . so I couldn't hear.'

'Yes. It was horrid. So will this be. The first demands are always the most frightening. The threats will be designed to pulverise. To goad Nerrity into paying anything, everything, very quickly, to save his little son. So dearest Alessia, take Miranda into the kitchen and eat cake.'

She smiled a shade apprehensively and walked over to Miranda, who was sobbing periodically in isolated gulps, like hiccups, but who agreed listlessly to making a cup of tea. The two girls went off to their haven, and Nerrity crunched back with a brown cardboard box.

Rightsworth importantly took charge of opening it, telling everyone else to stand back. Tony's eyebrows were sardonic. Rightsworth produced a pair of clear plastic gloves and methodically put them on before carefully slitting with a penknife the heavy adhesive tape fastening the lid.

Opening the box Rightsworth first peered inside, then put an arm in and brought out the contents: one cassette tape, in plastic case, as expected.

Nerrity looked at it as if it would bite and waved vaguely at an ornate stretch of gilt and padded wall unit, some of whose doors proved to be screening a bank of expensive stereo. Rightsworth found a slot for the cassette, which he handled carefully with the plastic gloves, and Nerrity pushed the relevant buttons.

The voice filled the room, harsh, thunderous, uncompromising.

'Now, you, Nerrity, you listen good.'

I took three quick strides and turned down the volume, on the grounds that threats fortissimo would sound even worse than threats should. Tony nodded appreciatively, but Rightsworth was irritated. The voice went on, more moderate in decibels, immoderate in content.

'We nicked your kid, Nerrity, and if you want your heir back in one piece you do what you're told like a good boy. Otherwise we'll take our knife out, Nerrity, and slash off something to persuade you. Not his hair, Nerrity. A finger maybe. Or his little privates. Those for sure. Understand, Nerrity? No messing about. This is for real.

'Now you got a horse, Nerrity. Worth a bit, we reckon. Six million. Seven. Sell it, Nerrity. Like we said, we want five million. Otherwise your kid suffers. Nice little kid, too. You don't want him screaming, do you? He'll scream with what we'll do to him.

'You get a bloodstock agent busy. We'll wait a week. One week, seven days. Seven days from now, you get that money ready in used notes, nothing bigger than twenty. We'll tell you where to leave it. You do what we tell you, or it's the castration. We'll send you a tape of what it sounds like. Slash. Rip. Scream.

'And you keep away from the police. If we think you've called in the Force, your kid's for the plastic bag. Final. You won't get his body back. *Nothing.* Think about it.

'Right, Nerrity. That's the message.'

The voice stopped abruptly and there was a numb minute of silence before anyone moved. I'd heard a score of ransom demands, but always, every time, found them shocking. Nerrity, like many a parent before him, was poleaxed to his roots.

'They can't . . .' he said, his mouth dry, the words gagging.

'They can,' Tony said flatly. 'but not if we manage it right.'

'What did they say to you this afternoon?' I asked. 'What's different?'

Nerrity swallowed. 'The . . . the knife. That part. Before, he just said "five million for your kid". And I said I hadn't got five million. . . . He said, "you've got a horse, so sell it." That was all. And no police, he said that too. Five million, no police, or the boy would die. He said he'd be getting in touch. I began to shout at him . . . he just rang off.'

Rightsworth took the cassette out of the recorder and put it in its box, putting that in its turn in the cardboard carton, all with exaggerated care in the plastic gloves. He would be taking the tape, he said. They would maintain the tap on Mr Nerrity's telephone, he said. They would be working on the case, he said.

Nerrity, highly alarmed, begged him to be careful; and begging didn't come easy, I thought, to one accustomed to bully. Rightsworth said with superiority that every care would be taken, and I could see Tony thinking, as I was, that Rightsworth was treating the threats too pompously and was not, in consequence, a brilliant detective.

When he had gone, Nerrity, his first fears subsiding, poured himself another stiff gin and tonic, again with ice and lemon. He picked the ice out of a bucket with a pair of tongs. Tony watched with incredulity.

'Drink?' he said to us as an afterthought.

We shook our heads.

'I'm not paying that ransom,' he said defensively. 'For one thing, I can't. The horse is due to be sold in any case. It's four years old, and going to stud. I don't need to get a bloodstock agent, it's being handled already. Some of the shares have already been sold, but I'll hardly see a penny. Like I said, I've got business debts.' He took a deep drink. 'You may as well know, that horse is the difference to me between being solvent and bankrupt. Biggest stroke of luck ever, the day I bought it as a yearling.' He swelled slightly, giving himself a mental pat on the back, and we could both see an echo of the expansiveness with which he must have waved many a gin and tonic while he recounted his good fortune.

'Isn't your business,' I said, 'a limited company? If you'll excuse my asking?'

'No, it isn't.'

'What is your business?' Tony asked him casually.

'Importer. Wholesale. One or two wrong decisions . . .' He shrugged. 'Bad debts. Firms going bankrupt, owing me money. On my scale of operations it doesn't take much of a recession to do a damned lot of damage. Ordinand will clear everything. Set me to rights. Fund me for future trading.

Ordinand is a bloody miracle.' He made a furious chopping gesture with his free hand. 'I'm damned if I'm going to throw away my entire life for those bloody kidnappers.'

He'd said it, I thought. He'd said aloud what had been festering in his mind ever since Miranda's 'phone call. He didn't love his son enough for the sacrifice.

'How much is Ordinand worth?' Tony said unemotionally.

'They got it right. Six million, with luck. Forty shares at a hundred and fifty thousand each.' He drank, the ice clinking.

'And how much do you need to straighten your business?'

'That's a bloody personal question!'

Tony said patiently, 'If we're going to negotiate for you, we have to know just what is or isn't possible.'

Nerrity frowned at his lemon slice, but then said, 'Four and a half, thereabouts, will keep me solvent. Five would clear all debts. Six will see me soundly based for the future.'

Tony glanced about him at the over-plush room. 'What about this house?'

Nerrity looked at him as if he were a financial baby. 'Every brick mortgaged,' he said shortly.

'Any other assets?'

'If I had any other bloody assets I'd have cashed them by now.'

Tony and I exchanged glances, then Tony said, 'I reckon we might get your kid back for less than half a million. We'll aim lower of course. First offer, a hundred thousand. Then take it from there.'

'But they won't . . . they said . . .' Nerrity stopped, floundering.

'The best thing,' I said, 'would be to get yourself onto the City pages of the newspapers. Go into print telling the world there's nothing like a Derby winner for keeping the bailiffs out.'

'But . . .'

'Yes,' I interrupted. 'Maybe not in the normal way good for business. But your creditors will be sure they'll be paid, and the kidnappers will be sure they won't. Next time they get in touch, they'll demand less. Once they acknowledge to themselves that the proceeds will be relatively small compared with their first demand, that's what they'll settle for. Better than nothing, sort of thing.'

'But they'll harm Dominic. . . .'

I shook my head. 'It's pretty doubtful, not if they're sure they'll make a profit in the end. Dominic's their only guarantee of that profit. Dominic, alive and whole. They won't destroy or damage their asset in any way if they're convinced you'll pay what you can. So when you talk to the press, make sure they understand – and print – that there'll be a margin over, when Ordinand is sold. Say that the horse will wipe out all your debts and then some.'

'But . . .' he said again.

'If you have any difficulty approaching the City editors, we can do that for you,' I said.

He looked from Tony to me with the uncertainty of a commander no longer in charge.

'Would you?' he said.

We nodded. 'Straight away.'

'Andrew will do it,' Tony said. 'He knows the City. Cut his teeth at Lloyds, our lad here.' Neither he nor I explained how lowly my job there had been. 'Very smooth, our Andrew, in his city suit,' Tony said.

Nerrity looked me up and down. I hadn't replaced my tie, although I'd long unrolled my trousers. 'He's young,' he said disparagingly.

Tony silently laughed. 'As old as the pyramids,' he said. 'We'll get your nipper back, don't you fret.'

Nerrity said uncomfortably, 'It's not that I don't like the boy. Of course I do.' He paused. 'I don't see much of him. Five minutes in the morning. He's in bed when I get home. Weekends . . . I work, go to the races, go out with business friends. Don't have much time for lolling about.'

Not much inclination, either, I diagnosed.

'Miranda dotes on him,' Nerrity said, as if that were no virtue. 'You'd have thought she could keep her eyes on him

161

for five minutes, wouldn't you? I don't see how she could have been so bloody stupid.'

I tried explaining about the determination of kidnappers, but it seemed to have no effect.

'It was her idea to have the kid in the first place,' Nerrity grumbled. 'I told her it would spoil her figure. She went on and on about being lonely. She knew what my life was like before she married me, didn't she?'

From the other side, I thought. From the office side, where his life was most intense, where hers was busy and fulfilled.

'Anyway, we had the kid.' He made another sharply frustrated gesture. 'And now . . . this.'

Miranda's mother arrived conveniently at that point, and shortly afterwards I put Alessia in my car and talked to Tony quietly in the garden.

'Thursday, tomorrow,' I said. 'Wittering's a seaside place. Good chance the same people will be on the beach tomorrow as today, wouldn't you think?'

'The Super in Chichester, would he buy that?' Tony asked.

'Yes, I'm sure.'

'I wouldn't mind a day myself of sitting on the effing pebbles.'

'The tide's going out in the mornings,' I said. 'How about if you take the stuff down to Eagler on the train, and I'll join you for a paddle when I've buzzed up the City?'

He nodded. 'See you at the Breakwater Hotel, then?'

'Yeah. Tell them at Reception that we're taking over Miranda's room. She's booked in until Saturday. Tell them the boy's ill, she's had to take him home, we're her brothers, we've come down to collect her clothes and her car . . . and pay her bill.'

'I don't know that sitting around in the Breakwater too long will do much good.'

I grinned in the darkness. 'Make a change from the switchboard, though.'

'You're an effing rogue, I always knew it.'

He vanished into the shadows without noise, departing on

foot to his distantly parked car, and I climbed in beside Alessia and pointed our nose towards Lambourn.

I asked if she were hungry and would like to stop somewhere for a late dinner, but she shook her head. 'Miranda and I ate cornflakes and toast until our eyes crossed. And you were right, she seemed a bit calmer by the time we left. But oh . . . when I think of that little boy . . . so alone, without his mother . . . I can't bear it.'

I spent the next morning in Fleet Street swearing various business-page editors to secrecy and enlisting their aid, and then drove back to West Wittering, reflecting that I'd spent at least twelve of the past thirty hours with my feet on the pedals.

Arriving at the Breakwater in jeans and sports shirt, I found Tony had checked in and left a message that he was out on the beach. I went down there and came across him sitting on a gaudy towel, wearing swimming trunks and displaying a lot of impressive keep-fit muscle. I dropped down beside him on a towel of my own and watched the life of the beach ebb and flow.

'Your Eagler already had the same idea,' Tony said. 'Half the holidaymakers on this patch of sand are effing plain clothes men quizzing the other half. They've been out here since breakfast.'

It appeared that Tony had got on very well with Eagler. Tony considered he had 'constructive effing ideas', which was Tony's highest mark of approval. 'Eagler's already sorted out what arson device was used to fire the dinghy. The dinghy was stolen, what a surprise.'

Some small children were digging a new sandcastle where Dominic's had been wiped out by the tide.

'A little girl of about eight gave Miranda the kidnapper's note,' I said. 'What do you bet she's still here?'

Without directly answering Tony rose to his feet and loped down onto the sand, where he was soon passing the time of day with two agile people kicking a football.

'They'll look for her,' he said, returning. 'They've found plenty who saw the boat. Some who saw who left it. The one with the green shorts has a stat of Giuseppe in his pocket, but no luck with that, so far.'

The two boys who had helped me carry the boat up from the grasp of the tide came by and said hello, recognising me.

'Hi,' I said. 'I see the boat's gone, what was left of it.'

One of them nodded. 'We came back along here after supper and there were two fishermen types winching it onto a pick-up truck. They didn't know whose it was. They said the coastguards had sent them to fetch it into a yard in Itchenor.'

'Do you live here?' I asked.

They shook their heads. 'We rent a house along there for August.' One of them pointed eastwards, along the beach. 'We come every year. Mum and Dad like it.'

'You're brothers?' I asked.

'Twins, actually. But fraternal, as you see.'

They picked up some pebbles and threw them at an empty Coke can for target practice, and presently moved off.

'Gives you a thought or two, doesn't it?' Tony said.

'Yes.'

'Eagler wanted to see us anyway at about five,' he said. 'In the Silver Sail café in that place the boy mentioned. Itchenor. Sounds like some disgusting effing disease.'

The football-kicker in green shorts was presently talking to a little girl whose mother bustled up in alarm and protectively shepherded her nestling away.

'Never mind,' Tony said. 'That smashing bit of goods in the pink bikini over there is a policewoman. What'll you bet green-shorts will be talking to her in two effing ticks?'

'Not a pebble,' I said.

We watched while green-shorts got into conversation with pink-bikini. 'Nicely done,' Tony said approvingly. 'Very natural.'

The pink-bikini girl stopped looking for shells exclusively and started looking for small girls as well, and I took my shirt off and began turning a delicate shade of lobster.

No dramas occurred on the beach. The hot afternoon warmed to tea-time. The football-kickers went off across the breakwaters and the pink-bikini went in for a swim. Tony and I stood up, stretched, shook and folded our towels, and in good holidaymaker fashion got into my car and drove westwards to Itchenor.

Eagler, inconspicuous in an open-necked shirt, baggy grey flannels and grubby tennis shoes, was drinking tea in the Silver Sail and writing a picture postcard.

'May we join you?' I asked politely.

'Sit down, laddie, sit down.'

It was an ordinary sort of café: sauce bottles on the tables, murals of sailing boats round the walls, brown tiled floor, plastic stacking chairs in blue. A notice by a cash desk stated 'The best chips on the coast' and a certain warm oiliness in the atmosphere tended to prove their popularity.

'My WPC found your girl child,' Eagler said, sticking a stamp on his postcard. 'Name of Sharon Wellor, seven years old, staying in a guest house until Saturday. She couldn't describe the man who asked her to deliver the note. She says he gave her some fruit pastilles, and she's scared now because her mother's always told her never to take sweets from strangers.'

'Did she know whether he was old or young?' I asked.

'Everyone over twenty is old to a seven-year-old,' Eagler said. 'She told my WPC where she's staying, though, so perhaps we'll ask again.' He glanced at us. 'Come up with any more ideas, have you?'

'Yeah,' Tony said. 'Kidnappers often don't transport their victims very far from their snatching point. Lowers the risk.'

'In holiday resorts,' I said mildly, 'half the houses are for rent.'

Eagler fiddled aimlessly with his teaspoon. 'Thousands of them,' he said dryly.

'But one of them might have been rented sometime last week.'

We waited, and after a while he nodded. 'We'll do the

legwork. Ask the travel agents, estate agents, local papers.' He paused, then said without emphasis, 'The kid may have been taken off in a boat.'

Tony and I paid fast attention.

'There was a motor-boat there,' Eagler said. 'One of those putt-putt things for hire by the hour. My detective constables were told that when the dinghy went on fire the other boat was bobbing round in the shallows with no one in it, but a man in swimming trunks was standing knee-deep in the water holding on to it by the bows. Then, our informants said, the dinghy suddenly went up in flames, very fast, with a whoosh, and everyone ran towards it, naturally. Our informants said that afterwards the motor-boat had gone, which they thought perfectly normal as its time was probably up.' He stopped, looking at us neutrally but with a smile of satisfaction plainly hovering.

'Who were your informants?' I asked.

The smile almost surfaced. 'A ten-year-old canal digger and his grandmother.'

'Very reliable,' I said.

'The boat was blue, clinker built, with a number seventeen in white on its bow and stern.'

'And the man?'

'The man was a man. They found the boat more interesting.' He paused again. 'There's a yard here in Itchenor with boats like that for hire. The trouble is they've got only ten. They've never had one with seventeen on it, ever.'

'But who's to know?' Tony said.

'Look for a house with a boat-shed,' I murmured.

Eagler said benignly, 'It wouldn't hurt, would it, to find the kid?'

'If they spot anyone looking they'll be off in a flash,' I said, 'and it would be dangerous for the boy.'

Eagler narrowed his eyes slightly at our alarm. 'We'll go round the agencies,' he said. 'If we turn up anything likely on paper we won't surround it without telling you first. How's that?'

We both shook our heads.

'Better to avoid raids and sieges if possible,' I said.

Tony said to Eagler, 'If you find a likely house on paper, let me suss it out. I've had all sorts of experience at this sort of thing. I'll tell you if the kid's there. And if he is, I'll get him out.'

twelve

There was an urgent message from the office at the Breakwater Hotel for me to telephone Alessia, which I did.

'Miranda's distracted . . . she's in pieces,' she said, sounding strung up herself beyond sympathy to near snapping point. 'It's awful. . . . She's telephoned me three times, crying terribly, begging me to get you to do something . . .'

'Sweet Alessia,' I said. 'Take three deep breaths and sit down if you're standing up.'

'Oh . . .' Her cough of surprise had humour in it, and after a pause she said, 'All right. I'm sitting. Miranda's dreadfully frightened. Is that better?'

'Yes,' I said, half smiling. 'What's happened?'

'Superintendent Rightsworth and John Nerrity are making a plan and won't listen to Miranda, and she's desperate to stop them. She wants you to make them see they mustn't.' Her voice was still high and anxious, the sentences coming fast.

'What's the plan?' I asked.

'John is going to pretend to do what the kidnappers tell him. Pretend to collect the money. Then when the pretend money is handed over, Superintendent Rightsworth will jump on the kidnappers and make them say where Dominic is.' She gulped audibly. 'That's what went wrong . . . with me . . . in Bologna . . . isn't it?'

'Yes,' I said, 'an ambush at the R.V. is to my mind too high a risk.'

'What's the R.V.?'

'Sorry. Rendezvous. The place where the ransom is handed over.'

'Miranda says John doesn't want to pay the ransom and Superintendent Rightsworth is telling him not to worry, he doesn't need to.'

'Mm,' I said. 'Well, I can see why Miranda's upset. Did she talk to you from the telephone in her own house?'

'What? Oh, my goodness, it's tapped, isn't it, with the police listening to every word?'

'It is indeed,' I said dryly.

'She was up in her bedroom. I suppose she didn't think. And, heavens . . . she said John was regretting calling in Liberty Market, because you were advising him to pay. Superintendent Rightsworth has assured him the police can take care of everything, there's no need to have outsiders putting their oar in.'

The phrase had an authentic Rightsworth ring.

'Miranda says John is going to tell Liberty Market he doesn't want their help any more. He says it's a waste of money . . . and Miranda's frantic.'

'Mm,' I said. 'If she telephones you again, try to remind her the 'phone's tapped. If she has any sense she'll ring you back from somewhere else. Then reassure her that we'll do our best to change her husband's mind.'

'But how?' Alessia said, despairing.

'Get our Chairman to frighten him silly, I dare say,' I said. 'And I never said that. It's for your ears only.'

'Will it work?' Alessia said doubtfully.

'There are also people who can overrule Rightsworth.'

'I suppose there are.' She sounded happier with that. 'Shall I tell Miranda to telephone directly to you in your office?'

'No,' I said. 'I'll be moving about. When you've heard from her, leave a message again for me to call you, and I will.'

'All right.' She sounded tired. 'I haven't been able to think of anything else all day. Poor Miranda. Poor, poor little boy. I never really understood until now what Papa went through because of me.'

'Because of your kidnappers,' I said, 'and for love of you, yes.'

After a pause she said, 'You're telling me again . . . I must feel no guilt.'

'That's right,' I said. 'No more guilt than Dominic.'

'It's not easy. . . .'

'No,' I agreed. 'But essential.'

She asked if I would come to lunch on Sunday, and I said yes if possible but not to count on it.

'You will get him back alive, won't you?' she said finally, none of the worry dissipated; and I said 'Yes,' and meant it.

'Goodbye, then . . .'

'Goodbye,' I said, 'and love to Popsy.'

Liberty Market, I reflected, putting down the receiver, might have an overall success rate as high as ninety-five per cent, but John Nerrity seemed to be heading himself perilously towards the other tragic five. Perhaps he truly believed, perhaps even Rightsworth believed, that an ambush at the drop produced the best results. And so they did, if capturing some of the kidnappers was the prime overriding aim.

There had been a case in Florida, however, when the police had ambushed the man who picked up the ransom and shot him down as he ran to escape, and only because the wounded man relented and told where his victim was a few seconds before he slid into a final coma, had they ever found the boy alive. He had been left in the boot of a parked car, and would slowly have suffocated if the police had fired a fraction straighter.

I told Tony of Nerrity's plans and he said disgustedly, 'What is he, an effing optimist?' He bit his thumbnail. 'Have to find that little nipper, won't we?'

'Hope to God.'

'Better chance in this country than anywhere else, of course.'

I nodded. Among well-meaning peoples, like the British,

kidnappers were disadvantaged. Their crime was reviled, not tolerated, and the population not afraid of informing. Once the victim was safely home, the trace-and-capture machinery had proved excellent.

Finding the hide-out before the pay-off was easier in Britain than in Italy, but still dauntingly difficult: and most successes along that line had come from coincidence, from nosey neighbours, and from guessing who had done the kidnap because of the close knowledge inadvertently revealed of the victim's private life.

'No one knew my daughter was going to be at that dance except her boy-friend,' one grief-stricken father had told us: and sure enough her apparently shattered boy-friend had organised the extortion – that time without the girl's knowledge, which wasn't always so. Collusion with the 'victim' had to be considered every time, human greed being what it was. The girl in that case had been found and freed without a ransom being paid, but she'd had a worse time in captivity than Alessia and the last I'd heard she was being treated for deep prolonged depression.

'I think I'll just mosey around a bit where the boats are,' Tony said. 'Can I borrow your car? You can use Miranda's if you're desperate. Do you mind if I go home later for some gear? I'll see you at effing breakfast.'

'Don't crunch it,' I said, giving him the keys.

'As if I would.'

I spent the evening eating the hotel's very reasonable dinner and packing Miranda's belongings. Dominic's clothes, quiet and folded, filled a neat small suitcase. I put his cuddly toys, a teddy and a Snoopy, in beside them, and shut the lid: and thought of him, so defenceless, so frightened, and knew that it was because of people like him and Alessia that what I was doing was a job for life.

In view of John Nerrity's change of heart I guessed he wouldn't be too pleased with the morning newspapers' money columns, where the financial editors had done him proud. The word

'Nerrity' sprang out in large black letters from every paper I'd visited, which were mostly of the sort that I guessed the writer of the kidnap note would read.

'Nerrity Home and Dried', 'Nerrity's Nag to the Rescue', 'Nerrity Floats on Stud' they said, and 'Nerrity Solvent by Short Head'. To kidnappers nervously scanning the press for signs of police activity, the bad news couldn't be missed. Creditors were zeroing in on the Ordinand proceeds, and there would be precious little left for other sharks.

Eagler telephoned me in Miranda's room while I was still reading. 'These papers. . . . Is this your doing?' he asked.

'Er, yes.'

He chuckled. 'I thought I detected the fine hand. Well, laddie, we're doing a spot of rummaging around the classifieds in the local rags of a week to two weeks ago, and we're checking through all the properties to rent. We'll have a partial list for you any time today.' He paused. 'Now I'm putting a lot of faith in your friend Tony Vine, and I want to be sure it's not misplaced.'

'He's an ex-S.A.S.,' I said. 'A sergeant.'

'Ah.' He sounded relieved.

'He prefers working at night.'

'Does he now?' Eagler was almost purring. 'I should have a fairly complete list for you by late this afternoon. Will you fetch it?'

We arranged time and place, and rang off; and when I went downstairs to breakfast Tony was walking in through the front door, yawning.

Over bacon, eggs and kippers he recounted what he'd found. 'Did you know there's a whole internal water system behind the coast here? Itchenor Creek goes all the way to Chichester. But there's a lock some way up, and our fellows didn't go through it.' He chewed. 'I hired a rowing boat. Sneaked around a bit. Reckon it's an effing needle in a haystack we're after. There's dozens, hundreds of likely houses. Holiday flats. Chalets. You name it. And on top of that the water goes clear to somewhere called Hayling Island, with thousands more little bungalows, and there are uncountable places where a car could have met the boat and taken the nipper anywhere.'

I gloomily ate some toast and told him about Eagler's impending list.

'OK then,' Tony said. 'I'll swim this morning, sleep this afternoon, work tonight, OK?'

I nodded and passed him one of the newspapers. Tony read the financial news over the rim of his cup of tea. 'You hit the effing bullseye. No one could miss it,' he said.

Nerrity himself certainly hadn't missed it. Gerry Clayton telephoned to say that Nerrity was furious and insisting we dropped the case. He wanted nothing more to do with Liberty Market.

'He admitted he'd agreed to your getting the story into the papers,' Gerry said. 'But he didn't think it would happen so quickly, and he had intended to cancel it.'

'Too bad.'

'Yes. So officially you and Tony can break off and come home.'

'No,' I said. 'We're working for Mrs Nerrity now. She specifically asked for us to continue.'

Gerry's voice had a smile in it. 'I thought you might, but it makes it all a damn sight more tricky. Both of you . . . take care.'

'Yeah,' I said. 'Fold some nice paper. Try a boat.'

'Boat?'

'A boat to thrust a small boy into so that you can put a tarpaulin or some such over him, a boat to chug noisily away over the breaking waves so that no one can hear him crying out.'

'Is that how is was done?' Gerry asked soberly.

'We think so, yes.'

'Poor little blighter,' Gerry said.

Tony and I in true holiday-making fashion spent the morning in or out of water, although the day was not so warm nor the beach so fruitfully crowded. The policewoman, now in a white bikini, came to splash with us in the shallows but said she hadn't been able to find anyone who had seen Dominic carried off. 'Every single person seems to have been looking at the dinghy,' she said disgustedly. 'And all we know about that is that it was stranded on the sand when the tide went out, and it had a large piece of paper taped to the seat saying "Don't touch the boat, we'll be back for it soon".'

'Didn't someone say they'd seen who left it?' I asked.

'Well, yes, but that was a boy playing up on the shingle, and all he could say was that they were two men in shorts and bright orange rainproof sailing jackets, who had pulled the dinghy up the sand a bit and been busy round it for a while and then had walked off north west along the beach. The boy went down to the dinghy soon afterwards and read the note, and after that he went off to get an icecream. He wasn't here in the afternoon when it went up in flames, much to his disgust. When he came back it was burnt and black.'

The policewoman was shivering in the rising breeze and turning a pale shade of blue. 'Time for a sweater and thick socks,' she said cheerfully. 'And I might as well chat up the ancient ladies living in the Haven Rest Home along there.' She pointed. 'They've nothing to do but look out of the windows.'

Tony and I picked up our belongings and moved to the shelter of the hotel, and in the afternoon while the clouds thickened overhead he slept undisturbed in Miranda's bed.

At five I drove to Chichester to collect the list of rentals from Eagler: he came to meet me himself, looking insignificant and slow, and climbed into the passenger seat at my side.

'These top eleven are the most promising,' he said, pointing. 'They are collected from all the agencies we could think of. They are all holiday homes on or near the water and they were all rented at the last minute. The weather was so bad in July and at the beginning of August that there were more properties than usual available, and then when it turned warmer there was a rush.'

I nodded. 'Miranda herself decided to come here only a few days in advance. The hotel had had cancellations because of the weather, and could take her.'

'I wonder what would have happened if she hadn't come?' Eagler said thoughtfully.

'They'd have grabbed him at home.'

'You'd have thought they'd have found it easier to wait until he was back there.'

'Kidnappers don't try to make things easy for themselves,' I said mildly. 'They plan to the last inch. They spend money. They're obsessional. There's never anything casual about a kidnap. Kidnappers would see a good chance of success while the child was in charge of his mother alone down here, and I bet once they'd done the planning they waited day after day for the right minute. If it hadn't presented itself they would have followed Miranda home and thought up a new plan. Or perhaps have reverted to a former plan which hadn't so far borne fruit. You never can tell. But if they'd wanted him, they would have got him in the end.'

'How would they have known she was coming here?' Eagler asked.

'Kidnappers watch,' I said. 'They're obsessional about that, too. What conclusion would you come to if you saw Miranda load suitcases and a beach chair into her car, strap Dominic into his seat, and drive away waving?'

'Hm.'

'You'd follow,' I said.

'I expect so.'

'Miranda in her nice red car, driving at a moderate speed, as mothers do with their children in the back.'

'True,' he said. He stirred. 'Anyway, the next bunch of houses on the list are all at least one street away from the water, and the last lot are further inland, but still in the coastline villages. Beyond that . . .' he stopped, looking doubtful. 'This whole section of Sussex is one big holiday area.'

'We'll try these,' I said.

'I've some good men,' Eagler suggested. 'They could help.'

I shook my head. 'They might just possibly enquire of one of the kidnappers themselves if they'd heard a child crying.

174

That's happened before. The kidnapper said no, and the child turned up dead on some waste ground a week later. It happened in Italy. The police caught the kidnappers in the end, and the kidnappers said they'd panicked when they found the police were so close to their hideout.'

Eagler stroked thumb and forefinger down his nose. 'All right,' he said. 'We'll do it your way.' He glanced at me sideways. 'But to be honest, I don't think you'll succeed.'

Tony, back at the hotel, wasn't particularly hopeful either. He looked judiciously at the first eleven addresses and said he would first locate them by land and then approach by rowing boat, and those eleven alone would take him all night. He said he would take my car, which still had his gear stowed in it, and he'd be back in the morning.

'Sleep tomorrow, try again tomorrow night,' he said. 'That brings us to Sunday. Hope those effing kidnappers meant it about giving Nerrity a week to collect the dough. They might be twitchy after the newspapers. Might advance the time of the drop. Hope effing not.'

He ate little for dinner and drove away when it was getting dark. I telephoned Alessia for news of Miranda, but except for her having come out of the house to call Alessia, nothing much had happened. Miranda continued to be distraught. The kidnappers had not been in touch again. John Nerrity still appeared to have faith in the ambush plan and had said he thought Miranda's near-collapse excessive.

'I wonder how he would have reacted if it had been Ordinand who'd been kidnapped?' I said.

Alessia nearly laughed. 'Don't talk of it. And it's been done.'

'Without success,' I agreed. 'Enough to put the horse-nappers off for life.'

'Would your firm work to free a horse?' she asked curiously.

'Sure. Extortion is extortion, however many legs the victim has. Ransoms can be negotiated for anything.'

'Paintings?'

'Anything anyone cares about.'

'Like "I'll give you your ball back if you pay me a penny"?'

175

'Exactly like that.'

'Where are you?' she said. 'Not at home . . . I tried there.'

'An evening off,' I said. 'I'll tell you when I see you.'

'Do come on Sunday.'

'Yes, I'll try.'

We spent more time than necessary saying goodbye. I thought that I could easily have talked to her all evening, and wished vaguely that she felt secure enough to travel and drive alone.

Tony came back soon after dawn, waking me from a shallow sleep.

'There are two possibles out of those eleven places,' he said, stripping off for a shower. 'Nine of them are occupied by bona-fide effing holidaymakers. I went into four to make absolutely sure, but there they were, tucked up nice and unsuspecting, dads, mums, grannies and kids, all regular law-abiding citizens.'

Tony's skill, as he immodestly said, would make any professional night burglar look like a herd of elephants. 'A creeper as good as me,' I'd heard him say, 'can touch a person in bed and get them to turn over to stop them snoring. I could take the varnish off their nails, let alone the wallets from under the pillows. Good thing I'm effing honest.'

I waited while he stepped into the shower and sluiced lavishly about. 'There's two of those places,' he said, reappearing eventually and towelling his sandy-brown hair, 'that gave me bad vibes. One of them's got some sort of electronic gadget guarding the door: it sent my detection gear into a tizzy. I'd guess it's one of those do-it-yourself alarms you can buy anywhere to stop hotel creepers fitting you up while you're sleeping off the mickey the barman slipped you.' He dried his neck. 'So I left a couple of bugs on that one, and we'll go back soon and listen in.'

He wrapped the towel round his body like a sarong and sat on Miranda's bed. 'The other one's got no electronic gadgets that I could see, but it's three storeys high. Boatshed on the ground floor. Empty. Just water and effing fish. Above that, rooms overlooking the creek. Above that, more rooms. There's a sort of scrubby paved garden on two sides. Not much cover. I didn't fancy going in. Anyway I stuck two bugs on it, one on each of the upper floors. So we'll listen to them as well.'

'Cars?' I said.

'Can't tell.' He shook his head. 'Neither place has a garage. There were cars along the streets.' He stood up and began to dress. 'Come on then,' he said. 'Get out of the effing pit, and let's go fishing.'

He meant it literally, it seemed. By eight-thirty we were out on Itchenor Creek in the chilly morning in his rented rowing boat, throwing lines with maggots on hooks over the side.

'Are you sure this is the right bait?' I said.

'Who cares? Bass swallow bare hooks sometimes, silly buggers.'

He paddled the boat along like a born waterman with one oar in a loop of rope over the stern. No creaking rowlocks, he explained. Ultra-silent travel: high on the S.A.S. curriculum.

'The tide was low at five this morning,' he said. 'You can't get a boat ashore at low tide in a lot of places, so if they landed the kid from that motor-boat it was probably somewhere where there's water at half-tide. Both our possibles qualify, just.'

Our rowing boat drifted along on slowly flooding water. The fish disdained the maggots and there was a salty smell of seaweed.

'We're just coming to the place with the electronic bulldog,' Tony said. 'Hold this aerial so it looks like a fishing rod.' He untelescoped about six feet of thin silvery rod and handed it over, and I found there was a line tied to the end of it with a small weight. 'Chuck the weight in the water,' he said, bending down to fiddle with the radio receiver in what looked like a fishing-gear box. 'Keep your eyes on the briny and pin back the lugs.'

I did all of those things but nothing much happened. Tony

grunted and did some fine tuning, but in the end he said. 'The lazy so-and-so's aren't awake. The bugs are working. We'll come back when we've checked the other house.'

I nodded and he paddled a good way northwards before stopping again to deploy the lines. Again we drifted on the tide, apparently intent on catching our breakfast, and Tony bent to his knobs.

The voice when it came nearly tipped me out of the boat.

'Give the little bleeder his breakfast and tape off his noise if he starts whining.'

The voice – unmistakably the voice – which we had heard on the tape in John Nerrity's house. Not over loud, but crystal clear.

'My God,' I said numbly, not believing it.

'Bingo,' Tony said with awe. 'Holy effing hell.'

A different voice on the tape said, 'He won't eat it. What's the point of taking it up there?'

'Son,' said the first voice with exaggerated patience, 'do we want our little goldmine to starve to death? No we don't. Take him his bread and jam, and shut up.'

'I don't like this job,' the second voice complained. 'Straight up, I don't.'

'You were keen enough when I put you up for it. Good work, you said; those were your words.'

'I didn't reckon on the kid being so . . .'

'So what?'

'So stubborn.'

'He's not that bad. Pining, most like. You concentrate on the payola and get up the bleeding stairs.'

Tony flipped a couple of switches and for a while we sat in silence listening to the faint slap of the water against our own drifting boat; and then the second voice, sounding much more distant, said, 'Here you are, kid, eat this.'

There was no audible reply.

'Eat it,' the voice said with irritation, and then, after a pause, 'I'd stuff it down your throat if you were mine, you snotty little sod.'

Tony said 'Charming' under his breath and began to pull in the lines. 'Heard enough, haven't we? That second bug is on the top floor, facing the street.'

I nodded. Tony reversed his switches and the second voice, downstairs again, said 'He's just lying there staring, same as usual. Gives me the willies. Sooner we're shot of him, the better.'

'Patience,' the first voice said, as if humouring an idiot. 'You got to let the man sell his horse. Stands to reason. One week we gave him. One week is what he'll get.'

'We're not collecting the five million, though, are we?' He sounded aggrieved. 'Not a chance.'

'We were never going to get five million, stupid. Like Peter said, you demand five to frighten the dads and take half a million nice and easy, no bones broken.'

'What if Nerrity calls in the Force, and they jump us?'

'No sign of them, is there? Be your age. Terry and Kevin, they'd spot the law the minute it put its size twelves over the doorstep. Those two, they got antennae where you've got eyes. No one at the hotel. No one at the house in Sutton. Right?'

The second voice gave an indistinguishable grumble, and the first answered. 'Peter knows what he's doing. He's done it before. He's an expert. You just do what you're bleeding told and we'll all get rich, and I've had a bellyful of your grousing, I have, straight up.'

Tony put the single oar over the stern of the boat and without fuss or hurry paddled us off towards where we'd set out, against the swirling incoming tide. I rolled up the fishing lines and unbaited the hooks, my fingers absentminded while my thoughts positively galloped.

'Don't let's tell Eagler until . . .' I said.

'No,' Tony answered.

He looked across at me, half-smiling. 'And let's not tell the Chairman either,' I said. 'Or Gerry Clayton.'

Tony's smile came out like the sun. 'I was afraid you'd insist.'

'No.' I paused. 'You watch from the water and I'll watch

179

from the land, OK? And this evening we'll tell Eagler. On our terms.'

'And the low profile can rest in effing peace.'

'You just get that vacuum pump purring like a cat and don't fall off any high walls.'

'In our report,' Tony said, 'we will write that the police found the hideout.'

'Which they did,' I said reasonably.

'Which they did,' he repeated with satisfaction.

Neither Tony nor I were totally committed to the advice-only policy of the firm, though we both adhered to it more or less and agreed that in most circumstances it was prudent. Tony with his exceptional skills tended always to be more actively involved than I, and his reports were peppered with phrases like 'it was discovered' and 'as it happened' and never with the more truthful 'I planted a dozen illegal bugs and heard . . .' or 'I let off a smoke canister and under its cover . . .'

Tony steered the boat back to where we'd left the car and rapidly set up a duplicate receiver to work through the car's aerial.

'There you are,' he said, pointing. 'Left switch for the lower floor bug, middle switch for the top floor. Don't touch the dials. Right switch, up for me to talk to you, down for you to talk to me. OK?'

He dug around in the amazing stores he called his gear and with a nod of pleasure took out a plastic lunch box. 'Long term subsistence supplies,' he said, showing me the contents. 'Nut bars, beef jerky, vitamin pills – keep you fighting fit for weeks.'

'This isn't the South American outback,' I said mildly.

'Saves a lot of shopping, though.' He grinned and stowed the lunch box in the rowing boat along with a plastic bottle of water. 'If the worst should happen and they decide to move the kid, we're in dead trouble.'

I nodded. Trouble with the law, with Liberty Market and with our own inescapable guilt.

'And let's not forget,' he added slowly, 'that somewhere around we have Terry and Kevin and Peter, all with their antennae quivering like effing mad, and you never know whether that crass bastard Rightsworth won't drive up to Nerrity's house with his blue light flashing.'

'He's not that crazy.'

'He's smug. Self satisfied. Just as dangerous.'

He put his head on one side, considering. 'Anything else?'

'I'll go back to the hotel, pay the bill, collect the cases.'

'Right. Give me a buzz when you're on station.' He stepped into the boat and untied its painter. 'And, by the way, do you have a dark sweater? Black, high neck?'

'Yes, I brought one.'

'Good. See you tonight.'

I watched him paddle away, a shortish figure of great physical economy, every movement deft and sure. He waved goodbye briefly, and I turned the car and got on with the day.

thirteen

The hours passed slowly with the mixture of tension and boredom that I imagined soldiers felt when waiting for battle. Half of the time my pulse rate was up in the stratosphere, half the time I felt like sleep. At only one point did the watch jerk from stand-by to nerve-racking, and that was at midday.

For most of the morning I had been listening to the bug on the lower of the two floors, not parking the whole time in one place but moving about and stopping for a while in any of the streets within range. The two kidnappers had repeated a good deal of what we'd already heard; grouse, grouse, shut up.

Dominic at one point had been crying.

'The kid's whining,' the first voice said.

I switched to the top floor bug and heard the lonely heart-breaking grizzle, the keening of a child who'd lost hope of being given what he wanted. No one came to talk to him, but presently his voice was obliterated by pop music, playing loudly.

I switched to the lower bug again and felt my muscles go into knots.

A new voice was speaking. ' . . . a bloke sitting in a car a couple of streets away, just sitting there. I don't like it. And he's a bit like one of the people staying in the hotel.'

The first-voice kidnapper said decisively, 'You go and check him out, Kev. If he's still there, come right back. We're taking no bleeding risks. The kid goes down the chute.'

The second-voice kidnapper said, 'I've been sitting at this ruddy window all morning. There's been no one in sight here, sussing us out. Just people walking, not looking.'

'Where did you leave the car?' Kevin demanded. 'You've moved it.'

'It's in Turtle Street.'

'That's where this bloke is sitting.'

There was a silence among the kidnappers. The bloke sitting in the car in Turtle Street, his heart lurching, started his engine and removed himself fast.

A red light on Tony's radio equipment began flashing, and I pressed the switch to talk to him. 'I heard,' I said. 'Don't worry, I'm on my way. Talk to you when I can.'

I drove a mile and pulled up in the car park of a busy pub, and bent my ears to catch the much fainter transmissions.

'The bloke's gone,' a voice eventually said.

'What do you reckon, Kev?'

The reply was indistinguishable.

'There hasn't been a smell of the Force. Not a flicker.' The first-voice kidnapper sounded as if he were trying to reassure himself as much as anyone else. 'Like Peter said, they can't surround this place without us seeing, and it takes eight seconds, that's all, to put the kid down the chute. You know it, I know it, we practised. There's no way the police would

182

find anything here but three blokes having a bleeding holiday and a little gamble on the cards.'

There were some more indecipherable words, then the same voice. 'We'll both watch, then. I'll go upstairs, ready. You, Kev, you walk round the bleeding town and see if you can spot that bloke hanging about. If you see him, give us a bell, then we'll decide. Peter won't thank us if we panic. We got to give the goods back breathing, that's what he said. Otherwise we get nothing, savvy, and I don't want to have gone through all this aggravation for a hole in the bleeding pocket.'

I couldn't hear the replies, but first-voice seemed to have prevailed. 'Right then. Off you go, Kev. See you later.'

I went inside the pub where I was parked and ate a sandwich with fingers not far from trembling. The low profile, I judged, had never been more justified or more essential, and I'd risked Dominic's life by not sticking to the rules.

The problem with dodging Kevin was that I didn't know what he looked like while he could spot me easily, and probably he knew the colour, make and number of my car. Itchenor was too small for handy hiding places like multi-storey parks. I concluded that as I couldn't risk being seen I would have to give the place a miss altogether, and drove by a roundabout route to reach Itchenor Creek at a much higher point, nearer Chichester. I could no longer hear the bugs, but hoped to reach Tony down the water; and he responded to my first enquiry with a faint voice full of relief.

'Where are you?' he demanded.

'Up the creek.'

'You've said it.'

'What's happened in the house?'

'Nothing. Whatever that chute is, the goods have not yet gone down it. But they're still quivering like effing jellyfish.' He paused. 'Effing bad luck, them having their car in that street.'

He was excusing me. I was grateful. I said, 'I'd been there only ten minutes.'

'Way it goes. Kev is back with them, incidentally.'

'I'll be here, if you need me.'

'OK,' he said. 'And by the way, it was the one called Peter who picked the goods up. Sweet as a daisy, they said. Peter 'phones them every day and apparently might go there himself tomorrow or the day after. Pity we can't wait.'

'Too risky.'

'Yeah.'

We agreed on a time and place for me to meet him, and switched off to conserve the power packs he had with him in the boat. Listening to the bugs was far more important and, besides, drained the batteries less.

There was always the slight chance with radio that someone somewhere would be casually listening on the same channel, but I reviewed what we'd said and thought it wouldn't have enlightened or alarmed anyone except the kidnappers themselves, even if we had, on the whole, sounded like a couple of thieves.

I stayed by the water all afternoon, in or near the car, but heard no more from Tony, which was in itself a sign that the status was still quo. At a few minutes to five I drove inland to the nearest telephone box and put a call through to Eagler.

He was off duty, the station said. What was my name?

Andrew Douglas.

In that case, would I ring the following number?

I would, and did, and he answered immediately. What a terrific change, I thought fleetingly, from my disaster with Pucinelli's second in command.

'Can your men work at night?' I said.

'Of course.'

'Tony found the kidnappers,' I said.

'I don't believe it!'

'It should be possible for you to arrest them.'

'Where are they?'

'Er,' I said. 'They are extremely alert, watching for any sign of police activity. If you turn up there too soon it would be curtains for the boy. So would you – um – act on our sugges-

184

tions, without questioning them, and positively, *absolutely* not altering the plan in any way?'

There was a fair pause, then he said, 'Am I allowed to approve this plan, or not?'

'Er . . . not.'

Another pause. 'Take it or leave it?'

'I'm afraid so.'

'Hm.' He deliberated. 'The kidnappers on your terms, or not at all?'

'Yes,' I said.

'I hope you know what you're doing, laddie.'

'Mm,' I said.

A final pause, then he said, 'You're on. All right. What's the plan?'

'You need enough men to arrest at least three people,' I said. 'Can you get them to your Chichester main police station by one in the morning?'

'Certainly.' He sounded almost affronted. 'Plain clothes or in uniform?'

'I don't think it will matter.'

'Armed or not?'

'It's up to you. We don't know if the kidnappers have guns.'

'Right. And where are my men to go?'

'I'll call you with directions after one o'clock.'

He snorted. 'Not very trusting, are you?'

'I do trust you,' I said. 'Otherwise I wouldn't be setting this up for you at all.'

'Well, well,' he said. 'The iron man in the kid glove, just as I rather suspected. All right, laddie, your trust won't be misplaced, and I'll play fair with you. And I'll tear the both of you to shreds if you bungle it.'

'It's a deal,' I said thankfully. 'I'll call you at the station.'

I went back to the water to wait but heard no squeak from Tony; and long after it had grown dark I drove to where we'd agreed to meet, and transferred him and his equipment from boat to car.

'They simmered down a bit in the house,' he said. 'They

had a 'phone call from Peter, whoever he is, and that seemed to steady them a bit. Pity I couldn't have fixed a tap on the telephone. Anyway, Peter apparently told them to carry on with the look-out and not dump the boy unless they could see the police outside.' He grinned. 'Which I hope they won't do.'

'No.' I stowed the power packs from the boat beside a large, amorphous canvas bag. 'Our friend Eagler promised. Also . . .' I hesitated, 'I've thought of another safeguard.'

'Tricky, aren't we?' Tony said, when I told him. 'But yes, we can't afford a balls-up. Want a nut bar? Good as dinner.'

I ate a nut bar and we sat quietly and waited, and a good while after one o'clock I telephoned Eagler and told him when and where to bring – and conceal – his men.

'Tell them to be silent,' I said. 'Not just quiet. Silent. No talking. No noisy feet. Absolutely silent.'

'All right.'

'Wait for us, for Tony and me. We will come to meet you. We may be a long time after you get there, we're not sure. But please wait. Wait in silence.'

'That's all you're telling me?' he said doubtfully.

'We'll tell you the rest when we meet you. But it's essential to get the timing right . . . so will you wait?'

'Yes,' he said, making up his mind.

'Good. We'll see you, then.'

I put the receiver down and Tony nodded with satisfaction.

'All right, then,' he said. 'How are your nerves?'

'Lousy. How are yours?'

'To be honest,' he said, 'when I'm doing this sort of thing I feel twice as alive as usual.'

I drove us gently back to Itchenor and parked in a row of cars round the corner from the kidnappers' house. There was only one street lamp, weak and away on a corner, which pleased Tony particularly, as he wanted time for us to develop night vision. He produced a tube of make-up and blacked his face and hands, and I tuned into the bugs again for a final check-up.

There was no noise from either of them.

I looked at my watch. Two-fifteen. Eagler's men were due to be in position by two-thirty. With luck the kidnappers would be asleep.

'Black your face,' Tony said, giving me the tube. 'Don't forget your eyelids. If you hear anyone walking along the street, squat in a corner and close your eyes. It's almost impossible to see anyone in the shadows who's doing that. Standing up and moving with your eyes open and gleaming, that's playing silly buggers.'

'All right.'

'And be patient. Silence takes time.'

'Yes.'

He grinned suddenly, the white teeth satanic in the darkened face. 'What's the good of years of training if you never put them to effing use?'

We got out of the car into the quiet deserted street, and from the large shapeless canvas bag in the boot Tony extracted his intricate and lovingly-tended harness. I held the supple black material for him while he slid his arms through the armholes and fastened the front from waist to neck with a zip. It changed his shape from lithe normality to imitation hunchback, the power packs on his shoulders lumpy and grotesque.

The harness itself was a mass of pockets, both patched on and hanging, each containing something essential for Tony's purpose. Everything was in pockets because things which were merely clipped on, as in a climber's harness, clinked and jingled and also threw off gleams of light. Everything Tony used was matt black and if possible covered in slightly tacky binding, for a good grip. I'd been utterly fascinated the first time he'd shown me his kit, and had also felt privileged, as he kept its very existence private from most of the partners, for fear they would ban its use.

'OK?' he said.

I nodded. He seemed to have no trouble breathing, but my own lungs appeared to have stopped. He had gone in, though, with his bare hands in many a land where to be discovered was death, and I daresay a caper in an English seaside village seemed a picnic beside those.

He pressed an invisible knob somewhere up by his neck, and there was a small muffled whine as the power came on, steadying to a faint hiss inaudible at two paces.

'Fine, then,' he said. 'Bring the bag.'

I took the canvas bag out of the boot and quietly shut and locked the door. Then without any fuss we walked in our black clothes as far as the corner, where Tony seemed to melt suddenly into shadow and disappear. I counted ten as agreed, slid to my knees, and with caution and thumping heart took my first dim view of the target.

'Always kneel,' Tony had said. 'Look-outs look at head height, not near the ground.'

The house's paved garden, weed-grown, was in front of me, but dimly perceived, even with night-accustomed eyes. 'Move to the house wall, on the right-hand side,' Tony had said. 'Bend double, head down. When you get there, stand up, face the wall, stay in any deep shadow you can find.'

'Right.'

I followed his instructions, and no one shouted, no one set up a clamour in the house.

Above me on the wall I could see, looking up, a dark irregular shadow where no one would expect a man to be. No one except people like Tony, who was climbing the bare walls with sucker clamps fastened on by a battery-powered vacuum pump. Tony – who could go up a tower block, for whom two storeys were a doddle.

I seemed all the same to wait for several centuries, my heart thudding in my chest. No one walked along the road; no insomniacs, no people humouring importunate dogs. Sussex-by-the-sea was fast asleep and dreaming, with only policemen, Liberty Market and perhaps kidnappers wide awake.

Something hit me gently in the face. I put my hand up to catch it and fastened my fingers round the dangling length of black nylon rope.

'Tie the bag on, give the rope two tugs, I'll pull it up,' Tony had said.

I obeyed his instructions, and the canvas hold-all disappeared into the darkness above.

I waited, heart racing worse than ever. Then suddenly the bag was down with me again, but heavy, not empty. I took it into my arms and gave two more tugs on the rope. The rope itself dropped down into the shadows round my feet, and I began to pull it in awkwardly, my arms full of bag.

I didn't hear Tony come down. His skill was truly amazing. One second he wasn't there, the next moment he was, stowing the last of the released clamps into voluminous pockets. He felt for the rope I was trying to wind in and had it collected into the holdall in a flash. Then he touched me on the arm, and we both left the scrubby garden, me hunched double over my burden and Tony already sliding out of his harness. Once in the road and out of any possible sight of the house I stood upright and grasped the bag by both handles, carrying it in one hand as one normally would.

'Here,' Tony said quietly, 'rub this over your face.' He gave me something moist and cold, a sort of sponge, with which I wiped away a good deal of the blacking, and I could see that he too was doing the same.

We reached the car on silent feet.

'Don't slam the doors,' Tony said, dumping his harness onto the front passenger seat. 'We'll close them properly later.'

'OK.'

I took the bag with me into the rear seats and removed its precious contents: one very small boy, knees bent to his chest, lying on his back, with coils of black nylon rope falling over his legs. He was more than normally asleep but not totally unconscious: unwakeably drowsy. Uncombed blond-brown curls outlined his head, and across his mouth there was a wide band of medicated sticky tape. I wrapped him in the rug I always kept in the car, and laid him along the back seat.

'Here,' Tony said, passing me a bottle and a tiny cloth over from the front seats. 'This'll clean the adhesive off.'

'Did they do this?' I said.

'No, I did. Couldn't risk the kid waking up and bawling.' He started the car and drove off in one fluid movement, and I pulled the plaster off gently and cleaned the stickiness away.

'He was asleep,' Tony said. 'But I gave him a whiff of ether. Not enough to put him right out. How does he look?'

'Dopey.'

'Fair enough.'

He drove quietly to where I'd told Eagler to take his men, which was to another of the eleven houses on his list; to the one which had had the electronic anti-burglar device, a good half-mile away.

Tony stopped the car short of the place, then got out and walked off, and presently returned with Eagler himself, alone. When I saw them coming I got out of the car myself, and for a moment in the dim light Eagler looked bitterly disappointed.

'Don't worry,' I said. 'He's here, in the car.'

Eagler bent to look as I opened a rear door gently, and then, relieved, straightened up. 'We're taking him straight to his mother,' I said. 'She can get her own doctor. One the boy knows.'

'But . . .'

'No buts,' I said. 'What he absolutely doesn't want is a police station full of bright lights, loud voices and assorted officials. Fair's fair, we got the boy, you get the kidnappers. You also get the media coverage, if you don't mind. We want our two selves and Liberty Market left out of it completely. We're useful only as long as we're unknown, both to the general public and especially to all prospective kidnappers.'

'All right, laddie,' he said, listening and capitulating paternally. 'I'll stick to the bargain. Where do we go?'

Tony gave him directions.

'I left a canister of tear-gas there,' he said cheerfully. 'I took it as a precaution, but I didn't need it myself. It had a timer on it.' He looked at his watch. 'I set it to go off seven minutes from now. There's enough in it to fill the house, more or less, so if you wait another five to ten minutes you should have a nice easy task. The air will be OK to breathe about then, but their eyes will be streaming . . . that is, if they haven't already come out.'

Eagler listened enigmatically, neither objecting nor commending.

'The kid was on the top floor,' Tony said. 'He was wearing one of those harness things they put in prams. He was tied to the bed with it. I cut it off him, it's still there. Also there's some floorboards up. Mind your PCs don't fall down the hole. God knows where they'd get to.' He fished into the car and brought five cassette tapes out of the glove compartment. 'These make good listening. You play them to your friends when you have them in the nick. No one's going to confess where they came from. Bugging other people's conversations ain't gentlemanly. Andrew and I never saw these recordings before.'

Eagler took the tapes, looking faintly bemused.

'That's about all then,' Tony said. 'Happy hunting.'

He slid into the car behind the steering wheel, and before I followed him, I said to Eagler, 'The kidnappers' leader is due to join them tomorrow or the day after. I don't suppose he'll come, now, but he might telephone . . . if the news doesn't break too soon.'

Eagler bent down as I manoeuvred myself into the rear seat. 'Thanks, laddie,' he said.

'And to you,' I answered. 'You're the best.'

Tony started the car, waved to Eagler as he closed the rear door, and without more fuss we were away and on the road, taking a direction opposite to the kidnappers' house, set fair for safety.

'Wow,' Tony said, relaxing five miles on. 'Not a bad bit of liberating, though I say it myself.'

'Fantastic,' I said, 'and if you go round any more corners at that speed Dominic will fall off the seat.'

Tony glanced back to where I was awkwardly jammed sideways to let Dominic lie stretched out, and decided to stop the car for rearrangements, which included removing more thoroughly the black from our faces and stowing Tony's gear tidily in the boot. When we set off again I had Dominic on my lap with his head cradled against my shoulder, and he was half grasping the cuddly teddy which I'd taken from his suitcase.

His eyes opened and fell shut occasionally, but even when it was clear the ether had worn off, he didn't wake. I wondered for a while if he'd been given sleeping pills like Alessia, but later concluded it was only the middle-of-the-night effect on the extremely young, because towards the end of the journey I suddenly found his eyes wide open, staring up at my face.

'Hello, Dominic,' I said.

Tony looked over briefly. 'He's awake?'

'Yes.'

'Good.'

I interpreted the 'good' to be satisfaction that the patient had survived the anaesthetic. Dominic's eyes slid slowly in Tony's direction and then came back to watch mine.

'We're taking you to your mother,' I said.

'Try mummy,' Tony said dryly.

'We're taking you to your mummy,' I said.

Dominic's eyes watched my face, unblinking.

'We're taking you home,' I said. 'Here's your teddy. You'll soon be back with your mummy.'

Dominic showed no reaction. The big eyes went on watching.

'You're safe,' I said. 'No one will hurt you. We're taking you home to your mummy.'

Dominic watched.

'Talkative kid,' Tony said.

'Frightened out of his wits.'

'Yeah, poor little bugger.'

Dominic was still wearing the red swimming trunks in which he'd been stolen away. The kidnappers had added a blue jersey, considerably too large, but no socks or shoes. He had been cold to the touch when I'd taken him out of the holdall, but his little body had warmed in the rug to the point where I could feel his heat coming through.

'We're taking you home,' I said again.

He made no reply but after about five minutes sat upright on my lap and looked out of the car window. Then his eyes came round again to look at mine, and he slowly relaxed back into his former position in my arms.

'Nearly there,' Tony said. 'What'll we do? It's only four. She'll pass effing out if we give her a shock at this time of night.'

'She might be awake,' I said.

'Yeah,' he said. 'Worrying about the kid. I suppose she might. Here we are, just down this road.'

He turned in through the Nerrity gates, the wheels crunching on the gravel: stopped right beside the front door, and got out and rang the bell.

A light went on upstairs and after a considerable wait the front door opened four inches on a chain.

'Who is it?' John Nerrity's voice said. 'What on earth do you want at this hour?'

Tony stepped closer into the light coming through the crack. 'Tony Vine.'

'Go away.' Nerrity was angry. 'I've told you . . .'

'We brought your kid back,' Tony said flatly. 'Do you want him?'

'What?'

'Dominic,' Tony said with mock patience. 'Your son.'

'I. . . .' he floundered.

'Tell Mrs Nerrity,' Tony said.

I imagined he must have seen her behind her husband, because very shortly the front door opened wide and Miranda stood there in a nightgown, looking gaunt. For a moment she hovered as if terrified, not daring to believe it, and I climbed out of the car with Dominic hanging on tight.

'Here he is,' I said, 'safe and sound.'

She stretched out her arms and Dominic slid from my embrace to hers, the rug dropping away. He wrapped his little

193

arms round her neck and clung with his legs like a limpet, and it was as if two incomplete bodies had been fused into one whole.

Neither of them spoke a word. It was Nerrity who did all the talking.

'You'd better come in, then,' he said.

Tony gave me a sardonic look and we stepped through into the hall.

'Where did you find him?' Nerrity demanded. 'I haven't paid the ransom . . .'

'The police found him,' Tony said. 'In Sussex.'

'Oh.'

'In conjunction with Liberty Market,' I added smoothly.

'Oh.' He was nonplussed, not knowing how to be grateful or how to apologise or how to say he might have been wrong in giving us the sack. Neither of us helped him. Tony said to Miranda, 'Your car's still at the hotel, but we brought all your gear – your clothes, chair, and so on – back with us.'

She looked at him vaguely, her whole consciousness attuned to the limpet.

'Tell Superintendent Rightsworth the boy's back,' I said to Nerrity.

'Oh . . . yes.'

Dominic, seen by electric light, was a nice-looking child with a well-shaped head on a slender stalk of a neck. He had seemed light in my arms but Miranda leant away from his weight as he sat on her hip, the two of them still entwined as if with glue.

'Good luck,' I said to her. 'He's a great kid.'

She looked at me speechlessly, like her son.

Tony and I unloaded their seaside stuff into the hall and said we would telephone in the morning to check if everything was all right; but later, when Nerrity had finally come up with a strangled thank you and shut his door on us, Tony said, 'What do you think we'd better do now?'

'Stay here,' I said decisively. 'Roughly on guard. There's still Terry and Peter unaccounted for, and maybe others. We'd look right idiots if they walked straight in and took the whole family hostage.'

Tony nodded. 'Never think the enemy have ceased hostilities, even though they've effing surrendered. Vigilance is the best defence against attack.' He grinned. 'I'll make a soldier of you yet.'

fourteen

For one day there was peace and quiet. Tony and I went to the office for a few hours and wrote a joint report, which we hoped would be acceptable to the assembled partners on the following morning. Apart from being misleading about the order in which Dominic's escape and the entry of the gladiators had occurred, we stuck fairly closely to the truth: as always it was in the wording itself that the less orthodox activities were glossed over.

'We deduced that the child was being held in the upper storey,' he wrote, without saying how the deduction had been made. 'After the child had been freed, Superintendent Eagler was of the opinion that he (the child) should be reunited with his parents as soon as possible, and consequently we performed the service.'

On the telephone Eagler had allayed our slightly anxious enquiries.

'Don't you fret. We took them without a fight. They were coughing and crying all over the place.' His voice smiled. 'There were three of them. Two were on the top storey running about, absolutely frantic, looking for the kid and not being able to see for tears. They kept saying he'd fallen down the chute.'

'Did you find the chute?' I asked curiously.

195

'Yes. It was a circular canvas thing like they have for escapes from aircraft. It slanted from the hole in the floorboards into a small cupboard on the floor below. The door of the cupboard had been bricked up and wallpapered and there was a wardrobe standing in front of it. All freshly done, the cement wasn't thoroughly dried. Anyway, they could have slid the boy down the chute and replaced the chunk of floorboards and put a rug over the trapdoor, and no ordinary search would have found him.'

'Would he have survived?' I asked.

'I should think so, yes, as long as they'd taken him out again, but to do that they'd have to have unbricked the doorway.'

'All rather nasty,' I said soberly.

'Yes, very.'

Tony and I put Eagler's account of the chute into our report and decided not to tell Miranda.

Eagler also said that none of the kidnappers was talking; that they were tough, sullen, and murderously angry. None of them would give his name, address or any other information. None of them had said a single word that could with propriety be taken down and used in evidence. All their utterances had been of the four-letter variety, and they had been sparing even with those.

'We've sent their prints to the central registry, of course, but with no results so far.' He paused. 'I've been listening to your tapes. Red hot stuff. I'll pry open these fine oysters with what's on them, never fear.'

'Hope they utter pearls,' I said.

'They will, laddie.'

Towards midday I telephoned to Alessia to postpone the lunch invitation and was forgiven instantly.

'Miranda telephoned,' she said. 'She told me you brought Dominic home. She can't speak for tears, but at least this time they're mostly happy.'

'Mostly?' I said.

'John and that policeman, Superintendent Rightsworth, both insisted on Dominic being examined by a doctor, and of

196

course Miranda didn't disagree, but she says they are talking now of treatment for him, not because of his physical state, which isn't bad, but simply because he won't talk.'

'What sort of treatment?'

'In hospital.'

'They can't be serious!' I said with alarm.

'They say Miranda can go with him, but she doesn't like it. She's trying to persuade everyone to let Dominic stay at home with her in peace for a few days. She says she's sure he'll talk to her, if they're alone.'

I reflected that once the news of his kidnap and return hit the public consciousness there would be little enough peace for a while, but that otherwise her instincts were right on the button.

I said, 'Do you think you could persuade John Nerrity, referring to your own experiences, that to be carted off to hospital among strangers would be desperately disturbing for Dominic now, even if Miranda went with him, and could make him worse, not better.'

There was a silence. Then she said slowly, 'If Papa had sent me to a hospital, I would have gone truly mad.'

'People sometimes do awful things with the best intentions.'

'Yes,' she said faintly. 'Are you at home?'

'No. In the office. And – about lunch, I'm very sorry . . .'

'Another day will do fine,' she said absently. 'I'll talk to John and ring you back.'

She telephoned back when Tony and I had finished the report and he'd gone home to a well-earned sleep.

'John was very subdued, you'd be surprised,' she said. 'All that self-importance was in abeyance. Anyway, he's agreed to give Dominic more time, and I've asked Miranda and Dominic down to Lambourn tomorrow. Popsy's such a darling. She says it's open house for kidnap victims. She also suggested you should come as well, if you could, and I think . . . I do think it would be the best ever thing . . . if you could.'

'Yes, I could,' I said. 'I'd like to, very much.'

'Great,' she said; then, reflectively, 'John sounded pleased, you know, that Miranda and Dominic would be out of the house. He's so odd. You'd think he'd be delirious with joy, having his son back, and he almost seemed . . . annoyed.'

'Think of your own father's state after you got home.'

'Yes, but . . .' she broke off. 'How very strange.'

'John Nerrity,' I said neutrally, 'is like one of those snow-storm paperweights, all shaken up, with bits of guilt and fear and relief and meanness all floating around in a turmoil. It takes a while after something as traumatic as the last few days for everything in someone's character to settle, like the snowstorm, so to speak, and for the old pattern to reassert itself.'

'I'd never thought of it like that.'

'Did he realise,' I asked, 'that the press will descend on him, as they did on you?'

'No, I don't think so. Will they?'

''Fraid so. Sure to. Someone down in Sussex will have tipped them off.'

'Poor Miranda.'

'She'll be fine. If you ring her again, tell her to hold onto Dominic tight through the interviews and keep telling him in his ear that he's safe and that all the people will go away soon.'

'Yes.'

'See you tomorrow,' I said.

Dominic was a big news item on breakfast television and near-headlines in the newspapers. Miranda, I was glad to see, had met the cameras with control and happiness, the wordless child seeming merely shy. John Nerrity, head back, moustache bristling, had confirmed that the sale of his Derby winner would go through as planned, though he insisted he was nowhere near bankruptcy; that the story had been merely a ploy to confound the kidnappers.

They all asked who had rescued his son.

The police, John Nerrity said. No praise was too high.

Most people in the office, having seen the coverage, read Tony's and my report with interest, and we both answered questions at the Monday session. Gerry Clayton's eyebrows rose a couple of times, but on the whole no one seemed to want to enquire too closely into what we had done besides advise. The Chairman concluded that even if Nerrity stuck to his guns and refused to pay a fee it shouldn't worry us. The deliverance of Dominic, he said contentedly, had been tidily and rapidly carried out at little cost to the firm. Liaison with the police had been excellent. Well done, you two chaps. Any more business? If not, we'll adjourn.

Tony adjourned to the nearest pub and I to Lambourn, arriving later than I would have liked.

'Thank goodness,' Alessia said, coming out of the house to meet me. 'We thought you'd got lost.'

'Held up in the office.' I hugged her with affection.

'No excuse.'

There was a new lightness about her: most encouraging. She led me through the kitchen to the more formal drawing room where Dominic sat watchfully on Miranda's lap and Popsy was pouring wine.

'Hello,' Popsy said, giving me a welcoming kiss, bottle in one hand, glass in the other. 'Out with the wand, it's badly needed.'

I smiled at her green eyes and took the filled glass. 'Pity I'm not twenty years younger,' she said. I gave her an 'oh yeah' glance and turned to Miranda.

'Hello,' I said.

'Hello.' She was quiet and shaky, as if ill.

'Hello, Dominic.'

The child stared at me gravely with the big wide eyes. Blue eyes, I saw by daylight. Deep blue eyes.

'You looked terrific on the box,' I said to Miranda. 'Just right.'

'Alessia told me . . . what to do.'

'Alessia told her to dress well, to look calm and to pretend everything was normal,' Popsy said. 'I heard her. She said it was a good lesson she'd learned from you, and Miranda might as well benefit.'

Popsy had made an informal lunch in the kitchen, of which Miranda ate little and Dominic nothing, and afterwards she drove us all up to the Downs in her Land Rover, thinking instinctively, I reckoned, that as it was there that Alessia felt most released, so would Dominic also.

'Has Dominic eaten anything at all since we brought him back?' I asked on the way.

'Only milk,' Miranda said. 'He wouldn't touch even that until I tried him with one of his old bottles.' She kissed him gently. 'He always used to have his bedtime milk in a bottle, didn't you, poppet? He only gave it up six months ago.'

We all in silence contemplated Dominic's regression to baby-hood, and Popsy put the brakes on up by the schooling fences.

'I brought a rug,' she said. 'Let's sit on the grass.'

She and the two girls sat, with Dominic still clinging to his mother, and I leaned against the Land Rover and thought that Popsy was probably right: the peace of the rolling hills was so potent it almost stretched out and touched you.

Miranda had brought a toy car, and Alessia played with it, wheeling it across the rug, up Miranda's leg and onto Dominic's. He watched her gravely for a while without smiling and finally hid his face in his mother's neck.

Miranda said, her mouth trembling, 'Did they . . . did they hurt him? He hasn't any bad bruises, just little ones . . . but what did they do, what did they do to make him like this?'

I squatted beside her and put an arm round her shoulder, embracing Dominic also. He looked at me with one eye from under his mother's ear, but didn't try to squirm away.

'They apparently kept him fastened to a bed with a sort of harness you get in prams. I didn't see it, but I was told. I don't think the harness would have hurt him. He would have been able to move a little – sit up, kneel, lie down. He refused to eat any food and he cried sometimes because he was lonely.' I paused. 'It's possible they deliberately frightened him more than they had to, to keep him quiet.' I paused again. 'There was a hole in the floorboards. A big hole, big enough for a child to fall through.' I paused again. 'They might have told Dominic that if he made a lot of noise they'd put him down the hole.'

Miranda's whole body shuddered and Dominic let out a wail and clung to his mother with frenzy. It was the first sound I'd heard him utter, and I wasn't going to waste it.

'Dominic,' I said firmly. 'Some nice policemen have filled up that hole so that no little boys can fall down it. The three men who took you away in a boat are not coming back. The policemen have locked them up in prison. No one is going to take you to the seaside.' I paused. 'No one is going to stick any more tape on your mouth. No one is going to be angry with you and call you horrid names.'

'Oh, darling,' Miranda said in distress, hugging him.

'The hole is all filled in,' I said. 'There is no hole any more in the floor. Nobody can fall down it.'

The poor little wretch would have nightmares about it perhaps all his life. Any person who could find a prevention for nightmares, I often thought, would deserve a Nobel prize.

I stood up and said to Alessia and Popsy, 'Let's go for a stroll,' and when they stood up I said to Dominic, 'Give your mummy lots of kisses. She cried all the time, when those horrid men took you. She needs a lot of kisses.'

She needed the kisses her husband hadn't given her, I thought. She needed the comfort of strong adult arms. She was having to generate strength enough to see herself and Dominic through alone, and it still seemed to me a toss up whether she'd survive triumphantly or end in breakdown.

Popsy, Alessia and I walked slowly over to one of the schooling fences and stood there talking.

'Do you think you did right, reminding him of the hole in the floor?' Popsy asked.

'Splinters have to come out,' I said.

'Or the wound festers?'

'Yes.'

'How did you know what they threatened?'

'I didn't know. I just guessed. It was so likely, wasn't it?

The hole was there. He was crying. Shut up you little bleeder or we'll put you down it.'

Popsy blinked. Alessia swallowed. 'Tell Miranda,' I said to her, 'that it takes a long time to get over something as awful as being kidnapped. Don't let her worry if Dominic wets the bed and clings to her. Tell her how it's been with you. How insecure it made you feel. Then she'll be patient with Dominic once the first joy of having him back has cooled down.'

'Yes, I'll tell her.'

Popsy looked from Alessia to me and back again, but said nothing, and it was Alessia herself who half smiled and gave voice to Popsy's thought.

'I've clung to you all right,' she said to me, looking briefly over to Miranda and then back. 'When you aren't here, and I feel panicky, I think of you, and it's a support. I'll tell Miranda that too. She needs someone to cling to herself, poor girl.'

'You make Andrew sound like a sort of trellis for climbing plants,' Popsy said. We walked again, as far as the next schooling fence, and stopped, looking out across the hills. High cirrus clouds curled in feathery fronds near the sun, omen of bad weather to come. We'd never have found Dominic, I thought, if it had rained the day after he was taken and there had been no canal-digger with his grandmother on the beach.

'You know,' Alessia said, suddenly stirring, 'it's time for me to go back to racing.' The words came out as if unpremeditated and seemed to surprise her.

'My darling!' Popsy exclaimed. 'Do you mean it?'

'I think I mean it at this moment,' Alessia said hesitantly, smiling nervously. 'Whether I mean it tomorrow morning is anyone's guess.'

We all saw, however, that it was the first trickle through the dike. I put my arms round Alessia and kissed her: and in an instant it wasn't a gesture of congratulation but something much fiercer, something wholly different. I felt the fire run through her in return and then drain away, and I let go of her thinking that the basement had taken charge of me right and proper.

I smiled. Shrugged my shoulders. Made no comment.

'Did you mean that?' Alessia demanded.

'Not exactly,' I said. 'It was a surprise.'

'It sure was.' She looked at me assessingly and then wandered away on her own, not looking back.

'You've pruned her off the trellis,' Popsy said, amused. 'The doctor kissed the patient; most unprofessional.'

'I'll kiss Dominic too if it will make you feel better.'

She took my arm and we strolled in comradely fashion back to the Land Rover and the rug. Miranda was lying on her back, dozing, with Dominic loosely sprawled over her stomach. His eyes, too, were shut, his small face relaxed, the contours rounded and appealing.

'Poor little sweetheart,' Popsy murmured. 'Pity to wake them.'

Miranda woke naturally when Alessia returned, and with Dominic still asleep we set off on the short drive home. One of the bumps in the rutted Down track must have roused him, though, because I saw him half sit up in Miranda's arms and then lie back, with Miranda's head bent over him as if to listen.

Alessia gave me a wild look and she too bent her head to listen, but I could hear nothing above the sound of the engine, and anyway it didn't seem to me that Dominic's lips were moving.

'Stop the car,' Alessia said to Popsy, and Popsy, hearing the urgency, obeyed.

Dominic was humming.

For a few seconds the low noise went on: randomly, I thought at first, though certainly not on one note.

'Do you know what that is?' Alessia said incredulously, when the child stopped. 'I simply don't believe it.'

'What, then?' I said.

For answer she hummed the phrase again, exactly as Dominic had done. He sat up in Miranda's arms and looked at her, clearly responding.

'He knows it!' Alessia exclaimed. 'Dominic knows it.'

'Yes, darling,' Popsy said patiently. 'We can see he does. Can we drive on now?'

'You don't understand,' Alessia said breathlessly. 'That's out of *Il Trovatore*. The Soldiers' Chorus.'

My gaze sharpened on her face. 'Do you mean . . .' I began.

She nodded. 'I heard it five times a day for six weeks.'

'What are you talking about?' Miranda asked. 'Dominic doesn't know any opera. Neither John nor I like it. Dominic only knows nursery rhymes. He picks those up like lightning. I play them to him on cassettes.'

'Holy hell,' I said in awe. 'Popsy, drive home. All is fine.'

With good humour Popsy restarted the car and took us back to the house, and once there I went over to my car to fetch my briefcase and carry it into the kitchen.

'Miranda,' I said, 'I'd like Dominic to look at a picture.'

She was apprehensive but didn't object. She sat at the kitchen table with Dominic on her lap, and I took out one of the photostats of Giuseppe and laid it face up on the table. Miranda watched Dominic anxiously for a frightened reaction, but none came. Dominic looked at the face calmly for a while and then turned away and leaned against Miranda, his face to her neck.

With a small sigh I put the picture back in the case and accepted Popsy's offer of a universal cup of tea.

'*Ciao, bambino*,' Dominic said.

My head and Alessia's snapped round as if jerked by strings.

'What did you say?' Alessia asked him, and Dominic snuggled his face deeper into Miranda's neck.

'He said "*Ciao, bambino*"' I said.

'Yes . . . that's what I thought.'

'Does he know any Italian?' I asked Miranda.

'Of course not.'

'Goodbye, baby,' Popsy said. 'Isn't that what he said?'

I took the picture of Giuseppe out of the case again and laid it on the table.

'Dominic, dear little one,' I said, 'what was the man called?'

The great eyes swivelled my way, but he said nothing.

'Was his name . . . Michael?' I asked.

Dominic shook his head: a fraction only, but a definite negative.

'Was his name David?'

Dominic shook his head.

'Was his name Giuseppe?'

Dominic's eyes didn't waver. He shook his head.

I thought a bit. 'Was his name Peter?'

Dominic did nothing except look at me.

'Was his name Dominic?' I said.

Dominic almost smiled. He shook his head.

'Was his name John?'

He shook his head.

'Was his name Peter?'

Dominic was still for a long time; then, slowly, very slightly, he nodded.

'Who's Peter?' Alessia asked.

'The man who took him for a ride in a boat.'

Dominic stretched out a hand and briefly touched the pictured face with one finger before drawing back.

'*Ciao, bambino*,' he said again, and tucked his head against his mother.

One thing was crystal clear, I thought. It wasn't Giuseppe–Peter who had most frightened Dominic. The baby, like Alessia herself, had liked him.

Eagler said, 'I thought the boy wouldn't talk. Superintendent Rightsworth told me he'd tried, but the child was in shock, and the mother was being obstructive about treatment.'

'Mm,' I said. 'Still, that was yesterday. Today Dominic has positively identified the photostat as being one of the kidnappers, known to him as Peter.'

'How reliable do you think the kid is?'

'Very. He certainly knew him.'

'All right. And this Peter – and I suppose he's the one the kidnappers are talking about on those tapes – he's Italian?'

'Yes. Dominic had learned two words from him: ciao bambino.'

'Luv-a-duck,' Eagler said quaintly.

'It seems also,' I said, 'as if Giuseppe–Peter has a fondness for Verdi. Alessia Cenci said her kidnappers played three of Verdi's operas to her, over and over. Dominic is humming the Soldiers' Chorus from *Il Trovatore*, which was one of them. Did you by any chance find a cassette player in that house?'

'Yes, we did.' He sounded as if nothing ever again would surprise him. 'It was up in the room where the kid was kept. There were only two tapes there. One was pop music, and yes, laddie, the other was Verdi. *Il Trovatore*.'

'It's conclusive, then, isn't it?' I said. 'We have a practitioner.'

'A what?'

'Practitioner. Sorry; it's what in Liberty Market we call a man who kidnaps on a regular basis. Like a safe-breaker or a con-man. His work.'

'Yes,' Eagler agreed. 'We have a practitioner; and we have you. I wonder if Giuseppe–Peter knows of the existence of Liberty Market.'

'His constant enemy,' I said.

Eagler almost chuckled. 'I dare say you made things too hot for him in his part of Italy, flooding the place with what is obviously a recognisable portrait. It would be ironic if he'd decided to move to England and came slap up against you all over again. He'd be speechless if he knew.'

'I dare say he'll find out,' I said. 'The existence of Liberty Market isn't a total secret, even though we don't advertise. Any kidnapper of experience would hear of us sometime. Perhaps one of these days there'll be a ransom demand saying no police and no Liberty Market either.'

'I meant you, personally, laddie.'

'Oh.' I paused. 'No, he wouldn't know that. He saw me once, in Italy, but not here. He didn't know then who I worked for. He didn't even know I was British.'

'He'll have a fit when he finds his picture all over England too.' Eagler sounded cheerfully smug. 'Even if we don't catch him, we'll chase him back where he came from in no time.'

'You know,' I said tentatively, 'you and Pucinelli might both flash that picture about among horse people, not just put it up in police stations. Many crooks are ostensibly sober citizens, aren't they? Both of the kidnaps that we're sure are his work are to do with racing. They're the people who'd know him. Someone, somewhere, would know him. Perhaps the racing papers would print it?'

'It's a pity I can't compare notes with your friend Pucinelli,' Eagler said. 'I sometimes think police procedures do more to prevent the exchange of information than to spread it. Even in England it's hard enough for one county to get information from another county, let alone talk to regional coppers in Europe.'

'I don't see why you can't. I can tell you his 'phone number. You could have an interpreter this end, standing by.'

'Ring Italy? It's expensive, laddie.'

'Ah.' I detected also in his voice the reluctance of many of the British to make overseas calls: almost as if the process itself was a dangerous and difficult adventure, not just a matter of pressing buttons.

'If I want to know anything particular,' Eagler said, 'I'll ask you to ask him. Things I learn from you come under the heading of information received, origin unspecified.'

'So glad.'

He chuckled. 'We had our three kidnappers in court this morning: remanded in custody for a week. They're still saying nothing. I've been letting them stew while I listened to all the tapes, but now, tonight, and with what you've just told me, I'll bounce them out of their socks.'

fifteen

Eagler opened his oysters, but they were barren of pearls. He concluded, as Pucinelli had done, that none of the arrested men had known Giuseppe–Peter before the day he recruited one of them in a pub.

'Does Giuseppe–Peter speak English?' I asked.

'Yes, apparently, enough to get by. Hewlitt understood him, right enough.'

'Who's Hewlitt?'

'Kidnapper. The voice on the ransom tape. Voice prints made and matched. Hewlitt has a record as long as your arm, but for burglary, not anything like this. The other two are in the same trade; housebreaking, nicking silver and antiques. They finally gave their names, once they saw we'd got them to rights. Now they're busy shoving all the blame onto Peter, but they don't know much about him.'

'Were they paid at all?' I asked.

'They say not, but they're lying. They got some on account, must have. Stands to reason.'

'I suppose Giuseppe–Peter didn't telephone the house in Itchenor, did he?'

There was dead silence from Eagler. Embarrassment, I diagnosed.

'He did,' I suggested, 'and got a policeman?'

'Well . . . there was one call from someone unknown.'

'But you got a recording?'

'All he said,' said Eagler resignedly, 'was "Hello". My young PC thought it was someone from the station and answered accordingly, and the caller rang off.'

'Can't be helped,' I said.

'No.'

'Did Hewlitt say how Giuseppe–Peter knew of him? I mean, you can't go up to a perfect stranger in a British pub and proposition them to kidnap.'

'On that subject Hewlitt is your proverbial silent stone. There's no way he's going to say who put him up. There's some things, laddie, one just can't find out. Let's just say that there are a lot of Italians in London, where Hewlitt lives, and there's no way he's going to point the finger at any of them.'

'Mm,' I said. 'I do see that.'

I telephoned Alessia to ask how she was feeling and found her full of two concerns: the first, her own plans for a come-back race, and second, the predicament of Miranda and Dominic.

'Miranda's so miserable and I don't know how to help her,' she said. 'John Nerrity's being thoroughly unreasonable in every way, and he and Miranda are now sleeping in different rooms, because he won't have Dominic sleeping in the room with them, and Dominic won't sleep by himself.'

'Quite a problem,' I agreed.

'Mind you, I suppose it's difficult for both of them. Dominic wakes up crying about five times every night, and won't go to sleep again unless Miranda strokes him and talks to him, and she says she's getting absolutely exhausted by it, and John is going on and on about sending Dominic to hospital.' She paused. 'I can't ask Popsy to have her here to stay. I simply don't know what to do.'

'Hm. . . . How much do you like Miranda?'

'Quite a lot. More than I expected, to be honest.'

'And Dominic?'

'He's a sweetheart. Those terrific eyes. I love him.'

I paused, considering, and she said, 'What are you thinking? What should Miranda do?'

'Is her mother still with her?'

'No. She has a job and doesn't seem to be much help.'

'Does Miranda have any money except what John gives her?'

'I don't know. But she was his secretary.'

'Yeah. Well . . . Miranda should take Dominic to a doctor I know of, and she should go and stay for a week near someone supportive like you that she can be with for a good deal of every day. And I don't know how much of that is possible.'

'I'll make it possible,' Alessia said simply.

I smiled at the telephone. She sounded so whole, her own problems submerged under the tidal wave of Dominic's.

'Don't let Miranda mention my name to her husband in connection with any plan she makes,' I said. 'I'm not in favour with him, and if he knew I'd suggested anything he'd turn it down flat.'

'But you brought Dominic back!'

'Much to his embarrassment. He'd sacked us two days earlier.'

She laughed. 'All right. What's the name of the doctor?'

I told her, and also told her I'd telephone the doctor myself, to explain the background and verify Dominic's need.

'You're a poppet,' Alessia said.

'Oh sure. What was it you said about going racing?'

'I rode out with the string today and yesterday, and I can't understand why I didn't do it sooner. I'm riding work for Mike Noland tomorrow, and he says if I'm fit and OK he'll give me a ride next week at Salisbury.'

'Salisbury . . . races?' I said.

'Yes, of course.'

'And, um, do you want an audience?'

'Yes, I do.'

'You've got it.'

She said goodbye happily and in the evening rang me at home in my flat.

'It's all fixed,' she said. 'Miranda said your doctor sounded a darling, and she's taking Dominic there first thing tomorrow. Then she's coming straight down here to Lambourn. I've got her a room in a cottage owned by a retired nanny, who I went to see, and who's pleased with the whole idea, and John raised no objections, absolutely the contrary, he's paying for everything.'

'Terrific,' I said, with admiration.

'And Popsy wants you down again. And so does Miranda. And so do I.'

'I give in, then. When?'

'Soon as you can.'

I went on the following day and also twice more during the following week. Dominic slept better because of a mild liquid sleeping draught in his nightly bottle of milk and progressed to eating chocolate drops and, later, mashed bananas. The ex-nanny patiently took away rejected scrambled eggs and fussed over Miranda in a way which would have worn my nerves thin but in that love-deprived girl produced a grateful dependency.

Alessia spent much of every day with them, going for walks, shopping in the village, all of them lunching most days with Popsy, sunbathing in the cottage garden.

'You're a clever clogs, aren't you?' Popsy said to me on my third visit.

'How do you mean?'

'Giving Alessia something so worthwhile to do.'

'It was accidental, really.'

'And encouraged.'

I grinned at her. 'She looks great, doesn't she?'

'Marvellous. I keep thinking about those first days when she was so deathly pale and shaky. She's just about back to her old self now.'

'Has she driven anywhere yet, on her own?'

Popsy glanced at me. 'No. Not yet.'

'One day she will.'

'And then?'

'Then she'll fly . . . away.'

I heard in my voice what I hadn't intended or expected to be there: a raw sense of loss. It was all very well mending birds' broken wings. They could take your heart off with them when you set them free.

She wouldn't need me, I'd always known it, once her own snowstorm had settled. I could have tried, I supposed, to turn her dependence on me into a love affair, but it would have been stupid: cruel to her, unsatisfactory to me. She needed to grow safely back to independence and I to find a strong and equal partner. The clinging with the clung-to wasn't a good proposition for long-term success.

We were all at that moment out in Popsy's yard, with Alessia taking Miranda slowly round and telling her about each horse as they came to it. Dominic by then had developed enough confidence to stand on the ground, though he hung onto Miranda's clothes permanently with one hand and needed lifting to her hip at the approach of any stranger. He had still not said anything else, but day by day, as the fright level slowly declined, it became more likely that he soon would.

Popsy and I strolled behind the two girls and on an impulse I squatted down to Dominic's height and said, 'Would you like a ride on my shoulders?'

Miranda encouragingly swept up Dominic and perched him on me with one leg past each ear.

'Hold on to Andrew's hair,' Alessia said, and I felt the little fingers gripping as I stood upright.

I couldn't see Dominic's face, but everyone else was smiling, so I simply set off very slowly past the boxes, so he could see the inmates over the half doors.

'Lovely horses,' Miranda said, half anxiously. 'Big horses, darling, look.'

We finished the tour of the yard in that fashion and when I lifted Dominic down he stretched up his arms to go up again. I hoisted him onto my left arm, my face level with his. 'You're a good little boy,' I said.

He tucked his head down to my neck as he'd done so often with Miranda, and into my receptive ear he breathed one very quiet word, 'Andrew.'

'That's right,' I said equally quietly, 'and who's that?' I pointed at Miranda.

'Mummy.' The syllables weren't much more than a whisper, but quite clear.

'And that?' I said.

'Lessia.'

'And that?'

'Popsy.'

'Very good.' I walked a few steps with him away from the

others. He seemed unalarmed. I said in a normal voice, 'What would you like for tea?'

There was a fairly long pause, then he said 'Chocolate,' still quietly.

'Good. You shall have some. You're a very good boy.'

I carried him further away. He looked back only once or twice to check that Miranda was still in sight, and I reckoned that the worst of his troubles were over. Nightmares he would have, and bouts of desperate insecurity, but the big first steps had been taken, and my job there too was almost done.

'How old are you, Dominic?' I asked.

He thought a bit. 'Three,' he said, more audibly.

'What do you like to play with?'

A pause. 'Car.'

'What sort of car?'

He sang, 'Dee-dah dee-dah dee-dah,' into my ear very clearly on two notes, in exact imitation of a police car's siren.

I laughed and hugged him. 'You'll do,' I said.

Alessia's return to race-riding was in some respects unpromising, as she came back white-faced after finishing last.

The race itself, a five furlong sprint for two-year-olds, had seemed to me to be over in a flash. Hardly had she cantered down to the start, a bent figure in shining red silks, than the field of eighteen were loaded into the stalls and set running. The red silks had shown briefly and been swamped, smothered by a rainbow wave which left them slowing in the wake. The jockey sat back onto her saddle the moment she passed the winning post, stopping her mount to a walk in a few strides.

I went to where all except the first four finishers were being dismounted, where glum-faced little groups of owners and trainers listened to tale after tale of woe and disaster from impersonal jockeys whose minds were already on the future. I heard snatches of what they were saying while I waited unobtrusively for Alessia.

'Wouldn't quicken when I asked him . . .'

'Couldn't act on the going . . .'

'Got bumped . . . shut in . . . squeezed out.'

'Still a baby . . .'

'Hanging to the left . . .'

Mike Noland, without accompanying owners, non-committally watched Alessia approaching, then patted his horse's neck and critically inspected its legs. Alessia struggled to undo the buckles on the girths, a service Noland finally performed for her, and all I heard her say to him was 'Thanks. . . .Sorry,' which he received with a nod and a pat on the shoulder: and that seemed to be that.

Alessia didn't spot me standing there and hurried away towards the weighing-room; and it was a good twenty minutes before she emerged.

She still looked pale. Also strained, thin, shaky and miserable.

'Hi,' I said.

She turned her head and stopped walking. Managed a smile. 'Hello.'

'What's the matter?' I said.

'You saw.'

'I saw that the horse wasn't fast enough.'

'You saw that every talent I used to have isn't there any more.'

I shook my head. 'You wouldn't expect a prima ballerina to give the performance of a lifetime if she'd been away from dancing for three months.'

'This is different.'

'No. You expected too much. Don't be so . . . so cruel to yourself.'

She gazed at me for a while and then looked away, searching for another face. 'Have you seen Mike Noland anywhere?' she said.

'Not since just after the race.'

'He'll be furious.' She sounded desolate. 'He'll never give me another chance.'

'Did he expect his horse to win?' I asked. 'It started at about twelve to one. Nowhere near favourite.'

Her attention came back to my face with another flickering smile. 'I didn't know you betted.'

'I didn't. I don't. I just looked at the bookies' boards, out of interest.'

She had come from Lambourn with Mike Noland, and I had driven from London. When I'd talked to her before she went to change for the race she'd been nervously expectant: eyes wide, cheeks pink, full of small movements and half smiles, wanting a miracle.

'I felt sick in the parade ring,' she said. 'I've never been like that before.'

'But you didn't actually vomit . . .'

'Well, no.'

'How about a drink?' I suggested. 'Or a huge sandwich?'

'Fattening,' she said automatically, and I nodded and took her arm.

'Jockeys whose talents have vanished into thin air can eat all the sandwiches they want,' I said.

She pulled her arm away and said in exasperation, 'You : . . you always make people see things straight. All right. I'll admit it. Not every vestige of talent is missing, but I made a rotten showing. And we'll go and have a . . . a small sandwich, if you like.'

Some of the blues were dispersed over the food, but not all, and I knew too little about racing to judge whether her opinion of herself was fair. She'd looked fine to me, but then so would almost anyone have done who could stand in the stirrups while half a ton of thoroughbred thundered forward at over thirty miles an hour.

'Mike did say something on the way here about giving me a ride at Sandown next week if everything was OK today, and I don't suppose he will, now.'

'Would you mind very much?'

'Yes, of course,' she said passionately. 'Of course I'd mind.'

She heard both the conviction and the commitment in her voice, and so did I. Her head grew still, her eyes became more peaceful, and her voice, when she spoke again, was lower in pitch. 'Yes, I'd mind. And that means I still want to be a jockey more than anything on earth. It means that I've got to work harder to get back. It means that I must put these last three months behind me, and get on with living.' She finished the remains of a not very good chicken sandwich and sat back in her chair and smiled at me. 'If you come to Sandown, I'll do better.'

We went eventually in search, Alessia said, of an honest opinion from Mike Noland; and with the forthrightness I was coming to see as normal among the racing professionals he said, 'No, you were no good. Bloody bad. Sagging all over the place like a sponge. But what did you expect, first time back, after what you've been through? I knew you wouldn't win. I doubt if that horse could have won today anyway, with Fred Archer incarnate in the saddle. He might have been third . . . fourth.' He shrugged. 'On the form book he couldn't have touched the winner. You'll do better next time. Sure to. Sandown, right?'

'Right,' Alessia said faintly.

The big man smiled kindly from the height of his fifty years and patted her again on the shoulder. 'Best girl jockey in Europe,' he said to me. 'Give or take a dozen or two.'

'Thanks so much,' Alessia said.

I went to Sandown the following week and to two more race meetings the week after, and on the third of those days Alessia won two races.

I watched the applause and the acclaim and saw her quick bright smiles as she unsaddled her winners, saw the light in her eyes and the certainty and speed of her movements, saw the rebirth of the skills and the quality of spirit which had taken her before to the heights. The golden girl filled to new stature visibly day by day and on the morning after her winners the newspapers printed her picture with rapturous captions.

She still seemed to want me to be there; to see me, specifically, waiting. She would search the surrounding crowds with her eyes and stop and smile when she saw me. She came and went from Lambourn every time with Mike Noland and spent her free minutes on the racecourse with me, but she no longer grasped me physically to save herself from drowning. She was afloat and skimming the waves, her mind on far horizons. She had begun to be, in the way she most needed to be, happy.

'I'm going home,' she said one day.

'Home?'

'To Italy. To see Papa. I've been away so long.'

I looked at the fine-boned face, so healthy now, so brown, so full of poise, so intimately known.

'I'll miss you,' I said.

'Will you?' She smiled into my eyes. 'I owe you a debt I can't pay.'

'No debt,' I said.

'Oh yes.' Her voice took it for granted. 'Anyway, it's not goodbye for ever, or anything dramatic like that. I'll be back. The Flat season will be finished here in a few weeks, but I'll definitely be riding here some of the time next summer.'

Next summer seemed a long way away.

'Alessia,' I said.

'No.' She shook her head. 'Don't say whatever's in your mind. You carry on giving a brilliant imitation of a rock, because my foundations are still shaky. I'm going home to Papa . . . but I want to know you're only a telephone call away . . . some days I wake up sweating . . .' She broke off. 'I'm not making sense.'

'You are indeed,' I assured her.

She gave me a brief but searching inspection. 'You never need telling twice, do you? Sometimes you don't need telling once. Don't forget me, will you?'

'No,' I said.

*

She went to Italy and my days seemed remarkably empty even though my time was busily filled.

Nerrity's near-loss of Ordinand had caused a huge flutter in the dovecotes of owners of good-as-gold horses and I, in conjunction with our chummy insurance syndicate at Lloyds, was busy raising defences against copy-cat kidnaps.

Some owners preferred to insure the animals themselves against abduction, but many saw the point of insuring their wives and children. I found myself invited to ring the front door bell of many an imposing pile and to pass on the Chairman's considered judgements, the Chairman in some erroneous way having come to consider me an expert on racing matters.

The Lloyds syndicate did huge new business, and into every contract they wrote as usual a stipulation that in the case of 'an event,' the advice of Liberty Market should be instantly sought. You scratch my back, I'll scratch yours: both the syndicate and Liberty Market were purring.

The Jockey Club showed some interest. I was despatched to their offices in Portman Square in London to discuss the problems of extortion with the Senior Steward, who shook my hand firmly and asked whether Liberty Market considered the danger a real one.

'Yes,' I said moderately. 'There have been three kidnaps in the racing world recently: a man in Italy who owned a race-course, Alessia Cenci, the girl jockey, whom you must know about, and John Nerrity's son.'

He frowned. 'You think they're connected?'

I told him how positively the latter two were connected and his frown deepened.

'No one can tell whether this particular man will try again now that the Nerrity venture has ended in failure,' I said, 'but the idea of forcing someone to sell a valuable horse may be seductive enough to attract imitators. So yes, we do think owners would be prudent to insure against any sort of extortion involving their horses.'

The Senior Steward watched my face unsmilingly. He was a thick-set man, maybe sixty, with the same natural assumption of authority as our Chairman, though not with the same overpowering good looks. Morgan Freemantle, Senior Steward, top authority of the huge racing industry, came across as a force of more power than charm, more intelligence than kindness, more resolution than patience. I guessed that in general people respected him rather than liked him, and also that he was probably good news for the health of the racing world.

He had said he had heard of our existence from a friend of his who was an underwriter at Lloyds, and that he had since made several enquiries.

'It seems your firm is well-regarded,' he told me austerely. 'I must say I would have seen no need for such an organisation, but I now learn there are approximately two hundred kidnaps for ransom in the world each year, not counting tribal disturbances in Africa, or political upheavals in Central and South America.'

'Er . . .' I said.

He swept on. 'I am told there may be many more occurrences than those actually reported. Cases where families or firms settle in private and don't inform the police.'

'Probably,' I agreed.

'Foolish,' he said shortly.

'Most often, yes.'

'I understand from the Police Commissioners that they are willing to work with your firm whenever appropriate.' He paused, and added almost grudgingly, 'They have no adverse criticisms.'

Bully for them, I thought.

'I think we can say, therefore,' Morgan Freemantle went on judiciously, 'that if anything further should happen to anyone connected with racing, you may call upon the Jockey Club for any help it is within our power to give.'

'Thank you very much,' I said, surprised.

He nodded. 'We have an excellent security service. They'll be happy to work with you also. We in the Jockey Club,' he informed me regretfully, 'spend a great deal of time confounding dishonesty, because unfortunately racing breeds fraud.'

There didn't seem to be an answer to that, so I gave none.

'Let me know, then, Mr . . . er . . . Douglas,' he said, rising, 'if your firm should be engaged by anyone in racing to deal with a future circumstance which might come within our province. Anything, that is to say, which might affect the stability of racing as a whole. As extortion by means of horses most certainly does.'

I stood also. 'My firm could only advise a client that the Jockey Club should be informed,' I said neutrally. 'We couldn't insist.'

He gave me a straight considering stare. 'We like to know what's going on in our own backyard,' he said. 'We like to know what to defend ourselves against.'

'Liberty Market will always cooperate as fully as possible,' I assured him.

He smiled briefly, almost sardonically. 'But you, like us, don't know where an enemy may strike, or in what way, and we find ourselves wishing for defences we never envisaged.'

'Mm,' I said. 'Life's like that.'

He shook my hand again firmly and came with me from his desk to the door of his office.

'Let's hope we've seen an end to the whole thing. But if not, come to see me.'

'Yes,' I said.

I telephoned to the Villa Francese one evening and my call was answered by Ilaria.

'Hello, Mr Fixit,' she said with amusement. 'How's it going?'

'Every whichway,' I said. 'And how are you?'

'Bored, wouldn't you know?'

Is Alessia there?' I asked.

'The precious girl is out visiting with Papa.'

'Oh . . .'

'However,' Ilaria said carefully, 'she should be back by ten. Try again later.'

'Yes. Thank you.'

'Don't thank me. She is out visiting Lorenzo Traventi, who has made a great recovery from his bullets and is now looking particularly ravishing and romantic and is kissing her hand at every opportunity.'

'Dear Ilaria,' I said. 'Always so kind.'

'Shit,' she said cheerfully, 'I might tell her you called.'

She did tell her. When I rang again, Alessia answered almost immediately.

'Sorry I was out,' she said. 'How's things?'

'How are they with you?' I asked.

'Oh . . . fine. Really fine. I mean it. I've ridden in several races since I've been back. Two winners. Not bad. Do you remember Brunelleschi?'

I thought back. 'The horse you didn't ride in the Derby?'

'That's right. Spot on. Well, he was one of my winners last week, and they're sending him to Washington to run in the International, and believe it or not but they've asked me to go too, to ride him.' Her voice held both triumph and apprehension in roughly equal amounts.

'Are you going?' I said.

'I . . . don't know.'

'Washington DC?' I asked. 'America?'

'Yes. They have an international race every year there at Laurel racecourse. They invite some really super horses from Europe to go there – pay all their expenses, and those of the trainers and jockeys. I've never been, but I've heard it's great. So what do you think?'

'Go, if you can,' I said.

There was a small silence. 'That's the whole thing, isn't it? If I can. I almost can. But I have to decide by tomorrow at the latest. Give them time to find someone else.'

'Take Ilaria with you,' I suggested.

'She wouldn't go,' she said positively, and then more doubtfully, 'Would she?'

'You can but ask.'

'Yes. Perhaps I will. I do wish, though, that you could go, yourself. I'd sail through the whole thing if I knew you were there.'

'Not a chance,' I said regretfully. 'But you will be all right.'

We talked for a while longer and disconnected, and I spent some time wondering if I could, after all, wangle a week off and blow the fare, but we were at that time very shorthanded in the office, Tony Vine having been called away urgently to Brazil and four or five partners tied up in a multiple mess in Sardinia. I was constantly taking messages from them on the switchboard in between the advisory trips to racehorse owners, and even Gerry Clayton's folded birds of paradise had given way to more orthodox paperwork.

Nothing happens the way one expects.

Morgan Freemantle, Senior Steward of the Jockey Club, went to Laurel for a week to be the guest of honour of the president of the racecourse, a courtesy between racing fraternities.

On the second day of his visit he was kidnapped.

Washington D.C.

sixteen

The Chairman sent me round to the Jockey Club, where shock had produced suspended animation akin to the waxworks.

For a start there were very few people in the place and no one was quite sure who was in charge; a flock without its leader. When I asked which individual had received the first demand from the kidnappers I was steered to the office of a stiff-backed middle-aged woman in silk shirt and tweed skirt who looked at me numbly and told me I had come at a bad time.

'Mrs Berkeley?' I enquired.

She nodded, her eyes vague, her thoughts elsewhere, her spine rigid.

'I've come about Mr Freemantle,' I said. It sounded rather as if I'd said 'I've come about the plumbing', and I had difficulty in stifling a laugh. Mrs Berkeley paid more attention and said, 'You're not the man from Liberty Market, are you?'

'That's right.'

'Oh.' She inspected me. 'Are you the person who saw Mr Freemantle last week?'

'Yes.'

'What are you going to do about it?'

'Do you mind if I sit down?' I asked, indicating the chair nearest to me, beside her polished desk.

'By all means,' she said faintly, her voice civilised upper class, her manner an echo of country house hostess. 'I'm afraid you find us . . . disarranged.'

'Could you tell me what messages you have actually received?' I said.

She looked broodingly at her telephone as if it were itself guilty of the crime. 'I am taking all incoming calls to the

Senior Steward's private number on this telephone during his absence. I answered. . . .There was an American voice, very loud, telling me to listen carefully . . . I felt disembodied, you know. It was quite unreal.'

'The words,' I said without impatience. 'Do you remember the words?'

'Of course I do. He said the Senior Steward had been kidnapped. He said he would be freed on payment of ten million English pounds sterling. He said the ransom would have to be paid by the Jockey Club.' She stared at me with the shocked glaze still in her eyes. 'It's impossible, you know. The Jockey Club doesn't have that sort of money. The Jockey Club are administrators. There are no . . . assets.'

I looked at her in silence.

'Do you understand?' she said. 'The Jockey Club are just people. Members. Of a club.'

'Rich members?' I asked.

Her mouth, half open, stopped moving.

'I'm afraid,' I said neutrally, 'that kidnappers usually couldn't care less where the money comes from or who it hurts. We'll get the demand down to far below ten million pounds, but it may still mean that contributions will be sought from racing people.' I paused. 'You didn't mention any threats. Were there any threats?'

She nodded slowly. 'If the ransom wasn't paid, Mr Freemantle would be killed.'

'Straight and simple?'

'He said . . . there would be another message later.'

'Which you haven't yet received?'

She glanced at a round-faced clock on a wall where the hands pointed to four-fifty.

'The call came through just after two,' she said. 'I told Colonel Tansing. He thought it might have been a hoax, so we telephoned to Washington. Mr Freemantle wasn't in his hotel. We got through to the public relations people who are looking after his trip and they said he hadn't turned up yesterday evening at a reception and they didn't know where he'd gone. Colonel Tansing explained about the ransom demand and they said they would tell Eric Rickenbacker – that's the president of the racecourse – and Mr Rickenbacker would get the police on to it straight away.'

'Was there any mention of not going to the police, on your ransom-demand call?'

She shook her head slowly. 'No.'

She had a firm, tidy-looking face with brown wavy hair greying at the sides: the sort of face that launched a thousand pony clubs and church bazaars, worthy, well-intentioned, socially secure. Only something of the present enormity could have produced her current rudderlessness, and even that, I judged, would probably transform to brisk competence very soon.

'Has anyone told the British police?' I asked.

'Colonel Tansing thought it best to contact your Chairman first,' she said. 'Colonel Tansing, you see, is . . .' She paused as if seeking for acceptable words. 'Colonel Tansing is the deputy licensing officer, whose job is mainly the registration of racehorse owners. No one of any seniority is here this afternoon, though they were this morning. No one here now really has the power to make top-level decisions. We're trying to find the Stewards . . . they're all out.' She stopped rather blankly. 'No one expects this sort of thing, you know.'

'No,' I agreed. 'Well, the first thing to do is to tell the police here and get them to put a tap on all the Jockey Club's telephones, and after that to get on with living, and wait.'

'Wait?'

I nodded. 'While the ransom negotiations go on. I don't want to alarm you, but it may be some time before Mr Freemantle comes home. And what about his family? His wife? Has she been told?'

She said glumly, 'He's a widower.'

'Children?'

'He has a daughter,' she said dubiously, 'but I don't think they get on well. I believe she lives abroad . . . Mr Freemantle never mentions her.'

'And, excuse me,' I said, 'is Mr Freemantle himself . . . er . . . rich?'

She looked as if the question were in ultra-poor taste but finally answered, 'I have no idea. But anyone who becomes Senior Steward must be considered to have personal funds of some sort.'

'Ten million?' I asked.

'Certainly not,' she said positively. 'By many standards he is moderate in his expenditure.' Her voice approved of this. 'He dislikes waste.'

Moderate spending habits and a dislike of waste turned up often enough in the most multi of millionaires, but I let it go. I thanked her instead and went in search of Colonel Tansing, who proved to be a male version of Mrs Berkeley, courteous, charming and shocked to near immobility.

In his office I telephoned the police and got things moving there and then asked him who was the top authority at the Jockey Club in Mr Freemantle's absence.

'Sir Owen Higgs,' he said. 'He was here this morning. We've been trying to reach him . . .' He looked slightly apprehensive. 'I'm sure he will agree we had to call you in.'

'Yes,' I said reassuringly. 'Can you arrange to record all calls on all your telephones? Separately from and in addition to the police?'

'Shall be done,' he said.

'We have a twenty-four hour service at Liberty Market, if you want us.'

He clasped my hand. 'The Jockey Club is one of the most effective organisations in Britain,' he said apologetically. 'This business has just caught us on the hop. Tomorrow everything will swing into action.'

I nodded and departed, and went back to the Liberty Market offices reflecting that neither the Colonel nor Mrs Berkeley had speculated about the victim's present personal sufferings.

Stunned disbelief, yes. Tearful sympathetic devotion; no.

*

Sir Owen Higgs having formally engaged Liberty Market's services, I set off to Washington the following morning, and by early afternoon, their time, was driving a rented car towards Laurel racecourse to talk to Eric Rickenbacker, its president.

The racecourse lay an hour's drive away from the capital city along roads ablaze with brilliant trees, golden, red, orange, tan – nature's last great flourish of trumpets before winter. The first few days of November: warm, sunny and windless under a high blue sky. The sort of day to lift the spirits and sing to. I felt liberated, as always in America, a feeling which I thought had something to do with the country's own vastness, as if the wide-apartness of everything flooded into the mind and put spaces between everyday problems.

Mr Rickenbacker had left instructions about me at the race-club entrance: I was to be conveyed immediately to his presence. Not so immediately, it transpired, as to exempt me from being stamped on the back of the hand with an ultraviolet dye, normally invisible to the eye but transformed to a glowing purple circular pattern under special lamps. My pass into the Club, it was explained: without it I would be stopped at certain doorways. A ticket one couldn't lose or surreptitiously pass to a friend, I thought. It would wash off, they said.

Mr Rickenbacker was in the president's domain, a retreat at the top of the grandstand, reached by elevator, hand-checks, a trudge through the Members' lounges, more checks, an inconspicuous doorway and a narrow stair. At the top of the stair, a guardian sitting at a table. I gave my name. The guardian checked it against a list, found it, ticked it, and let me through. I went round one more corner and finished the journey. The president's private dining room, built on three levels, looked out across the course through acres of glass, with tables for about a hundred people; but it was almost empty.

The only people in the place were sitting round one of the furthest tables on the lowest level. I walked over and down, and they looked up enquiringly at my approach. Six men, four women, dressed for tidy racing.

'Mr Rickenbacker?' I said generally.

'Yes?'

He was a big man with thick white hair, quite clearly tall even though sitting down. His eyes had the reflecting brilliance of contact lenses and his skin was pale and smooth, immensely well-shaven.

'I'm Andrew Douglas,' I said briefly.

'Ah.' He stood up and clasped my hand, topping me by a good six inches. 'These are friends of mine.' He indicated them with a small gesture but made none of the usual detailed introductions, and to them he said, 'Excuse me, everyone, I have some business with Mr Douglas.' He waved to me to follow him and led the way up deep-carpeted steps to a yet more private eyrie, a small room beyond, above, behind his more public dining room.

'This is a goddam mess,' he said forcefully, pointing me to an armchair. 'One minute Morgan was telling me about John Nerrity's troubles, and the next . . .' He moved his arms frustratedly. 'We've heard nothing ourselves from any kidnappers. We've told the police both here and in Washington of the ransom demand received in London, and they've been looking into Morgan's disappearance. How much do you know about that?'

'Nothing,' I said. 'Please tell me.'

'Do you want a drink?' he said. 'Scotch? Champagne?'

'No, thank you.'

'We have a public relations firm that handles a lot of things here for us. This is a social week, you follow me? We have a lot of overseas visitors. There are receptions, press conferences, sponsors' parties. We have guests of honour – Morgan was one of those – for whom we arrange transport from the hotel to the racecourse, and to the various receptions, you follow?'

I nodded.

'The public relations firm hires the cars from a limousine service. The cars come with drivers, of course. The public relations firm tells the limousine service who to pick up from where, and where to take them, and the limousine service instructs its drivers, you follow me?'

'Yes,' I said.

'Morgan was staying at the Ritz Carlton, you follow? We put him in there, it's a nice place. The racecourse is picking up the tab. Morgan was supposed to join us at a reception in Baltimore the evening before last. The reception was for the press . . . many overseas sportswriters come over for our big race, and I guess we do everything we can to make them feel welcome.'

'Mm,' I said, understanding. 'World coverage of a sports event is good for the gate.'

He paused a fraction before nodding. Maybe I shouldn't have put it so baldly; but the public-relations-promotions bandwagon generated business and business generated jobs, and the artificial roundabout bought real groceries down the line.

'Morgan didn't arrive at the reception,' Rickenbacker said. 'He was expected . . . he had assured me he would be there. I know he intended to say he was glad to be representing British racing, and to tell the press of some of the plans the English Jockey Club is making for the coming year.'

'He was going to speak?' I said. 'I mean, make a speech?'

'Yes, didn't I make that clear? We always have three or four speakers at the press party, but very short and informal, you follow, just a few words of appreciation, that sort of thing. We were surprised when Morgan didn't show, but not disturbed. I was myself surprised he hadn't sent a message, but I don't know him well. We met just three days ago. I wouldn't know if he would be careful about courtesies, you follow?'

'Yes,' I said. 'I follow.'

He smoothed a muscular hand over the white hair. 'Our public relations firm told the limousine service to pick Morgan up from the Ritz Carlton and take him to the Harbor Room in Baltimore.' He paused. 'Baltimore is nearer to this racetrack than Washington is, you follow me, so a majority of the press stay in Baltimore.' He paused again, giving me time for understanding. 'The Ritz Carlton report a chauffeur coming to the front desk, saying he had been assigned to collect Morgan. The front desk called Morgan, who came down, left his key, and went out with the chauffeur. And that's all. That's all anyone knows.'

'Could the front desk describe the chauffeur?' I asked.

'All they could positively remember was that he wore a chauffeur's uniform and cap. He didn't say much. They think he may have spoken with some sort of non-American accent, but this is a polyglot city and no one took much notice.'

'Mm,' I said. 'What happened to the real chauffeur?'

'The real . . . ? Oh, no, nothing. The Ritz Carlton report a second chauffeur appeared. They told him Morgan had already been collected. The chauffeur was surprised, but not too much. With an operation of this size going on there are always mix-ups. He reported back to his service, who directed him to another assignment. The limousine service thought Morgan must have taken a ride with a friend and not told them. They were philosophical. They would charge the racetrack for their trouble. They wouldn't lose.'

'So no one was alarmed,' I said.

'Of course not. The public relations firm called the Ritz Carlton in the morning – that was yesterday – and the front desk said Morgan's key was there, he must already have gone out. No one was alarmed until we had the call from your Colonel Tansing asking about a hoax.' He paused. 'I was at home eating breakfast.'

'Rather a shock,' I said. 'Have all these pressmen woken up yet to the story under their noses?'

With the first faint glimmer of humour he said that things were at the unconfirmed rumour stage, the whole hive buzzing.

'It'll put your race on the world map like nothing else will,' I said.

'I'm afraid so.' He looked undecided about the worth of that sort of publicity, or more probably about the impropriety of dancing up and down with commercial glee.

'You told the police,' I said.

'Sure. Both here in Laurel and in Washington. The people in Washington are handling it.'

I nodded and asked which police, specifically: there were about five separate forces in the capital.

'The Metropolitan Police,' he said. 'Sure, the FBI and the Missing Persons Bureau have taken an interest, but they've sorted it out that it's the Metropolitan Police's baby. The man in charge is a Captain Kent Wagner. I told him you were coming. He said I could send you along, if you wanted.'

'Yes, please.'

He took a wallet from an inner pocket and removed a small white card. 'Here you are,' he said, handing it over. 'And also . . .' he sorted out another card, 'this is my home number. If I've left the racetrack, you can call me there.'

'Right.'

'Tomorrow morning we have the Press Breakfast,' he said. 'That's when all the overseas owners and trainers and jockeys meet downstairs here in the club.' He paused. 'We have a Press Breakfast before most big races in America . . . have you been to one before?'

'No,' I said.

'Come tomorrow. You'll be interested. I'll arrange passes for you.'

I thanked him, not sure whether I could manage it. He nodded genially. A small thing like the abduction of Britain's top racing executive was not, it seemed, going to dent the onward steamrollering of the week's serious pleasures.

I asked him if I could make a call to Liberty Market before I went to the police in Washington, and he waved me generously to the telephone.

'Sure. Go right ahead. It's a private line. I'll do everything possible to help, you know that, don't you? I didn't know Morgan himself real well, and I guess it couldn't be thought this racetrack's fault he was kidnapped, but anything we can do . . . we'll give it our best shot.'

I thanked him and got through to London, and Gerry Clayton answered.

'Don't you ever go home?' I said.

'Someone has to mind the store,' he said plaintively: but we all knew he lived alone and was lonely away from the office.

'Any news from the Jockey Club?' I asked.

'Yeah, and how. Want me to play you the tape they got by Express Mail?'

'Fire away.'

'Hang on.' There was a pause and a few clicks, and then an American voice, punchy and hard.

'If you Brits at the Jockey Club want Freemantle back, listen good. It's going to cost you ten million English pounds sterling. Don't collect the money in notes. You're going to pay in certified bankers' checks. You won't get Freemantle back until the checks are clear. You've got one week to collect the bread. In one week you'll get more instructions. If you fool around, Freemantle will lose his fingers. You'll get one every day, Express Mail, starting two weeks from now.

'No tricks. You in the Jockey Club, you've got money. Either you buy Freemantle back, or we kill him. That's a promise. We take him out. And if you don't come up with the bread, you get nothing, you don't even get his corpse. If we kill him, we kill him real slow. Make him curse you. Make him scream. You hear us? He gets no tidy single shot. He dies hard. If we kill him, you'll get his screams on tape. If you don't want that, you're going to have to pay.

'Freemantle, he wants to talk to you. You listen.'

There was a pause on the line, then Freemantle's own voice, sounding strong and tough and incredibly cultured after the other.

'If you do not pay the ransom, I will be killed. I am told this is so, and I believe it.'

Click. 'Did you get all that?' Gerry Clayton's voice said immediately.

'Yeah.'

'What do you think?'

'I think it's our man again,' I said. 'For sure.'

'Right. Same feel.'

'How long will you be on the switchboard?' I asked.

'Until midnight. Seven p.m., your time.'

'I'll probably ring again.'

'OK. Happy hunting.'

I thanked Rickenbacker and drove off to Washington, and after a few false trails found Captain of Detectives Kent Wagner in his precinct.

The Captain was a walking crime deterrent, big of body, hard of eye, a man who spoke softly and reminded one of cobras. He was perhaps fifty with flat-brushed dark hair, his chin tucked back like a fighting man; and I had a powerful impression of facing a wary, decisive intelligence. He shook my hand perfunctorily, looking me over from head to foot, summing up my soul.

'Kidnappers never get away with it in the United States,' he said. 'This time will be no exception.'

I agreed with him in principle. The American record against kidnappers was second to none.

'What can you tell me?' he asked flatly, from his look not hoping much.

'Quite a lot, I think,' I said mildly.

He eyed me for a moment, then opened the door of his glass-walled office and called across an expanse of desks, 'Ask Lieutenant Stavoski to step in here, if you please.'

One of the many blue-uniformed men rose to his feet and went on the errand, and through the windows I watched the busy, orderly scene, many people moving, telephones ringing, voices talking, typewriters clacking, computer screens flicking, cups of coffee on the march. Lieutenant Stavoski, when he came, was a pudgy man in the late thirties with a large drooping moustache and no visible doubts about himself. He gave me a disillusioned stare; probably out of habit.

The Captain explained who I was. Stavoski looked unimpressed. The Captain invited me to give. I obligingly opened my briefcase and brought out a few assorted articles, which I laid on his desk.

'We think this is definitely the third, and probably the

fourth, of a series of kidnappings instigated by one particular person,' I said. 'The Jockey Club in England has today received a tape from the kidnappers of Morgan Freemantle, which I've arranged for you to hear now on the telephone, if you like. I've also brought with me the ransom-demand tapes from two of the other kidnaps.' I pointed to them as they lay on the desk. 'You might be interested to hear the similarities.' I paused slightly. 'One of the tapes is in Italian.'

'Italian?'

'The kidnapper himself is Italian.'

Neither of them particularly liked it.

'He speaks English,' I said, 'but in England he recruited an English national to utter his threats, and on today's tape the voice is American.'

Wagner pursed his lips. 'Let's hear today's tape then.' He gave me the receiver from his telephone and pressed a few preliminary buttons. 'This call will be recorded,' he said. 'Also all our conversations from now on.'

I nodded and got through to Gerry Clayton, who gave the kidnapper a repeat performance. The aggressive voice rasped out loudly through the amplifier in Captain Wagner's office, both the policemen listening with concentrated disgust.

I thanked Gerry and disconnected, and without a word Wagner held out a hand to me, his eyes on the tapes I'd brought. I gave him the Nerrity one, which he fitted into a player and set going. The sour threats to Dominic, the cutting off of fingers, the screams, the non-return of the body, all thundered into the office like an echo. The faces of Wagner and Stavoski both grew still and then judicious and finally convinced.

'The same guy,' Wagner said, switching off. 'Different voice, same brain.'

'Yes,' I said.

'Get Patrolman Rossellini in here,' he told the Lieutenant and it was Stavoski, this time, who put his head out of the door and yelled for the help. Patrolman Rossellini, large-nosed, young, black-haired, very American, brought his Italian grand-

234

parentage to bear on the third of the tapes and translated fluently as it went along. When it came to the last of the series of threats to Alessia's body his voice faltered and stopped, and he glanced uneasily around, as if for escape.

'What is it?' Wagner demanded.

'The guy says,' Rossellini said, squaring his shoulders to the requirement, 'well, to be honest, Captain, I'd rather not say.'

'The guy roughly said,' I murmured, coming to the rescue, 'that bitches were accustomed to dogs and that all women were bitches.'

Wagner stared. 'You mean–?'

'I mean,' I said, 'that that threat was issued to reduce her father to pulp. There seems to have been no intention whatsoever of carrying it out. The kidnappers never threatened anything like it to the girl herself, nor anything indeed about daily beatings. They left her completely alone.'

Patrolman Rossellini went away looking grateful, and I told Wagner and Stavoski most of what had happened in Italy and England and in what ways the similarities of the two kidnappings might be of use to them now. They listened silently, faces impassive, reserving comments and judgement to the end.

'Let's get this straight,' Wagner said eventually, stirring. 'One: this Giuseppe–Peter is likely to have rented a house in Washington, reasonably near the Ritz Carlton, within the last eight weeks. That, as I understand it, is when Morgan Freemantle accepted Eric Rickenbacker's invitation.'

I nodded. 'That was the date given us by the Jockey Club.'

'Two: there are likely to be at least five or six kidnappers involved, all of them American except Giuseppe–Peter. Three: Giuseppe–Peter has an inside edge on racecourse information and therefore must be known to people in that world. And four,' with a touch of grim humour, 'at this moment Morgan Freemantle may be getting his ears blasted off by Verdi.'

He picked up the photocopy likeness of Giuseppe–Peter.

'We'll paper the city with this,' he said. 'If the Nerrity kid recognised him, anyone can.' He gave me a look in which, if there wasn't positive friendship, one could at least read a sheathing of poison fangs.

'Only a matter of time,' he said.

'But . . . er . . .' I said diffidently, 'you won't, of course, forget that if he sees you getting close, he'll kill Morgan Freemantle. I'd never doubt he means that part. Kill him and bury him. He'd built a tomb for little Dominic that might not have been found for years.'

Wagner looked at me with speculation. 'Does this man Giuseppe–Peter frighten you?'

'As a professional adversary, yes.'

Both men were silent.

'He keeps his nerve,' I said. 'He thinks. He plans. He's bold. I don't believe a man like that would turn to this particular crime if he were not prepared to kill. Most kidnappers will kill. I'd reckon Giuseppe–Peter would expect to kill and get away with it, if killing were necessary. I don't think he would do it inch by inch, as the tape threatened. But a fast kill to cut his losses, to escape, yes, I'd bet on it.'

Kent Wagner looked at his hands. 'Has it occurred to you, Andrew, that this Giuseppe–Peter may not like you personally one little bit?'

I was surprised by his use of my first name but took it thankfully as a sign of a working relationship about to begin; and I answered similarly, 'Kent, I don't think he knows I exist.'

He nodded, a smile hovering, the connection made, the common ground acknowledged.

seventeen

Silence from the kidnappers, indignation from the about-to-be-dunned members of the Jockey Club and furore from the world's sporting press: hours of horrified talk vibrating the air-waves, but on the ground overnight a total absence of action. I went to the Press Breakfast in consequence with a quiet conscience and a light heart, hoping to see Alessia.

The raceclub lounges were packed when I arrived, the decibel count high. Glasses of orange juice sprouted from many a fist, long-lensed cameras swinging from many a shoulder. The sportswriters were on their feet, moving, mingling, agog for exclusives, ears stretching to hear conversations behind them. The majority, knowing each other, clapped shoulders in passing. Trainers held small circular conferences, the press heads bending to catch vital words. Owners stood around looking either smug or bemused according to how often they'd attended this sort of shindig; and here and there, like gazelles among the herd, like a variation of the species, stood short light-boned creatures, heads thrown back, being deferred to like stars.

'Orange juice?' someone said, handing me a glass.

'Thanks.'

I couldn't see Rickenbacker, nor anyone I knew.

No Alessia. The gazelles I saw were all male.

I wandered about, knowing that without her my presence there was pointless; but it had seemed unlikely that she would miss taking her place among her peers.

I knew she'd accepted Laurel's invitation, and her name was plainly there at the breakfast, on a list pinned to a notice board on an easel, as the rider of Brunelleschi. I read through the list, sipping orange juice. Fourteen runners; three from Britain, one from France, one from Italy, two from Canada, two from Argentina, all the rest home-grown. Alessia seemed to be the only jockey who was a girl.

Presumably at some sort of signal the whole crowd began moving into a large side room, in which many oblong tables were formally laid with flowers, tablecloths, plates and cutlery. I had vaguely assumed the room to be made ready for lunch, but I'd been wrong. Breakfast meant apparently not orange juice on the wing, but bacon and eggs, waitresses and hot breads.

I hung back, thinking I wouldn't stay, and heard a breathless voice by my left ear saying incredulously, 'Andrew?' I turned. She was there after all, the thin face strong now and vivid, the tilt of the head confident. The dark bubble curls shone with health, the eyes below them gleaming.

I hadn't been sure what I felt for her, not until that moment. I hadn't seen her for six weeks and before that I'd been accustomed to thinking of her as part of my job; a rewarding pleasure, a victim I much liked, but transient, like all the others. The sight of her that morning came as almost a physical shock, an intoxicant racing in the bloodstream. I put out my arms and hugged her, and felt her cling to me momentarily with savagery.

'Well. . . .' I looked into her brown eyes. 'Want a lover?'

She gasped a bit and laughed, and didn't answer. 'We're at a table over there,' she said, pointing deep into the room. 'We were sitting there waiting. I couldn't believe it when I saw you come in. There's room for you at our table. A spare place. Do join us.'

I nodded and she led the way: and it wasn't Ilaria who had come with her from Italy, but Paolo Cenci himself. He stood up at my approach and gave me not a handshake but an immoderate Italian embrace, head to head, his face full of welcome.

Perhaps I wouldn't have recognised him, this assured, solid, pearl-grey-suited businessman, if I'd met him unexpectedly in an American street. He was again the man I hadn't known, the competent manager in the portrait. The shaky wreckage of five months earlier had retreated, become a memory, an illness obliterated by recovery. I was glad for him and felt a stranger with him, and would not in any way have referred to the anxieties we had shared.

He himself had no such reservations. 'This is the man who brought Alessia back safely,' he said cheerfully in Italian to the three other people at the table, and Alessia, glancing briefly at my face said, 'Papa, he doesn't like us to talk about it.'

'My darling girl, we don't often, do we?' He smiled at me with intense friendship. 'Meet Bruno and Beatrice Goldoni,' he said in English. 'They are the owners of Brunelleschi.'

I shook hands with a withdrawn-looking man of about sixty and a strained-looking woman of a few years younger, both of whom nodded pleasantly enough but didn't speak.

'And Silvio Lucchese, Brunelleschi's trainer,' Paolo Cenci said, introducing the last of the three.

We shook hands quickly, politely. He was dark and thin and reminded me of Pucinelli; a man used to power but finding himself at a disadvantage, as he spoke very little English very awkwardly, with an almost unintelligible accent.

Paolo Cenci waved me to the one empty chair, between Alessia and Beatrice Goldoni, and when all in the room were seated a hush fell on the noisy general chatter and Rickenbacker, followed by a few friends, made a heralded entrance, walking in a modest procession down the whole room, heading for the top table facing everyone else.

'Welcome to Laurel racecourse,' he said genially, reaching his centre chair, his white hair crowning his height like a cloud. 'Glad to see so many overseas friends here this morning. As I expect most of you have now heard, one of our good friends is missing. I speak of course of Morgan Freemantle, Senior Steward of the British Jockey Club, who was distressfully abducted here two days ago. Everything possible is being done to secure his early release and of course we'll keep you all informed as we go along. Meanwhile, have a good breakfast, and we'll all talk later.'

A flurry of waitresses erupted all over the place, and I suppose I ate, but I was conscious only of my stirred feelings for Alessia, and of her nearness, and of the question she hadn't answered. She behaved to me, and I dare say I to her, with civil calm. In any case, since everyone else was talking in Italian, my own utterances were few, careful, and limited in content.

It seemed that the Goldonis were enjoying their trip, though one wouldn't have guessed it from their expressions.

'We are worried about the race tomorrow,' Beatrice said. 'We always worry, we can t help it.' She broke off. 'Do you understand what I'm saying?'

'I understand much more than I speak.'

She seemed relieved and immediately began talking copiously, ignoring repressive looks from her gloomier husband. 'We haven't been to Washington before. Such a spacious, gracious city. We've been here two days . . . we leave on Sunday for New York. Do you know New York? What should one see in New York?'

I answered her as best I could, paying minimal attention. Her husband was sporadically discussing Brunelleschi's prospects with Lucchese as if it were their fiftieth reiteration, rather like the chorus of a Greek play six weeks into its run. Paolo Cenci told me five times he was delighted to see me, and Alessia ate an egg but nothing else.

An ocean of coffee later the day's real business began, proving to be short interviews with all the trainers and jockeys and many of the owners of the following day's runners. Sportswriters asked questions, Rickenbacker introduced the contestants effusively, and everyone learned more about the foreign horses than they'd known before or were likely to remember after.

Alessia interpreted for Lucchese, translating the questions, slightly editing the answers, explaining in one reply that Brunelleschi didn't actually mean anything, it was the name of the architect who'd designed a good deal of the city of Florence; like Wren in London, she said. The sportswriters wrote it down. They wrote every word she uttered, looking indulgent.

On her own account she said straightforwardly that the horse needed to see where he was going in a race and hated to be shut in.

'What was it like being kidnapped?' someone asked, transferring the thought.

'Horrible.' She smiled, hesitated, said finally that she felt great sympathy for Morgan Freemantle and hoped sincerely that he would soon be free.

Then she sat down and said abruptly, 'When I heard about Morgan Freemantle I thought of you, of course . . . wondered if your firm would be involved. That's why you're here, isn't it? Not to see me race.'

'Both,' I said.

She shook her head, 'One's work, one's luck.' She sounded merely practical. 'Will you find him, like Dominic?'

'A bit unlikely,' I said.

'It brings it all back,' she said, her eyes dark.

'Don't . . .'

'I can't help it. Ever since I heard . . . when we got to the track this morning . . . I've been thinking of him.'

Beatrice Goldoni was talking again like a rolling stream, telling me and also Alessia, who must have heard it often before, what a terrible shock it had been when dear Alessia had been kidnapped, and now this poor man, and what a blessing that I had been able to help get dear Alessia back . . . and I thought it colossally lucky she was speaking in her own tongue, which I hoped wouldn't be understood by the newspaper ears all around.

I stopped her by wishing her firmly the best of luck in the big race, and by saying my farewells to the whole party. Alessia came with me out of the dining room and we walked slowly across the bright club lounge to look out across the racecourse.

'Tomorrow,' I said, 'they'll be cheering you.'

She looked apprehensive more than gratified. 'It depends how Brunelleschi's travelled.'

'Isn't he here?' I asked, surprised.

'Oh yes, but no one knows how he feels. He might be homesick . . . and don't laugh, the tap water here tastes vile to me, God knows what the horse thinks of it. Horses have their own likes and dislikes, don't forget, and all sorts of unimaginable factors can put them off.'

I put my arm round her tentatively.

'Not here,' she said.

I let the arm fall away, 'Anywhere?' I asked.

'Are you sure . . . ?'

'Don't be silly. Why else would I ask?'

The curve of her lips was echoed in her cheekbones and in her eyes, but she was looking at the track, not at me.

'I'm staying at the Sherryatt,' I said. 'Where are you?'

'The Regency. We're all there: the Goldonis, Silvio Lucchese, Papa and I. All guests of the racecourse. They're so generous, it's amazing.'

'How about dinner?' I said.

'I can't. We've been invited by the Italian ambassador . . . Papa knows him . . . I have to be there.'

I nodded.

'Still,' she said. 'We might go for a drive or something this afternoon. I don't truthfully want to spend all day here on the racecourse. We were here yesterday . . . all the foreign riders were shown what we'll be doing. Today is free.'

'I'll wait for you here, then, on this spot.'

She went to explain to her father but returned immediately saying that everyone was about to go round to the barns and she couldn't get out of that either, but they'd all said I was very welcome to go with them, if I'd like.

'Barns?' I said.

She looked at me with amusement. 'Where they stable the horses on American racecourses.'

In consequence I shortly found myself, along with half the attendance from the breakfast, watching the morning routines on the private side of the tracks; the feeding, the mucking-out, the grooming, the saddling-up and mounting, the breezes (short sharp canters), the hot-walking (for cooling off from exercise), the sand-pit rolling, and all around, but constantly

242

shifting, the tiny individual press conferences where trainers spoke prophesies like Moses.

I heard the trainer of the home-based horse that was favourite saying confidently 'We'll have the speed all the way to the wire.'

'What about the foreign horses?' one of the reporters asked. 'Is there one to beat you?'

The trainer's eye wandered and lit on Alessia, by my side. He knew her. He smiled. He said gallantly, 'Brunelleschi is the danger.'

Brunelleschi himself, in his stall, seemed unimpressed. Silvio Lucchese, it appeared, had brought the champion's own food from Italy so that the choosy appetite should be unimpaired. And Brunelleschi had, it seemed, 'eaten up' the evening before (a good sign), and hadn't kicked his stable-lad, as he did occasionally from displeasure. Everyone patted his head with circumspection, keeping their fingers away from his strong white teeth. He looked imperious to me, like a bad-tempered despot. No one asked what he thought of the water.

'He's nobody's darling,' Alessia said out of the owners' earshot. 'The Goldonis are afraid of him, I often think.'

'So am I,' I said.

'He puts all his meanness into winning.' She looked across with rueful affection at the dark tossing head. 'I tell him he's a bastard, and we get on fine.'

Paolo Cenci seemed pleased that Alessia would be spending most of the day with me. He, Lucchese and Bruno Goldoni intended to stay for the races. Beatrice, with a secret, sinful smile of pleasure, said she was going to the hotel's hairdresser, and, after that, shopping. Slightly to my dismay Paolo Cenci suggested Alessia and I should give her a lift back to Washington to save the limousine service doubling the journey, and accordingly we passed the first hour of our day with the voluble lady saying nothing much at great length. I had an overall impression that separation, even temporary, from her husband, had caused an excited rise in her spirits, and when

243

we dropped her at the Regency she had twin spots of bright red on her sallow middle-aged cheeks and guilt in every line of her heavy face.

'Poor Beatrice, you'd almost think she was meeting a lover,' Alessia said smiling, as we drove away, 'not just going shopping.'

'You, on the other hand,' I observed, 'are not blushing a bit.'

'Ah,' she said. 'I haven't promised a thing.'

'True.' I stopped the car presently in a side street and unfolded a detailed map of the city. 'Anything you'd like to see?' I asked. 'Lincoln Monument, White House, all that?'

'I was here three years ago, visiting. Did all the tours.'

'Good . . . Do you mind then, if we just drive around a bit? I want to put . . . faces . . . onto some of these street names.'

She agreed, looking slightly puzzled, but after a while said, 'You're looking for Morgan Freemantle.'

'For possible districts, yes.'

'What are possible?'

'Well . . . not industrial areas. Not decayed housing. Not all-black neighbourhoods. Not parks, museums or government offices. Not diplomatic residental areas . . . embassies and their offices. Not blocks of flats with janitors. Not central shopping areas, nor banking areas, nor schools or colleges, nowhere with students.'

'What's left?'

'Private housing. Suburbs. Anywhere without prying neighbours. And at a guess, somewhere north or west the centre, because the Ritz Carlton is there.'

We drove for a good long while, methodically sectioning the sprawling city according to the map, but concentrating most and finally on the north and west. There were beauties to the place one couldn't guess from the tourist round, and miles and hosts of residential streets where Morgan Freemantle could be swallowed without trace.

'I wonder if we've actually been past him,' Alessia said at one point. 'Gives me the shivers, not knowing. I can't bear to

244

think of him. Alone . . . dreadfully alone . . . somewhere close.'

'He might be further out,' I said. 'But kidnappers don't usually go for deserted farmhouses or places like that. They choose more populated places, where their comings and goings aren't noticeable.'

The scale of it all, however, was daunting, even within the radius I thought most likely. Analysis of recent rentals wouldn't come up this time with just eleven probables: there would be hundreds, maybe one or two thousand. Kent Wagner's task was impossible, and we would have to rely on negotiation, not a second miracle, to get Morgan Freemantle safe home.

We were driving up and down some streets near Washington Cathedral, simply admiring the houses for their architecture: large old sprawling houses with frosting of white railings, lived-in houses with signs of young families. On every porch, clusters of Halloween pumpkins.

'What are those?' Alessia said, pointing at the grinning orange faces of the huge round fruits on the steps outside every front door.

'It was Halloween four days ago,' I said.

'Oh yes, so it was. You don't see those at home.'

We passed the Ritz Carlton on Massachusetts Avenue and paused there, looking at the peaceful human-scaled hotel with its blue awnings from where Morgan had been so unceremoniously snatched, and then coasted round Dupont Circle and made our way back to the more central part. Much of the city was built in radii from circles, like Paris, which may have made for elegance but was a great recipe for getting lost: we'd chased our tails several times in the course of the day.

'It's so vast,' Alessia said, sighing. 'So confusing. I'd no idea.'

'We've done enough,' I agreed. 'Hungry?'

It was three-thirty by then, but time meant nothing to the Sherryatt Hotel. We went up to my room on the twelfth floor of the anonymous, enormous, bustling pile and we ordered

245

wine and avocado shrimp salad from room service. Alessia stretched lazily on one of the armchairs and listened while I telephoned Kent Wagner.

Did I realise, he asked trenchantly, that the whole goddam population of North America was on the move through Washington, D.C., and that a list of rentals would bridge the Potomac.

'Look for a house without pumpkins,' I said.

'What?'

'Well, if you were a kidnapper, would you solemnly carve Halloween faces on pumpkins and put them on the front steps?'

'No, I guess not.' He breathed out in the ghost of a chuckle. 'Takes a limey to come up with a suggestion as dumb as that.'

'Yeah,' I said. 'I'll be at the Sherryatt this evening and at the races tomorrow, if you should want me.'

'Got it.'

I telephoned next to Liberty Market, but nothing much had developed in London. The collective fury of the members of the Jockey Club was hanging over Portman Square in a blue haze and Sir Owen Higgs had retreated for the weekend to Gloucestershire. Hoppy at Lloyds was reported to be smiling cheerfully as in spite of advising everyone else to insure against extortion the Jockey Club hadn't done so itself. Apart from that, nix.

The food arrived and we ate roughly jockey-sized amounts. Then Alessia pushed her plate away and, looking at her wine glass, said, 'Decision time, I suppose.'

'Only for you,' I said mildly. 'Yes or no.'

Still looking down she said, 'Would no . . . be acceptable?'

'Yes, it would,' I said seriously.

'I . . .' She took a deep breath. 'I want to say yes, but I feel . . .' She broke off, then started again. 'I don't seem to want . . . since the kidnap . . . I've thought of kissing, of love, and I'm dead. . . .I went out with Lorenzo once or twice and he wanted to kiss me . . . his mouth felt like rubber to me.' She

246

looked at me anxiously, willing me to understand. 'I did love someone passionately once, years ago, when I was eighteen. It didn't last beyond summer. . . . We both simply grew up . . . but I know what it's like, what I should feel, what I should want . . . and I don't.'

'Darling Alessia.' I stood up and walked to the window, thinking that for this battle I wasn't strong enough, that there was a limit to controlled behaviour, that what I myself longed for now was warmth. 'I do truly love you in many ways,' I said, and found the words coming out an octave lower than in my normal voice.

'Andrew!' She came to her feet and walked towards me, searching my face and no doubt seeing there the vulnerability she wasn't accustomed to.

'Well . . .' I said, struggling for lightness; for a smile; for Andrew the unfailing prop. 'There's always time. You ride races now. Go shopping. Drive your car?'

She nodded.

'It all took time,' I said. I wrapped my arms around her lightly and kissed her forehead. 'When rubber begins feeling like lips, let me know.'

She put her head against my shoulder and clung to me for help as she had often clung before; and it was I, really, who wanted to be enfolded and cherished and loved.

She rode in the race the next day, a star in her own firmament.

The racecourse had come alive, crowds pressing, shouting, betting, cheering. The grandstands were packed. One had to slide round strangers to reach any goal. I had my hand stamped and checked and my name taken and ticked, and Eric Rickenbacker welcomed me busily to the biggest day of his year.

The president's dining room, so echoingly empty previously, spilled over now with chattering guests all having a wow of a time. Ice clinked and waitresses passed with small silver trays and a large buffet table offered crab cakes to aficionados.

Paolo Cenci was there with the Goldonis and Lucchese, all

247

of them looking nervous as they sat together at one of the tables. I collected a glass of wine from an offered trayful and went over to see them, wishing them well.

'Brunelleschi kicked his groom,' Paolo Cenci said.

'Is that good or bad?'

'No one knows,' he said.

I kept the giggle in my stomach. 'How's Alessia?' I asked.

'Less worried than anyone else.'

I glanced at the other faces; at Lucchese, fiercely intense, at Bruno Goldoni, frowning, and at Beatrice, yesterday's glow extinguished.

'It's her job,' I said.

They offered me a place at their table but I thanked them and wandered away, too restless to want to be with them.

'Any news from London?' Eric Rickenbacker said in my ear, passing close.

'None this morning.'

He clicked his tongue, indicating sympathy. 'Poor Morgan. Should have been here. Instead . . .' he shrugged resignedly, moving away, greeting new guests, kissing cheeks, clapping shoulders, welcoming a hundred friends.

The Washington International was making the world's news. Poor Morgan, had he been there, wouldn't have caused a ripple.

They saved the big race until ninth of the ten on the card, the whole afternoon a titillation, a preparation, with dollars flooding meanwhile into the Pari-mutuel and losing tickets filling the trashcans.

The whole of the front of the main stands was filled in with glass, keeping out the weather, rain or shine. To one slowly growing used to the rigours of English courses the luxury was extraordinary but, when I commented on it, one of Rickenbacker's guests said reasonably that warm betters betted, cold betters stayed at home. A proportion of the day's take at the Pari-mutuel went to the racecourse: racegoer comfort was essential.

For me the afternoon passed interminably, but in due course

248

all the foreign owners and trainers left the president's dining room to go down nearer the action and speed their horses on their way.

I stayed in the eyrie, belonging nowhere, watching the girl I knew so well come out onto the track; a tiny gold and white figure far below, one in a procession, each contestant led and accompanied by a liveried outrider. No loose horses on the way to the post, I thought. No runaways, no bolters.

A trumpet sounded a fanfare to announce the race. A frenzy of punters fluttered fistfuls of notes. The runners walked in procession across in front of the stands and cantered thereafter to the start, each still with an escort. Alessia looked from that distance identical with the other jockeys: I wouldn't have known her except for the colours.

I felt, far more disturbingly than on the English tracks, a sense of being no part of her real life. She lived most intensely there, on a horse, where her skill filled her. All I could ever be to her as a lover, I thought, was a support: and I would settle for that, if she would come to it.

The runners circled on the grass, because the one and a half mile International was run on living green turf, not on dirt. They were fed into the stalls on the far side of the track. Lights still flickered on the Pari-mutuel, changing the odds: races in America tended to start when the punters had finished, not to any rigid clock.

They were off, they were running, the gold and white figure with them, going faster than the wind and to my mind crawling like slow motion.

Brunelleschi, the brute who kicked, put his bad moods to good use, shouldering his way robustly round the first bunched-up bend, forcing himself through until there was a clear view ahead. Doesn't like to be shut in, Alessia had said. She gave him room and she held him straight: they came past the stands for the first time in fourth place, the whole field close together. Round the top bend left-handed, down the back stretch, round the last corner towards home.

Two of the leaders dropped back: Brunelleschi kept on

going. Alessia swung her stick twice, aimed the black beast straight at the target and rode like a white and gold arrow to the bull.

She won the race, that girl, and was cheered as she came to the winners' enclosure in front of the stands. She was photographed and filmed, her head back, her mouth laughing. As Brunelleschi stamped around in his winner's garland of laurels (what else?) she reached forward and gave his dark sweating neck a wide-armed exultant pat, and the crowd again cheered.

I wholeheartedly shared in her joy: and felt lonely.

They all came up to the dining room for champagne – winners, losers and Eric Rickenbacker looking ecstatic.

'Well done,' I said to her.

'Did you see?' She was high, high with achievement.

'Yes, I did.'

'Isn't it fantastic?'

'The day of a lifetime.'

'Oh, I do love you,' she said, laughing, and turned away immediately, and talked with animation to a throng of admirers. Ah, Andrew, I thought wryly, how do you like it? And I answered myself; better than nothing.

When I finally got back to the hotel the message button was flashing on my telephone. My office in England had called when I was out. Please would I get through to them straight away.

Gerry Clayton was on the switchboard.

'Your Italian friend rang from Bologna,' he said. 'The policeman, Pucinelli.'

'Yes?'

'He wants you to telephone. I couldn't understand him very well, but I think he said he had found Giuseppe–Peter.'

eighteen

By the time I got the message it was three in the morning, Italian time. On the premise, however, that the law neither slumbered nor slept I put the call through straightaway to the carabinieri, and was answered by a yawning Italian who spoke no English.

Pucinelli was not there.

It was not known when Pucinelli would be there next.

It was not known if Pucinelli was in his own house.

I gave my name, spelling it carefully letter by letter but knowing it would look unpronounceable to most Italians.

I will telephone again, I said; and he said, 'Good.'

At one in the morning, Washington time, I telephoned Pucinelli's own home, reckoning his family would be shaping to breakfast. His wife answered, children's voices in the background, and I asked for her husband, in Italian.

'Enrico is in Milan,' she said, speaking slowly for my sake. 'He told me to give you a message.' A short pause with paper noises, then: 'Telephone this house at fourteen hours today. He will return by that time. He says it is very important, he has found your friend.'

'In Milan?' I asked.

'I don't know. Enrico said only to ask you to telephone.'

I thanked her and disconnected, and slept fitfully while four thousand miles away Pucinelli travelled home. At fourteen hours, two p.m. his time, eight a.m. in Washington, I got through again to his house and found he had been called out on duty the minute he returned.

'He is sorry. Telephone his office at seventeen hours.'

By that time, I reckoned, my fingernails would be bitten to the knuckle. My stomach positively hurt with impatience. I ordered breakfast from room service to quieten it and read the Washington Sunday papers and fidgeted, and finally at eleven I got him.

'Andrew, how are you?' he said.

'Dying of suspense.'

'What?'

'Never mind.'

'Where are you?' he said. 'Your office said America.'

'Yes. Washington. Have you really found Giuseppe–Peter?'

'Yes and no.'

'What do you mean?'

'You remember,' he said, 'that we have been enquiring all the time among horse people, and also that we were going to try some students' reunions, to see if anyone recognised him from the drawing.'

'Yes, of course,' I said.

We had drifted automatically into our normal habit of speaking two languages, and it seemed just as satisfactory as ever.

'We have succeeded in both places. In both worlds.' He paused for effect and sounded undeniably smug. 'He lives near Milan. He is thirty-four now. He went to Milan University as a student and joined radical political groups. It is believed he was an activist, a member of the Red Brigades, but no one knows for sure. I was told it was a fact, but there was no true evidence. Anyway, he did not continue in political life after he left university. He left without sitting his final examinations. The university asked him to leave, but not because of his radical opinions. They made him leave because he forged cheques. He was not prosecuted, which I think is a mistake.'

'Mm,' I agreed, riveted.

'So then I had his name. And almost immediately, the same day that I learned it, we had the information from the horse people. They say he is not well known in the horse world, he never goes to the races, he is the black sheep of a well-regarded family, and is banished from their house. No one seems to be absolutely certain in detail why this is, but again there are many rumours that it is to do with fraud and forging cheques. Everyone believes the father repaid every penny to keep the family name out of the disgrace.'

252

'But the horse world told you this?'

'Yes. In the end, someone recognised him. Our men were very diligent, very persistent.'

'They're to be congratulated,' I said sincerely.

'Yes, I agree.'

'What is his name?' I asked. It hardly seemed to matter, but it would be tidier to give him the proper label.

'His father owns racehorses,' Pucinelli said. 'His father owns the great horse Brunelleschi. Giuseppe–Peter's real name is Pietro Goldoni.'

Washington D.C. seemed to stand still. Suspended animation. I actually for a while stopped breathing. I felt stifled.

'Are you there, Andrew?' Pucinelli said.

I let out a long breath. 'Yes. . . .'

'No one has seen Pietro Goldoni since the summer. Everyone thinks he went abroad and hasn't come back.' He sounded pleased. 'It fits the timetable, doesn't it? We chased him out of Italy and he went to England.'

'Er . . .' I said faintly, 'have you heard about Morgan Freemantle? Did you read anything in the papers yesterday or today, see anything on television?'

'Who? I have been so busy in Milan. Who is Morgan Freemantle?'

I told him. I also said, 'Bruno and Beatrice Goldoni have been here all this week in Washington. I have talked to them. Brunelleschi won the big International race here yesterday afternoon. Alessia Cenci rode it.'

There was the same sort of stunned breathless silence from his end as there had been from mine.

'He is there,' he said finally. 'Pietro Goldoni is in Washington.'

'Yeah.'

'You of course knew that.'

'I assumed that Giuseppe–Peter was here, yes.'

He paused, considering. 'In what way is it best that I inform the American police of his identity? It may be that my superiors would want to consult . . .'

'If you like,' I said politely, 'I myself will first tell the police captain in charge of things here. The captain might be pleased to talk to you then direct. There's an Italian-speaker in his force who could translate for you both.'

Pucinelli was grateful and careful not to sound it. 'That would be excellent. If you would arrange it, I am sure it would be helpful.'

'I'll do it at once,' I said.

'It is Sunday,' he said, almost doubtfully.

'But you yourself are working,' I pointed out. 'And I'll reach him, somehow.'

He gave me his schedule of times on and off duty, which I wrote down.

'You've done marvels, Enrico,' I said warmly, near the end. 'I do congratulate you. It must be worth promotion.'

He laughed shortly, both pleased and unhopeful. 'This Goldoni has still to be caught.' A thought struck him. 'In which country, do you think, will he be brought to trial?'

'On his past record,' I said dryly, 'nowhere. He'll skip to South America as soon as the police get near him here, and next year maybe a polo player will be snatched from out of a chukka.'

'What?'

'Untranslatable,' I said. 'Goodbye for just now.'

I telephoned immediately to Kent Wagner's headquarters and by dint of threats and persuasion finally tracked him to the home of his niece, who was celebrating her birthday with a brunch.

'Sorry,' I said; and explained at some length.

'Jesus Christ,' he said. 'Who is this guy Pucinelli?'

'A good cop. Very brave. Talk to him.'

'Yeah.'

I gave him the telephone numbers and Enrico's schedule. 'And the Goldonis are going to New York,' I said. 'Mrs Goldoni told me. I think they're going today. They've been staying here at the Regency.'

'I'll get onto it at once. Will you be at the Sherryatt still?'

'Yes, I'm there now.'

'Stay by the 'phone.'

'OK.'

He grunted. 'Thanks, Andrew.'

'A pleasure, Kent,' I said, meaning it. 'Just catch him. He's all yours.'

As soon as I put the receiver down there was a knock on the door, and I was already opening it before it occurred to me that perhaps I should start to be careful. It was only the maid, however, on my doorstep; short, dumpy, middle-aged and harmless, wanting to clean the room.

'How long will you be?' I said, looking at the trolley of fresh linen and the large vacuum cleaner.

She said in Central-American Spanish that she didn't understand. I asked her the same question in Spanish. Twenty minutes, she said stolidly. Accordingly I lifted the telephone, asked the switchboard to put any calls through to me in the lobby temporarily, and went downstairs to wait.

To wait . . . and to think.

I thought chiefly about Beatrice Goldoni and her excited guilt. I thought of her son, banished from his father's house. I thought it highly likely that it wasn't a lover Beatrice had been sneaking off to meet in Washington that Friday, but a still-beloved black sheep. He would have set it up himself, knowing she was there for the race, and still feeling, on his part, affection.

For a certainty she didn't know he was the kidnapper of Alessia and Freemantle. She hadn't that sort of guile. She did know, however, that it had been I who'd negotiated Alessia's ransom, because at that Friday breakfast Paolo Cenci had told her. What else he had told her, heaven knew. Maybe he had told her also about Dominic: it wouldn't have been unreasonable. Many people didn't understand why Liberty Market liked to keep quiet about its work, and saw no great harm in telling.

I had myself driven Beatrice into Washington; and she talked, always, a lot. Chatter, chatter . . . we're here with the

255

Cencis, you remember Alessia who was kidnapped? And there's a young man with her, the one who came to Italy to get her back safely . . . he's here because of this other kidnapping . . . and Paolo Cenci told us he rescued a little boy Dominic in England . . . Alessia was there too . . . chatter, chatter, chatter.

I stood up from the lobby sofa, went to the desk, and said I was checking out; would they please prepare my bill. Then I got through again to Kent Wagner, who said I'd just caught him, he was leaving the brunch.

'You sure as hell broke up my day,' he said, though sounding philosophical. 'Thought of something else?'

I said I was leaving the Sherryatt, and why.

'Jee-sus' he said. 'Come down to headquarters; I'll put you into a good place where Goldoni would never find you. It's sure prudent to assume that he does now know you exist.'

'Might be safer,' I agreed. 'I'm on my way.'

The desk said my account would be ready when I came down with my gear. The twenty minutes was barely up, but when I stepped out of the lift I saw the maid pushing her trolley away down the passage. I unlocked my door and went in.

There were three men in there, all in high-domed peaked caps and white overalls, with International Rug Co. Inc. on chests and backs. They had pushed some of the furniture to the walls and were unrolling a large Indian-type rug in the cleared free centre.

'What. . . .' I began. And I thought: it's Sunday.

I spun on my heel to retreat, but it was already too late.

A fourth man, International Rug Co. Inc. on his chest, was blocking the doorway; advancing, stretching out his arms, thrusting me forcefully backwards into the room.

I looked into his eyes . . . and knew him.

I thought in lightning flashes.

I thought: I've lost.

I thought: I'm dead.

I thought: I meant to win. I thought I would win. I thought

256

I'd find him and get him arrested and stop him, and it never seriously occurred to me it could be this way round.

I thought: I'm a fool, and I've lost. I thought I would win, and Brunelleschi . . . the danger . . . has beaten me.

Everything happened very fast, in a blur. A sort of canvas bag came down over my head, blocking out sight. I was tripped and tossed by many hands to the floor. There was a sharp sting in my thigh, like a wasp. I was conscious of being turned over and over, realised dimly that I was being rolled up like a sausage in the Indian rug.

It was the last thing I thought for quite a long while.

I woke up out of doors, feeling cold.

I was relieved to wake up at all, but that said, could find little else of comfort.

For a start, I had nothing on.

Sod it, I thought furiously. True to bloody form. Just like Alessia. Morgan Freemantle – he too, I dared say, was currently starkers.

Liberty Market's own private unofficial training manual, issued to each partner on joining, spelled it out: 'immediate and effective domination and demoralisation of the victim is achieved by depriving him/her of clothes'.

Dominic had had clothes; they'd even added a jersey to his tiny shorts. Dominic, on the other hand, was too little to find anything humiliating in nakedness. There would have been no point.

The only thing to do was to try to think of myself as dressed.

I was sitting on the ground; ground being loamy earth covered with fallen leaves. I was leaning against the tree from which most of the said leaves appeared to have descended: a small tree with a smooth hard trunk no more than four inches in diameter.

The view was limited on every side by growths of evergreen; mostly, it seemed to me ironically, of laurel. I was in a small clearing, with only one other youthful tree for company. Beech trees, perhaps, I thought.

257

The main and most depressing problem was the fact of being unable to walk away on account of having something that felt like handcuffs on my wrists, on the wrong side of the tree trunk, behind my back.

It was quiet in the clearing, but beyond I could hear the muffled, constant roar which announced itself as city. Wherever I was, it wasn't far out. Not nearly as far, for instance, as Laurel. More like a mile or two . . . in a suburb.

I opened my mouth and yelled at the top of my lungs the corny old word 'Help.' I yelled it many times. Consistently negative results.

The sky, so blue for the race-week, was clouding over: grey, like my thoughts.

I had no idea what time it was. My fingers, exploring discovered I had no watch.

I could stand up.

I stood.

I could kneel down: didn't bother.

I could circle round the tree.

I did that. The surrounding greenery was similar from all angles.

The branches of the tree spread from just above my head, narrow hard arms ending in smaller offshoots and twigs. A good many tan-coloured leaves still clung there. I tried shaking them off, but my efforts hardly wobbled them and they stubbornly remained.

I sat down again and thought a good many further unwelcome thoughts, chief among them being that in the Liberty Market office I would never live this day down . . . if ever I lived to tell.

Getting myself kidnapped . . . bloody stupid.

Embarrassing to a degree.

I thought back. If Pucinelli had been easier to reach I would have learned about the Goldoni family sooner, and I would have been long gone by the time the International Rug Co Inc. arrived at the Sherryatt with their rug.

If I hadn't gone back upstairs to fetch my things . . .

If, if, if.

I thought of the face of Giuseppe–Peter-Pietro Goldoni coming through my bedroom door: intent, determined, a soldier in action, reminding me in his speed and neatness of Tony Vine. He had himself taken Dominic from the beach, and in a mask had been there personally to seize Alessia. It was possible to imagine that it had been he who had announced himself as the chauffeur to collect Morgan Freemantle; and if so the actual act of successful abduction could be almost as potent a satisfaction to him as the money it brought.

If I understood him, I wondered, would I be better equipped? I'd never negotiated face to face with a kidnapper before: always through proxies. The art of coercive bargaining, Liberty Market training manual, chapter six. Hard to be coercive while at the present disadvantage.

Time passed. Aeroplanes flew at intervals overhead and a couple of birds came crossly to inspect the stranger in their territory. I sat, not uncomfortably, trying to shape my mind to the possibility of remaining where I was for some time.

It began to rain.

The tree gave little shelter, but I didn't particularly mind. The drops spattered through the dying leaves in a soft shower, fresh and interesting on my skin. I'd never been out in the rain before with no clothes on, that I could remember. I lifted my face up, and opened my mouth, and drank what came my way.

After a while the rain stopped, and it grew dark. All night, I thought coldly.

Well. All night, then. Face it. Accept it. It's not so hard.

I was strong and healthy and possessed of a natural inborn stamina which had rarely been tested anywhere near its limits. The restriction to my arms was loose and not unbearable. I could sit there for a long time without suffering. I guessed, in fact, that I would have to.

The greatest discomfort was cold, to which I tried to shut my mind, joined, as the night advanced, by a desire for a nice hot dinner.

I tried on and off to rub the handcuffs vigorously against the treetrunk to see if the friction would do anything spectacularly useful like sawing the wood right through. The result of such labours was a slight roughening of the tree's surface and a more considerable roughening of the skin inside my arms. Small the treetrunk might be, but densely, forbiddingly solid.

I slept, on and off, dozing quite deeply and toppling sideways once, waking later with my nose on the dead leaves and my shoulders stretched and aching. I tried to find a more comfortable way of lying, but everything was compromise: sitting was the best.

Waiting, shivering, for dawn, I began to wonder seriously for the first time whether he intended simply to leave me to the elements until I died.

He hadn't killed me in the hotel. The injection in my thigh which had put me unconscious could just as easily have been fatal, if death had been what he intended. A body in a rug could have been carried out of a hotel as boldly dead as unconscious. If he'd simply wanted me out of his life, why was I still in it?

If he'd wanted revenge . . . that was something else.

I'd told Kent Wagner confidently that Giuseppe–Peter wouldn't kill by inches . . . and perhaps I'd been wrong.

Well, I told myself astringently, you'll just have to wait and see.

Daylight came. A grey day, the clouds lower, scurrying, full of unhappy promise.

Where's the Verdi?, I thought. I wouldn't mind an orchestral earful. Verdi . . . Giuseppe Verdi.

Oh well. Giuseppe . . . It made sense.

Peter was his own name – Pietro – in English.

Coffee wouldn't be bad, I thought. Ring room service to bring it.

The first twenty-four hours were the worst for a kidnap victim: chapter one, Liberty Market training manual. From my own intimate viewpoint. I now doubted it.

260

At what would have been full daylight except for the clouds, he came to see me.

I didn't hear him approach, but he was suddenly there, half behind me, stepping round one of the laurels; Giuseppe–Peter-Pietro Goldoni, dressed in his brown leather jacket with the gold buckles at the cuffs.

I felt as if I had known him forever, yet he was totally alien. There was some quality of implacability in his approach, a sort of mute violence in the way he walked, a subtle arrogance in his carriage. His satisfaction at having brought me to this pass was plain to see, and the hairs rose involuntarily all up my spine.

He stopped in front of me and looked down.

'Your name is Andrew Douglas,' he said in English. His accent was pronounced, and like all Italians he had difficulty with the unfamiliar Scots syllables, but his meaning was clear.

I looked back at him flatly and didn't reply.

Without excitement but with concentration he returned me look for look, and I began to sense in him the same feeling about me as I had about him. Professional curiosity, on both sides.

'You will make a tape recording for me,' he said finally.

'All right.'

The ready agreement lifted his eyebrows: not what he'd expected.

'You do not ask . . . who I am?'

I said, 'You're the man who abducted me from the hotel.'

'What is my name?' he asked.

'I don't know,' I said.

'It is Peter.' A very positive assertion.

'Peter.' Inclined my head, acknowledging the introduction. 'Why am I here?'

'To make a tape recording.'

He looked at me sombrely and went away, his head round and dark against the sky, all his features long familiar because of the picture. I'd nearly got him right, I thought. Maybe in

261

the line of the eyebrows I'd been wrong: his were straighter at the outer edge.

He was gone for a period I would have guessed at as an hour, and he returned with a brown travelling bag slung from one shoulder. The bag looked like fine leather, with gold buckles. All of a piece.

From his jacket he produced a large sheet of paper which he unfolded and held for me to read.

'This is what you will say,' he said.

I read the message, which had been written in laborious block capitals by an American, not by Giuseppe–Peter himself. It said:

I AM ANDREW DOUGLAS, UNDERCOVER COP. YOU IN THE FUCKING JOCKEY CLUB, LISTEN GOOD. YOU'VE GOT TO SEND THE TEN MILLION ENGLISH POUNDS, LIKE WE SAID. THE CERTIFIED CHECK'S GOT TO BE READY TUESDAY. SEND IT TO ACCOUNT NUMBER ZL327/42806, CREDIT HELVETIA, ZURICH, SWITZERLAND. WHEN THE CHECK IS CLEARED, YOU GET FREE-MANTLE BACK. NO FINGERS MISSING. THEN SIT TIGHT. IF ANY COPS COME IN, I WON'T BE MAKING IT. IF EVERYTHING IS ON THE LEVEL AND THE BREAD IS SATISFACTORY, YOU'LL BE TOLD WHERE TO FIND ME. IF ANYONE TRIES TO BLOCK THE DEAL AFTER FREEMANTLE GOES LOOSE, I'LL BE KILLED.

He tucked the paper inside the front of his jacket and began to pull a tape recorder from the leather bag.

'I'm not reading that,' I said neutrally.

He stopped in mid-movement. 'You have no choice. If you don't read it, I will kill you.'

I said nothing, simply looked at him without challenge; trying to show no worry.

'I will kill you,' he said again: and I thought yes, perhaps, but not for that.

'It's bad English,' I said. 'You could have written it better yourself.'

He let the tape recorder's weight fall back into the bag. 'Are you telling me,' he asked with incredulity, 'that you are not reading this because of the style literary?'

'Literary style,' I said. 'Yes.'

He turned his back on me while he thought, and after a while turned back.

'I will change the words,' he said. 'But you will read only what I say. Understand? No . . .' he searched for the words but said finally in Italian, 'no code words. No secret signals.'

I thought that if I kept him speaking English it might fractionally reduce my disadvantage, so I said, 'What did you say? I don't understand.'

He narrowed his eyes slightly. 'You speak Spanish. The maid at the hotel said you were a Spanish gentleman. I think you also speak Italian.'

'Very little.'

He pulled the paper from his jacket and found a pen, and, turning the sheet over, began to write a new version for me, supporting it on the bag. When he'd finished, he showed it to me, holding it so that I could read.

In elegant handwriting the note now said:

I AM ANDREW DOUGLAS. JOCKEY CLUB, COLLECT TEN MILLION ENGLISH POUNDS. TUESDAY, SEND CERTIFIED BANKER'S DRAFT TO ACCOUNT NUMBER ZL327/42806, CREDIT HELVETIA, ZURICH, SWITZERLAND. WHEN THE BANK CLEARS THE DRAFT, MORGAN FREEMANTLE RETURNS. AFTER THAT, WAIT. POLICE MUST NOT INVESTIGATE. WHEN ALL IS PEACE, I WILL BE FREE. IF THE MONEY IS NOT ABLE TO BE TAKEN OUT OF THE SWISS BANK, I WILL BE KILLED.

'Well,' I said. 'It's much better.'

He reached again for the tape recorder.

'They won't pay ten million,' I said.

His hand paused again. 'I know that.'

'Yes. I'm sure you do.' I wished I could rub an itch on my nose. 'In the normal course of events you would expect a letter to be sent to your Swiss account number from the Jockey Club, making a more realistic proposal.'

He listened impassively, sorting the words into Italian, understanding. 'Yes,' he said.

'They might suggest paying a ransom of one hundred thousand pounds,' I said.

'That is ridiculous.'

'Perhaps fifty thousand more, to cover your expenses.'

'Still ridiculous.'

We looked at each other assessingly. In the normal course of events negotiation of a ransom price was not conducted like this. On the other hand, what was there to prevent it?

'Five million,' he said.

I said nothing.

'It must be five,' he said.

'The Jockey Club has no money. The Jockey Club is just a social club, made up of people. They aren't all rich people. They cannot pay five million. They do not have five million.'

He shook his head without anger. 'They are rich. They have five million, certainly. I know.'

'How do you know?' I asked.

His eyelids flickered slightly, but all he said again was, 'Five million.'

'Two hundred thousand. Positively no more.'

'Ridiculous.'

He stalked away and disappeared between the laurel bushes, and I guessed he wanted to think and not have me watch him at it.

The Swiss bank account was fascinating, I thought: and clearly he intended to move the money more or less at once from ZL327/42806 to another account number, another bank even, and wanted to be sure the Jockey Club hadn't thought of a way of stopping him or tracing him, or laying a trap. As some of England's top banking brains could be found either in or advising the Jockey Club, his precautions made excellent sense.

One victim in return for the ransom itself.

One victim in return when the ransom had disappeared into further anonymity.

Morgan Freemantle for money, Andrew Douglas for time.

No drops to be ambushed by excitable carabinieri: no stacks of tatty – and photographed – notes. Just numbers, stored electronically, sophisticated and safe. Subtract the numbers from the gentlemen of the Jockey Club, add the total, telex it to Switzerland.

With his money in Zurich, Giuseppe–Peter could lose himself in South America and not be affected by its endemic inflation. Swiss francs would ride any storm.

Alessia's ransom, at a guess, had gone to Switzerland the day it had been paid, changed into francs, perhaps, by a laundryman. Same for the racecourse owner, earlier. Even with the Dominic operation showing a heavy loss, Giuseppe–Peter must have amassed an English million. I wondered if he had set a target at which he would stop, and I wondered also whether once a kidnapper, always a kidnapper, addicted: in his case, for ever and ever.

I found I still thought of him as Giuseppe–Peter, from long habit. Pietro Goldoni seemed a stranger.

He came back eventually and stood in front of me, looking down.

'I am a businessman,' he said.

'Yes.'

'Stand up when you talk to me.'

I thrust away the first overwhelming instinct to refuse. Never antagonise your kidnapper: victim lesson number two. Make him pleased with you, make him like you; he will be less ready to kill.

Sod the training manual, I thought mordantly: and stood up.

'That's better,' he said. 'Every time I am here, stand up.'

'All right.'

'You will make the recording. You understand what I wish to say. You will say it.' He paused briefly. 'If I do not like what you say, we will start again.'

I nodded.

He pulled the black tape recorder from the leather bag and

switched it on. Then he plucked the sheet of instructions from his jacket pocket, shook it open, and held it, with his own version towards me, for me to read. He gestured to me to start, and I cleared my voice and said as unemotionally as I could manage:

'This is Andrew Douglas. The ransom demand for Morgan Freemantle is now reduced to five million pounds—'

Giuseppe–Peter switched off the machine.

'I did not tell you to say that,' he said intensely.

'No,' I agreed mildly. 'But it might save time.'

He pursed his lips, considered, told me to start again, and pressed the record buttons.

I said:

'This is Andrew Douglas. The ransom demand for Morgan Freemantle is now reduced to five million pounds. This money is to be sent by certified banker's draft to the Credit Helvetia, Zurich, Switzerland, to be lodged in account number ZL327/42806. When that account has been credited with the money, Morgan Freemantle will be returned. After that there are to be no police investigations. If there are no investigations, and if the money in the Swiss bank has been paid clear of all restrictions and may be moved to other accounts without stoppage, I will be freed.'

I halted. He pressed the stop buttons and said, 'You have not finished.'

I looked at him.

'You will say that unless these things happen, you will be killed.'

His dark eyes looked straight at mine; level, at my own height. I saw only certainty. He pressed the start buttons again and waited.

'I am told,' I said in a dry voice, 'that unless these conditions are met, I will be killed.'

He nodded sharply and switched off.

I thought: he will kill me anyway. He put his tape recorder into one section of his bag and began feeling into another section for something else. I had the most dreadful lurch of

266

fear in my gut and tried with the severest physical will to control it. But it wasn't a gun or a knife that he brought out of the bag: it was a cola bottle containing a milky-looking liquid.

The reaction was almost as bad. In spite of the chilly air, I was sweating.

He appeared not to have noticed. He was unscrewing the cap and looking in the bag for what proved to be a fat, plastic, gaily-striped drinking straw.

'Soup,' he said. He put the straw into the bottle and offered it to my mouth.

I sucked. It was chicken soup, cold, fairly thick. I drank all of it quite fast, afraid he would snatch it away.

He watched without comment. When I'd finished he threw the straw on the ground, screwed the top on the bottle and replaced it in the bag. Then he gave me another long, considering, concentrated stare, and abruptly went away.

I sat down regrettably weakly on the loamy ground.

God dammit, I thought. God dammit to hell.

It is in myself, I thought, as in every victim; the hopeless feeling of indignity, the sickening guilt of having been snatched.

A prisoner, naked, alone, afraid, dependent on one's enemy for food . . . all the classic ingredients of victim-breakdown syndrome. The training manual come to life. Knowing so well what it was like from other people's accounts didn't sufficiently shield one from the shock of the reality.

In the future I would understand what I was told not just in the head but with every remembered pulse.

If there were a future.

nineteen

Rain came again, at first in big heavy individual drops, splashing with sharp taps on the dead leaves, and then quite soon in a downpour. I stood up and let the rain act as a shower, soaking my hair, running down my body, cold and oddly pleasant.

I drank some of it again, getting quite good at swallowing without choking. How really extraordinary I must look, I thought, standing there in the clearing getting wet.

My long-ago Scottish ancestors had gone naked into battle, whooping and roaring down the heather hillsides with sword and shield alone and frightening the souls out of the enemy. If those distant clansmen, Highland-born in long-gone centuries, could choose to fight as nature made them, then so should I settle for the same sternness of spirit in this day.

I wondered if the Highlanders had been fortified before they set off by distillations of barley. It would give one more courage, I thought, than chicken soup.

It went on raining for hours, heavily and without pause. Only when it again began to get dark did it ease off, and by then the ground round the tree was so wet that sitting on it was near to a mud bath. Still, having stood all day, I sat. If it rained the next day, I thought wryly, the mud would wash off.

The night was again long and cold, but not to the point of hypothermia. My skin dried when the rain stopped. Eventually, against all the odds, I again went to sleep.

I spent the damp dawn and an hour or two after it feeling grindingly hungry and drearily wondering whether Giuseppe–Peter would ever come back: but he did. He came as before, stepping quietly, confidently, through the laurel screen, wearing the same jacket, carrying the same bag.

I stood up at his approach. He made no comment; merely noted it. There was a fuzz of moisture on his sleek hair, a matter of a hundred per cent humidity rather than actual drizzle, and he walked carefully, picking his way between puddles.

It was Tuesday, I thought.

He had brought another bottle of soup, warm this time, reddish-brown, tasting vaguely of beef. I drank it more slowly than on the day before, moderately trusting this time that he wouldn't snatch it away. He waited until I'd finished, threw away the straw, screwed the cap on the bottle, as before.

'You are outside,' he said unexpectedly, 'while I make a place inside. One more day. Or two.'

After a stunned moment I said, 'Clothes . . .'

He shook his head. 'No.' Then, glancing at the clouds, he said, 'Rain is clean.'

I almost nodded, an infinitesimal movement, which he saw.

'In England,' he said, 'you defeated me. Here, I defeat you.'

I said nothing.

'I have been told it was you, in England. You who found the boy.' He shrugged suddenly, frustratedly, and I guessed he still didn't know how we'd done it. 'To take people back from kidnap, it is your job. I did not know it was a job, except for the police.'

'Yes,' I said neutrally.

'You will never defeat me again,' he said seriously.

He put a hand into the bag and brought out a much-creased, much-travelled copy of the picture of himself, which, as he unfolded it, I saw to be one of the original printing, from way back in Bologna.

'It was you, who drew this,' he said. 'Because of this, I had to leave Italy. I went to England. In England, again this picture. Everywhere. Because of this I came to America. This picture is here now, is it not?'

I didn't answer.

'You hunted me. I caught you. That is the difference.'

He was immensely pleased with what he was saying.

'Soon, I will look different. I will change. When I have the ransom I will disappear. And this time you will not send the police to arrest my men. This time I will stop you.'

I didn't ask how. There was no point.

'You are like me,' he said.

'No.'

'Yes . . . but between us, I will win.'

There could always be a moment, I supposed, in which enemies came to acknowledge an unwilling respect for each other, even though the enmity between them remained unchanged and deep. There was such a moment then: on his side at least.

'You are strong,' he said, 'like me.'

There seemed to be no possible answer.

'It is good to defeat a strong man.'

It was the sort of buzz I would have been glad not to give him.

'For me,' I said, 'are you asking a ransom?'

He looked at me levelly and said, 'No.'

'Why not?' I asked; and thought, why ask, you don't want to know the answer.

'For Freemantle,' he said merely, 'I will get five million pounds.'

'The Jockey Club won't pay five million pounds,' I said.

'They will.'

'Morgan Freemantle isn't much loved,' I said. 'The members of the Jockey Club will resent every penny screwed out of them. They will hold off, they'll argue, they'll take weeks deciding whether each member should contribute an equal amount, or whether the rich should give more. They will keep you waiting . . . and every day you have to wait, you risk the American police finding you. The Americans are brilliant at finding kidnappers . . . I expect you know.'

'If you want food you will not talk like this.'

I fell silent.

After a pause he said, 'I expect they will not pay exactly five million. But there are many members. About one hundred. They can pay thirty thousands pounds each, of that I am sure.

That is three million pounds. Tomorrow you will make another tape. You will tell them that is the final reduction. For that, I let Freemantle go. If they will not pay, I will kill him, and you also, and bury you here in this ground.' He pointed briefly to the earth under our feet. 'Tomorrow you will say this on the tape.'

'Yes,' I said.

'And believe me,' he said soberly, 'I do not intend to spend all my life in prison. If I am in danger of it, I will kill, to prevent it.'

I did believe him. I could see the truth of it in his face.

After a moment I said, 'You have courage. You will wait. The Jockey Club will pay when the amount is not too much. When they can pay what their conscience . . . their guilt . . . tells them they must. When they can shrug and grit their teeth, and complain . . . but pay . . . that's what the amount will be. A total of about one quarter of one million pounds, maximum, I would expect.'

'More,' he said positively, shaking his head.

'If you should kill Freemantle, the Jockey Club would regret it, but in their hearts many members wouldn't grieve. If you demand too much, they will refuse, and you may end with nothing . . . just the risk of prison . . . for murder.' I spoke without emphasis, without persuasion: simply as if reciting moderately unexciting facts.

'It was you,' he said bitterly. 'You made me wait six weeks for the ransom for Alessia Cenci. If I did not wait, did not reduce the ransom . . . I would have nothing. A dead girl is no use. . . . I understand now what you do.' He paused. 'This time, I defeat you.'

I didn't answer. I knew I had him firmly hooked again into the kidnapper's basic dilemma: whether to settle for what he could get, or risk holding out for what he wanted. I was guessing that the Jockey Club would grumble but finally pay half a million pounds, which meant five thousand pounds per member, if it was right about their numbers. At Liberty Market we would, I thought, have advised agreeing to that

271

sort of sum; five per cent of the original demand. The expenses of this kidnap would be high: trying too hard to beat the profit down to zero would be dangerous to the victim.

With luck, I thought, Giuseppe–Peter and I would in the end negotiate a reasonable price for Morgan Freemantle, and the Senior Steward would return safely home: and that, I supposed, was what I had basically come to America to achieve. After that . . . for myself . . . it depended on how certain Giuseppe–Peter was that he could vanish . . . and on how he felt about me . . . and on whether he considered me a danger to him for life.

Which I would be. I would be.

I didn't see how he could possibly set me free. I wouldn't have done, if I had been he.

I thrust the starkly unbearable thought away. While Morgan Freemantle lived in captivity, so would I . . . probably.

'Tomorrow,' Giuseppe–Peter said, 'when I come, you will say on the tape that one of Freemantle's fingers will be cut off next week on Wednesday, if three million pounds are not paid before then.'

He gave me another long calculating stare as if he would read my beliefs, my weaknesses, my fears, my knowledge; and I looked straight back at him, seeing the obverse of myself, seeing the demon born in every human.

It was true that we were alike, I supposed, in many ways, not just in age, in build, in physical strength. We organised, we plotted, and we each in our way sought battle. The same battle . . . different sides. The same primary weapons . . . lies, threats and fear.

But what he stole, I strove to restore. Where he wantonly laid waste, I tried to rebuild. He crumbled his victims, I worked to make them whole. His satisfaction lay in taking them, mine in seeing them free. The obverse of me . . .

As before he turned away abruptly and departed, and I was left with an urge to call after him, to beg him to stay, just to talk. I didn't want him to go. I wanted his company, enemy or not.

I was infinitely tired of that clearing, that tree, that mud, that cold, those handcuffs. Twenty-four empty hours stretched ahead, a barren landscape of loneliness and discomfort and inevitable hunger. It began raining again, hard slanting stuff driven now by a rising wind, and I twisted my hands to grip the tree, hating it, trying to shake it, to hurt it, furiously venting on it a surge of raw, unmanageable despair.

That wouldn't do, I thought coldly, stopping almost at once. If I went that way, I would crack into pieces. I let my hands fall away. I put my face blindly to the sky, eyes shut, and concentrated merely on drinking.

A leaf fell into my mouth. I spat it out. Another fell on my forehead. I opened my eyes and saw that most of the rest of the dead leaves had come down.

The wind, I thought. But I took hold of the tree again more gently and shook it, and saw a tremor run up through it to the twigs. Three more leaves fell off, fluttering down wetly.

Two days ago the tree had immovably resisted the same treatment. Instead of shaking it again I bumped my back against it several times, giving it shocks. I could feel movement in the trunk that had definitely not been there before: and under my feet, under the earth, something moved.

I scraped wildly at the place with my toes and then circled the tree and sat down with a rush, rubbing with my fingers until I could feel a hard surface come clear. Then I stood round where I'd been before, and bumped hard against the trunk, and looked down and saw what I'd uncovered.

A root.

One has to be pretty desperate to try to dig up a tree with one's fingernails, and desperate would be a fair description of Andrew Douglas that rainy November morning.

Let it pour, I thought. Let this sodden soaking glorious rain go on and on turning my prison into a swamp. Let this nice glorious fantastic loamy mud turn liquid. . . . Let this stubborn little tree not have a tap root its own height.

It rained. I hardly felt it. I cleared the mud from the root

273

until I could get my fingers right round it, to grasp. I could feel it stretching away sideways, tugging against my tug.

Standing up I could put my foot under it; a knobbly dark sinew as thick as a thumb, tensing and relaxing when I leant my weight against the tree trunk.

I've got all day, I thought, and all night.

I have no other chance.

It did take all day, but not all night.

Hour by hour it went on raining, and hour by hour I scraped away at the roots with toes and fingers, baring more of them, burrowing deeper. The movement I could make in the trunk slowly grew from a tremble to a protesting shudder, and from a shudder to a sway.

I tested my strength against the tree's own each time in a sort of agony, for fear Giuseppe–Peter would somehow see the branches moving above the laurels and arrive with fearsome ways to stop me. I scraped and dug and heaved in something very near frenzy, and the longer it went on the more excruciatingly anxious I became. Given time I would do it. Given time . . . Oh God, give me time.

Some of the roots tore free easily, some were heartbreakingly stubborn. Water filled the hole as I dug, blocking what I could see, hindering and helping both at the same time. When I felt one particularly thick and knotty root give up the contest the tree above me lurched as if in mortal protest, and I stood up and hauled at it with every possible muscle, pushing and pulling, wrenching, thudding, lying heavily against the trunk, digging in with my heels, feeling the thrust through calves and thighs; then yanking the tree this way and that, sideways, like a pendulum.

A bunch of beleaguered roots gave way all together and the whole tree suddenly toppled, taking me down with it in rough embrace, its branches crashing in the rain onto a bed of its own brown, leaves, leaving me breathless and exultant . . . and still . . . still . . . fastened.

Every single root had to be severed before I could get my

274

arms out from under them, but I doubt if barbed wire would have stopped me at that point. Scratching and tugging, hands down in water, kneeling and straining, I fought for that escape as I'd never thought to fight in my life; and finally I felt the whole root mass shift freely, a tangled clump of blackly-sprouting woody tentacles, their grip on the earth all gone. Kneeling and jerking I got them up between my arms, up to my shoulders . . . and rolled free into a puddle, ecstatic.

It took not so very much longer to thread myself through my own arms, so to speak, bottom first then one leg at a time, so that I ended with my hands in front, not behind my back; an unbelievable improvement.

It was still raining and also, I realised, beginning to get dark. I went shakily over to the laurels on the opposite side of the clearing from where Giuseppe–Peter had appeared, and edged slowly, cautiously, between two of the glossy green bushes.

No people.

I took a deep breath, trying to steady myself, trying to make my knees work efficiently instead of wanting to buckle. I felt strained and weak and in no shape for barefoot country rambles, but none of it mattered. Nothing mattered at all beside the fact of being free.

I could hear only wind and rain. I went on and came shortly to a sketchy fence made of strands of wire strung between posts. I climbed through and walked on and suddenly reached the top of an incline, the wood sloping away in front: and down there, through the trees, there were lights.

I went down towards them. I'd been naked so long that I'd stopped thinking about it, which was somewhat of a mistake. I was concerned only to get away from Giuseppe–Peter, feeling that he still might find me gone and chase after. I was thinking only, as I approached what turned out to be a very substantial house, that I'd better make sure it wasn't where Giuseppe–Peter was actually staying before I rang the doorbell.

I didn't get as far as ringing the bell. An outside light was suddenly switched on, and the door itself opened on a chain.

A pale, indistinguishable face inspected me and a sharp, frightened female voice said 'Get away. Get away from here.'

I started to say 'Wait,' but the door closed with a slam, and while I hovered indecisively it opened again to reveal the business end of a pistol.

'Go away,' she said. 'Get away from here, or I'll shoot.'

I thought she might. I looked down at myself and didn't altogether blame her. I was streaked with mud and handcuffed and bare: hardly a riot as a visitor on a darkening November evening.

I backed away, looking as unaggressive as I could, and presently felt it safe to slide away again into the trees and reconsider my whole boring plight.

Clearly I needed some sort of covering, but all that was to hand easily were branches of evergreen laurel. Back to Adam and Eve, and all that. Then I'd got to get a householder – a different one – to talk to me without shooting first. It might not have been too difficult in the Garden of Eden, but in twentieth-century suburban Washington D.C., a proper poser.

Further down the hill there were more lights. Feeling slightly foolish I picked up a twig of laurel and held it, and walked down towards the lights, feeling my way as it grew darker, stubbing my toes on unseen stones. This time, I thought, I would go more carefully and look for something to wrap round me before I tackled the door: a sack, a trash bag . . . absolutely anything.

Again events overtook me. I was slithering in darkness under a sheltering canopy-roof past double garage doors when a car came unexpectedly round a hidden driveway, catching me in its lights. The car braked sharply to a stop and I took a step backwards, cravenly ready to bolt.

'Stop right there,' a voice said, and a man stepped out of the car, again bearing a pistol. Did they all, I thought despairingly, shoot strangers? Dirty naked unshaven handcuffed strangers . . . probably, yes.

This native wasn't frightened, just masterful. Before he

could say anything else I opened my mouth and said loudly, 'Please get the police.'

'What?' He came three paces nearer, looking me up and down. 'What did you say?'

'Please get the police. I escaped. I want . . . er . . . to turn myself in.'

'Who are you?' he demanded.

'Look,' I said. 'I'm freezing cold and very tired, and if you telephone Captain Wagner he'll come and get me.'

'You're not American,' he said accusingly.

'No. British.'

He came nearer to me, still warily holding the gun. I saw that he was of middle age with greying hair, a worthy citizen with money, used to decision. A businessman come home.

I told him Wagner's telephone number. 'Please,' I said. 'Please . . . call him.'

He considered, then he said, 'Walk along there to that door. No tricks.'

I walked in front of him along a short path to his impressive front door, the rain stopping now, the air damp.

'Stand still,' he said. I wouldn't have dreamt of doing anything else.

Three orange pumpkin faces rested on the steps, grinning up at me evilly. There was the sound of keys clinking and the lock being turned. The door swung inward, spilling out light.

'Turn round. Come in here.'

I turned. He was standing inside his door, waiting for me, ready with the gun.

'Come inside and shut the door.'

I did that.

'Stand there,' he said, pointing to a spot on a marble-tiled hallway, in front of a wall. 'Stand still . . . wait.'

He took his eyes off me for a few seconds while he stretched a hand through a nearby doorway; and what it reappeared holding was a towel.

'Here.' He threw it to me; a dry fluffy handtowel, pale green with pink initials. I caught it, but couldn't do much with it, short of laying it on the ground and rolling.

He made an impatient movement of his head.

'I can't . . .' I said, and stopped. It was all too damn bloody much.

He parked the pistol, came towards me, wrapped the towel round my waist and tucked the ends in, like a sarong.

'Thank you,' I said.

He put the pistol near an adjacent telephone and told me to repeat the number of the police.

Kent Wagner, to my everlasting gratitude, was in his headquarters half an hour after he should have gone off duty.

My unwilling host said to him, 'There's a man here says he escaped . . .'

'Andrew Douglas,' I interrupted.

'Says his name is Andrew Douglas.' He held the receiver suddenly away from his ear as if the noise had hurt the drum. 'What? He says he wants to give himself up. He's here, in handcuffs.' He listened for a few seconds and then with a frown came to put the receiver into my hands. 'He wants to talk to you,' he said.

Kent's voice said into my ear, 'Who is this?'

'Andrew.'

'Jee . . . sus.' His breath came out wheezing. 'Where are you?'

'I don't know. Wait.' I asked my host where I was. He took the receiver temporarily back and gave his address, with directions. 'Three miles up Massachusetts Avenue from Dupont Circle, take a right onto 46th Street, make a right again on to Davenport Street, a quarter mile down there, in the woods.' He listened, and gave me back the receiver.

'Kent,' I said, 'bring some men and come very quietly. Our friend is near here.'

'Got it,' he said.

'And Kent . . . bring some trousers.'

'What?'

'Pants,' I said tersely. 'And a shirt. And some shoes, size ten English.'

He said disbelievingly, 'You're not . . . ?'

'Yeah. Bloody funny. And a key for some handcuffs.'

My host, looking increasingly puzzled, took the receiver back and said to Kent Wagner, 'Is this man dangerous?'

What Kent swore afterwards that he said was, 'Take good care of him,' meaning just that, but my host interpreted the phrase as 'beware of him' and kept me standing there at gunpoint despite my protestations that I was not only harmless but positively benign.

'Don't lean against the wall,' he said. 'My wife would be furious to find blood on it.'

'Blood?'

'You're covered in scratches.' He was astonished. 'Didn't you know?'

'No.'

'What did you escape from?'

I shook my head wearily and didn't explain, and waited what seemed an age before Kent Wagner rang the doorbell. He came into the hall half grinning in anticipation, the grin widening as he saw the pretty towel but then suddenly dying to grimness.

'How're you doing?' he said flatly.

'OK.'

He nodded, went outside and presently returned with clothes, shoes and impressive metal cutters which got rid of the handcuffs with a couple of clips. 'These aren't police issue handcuffs,' he explained. 'We've no keys to fit.'

My host lent me his cloakroom to dress in, and when I came out I thanked him, handing over the towel.

'Guess I should have given you a drink,' he said vaguely; but I'd just seen myself in a looking glass, and I reckoned he'd dealt with me kindly.

twenty

'You're not doing that,' Kent said.

'Yes I am.'

He gave me a sidelong look. 'You're in no shape . . .'

'I'm fine.' A bit tattered as to fingers and toes, but never mind.

He shrugged, giving in. We were out in the road by the police cars, silent as to sirens and lit only by parking lights, where I'd been telling him briefly what had happened.

'We'll go back the way I came,' I said. 'What else?'

He told his men, shadowy in the cars, to stay where they were and await orders, and he and I went up through the woods, up past the house I'd waited in, and up past the one with the frightened lady: up to the top of the slope, over onto flat ground and through the wire fence.

We were both quiet, our feet softly scuffling on the sodden leaves. The rain had stopped. Behind broken clouds the moon sailed serene. The light was enough to see by, once we were used to it.

'Somewhere here,' I said, half whispering. 'Not far.'

We went from laurel clump to laurel clump and found the familiar clearing. 'He came from that way,' I said, pointing.

Kent Wagner looked at the uprooted tree for a frozen moment but without discernible expression, and then delicately, cautiously, we passed out of the laurel ring, merging with the shadows, a couple of cats stalking.

He wasn't as good as Tony Vine, but few were. I was conscious just that he would be a good companion in a dark alley, and that I wouldn't have gone back up there without him. He, for his part, had explained that his job was chiefly indoors now, in his office, and he was pleased for once to be outside with the action.

He was carrying a gun like a natural extension of his right

280

hand. We went forward slowly, testing every step, aware of the chance of trip-alarms. There were a good many laurels here among a whole bunch of younger trees and we could get no distant view, but approximately fifty paces from the clearing we caught a glimpse of a light.

Kent pointed to it with the gun. I nodded. We inched in that direction, very careful now, conscious of risk.

We saw no look-outs, which didn't mean there weren't any. We saw the front of a modern split-level house looking perfectly harmless and ordinary, with lights on downstairs and curtains half drawn.

We went no closer. We retreated into the first line of trees and followed the line of the driveway from the house to the road. At the roadside there was a mailbox on a post, the mailbox bearing the number 5270. Kent pointed to it and I nodded, and we walked along the road in what he confidently assured me was the direction of the city. As we went he said, 'I heard the tape you made. Your company relayed it to us from London this morning. Seems the Jockey Club had got it by express courier.'

'My company,' I said wryly, 'were no doubt displeased with me.'

'I talked with some guy called Gerry Clayton. All he said was that while you were alive and negotiating it was OK.'

'Nice.'

'They did seem to want you back; can't think why '

We walked on, not hurrying.

'I talked to the Goldonis,' he said. 'Parents.'

'Poor people.'

I felt him shrug. 'He was furious. She was all broken up. Seems she did see her son, did tell him about you. But no use to us. She met him by the Potomac, they walked about a bit, then went to some quiet restaurant for lunch. He'd telephoned her in their hotel to fix it . . . never told her where he was staying, himself.'

'It figured.'

'Yeah.'

A step or two further on he stopped, parked the gun in his belt and unclipped a hand radio instead.

'Turn around,' he said to his men in the police cars. 'Go back to 45th Street, make a left, make another left into Cherrytree, and crawl along there until you reach me. No sirens. No, repeat, no noise. Understood?'

The policemen answered in regulation jargon and Kent pushed down the telescopic aerial of his radio and stuck the black box on his belt.

We stood waiting. He watched me calmly in the moonlight, a hard man offering parity. I felt at ease with him, and grateful.

'Your girl-friend,' he said casually, 'will be one happy lady to have you back.'

'Alessia?'

'The jockey,' he said. 'White face, huge eyes, hardly could speak for crying.'

'Well,' I said, 'she knows what it's like to be kidnapped.'

'Yeah, so I heard. I was talking to her this afternoon. In addition she said she didn't know she loved you that way. Does that make sense? She said something about regretting saying no.'

'Did she?'

He glanced with interest at my face. 'Good news, is it?'

'You might say so.'

'Something about prisoners coming home impotent from Vietnam.'

'Mm,' I said, smiling, 'I told her that.'

'Glad it makes sense to you.'

'Thanks,' I said.

'She's still at the Regency Hotel,' Kent said. 'She said she wasn't leaving until you were free.'

I made no immediate reply, and after a pause he said, 'I didn't tell her you wouldn't make it. That if you did, it would be a miracle.'

'They happen,' I said; and he nodded.

'Once in a while.'

We looked back along the road to where I'd escaped from.

'The house back there is three and a half miles in a pretty direct route from the Ritz Carlton,' he said. 'And . . . did you notice? No pumpkins.' He was smiling in the semi-darkness, his teeth gleaming like Halloween.

He checked things pretty thoroughly, however, when his cars came, climbing into the back of one of them, with me beside him, and flicking through sheets and sheets of computer print-out. The print-out, I discovered, was of properties offered for rental, or rented, during the past eight weeks, not only in the District of Columbia itself but in adjacent Arlington and parts of Maryland and Virginia. It seemed to me to have entailed a prodigious amount of work: and again, like Eagler's efforts, it produced results.

Kent growled a deep syllable of satisfaction and showed me one particular sheet, pointing to the lines:

. 5270 Cherrytree Street, 20016, Rented October 16, period 26 weeks, full rental prepaid.

He picked up a map already folded to the right page and showed me where we were.

'There's the house you called from, on Davenport Street. We walked a block up diagonally through the woods to Cherry-tree, which is parallel with Davenport. The woods are part of American University Park.'

I nodded.

He heaved himself out of the car to talk to his men, and presently we were riding back in the direction of 5270, driving slowly with side lights only.

Kent and Lieutenant Stavoski, who'd come in the second car, were in full agreement with each other that a sudden all-out raid was best, but a raid on their own well-prepared terms. They sent two policemen through the woods to approach from the rear but stay out of sight, and positioned the cars also out of sight of the house, but ready.

'You stay out here,' Kent said to me. 'You keep out, understand?'

'No,' I said. 'I'll find Freemantle.'

He opened his mouth and closed it again, and I knew that like all policemen he'd been concentrating almost exclusively on capturing the villains. He looked assessingly at me for a moment and I said, 'I'm going in, don't argue.'

He shook his head in resignation and didn't try any further to stop me, and it was he and I, as before, who made the first approach, quiet as cobwebs, to the house with no pumpkins.

In the shadow of a laurel I touched his arm and pointed, and he stiffened when he saw what I was showing him: a man standing in an upstairs unlit window, smoking a cigarette.

We stayed quiet, watching. So did the man, unalarmed.

'Shit,' Kent said.

'There's always the back.'

Behind bushes we slithered our way. The windows facing rearwards to the woodland looked merely blank.

'What do you think?' I asked.

'Got to be done.' The gun was back in his hand, and there was both apprehension and resolution in his voice. 'Ready?'

'Yes.'

Ready, if that included a noisy heart and difficulty in breathing.

We left the shelter of the bushes at the nearest point to the house and crept from shadow to shadow to what was evidently the kitchen door. The door was double; an outer screen against insects, an inner door made half of glass. Kent put his hand on the screen door latch and pulled it open, and tried the handle of the main door beneath.

Unsurprisingly, locked.

Kent pulled the radio from his belt, extended the aerial, and said one single word, 'Go.'

Before he'd finished returning the radio to his belt there was a sudden skin-crawling crescendo of sirens from in front of the house, and even at the rear one could see the reflections of the revolving lights racing forwards. Then there were search-lights flooding and voices shouting incomprehensibly through megaphones: and by that time Kent had smashed the glass panel of the door and put a hand inside to undo the lock.

There was pandemonium in the house as well as out. Kent and I with the two rear patrolmen on our heels raced through the kitchen and made straight for the stairs, sensing as much as seeing two men pulling guns to oppose the invasion. Stavoski's men seemed to have shot the lock off the front door: in a half glimpse after the staccato racket I saw the blue uniforms coming into the hall and then I was round the bend of the stairs, heading for the upper level.

Still quiet up there, comparatively. All doors except one were open. I made for it, running, and Kent behind me cried agonisedly, 'Andrew, don't do that.'

I looked back for him. He came, stood out of the line of fire of the door for a second, then leaped at it, giving it a heavy kick. The door crashed open, and Kent with gun ready jumped through and to one side, with me following.

The light inside was dim, like a child's nightlight, shadowy after the bright passage outside. There was a tent in the room, greyish-white, guy ropes tied to pieces of furniture: and standing by the tent, hurrying to unfasten the entrance, to go for his hostage, stood Giuseppe–Peter.

He whirled round as we went in.

He too held a gun.

He aimed straight in our direction, and fired twice. I felt a fierce sting as one bullet seared across the skin high on my left arm, and heard the second one fizz past my ear . . . and Kent without hesitation shot him.

He fell flat on his back from the force of it, and I went over to him, dropping to my knees.

It was Kent who opened the tent and went in for Morgan Freemantle. I heard the Senior Steward's slow sleepy voice, and Kent coming and saying the victim was doped to the eyeballs and totally unclothed, but otherwise unharmed.

I was trying with no success at all to wad a handful of folded tent against my enemy's neck, to stop the scarlet fountain spurting there. The bullet had torn too much away; left nothing to be done.

His eyes were open, but unfocused

He said in Italian, 'Is it you?'

'Yes,' I said, in his tongue.

The pupils slowly sharpened, the gaze steadying on my face.

'I couldn't know,' he said. 'How could I have known . . . what you were. . . .'

I knelt there trying to save his life.

He said, 'I should have killed you then . . . in Bologna . . . when you saw me. . . . I should have put my knife . . . into . . . that Spanish . . . chauffeur.'

'Yes,' I said again. 'You should.'

He gave me a last dark look, not admitting defeat, not giving an inch. I watched him with unexpected regret. Watched him until the consciousness went out of his eyes, and they were simply open but seeing nothing.

Dick Francis
Special limited edition
Hot Money / In the Frame £4.99
Two bestsellers for the price of one!

'Dick Francis at his brilliant best . . .'
Sporting Life

From Dick Francis – undisputed champion of the racing crime mystery – two more classic tales of skulduggery and intrigue set against the colourful background of the sport of kings . . .

Financial whizz-kid Malcolm Pembroke finds a new gambling outlet for his hard-earned millions – the international bloodstock market. But playing for fortunes means danger; and *Hot Money* could cost him his life . . .

The trail of a ruthless gang carrying on a lucrative business in forged paintings leads to Melbourne during the razzmatazz of Cup Week. Enter a steely-nerved English painter, ready to expose the killers for a place *In the Frame* . . .

'The plot, the characters and the excitement are the best yet'
Daily Mirror

'When the gloves are off it's very gritty indeed'
Daily Telegraph

All Pan Books are available at your local bookshop or newsagent, or can be ordered direct from the publisher. Indicate the number of copies required and fill in the form below.

Send to: Pan C. S. Dept
            Macmillan Distribution Ltd
            Houndmills Basingstoke RG21 2XS

or phone: 0256 29242, quoting title, author and Credit Card number.

Please enclose a remittance* to the value of the cover price plus £1.00 for the first book plus 50p per copy for each additional book ordered.

*Payment may be made in sterling by UK personal cheque, postal order, sterling draft or international money order, made payable to Pan Books Ltd.

Alternatively by Barclaycard/Access/Amex/Diners

Card No.

Expiry Date

_____
                    Signature

Applicable only in the UK and BFPO addresses.

While every effort is made to keep prices low, it is sometimes necessary to increase prices at short notice. Pan Books reserve the right to show on covers and charge new retail prices which may differ from those advertised in the text or elsewhere.

NAME AND ADDRESS IN BLOCK LETTERS PLEASE

. . . .

Name _____

Address _____

_____

_____

_____

6/92